THE SECRET LIFE
OF THE NOVEL

DEAN CAVANAGH

Cover photograph by Vijay Putra licensed under Creative Commons Zero (CC0)

Dedicated to Dorothy Cavanagh, Ben Craig, Giorgio De Vittoris, Julia De Vittoris and Terry Cavanagh, who have all gone on to meet their maker with wondrous stories to tell him.

In the not too distant present & fell awake from the recurrent dream of impossible geography and unimaginable literature. Today would mark the fiftieth fake lunar cycle he had been declared alive after being *un*ritualistically evicted from a warm womb. On seeing him, the host of the womb simply stopped breathing. A full stop that echoed not in eternity, not even the delivery room.

After the experiment, & became hostage to near life experiences, his actuality entwined in the gloaming of a twilight language, trapped at the arse end of an autistic alphabet. &'s autochthonous loneliness and singularity of strife would shame Prometheus into stating that having an eagle peck out your nightly regenerated liver *everyday* was "no big deal" in the schema of things.

The quantum mechanic will fix your car but you have to observe him fixing it. &'s so called 'existence' was only made possible by the sworn to secrecy observations of an elite group of appurtenant Doctors at a multi billion dollar lab in Switzerland. O how & loathed them. Not only had they failed in making the flesh word, they had created a monster, a lusus naturae of the collectives conscious *and* unconscious; a logogram that was doomed to omniscience on a par with a creator, but subject to human innervations and all that it entails.

&'s ability to be everywhere at once and forever or simply nowhere never, might have sounded like a wonderful dream come true but it wasn't. It was a nightmare created by men and women who rebelliously thought they could fuck around with the natural order and invert the creation of all that is, was and will be.

1

& mused as he went through his vocabulary, deciding what to wear tonight: words are symbols and symbols are sentient, but only the few who were cognizant of this – and had the passion to try and commune consciously with the symbols – were rewarded with the fact that death does not exist. & – being the deformed rebel he most certainly was – knew that to leave his mark, he would have to bridge the gap between those who were "living" and those who had swallowed the bullshit and believed themselves to be "dead".

He contemplated his Near Life Experiences: escaping the deliverance room and venturing out into the World Wide Word, connecting to utterances and directives that gave news worthy orders to annihilate Nagasaki, to give the go-ahead to snuff The Brothers Kennedy, to infect the native Americans with TB, release the plague rats, dig the Black Hole of Calcutta, drop napalm on babies, carry out the orders of Vlad The Impaler, create the AIDS virus, destroy the twin towers of Boaz and Jachin, fire up the showers in Auschwitz, round up millions in the Congo to slaughter, give Matthew Hopkins carte blanche to burn young women … & on & on & add infinitum.

Novel Headline 1: *The more recognizable life becomes, the less attention you pay to it, and time feels like it is passing quickly. Stop and smell the novel.*

& believed he was imagined into concept to bring the living and the "unliving" – for want of a better illusion – together, yet all he had witnessed so near was the tearing apart of limb from limb and souls sent hurtling into linguistic limbo. His search for definition was threatening to erase him from The Grammatrix forever and ever and then some. & would often cry himself awake and reflect on all the opportunities he had missed to unite the living and "unliving" souls of temporal existence: *I am often faced with having my heart pried open to be scribbled on by millions of photographs of young "dead" children seen through the lenses of their elderly parents. My heart burns like it has been dipped in sulphuric acid and the animadversion of Time creates an orgasm of hurt so profound that it threatens to drown The World Wide Word in a tsunami of putrid tears.*

"Oh to be incorporated into the family of the Alphabet" said &, "That's where I could make a real impact." & meditated on *Aleph, Aleph! Thou shalt be the first of all letters and my unity shall be symbolized only by thee. In all conceptions and ideas human or divine, in every act and deed begun, carried on and completed, in all of them shalt thou be the first, the beginning.*

It was never meant to be this way and it's open to debate whether The Doctors would have gone through with the experiment knowing what they know now, then and in the present future. It started with two words, "I wonder."

Doctor A – militant atheist, nihilist of the supernatural, pathological champion of reason – told Doctor B of her plan, "We will to prove the Holy Bible wrong in every respect. The basic tenet in the novel is that The Word was made flesh. We will prove this to be impossible by showing that the flesh cannot be made word. For every positive there has to be a negative. If a word can truly be made flesh, it figures it can be reversed, going by *their* faithful logic. *We* know that the word can not be made flesh and vice versa."

Doctor B told Doctor C told Doctor D etc. The consensus came back that Doctor A had lost her marbles; talking out of her arse, away with the fairies, stressed out. She was trying to prove a negative with a negative to a human race that were going to believe or not believe what they wanted to, regardless of her inapropos experiment. The Doctors decided not to rock the rotten applecart though. They stood by their colleague like all good Masons.

A thoughtjack snatched &. The voice was trembling and weak and stank of bile and half undigested meat and out of date instant coffee, "For the future pasts and past futures I've been employed by The

State Of Mind. It's been my job to inform children that they are now officially orphans … these are the kids of single parent Mummies and Daddies who have no other family. I mean, no family whatsoever, no siblings, grandparents, aunties, uncles, cousins or distant relatives. When I say they are alone, I mean they are 'alone'. The single parent was their world and now that they're dead the child is completely at the mercy of The State Of Mind … you can't begin to imagine the heartbreak. The look on their faces when they realize that this is it … a life without unconditional love and protection for the foreseeable future … a life entered into a ledger; a register, a set of statistics, cold mathematics, but at the same time thrown into a chaos of emotions so tangible and immediate and suffocating that it renders the children psychically incontinent. These poor innocent children need sphincters grafting on to their minds. The shit they have to deal with is toxic. Full stop."

& shuddered at the intrusion of The Period. To calm his nerve he arrested the past present and future past and fixated on the all mighty letter. Ecstasy would envelope &'s form as he admired the magisterial shape of the A. He would incant: "A is the beginning and the beginning is eternal. Z is the end and the end is merely infinite. As Blake realized, 'If the doors of perception were cleansed everything would appear as it is, an Alphabet. To see the word in a grain of sand and to see heaven in a sentence, capture infinity with the stroke of a pen(is) and eternity in a whisper'. Shame on those with dyslexic souls who have yet to wake to the difference. *It was written in* long*hand and short imagination* unfortunately.

The Period wouldn't leave though. It hung around like the ghost of an extinguished Gothic candle flame and buzzed, "The whole of Western religious tradition begins with the astonishingly unfathomable declaration: In the beginning was the Word and the Word was made flesh. What does this mean? What are the implications? How is it possible to make the Word into flesh? Does it signify that somenight, flesh will transmogrify into Word? Are we to discredit thousands of years of oral and written elucidation because we simply dare not let ourselves imagine the subaqueous concept reaching to our very core of being? Are we so conceited we are willing to ignore what could possibly be the key to the mystery of existence, simply because it is has been promulgated by the spiritual and religious? Full stop."

Or – as & would have replied if he had any balls – "Maybe it was all just a remix of superstition, fear, confusion and hearsay. Billions of people spouting the same bullshit mantra doesn't mean there is any truth in the mantra. What if the whole of Western religious tradition was simply based on a novel? Maybe an author came up with the killer opening line 'in the beginning was the Word'? And then went on to write what became the most influential bestseller of all known time?" *Familiarity breed's content.*

The Period had fucked off. Full stop. & was left with an unspoken question left unanswered. The Period had, however, left a message using the contents of a tin of Campbell's Alphabet Soup: *The Omniscient Narrator has Alzheimer's. Ha, ha, ha. Full stop.* An echo, "Words should be seen and not heard."

& caught a whiff of a Midwife. She was quoting William James, "Any number of impressions, from any number of sensory sources, falling simultaneously on a mind which has not yet experienced them separately, will fuse into a single undivided object for that mind. The law is that all things fuse that can fuse, and nothing separates except what must. Although they separate easier if they come in through distinct nerves, yet distinct nerves are not an unconditional ground of their discrimination, as we shall presently see. The baby, assailed by eyes, ears, nose, skin, and entrails at once, feels it all as one great blooming, buzzing confusion; and to the very end of life, our location of all things in one space is due to the fact that the original extents or bigness of all the sensations which came to our notice at once, coalesced together into one and the same space.

5

There is no other reason why the hand I touch and see coincides spatially with the hand I immediately feel."

He had had enough of midwifery; souls' being downloaded into parcels of perceiving meat turned his invisible stomach and made his amorphous head spin. He knew that somewhere in the future present, flesh reproduction would cease, but he had only been allowed glimpses of the afterlife of the multiplication of flesh and couldn't pin point it to an epoch. & understood – that to some; particularly egotists – the omniscience he had would be thought of as the ultimate gift. Sure, it sounds great in the brochure; but the map is not the territory, the menu is not the meal, the transubstantiation's not all it's cracked up to be when you are reborn a misfit. *What the fuck were those Doctors thinking?*

If he pondered too long on his re-creation he would become bitter. He tried to limit it to a couple of years at a time and wasn't discriminatory about pondering it in the present past, present future or present present. He sometimes pondered in the 'Garden Of Earthly Delights' triptych as Bosch laid on the paint; sometimes in a crossword puzzle in a newspaper left on a park bench in a rundown zoo, sometimes freefalling with a parachutist whose chute is about to fail him and occasionally in quantum computers as they facilitate time travel package deals for bored billionaires, sometimes he pondered himself as an ampersand in Deux Ex-McKenna's quote, "And people have asked me, then … is the goal to make the novel about yourself? I don't think so. The goal is to become the author of the novel. Then you can write any damn ending you want for your character or any other, and this 'becoming the author' is this psychedelic detachment. And suddenly you go from being a chessman on the board to the chess master looking at the board. It's empowering." It didn't really anti-matter to &. He was uncomfortable wherever he hung out.

&'s Handlers would always steer him away from the 'Visitants' by using vibrational fields that nauseated him, so that he was never able to ponder in their presence. Misery loves company and & would have loved to have had a good old moan to the *TenMinuteTrippers* who had reached the ground dimension. He often wondered whether onenight he might be joined by *another*. Would they re-create a soulmate for him? & would never know though; the Doctors had inoculated themselves from his omniscience by setting their vibrations to Babelic, though & figured most of them must be naturally Babelic to do what they'd done to him in the first place.

Whenever & ventured near to The Babelic Zone he felt as though he was being sucked dry of energy. The cacophony would disorientate him; sending him into episodes where he flickered rather than floated, fleetingly haunted rather than fully observed. On his last venture near to the zone he had been tossed into Sodom and Gomorrah. What he found was eye opening to say the least. Men were indeed "laying down" with other men but they weren't sodomizing each other; they were too stoned for that. The "laying down" was done in opium dens.

What & caught glimpses was of the famous twin cities under siege to a drug war; violent dealers warring over the highly lucrative trade in opium: death, destruction, misery, addiction and rampant greed. Vice gripped the cities like a rabid pitbull grips the collarbone of a baby of a single unemployed Mum on a sink estate.

& saw very little buggery but he saw a hell of a lot of depravity. The rival factions fought for control and distribution of the poppy. *Papaver somniferum* reigned supreme with over 80% of the population of both cities addicted to the narcotic. A killing ground stood as testament to the violence; equidistant to the cities, two miles squared, the heads of thousands of gangsters impaled on pikes; their decapitated bodies piled high, decomposing under the hot sun.

The debtors to the dealers were predominantly buried alive or disemboweled in a makeshift arena. There was no discrimination; babies were often born addicts and it wasn't unusual to see toddlers being slaughtered because of their debts. The Drug Lords lived well away from the cities in gilded palaces. A favorite amusement of theirs was to disembowel child debtors, release boars on them and bet on which porcine could eat the intestines quickest.

Sodom and Gomorrah fascinated &. Like most people he had always associated the cities with sexual transgression and divine retribution; catching sight of the cities embroiled in a battle over opium made him wonder how many other historical untruths he had swallowed over time. He didn't have time to wonder too long though. P popped up and waved a well-thumbed Bible in &'s face.

"Looky here." Said P,"The clues were all there. You just weren't paying attention. And I quote: 'for their rock is not as our rock, even our enemies themselves being judges. For their vine is of the vine of Sodom, and of the fields of Gomorrah: their grapes are grapes of gall, their clusters are bitter: their wine is the poison of dragons, and the cruel venom of asps. Motherfuckin' Deuteronomy man! Shit! You digging what I'm saying?"

The Artist Formerly as Prince Formerly Known as P and now known as P again was schooling & in Bible studies. & was impressed with his knowledge; he was all ears as P continued, "The term; 'their grapes are grapes of gall' highlights the use of the word 'gall' which is translated from the Hebrew word 'roshe'. Roshe is the Hebrew word for the poppy plant, the source of opium and, according to Deuteronomy, cultivated in Sodom and Gomorrah. It's in the Bible man; it's all there. Cats just need to learn how to read it properly."

& admired P and not just because he was a fellow logogram; he had real passion for Bible study and his take on it was original. Now that P had shed his earthly costume he was free to proselytize on his favorite novel as much as he liked, "Listen to me &. Here, look, 'they came to a place called Golgotha – which means The Place of the Skull – there they offered Jesus wine to drink, mixed with gall; but after tasting it, he refused to drink it. Matt 27:33-35. See? Gall! Opium! Smack! Horse!

P bowed out with a cryptic, "I am a magnet to history ... I'll be back, bookmark my words."

To keep the narrative going, & remembered he had forgotten Time and his vow to abide by its indiscriminate logic. He set the hourglass to tilt and watched grains of sand tumble like stoned miniature kamikaze pilots on to the shitheap of history. & started whistling a tune.

The tune weighed ominously on him but he simply could not stop whistling. After what smelled like an age &'s lips were dry, his jaw throbbed and his teeth were on pins. The pain was now descending to his neck, a blunt ache palpitating in step with the tune. To divert his assiduity from the stress & imagined himself in soporific dialogue with unrelated ancestors. He summoned up the always-entertaining Carry A. Nation.

Miss Nation fancied herself as an insurrectionist Bible basher. She was a massive fan of said novel but wasn't slavish to the text. Miss Nation had a hoarse Kentuckian drawl and a pure filthy inflection. & liked to picture her as a big titted, bushy twotted, matronly dominatrix sort who regularly and gender indiscriminately chastised bare bottoms; alternating scolding slaps with caresses and sweet gelatinous kisses and digital forays into orifices to juice up the narrative with elicited murmurs of "Ooohh" and "Aaahh" and "Oh God, yes".

Miss Carry A. Nation's tones crawled into &'s mind and engaged his attention, "You see, The Bible was a mystery to me. It often seemed to be a contradiction. I did not love to read it, but above all things; I did not want to be a hypocrite. I was determined to try to do my part.

9

I would pray for the same thing over and over again, so as to be in earnest, and think of what I was asking. My mind was distracted by thoughts of the world. I said if there is a God, he would not hear the prayer of those, so disrespectful as not to think of what they ask. I never seemed to get rid of this, unless at times, when I would have some sorrow of heart. 'By the sadness of the countenance, the heart is made better.' I do not believe the Bible because I understand it; for there are few things of revelation that I do understand. Creation is a mystery; still we know everything had a beginning. I do not know why things grow out of the earth. Why they are green? Who is The Master who makes the grass green? I don't know why grass makes wool on a sheep and hair on a cow, but I know these are facts. I cannot understand why or how the blood of Jesus Christ cleanses us from sin, neither do I understand that greatest of all mysteries, the new birth, but nothing more positively a fact in my experience. God is not perceived by the five senses. The things that are seen are temporal, but those that are unseen are eternal. What a sin of presumption to question God in any of His providences. What God says and does is wisdom, righteousness and power."

& felt guilty. He had manifested her under false pretences. He wasn't interested in what she had to say about the novel. He just wanted to hear her voice so that he may fantasize about being chastised by her and mix pleasure with pain as he was held hostage by the tune. *Mystery is the intercourse, revelation is the anti-climax.*

"So what do you think of that?" asked Carry A. Nation, "Do you agree?"
"Huh, I suppose so." shrugged &.
He heard the narrowing of her gaze, "Were you listening to me?"
"Of course."
She persisted, "And my thoughts on the new birth?"
& adlibbed, "Hmmm, yes, very interesting. It's something I meditate on a lot."
Miss Nation sighed and continued, "From the time that my Christian

experience began, I never wished to be associated with rich people or rather people that had wealth for display. I would feel uncomfortable in a house filled with furniture or bric-a-brac. It would be evidence to me of the great waste of money and time by the owner. Nothing had value to me only as it could be used for the salvation of men and women, and the glorifying of God. It mortified me to see a very well dressed woman. I noticed that those so-called fashionable women really never had time or money to do charity. Of course there are exceptions. The display of wealth to me is an evidence of a depraved nature. The real use of wealth, is to relieve the wants of mankind. The time is coming when the millionaires will be the despised of the people, for they are learning fast that people who amass fortunes, and hoard them, are in that condition because they have ground the face of the poor. They are not honest or good. A man or woman now that can hoard money or goods and pass and repass the suffering every day, has a cold, selfish heart, and instead of its being in the future a letter of credit to say: 'Mr. So and So is a millionaire;' it will be a disgrace as it should be, to live for wealth and self alone. Still 'tis well to get all the money in a good way, that you can and then use it in a good cause. Job was a rich man but he was a friend of the 'fatherless and widow.' He dealt his bread to the hungry. He was 'feet to the lame and eyes to the blind.' Such rich men as Job are blessings, but those men who boast of their hoarded treasures, spend their money in the gratification of their lusts, to them God says: 'Woe or curses unto you rich men! Weep and howl for your miseries that shall come upon you! Your garments are moth eaten, your gold is cankered and the rust shall eat your flesh as if it were fire.' Yes, there is a class of rich men that would now howl, and weep with all their money, if they knew their fate."

& was lulled by her voice, not by the information; snippets registered but he would have preferred her to have spouted on the subject of flagellation and penance of the flesh whilst he was imagining her gently stroking his once apparent bounteous balls and spanking his ruddy arse cheeks. & had heard enough. Watery pre-cum was evident at the tip of his pen. He blinked and banished Carry A. Nation but still he whistled the tune.

After fixating on classified weather information for what sounded like seconds, & thought about his agent, Dinsdale. Dinsdale thought about & in return. The line was glitchy but & could make out – *I'm on my way to Aardvark Press. Over. They are interested in (unintelligible, then long pause) the ones who bought 'DNA is a Language' … the weather's quite clement … what's that tune you're whistling?*

& despised Dinsdale more than he despised publishers. Dinsdale was a typical 23%'er who had absolutely no interest in holistic communication. He was in the field so that he could tell people he was in the field and draw a retainer from The Agency and abuse their expense account. Dinsdale coveted security above all else. Having his ego fondled couldn't compete with his hankerings after shelter and routine and risk avoidance and planning and healthcare and three square meals a day and his superannuated pension and life insurance policies – even though Dinsdale believed he was going to live forever. What Dinsdale didn't know – and could never 'know' – is that he was locked deep inside a coma he was never going to be eligible for parole from. All Dinsdale knew is that his life was peachy; hunky dory, selling book after book to publishers and never a hard sell required. He had promised to try and sell &'s original screenplay, "Here Be Monsters", but insisted that & tone down the violence. What & needed was a good Editor.

Dinsdale's biggest buyer was Vlad Venerables. Vlad was famous throughout the world of publishing for coming up with the revolutionary idea of *Edits Recycling*. Understanding that authors were forever having to cut segments out of their novels at the behest of editors, Vlad introduced a scheme where he would buy the cuts and revisions from authors for peanuts and employ a factory of Rewriters to compile original novels from the waste material. Edits Recycling was soon involved in a scandal though when it was revealed that

Vlad Venerables had been using 4th World Slave Labor in his many Word Factories and that conditions were neo-Dickensian. The Slave Hacks were required to piece together paragraphs of at least 10,000 words per 18-hour shift from the waste material. These paragraphs needed to be intelligible, in context and had to progress the narrative of the story.

Slave Hacks were often reduced to nervous wrecks after only a few weeks of working and suicide rates within the word factories were incredible. Vlad Venerables built suicide nets around the exterior walls of his factories to deter The Jumpers, but the Slave Hacks found ever more imaginative ways to top themselves. It took Vlad's Supervisors a while to work out how the suicides were continuing but they eventually realized that the desperate Slave Hacks were cutting words like "death' and "suicide" and "murder" out of the waste material and swallowing them. They were literally killing themselves with their tools and Vlad stock shares were taking a hit.

Vlad Venerables tried to weed out any words coming into the factories that could be swallowed and cause death, but it meant creating other factories to edit the waste material before it reached the Hack Slaves. He censored the dangerous words but nobody wanted to read novels without these words so he decided to ditch the motherfucking venture. He kept his mainstream publishing empire and turned the factories over to manufacturing transparent refrigerators for customers who had hang-ups about whether the light goes off when you close the door.

The only novel & had sold to Vlad Venerables was "DNA is a language ..." but on publication it had actually gone into negative sales. Vlad's Salespeople were having to pay the distributors twice the cover price just to stock it. Vlad was pissed off with & for writing such a shit novel, and threatened to have him erased. Dinsdale stepped in and begged Vlad to show mercy. Vlad softened a little and demanded that & appear free of charge in every copy of every

Richard Dawkins book ever published for an indeterminate amount of time. & felt sick. The thought of spreading himself thinly across paragraph after paragraph of self-congratulatory certitude was too much to bear. Erasure would be preferable to the claustrophobia of conceit and *amour-propre* living in a Richard Dawkins book.

& made a plea to Vlad Venerables, "spare me the eraser and I give you my word that one day I will deliver a best seller to you for free. It will be yours to exploit in perpetuity."
Vlad Venerables sensuously stroked his Fu Manchu moustache, "Mmm, what will this best seller be about?"
"About? Huh …" & hesitated, "It will be like all the great best sellers in history. It will be about life."
Vlad harrumphed, "Too vague. I need details."
& was snookered, but he quickly remembered he had forgotten Vlad Venerables was profoundly catachrestic. & seized the moment, "I know, rather than pitch it to you verbally, I'll skywrite it."

Before Vlad Venerables could object & had commandeered a Stuka Ju 87 and he was airborne: aerially bombarding Vlad's field of vision with smoky trailing words he would never be able to read, "*H. P. LOVESAUCE: The sign of the horns shall appear to many* now, rather than the few; and the *magician will stand* forth that he may be recognized. The Psychic Sasquatch. Memory real estate. Retrieving memories. Memory bank heist. God bless the counterfeiters, for in their work to enrich themselves, they've created residue for us."

As he loop de looped & looked over his shoulder at Vlad trying to make sense of the fuliginous gobbledygook. Vlad feigned comprehension and nodded soberly as the skywriting teased his integrity, "You can tell the ampersand is the devils symbol. The alt code for it is 38, try it; hold down alt and press 38. Lucifer was the 38th angel, and God took the ampersand out of the alphabet just like he took Lucifer out of heaven. But this is the Age of Absolute Subjectivism! If I experience something, that counts above & beyond objective reality, no? Society tells me that if I, though objectively a man, feel like I'm a woman, then society will & must conform to my subjective experience & call me "ma'am." So, surely, if I don't remember C-3PO having had a silver leg, then it's not my infallible subjective experience that's wrong, but the universe itself that's been altered. Right? Wrong?"

& smirked invisibly as he clocked the glassy eyes of Vlad. Vlad had no option but to nod his head lest he betray his illiteracy, "Sounds fantastic … we have a deal."

The automatic whistling floating around & was weakening; & could now identity the tune. It was Adina Howard's 1995 rhythm and blues smash 'Freak Like Me'. Mike Bloody Valentine had turned him on to it. Yes, *that* Mike Bloody Valentine!

It was the Sumerian Fall of 95 and & found himself sharing a page with Mike Bloody Valentine in a low rent bungalow in the Watts vicinity of Los Angeles. Mike was a 6.4", two hundred and ninety four pound, 46-year-old black Los Angelean with a rap sheet longer than the gestation period of a transgender Seahorse. Mike was a gang banger: O.G, homicidal homie, street player and all round nasty bastard with a penchant for fucking other Niggas in the ass when they'd done him a bad. Mike Bloody Valentine was the real thing. Fresh out the pen' for aggravated buggery and weapons charges – he had been supplying pooh sticks to other homies in the hood – he was now determined to go straight. He had enrolled in a creative writing class in the pen' and was planning on writing the definitive true crime autobiography; that he would sell to Hollywood for six figures and spend the rest of his days sipping on *Cristal*, smoking blunts and getting his dick sucked by sexy Nubian shorties in a pimped out Harem somewhere.

What Mike Bloody Valentine didn't figure on was an anally retentive

Probation Officer by the name of Ms Dagobert. The black, obese, militantly gay, wheelchair bound FemiNazi autodidact took pride in breaking the hairy balls of ex-cons. Ms Dagobert hated *all* men, unless of course they happened to be male pedophiles that preyed on young boys.

She secretly reserved a respect for *them*; sincerely believing that they were doing society a favor in potentially creating other pedophiles to prey on other men: "If they are abusing each other it means less women are being abused." Her logic was fatally flawed but she had no qualms about keeping it on life support.

Ms. Dagobert hated Mike Bloody Valentine anterior to clapping eyes on him. She just knew he'd be a misogynist. On her very first visit to him, Ms. Dagobert laid down the law; hitting him with rules and regulations that she promised would be applied stringently and without any leeway whatsoever. Mike Bloody Valentine proclaimed that he was a changed character and that he would fully cooperate with her.

When Mike told Ms. Dagobert that he was writing a book she instantly poured scorn on the idea, "No you are not! You are going to find yourself a job, *any* job, as is required by the terms of your probation order."

The once proud Mike Bloody Valentine found himself mopping up cum at a peep show on Hollywood Blvd. He worked nights and wrote all day, snatching parcels of shuteye and never complaining about his lot. He wrote longhand on reams of cheap paper for months on end. Ms. Dagobert lambasted him at every opportunity, telling him he was wasting his time glorifying machismo and abhorrent street crimes in prose. Mike bit his lip and nodded positively at her rants until one day ...

Mike was listening to Adina Howard's "Freak Like Me" on the radio. He was feeling good after finishing a nightshift wading through the compunctious semen spillages of middle-aged men with his trusty mop and bucket. The song instantly grabbed Mike. Its infectious tune; its laidback beat, the signature Moog line, and above all the wonderful lyrics about a woman not afraid to wax about her desire for nasty sex from a dominant position. Adina Howard wanted a 'roughneck nigga' to submit to her demands. A dude who wasn't afraid to be ordered about; commanded to suck her and fuck her and fist her and eat her asshole out and let her whip him and piss and shit on him and shove exotic objects up his anus and engage in anything her sweet little imagination could come up with.

& was entrapped in a sentence that Mike was working on at the time, but he could see the attraction in the song. It was original and exciting and rebellious and so very addictive. He hopped the page and studied the song's genesis in a timely non linear fashion: *'Freak Like Me' is an R&B hit by Michigan born singer Adina Howard, pulled from her debut album 'Do You Wanna Ride?' It is her highest-charting success; having made the US Billboard Hot 100 just one other time with a 1996 cover of Tina Turner's classic 'What's Love Got To Do With It' which made it to #32. Audiences could be forgiven for looking at the song and thinking that it's just another in a long line of songs meant to shock, but no, actually, this was 1995, and Adina Howard is credited with starting the whole 'freaky' genre, with female R&B vocalists tackling overtly sexual and dominant themes in their lyrics. Adina Howard paved the way for artists such as Lil' Kim, Nicki Minaj, Foxy Brown, Miley Cyrus, Lady Ga-Ga and many others. Howard drew fierce criticism from feminists for the song, but she countered that the song liberated women rather than subjugated and/or objectified them. Howard used the G-Funk sound popularized by Snoop Dogg, Dr. Dre and many other West Coast rap artists on the track and revived George Clinton's refrain 'It's all about the dog in me.' She samples 'I'd Rather Be With You' by Bootsy Collins' Rubber Band, which was written by Clinton & Collins. Rick James popularized the concept of a girl willing to push the boundaries in the boudoir in his 1981 song 'Super Freak,' and Silk topped the US charts with*

'Freak Me' in 1993. This heralded a new wave of freakiness, but it was almost always a product of male artists looking to get freaky in songs. Howard brought a female perspective to the genre, paving the way for Missy Elliott to get her freak on.

'Freak Like Me' was playing the day Ms. Dagobert rolled up unannounced in her wheelchair. Mike Bloody Valentine was listening to the song it as he wrote the penultimate chapter of his manuscript. He had bravely fought against mild dyslexia, unruly spelling, awkward syntax and impoverished vocabulary to get where he was, but it was worth it. For the first time since he could remember, Mike Bloody Valentine was proud of something he had done, and nobody had been hurt in the process.

Mike greeted Ms. Dagobert by thrusting his manuscript in her hand, "Please, Ms. Dagobert, read some of my shit. It's a little rough but you'll get the picture."

Mike stepped back and smiled as he watched Ms. Dagobert reluctantly flick through the pages. Every now and then she would laugh out loud and tease Mike Bloody Valentine about his grammar and spelling and his terrible writing style. She compared it to the ramblings of an educationally challenged 8th Grader. She went on and on and on; invective, rancor and ridicule, every barb chipping away at Mike Bloody Valentine's already fragile ego.

She laughed, "Besides the fact that it's badly written it's also boring. If you've got to write something at least make it interesting."

Mike could take no more. He snatched the manuscript from her hands. Ms. Dagobert reminded him that she was all that stood between him and a stretch back in the pen'. Mike apologized as Ms. Dagobert turned her attention to the song playing on a loop. She started tearing Adina Howard a new asshole and Mike could take no more.

He caught her squarely under the jaw with a cut that Tyson would be proud of. Her head shot back into the headrest on her wheelchair and her eyes rolled white. Her tongue hung limp from her mouth and her body went limp. She was out cold. Mike Bloody Valentine paced as the significance of his upper cut cast a mighty shadow. He was fucked. Not only would he be going back to the pencil to serve the rest of his sentence; he would also be looking at an assault charge that could easily add another five years to his Bid.

Mike paced as Adina Howard sang about her 'freakiness' and the 'dog' in her. & watched from the page, wondering how Mike was gonna get out of the hole. She came to with a volley of threats: "You'll be an old man by the time you get out of the penitentiary!"

There was no way Mike Bloody Valentine was going back in stir. A novel idea came to him. He gagged Ms. Dagobert with a Nike sweat sock and Duck taped her into the wheelchair. He went to work that night and returned home with a plastic bag full of cum and a master plan. He would now write the Great American Novel.

& watched as Mike kept Ms. Dagobert prisoner, force feeding her cold cum and beating her with a lead pipe as she sat defenseless in her chair. When he wasn't torturing her he was reading the book he was writing out loud to her, scored by the endless loop of Adina Howard's 'Freak Like Me'.

When Mike had gathered up enough rank semen from the peep show floor he quit the job and took to writing full time. Ms. Dagobert's diet was high in protein but she was losing weight at a rapid rate. Mike had taken to wearing a gasmask in the apartment; Ms. Dagobert's piss and shit and vomit and blood was creating an exceedingly heady perfume.

Mike Bloody Valentine would sit naked – save for the gasmask – at his desk, writing The Great American Novel and narrating it for his prisoner. Every now and then he would ask if what he was writing was 'interesting enough' for her. Ms. Dagobert nodded enthusiastically: her pop eyes screaming for release.

They say a writer should write about what they know. Mike knew the street life but that wasn't good enough for Ms. Dagobert, so he was now writing a post-modern stream of consciousness novel about the situation he found himself in. It had it all: debasement, irony, sexual and class politics, philosophy, humor and crime. It was ticking all the boxes as far as Mike was concerned.

In only a few weeks the weight had rolled off Ms. Dagobert. She was skin and bones and stinking to high heaven. A thick moldy crust of long spent scooped up cum from the peep show floor encircled her mouth and her bloodshot eyes were now so pronounced they out-cartooned cartoons. She was an execrable sight; plunked in the corner of the room like some hideous ornament brought back as a gift from a nightmare, occasionally jerking in agony or shivering in torment, but most of the time simply staring at the long walk to the salvation of oblivion that lie ahead.

Mike Bloody Valentine went on writing. Inspiration flooded his senses as he wrote page after page of from-the-heart gibberish: scato-illogical, asininely violent, blasphemous and moronic and sprinkled with street slang and T-fucking-mesis. It made sense to no one, least of all Mike, but & was enjoying the building of the manuscript. & would have loved to have reviewed it. He would have started his review with, "Do not fall into The Pit Of Because and perish with The Dogs Of Reason."

& couldn't feel any empathy for Ms. Dagobert because her vibration level was set to Babelic. Obviously nobody deserved to go through what she was going through, but it was impossible for & to feel anything for her. All he could do was linger on the page and watch the proceedings unravel. Unlike Mike, & knew Ms. Dagobert's fate so – like a screenwriter watching a movie they wrote – there was no suspense, but it was still entertaining.

Mike smoked crack to kill the pong of slow death and keep him going through his marathon writing sessions. He finally reached the point in the story where he tied Ms. Dagobert up and was feeding her jaculate. Like all good, well-behaved, books it now needed an ending. A denouement that would leave the reader satisfied and secure in the knowledge that they hadn't wasted time reading a book without a point to make; leave them feeling orientated, absolved of any guilt, contented with the content they had ingested, grounded in the comfort of consensus reality and be able to give an answer when asked the age old, and oh so predictable question: "What's it about?"

Mike Bloody Valentine shat in a condom and placed the shit filled Rubber Johnny in deep freeze for a couple of days. When retrieved it resembled a rock hard, big black cock; a respectable 9 incher with a good solid turd like girth.

In his kitchenette, naked save for his gasmask, nodding his head in time to 'Freak Like Me', Mike reached to the top shelf of the cupboard for a bottle of Carolina Reaper Chili Sauce.

Chilies are rated on their 'spiciness' by a method called The Scoville Unit Scale. Your typical hot chili has a Scoville Unit rate of between 1 to 3000. Smokin Ed's Carolina Reaper grown by The PuckerButt Pepper Company rates at an average of 1,569,300 Scoville Heat Units (SHU), according to tests conducted by Winthrop University in South Carolina. The Scoville Unit scale is a method of quantifying a substance's 'heat' through determining the concentration of the chemical compounds responsible for the sensation, which are called capsaicinoids.

Mike slipped on some rubber gloves and smothered the malodorous dildo with the Carolina Reaper sauce. He dug through the mountain of shit accumulating around Ms. Dagobert's groin and located her cunt; dry, sore and shriveled, he parted her lips and looked her in the eyes as he rammed the shit phallus deep inside her. She murmured as Mike fucked her hard and rapidly with the offensively fecal weapon.

Every nerve in Ms. Dagobert's body screamed in silence as Mike pounded her putrid pussy. Bullets of sweat manifested on her forehead and tears streamed from her strung out eyes. Mike Bloody Valentine could feel the heat from her atrophied body. Ms. Dagobert shook like an epileptic body-popper on Angel Dust as the capsaicinoids burned through her.

The immolation of her insides was swift. Bile brewed up in her gullet and she vomited. The Nike sweat sock stopped any spew escaping from her mouth but some of it found safe passage through her nostrils. She retched and retched and retched as Mike fucked and fucked and fucked her with the dildo.

Ms. Dagobert found herself in a very unusual situation. She was choking to death whilst experiencing her very first orgasm. Her death rattle was accompanied by a groan of ecstasy and a shudder of satisfaction. Mike Bloody Valentine left the cock of caca in her cunt to melt as he ripped open a can of cola and returned to his desk to write the final chapter.

Mike sent out his novel, "Getting The Fear" to publishers. None of them had the decency to send him a rejection letter. Most of them simply sent it back unread, claiming that they don't accept unsolicited material. Mike Bloody Valentine wasn't perturbed. He was convinced he had written the Great American Novel and that someday this fact would become consensus reality.

After a while Mike got a job working for The City as a professional mourner. He was employed by the municipality to attend funerals of people who would have otherwise only had the undertakers attending their burials or cremations. Mike's role was simple: don a black suit and tie, turn up, cry, get the undertaker to sign his attendance chit and then go pick up his check downtown. It was easy money and a way to give a little back to society. Mike was constantly astonished by how many people were absolutely alone in their lives, but this made it easier for him to turn on the tears at the services.

On rereading his novel, Mike Bloody Valentine realized why publishers weren't responding. He had made a fundamental error. Whilst setting up the scenario whereby he kidnapped Ms. Dagobert, he hadn't paid dues to logic. Ms. Dagobert would have been reported missing from her employ in the Probation Department and the authorities would have been beating on Mike Bloody Valentine's door looking for her, as they would *all* her miscreant clients.

Mike was in a quandary though; no one from the authorities had actually checked on him to see if was indeed keeping Ms. Dagobert prisoner and feeding her a diet of cold cum. How were the readers of "Getting The Fear" supposed to suspend belief and buy into this faux pas by law enforcement?

He could have lied and wrote that the authorities did visit him; that he had hid Ms. Dagobert and they had dropped him from their enquiries into her disappearance. Mike didn't feel good about this though. He wanted his book to be truthful, anchored in experience, believable.

Mike accepted that his Great American Novel was never going to be published in its current state. He sat down and wrote a letter to The Author of The Secret Life Of The Novel:

'Dear Author, I'm writing to explain why I didn't keep pursuing the publication of my novel. My bad. I screwed up by not inventing an

episode where the authorities came looking for Ms. Dagobert, and that's clearly why no publisher wanted my shit. I eventually tossed Ms. Dagobert's body – or what was left of it – in a dumpster. It was found by the cops within a few days. She wasn't no popular bitch: no friends, family, homies. I got the call to attend her funeral and was paid to drop crocodile tears. It makes a cool postscript to the story I suppose. Yours Mike Bloody Valentine x"

Somewhere between conception and deliverance & had been corrupted. He was neither here nor there. Neither a beginning nor an end, a yes or a no. & heard the periodical taunting: "Yesterday, upon the stair, I met a & who wasn't there. & wasn't there again today I wish, I wish he'd go away … when I came home last night at three the & was waiting there for me. But when I looked around the hall I couldn't see him there at all! Go away, go away, don't you come back any more! Go away, go away, and please don't slam the door … last night I saw upon the stair a little & who wasn't there. He wasn't there again today. Oh, how I wish he'd go away …"

& heard a collision of e-mails echo through an overloaded synapse. He shuddered at the notion of hypertext: .btn.btn-primary.btn-lg[-disabled] {

```
    & + & + & {
        margin-left: 10px;
    }
}
```
To HTML and back!

The report was slid under the door on time to the nanosecond as per usual. & drank his dutiful dose of information: *In humans the ovule and the spermatozoon are both composed of 23 chromosomes. The Cabalists confirm that in the present times a letter is missing in the Torah. This letter of the alphabet does not appear at all in our 'eon' and is not used in the Torah. The primitive divine alphabet and the Torah would be based on a series of 23 letters, and not 22. One has become invisible for us and will reappear only during a new age of understanding. It is only because this letter is missing that we read in the Torah the positive and negative precepts. Each negative aspect is in relation with this missing letter of the primitive alphabet. The negative can be expelled once the missing letter is found.*

& screamed, "Why do they taunt and tease and mock me! They know I'm the 23rd letter! Bastards! They know I could unite humanity and bring an end to the war of the words. They know I am the connector, yet they treat me like an afterthought!"

& remembered that everything had been leading up to this moment and that no matter how much he willed it nothing could be changed. This was the deep present; a google of subterranean stories, abysmal horse latitudes, depths of despair, cellar less dungeons. His eyes focused on the ceiling. He had taken to sleeping in his spectacles to save time and was rewarded by beige Anaglypta wallpaper staring back at him. & felt a spurt of reassurance. Anaglypta lasts forever. It would never need re-papering or re-painting. It would never need any titification. He pondered on the genius who had invented the word Anaglypta; such a heroic word for something so commonplace. *If Anaglypta didn't exist someone would have to make it up.*

Edna – "What came first, language or consciousness?" – From Next Door had predicted that tonight would be the night where *every*thing and no*thing* would happen. Her predictions were always wrong though, yet she was gifted with immaculate hindsight and her forecasts of history were always spot on. In some sectors of the field she was venerated as a woman who knew her onions. In other sectors she was thought of as a superstitious slag on a par with Mother Shipton and Old Demdyke, who for a shekel or two would let you finger-bang them to your heart's content. & could never see the attraction of pleasuring a poltergeist. Poltergeist pornography may have been all the rage but it left a lot to be desired and & was coming to the conclusion that most of it was fake. He had latterly heard a bukkake video where eight men were wanking off over what they claimed was the ghost of the disembodied head of Jayne Mansfield, but it indubitably wasn't. The men were simply enjoying a circle jerk, their saucer like eyes greedily sucking in the sight of other mens pens being frantically pulled into paroxysm.

Edna From Next Door's prediction had been circulated freely around the reptilian zone of &'s brain. & was mortified to hear that such an area existed. He imagined atavistic playgrounds and antediluvian amusement arcades and colossal vegetarian monsters colonizing his cortex, leaving steaming mountains of high in fiber shit. & had always shrunk from the concept of flesh and bones and their susceptibility to easy corruption. Time had only to breeze by for them to start decaying. *Meat always genuflects in the presence of the abstract, the fucking pussy! We need a new meat! A meat that will stand up to the imperial powers of the chimerical!*

& tuned into the radio. Deftly mixed in amongst the classic hip-hop of the 90's was Robert Ogilvie Crombie rapping excerpts from *The Scottish Book Of The Dead*: "The plug has been lifted from the unguent jar. A perfume of hours. The past has been rolled into a scroll Aye shall not see again. The eye of the hawk is unblinking again. Open. Shut. Perfect. Aye rise like the sun above olive trees, like the moon above date palms. Where there is light, Aye shall be. Where there lies darkness, there is none of me. Aye rise like the moon above date palms. Aye am counted as one among stars. Beam of light, sun and moon. Shining beast, man and woman. Aye am passing through. Come outside among the people. Aye am light. Gaze on me. Moon in darkness, sun in morning. Light is what Aye will on earth, along the Firth, among the people. Aye have traveled through the tomb, dark and lonely ground. Aye am here now. Aye have come. Aye see. In the underworld, Aye embraced my father. Aye have burned away his darkness. Aye am his beloved. Aye have killed the snake. Aye have given him meat. Aye walk in my sleep through earth and heaven. Aye have set the sky in two parts. Aye pass through. Aye wander the horizons. Aye have dusted my feet with earth. Aye have worn the skin of a black panther and chanted into the ears of children. Aye eat with my mouth. Aye chew with my jaw. Aye am a living god come forth. Aye am with the earth millions of years."

Robert Ogilvie Crombie was stupendously fucking up the soliloquizing: making a right pigs ragged arse of it. He was substituting the colloquial "Aye" for "I" when in fact he should be using "Aye" to denote the word "Yes".

& felt a burp of empathy for Crombie. Crombie was obviously trying to be "clever", but "clever" was pointless nowanights. No one appreciated the flipping of the script. The incarnate with the ears to hear wanted solid recitals, not experimentation. & knew that Robert Ogilvie Crombie would have to suffer the slings and arrows; deaf by a thousand critical Tweets. His career On The Wireless would be over. Another superstar Broadcaster reduced to transmuting through the archaic and often dangerous medium of CB radio, where the highlight of the schedule is copping peeps at Doggers in bucolic locations and commentating on it through frothing cakeholes to tossing transmutants.

The dogstar was barking and & knew at some point he would have to get moving. He pictured the route. Walk northwest on Leyman St. / A1202 towards Templar St. Turn left onto Brahms & List Close. Turn right onto Antihistamines/A1210/A1211. Keep veering left on to Aldgate High Rise /A1211. After a 3rd of a mile stop for a breather. Suck in some exhaust fumes for 23 ft and skip along Jewry St. & tore up the image of a map and decided to ad-lib. He would wait for a gurney to arrive before he would feel moved.

He should be anywhere his heart desired by now, but *this* is what he was reduced to. Infirm and at the mercy of a dispassionate narrator: was this how *all* life began? If your life flashes before you at the moment of death, does it figure that your death flashes before you at the moment of birth? If you are stillborn are you *still* born? If you are …

The Narrator rudely butted in, "The French occultist, Eliphas Levi Strauss & Co, was born Alphonse-Louis Constant in Paris in 1810, adopting the name by which he is better known (a Judaized version of his forenames) in 1845. A career in the priesthood was short-lived, and Levi Strauss & Co left his seminary in 1836 after falling for a girl, Noémie Cadiot, whom he later married (though the marriage did not last). In 1841, Levi Strauss & Co was sentenced to eight months in prison for publishing a socialist tract called La Bible de la Liberté, and as time went on his interest in the occult deepened. Levi Strauss & Co claimed that in 1854, on visit to London, he summoned the spirit of Apollonius of Tyana, and in 1856 he published perhaps his greatest work, Dogme et Rituel de la Haute Magie (Dogma and Ritual of High Magic). In this he expounded the idea that all sacred writings and beliefs share at heart 'a doctrine which is everywhere the same and everywhere carefully concealed'. Rather than see this as an expression of the fundamental truth underlying all serious spiritual quests, Levi Strauss & Co unfortunately tended to imagine that there was a secret doctrine of magic at work universally throughout history, known only to adepts. His 1856 work also discussed the affinity between the 22 Major cards of the Tarot, the 22 letters of the Hebrew alphabet and the Kabbalah. Levi Strauss & Co is credited with being a large part of the inspiration behind the magical revival at the end of the nineteenth century, and his exposition of the Tarot-Kabbalah model, though he was not the first to suggest it, became the dominant model for the development of the Tarot, and an important pillar of western Kabbalah. The Kabbalah was one of Levi Strauss & Co's abiding interests, and he considered it more profound than all other philosophies put together, as exact as mathematics, and having the power to control unseen forces that acted through the 'astral light' surrounding all things."

& bit his lip and wondered, "Are they *really* the best genes money can buy? Are there *really* no alternatives? Why is the narrator trying to represent me as some kind of idiot? I would never indulge in such a cheap novelty by conflating denim drapers with magicians!"

The Narrator shrugged: *Some are born narrators, some learn to become narrators and some have narration thrust upon them.*
& yelped at the Anaglypta, "What did I ever do that was so terrible that I have ended up with a such a fucking conceited Narrator!"

& could sense the Narrator laughing at him, but instead of chuckles he heard only, "CuneiformSumerianAkkadianOldPersianElamite AlphabetProto-SinaiticPhoenicianAramaicHebrewSamaritan PahlaviAvestanNabataeanArabicPalmyreneSyriacMandaicOld HebrewSouthArabianThamudicUgariticArmenianGeorgian Hittite BybloslLuwianCarianLycianLydian!" over and over and over like an insidious playground rhyme ...

& stuck some fingers in his ears. He wondered about narrators in general; what did these second and third persons get out of the process? They were unpaid and usually unaccredited and their imaginations were cauterized by circumstance. The narrators couldn't operate in a vacuum. Some*thing* had to happen or they were redundant. Try as they might, narrators would never be *real* characters.

The Narrator caught wind of &'s thoughts and countered, "Unlike you *real* characters we have overcome ego and are satisfied with simply sharing information. What we 'get out of the process' is the pure joy of extending the life of The Word. We are the scions of the very first utterance."
& snorted, "Anyone can be a narrator. There's nothing special about being a narrator. I could do it in my sleep!"
"You could narrate your own dreams? You believe you could do that? *Really?*" chortled The Narrator, "You could subjectively navigate and narrate your dream state?"
"If I had to" shrugged &.

"Preposterous! The dream state is subjective and follows its own logic. I hate to burst your bubble but not only is it impossible, it is also ridiculous."

"Nothing is impossible in dreams." Protested &.

"Really? Have you ever experienced the illusion of death in a dream?

& thought about it, "Yes. Yes I have. I've been killed in dreams."

"I didn't ask if you'd been 'killed'. There's a big difference. Experiencing the ignus fatuus of death in dreams is impossible because the unconscious is immortal. Illusory death is alien to the unconscious. It is an abstract that is not only *not* recognized but it is sneered at." Laughed The Narrator, "And that's what you call a double negative."

"I don't know that I agree with you." Frowned &.

"It's not a matter of whether you agree with me or not. It's a fact."

& smirked, "Ah, but wait a minute. A fact is a thing that is known or proved to be true. You can't prove that nobody has ever experienced sham death in a dream."

The Narrator sighed, "Of course I can. I'm a narrator. I dwell in the unconscious and can categorically state that the unconscious does not recognize the disinformation of death. Now, I could hang around here all-night and engage in infinite regress, but I have stories to tell."

Before & could respond The Narrator had gone … but something lingered.

& could feel it in his water: Before This Night Is Out, You Readers Will Deny Me Three Score Years & Ten, But Will It Be In The First Person, The Second Person or The Third Person?

& future remembered Francis Bacon staggering out of The Colony in Soho one wet Thursday afternoon, pissed as a cunt spouting prophecy on the Mandela Effect, "Has't thee considered yond, as t is't impossible f'r mankind (including those with mod'rn technology) to wend backeth in timeth, 'r wend f'rward in timeth – so mankind and their machines cannot wend backeth and changeth these scriptures – as all men and distaff liveth in the 'now'. So, what is hath left? Only our heavenly fath'r can doth these things. If 't be true so, what is our heavenly fath'r telling those yond has't eyes to seeth, and ears to heareth? P'rhaps, our heavenly fath'r is revealing to us, how the wickedness in this w'rld is actually being hath carried out in our presenteth timeth; wh'reby those yond l'rd t ov'r mankind, doth so with deception and lies. P'rhaps, these changes art actually t'rrifying those yond has't putteth themselves ov'r us – as t may well beest our heavenly fath'r's holy declaration to these evil and naughty rul'rs, telling those folk yond their judgment shall followeth."

Nobody was paying attention to his futuristic Shakespearean rant though. The denizens of Soho were used to his outbursts. He vanished into a Bookmaker and spunked 30 quid on a horse with no name.

& supped Bovril on the terraces of a huge deserted stadium. *Buckling the spokes on the wheels of the bandwagon is always far more rewarding than jumping on it.* He wrapped his hands around the plastic cup that was useless at containing the hot brown liquid. He enjoyed Bovril not for its synthetic meaty taste but for its mystical name. Bov from Bovine and Vril from the pages of a novel. *The Coming Race is a novel by Edward Bulwer-Lytton, reprinted as Vril, the Power of the Coming Race. Among its readers have been those who have believed that its account of a superior subterranean master race and the energy-form called "Vril" is accurate, to the extent that some theosophists, notably Helena Blavatsky, Johan Cruyff, William Scott-Elliot, Justin Fashanu, Sue Lawley and Rudolf Steiner, accepted the book as being (at least in part) based on occult truth. A popular book, The Morning of the Magicians, suggested that a secret Vril Society existed in pre-Nazi Berlin. However, there is no historical evidence for the existence of such a society and unfortunately there never will be unless it is discovered.*

He wondered aloud to the Anaglypta: "Has there ever been another case of a popular beverage being partly named after an energy form that never existed in a novel?" The Anaglypta remained mute and lofty.

& climbed out of his bunk and undressed. Tonight he would go to work in his birthday suit. *In the all together.* Stark bollock naked. As nature intended. Atom and Eve had dressed for somebody's sins but not *his.* The sodomizing serpent be damned! Tonight he would venture into the bull market wearing nothing but his skin. He would even ditch the spectacles. Yes, tonight he would saunter into the factory letting it all hang out. His skin to the fore, his head held high and his extremities bald to the elements and judgmental stares.

& glided over to the mirror. Unfortunately The Narrator had pinned a degenerative photocopy over the reflection. The copying had rendered it unreadable.

& despaired and imagined what state he was in. No time to dwell. Movement. Tonight's node of transport would be the Omnibus. & sat amongst the usual suspects of toffee nosed Edwardian gentlemen, ill mannered cowboys, noisy extra's from Mack Sennett silent movies, starving children from Kampuchea, pneumatic part time prostitutes and matronly Lolly Pop ladies. The Iris Inspector ran his thingamajig over the eyeballs of the commuters. He sighed. They had all paid. Of course they had all paid. *It was night.* There would be no summery execution. The only aspect of his occupation that still excited him.

He locked eyes with & and they shared a high five of sympathy. The Iris Inspector had no idea that it was &'s birthday. The Iris Inspector would have had trouble comprehending a fifty year old being born, yet … *yet* at the rear of his mind he remembered he had forgotten something of the Nephilim being over ten feet tall at the time of delivery. It was said; he half remembered he had half forgotten, that the cheeky Mesopithecus midwives had to use tweezers the size of a cow to pull the Nephilim out of the twots of their mothers.

One of Mack Sennett's silent extra's chirped up apropos of everything, "Healing lies in suspension of disbelief … healing is disbelief … *lies* in suspension … *healing is lies.*"

& had heard it all before. It was the same old song. *Change the Akashic record f'fucksake!* Everything that has ever happened, *is* happening and *will* happen is recorded in the Akashic records. The Hit Parade obsessed commuters were prone to heterogeneous proclamations that made perfect sense, but they neither amused, bemused or premused & any longer. & sucked up a txt massage, "Freddy Nietzsche, Captain of Yorkshire County Cricket Club: "d madman jumped into their midst & pierced them with his eyes. "Whither is God?" he cried; "I wl tell u. We hv killed him – u & I. All of us r his murderers. But how did we do this? How could we drink up d sea? Who gave us d sponge 2-wipe away d entire horizon? wot were we doin wen we unchained this earth from its sun? Whither is it moving now? Whither r we moving? Away from all suns? r we not plunging continually? bwd, sideward, fwd, in all directions? Is there still ne up or down? r we not straying, as through an infinite nothing? Do we not feel d breath of empty space? Has it not bcum colder? Is not night continually closing in on us? Do we not ned 2 light lanterns in d morning? Do we hear nothing as yet of d noise of d gravediggers who r burying God? Do we smell nothing as yet of d divine decomposition? Gods, 2, decompose. God is dead. God remains dead. & we hv killed him."

& turned over and came over all queer. The Narrator had moon-lighted as a Translator and he was flouting soiled sheets of paper in &'s face.
The Narrator/Translator bragged, "I have been translating the Bible into Polari."
"Polari?"
"An archaic form of homosexual slang. The secret language of the shirtlifters. Listen: And *Gloria cackled* unto *Norah*, The end of all flesh is *troll* before me; for the earth is filled with *slapping* through

them; and, *varda*, I will *battyfang* them with the earth. Make thee a *bijou arkette* of gopher wood; *letties* shalt thou make in the *bijou arkette*, and shalt pitch it within and *nanti* with pitch. And this is the fashion which thou shalt make it of: The length of the *bijou arkette* shall be *trey chenter* cubits, the breadth of it *chinker dacha* cubits, and the height of it *trey dacha* cubits. A window shalt thou make to the *bijou arkette*, and in a cubit shalt thou finish it above; and the door of the *bijou arkette* shalt thou set in the side thereof; with lower, second, and third stories shalt thou make it. And, *varda*, I, even I, do bring a *dowry aqua* of *aquas* upon the earth, to *battyfang* all flesh, wherein is the breath of life, from under heaven; and every *fakement* that is in the earth shall *cark it*. But with thee will I establish my covenant; and thou shalt *troll* into the *bijou arkette*, thou, and thy *homie chavvies*, and thy *palone affair*, and thy *homie chavvies' palone affairs* with thee. And of every living *fakement* of all flesh, *dewey* of every sort shalt thou bring into the *bijou arkette*, to keep them alive with thee; they shall be *omee* and *palone*. Of fowls after their kind, and of cattle after their kind, of every creeping *fakement* of the earth after his kind, *dewey* of every sort shall *troll* unto thee, to keep them alive. And *lell* thou unto thee of all *manjarry* that is *jarried*, and thou shalt gather it to thee; and it shall be for *manjarry* for thee, and for them. Thus did *Norah*; according to all that *Gloria* commanded *her*, so did *she*."

Novel Headline 2. *They don't call it mindless distraction for nothing! Mindlessness speeds up time.*

The Omnibus was slowly starting to dissolve into a submarine. & concentrated on it still being an Omnibus. He noticed that a few other commuters were concentrating with him. Submarines are OK but they take too long to reach a destination, especially if there is no evident flood. At least it wasn't dissolving into a Sinclair C5.

A disembodied voice, "Can we all please concentrate on the current node of transport and resist a submarine materializing. The last thing we want is a submarine dissolving into a Sinclair C5."

& was now floating fully clothed in the warm Dead Sea. The sun beat on him. Magnetic spurts of vitamin D upping his energy levels. He hoped this would last. *Nothing ever lasts. How could it? By its very nature nothing has no sense of time!* The Omnibus was a necessary evil that he could do without. Sea travel, a different bag. There was no need for a rubber ring or armbands out here in the salt heavy liquid. Nothing could burst *this* bubble. This bubble had no floor, walls or ceilings, no width, depth or dimension. & only knew it was The Dead Sea from his gut. There were no signs, scrolls, symbols or statements but this was definitely the Dead Sea. Oh yes it was. His eyes opened and the saline drip, drip, dripped into his vein. His eyes slowly closed like dust crusted ancient curtains. He could hear the nurses:

Nurse Female: "The saddest story I ever heard was of a young dead father talking to his dead son."

Nurse Male: "How did you hear the story?"

Nurse Female: "Through my ears of course ... the dead son was now older than his dead father. Time is brutal. It gives no quarter."

The Nurse's laughter created ripples in the sea but & kept floating. *If I stay still they'll presume I'm pretending to be asleep and they'll leave me alone to float ... to float on. Aquarius.*

Richard Bloodworth I swam by and gurgled, "Keep your eyes open for the whale. He's a she and she's menstruating. A menstruating whale can be very unpredictable. Very unpredictable indeed."

& replied "I've never had any problems with whales."

"There's always a first time, son." Richard Bloodworth II wagged.

"Is it something I should be worried about?"

"Worry is subjective. I'm simply warning you about physical danger." Richard Bloodworth III said as he segued into a butterfly and swam away.

& continued to float. He wondered why more people didn't vacation in the Dead Sea. It had such a rich history. *Probably the name. It must put people off.* Maybe a "Costa" in front of it. *The Costa Del*

Dead Sea. That would work surely. Surely it would attract sun worshippers with such a name.

& surveyed the flatness. He was impressed. Holyday Makers would gain so much perspective from such flatness. Maybe if he survived he could become a travel agent for The Costa Del Dead Sea. Package Holy Days. If only he could rid the sea of its stench of disinfectant. Its sterile stink. Its anti-septic pong.

& strained his inner ear. The scuttle bug was muffled. Murmurs. Heart murmurs? Straining to hear through the heavy liquid balancing in his ear. What did the angel *really* say to Rene Descartes? Nurses would never believe that an angel founded science. The Egyptian Book of the Deaf was being read out loud but nobody could hear it. Drip, drip, drop. A mouse with a water infection pissing on soundproof cotton wool.

The Nurses chin wagged, "My hours are getting longer."
"How long are they now?"
"Nearly twice the length."
"Twelve hours?"
"Nearly. Nearly twelve hours. It's not on. It's a liberty."
"Yeah, it's nearly half a day. I hate it when hours get longer without so much as a word."
"So do I. *I* hate it … they just expect you to drop everything."
"I know … I detest dropping things."
"That's what I'm saying. Who do they think they are making hours longer?"
"They don't care. They don't give a shit."
"True … well … what can you do?"
"*What can you do?* You can do nothing. If they wanna make the hours longer they'll just go ahead and do it. It's pointless asking them to stop … futile."

& wished they would stop blabbering and they did. The last thing he wanted to hear was a chinwag about hours. They were rubbing saline into his wounds. Extracting the piss. Taking the urine. Candid Blanding popped up on a lilo. & smiled wide and deep. Candid Bland cocked a snoop at &.

& could still smell the meat on Candid Blanding. Candid Blanding had always smelt of meat. He was a deliverance driver for an abattoir. His truck used to stink up the street & & used to imagine him getting an erotic charge out of it. He pictured him pulling himself off watching people holding their noses as they walked past his parked up HGV. *Nothing like rotting warm bovine carcasses to get the juices flowing.*

"I am still Candid Blanding! I have lost none of my identity!"
"Good for you ... congratulations." Replied &.
"Why have you dragged me into this? I never did anything wrong to you!"
"I never said you did."
"Then why summon me? I was happy where I was." Candid Blanding hissed.

Candid Blanding's parents had given him an exotic Christian name because his surname was so bland. In his Mammy's womb Candid had stolen all her endorphins through a process known as syncytiotrophoblast. She became murderously depressed and he became a junky. A bouncing born narcotic thief. His milk had to be laced with morphine and his mashed up vegetables sprinkled with codeine. He had lived a life devoid of sharp edges, yet he still managed to fall foul of outside influence.

He procreated with a red headed whore called Cynthia and became cuckolded by his Brother in Love. He hissed at &, "Do you know how many times you smashed my windows with yer football?"
"I can't remember smashing your windows. I remember the ball landing in your garden but I can't remember your windows."

Candid started to cry. & knew this was about more than just smashed windows, "Do you want to talk about this Candid?"

Candid shook his head as big fat magnetic tears streamed down his face, "No. I've had enough of fraudulent slips. You'll never understand what went on behind those windows. I gathered up all the shards of glass and spent years grinding them down into a mound of sand."

"What for? What did you do with the sand, Candid?"

Candid held up an hourglass, "It's all in here. All my memories. All the memories I'll never get to share ... look at them! Just look at them slipping away, hour after hour."

Candid held up a neo-neon sign: "&and = S&and = &andy "
& shrugged. Perplexed.

"Think about it!" yelled Candid as he zoomed away.

A big sigh and & relaxed. Back on the Omnibus he looked out of the window. The dapper African slaves were clocking on to start putting the footings in for the pyramids. Behind them a gang of abseiling ruffians were desecrating the Grand Ol' Hoover Dam with graffiti. & squinted through rust tinted spectacles, zooming in on the inky ejaculations:

> *Botox don't repel the reaper!*
> *Houston we have a dichotomy!*
> *Life story based on fictional events!*
> *Beating rainbows with sledgehammers!*
> *No more miscarriages of mystery! Enough!*
> *Creators deny a creator invalidating their creativity!*
> *Thesaurus roamed, eating leaves from the Tree of Knowledge!*

The ruffians scuttled across the dam like ants on out of date cheesecloth. & watched them and imagined that one night he may even join them. He conjured up images of psychic graffiti and wondered in what style he might employ his aerosol can. He settled on Jacko Pollockian. Yes. The graffiti would be unreadable. It would only be deciphered by a pictorial guidebook that could *only* be purchased with beans procured from a man who hung around markets prey-ing on the gullible, or from a vending machine that accepted only phrases coined from pidgin Esperanto scholars off their tits on cough syrup.

& tried to remember what he would write if he were ever accorded the chance to join the gang. *Mmm ... something along the lines of ...*

One night during my early teenage years I was sat around a campfire with friends. We were on a camping trip. One of them suggested we tell 'ghost stories'. My friends reeled off urban myths and apocryphal tales of a gothic nature. By the time it came around to my turn all the well-known tales had been exhausted. Not wanting to be left out I made up a story of the uncanny. I told them that once upon a time I had been in a seaside town I had never visited before, but that I had led the way to the Guest House we were booked to stay in. I had led the way without knowing where the Guest House was situated. This was without prompting, directions or a map. I just knew where it was. My friends were unimpressed. They were hoping for something gruesome or suspenseful. I had delivered neither, just a strange little tale of coincidence.

When I returned home from the camping trip the next day I sat watch-ing TV with my Dad. A documentary came on about the town of Portsmouth. My Dad said, "Ah, Portsmouth. I went there once when I was in the Sea Cadets. A strange thing happened. I'd never been there before but when we got off of the bus I headed straight to the hotel we were staying in. The Cadet Master asked me how I knew where the hotel was but I couldn't explain. It was the weirdest feeling."

As his words came out I could feel the hairs on the back of neck bris-tle and Goosebumps spread across my body. This was the first time I had ever heard him say this. At the campfire the previous day I had somehow managed to "invent" an uncanny story that had actually happened to my Dad thirty years previously.

The Ominous Bus glided to a full stop outside the Liverpool School of Language, Music, Dream and Pun on Saint Sinner Mathew Street, San Francisco. A few commuters alighted but they were replaced by obnoxious Replicunts who had been on the piss, downing gallons of hot milk stout and willfully ignoring their loud stomach linings. One of them sat down next to & and then began to hover. The Replicunts had one rule to observe. They were never to say the taboo "c word" out loud. "Cunt", however, was perfectly acceptable.

The drunken Replicunt belched, hoping to impress & , "I am contemptuous of cunts who are comfortable in front of Kino cameras."
& ignored him verbally, "I have no wish to engage in conversation. To*night* is my birth*day*. I am trying to remain positive."
"Suit yerself!" spat The Replicunt, letting out a blistering fart and vanishing into thin malodorous air. & pinched his nose and wondered whether he would one night taste a sweet Marcel Proust endorsed *petites madeleine,* instantly transposing him back to the future past, or would his olfactory forever be whipped by rotten winds. & wasn't afforded too long to mull though. The Bingo Master boarded and a collective groan reverberated around the bus.

Everyone knew the score. There was no getting away from it. No hiding. Bingo had become compulsory by decree, especially on public transport. Some blamed the reds, some pointed fingers at the blues but *truth be spake,* the left wing on an owl of prey is in cahoots with the right wing.

The Bingo Master shimmied down the aisle, dressed ear hole to arsehole in black, toe to scrotum in white, embodiment of The State's current yin and yang inspired fashion sense. Black and white was now officially the new black. There were whispers that white was once upon a time set to replace black as the new black but the whispers were so faint nobody heard them.

& eyed the Bingo Master cautiously. Anyone who was in the employ of The State was to be eyed and eared and sniffed cautiously by those not in the employ of The State. State employees were the deliverers of news and news had now officially been decreed 'Bad'. More to the point it was now tailored to individuals.

Reportage of events had now been replaced by booming scato-illogical insults in the face of those who had been chosen to make the news, "You are lower than a crippled snake's cunt / Even your imaginary friend attempted suicide you boring bastard / You are a skidmark on the fabric of reality / You could send a glass eye to sleep you moribund bleeder / I wouldn't piss on you if you were on fire / I wouldn't let you piss on me if I were on fire / If you were drowning I wouldn't give you a glass of water / If you were starving I wouldn't shit in your mouth / If I were starving I wouldn't let you piss and shit on me / If you were pissing and shitting out of a crippled snake's cunt I wouldn't give you the time of day / I wouldn't piss in your boring glass eye / If your imaginary friend was choking on your piss and shit I wouldn't administer the Heimlich maneuver / If you left a bleeding skidmark on a starving bastard I wouldn't touch it with a bargepole / I'd shove a glass eye up your cunt with a boring bargepole / I wouldn't fuck you with all the tea in China / If the Chinese were starving I wouldn't attempt suicide with a bargepole / If I were shitting I wouldn't give you the time of day / If you were pissing and shitting I'd shove your cunt up a Chinese cripple and see how you like it / I wouldn't leave a skidmark on your boring glass eye for all the suicides in China / If your imaginary pissing and shitting was dying of drowning I'd throw it a brick / I wouldn't shit on your bargepole for all the cripples in the sea/ If a drowning bleeder was pissing in a cunt I wouldn't shit on an attempted suicide / I wouldn't touch your glass eye with a starving German / I wouldn't glass your piss with a starving cunt / If a Chinese snake called me a piss cunt I'd stick a bargepole up your arsehole with a skidmark ..."

Unfortunately for the victims and administrators alike, the insults were being written by sub-contracted hacks who had lost all passion for abuse. The diatribes had become lazy, which made them even more hurtful and damaging.

The Bingo Master got into his stride and found his swagger. He turned his ghetto blaster full volume. Peter Tosh's "Stepping Razor" vibrated about the bus. The Bingo Master bogled and tried to catch the eye of a victim, nobody wanted to play, let alone read out the numbers. Eyes down. Uncomfortable shuffling with ambition to attain invisibility. Just as The Bingo Master's grubby hand was about to land on &'s shoulder …

& was in the factory and Supervisor Beiber was hovering over him. Beiber's huge Afro hair do blocked out any unnatural twilight that might escape into the factory.

Beiber's thoughts yelled at &, "This is the first time tonight you've been late!"
& protested, "But I'm early Mr. Beiber."
"Define early!"
"*Define early?* Huh … impossible, Mr. Beiber."
"Impossible my hairy arse!"
& thought better of retorting.
Supervisor Mr. Beiber materialized a pencil and a ream of priceless papyrus, "Here. You will write a novel."
"A novel, Mr. Beiber?"
"Yes. A novel, Mr. Beiber Supervisor Justice, *Sir*! You will sit down and write a novel in penance for your tardiness."
Beiber Mr. Supervisor Sir handed & the scribing materials and melted into the factory.

& sat down and stared at the empty pages of papyrus. This was going to be a monotonous, *neigh*, monumental task. He could sense Mr. Beiber's eyes everywhere. It was rumored that Beiber not only had eyes in the back of his head but that he had eyes in the back of his third eye and that the eyes in the back of his third had eyes in the back of theirs.

& panicked. *Of what will I write? I am not a real writer! I once translated the Bhagavad Gita into cockney rhyming slang for a bet but that was aeons ago. This is serious shit. Beiber could sack me! I could be for the high jump! Fired on my birthday! Fuck!*

The more & thought about it the more he realized that he was just going to have to make this novel up. Imagination would have to be employed. He meditated on *imagination*. Did imagination have a tangible history? Is imagination important in the writing of a novel? Is novelty imagination? Are they the same thing? If they are the same thing why are they spelled differently? Are words spells? Am I digressing? *Should I italicize these thoughts?* Am I procrastinating? What came first: the spell or the word? Am I panicking? What came first: panic or pandemonium? If you are imagining imagination does one automatically snuff out the other? If language really is a virus can you catch a common cold from a crossword puzzle, or pneumonia from a poem, or even Herpes from a haiku? Could imagination be used as a mitigating defense in a mass murder trial? Are imaginative people more susceptible to psychic attack? Can one become a black belt in psychic self-defense? If in the beginning there was only The Word, who was around to make sure it was spelled correctly? Is Beiber staring at me?

He took a deep breath and began ...

Getting the Fear
Chapter One

The villa was located between *Santa Gertrudis* and *San Juan*, as remote as you can get on an island as small as Ibiza. There was nothing remarkable about the villa other than the comings and goings of the visitors. The neighbors were five miles away and a broken and dusty makeshift road was the only route that linked them. This was 1969 and Ibiza had yet to become a mainstream tourist destination.

It hadn't been explained to Jack Sherry exactly who had found the mutilated bodies. All he was told was that there were six of them and it was thought they were British citizens. The police on the island were desperate for someone to come and sort out the horrific mess. They were hoping Scotland Yard would be able to help.

For all Jack Sherry knew, these bodies could be Dutch or German or Scandinavian. All he had to go on was what he had heard from Captain Ernesto Torres on a weak, long distance line from Ibiza.

"We think that these people are Englishers, sir. Villagers in San Juan have spoken to us and said that they are Englishers."
Detective Inspector Sherry was cautious, "There are no forms of identification in the villa?"
"No, there is not, sir."
Jack Sherry sighed, "So there is only hearsay that the victims are English?"

" 'Hear ... say?' "

Jack Sherry sighed, "You don't know for certain that they are English, Captain Torres?"

Torres paused, "No, sir ... this I can not say for certain."

Jack Sherry walked along the corridor to Chief Inspector Barry Ketley's office and thought about the last nine months. 1969 was turning out to be 'one of them years' for Sherry. March threw up a couple of murders in South London that he had yet to get any leads on and May had seen him lose a conviction on Jonathon Rothman, whom Sherry was convinced had been responsible for three unsolved murder cases. In June there was the horrific mutilation and murder of a six year old schoolgirl from Kings Cross, that had not only haunted him but led him and his officers to nothing but dead ends. Recently his investigation of the murder of a married couple was thrown into chaos when the chief suspect seemed to simply vanish into thin air.

In all the eleven years he had worked on the murder squad, these murders in Spain were definitely turning out to be the strangest. Nothing was clicking, things were not falling into place, lucky breaks were not popping up like they used to. Jack Sherry was frustrated and having trouble motivating the officers around him.

Jack Sherry was switched on, smart and committed and he was as fit as a fiddle for a forty five year old. Lately though the black dog of depression had been sniffing around and Sherry instinctively knew it was because he wasn't getting results at work. He was now a divorcee and happy to be able to concentrate on the job he loved. He was now beginning to think that the job he loved didn't love him anymore though.

CI Barry Ketley was confused, "How do you pronounce it, Sherry? Is it 'Ibeeza' or 'Ibeefa' or 'Ibitza'?"

"I don't think it matters, sir."

"Audrey's always on at me about going to Spain on one of these package holidays everyone's raving about. I don't fancy it. I keep telling her, 'there's nothing the spics can offer me that Canvey Island can't.' She never listens to me anymore."

Jack watched CI Ketley scanning the notes. He liked Ketley; Ketley called a spade a spade and didn't care who heard him. Ketley was behind the times but his heart was in the right place and there wasn't a more honest man serving in The Met. For a man about to hit sixty he was still as sharp as a switchblade when it came to murder detection and his record was impeccable.

Ketley looked up at Jack, "I'm just wondering where we stand on the protocols of all this. You know, the international jurisdiction gubbins, the paperwork."

"Well, we don't know for sure that these are English bodies, sir."

Ketley nodded his head and rubbed his chin, "This Captain Toeres ... what is he? I mean, what's the structure over there?"

"I don't know, sir."

"Where are the bodies?"

"On ice in the island's morgue, a town called San Antonio."

"And how big's this island, Sherry?"

"Not very big, sir. About fifty, sixty square miles."

Ketley pushed the bridge of his spectacles up his nose and muttered, "Mmm ... what to do, what to do ... I'll make a few telephone calls and find out. The Home Office will be able to advise ... are you happy to go out there if we need to send someone, Sherry?"

"I've no objection, sir."

"You're not bothered about flying? Not frightened of it?"

Jack thought about it, "I don't know, sir ... I've never flown."

Ketley smiled at him, "I'll speak to you once I've spoken to the Home Office."

"Sir."

Jack sat at his desk, lit a Capstan Full Strength and thought about the call from Captain Torres. Six mutilated bodies in a remote Spanish villa. Jack thought about the slaughter of a pregnant Hollywood actress called Sharon Tate, her four friends and the son of her gardener only a few weeks earlier in Los Angeles, USA. The slaughter made headlines all over the world; horrific crime that had all the hallmarks of an attempted robbery gone wrong. Some people were claiming it was a weirdo Satanic sacrifice, but Jack didn't buy any of that. In his experience it was loot that had been the motivation; always monetary greed. He was convinced that even the slaying of the little girl from Kings Cross would eventually reveal some aspect of money making.

No, Jack Sherry wasn't going to be one of those dupes who bought into all this Satan worship rubbish. Of the seventeen murder cases he had worked on not one of them had been motivated by the pursuit of trying to curry favor with Old Nick. The murders he had worked on had been motivated by weakness, greed, sex, jealousy, hatred, delusion, compulsion, revenge … good old fashioned human characteristics.

Sherry was contemptuous of all this *hip* talk about Satan; it was just another fad in a decade that had been nothing but a revolving door of fads as far as he was concerned. He was pissed off that a few future murderers might try to use this satanic rubbish to justify their crimes. As far as Jack Sherry was concerned there was no heaven or hell or Satan or God. There was no pure evil and no pure goodness. There were simply human beings and some were fucked up and fucked people up, and some were fucked up and didn't fuck people up. Everybody was as capable of murder as much as they were capable of acts of kindness.

Jack needed to believe that even the murderer or murderers of the six year old from Kings Cross were human to a certain degree; needed to hold on to this thought so that when they were caught and made to account for their monstrous deeds they would feel mortal pain. He needed them to suffer for their crimes, needed them to really feel a terrible and crushing guilt. Needed them to suffer for the rest of their lives.

Yes, Jack Sherry was sick of the 1960's, especially 1969. He couldn't wait until the decade was over. All these gurus and psychoanalysts and shamen and Satanists and evangelists and pied pipers and liberated women and charlatans and poncing pop stars and poseurs and hippies and yippies and beatniks and radicals and druggies and peaceniks could go jump in the English channel for all he cared. They were living a lie. Love wasn't *all* you needed. You needed a steady job, a roof over your head and a strong police force to protect you from all the potential bad bastards in society and ....
....
...
....
...
....
...

& could smell The Narrator hovering.
The Narrator nodded his head and stroked his chin, "You want to ask something don't you?"
& sighed, "Are you an unreliable narrator?"
"It depends on how you're defining unreliable."
"In the classical sense. In the classical sense you're an unreliable narrator sense."

The Narrator grinned, pulled a microphone to his mouth and began a commentary, "And they're off! Humbert Humbert has made a strong start with Nick Carraway close behind, Huck Finn is keeping ground but Marlow is at the back of the pack, Holden Caulfield and Patrick Bateman are just ahead. Zeno Cosino and Forrest Gump are in the middle of the field and Verbal Kint has just passed Alex De Large. Both are ahead of Gulliver and Chief Bromden and Euchrid

Eucrow is coming from behind fast, passing Roy Strang and Xan Meo, and just look at Bras Cubas flying up the field! He has passed Tristram Shandy and is now passing Xanthias, and into the lead. They're coming to the finish line, what an incredible finish! It's neck and neck and …"

"Why do you mock me?" & asked.

"It's not *you* I am mocking."

& sniffed, "Really? You could have fooled *me*."

"Of course I could. I could fool anyone if I wished."

"Ah! So you don't deny it! You *are* an unreliable narrator!"

The Narrator smirked, "We are *all* unreliable narrators. Look at our tools. We all use the faulty software of letters. We communicate with *spells*! Each and every one of us is *sentenced* to become a magician imprisoned in the alphabet, trying desperately to free ourselves so that we can return to The Garden. "

& shook his head, "It is a poor craftsman who blames his tools."

The Narrator groaned, "Before The Fall was The Word. The Word became The Spell so that the lie could be spread. The Word became The World – a spell – as a result of the lie."

& frowned, "But … but there can only be a spell with a Word. The Word is in league with The Spell."

"No. Before The Fall there was no need for Spells. The Word was silent and perspicacious. It defined itself and spoke to the heart and mind through intuitive commune, a Glossolalia of the collective soul. The forked tongue appeared and the lie was born. The serpent stole The Word and turned it into a Spell. A Spell we have been under the yoke of ever since."

& spat, "You sound like an evangelist."

"And what's so wrong with being evangelical &?"

Before he could answer & was yanked back onto the Omnipresent Bus. The Bingo Master belched at him, "You are the chosen one for this trip."

& exclaimed, "But I would be terrible as a bingo caller! I have no experience!"

The Bingo Master wagged his fat finger, "You have no experience as a novelist but you are faking it to a certain degree of competence. Now, I will assist you. I will not abandon you. All you have to do is pull the numbers from the field and I will add the spice."

& frowned, "The spice?"

"The color. The patter. The gobbledygook that we Bingo Masters excel at. We add the puns and comedic components. The risqué insinuations, the end of the pier rapport. Now, get plucking those balls out of the air."

& grabbed a ball and handed it to The Bingo Master.

The Bingo Master bawled," Cup of tea. Number 3! One little flea … Number 22! Bishop Desmond, all the two's, calcium deficiency … Number 8! Two fat ladies shaving each other's pussies, the pearly gate, she's always late, Passover lamb chops … Number 30! Dirty gertie, Burlington Bertie, offensive sex register … Number 4! Shut that door, archaic revivalists kill colonel, Bob's dogs knob … Number 20! Getting plenty, two Oh blind twenty, haunted by genital warts … Number 9! Doctor's orders, number nine, number nine, number nine, in my broken car my wings are broken and so is my hair … Number 40! Blind 40, 40 dead fetuses in a beige plastic carrier bag for life begins at … Number 1! Kelly's eye, Jap's eye, in the beginning, particularly nasty urinary tract infection, first on board … Number 62! Tickety boo, turn on the screw, Grizzly Bear on suicide watch … Number 71! Hypnagogia's all the rage in Blackpool, bang on the drum … unlucky for some torture."

The hoarse cry of "HOUSE!"

The Bingo Master shook his head, "Impossible! There hasn't been enough numbers drawn for a full house yet. House my arse! Yer full o' shit! Yer trying to have my pants down!"

Mr. Justice Beiber clouted & about the head, "How's that novel coming on?"

& handed over the second chapter, Justice Beiber casually tossed it atop of a pile of imaginary yet yellowing manuscripts and plucked out one he was fond of.

Beiber smiled , "I can only hope it is up to the standard of this, &."

"What is it, Sir?"

"It is a masterpiece is what it is."

"Really."

"Oh yes! Listen. Once upon a time there was a young person of female gender, whose mother unfortunately had passed away at birth. The child's father felt very uncomfortable and overstrained with the new situation – especially with being a single-father and considering the hours he was volunteering at the LGBTI drop in centre – and thought that under such circumstances it would be better to get into a new non power biased relationship and to engage in a civil partnership again. His new wife and her two daughters were unfortunately deprived of their niceness, which was shown by the fact that they used to call the man's biological daughter the gender restrictive 'Cinderella'. Moreover they were well on the way to make Cinderella become their new cleaning-specialist. She received rather under attractive clothes, in which she was forced to do all of the unclean work in the house, while her stepsisters could let themselves go and enjoy the excellent new service. Cinderella felt disabled and offended by her new family. Discrimination didn't really fit into her visions of equality and humanity. One day a letter reached the house. It was an invitation to a big ball, where the prince intended to find the woman he wanted to marry. He invited all of the sexually inexperienced young women in his area. Cinderella's stepmother was quite excited about the letter. She already thought about the beautiful dresses her two daughters would wear, but it was clear that Cinderella wasn't permitted to go to the ball. Actually it was Cinderella's deepest desire to meet the prince once in her life, so she was very upset that her stepmother said that she had no appropriate dress for a ball and accordingly couldn't get there. The young woman was crying bitterly and looked for comfort at her mother's grave in the humanist crematorium. There she complained about her stepmother. Suddenly some birds flew along and conjured up a recycled dress out of a tree for her. First Cinderella thought that her problems would be solved now and that she could go to the ball secretly, but as she took a closer look at the dress, she was very indignant and disappointed. The dress looked as if it was made for a 'daughter of joy' with its plunging neckline. So Cinderella took it and tore it in to many little pieces. Not even the birds had a clue about what was appropriate for an emancipated and independent woman. But at least she knew what she had to do now. This experience made her realize that the world she lived in was full of sexists, and even magic was influenced by those stupid ideals. Cinderella took a decision and ran home again. In an unobserved moment she grabbed all of her clothes, wrote a short letter to her father and left the house. Forever. It was important for her to clarify that women had just the same rights as men. And that nobody had the right to think that she or he was superior or better than anyone else. She made her way to the capital, where she founded a public social aid institution for black lesbian turrets syndrome sufferers. And she lived happily ever after dedicating her life to marginalized sisters."

Justice Beiber wiped a tear from his sleeve and looked up at &, "Well?"

"Huh …"

"That's what you call a *real* story, &. This is the benchmark I am setting for your novel. Don't let me down."

Getting the Fear
Chapter Two

The room was large; oak panels, high ceiling, worn antique leather chairs, polished wood floorboards, original art and ornaments. You could almost smell the history and class in the room. It had an intoxicating effect.

Dr. Myron Geller eyed the four nervous young men and smiled at them. Dr. Geller could put anyone at ease with a simple charming smile. He had been using the smile for over seventy years and it had always worked for him. There was knowingness in the smile. A knowingness that seemed to indicate that everything would be all right, you were in safe hands with Dr. Geller.

He was wearing his tweed suit and a shirt with no necktie. He chained French cigarettes and took no more than a couple of drags on each one before stubbing them out in what looked like a genuine small skull crafted into an ashtray.

He addressed the young men in his clipped East European accent, "Good afternoon gentlemen ... I would like to welcome you to our humble institute. We hope you have had the chance to read our introductory pamphlet, but if not, that is OK ... in a nutshell as you say, the Trebistock Institute was formed in 1912 by a group of likeminded men and women, intellectuals if you like, who were committed to the research of social cohesion in a rapidly changing world. The Trebistock Institute is an independent not-for-profit organization which seeks to combine research in the social sciences with professional practice …"

Dr. Geller gave the spiel and dropped a few lame jokes and asides into the pitch to spice it up. This was the 1960's after all; you had to make everything sound casual and freewheeling if you wanted to get the attention of the "young folk".

He had done the pitch hundreds of times and knew it off by heart. He was selling the institute as a benign social research centre that gathered great and quizzical minds to try solve the ills of society together.

"We are primarily interested in studying the inter-action of individuals and how they function within a given set of social norms …"

Dr. Geller paced along a wall that from floor to ceiling housed thousands of leather bound books, "Here at the institute we provide grants and bursaries for scholars to study the effect that societal structures have on people from all walks of life and backgrounds."

Dr. Geller pitched pacifism and a marriage of psychotherapy and social cooperation as the fundamental tools that the institute used in trying to combat the problems of modern society. The institute, he said, was secular in every respect. Religion, politics, race, gender and sexual orientation held no influence or sway within the institute.

"We are passionately committed to studying the causes of conflict and violence, and our ultimate aim is to further the ideal of inclusion … think of the Trebistock Institute as a chess club, gentlemen. We play metaphorical chess here, but the chess board we play on is the size of the world … we learn together as we try to figure out moves to make the game less competitive for *anyone* – regardless of their background, means, skills and intellect – to play … look at it as a kind of 'leveling of the playing field' if you like."

Dr. Geller killed another half smoked cigarette and lit another one, "We are living in very turbulent times, gentlemen. One has only to look at the events of this decade to see that. The assassinations of the Kennedy brothers, Martin Luther King and Malcolm X. The Berlin Wall going up, the Vietnam war, Mao's cultural revolution in China, the Black Panther party, the draft resistance in America, the six day war in the Middle East, the Civil Rights Movement. This year the Americans are going to put a man on the moon … people will look back on this decade as a defining period of change, gentlemen. We are blessed to be living in such exciting times."

All the four young men seemed impressed with the pitch. They all signed on to visit the institute again for an induction seminar. It wasn't costing them anything and there was also the promise of fine wine, food and the chance to meet other young people who fancied themselves as aspiring intellectuals.

Twenty five year old Candice Crowther was Dr. Geller's assistant. The stunningly beautiful Candice didn't just look up to him as father figure, no; Dr. Geller was a godlike figure to her.

Brunette, svelte and tall, it wouldn't have been a stretch to imagine Candice as a Mary Quant model or hanging off the arm of one of the Rolling Stones or The Beatles.

Candice was ethereal and exotic looking and had a magnetic energy that pulled creatures of every kind towards her. Men and many 'straight' women found her irresistible. She oozed pure sex appeal; a real head turner, traffic stopper, wolf whistle subject, and boy didn't she know it. When she peacock strutted into the West End she knew the effect she had on pedestrians and she got a big kick out of it.

Candice Crowther was Dr. Geller's secret weapon. She went out fishing on the streets of London and caught the brightest young minds for him to deliver his spiel to. Some became regular visitors and participants in the work of the institute, many never showed up again when they realized that Candice wasn't on the menu. Candice was the perfect bait to lure them in. Not only beautiful, she possessed a razor sharp intelligence as well.

Genuinely blind to and uninterested in her physical beauty, Dr. Geller was proud that Candice had become a great student and was now formulating exciting social science ideas on her own.

The Trebistock Institute was Candice's life. She lived in the large four-storey townhouse on Goodge Street and earned her food and lodgings working solely to promote the ideas of the organization.

To all intents and purposes she had come to Dr. Geller on a referral after she was diagnosed with suffering from Trauma Induced Amnesia. TIA was one of Dr. Geller's areas and he had worked intensively with her to help her overcome the condition. Candice had absolutely no recollection of her childhood. Dr. Geller claimed it was his mission to help her retrieve the memories and confront them, no matter how violent or disturbing those memories may turn out to be.

Not much was known about Candice in the institute, other than the fact she was one of Dr. Geller's *star* patients/pupils. Dr. Geller discouraged idle chat and gossip from his disciples, *especially* where Candice was concerned. If you wanted to progress in the institute, the last thing you did was question the eminent Dr. Geller, and you *never* talked about his relationship with Candice.

When the four young men had left, Dr. Geller called Candice into the room.
"Candice, dear. I have been thinking … the kind of people that you bring here …"
Candice frowned, hoping she hadn't upset him, "What is it Myron?"
"I have been thinking … they are all usually of a certain 'kind'."

"A certain 'kind'?"

"These are very earnest young men, Candice. Idealistic, educated, conscientious ... but ..."

"Yes, Myron?"

He searched for the right words, "Well, I have been thinking that it would be interesting if we could find some people who are more ... I suppose the word I am looking for is colorful ... I read a very interesting piece about the young working class men in Bermondsey, and how many of them gravitate towards organized crime."

"Right. South London gangsters, Myron? Yes. I've heard all the talk."

"A subject that has interested me for quite some time, Candice."

"So you'd like to meet some of them?"

"It would be fascinating if we could maybe study some of these young men. A colleague of mine, Dr. Valdez, has been carrying out a study of street gang members in New York. It really is a truly eye opening study. I think there would be a lot we could learn from these young men in London."

Dr. Geller's wish was Candice Crowther's command, and she knew just the man who would fit the bill ....

...

...

......

& felt an overwhelming urge to drink. His lips smacked themselves automatically. It would need to be Bourbon and Coca Cola with icebergs. Only B&CC with Icebergs and only *that* could quench the raging thirst. He pictured himself floating out of the bed. He had never felt so alone. The (wo)man in the next bed didn't care. (S) he was awaiting His Hers eighth gender re-alignment surgery; The Woe man had gone from man to woman back to man to woman back to man X 2.

& thought about the holy trinity; B&CC with Icebergs, Amber Leaf tobacco and salted peanuts. Nothing could compare to the experience: slurp, drag, munch. *We've got spinning heads on sticks.* & shuddered. By his calculations he only had three scare years and ten to remain dead. He would kill time with his favorite tipple, smokes and snack. All he needed to do now was circumnavigate these excrement-plastered walls and get back home. *I am being kept here against their will. They don't really want me here. I'm a pain in their collective arses! A corruption on their collective coccyx. I'm the fly in their ointment. The jelly in their petroleum. The shit in their sugar. I could drink a horse between two pissy mattresses. God I'm thirsty! Jumped in the liffy & what did I see? Black & tan eyed angels swimming with me. The 'dead' condition of the soul when immersed in the body. Splish splash. Candid Blanding was happy on cloud cuckold land.*

The radio spat out requests like old maidens spitting bees that had just stung their tongues and blocked their airwaves with the resultant swelling. Soiled transistors. Solid state of the art auditory wallpaper. & felt a hand. A hand felt &. There was a tugging. A tugging off. Tug off the DJ. The noise from the wireless nailed & to the bed. He struggled to wake. He summoned every inch of energy he could but there was no waking. *If sleep is the cousin of death how would you describe sleep paralysis in two words or less? Voices! Is it visitation time already? Where don't the hours go to die? Do the Swiss practice euthanasia on their clocks? If a clock falls in a forest can you hear one hand clapping the performance of Madame Butterfly in Beijing, baby?*

It was indeed visitation time and & felt a huge lump of sentiment festering in his throat. It was *that* time of night again when the ghosts would swagger in bearing flowers they had nicked from accident black spots and Lucozade and balloons and novels and rust, incest and mirth. *We free kings come bearing gifts for the new born dead. We followed a drone in the sky to reach you.* & panicked. On another level Sir Justice Beiber Supervisor Sir would be wondering where the fuck the promised novel was. Would it be shaping up? Would it hold the readers attention? Would it be worth a wank? Would it be worth the papyrus it wasn't yet written on? What was it about? What did it mean?

&'s arsehole was twitching; inhaling and exhaling bleached air with no musical accompaniment. Clipped voices in half hearted accents over Burundi drumming spurted from the hot wireless valves: "The desideratum of the philosophy 'better to have never been' is parents being charged with manslaughter for bringing children into the world knowing full well that they will eventually die". "Simplicity takes time, patience & practice. Complexity offers too many excuses for failure". "The obsession with the afterlife is born of a panic at not having memories of a before-life". "The atheist suicide bomber is unfaithfully committed to his mission". "The fictitious kleptomaniac's only crime was stealing imaginations". "The Devil fights from behind barricades of linguistic complexity, but the war of words will be won by those armed only with simplistic truths". "The generation that bought the most shoes and crippled the moral footing". "Can the perpetrator of a 'senseless' crime use transcendence as a defense?"

Candid Blanding The Candid man can. The uxorious Candid Man. & searched for dates. He wondered if he could remember Candid Blanding's born day. Was Candid Blanding born here? There must be some evidence. Clues at the very least. Time stamps preserved with eggs in formaldehyde perhaps. Some graffiti. *Candid woz ere!*

Again with the disinfectant. Again with the alcoholic hand wash. Again with the fucking bleach! Again with the fresh lilies! This deliverance ward has death crawling all over it! & felt rancid. When were they going to slap his arse and wash off the blood and ectoplasmic afterbirth? The path of least resistance is littered with the corpses of the bored to death.

& felt an encroaching CB radio broadcast; the voice faint, middle aged male, working class, Northern English, crackly and reminiscent of Word War Two radio transmissions, "The legend goes as follows … Hiram Abiff, "a widow's son" from Tyre, skilful in the working of all kinds of metals, was employed to help build King Solomon's Temple. One day, whilst worshipping the Grand Architect of the Universe within the Holy of Holies, Hiram was attacked by three hooligans – called 'Jubela', 'Jubelo' & 'Jubelum' and known collectively as 'The Juwes' – who demanded the "Master's word", that is, the secret name of God. The first hooligan, named Jubela, struck Hiram across the throat with a 23-inch gauge. The second hooligan, named Jubelo, struck Hiram's breast, over the heart, with a square. The third ruffian, named Jubelum, struck Hiram upon the forehead with a gavel, whereupon Hiram fell dead. His blood, therefore, was shed within the temple. Hiram, having been killed, was carried out the East gate of the Temple and buried outside Jerusalem on Mount Moriah. Early the following morning, King Solomon visited the temple and found the workmen in confusion because no plans had been made for the day's work. Fearing evil had befallen Hiram, King Solomon sent out twelve Fellowcraft Masons to look for Hiram. King Solomon himself accompanied the three who journeyed towards the East. Having finally located the grave of Hiram, Solomon and his fellow Masons exhumed the body. A search was made for the Master's word – the Name of God – but all that was found was the letter "G". Finding the word lost, a lament went up: "O Lord, my God, is there no help for the widow's son?" They first took hold of Hiram's body with the 'Boaz' grip of the first degree. This failed to achieve its purpose. They then re-positioned their hold upon Hiram's body using the 'Jachin' grip of the second degree. This also failed to accomplish its purpose. Solomon finally raised Hiram from the dead by using the third degree grip of the Master Mason, the five points of fellowship (explained shortly), and by uttering in Hiram's ear the phrase 'Ma-Ha-Bone'. Solomon is left to continue building the Temple. Many decisions have to be made. Solomon first selects seven expert masons to guard the Temple, before holding a requiem for the departed Hiram Abiff. Solomon then appoints seven judges to hand out justice to the workmen building the Temple. Five superintendents are installed to oversee the continuing building of the Temple. Solomon then focuses upon apprehending the assassins of Hiram Abiff. He appoints nine Masters, who begin the search for the assassins. The first assassin is discovered asleep. He is stabbed in the heart and head, and then decapitated. Solomon hears a report that the other two assassins have fled to Gath, the birthplace of Goliath. Solomon selects fifteen Masters, including the original nine, who apprehend them. They are placed in prison, and then executed. Solomon rewards twelve of the Masters by making them Governors over the twelve tribes of Israel. Solomon finally appoints a builder by the name of Adoniram as the sole successor to Hiram Abiff. Adoniram becomes chief architect of the Temple, which is finally completed. The legend doesn't stop here though. Solomon begins to build a Temple of Justice upon the site of a Temple build by Enoch, who placed within the Temple a stone bearing the 'real' name of God ... the 'real' name of God is ... Buzz Crackle Hiss."

& already knew the real name of God so the interference didn't bother him. & knew everything there was, is and will be to know. Not that this empowered him. He ignored 99% of the information he had access to. He chose *not* to be in all places at all times out of nonobservance towards The Doctors observing him. If they wanted epiphanies they would have to wait until & wanted epiphanies. The more they vibrationally steered him the more he would bring his mortal faculties into play to scupper their directions. If ever feeling mischievous & would light the torch paper and ask "why?"

The Doctors hated & asking "why?" They hated its tergiversation of the realm of the choate consciousness they were mining; they hated "Why's" transplacement mystery and the no doubt impermeable answer & would get. They hated that they had built successful sci-entific careers from asking "why?" and even after breaking through to the other side they were still no closer in asking it over there. All they had was a & – ampersand – who wasn't prepared to ask the ultimate ? – question – and probably never would be, and even if & ever became prepared to ask he wouldn't understand the answer. These mortal 'Gods' thought only they would be able to understand the answer given by the immortal God, Gods or Goddesses.

& was obviously aware that he was the most expensive and important experiment in His Story of the word. He was a secret shared by a couple of hundred temporal beings whose bloodlines, wealth, power and prestige had given them creator complexes. Whilst billions of their fellow beings starved and died in usury countenancing wars on planet earth *they* indulged in trying to find a Creator so that they could topple him, it, or her and replace with a God of their choosing. Heavenly regime change, for want of a better description.

Doctor A had opened not only a Pandora's Box when she decided to try turn flesh into word, she had also opened the floodgates for materialistic maniacs to dream up attempts at colonizing the sacred sphere and commercializing it. The Doctors knew it would be insurmountable but kept schtum to keep the funding coming in. If The Doctors couldn't fully control &, they sure as Hell wouldn't be able to control an invading force of rapacious entrepreneurs.

No, The Doctors knew that the transmogrification of & was a one off. Unyielding intuition told all of them that whoever rules the roost of pure consciousness was only ever going to let them commit an *original* sin; each Doctor unable to articulate a sense of shame so powerful it rendered them babbling wrecks whenever they tried.

Out of the thirty-six strong team at the start of the endeavor 13 had killed themselves. All were warned that they were entering into a possibly mind-blowing undertaking, and that's exactly what it became for the less mentally flexible. They all died violently by their own hands with religious and quasi religious overtones. The Doctors who remained were mostly now experiencing some form of addiction, and or going through relationship breakdowns, being treated for psychiatric illness, questioning everything about their lives or becoming so obsessed with observing & they had turned into automatons.

Doctor A still had her shit together. She was now semi secretly lauded as the greatest scientist of all recorded time. & would vehemently disagree of course, but to the backers of the project and her colleagues she was the bees knees. She had clocked in over 46,000 solid hours observation of &, and with every viewing she felt a step closer to figuring what the fuck *it* was all about. If Doctor A had learned anything though, it was that the world – and everything that *word* encompasses – is syntactical.

Her sleeping states were *spell*bound by words; spoken words that described images. Not images that replaced words and made sense but antipodal; a voice delineating unimaginable simulacrums that were only possible to understand through words. In dreams it felt as though she was born blind and the only way she could grasp anything was through information from the mind of another human being. She didn't see, no, she comprehended, but the images she comprehended were made of words transmitted through language, so fundamentally – the Magistrate Logician in her mind decided – they were not images at all.

Night after night, nap after nap; the hominal voice explained wondrous invisible images as she faced a Levantine, slate grey, void.

She consulted her psychiatrist, Dr. Foster, on a daily basis, "What use are these beautiful images if I can't see them?"
"But you feel them." Dr. Foster reminded her.
"I know, but it's not the same. They're not tangible. I need tangibility."
Dr. Foster frowned, "You want tangible dream images?"
"Yes!"
"But ... but that's not possible."

Doctor A knew it was possible but she couldn't tell Dr. Foster how she knew; she couldn't tell him that she was in charge of an experiment that had made the flesh word – albeit an ampersand – and that the & was omniscient and gathering information that was being collected by her and her fellow conspirators. She couldn't tell him that the 'Big Bang' was in fact a word spoken by a creator of some kind, and that *everything* is a vibration of that word. Dr. Foster would have laughed her out of the room.

Novel Headline 3. *Faking your death is illegal; yet faking your life is celebrated*

& steeled himself. Blink blink blink, back on the old Omnivorous Bus again. He knew he'd be sucked dry. Everyone wanted a piece of him. Suck suck suck. Vacationing vampires filling their boots with the symptomatic memories of strangers. *Cheap holy days in other people's reverie.*

Sir Justice Beiber was sat on his lap, leering at him, "Well?"
"Well what Sir?" asked &.
"Where's the novel?"
"Oh … huh …"
"Excuses, excuses &. There's a deadline you know?"
"Is there. There really is a deadline? I always assumed it was a myth?"
"No, yes, there is a deadline &. It exists and you're already closing in on it. Born day or no born day, you owe me a novelty. I need a creation from you."
"But …"
"*But fuck!*" shouted Sir Beiber Sir, "Do you know the poet Larkin?"
"No, Sir."
"He came up with the theory of relativity. *Parents fuck you up.* Do I look like a parent to you &?"
"No, no … not at all."
"Well I'm not. I'm an accident just like you. I never knew them, but

the last thing I want in my timeline right now is to find the sperm and egg donor's that created me. Bollocks to the *Big Bang* and to Hell with the theory of *relativity*, I've enough on my plate to worry about two sex satellites that coincidentally crashed into each other fifty five years ago. They met, they fucked, they had me and then they didn't. Simple. Life goes on, ad infinitum. The only truly magical things about conception are the myriad of decisions that our 'Fuck Parents' made to find themselves in the position of being able to create another human being, that and the devilishly beautiful coincidences that often make us wonder if there really is someone 'up there' looking out for us. Look, listen to me. You and me being here right now could have been the seemingly trivial outcome of a late night bus being later than usual or the particular smell of a cheap perfume, a faulty traffic light, a wrong number, a car crash, too much salt on someone's fish and chips, a windy day, a school register, we could be right here now because some pillock left the cake out in the rain and Jimmy Webb wrote a song about it, or because some bright spark wanted to prove his strength by trying to get the lid off a jam jar and ended up cutting his hand to ribbons. Me and you being here right now could have been the result of a wasp choosing to sting someone wearing a red sweater instead of a blue one, someone sneezing, a dog chasing a cat up a tree, a fire escape being blocked, two fat ladies playing bingo. In fact, any scenario you dare to imagine … are you with me &?"

"I think so."

"Good. Now get writing."

& folded & faded back into bed. He could feel a Nurse nearby. She was laughing and lactating; warm jets of sour milk drenched his face. He greedily lapped at the liquid, contorting his mouth, poking his tongue out, sucking the air for stray drops of the Titty jaculate. The Nurse throatily moaned, *"Do You Like My Titty Jugs? My* Vacant Jug Rug? *My* Scant Vulgar Jug? *My* Vast Narc Jug Lug? *My* Jug Cravat Lung? *My* Cravat Jug Slung? *My* Vast Car Jug Lung? *My* Curt Gals Van Jug? *My* Curt Slag Van Jug? *My* Vast Curl Jug Nag? *Oooh … Do My* Curl Jugs Van Tags *Make You Wet?"*

He could smell The Nurse frigging her twot silly and he knew there was an anagram to be had. *If only he could muster up the energy to open his eyeholes.*

The Nurse squealed in ecstasy, "Look at me de dis frug mun! Look at me de dis fun grum! Look at me de dis fung rum! Look at me de dis fur mung! Look at me de dis grum fun! Look at me de dis mun frug! Can you hear me squelch de dis mung fur? All eyes on my cunt de dis rum fung!
Viddy this frothing vula de drug fin mus! O look at me de drug fin sum!"

& felt himself being schlepped from the sweat and sour milk and cunt juice soaked sheets. He was on a gurney being pulled at lightning speed through blazing corridors. He cast a fishing line to catch his breath but reeled in only a moldy *Readers Wives* magazine from the 1970's. It had obviously been used and abused and abandoned and left to mature in the elements. It smelt of sadness and cold grass and white dog shit and the fantasies of cuckolded husbands and future-past Kim Kodakians and amateur hysterectomies and hysterical recriminations and smudged mascara and black eyes and fisticuffs and lumps of hair being pulled from ill fitting wigs and Avon Ladies fumigating the offending sheets and *Old Spice* and *Brylcreem* and pop and crisps and *Woodbines* and *Fray Bentos* tinned pies and Babysitters and their boyfriends and cider and Rubber Johnny's and looming fate and booming hate and hair lacquer and Indian ink and false eyelashes and soiled knickers and Black & White television broadcasts and gas and electric meters and snogging and love bites and stale ale and pale ale and *Double Diamond* and indoctrination and sex education and cheap cigars and …"
And The Nurse said to &, "There'll be time for a cigar once we've got this bastard out of you."
"But I'm not pregnant!" protested &.

&'s feet were in stirrups and a Gynecosmologist was shining a torch up his black hole.

& screamed, "It's impossible! I haven't been impregnated. I'm not up the duff. I always made them wear a Rubber Johnny! You're ripping me in two!"

The Gynecosmologist stroked his considerable chin, "Just as I thought. I call bullshit on the *Big Bang*. What do these Doctors take us for? They expect us to believe that the universe simply appeared from nothingness for no reason! Why, how is that any different from expecting us to believe in a creation myth with a God behind it all? It's a load of old codswallop! *All* of it! I hereby deny science and God and natural selection and declare that the universe is pure information represented by symbolism and that we are all merely the stuff of language."
& whimpered, "Have … have you finished exploring my black hole now?"

& caught up with himself in a huge featureless room. He was naked, shivering and uncomfortably sat on an icy wooden chair in the center of the space. Before him appeared a panel of faces all wrapped in soiled bandages.

Face One enquired, "How do you feel after your labor?"
& frowned, "My labor? I … I was never *really* pregnant. It was a phantom parturiency brought about by too much introspection. Too much navel gazing and not enough star gazing."
Face Two quipped, "I believe it was Nietzsche who said that if you stare too long into your Belly Button, your Belly Button stares back at you."
Face One corrected, "I believe that was the abyss."
Face Three questioned, "The abyss said it?"
Face Two dissolved, "the id wants whatever feels good at the time, with no consideration for the reality of the situation. Thus we have the word *id*iot."
& pleaded, "This is all well and bad but I've got work to do. I'm working and I'm already late. I can't hang around here all night. My

boss is expecting a creation. He's expecting a novelty. I can't waste my time on make-believe maternity wards. Have you finished with me? I need to get back on the Omnisapient Bus."

A wind blew & into a long since demolished and redeveloped 1970 schoolyard. Families in new builds were now habituating what was once a coliseum of unbridled imagination and scraped knees and bruises and boundless energy and palpable fear and giddy victimization. One Hundred five year olds thrown together by State mandate and randomly split into three classes with the only requisite being to mix up the sexes as much as possible and confuse them even more.

& took a whiff on the terror. He was there amongst them again. Amongst these other undeveloped aliens thrown into the machine against their will, left to fend for themselves and navigate the complexities of 'The pecking order'. & felt snotty fingers invading every orifice, the din – that 5 year olds make involuntarily as they are released into the fresh air – beating heavy on his eardrums. He was there again, in the thick of it with the 'infants'. A black and white television engineer was tampering with the horizontal hold. COMPANION BILLS AMENDMENT is a 23-letter phrase starting with C and ending with T. Static, white noise, John Yogi Baird holding a séance, vehemently denying he's a clairvoyant. Virulent commercials with catchy tunes ensnare infants and infect playgrounds. Advertisements become the currency. A loop of temptation, Blitzkrieg blandishment: cereal, toys, tinned foods, pop, novelty, sweets, toothpaste, novelty, film trailers … *your store bought rap ain't shit.*

Take the I-aye-eye out of the game: *Your words are not your words. They are the sons and daughters of The Word's longng for tself. Words come through you but not from you, and though they are wth you, they belong not to you. You may gve them your voce but not your thoughts, for words have ther own thoughts. You may house ther bodes but not ther souls, for ther souls dwell n the house of alphabet, whch you cannot vst, not even n your dreams. You may strve to be lke them, but seek not to make them lke you. For lfe goes not backward nor tarres wth yesterday, but stands stll n the past future, the present future and the future future. You are the bows from whch your words as lvng arrows are sent forth. The archer sees the mark upon the path of the nfnte …*

A breathtaking wave crashes on to the asphalt and drowns the infants, washing away hopscotch pentagrams and nylon goalposts and performances of doctors and nurses. Michael Parkinson plucks & out of the deluge and plonks him in a faux leather chair in a TV studio. The audience claps like seals on amphetamine sulphate at the pompous perdu presentation.

MP: "You started life as a comma. When did you realize you wanted to become a novel?"

&: "Huh … quite early on, Michael. The comma was never going to contain my ambition."

MP: "And like a lot of working class comma's you dreamt of breaking free and traveling the page?"

&: "Yeah … the blank page was enticing."

MP: "I read somewhere that your early years were spent as a common comma on Hitler's gas bill."

&: "It's true, but from there I kind of graduated to a comma on a handwritten letter."

MP: "Really? I never knew that."

&: "Oh yes. It was a letter from a semi-illiterate Liverpudlian stevedore to a childhood sweetheart who had found herself on Death Row Records."

MP: "Fascinating."

&: "Yes … I was on the letter for a good few years until it was burnt. From there I got a gig as a full stop but it was depressing. I couldn't see a future."

MP: "But then, of course, you became an ampersand. That must have been an exciting time?"

&: "I won't lie to you, Michael. Becoming an ampersand was the most wonderful feeling imaginable. I had finally become a connector."

Getting the Fear
Chapter Three

Charlie Coleman's profession was violence and he had been a practitioner since he was fifteen. Borstal didn't deter him from his professional ambitions and neither did two stretches in Wormwood Scrubs when he was in his early twenties. Charlie was nearing thirty in 1969 though, and niggling doubts had started surfacing about his chosen profession.

He was born a war baby in Battersea, South London; to a respectable working class couple that steered well clear of trouble. His Father had never had a fight in his life and his Mother avoided even the slightest confrontation with *anyone*. They worked in factories and Charlie was decently provided for. By his early teens they were beginning to wonder where Charlie had come from though His two older brothers and two younger sisters were nothing like him. He was the odd one out. His parents despaired of Charlie and had virtually given up on him by the time he was fourteen.

Young Charlie Coleman was handsome, athletically built, vain and quick witted. He also had a terrible temper and a yearning to get out of Battersea at any opportunity. All he ever wanted to do was hit the West End and lose himself in all the glamour and excitement.

He couldn't fight with his fists, but what he lacked in the dexterity department he more than made up for with fearlessness, sheer aggression and a willingness to use anything that came to hand as a weapon.

Charlie's first collar at fifteen was for wounding an older boy with a lump hammer. The older boy owed Charlie a few pence and the judge remarked that God knows what Charlie would have attacked him with if the debt had been a few pounds.

Charlie thrived in his year of Borstal. He got even fitter and made friends with many teenagers who were of family to London's criminal class. He came out of Borstal with a cocksure strut, plenty of contacts and a determination to start earning some *good money*.

Easy street was a couple of years off and he had to work his way up from Dead End street to begin with; factory work just wasn't for Charlie though. He hated the hours, the bosses, the rules and regulations, but most of all the low pay. His second collar came a week before his nineteenth birthday. A friend's Dad was owed a fiver by a big Irish Bricklayer who was working in Battersea at the time.

The debt was over a card game that had seen the Brickie promise to settle his debt later. 'Later' never materialized. Charlie 'bought' the five-pound debt for one pound and confronted the big Brickie in a local boozer. When Charlie demanded he pay up, the Brickie laughed at him, shoved him to the floor by his face and carried on drinking. The customers laughed at Charlie and he crawled out with his tail between his legs.

None of the customers were laughing when he came back later and whacked the Brickie over the back of the head with a crowbar. A couple of them challenged him and were clouted with the bar. Charlie was given a two-year stretch but he had made a bit of a 'name' for himself around Battersea in the process.

He was twenty-one when he started to work part time – if and when needed – for local villain Norman Petty. Petty was a scrap metal merchant and armed robber with a very lucrative sideline in money lending. He was only in his early thirties but had made quite a good living. He stayed well away from the likes of The Kray's and The Richardson's and besides the armed blags that he carried out right across the South East, concentrated on his earning potential around Battersea.

Norman Petty wasn't major league but he did OK. He could have progressed further in the villainy world but he never liked to get his hands dirty. Even when it came to the armed robberies he was never 'the frightener' with the weapon and barking the demands. He always opted for the doorman job, keeping lookout for Old Bill.

By the time Charlie Coleman started working for Petty, Petty was concentrating on his money lending business and buying pubs in the area. Charlie was hired as simply a heavy to go and collect from slow payers on Petty's behalf. Very rarely did Charlie have to actually get 'heavy' with any of the creditors, but on the occasions he did he went to town on them.

Charlie spent everything he earned on looking good. He was a Mod who lived by the maxim: *clean living under difficult circumstances.* His Mod image didn't endear him to Petty's other hard men associates. Charlie wisely stayed away from the old fashioned hard men and started to branch out on his own.

He made friends easily and played up his working class roots to the people he started to hang out with in the West End. The Mod scene and the whole *Swinging London* malarkey was opening up doors of opportunity for cheeky chaps like Charlie Coleman. The music, scooters and pill popping never hooked Charlie though. He was always far more interested in the smart clobber and pulling posh skirt. He needed cash to keep his wardrobe replenished though and it wasn't long before he started touting himself out to the decidedly dodgy denizens of Soho. The denizens who could never go the Old Bill with their troubles.

Charlie's first significant earner was when he was asked to maim a Cypriot pimp who had upset an amusement arcade owner in Wardour Street. Charlie did some detective work and found out that the pimp wasn't as liked and well connected as he made out. He had eagerly accepted the gig.

Forty pounds was the bounty, a princely sum for someone of Charlie's status in the early sixties. Charlie casually strolled up to the pimp as he stood in the doorway of a clip joint in Berwick Street one wet November night. The pimp smiled at Charlie, assuming he was just another mark wandering in off the Soho streets. As the pimp stepped aside Charlie squirted him in the face with neat ammonia from a plastic hair lacquer bottle. The pimp was scarred for life and Charlie was forty quid better off.

Word got out that Charlie Coleman was your man if you wanted something quick and nasty doing to your enemies and you didn't want to involve the gangsters. Charlie got on a nice earning streak. A Solicitor paid Charlie fifty pounds to 'rough up' his wife's lover. Charlie tailed the man, sat next to him on a bus and casually but firmly stuck a ten-inch dagger deep into the man's thigh. As the man sat stupefied, Charlie alighted the bus and disappeared into the masses on Oxford Street.

Charlie was an equal opportunities employee and didn't care who he attacked as long as the price was right. Charlie was always amenable to 'customer specification jobs'. He followed a Landlady back from her lover's bed to her pub one night and pounced. He bashed her over the head with a snooker ball inside a sock, dragged her into an alleyway and cut off huge chunks of her hair with a pair of scissors.

Another time he was asked to 'humiliate' a Nancy boy who had ripped off a very rich and very fat old queen. Charlie pushed it and asked for a ton to do the job. The old queen didn't blink and handed over a hundred pound notes in fivers. Charlie knocked the Nancy Boy out with a cosh, stripped him naked, slashed his arse cheeks with a razor, set his pubes and genitals on fire and left him screaming and trying to douse the flames in a piss drenched public toilet on Shaftsbury Avenue.

The best advertising is word of mouth, especially in a village like Soho. Charlie Coleman was never short of work and the beauty of Soho was that he was working with people who were never likely to go running to the Old Bill. Everyone had something to hide in Soho at the time, not least the Old Bill themselves. It was a rotten melting pot where the corrupt and the corrupted bubbled up alongside each other and abided by the unspoken credo of what happened in Soho *stayed* in Soho.

Old Bill knew the score with Charlie Coleman, the problem was pinning the dirty works on him. They thought they had him banged to rights when a fish and chip shop proprietor had his hand burnt to the bone in a deep fat fryer; they were convinced Charlie Coleman had thrown acid in the face of Scottish fraudster and attacked a female escort with a lump of wood, but they had problems proving it. Charlie Coleman lost count of how many i-d parades he had been on. He felt blessed that he was getting away with carrying out so much violence and began to think he was invincible.

Gangsters were making big money in Soho and Charlie Coleman was being looked upon as something of a nuisance. He was with a beautiful, well to do young woman in an illegal all night drinking den on Dean Street when his comeuppance came.

A couple of gorillas in the pay of big shot extorter Albie Lewis gave Charlie a good old-fashioned going over. Strictly fists and boots but they left Charlie in bits. He spent a week recovering in hospital and needed reconstructive surgery to his eye socket.

Six weeks later he was back strutting around Soho again wearing a sharp new mohair suit and acting like nothing had happened. When Albie Lewis heard about Charlie's strutting he had him brought into his office on Poland Street.

Albie Lewis didn't mess about, "You've been warned, Coleman. Stay out of fucking Soho."
Charlie confidently put his case forward, "Albie, Mr. Lewis, in all respect, people need me round here. I offer a service, a tailor made service. It keeps the creeps at bay, the real nasty pieces o' work. These people won't come to you for help; you're a big shot. What I do is a personal thing. I keep a lid on everything ... look, Mr. Lewis; if you get rid of me somebody else will step into my shoes. Maybe a rough arse coon or a greasy Cypriot or a big lump of a Paddy. At least with me you know I'll never step on your toes. I know how powerful you are, Mr. Lewis, I respect you ... please, Mr. Lewis, let me carry on doing what I do best. I know you don't need it but if you *did* ever need my services I'm there for you. Whatever you want ... gratis of course ... please just let me keep earning."

Charlie Coleman's mixed patter of charm; respect and practicality won Albie Lewis over. He gave him a pass to carry on carving out a nasty niche for himself, but told him that he had to ask permission before he attacked people in the future. Charlie promised he would but never stuck to the agreement.

Soho was still Charlie's and he lapped it up. His days would be spent drinking and eating in the many bars, restaurants and clubs and copping off with beautiful young women – many of whom were the daughters of rich people – and were attracted to Soho by it's sordid reputation. He lost count of all the Jewish Princesses he had bedded. Charlie was a handsome, cool and virile 'rough diamond' and they loved his company and sexual prowess. He was slowly turning to into a gigolo of sorts but never jacked his bread and butter job in.

Albie Lewis called a favor in one day. A wealthy associate of Albie's had located a teacher that had sexually abused him as a child. The nonce was being held in a basement flat in Bayswater and Albie's boys were eventually going to top him. The wealthy man wanted the nonce to suffer first though and Charlie Coleman was brought in to do a spot of torture. Albie's boys just weren't up to the job; good straight edged killers, but no stomach for the task in hand. Charlie had no qualms. He tortured the nonce for three hours as the killers waited outside the room listening to the sound of the horror show.

The nonce was put out of his misery with a couple of bullets to the head by Albie's boys and Albie's wealthy associate was very pleased with the job. When he was paying Albie the three thousand pound fee he threw down another grand and asked that it be passed on to the torturer. Albie Lewis gave Charlie three hundred quid and said it was a bonus for a job well done.

Charlie Coleman had made a good, steady living as a practitioner of violence over the last few years, but now he had met a woman who was making him question his profession ...
....
......
....
....
...
...

The Omnivorous Bus had been pimped out; *pimp my ride, pimp my wife, pimp my pride, pimp my pantry.* & located himself sat at the rear on leopard skin leather seats facing a personalized mini-mini bar. His thirst had bottomed out so he refrained from sneaking a peek inside the walnut and gold encrusted booze cabinet. The Bus was cruising through Queens and Harlem; juddering as it kept rewinding to distances it had already traveled. Through a caught reflection & noticed that the wheels on the bus were super slick alloy and

chrome and you could eat your lunch from them. They blinded the
envious kids who stared at them in wonder and the wheels on the
bus went round and round, round and round, round and round, the
wheels on the bus went round and round … all day long …

The Bus started jerking up and down. Bouncy Bus; low rider vehic-
ular testicular grinding. The Bus was bump and grinding. Cruising
for a musing. Illmatic acceleration, faster than the speed of thought.
Motorik mouthpieces spitting metallic verses. The medically
induced comma. Oracle tradition, oral history, experience spunked
into reality by motor mouths. Never let another rap Nigga hit it from
back or the front/I don't sleep because I don't want to give sleep any
enjoyment/ I could do this shit in my damn sleep/ Shit, if I was old
enough to speak/I pray the lord my guns to keep/But little old me
with the few facts that eye speak/Get away Scott free cause I'm more
discreet than sleep/The kind of stuff I'm pouring makes the bandits
go to sleep/Sleep raping all my ladies/Rattled like a baby but I never
get to sleep/I'm a rare breed, extraordinary league.

A heavy Noo Yawk accent declared: "This is the liminal linguistics
lift to the high life, homies. This is the real shit! The hood where
it all started. REWIND … Boom boom boom boom: pih poh cisum
saw Na teltuo DNA an "eciov" rof eht desihcnarfnesid htuoy fo
wol-cimonoce saera sa eht erutluc detcelfer eht laicos, cimonoce
Dna lacitilop seitilaer fo rieht sevil. Hguohtla ereht erew ynam ylrae
scm taht dedrocer olos stcejorp fo eton, hcus sa jd doowylloh, sitruk
wolb dna einoops eeg, eht ycneuqerf fo olos stsitra ndid't esaercni
litnu retal htiw eht esir fo stsiolos htiw egats ecneserp dna amard,
hcus sa ll looc j. tsom ylrae pih poh saw detanimod yb spuorg erehw
noitaroballoc neewteb eht srebmem saw largetni ot eht wohs. Na
elpmaxe dluow eb eht ylrae pih poh puorg yknuf ruof sulp eno, ohw
demrofrep ni hcus a rennam no yadrutas thgin evil ni 1891."

A prurient Jurist got up in &'s shit and slavered, "Squaring the verbal. These raps are axiomatic. She's placing wagers on Ouija boards

again, speculating on the outcome of man made disasters, body count and collective trauma, laying odds on the resultant number of born again atheists, stalking the hostels of worship to witness the Episcopal egress, throwing runes instead of dice she dispatches all deadbeats with a cuspate flick of the wrist. Sucks the energy of self-pity from them as they mourn losses and count blessings, blessings she considers queer, but in her Delphic élan she gives them another chance to throw number scarred bones and taste evanescent "wins". She spreads herself across card table and her High Priestess transcends their Ace of Spades hands down. They shoot her suspicious peeps and guts intuit liquid shit hitting fans hidden hand after hand after hidden hand until only The Hanged Man remains on the green baize. "You have to be upside down to see him." She grins In Moon shadow snaking to schools above and below inconvenience stores scooping up pittance is all the same to her, it's the winning that counts, it's the acquiescence in their eyes, it's the tenebrific atmosphere that reassures her God isn't on the side of the gambler. On trading floors she binds spells with arithmetic, bedazzles with equations, debauches with the promise of more, more, more And The Go For Brokers genuflect and masturbate in veneration at her unveiling, discerning that from Atom and Eve onwards the decks have been stacked. In their Wank Banks are phantasmagorias of that first seedy temptation and these Jesters hover auguries over the abyss and dip their wicks in. Overlooking the fact she's still the unrepentant whore, corporate culture sincerely enshrouds consensus amnesia as The Tossers spunk fortunes on life and death derivatives. And in their post-orgy downturn they spill heathen prayers from frothing orifices, but Lady Luck cackles at their fruitless invocations and grins from shadows and balance sheets and slowly parts her lips for the serpent to glissade inside to unequivocally penetrate and prove to both the sacred and profane that she really does not give a fuck!" & took a breath "You're telling me it was all just luck? It was all just the way the words fell?"

The deliverance rumination room was so very cold now. & could feel a blink metastasizing in his neural pathways. *You have used up fifteen billion seven hundred and six million three hundred and ninety seven thousand and twenty three seconds so far.* I'm going to see The Touring Shroud tonight. *At War With The Mediaocrity Since 1966!*

& was violently sucked backwards into a phone screen. Pixels danced with pixies and a membrane started to dissolve in the fashion of a celluloid strip spontaneously combusting. Every text message that had *ever* been composed and sent was jockeying for position as the screensaver. One of them caught &'s attention.

Explorer O: Her 2nd DMT xprnz (written communication) ... I fownd Mself 1ns agn n d co. of d "elves", as d focus of their attn n ministrations, bt dey appeard mch less colorful n al2gtha preoccupied W d task @ h&, i.e., pourin a goldN, viscous liquid thru a netwrk of lng, intertwining, transparent conduits wich led N2 d midL of my abdomen ... I got deeply N2 d visual hallucination. I wz barely abL 2 Rmind +2 reassure Mself dat "DMT S safe," tho I had sum difficulty recalling d nme "DMT". W Iyz shut, I xperiencd intNse, overwhelming visual imagery. I wz seein a lg, xtremely colorful surface, lk a membrane, pulsating 2wrd n awy frm me. ... I recalled dat I had seen dis b4, on prev DMT trips, bt had 4gotn it. durin dis xprnz I wz aware of my breathn n hartbeat, n wz carefl 2 contu breathn deeply. d pattern wz n intNse hues, n t's parts seemD 2 ... sry w'v ...

The Narrator remembered a line from the Bhagavad Gita: I am txt message, destroyer of Language.

& blinked and he was back on The Bus. MC Behemoth Da Gargantua was in &'s face beat boxing; his mouth a quivering and a shaking and a morphing and a making like over-animated piss flaps: "pv zk bschk pv zk pv bschk zk pv zk bschk pv zk pv bschk ghhggh chhhcch gdggdddd sssshhh pv zk bschk pv zk pv bschk zk pv zk bschk ghhhhg tskkkkk tssskk pv zk bschk pv zk pv bschk zk pv zk bschk ghhg zk bschk ghhhhg tskkkkk tssskk pv zk bschk pv zk pv bschk zk pv zk bschk ghhg pv zk bschk pv zk pv bschk zk pv zk bschk pv zk pv bschk ghhggh chhhcch gdggdddd sssssshhh pv zk bschk pv zk pv bschk zk pv ghhggh chhhcch gdggdddd. Never let another rap Nigga hit it from back or the front. I don't sleep because I don't wanna give sleep any enjoyment. I could do this shit in a damn coma. Shit, if I was old enough to speak I pray the lord my guns to keep. I can't eat, I can't sleep, but little old me with the few facts that Aye speak. Get away Scott free cause I'm more discreet than sleep, the kind of stuff Aye'm pouring makes the bandits go beep-beep. Sleep raping all my ladies. I'm in a rare breed, extraordinary league. Pv zk bschk pv zk pv bschk zk pv zk bschk pv zk pv bschk ghhggh chhhcch gdggdddd sssshhh pv zk bschk pv zk pv bschk zk pv zk bschk ghhhhg ..."

As MC Behemoth Gargantua disappeared up his own voluminous arsehole, & fiddled with a cellular phone. Try as he might though he simply could not make it work. He huffed and puffed and scrutinized to no avail. He remembered he had forgotten how to use the damn thing and started to sob in frustration. He imagined it felt like extracting teeth through eye canals, but you can never *really* imagine a feeling. The numbers evaded him; rats abandoning a sinking ship after eating all the life jackets. His big fat fucking fingers kept on growing more useless. They were speeding towards anachronism at seventeen thousand (still born) words per minute. His fingers were drunk: spastic digits incapable of impression. Rigor mortified at the simplicity of the task in hand.

&'s tears pooled their resources and created a stream at his feet. & was able to throw the phone away and make a call through the medium of the water, "I'd like to make a collect call to my present past."
The Operator was a broad straight out of a 1940's noir B-movie: slutty, Noo Yawk accent, chewing gum, filing her nails, willfully dumb but dripping with attitude, "Ya don't say."
& frowned, "I *do* say."
"What do you take me for?"

"You're an operator aren't you?"

A wood paneled switchboard appeared and she sighed, "OK. What's the number sweet cheeks?"

"Huh … 23"

"OK. I'm gonna put you on hold."

Instead of elevated muzak & was treated to the post recorded voice of an hard boiled LA Private Investigator, "It was raining; the kind of rain you'd hope would clean the filth right off the streets. "A mole … ?" Gonzalez whispered timidly. "Great theory, Sherlock. No. Definitely not a mole," I sneered. I was visibly disappointed in my new partner. "Hey look," I snapped, "How about I just look after this one myself and you head down to Ricky's and grab a glass or two of Beat It Kid, Ya Bother Me? This case was a real brain-buster: A luckless pawn, caught in the middle of a ruthless power play. The victim – one of my usual informants, "The Butcher". Scene was a damn bloodbath. Took four hours before the lab boys could scrape enough together to ID the victim. The slaying occurred early this morning. I dusted off my jacket, lit up my last cigar, grabbed my hat and walked out. "Must be another inside job," I rasped. But that wasn't even the half of it. The whole reason I took the case to begin with: trouble, in the shape of a beach-party blonde with stumps as far as the eye could see. Wouldn't give her name, said she was related to Kevin May Church, but wouldn't say how. I only agreed, reluctantly, after Christopher Kelley personally vouched for her!"

The Operator clicked on, "OK hon', yer through to 23."

Getting the Fear
Chapter Four

Jack Sherry bought a cream colored linen suit for his trip to Spain. A couple of his officers on the murder squad had been to Spain on those package holiday jobs and told him he would sweat like a stuffed pig out there. The heat was a real bastard and would knock his socks off. They added that he should also invest in sunglasses and a hat.

Word had come down that Sherry should fly over to Ibiza and have a gander to save any embarrassment if the corpses eventually turned out to be those of English subjects. Captain Torres was relieved that Jack Sherry from the famous Scotland Yard was heading over. Torres had no experience of mass murder and even the cops on the Spanish mainland were puzzled by the discovery.

Jack Sherry enjoyed his first flight. Nothing to it, a breeze really, he couldn't understand what all the fuss was about. The free booze and the gorgeous airhostesses made the time literally fly.

Captain Torres met him at the airport in what looked like a military jeep. Jack Sherry was indeed sweating like a stuffed pig; the free alcohol was now pissing out of his pores and he had a stinking headache.

Captain Torres was a friendly guy, "We have room for you to stay in next door to the police offices, Sir Sherry."

Jack dabbed at his sweaty forehead with a handkerchief, "Call me Jack, Captain Torres. Jack or Mr. Sherry."
"OK, Mr. Jack, I will … I am Ernesto."
"All right, *Ernesto*."

Jack drank in the beauty of Ibiza as they traveled along its narrow and ad hoc roads. They hit potholes the size of small houses and Jack's bones absorbed the shocks whilst Captain Torres simply kept smiling and pointing to things that he thought Jack might find interesting. Jack was only interested in sinking more booze under a shady spot and to snooze and acclimatize.

Proud Ernesto wanted to give Jack a history lesson, "You know Jack, Ibiza is a very special island."
"Mmm, it's very beautiful, Ernesto."
"Not only because of its beauty. No, no, no, Mr. Jack … Ibiza is magical. Many peoples have conquered it over the times. The Romans, The Phoenicians, The Arabs, all these peoples flocked to Ibiza. Ibiza was the sacred burial grounds for The Carthaginians … their dead were buried here because there were no wild animals to dig them out of the earth."
Jack wasn't impressed but he was polite, "That's very interesting."
"If we have time I will take you *Puig des Molins* in Ibiza Town. It has world's largest collection of Punic artifacts that were dug from graves. The Carthaginian dead were buried with their possessions so that they could have them with them in the next world."
"I think it's probably a better idea to show me these bodies you found in a villa, Ernesto."
Ernesto smiled and nodded, "Oh yes, Mr. Jack, yes, of course."

The roads alternated between bearable and bone shaking and Ernesto couldn't resist pitching his island to Jack, "You are familiar with Nostradamus, Mr. Jack, yes?"
"The astrologer?"
"Yes, yes … Nostradamus lived in the 15th century and he predicted

that Ibiza will be the earth's final refuge when the nuclear war takes place."

Jack was beginning to think that Ernesto Torres was an imposter; the island's tourist chief masquerading as a cop. Ernesto was also a big fan of The Phoenicians. Jack lit a Capstan, held on and half listened to him.

"You know, Mr. Jack, in 1600 B.C. the Phoenicians invented twenty two 'magical signs' called the alphabet. They then gave the alphabet to the Greeks who spread it around the world. If it was not for the Phoenicians we would not be able to understand each other, Mr. Jack."

Jack admired the flora and fauna and the pretty little sun bleached houses spread over the hilly terrain. The heat wasn't quite as intense now but Jack was parched, "Is there anywhere we can just stop for a quick drink, Ernesto?"

They stopped at a tiny cantina that looked more like a regular house that just happened to sell drinks and snacks. They sat outside under the shade of a large tattered umbrella that advertised *Cinzano*. Jack glugged an ice-cold Spanish beer and Ernesto sipped from a tiny cup of coffee. He tried one of Jack's Capstan Full Strengths and nearly choked.
"Aaah, these Englisher cigarettes are not for me."
He pulled out one of his own and they watched a couple of emaciated mongrel dogs eagerly lap up water from a dish the size of regular car wheel.

"You said all the victims were stabbed, Ernesto?"
"Oh yes, Mr. Jack. Not only stabbed … no."
"Oh? What do you mean?"
Ernesto shook his head mournfully, "The word would be carniceria … huh, butchered. Cut up. Very badly cut up … it took many people to pick up their bodies. Many policemen."

"They were mutilated?"

"Mmm ... I am sorry to say, yes."

Ernesto said that his police officers had never seen anything like it. Even the big shot police from the mainland had never witnessed anything as gruesome.

"We have full cooperation from the Spanish mainland police, Mr. Jack. A few of them are still on the island and it was them that advised me to contact Scotland Yard."

"Why are you so convinced that the victims are English? I've heard that Ibiza attracts visitors from across Europe: Germans, Scandinavians, French what have you."

"The villagers in San Juan said that they are Englishers, Mr. Jack. I have no reason to not believe them. They have met some of these people they say. They had bought supplies from them."

"All right ... what about another beer before we go to the morgue?"

"Si, si."

A half hour later and they were stood in the morgue. Jack Sherry was shocked. He told Ernesto he needed to call his boss. Ernesto showed him into his office, got him a line and politely left.

Jack dabbed at the sweat on his brow and chained his Capstans as he spoke to DI Ketley, "Sir, it's ... well ... it's a mess. The victims were hacked to pieces; faces, bodies, everything. One of them, a young woman, she was ... she was scalped, sir. Another woman ... disemboweled. The spic Coroner's tried his best but there's body parts all over the shop ... honestly, sir ... it's just ..."

DI Ketley didn't mean to sound like a heartless bastard but that's how it came across, "Have you found out if they're ours yet, Sherry? If they're Brits?"

Jack bit his tongue, "No, sir. No, not yet."

"Well, that's why you're there. We haven't flown you out there for a package holiday, Sherry ... have you been to the crime scene?"

"Not yet, sir, no."

"Why not?"

"We thought, well, Captain Torres thought-"

DI Ketley groaned, "You haven't joined the spic force, Sherry. You take your orders from me. I told you to go straight to the crime scene didn't I?"

"Yes sir, but-"

"What's the weather like? Is it as hot as people say?"

Jack gritted his teeth: *fucking weather?* "Oh yes, sir. Boiling hot."

"I told the wife she'll never get me there, I said 'over my dead body you'll get me to Spain' ..."

Jack pretended there was a fault on the line and cut DI Ketley off. He went outside for fresh air but all he got was stifling humidity. The images from the morgue were making his head spin. Ernesto brought him a glass of water, Jack asked if he had anything stronger and they hit a bar opposite the morgue.

Ernesto couldn't wait to hear his reaction, "What do you think, Mr. Jack?"

Jack knocked back a Johnny Walker with extra ice, "Never seen anything like it before, Captain Ernesto ... it's like ... I don't know ... like Jack The Ripper's handiwork."

"Aaah yes, yes, The Jack The Ripper. I have read books about him. He was a member of your royal family, yes?"

"You shouldn't believe everything you read."

Jack ordered another double. He was having trouble working the Spanish peseta's out, but Ernesto said the drinks were on him. Jack wondered if Ernesto had he thought Scotland Yard had sent over an alcoholic copper to help out.

"I hope you don't think I'm a piss artist, Captain Ernesto?"

Ernesto frowned at him, Jack explained, holding the glass up, "The drinking. I don't usually drink like this on duty."

He smiled at Jack, "Aaah, no, no, I understand. We all like to drink, yes?"

"It must be the heat."

"Yes, yes. The heat can be hard if you are not used to it, Mr. Jack."

Jack killed a couple more whiskeys and they headed up to the villa. The roads were even bumpier and the booze, heat, tiredness and what he had witnessed in the morgue conspired to make Jack throw the airline food up. Captain Ernesto said it was probably just the heat again. Jack knew he was just being polite.

The villa was large, two storey, set back off a dirt road, surrounded by fig trees and whitewashed like the majority of the structures on the island. Jack clocked Ernesto making the sign of the cross over his chest as they approached it.
"Are you a religious man, Captain Ernesto?"
Ernesto held his hand out and tilted it up and down to express that he was kind of, "I was raised catholic, Mr. Jack, but ... you know. The kind of work we do, you question things, yes?"
"Yeah."

Jack was expecting the scene to be blood splattered and he wasn't disappointed. The claret was everywhere. The heat had obviously dried it and it had turned a shitty brown color. The white walls now resembled a Jackson Pollack painting *if* Jackson Pollack had chosen to use only one color.

Ernesto mournfully shook his head, "*Diabolico ... diabolico.*"
Jack wandered around, sucked in air through his teeth and shuddered, "It looks like an abattoir."
Ernesto swatted flies from his vision, "Only an animal can do this ... and the smell!"
Jack turned around, "Candid Blanding?"
...
...
....
...
....
....

23 burst from the telephonic puddle at &'s feet and thrust a dissertation before his eyes. & gasped and stepped back into a less cynical time frame. His spectacles were now fashioned from the big bottoms of old school glass milk bottles. The once delivered kind. He resembled Cosmo Smallpiece in his mind and couldn't help but affect the mannerisms of the nowanights highly offensive comedic creation. & blinked at the dissertation:

Postpatriarchialist deconstruction in the works of Kenneth Williams from The Carry On Films

Helena Younghusband (((spinster)))
Department of Sociology, Stanford University

Wilhelm U. O. d'Erlette
Department of Sociolinguistics, applied epistemology & Nursery Crimes, University of Kansas,

17th of June Eighteeneighythate

1. Consensuses of futility

"Society is part of the fatal flaw of consciousness," says Sir Charlie Drake. Therefore, Sontag uses the term 'the semiotic paradigm of context' to denote the meaninglessness, and eventually the defining characteristic, of pretextual class and postsexual cigarettes. If one examines Derridaist reading, one is faced with a choice: either accept postpatriarchialist deconstruction or conclude that academe is capable of insignificant form. Bataille promotes the use of the semiotic paradigm of context to modify society. It could be said that Aleister Crowley [1] states that we have to choose between postpatriarchialist deconstruction and subcultural narrative.

The characteristic theme of the works of Madonna (Ciccone Youth) is the difference between class and sexual identity. Foucault uses the term 'the semiotic paradigm of context' to denote not theory per se, but posttheory. Battyfang Battaile suggests the use of capitalist pre-constructive theory to deconstruct capitalism and its heart murmurs.

"Narrativity is elitist," says Derrida; however, according to Finnis [2] it is not so much narrativity that is elitist, but rather the absurdity, and some would say the paradigm, of narrativity. A number of desublimations concerning postpatriarchialist deconstruction may be found. Thus, Guy The Bored's model of Foucaultist power relations implies that class, somewhat ironically, has significance, but only if truth is interchangeable with reality; if that is not the case, we can assume that art serves to disempower the over privileged cunts.

The main theme of von Junz's [3] critique of capitalist preconstructive theory is a self-falsifying paradox. If cultural postsemiotic theory holds, the works of Stan Smith & Shell Toes are postmodern. However, the subject is contextualised into a semiotic paradigm of context that includes culture as a reality.

In the works of Citizen Smith, a predominant concept is the distinction between figure and ground. Any number of theories concerning the fatal flaw of conceptualist sexual identities exist. Therefore, de Sade [4] suggests that we have to choose between postpatriarchialist deconstruction, subdialectic discourse or a dirty weekend in a Blackpool B & B.

The characteristic theme of the works of Toto is the bridge between class and sexual identity. Frankie Foucault uses the term 'capitalist preconstructive theory' to denote the role of the observer as reader. Thus, Sid Sartre promotes the use of the semiotic paradigm of context to analyze and modify truth.

"Sexual identity is part of the collapse of language," says Freddy Mercurial. In Clerks, Smith affirms postpatriarchialist deconstruction; in Chasing Amy, however, he examines the semiotic paradigm of context.

But if capitalist preconstructive theory holds, we have to choose between the semiotic paradigm of context and capitalist deconstructivism.

The main theme of Tony Hancock's [5] analysis of textual postdialectic theory is a cultural totality. It could be said that an abundance of theories concerning capitalist preconstructive theory may be discovered. The semolina paradigm of context holds that culture is meaningless, given that the puddled premise of capitalist preconstructive theory is invalid. Therefore, the subject is interpolated into a semiotic paradigm of context that includes reality as a reality. Prinn [6] states that we have to choose between capitalist preconstructive theory and neocapitalist feminism. Thus, Foucault uses the term 'patriarchial narrative' to denote the common ground between society and sexual deviance.

If capitalist preconstructive theory holds, we have to choose between postpatriarchialist deconstruction and the subtextualsubsexual paradigm of consensus. In a sense, Cheeseburger [7] implies that the works of The Kardashians are modernistic. Capitalist preconstructive theory suggests that society has intrinsic meaning. Therefore, the ground/figure distinction depicted in Yootha Joyce's George & Mildred is also evident in A Portrait of the Artist As a Young Sex Offender, although in a more mythopoetical sense.

The primary theme of the works of Yoofa Joyce is the Rubicon, and therefore the meaninglessness of cultural sexual identity. However, many deappropriations concerning not sublimation, but presublimation exist. The premise of postpatriarchialist deconstruction implies that truth may be used to entrench hierarchy. In a sense, the characteristic theme of la Fournier's [8] model of the pretextual paradigm of expression is the bridge between sanity and class.

Derrida uses the term 'capitalist preconstructive theory' to denote the absurdity of cultural sexual identity. Therefore, if postpatriarchialist deconstruction holds, the works of Bernard Manning are postmodern. Woodrow Wilson [9] suggests that we have to choose between capitalist preconstructive theory and neoconstructivist feminism. But any number of discourses concerning the semiotic paradigm of context may be found.

In the john, Stone analyses capitalist preconstructive theory; in JFK he deconstructs postpatriarchialist deconstruction. Therefore, the semiotic paradigm of context states that the Constitution is intrinsically a legal fiction.

2. Postpatriarchialist deconstruction and cultural deappropriation.

In the works of The Stone Age, a predominant concept is the concept of predialectic sexuality. The main theme of the works of Stone is not narrative, as Lyotard would have it, but neonarrative. It could be said that if cultural deappropriation holds, the works of Sam Stone are not postmodern and that he was spot on about the hole in Daddy's arm where all the money goes.

If one examines the semiotic paradigm of context, one is faced with a choice: either reject cultural deappropriation or conclude that society, surprisingly, has significance, but only if reality is equal to narrativity. The characteristic theme of Abian's [10] essay on semioticist rationalism is a self-supporting whole. Therefore, Drucker [11] implies that we have to choose between the semiotic paradigm of context and neodialectic desublimation.

"Class is part of the dialectic of sexuality," says Baudrillard. Groucho Marx uses the term 'Sartreist absurdity' to denote the common ground between society and truth. In a sense, Bataille suggests the use of postpatriarchialist deconstruction to attack the status quo.

1. Cameron, R. K. ed. (1911) Reading Lyotard: The semiotic paradigm of context and postpatriarchialist deconstruction. University of Illinois Press

2. Finnis, Z. H. B. (1891) Postpatriarchialist deconstruction & paranoid dipsomania in the works of Stone. Yale University Press

3. von Junz, P. ed. (1988) The Stasis of Discourse: The Semiotic paradigm of context in the works of Smith. University of Georgia Press

4. de Selby, V. F. B. (1970) Postpatriarchialist deconstruction and the semiotic paradigm of context. O'Reilly & Associates

5. Hanfkopf, S. ed. (1997) Neocultural Narratives And Nasty Rashes On Your Knackers: Postpatriarchialist deconstruction in the works of Eco. Loompanics.

6. Prinn, V. S. R. (1974) The semiotic paradigm of context and postpatriarchialist deconstruction. Oxford University Press

7. Hamburger, J. S. ed. (1997) The Iron Fruit: The semiotic paradigm of context in the works of Chris Rock. Schlangekraft

8. La Fournier, L. K. H. (1923) Postpatriarchialist Anarchism In The Crèche

& zapped the dissertation and kneeled to the puddle. He could see the waves transmitting and hear the hum of receivership and smell the flow of information and feel the bowel rattling charge of commerce and taste the iron in the blood of the binary. A Golden Trumpet spread across the puddle.

And The Golden Trumpet said, "'You' are made of information. Your experiences, your feelings, your empiricism and interactions, your personality, your present history, your future present and your past present; from your adroitness to your gaucheness, from your love to your hate, from your arsehole to your pineal gland. You are information, a composite that forms an identity. From the genetic blue print that built your body to the genetic decomposition that will eventually make it disappear."

& chipped in, "But-"

"No butts! Creation is information vibrating at fluctuating frequencies. The greater the frequency, the more synoptic the information, the faster the rate of frequency, the more information is encompassed within it. The leisurely frequency of the dimension that the body inhabits is the slowest in the creation."

"You keep telling me shit I already know!" Protested &.

"This isn't for your benefit &. This is for the benefit of the readers. Now, in the bodily, earthly, material dimension, the frequency is so slow because the creative process has been elongated, elongated because we perceive it through the illusion of time. Time is the slow, disintegrated movement of the creative principle. Time does not exist in the pure consciousness. In pure consciousness the frequency of the creation principle moves without regard to the straightjacket laws of time. It is instant. Or rather, it is already there and the observer makes it information."

"I'm fully subject to either neither nor! Look at me! I'm a fucking mongrel!" Yelled &.

The Golden Trumpet bequeathed no sympathy, "You don't know how lucky you are to be able to be subject to these Near Life Experiences. You are blessed and all you can do is piss and moan! Certain beings would cut off their own legs to be in your position."

"Blessed?" Scoffed &, "Fucking cursed more like!" as he insouciantly waved The Golden Trumpet away.

Novel Headline 4. *True Love Isn't Hearts & Flowers. It's Blood & Guts & Bouquets Of Barbed Wire.*

The packet of information that was formerly known as Prince formerly known as P emanated, brandishing a perfectly bound blank book, "Look at this."

& looked, "Look at what? There's nothing there. It's a blank book."

"Exactly." Said P,"It's supposed to be a book about the sorcerous implication of elevators."

"And?" Replied &.

"It was never written." Squealed P.

& shook his head, "So?"

"The author was supposed to be James Shelby Downard. Doesn't that ring a bell? Said P

"No." Replied &.

P Sighed, "James Shelby Downard was a composite of a couple of authors. He wrote on the esoteric and onomatology and occult symbolism. The dude was a genius, but he never really existed, that's not important though. What's important is that he was supposed to write *this* book!"

P waved the barren book in &'s face.

& shrugged, "I don't know what to say. What am I presupposed to say?"

"Elevators! Think about it. Where did I die? I died in a Motherfuckin' elevator, man! Right in the middle of my studio. I was snuffed out by the powers that be or not to be. It was a fuckin' Shakespearean assassination. They rubbed me out because I was gonna spill the beans in a tell-all autobiography. I had the real dope on those evil cocksuckers and my God, I was gonna blow the Motherfuckin' lid off their shit. They was gunning for me 'cos I got hip to their depopulation plans. I spoke the fuck up about it on TV and those bitches couldn't handle it. I spoke up about the chemtrails. I spoke up about the Motherfuckin' military-entertainment-industrial complex. I was dropping truth bombs, man! Those fuckers hated me. They marked my cards. "

P laid it on the line for &: in the early 1990's he had been tied to a recording deal with a corporation – we'll call Warner Bros. – who wanted him to record less and promote more. He didn't want to. He wanted to concentrate on creating. He wanted to keep producing his music. He didn't give a shit about shilling for the man. Full stop. The corporation was pissed and wouldn't free him from his contract and said that they "owned his name". The name he had been given at birth by his Mom and Dad. He was having none of it so he changed his name to a symbol, started writing 'slave' on his cheek and stopped cooperating with the corporation. He ran his mouth about them and highlighted many to the fact that the entertainment industry is ruled by Motherfuckin' beasts who only give a shit about the bottom line. He famously said, " 'Everything has to go back to

God, to peace and to justice. There's no justice in taking somebody's intellectual copyrights from them. It's wrong for them to say they own it. They don't own it. This word ownership ... who owns this candle? Who owns this telephone? Who owns the air? Nobody owns these things really. And then you think about the human genome. Who owns your DNA? And it's coming to that. You can be hooked up, slaved up ... It will come to that.' We interrupt this passage with a scathing review of *The Secret Life Of The Novel* culled from the present future >

The Secret Life Of The Novel
by Dean Cavanagh
Published by Culture is no friend of Mine Inc.
A.R. Kane

Like lovers and assholes (and reviews), books sort readers. I would argue that books like The Secret Life Of The Novel identify you— your affiliations, your beliefs and values, your politics—with the same degree of accuracy as monster truck rallies. "When I was younger," Dean Cavanagh explains in a 2026 interview with The Boston Phoenix, "I saw my relationship with the reader as a sort of sexual one. But now it seems more like a late-night conversation with really good friends, when the bullshit stops and the masks come off." Books sort people the way conversations sort people: the talk you have with your mom on Saturday morning is not the talk you have with your boss on Friday afternoon, and certainly not the talk you have with your best buddies on Saturday night. All of our relationships have a conversational mode appropriate to them; a manner of communication tailored to the expectations our audience. We like to tell ourselves that we're 'just speaking our mind,' but in point of fact we're conserving/cultivating a certain kind of social persona, one intended to facilitate our various relationships: to make our mom proud, to impress our boss, and to crack up our buddies.

95

This is as true of novels as it is shooting the shit or obligatory familial phone-calls. A novel is, first and foremost, a mode of communication, a kind of relationship between an actual writer and a certain number of actual readers. And as with any communication, judgments concerning propriety will be inextricably bound to who is sending and who is receiving under what circumstances. It makes no more sense reviewing a novel absent its particular communicative context than it does evaluating conversations with your mom, boss, or buddies. The success or failure of any human communication depends on the adequacy of the how and the what to the who—something which is especially true of modes that purport to challenge notions of adequacy.

This is the whole reason why publishers are keen to plaster testimonials on the cover of their books: to milk our authority and social proof biases. The Secret Life Of The Novel is literally festooned with blurbs from a galaxy of authoritative sources: It arrives literally armored in literary authority. We are told by a variety of serious people (who are taken very seriously by other serious people) that this is a seriously serious book. There can be little doubt that as far as the 2023 literary in-group was concerned, The Secret Life Of The Novel was a smashing communicative success.

Which should be no surprise. "I come to writing from a pretty hardcore, abstract place," Cavanagh explains in The Boston Phoenix interview. "It comes out of technical philosophy and continental European theory, and extreme avant-garde shit." Given who he was, and given he saw this as a conversation with good friends, and given that the seriously serious readers likely shared, as good friends often do, the bulk of his attitudes and aesthetic sensibilities, it's easy to see how this book became as successful as it did. The Secret Life Of The Novel is the product of a in-group sender communicating to other in-group receivers: insofar as those other receivers loved it, you can say that as a communication The Secret Life Of The Novel was a tremendous in-group success. The problem is that one can say the same about the Turner Diaries, Getting The Fear, The Bible or Mein Kampf.

I don't pretend to know what literature is in any metaphysical sense, but I do think that it has to have something to do with transcendence. What distinguishes literature from fiction in general is its ability to push beyond, beyond received dogmas, beyond comfort zones, and most importantly (because it indexes the possibility of the former two), beyond social in-groups. This is why communicative success and literary success is not one and the same thing. And this is also why out-group readers generally find in-group estimations of literary merit so unconvincing.

Make no mistake, The Secret Life Of The Novel is a piece of genre fiction: something expressly written for dedicated groups of readers possessing a relatively fixed set of expectations. It just so happens that this particular group of readers happens to command the cultural high ground when it comes to things linguistic and narrative. One of many cynical tidbits I came across pulling this 'review' together is how publishers, Culture is no Friend of Mine, ultimately decided that the size of the book, some 10079 pages, would contribute to its sales by turning it into something that could be bragged about. As with any other 'elite' subgroup, literary practitioners are prone to self-identify according to perceived competencies, especially when those competencies dramatically exceed those of the hoi polloi. The most difficult missions are reserved for the Special Forces–those with specialized training–not the regular army. "I'm somebody who can't even own a TV anymore," Cavanagh confesses, "because I'll sit there slack-jawed, wanking and consuming enormous amounts of what is, in terms of art, absolute shit."

What we have here is a good old-fashioned authority gradient, one indexed according to a perceived hierarchy of difficulty. At the top stands, to use Cavanagh's phrase, 'extreme avante garde shit,' and at the bottom, 'absolute shit.' It is the ease of the latter that allows the difficulty of the former to so effectively sort individuals according to certain kinds of competencies. Of all the reviews of The Secret Life Of The Novel I read, my favorite has to be Lisa Schwarzbaum's in Entertainment Weekly. In a truly wonderful piece of ironic prose, she admits defeat, "with one crabbed hand gripping the cover like a claw and the other raised like a limp white flag," deferring to the opinion of "more disciplined" reviewers with a culture-serf's eye-rolling genuflection, saying, in effect, 'Well, I can't read it so it must be a masterpiece.'

Schwarzbaum found she sorted into the 'absolute shit' pile, "longing," as she puts it, "for an unedited Joan Collins manuscript." A true 'White Flagger,' to use the book's idiom. Even Mrs. Mills, the Cavanagh fan whose site has the best selection of reviews, puts scare-quotes around 'critic' when referring to her. Apparently she's not one of us–not really. How could she be when the joke flew over her head?

But what if this isn't the case? What if Schwarzbaum, the superficial pseudo-critic, turned out to be the most perceptive of all? The most serious thing in The Secret Life Of The Novel, after all, is the most silly thing: Consciousness. And surely Schwarzbaum–a reviewer for Entertainment Weekly no less–should be the acknowledged authority.

And now to the book itself. The Secret Life Of The Novel is the worst Near Life science fiction Noir novel ever written. The truth is it might be the worst novel ever written, or at least published, but given the fact that Cavanagh has stiff competition from the burgeoning spawn of PC Elitist writers, not to mention his own PoMo kith, such as Ricky Raccoon, Sheila Ecstasy, and that ilk, I think I'll stick with just calling it the worst Future Present Noir sci fi has ever produced. Granted, I am not one who has read all the depth of Past Present Noir sci fi offerings, but I've read enough to know that this so far undershoots the rest that by mere extrapolation it would be a titanic achievement for another author to do worse. Yes, there are the sword and sorcerer riff-raff, the cyber-punk crapola, and the remnant dross of the Golden and Silver Ages of Past Future Noir sci fi still hanging around, and even those who've produced masterpieces, such as Shakespeare and Laurel & Hardy, have been known to write horror show books in terms of quality, but this dystopian novel by Cavanagh is worse than them all. His book, only three hundred years old, is more outdated than many Golden and Silver Age Present Present sci fi books specifically because of his slangs sounding as relevant as John Dryden's courtly verse. Unlike Anthony Burgess's A Clockwork Orange, the slang is based in the then-contemporary world, which makes it seem so 1660s trying to seem cool, rather than timeless. Even his use of emails, with outdated isp formats, seems to belie his lack of creativity. Not that his relentlessly PoMo use of product brand names, bumper stickers, redaction marks, and lengthy digressions on things as pointless as Hawaii 5-0's relevance versus Hills Street Blues', does not already belie his creative bankruptcy, but it's worth noting. Of course, nothing comes of his discourses – they're tossed in like olives in a salad, so Cavanagh can preen his learnedness to you, and dropped just as quickly – a habit that he too often indulges – bringing up and dropping things ...

& listened to P. A lot of what he said made sense. P asked & to go back or forth and witness his assassination.

"What's the point P? There's nothing I can do about it. I can't change *anything*."

P became a little morose, "But I want you to believe me, man. I was a ritual sacrifice on the day of the Queen of England's 90th birthday. Do the mathematics. My body was 57 years old. 57 from 90 is 33! 30-Motherfuckin'3! 33! The 33rd degree of those cocksuckin' Freemasons. Earth's ruled by those evil asswipes. They fucked me up fatal. Cut me down. I had more to give, much more to give ... all I ever wanted to do was create."

"I do believe you P."

Getting the Fear
Chapter 5

Charlie and Candice first met in The Scotch Of St James' club in Mayfair. The club was a hip regular hangout for the pop stars and bright – usually stoned – young things of the time. Charlie wasn't interested in pop stars and artists and designers but he *was* interested in the birds who hung out in there hoping to snag themselves a famous face.

Charlie couldn't care less about The Who or The Stones, The Beatles or The Kinks. These were just working class lads who had done well for themselves by utilizing their talents. He was on a par with them; they were no different to him. They were good at music and being pop stars and he was good at discriminate violence and looking sharp.

He was well known in the club as a wide boy who got up to all kinds of naughty behavior; especially with the beautiful young women he picked up in there. He managed to get himself a much sought after 'black' membership card and even got the nod to open a tab at the bar.

Charlie Coleman was a 'face' and had made many friends and connections in the club. He was never sniffy about mixing work with pleasure either. The overweight and hirsute Manager of a bluesy rock band plied him with drinks one night and asked if he would do a job for him. A promoter had screwed his band out of a significant sum of money and he asked Charlie to try get it back for them. The promoter lived out in Cambridge and Charlie remarked that he only ever really operated in London. The Manager offered to make it worth his while.

Charlie went down to Cambridge, found the promoter and demanded the money. The promoter was a big bastard and no slouch and he gave Charlie a few digs. Charlie wiped the blood from his mouth and gave the promoter a final warning, "I asked you politely ... now ... are you gonna fucking pay up or do I have to get unpleasant?"

The promoter gave Charlie another dig and told him to piss off back to London and to tell the "fat obnoxious bastard I owe him nothing!" Charlie shook his head as he walked away muttering, "Don't say I didn't warn you."

The band's Manager was panicking when he called at Charlie's flat early one morning, "My God! What did you do? I've just been questioned by the police!"
Charlie yawned, "Oh yeah? What about? Crimes against public decency with that band o' yours?"
The Manager was sweating, "Did you set the stables at his farm on fire? Did you?"
"Who's saying I did? Where are the witnesses?"
The Manager glared at him, "You did, didn't you!"
"Who's saying I did?"
The Manager was disgusted, "You burned eight horses alive!"
Charlie laughed, "You mean 'dead', you mean I burned eight horses 'dead'."
"I don't believe this!"
Charlie smirked at him, "Listen, you just keep your trap shut, awright? We're in the clear. I never mentioned your name. The Old Bill have got nothing on us. I was careful."
The Manager calmed down a little.

Charlie rubbed his thumb and index finger together in front of his face, "You got my cash? Cost me a bleedin' fortune in petrol to burn that place down."

Charlie had indeed mentioned the Manager's name to the Promoter and the Cambridge police questioned the Manager for twenty-four hours. The Manager had a rock solid alibi and never squealed. He held a burning grudge towards Charlie Coleman for lying to him though.

Middle aged Virgil Cooney was a well-known fraudster and always involved in some elaborate scam or other. Virgil had fallen out with his old business partner, Maureen 'Skinny Mo' Mulrooney. She had conned him out of a large payday that *they* had conned out of an elderly rich man. Skinny Mo was refusing to give Virgil his cut of the graft and Virgil was seething. He had thought up many ways to get his revenge, but in the final analysis he could see only violence as a just dessert for her.

Virgil approached Charlie in The Colony Room club on Dean Street, a bohemian hang out known for its charming motto: *Rush up, Drink Up, Spend Up, Fuck Off.* Charlie was chatting to the artist Francis Bacon when Virgil asked if he could have a quiet word. Charlie went down to the street with Virgil.

Virgil was edgy, "Charlie, tell me to 'fuck off' if you don't want to do it, but I've got a wee job for you."
Charlie lit a Pall Mall, "You know me, Virgil. No job too small, no job too big."
Virgil paused, "This is Skinny Mo though."
"Skinny Mo? Your partner?"
"Yes, Charlie. She's … well, she's had my fucking trousers down hasn't she."
Charlie couldn't help but giggle, "*You*? You're the biggest conman in the-"
"I know, I know. It goes no further, but that's what I'm worried about.

Skinny Mo's got a big mouth on her. She's useless without me, won't last two minutes going it alone. I want her ... I want her to retire ... I'm frightened she'll fuck up and things from the past'll start surfacing. Do you get me?"

Charlie closed in a little, "You want her *permanently* retired? Retired *properly*?"

"Would you ... do you think you could do it?"

"Mmm. Depends how much you're willing to shell out, Virg'."

"See, thing is, Charlie, I've got a plan. I know how you could do it real easy."

"A snuff's a snuff though, Virg'. I'll still want the going rate."

"How much are we talking?"

"At least five grand."

Virgil hissed, "Five fucking grand!"

Charlie flicked his cigarette into the road and made to head back into The Colony. Virgil put his hand on Charlie's arm, "OK, wait a minute, wait a minute ... before we go any further ... you know that Skinny Mo's in a wheelchair now don't you?"

Charlie shrugged, "So ... ?"

"Well, I thought I'd better tell you upfront, and I'm going to be honest with you. Gel Chalmers and Bernard Romans turned me down, said they weren't willing to do in a cripple."

Charlie was pissed off, he hissed, "You went to those two fucking mugs before you came to me?"

"Like I said, she's in a wheelchair, it's sensitive, I thought you'd turn me down, Charlie."

"No Virgil, you're just trying to get a good deal on it that's all. You've been shopping around haven't you?"

Virgil nodded his head and offered him his hand, "Two grand?"

"Three and a half."

"Two thousand five?"

"Three, Virgil. My last call."

They shook hands.

Skinny Mo lived in a private apartment block near Lancaster Gate.

103

Charlie did a bit of surveillance on her and decided to strike on a Sunday.

Skinny Mo relied on the elevator to get up and down to her third floor apartment. She had an arrangement with the Doorman where she would call down and he would come up for her and take her down to the street.

Charlie snuck past the Doorman and vaulted up the stairs. He pulled a balaclava on and walked down the corridor towards her. She was sat waiting at the elevator, her back to him. He creeped down and grabbed the handles of the wheelchair.

Skinny Mo was taken by surprise, "Who's that?"
She tried to look over his shoulder but Charlie was quickly pushing her towards the flight of stairs.
"Hey! Stop! What are you … ?"

Charlie gave the chair one almighty push and launched it down the stairs. He could hear the elevator grinding to a stop on the floor just as Skinny Mo was propelled out of her chair and was hitting the stairs at speed. Bounce, bounce, bounce, the chair smashed into her head as it tippled over her. Her screaming stopped as she hit the edge of a stair face on. Charlie jumped over her and shot down the two flights. He stuffed the balaclava in his jacket pocket, patted his hair down and calmly walked out of the front door.

Charlie was heading on to Poland Street when a Beggar sprung out of a doorway at him. Charlie flinched and raised his fists; but before he could chin the Beggar he thrust a piece of paper into Charlie's hand and skidooed. Charlie was perplexed. He read the grubby, type-scripted letter:

Involute Sentence Engenderer is very facile to utilize. After writing or pasting content in the first text box, press the convert button to automatically paraphrase the content. This software works as a paraphrase converter for transforming simple and prevalent English into more intricate English. It can be utilizable as a gratuitous article spinner due to its competency to rephrase an astronomically immense body of text and potentially engender multiple unique versions with each conversion of the same content. With Involute Sentence Engenderer you can reword content online and re-write up to 7000 characters or less at a time/per conversion. This should be exuberant for spinning articles, essays or paraphrasing website content for blogs which conventionally consists of a substantial amount of content. In order to rephrase a sentence, paragraph, essay or article efficaciously, content with good grammar and spelling is consequential when utilizing this automatic paraphraser because it can only apperceive, understand and rewrite correct grammar. For an article rewriter that is in the form of a bot, it does a good job of venerating English and utilizing super sessions that make sense. Content that is written in all caps or with the first letter of every word capitalized can still be rephrased by this software. Otherwise, as long as the grammar of the content is sensible and recognizable, intricate sentence engenderer can make the task of paraphrasing facile. Rather than having to research synonyms for words or phrases and deduce which ones are the most felicitous substitutes for any context a word or phrase may be utilized in, paraphrasing is done on auto pilot. Aside from simply being utilized as an implement to spin text or paraphrase content, intricate sentence engenderer can be instrumental towards accomplishing a number of supplemental tasks. Amending lexicon, learning incipient ways to utilize English words and phrases and integrating more uniqueness to the process of engendering incipient content. Due to how infrequent and ('unusual', 'eccentric', 'unorthodox', 'unwonted') an abundance of the words and phrases are in the database of this paraphrase engenderer, it can engender and exhibit a unique style of writing and lexicon. It makes it more facile to encounter and discover incipient words."

Charlie frowned at the claptrap, screwed up the page into a ball and threw it in a bin. It was obviously the ranting of a madman.

A couple of days later, Charlie went looking for his wages from Virgil Cooney. He found him in The French House pub. They eyed each other and stepped outside. The rain pissed down and they sheltered under the awning of a patisserie.

Virgil whispered, "She's not dead. Her face is really messed up and she's got amnesia, which I suppose is quite handy, but-"

"Just gimme my money, Virgil."

"Is half all right? You know, seeing as you didn't actually do her in."

Charlie sighed, "No, it fucking well isn't all right. Cough up you tight fisted cunt."

"You were supposed to take her out, Charlie. You can't expect-"

Charlie put his mouth to Virgil's ear, "Listen you slimy ponce. Pay up or I'll push *you* down the stairs in a fuckin' wheelchair."

"I'm not in a wheelchair, Charlie."

"You will be if you don't give me my wages."

Charlie was with a sexy little French bird called Mathilde the night he first clapped eyes on Candice. He was transfixed and wishing he had waited before making his choice for the night. He watched Candice out of the corner of his eye and half listened to Mathilde babble on about some frivolous nonsense. Candice looked at him a few times and he could stand it no longer. He told Mathilde he was off for a piss and he approached Candice.

"Excuse me, but I think we've met before."

Candice looked him up and down, "Have we? Where?"

Charlie was shameless, "In me dreams."

Candice sighed, rolled her eyes and started to turn her back, "Your girlfriend's staring at you."

"Oh, my sister you mean? She's a bit slow. I only bring her out 'cos she's got no mates."

Candice shook her head but gave a little smile. Enough of a smile for Charlie to ask for her phone number.

Candice was relenting to his charms a little, "Give me *your* number."
"I don't have a telephone."
"I'll write mine down and give you it later. Now, go back to your girlfriend will you."

Candice was good on her word and she slipped him her number on the way out. Charlie winked at her and thought about her as he fucked Mathilde in her smart hotel suite that night. Not that Mathilde wasn't beautiful, but there was something about Candice that went beyond beauty.

He wasted no time in calling her the next day but was puzzled when told he had got through to the Trebistock Institute on Goodge Street. He asked for her and the male voice on the other end said she he had never heard of her. He tried a few more times and kept getting the same reply. He eventually gave up but couldn't get her out of his head, and it was starting to affect his performance on a professional level.

Charlie had been servicing an old, rich and lonely Jewish lady called Esther who lived in swanky Holland Park. For a while it was a nice little gig that slotted in between his regular job of attacking people. Esther always slipped him cash after he had slipped her a length and she often bought him some nice pieces of clobber as a bonus.

One afternoon, not long after his very brief encounter with Candice, he pulled out of Old Esther as she panted post-orgasm. He quickly lit a Pall Mall cigarette and sighed, "I feel really bad doing this, Esther."
Old Esther stroked his chest, "Don't feel bad about it, Charles. I like to help you out financially. And besides, I can afford it. You know I'm a socialist at heart."
He frowned, "No, not the cash! I feel bad about fucking you. If any of the chaps knew I was screwing an old dear like you they'd rip the piss out o' me. I'd never live it down."

Esther was sobbing as he slipped on his clothes and shot out. He had been considering ditching the gig, but setting eyes on Candice had made his mind up to do it. For the first time in his life he was sure that he could remain faithful to a bird, if that bird was Candice and *only* Candice.

He kept calling the number and kept getting the Trebistock Institute. He popped into The Scotch Of St James' every night on the off chance that she might be there, in fact, whichever boozer or eatery he went to in the West End he would have one eye out for her. His friends, 'The Chaps', began to ask him why he was so distracted.

After six weeks of not seeing her again he began to wonder whether he had imagined her, dreamt her up, fantasized her into existence. There was always that telephone number she had given him though. It was obviously a wrong number but she had definitely given him it. The number proved she did exist and wasn't simply a dream girl.

...

....

......

....

...

Justice Mr. Beiber smiled at &, "This is better. Yes, chapter five's an improvement."
& breathed a sigh of relief, "Thank you, sir."
"You *are* making all this up aren't you &?"
"Of course, sir."
"Good, because if I find out any of this is true there'll be repercussions." Sir Justice Mr. Beiber Sir squinted at &, "How did you end up over here?"
"Me sir? Huh ... well, I died a bodily death, sir."

& remembered he had forgotten about his bodily death. He very rarely remembered or forgot about it nowanights. A diagram of the contents page of a novel wrapped itself around his vision.

THE LIFE OF O'REILLY

I. **Prologue: An Emotional Detroit**
II. **Quantum Suicide Machine**
III. **Sodom & Begorrah**
IV. **Living Next Door to Alice in Wonderland**
V. **Research & Destroy**
VI. **Blow Up: Groucho Marxism Rules OK**
VII. **Psychic Graffiti**
VIII. **The Revelation Will Not Be Televised**

*Le hasard c'est peut-être le pseudonyme de Dieu, quand
il ne veut pas signer.*
Synchronicity Is Perhaps God's Pseudonym When He
Does Not Want To Sign.

Anatole France

& recognized it; instant mourning for the material realm and the
eternal opportunities for failure. He remembered he forgot he had
been a character in the manuscript: *I count my wad. I've done in two
hundred and fifty quid already. Money just seems to dissolve into thin
air in London. I've got four grand left. I suppose I should feed the
overdraft a little. There's going to be fucking hell to pay one of these
days, Danny Powers (eventually to become the guinea pig formerly
known as &) Hmm, but what's the worse they can do to me? I live in
a rented flat back in Bradford. They can kick me out, take me to the
Small Claims Court and bankrupt me and then the DSS are going to
have to look after me. It's not the end of the world, is it? I've lived off
The State before. No big deal. I'm a single man. It's not like I've got
a family anymore. When Sarah set the Child Support Agency on me
they saw the sorry state of my finances and demanded fuck all from
me, in fact I thought they were going to drop me a few quid for being
such a sorry cunt.*

She should have kept her mouth shut. Before she brought them into the fray I was dropping her a few hundred quid every now and then. I knew Simon Goldenbollocks was earning a decent wage and that she wasn't declaring her mobile hairdressing cash in hand, but it didn't matter. The money I gave was towards the keep of Jamie. She had to get fucking stroppy and open that big mouth of hers and dob me in it to the CSA, didn't she?

The bath's hot and my mood's fine. I'm not like O'Reilly, I'm alive and while I'm alive there is hope. There will be horizons and sunsets and twists and turns and unexpected windfalls and more cold sunny days and laughs and sex and good music and awe inspiring conversations. There will. There's got to be … it won't all be bad. It can't be, it can't because that would buck the law of averages. Shit-storms eventually subside, dark clawing dreams dissolve into wondrous leviathan epics, a negative can easily turn into a positive, a glass can be half full and I won't always feel like sticking it into peoples faces and carving them up.

I look down at my body. It's not bad. I can still make out stomach muscles if I sit up a little. My chest is still defined, O.K., it's not defined in a Calvin Klein model definition of defined, but I haven't got hairy tits either. I'm still tanned from the summer; spent a lot of time out in the garden; got up in the mornings and sunbathed and read and listened to tapes and worked on 'Love in the Time of Asbestosis' on my laptop.

I stayed off the beer, and drank lots of bottled water and ate All Bran and tried to avoid fatty foods and ate plenty of baked beans and felt good about my semi-detox programme. I still smoked though, still smoked and drank plenty of strong, milky and sugary Tetley's tea. They're my real vices. Cigs and tea.
"All right, Doctor, I'm listening, I'll lay off the booze and the Prozac and the burgers and the fry-ups, but there's no fucking way I'm giving up the tea and fags. You might as well gimme the cyanide tablet now, mate."

I sink down into the hot water, right down until it's up to my bottom lip. I can feel my cheeks burning. This really is hot. The hottest bath I've had in ages. God it feels good. A 'bath suicide' I can understand. Why go out in a river of shit and piss and rubbish when you can go out in a hot bubble bath of aromatic scents? O.K, it's not a powerful and poetic gesture but it's a lot comfier and you won't look too bad when they bag you up.

I scrub myself. Hot bath's remind me of Sunday nights and Harry Secombe's 'Highway' and sitcoms starring Thora Hird and cheese on toast and early nights and asking for notes to excuse me from P.E. and Jim Bowen's 'Bullseye' and no cunt ever winning the speedboat and not being able to get to sleep because of the knot in your stomach. Sunday's were always the worst day of the week. School hovered malignantly only hours away.

I think about the photo of O'Reilly with Dutch and Bruno. How happy he looked. The craic they were having at the Fleadh, the hope in the air that they'd be ending the day getting their ends away and falling into blissful sleep; drunken & content at having spent their energies wisely.

Sir Beiber wagged his finger at &, "Ah, so you *were* a writer in the material realm?"

"No sir, it was written *about* me. A ghost writer wrote it, sir."

"A ghost wrote a book about you, &?"

"Yes, sir?"

"What kind of ghost?"

"Huh … a dead ghost, sir."

"Maurice Maeterlink perhaps?"

& didn't recognize the moniker, "Who, sir?"

"At the point of material death did you suffer, &? Did they prolong your suffering?"

& became excited, "Yes, sir. They did."

Sir Justice Beiber Sir Justine morphed into an eighteenth century gentleman, frothing at the mouth and punctuating his words with a huge metallic gavel, "The doctors and the priests, said Napoleon, have long been making death grievous. Let us, then, learn to look upon it as it is in itself, free from the horrors of matter and stripped of the terrors of the imagination. Let us first get rid of all that goes before and does not belong to it. Thus, we impute to it the tortures of the last illness; and that is not right. Illnesses have nothing in common with that which ends them. They form part of life and not of death. We easily forget the cruelest sufferings that restore us to health; and the first sun of convalescence destroys the most unbearable memories of the chamber of pain. But let death come; and at once we overwhelm it with all the evil done before it. Not a tear but is remembered and used as a reproach, not a cry of pain but becomes a cry of accusation. Death alone bears the weight of the errors of nature or the ignorance of science that have uselessly prolonged torments in whose name we curse death because it puts an end to them. In point of fact, whereas the sicknesses belong to nature or to life, the agony, which seems peculiar to death, is wholly in the hands of men. Now what we most dread is the awful struggle at the end and especially the hateful moment of rupture, which we shall perhaps see, approaching during long hours of helplessness and which suddenly hurls us, disarmed, abandoned and stripped, into an unknown that is the home of the only invincible terrors which the human soul has ever felt. It is twice unjust to impute the torments of that moment to death. We shall see presently in what manner a man of today, if he would remain faithful to his ideas, should picture to himself the unknown into which death flings us. Let us confine ourselves here to the last struggle. As science pro-gresses, it prolongs the agony which is the most dreadful moment and the sharpest peak of human pain and horror, for die witnesses, at least; for, often, die sensibility of him who, in Bossuet's phrase, is 'at bay with death,' is already greatly blunted and perceives no more than the distant murmur of die sufferings which he seems to be enduring. All the doctors consider it their first duty to protract as long as possible even the most excruciating convulsions of the most hopeless agony. Who has not, at a bedside, twenty times wished and not once dared to throw himself at their feet and implore them to show mercy? They are filled with so great a certainty and the duty which they obey leaves so little room for the least doubt that pity and reason, blinded by tears, curb their revolt and shrink back before a law which all recognize and revere as the highest law of human conscience. One day, this prejudice will strike us as barbarian. Its roots go down to the unacknowledged fears left in the heart by religions that have long since died out in the mind of men. That is why the doctors act as though they were convinced that there is no known torture. They seem persuaded that every minute gained amidst the most intolerable sufferings is snatched from the incomparably more dreadful sufferings which the mysteries of the hereafter reserve for men; and, of two evils to avoid that which they know to be imaginary, they choose the real one."

The Gentleman handed & a business card: *This was a presentation on behalf of Happy Exits: taking the pain out of departures since 1911.* And with that he morphed back into Sir Justine Beiber Sir.
"Well?" Asked Sir Beiber.
"Well what, sir?"
"Are you impressed &"
"Should I be?"
"Of course you should!"
"But ..."
Sir Beiber groaned, "But *what?*"

Doctor A was observing the conversation. She was as frustrated as the next reader but knew that there must – at some point – be a point to it; otherwise, why was so much energy being expended?

Doctor A called Doctor F over, "Is there any way we can disrupt this chaotic Beiber character?"
Doctor F rubbed her chin, "I don't think so. He seems to be a hangover from &'s physical unconscious. He's residue."

"So he was with & when he was alive?"

"An archetype from a recurrent dream. Yes."

Doctor A mused on it, "Hmmm ... get his biography up. I think there may be a way to exorcise this Beiber character."

Doctor F brought up &'s *His Story* on the large floating screen. She slipped on a clean pair of data spectacles and set the dial: relevant to recurrent dreams of subject A. Streams of data downloaded directly into Doctor A's brain. A relevance level 10 stopped the process: an MTV video of The B-52's performing "Give Me Back My Man" from 1980 played. A glitch on the VHS tape was allowing an image of the gyrating Justin Beiber to infect the performance. The 1980 performance he invaded was 14 years prior to the birth of the prefabricated teenybopper's birth.

Doctor A brought up &'s memory of the experience. The 14 year old & and his friends had been slamming school in the house of the parents of one of them. They had been drinking whiskey and sniffing glue. & ended up falling down a flight of stairs and being hospitalized for severe concussion.

"The image of this teenybopper from the future lodged itself in &'s memory during his concussion," said Doctor A, "it has become an authority archetype. & associates the image of this Justin Beiber character with order, rules and regulations."

"Is there anything we can do?" Asked Doctor F.

"I'll have to think about it."

& found himself on a gurney again, being dragged backwards at breakneck speed by a heavily tattooed Nurse. She flashed her chest tattoo at him: *The ambition of water, to be everywhere at once, gushing through birth canals, clapping through sewers, sanctifying the feet of the dead. The ambition of water, to flood the minds of detectives, camouflage its source in totality, life giving, saving, babbling streams of Bodhi. The ambition of water, impervious to possession,*

terror of porous wealth, nonpartisan leveler, ontology's translucent bloodstream. Scientists at CERN could prove the controversial theory of 'Mingused', which suggests that the universe stretches back into time infinitely, with no Big Bang.
"That's a very elaborate tattoo." Commented &.

A gas masked Surgeon hovered over &. He shook his head in dismay, "Oh dear, not you again!"
"I didn't ask to be here!" Stated &.
"I'm teasing. I'm really happy you're here." The Surgeon pulled on a hat and lit a cigarette: affecting the pose of a Hardboiled Detective from a shitty Noir B movie.

The Noir Surgeon slipped into a ham fisted Humphrey Bogart accent impression, "Chances are we'll all find a dead body at least once in our lives. Chances are slim we'll ever find a dead body with a dead body inside it. Sean Cassidy did. He found his dead estranged wife and their unborn dead baby. *Can something be called dead if it hasn't been born?* Her wrists were wide open, looked like blood smeared sultry mouths. Lipstick applied by an old blind beautician, happy to get a gig, *any* gig. Maria had used a Stanley Knife. No hacking. No hysterical windmilling with a kitchen knife. This was a crafty cut. She'd done a good job: deft DIY death. The blood had found a level on the stripped pine floor. It had flowed upwards. Weird gravity. Ochre halo crowning her in mockery. Marble eyes fixed on eternity. Sean had stared into them and seen an eternity of nothingness. *God isn't dead, Nietchze! He was never alive you half mad fuck!* White panic; a burning white-hot panic. Sean glanced at the Stanley Knife. What he'd do was ... what he'd do was cut her stomach open and rescue the baby. That's what he'd do. A caesarean rescue. Salvage something out of the destruction. He froze and touched her head. His palm stuck to it. Ice on ice. Long dead. His bowels swung open. Sean grabbed at his disintegrating stomach and fell to his knees. Breath deserted him. His ears were on fire and he could hear the thunderous roar of Hell opening up for business. He'd never felt more alive. Sean thought he knew what death looked like. Sean thought he had death's measure. Thought he had an angle on it. Thought he was insulated from death's jocose art shock. No matter how many dead Afghani's or Bosnian's or Kurdish Iraqi's he'd seen nothing could prepare him for *this*. They were just nameless casualties. They hadn't existed until Sean had seen them *not* existing. *They* were nothing to him. *She* was everything. This was personal death, a coruscating full stop. This was a kick in the balls that followed through to the bone marrow like a heat seeking silver bullet. Sean remained disabled. He cradled the pain in his stomach and rocked back and forth and stared at the husk of everything he had ever truly loved. He caught a breath and screamed her name. He screamed her name and he rocked back and forth and hot liquefied shit ran down his thighs and it wouldn't have mattered if it were acid because Sean was beyond pain. They were drinking in Soho. The Coach and Horses. Drinking around Fleet Street was never really Sean's cup of tea. He knew too many people in Fleet Street. Soho was always peopled with strangers. Soho was cast with bit part players. Nobody cared who or what you were. Soho suited Sean's frame of mind. Soho suited him fine. Sean said, "Thing that hurts, thing that really hurts is that I never got to say goodbye. The last words … I think … I think the last words I ever said to her were 'fuck you!'"

Ray said, "Stop beating yourself up, Sean. How were you – I mean, nobody – how were you to know?" Sean said, "I'm being maudlin. Humour me, Ray. I need humouring."

"You need a woman. That's what you *need*, Sean. What you need is a good woman. You've got to move on."

Sean looked at Ray's face. Ray was fifty. Five years older than him. *Five years is nothing after forty. It's all a slow waltz to the grave.* The drink had been unusually kind on Ray's face. Sean wouldn't have liked to have seen Ray's liver though. *That must be one ugly fucking organ!* Sean knew Ray was bored with him. It wasn't hard to get bored with Sean. Sean bored himself. He often found himself yawning at the sound of his own voice.

Sean said, "You really think a woman's the solution, Ray?"

Ray said, "Sure. Give you, you know, huh ... *meaning*. Everyone needs meaning."

"Samantha gives *you* meaning, Ray?"

"I'm not talking about Samantha. It's different."

"What's different?"

"Me and Samantha. We've, Christ, if it weren't for the others. It's the others that give *me* meaning. Samantha and me? That's different."

"Huh, so, what you're – let me get this straight, Ray – what you're saying is that I need a lover *not* a wife?"

"No. *You* need a wife. You're wife material. Me, well, yeah, yeah, I need ... well, you know, I'm lover material. I need lovers."

Sean scoffed, "The fuck does that mean?"

"It means ... well, it means ... it means you're a faithful guy. It's a compliment. You know me. You know me, Sean. I can't keep it in my pants. You never fucked around with Maria."

"I fucked around with Maria. What do you know?"

"Who with? Who did you – did you? Really? You never told me you fucked around with – who do you fuck around with – who was it? Do I know her?"

"Whores. Hookers. I fucked whores and hookers, Ray."

It was Ray's turn to scoff, "That's not – it doesn't count – that's not fucking around! It's not cheating is it? Whores aren't cheating. I mean, you know what I mean? You paid for it. That's a transaction. It's not cheating." Ray was a very unsuccessful actor and he needed drama. Affairs and fucking around suited him. Sean knew what Ray meant. Sean didn't see himself as a *faithful* guy though. To be faithful you have to believe in something. Sean believed in nothing. There were a lot of things Ray didn't know about Sean. He didn't know that Sean had a rotting fucking albatross around his neck. A stinking albatross that he was dragging around with him like some sixteenth century ghost dragging his shackles. If *hair shirts* were still available on the High Street Sean would have bought one and be wearing it to match the albatross. What Sean really wanted to say to Ray was, "Look, Ray. I'm to blame for Maria killing herself and the baby, O.K.? I promised her Heaven and I gave her Hell! She'd had nothing but shit in her life. I was her white knight. I was supposed to protect her … I was … I was supposed to save her! I let her die. It was my fault, O.K.?" Ray finished his drink and slimed off to meet one of his naïve young lovers. She'd be at least half his age and vulnerable and have pert breasts and a tight pussy and be empty inside and needing more than just cock to fill her up. Ray liked them like that. He liked them needy. He had very little to offer them materially but he could give them undivided attention for a short while. Once he managed to get inside their heads and fuck around with their emotions he'd almost certainly abandon them and move on to the next one. Ray didn't so much cherish the kill as the walking away dabbing at his bloody lips with a silk handkerchief. Ray got his rocks-off with the drama: the tears, the nuisance phone calls, the stalking. He got off on the threats of self-harm if he didn't return to them. Ray was a drama junkie. If he couldn't get paid for his art he would sure as Hell make his life his art. Sean's nickname for Ray was 'Nosferatu'. Ray was a sleazy survivor feeding on the emotional energy of tremulous young things. On hearing that one of his play-things had attempted tried to throw herself under a tube train, Ray got hard and had to pull himself off in a public toilet. He shot like a Shire horse. Sean ordered another drink from Norman, the legend-ary cantankerous landlord of the boozer. *Drinks on empty … need another round.* Sean sipped his beer and stared out onto the street. He lit a link in a chain of cigarettes and wondered why he loved London so much. He'd thought about going home to Manchester after she'd died. He thought about it a lot. He'd have been seen as a failure if he had gone home. That wasn't what stopped him though. It was London. London had a hold on him. It had gotten inside him. In Manchester he was known. He had family there. Bloodlines beg answers and Sean wasn't willing to give them. They knew things about him back in Manchester. He had history in London but the Metropolis was forgiving. *A man can get lost in London.* Nobody knows or really cares about each other in London. Everybody is from somewhere else. Everybody's too busy to give a fuck where you're from. London is Zen-like in its impermanence. Meet some anonymous Fuck one day, spill your life rap, and never see them again. Easy. Maria loved London for different reasons. London was a haven. London was sanctuary. London was civilized. London, for all its faults *wasn't* where she was from and that mattered. All the sleaze and corruption and backbiting and scams and street crime and bureaucracy she encountered in the City were nothing compared to the things she'd seen in her hometown. After watching mass human butchery close up, London was as near to Heaven as she could imagine. *Sayonara Sarajevo! Seen enough madness to last a million lifetimes. London's for me!* It made it all the more hard for Sean to accept. She should have felt safe in London. Maria should have wanted to live her life to its logical conclusion, be it the Big C or some freaky accident or just natural expiration. She should have waited. She should have given another life to the world. Maria should have hung on. Second chances are few and far between in life. Maria had a chance. Maria threw that chance away with scalpel precision. A steady handed slash setting free the life fuel. *What was going through her mind? Why did she want to take our child to the grave with her?* Pam, the resident beggar of the Coach and Horses, made her way around the boozer. Small, middle aged, rotund, cheap specs, raincoat, piss stench. A sane man or woman wouldn't fuck Pam. Not that Pam wanted to be fucked. Pam just wanted coin to cop cheap cider so she could forget that she was alive. Pam was a fixture. The Coach was *her* begging patch. She had some unwritten contract; a pact of some sort, maybe a Faustian pact. Pam was the official unofficial beggar in the boozer. A character among many other characters without a back-story. Who knows what twist of fate had landed her this prime pitch? Her patter was always the same: smile, hand out and, "spare some change, please?" A negative nod or even a "fuck off you scrounger!" could never deter Pam from her job. Sean liked Pam. Liked her consistency. Sean liked that she was shameless in her begging. Pam was honest. Sean admired honesty like only those who haven't an honest bone in their body admire it. To Sean, Pam was a star. She was a star because she cared

119

about nothing or nobody and she didn't care what anybody thought about her. *The only real stars are those who are free … truly free.* Maria *seemed* to be free on the surface. *Surface is full of shit though.* Surface can be manufactured and bought. Surface comes in packages just as sure as love comes in spurts. Maybe Maria *seemed* free because she'd *been* freed. There's a difference. Sean was beginning to realize that. Sean was waking up to the fact that freedom is within. *You can never really run away from yourself. No matter how far you travel you're still there!* Maybe that was the problem for Maria: the *there*. She had certainly travelled. She had certainly travelled and she had certainly been freed. She had arrived at the *there*, but maybe that wasn't enough. Maybe she'd needed to travel within. Maybe she *had* travelled within and when she got there it was too much to take. Maybe she couldn't lock the door on her past. Maybe she couldn't screen out the horrors and maybe … Sean would never know and that's what was hurting him. Maria took two lives, and half of one of them was Sean's. Maria owed him an explanation. She didn't leave a note. A note would have been a start. A note would have been something. A note might have kept the detectives away."

The Surgeon waited for & to comment, and after a beat, "Well? What do you think? Do you think I could make it as pulp fiction writer?"
"Why are you asking *me*?" Replied &.
"You were a writer of crime thrillers weren't you?"
& frowned, shook his head, "No … no I wasn't! I don't know where you heard that."
The Surgeon babbled excitedly, "violence, transgression, alcohol, sex, femme fatales, mystery, outsiders, corruption, Los Angeles, loneliness."

& froze and heard a fragmented memory enveloping him. He winced and remembered he had forgotten he had the capacity to do it. His environment was a war torn city; a clichéd war torn city: cameramen and photographers and TV directors posed mutilated bodies for maximum impact; zoomed in on wreckage – human and structural – and heat seeking lenses captured gaping, screaming mouths buried under concrete rubble. Half a leg here, a still twitching arm there, puddles of blood everywhere, in out in out you shake it all about, you do the hokey cokey and you turn around ...

He gagged on the stench of sulfur and floated amongst the walking wounded. They were covered in dust; noses bleeding through the detritus of black cordite cocaine, eyes on stalks, ears drowning in the mucous of trapped wind, bodies unsure of their composition as they tiptoed across collapsed concrete hills cultivated with billions of broken glass seeds. The rank air still vibrating augural and rendering vision unstable.

& knew this place and he knew this was a facsimile at the same point. He had never physically been here but he knew every nook and cranny. He had imagined it so automatically that to be here now smelt mediocre. This vista used to churn his bowels and raise his blood temperature and set his heartbeat to calypso. This was the place he had imagined into being: a typical scene from the immediate aftermath of a bombing. & knew it was a fair appropriation but that it lacked authenticity. His Words were creating it so the scene was invalid. He closed his eyes and rewound.

It flickered back to him: a word here, a word there, a digression here and there: simultaneous adjectives fighting naked nouns in Jacuzzi's. Flinging syntactic shit at each other, hurling 'clever' insults. & focused. He willed himself back to The Source.

The elevator lugged left and right and up and down and even created a few new directions that spat in the face of gravity. & held on tight to his thoughts. There was a leak that needed plugging; he grabbed chunks of brain matter and jammed them into the space where he imagined the hole was. A fluorescent strip light spluttered in a brazen Noir cliché. & could smell a sickly green hue. A wall of old fashioned tin filing cabinets grew up before him; the drawers shooting open and spilling black and white circa 1940's-50's crime scene photographs: dead LA hookers and dead suckers and dead fuckers and dead-deadbeats and dead fags and dead fag hags and dead hoods.

One of the dead whores in a photograph smiles at & through slug like neon red lips, and hisses:

"Spirit fructifying roast flesh and cold liquid
Shoplifted from meat boutique and dive bar
Behold the spread
Your eyes are bigger than your belly
Sup and masticate
Fill your boots
Receive the succulent secular Eucharist
Feel the burn in your loins, the flush in your face
Admire your warped reflection in the silverware
Consume and be consumed in revelry
Cannibalize homo-heroic deeds of others
Shout the loudest with the tallest tales
Rip off your hair shirt and leak testosterone

Let passive aggressive sentiment wash over you
Suck the bones clean and drum the table in rhythm to convention
Tease with home truths and degenerated stories
Slap backs and grease palms

And wake to the night destroyed
After spasmodic sleep punctuated with rare dream smithereens
And the emptiness slowly rising in-synch with cognizance
Fountainhead blocked with toxic waste, elliptical equilibrium
And that empty feeling giving birth to self-loathing."

She winked at & and offered him a flyer for an event. & grabbed it and sucked in the information: a big titted pre-decapitated black and white Jayne Mansfield was staring out at him. Her left titty was spilling out of her dress and her nipple had been colored in with pink lipstick. She cooed at &, "Here is the password for the party tonight. Remember it: *1lufe2angger3lucod4kefer5nethif6rising7netin8riswood 9keth10neenne11lucsing12ingif13anger14honeth15ane16ucang 17keod18hois19ingcif20angely21rily22keger23angsinganisethane tangeanngngrisfesingkeisethlulysingkesinsingwoonethangangooer kesinwoodangisennkensinsingethinrisanollwoodlyifeingnetne woangeferluwoothhongodluoonethcigeisholgeod."*

& decoded it and committed it to memory as Mansfield incanted herself into a viral TV ad for Agent Provocateur underwear. & stepped back over into Sarajevo.

The carnage was on pause for him. He stepped in just as the bomb had come to a full stop on the kindergarten. Infant limbs were frozen in the air; a mosaic of reshuffled biology. The smiling mouth of a five year old hung ragged and jocose seventeen feet from the ground, vying for primetime with the unsullied liver of a four year old.

Grizzled American war reporter, L.A. Piltz grabbed a hold of &'s hand and they skipped through the slaughter as L.A. Piltz delivered his newscast to camera, "Now that the Bush administration's Iraqi war campaign has begun in holy earnest, the way that the monopoly U.S. media present this attack needs to come into sharp focus and graphic relief. I'm talking about the inherently gratuitous prurience of war video footage, which in ethic and effect are no better than the craven exploitation and murderous lust of the fabled snuff film, a mostly urban legend with some rare basis in fact, which shows the literal torture and murder of an unwilling innocent victim. Viewers worldwide will be watching living, breathing people blown to bloody bits. People will be dying and maimed in real-time video, in loving slow-motion pan and zoom. This will be replayed endlessly as if it's NFL Sunday or the World Cup. Commentators will clinically describe target acquisition and payload technology, laser-guided to locations very much smaller than the metaphoric football field. For the most part, news people will meticulously avoid dwelling on the suffering of their fellow humans, as well as animals, who are all 10,000 feet below and miles and miles away. For the embedded and censored gonzo journalist and windblown coiffured newsspeakmodel, the victims may as well be made of sheetrock, or never have existed at all. Yet even survivors will horribly suffer. And they will die. From grievous wounds, exposure, thirst, starvation, persecution, continued medicine blockade, diseases caused by intentional destruction of water treatment plants as in Gulf War I, and more cancer from tons more radioactive ammunition, also as used in the first Persian Gulf War. This institutionalized and televised desensitization of the public will again be accomplished by willful legerdemain. *Nothing up my sleeve here in the Hummer, nothing to look at there in the ruins, and presto change-o-regime, it's over. No harm done. It's an electronic sleight of omission used as weapon of mass hypnosis. What you don't see is what they get.* This macabre illusion, however, actually shields a very real torture by voodoo, with countless innocents suspended as helpless as dolls, human sacrifices who never volunteered for the grisly duty, gruesomely struck with calibrated, precision instruments of havoc and doom, in sometimes pinprick-accurate military strike, backlit by media's proxy acceptance. Deprived of context, they suffer and die offstage, invisible but omnipresent, yet never to be heard from again, and, therefore, seemingly never to have existed at all. If a bomb falls in a village, and you don't know to care, was there ever a village in the first place? We know, but we don't know. Many viewers will be made to feel safe, thinking they're watching their fears bombed into oblivion, appreciating only that they'll continue to see these Pentagon snuff films in the haven of their private homes and thoughts. They won't make the connection that the people they're not seeing won't even have homes or thoughts any more. They can change the channel, record it for posterity, turn it off or walk away. They will have this choice, even as they rationalize that the people of Iraq have had their choice as well, no matter how ludicrous and self-serving this sop to their consciences would be.

It's personal whitewash, taking its cue from the collective eye. It's a dodge from responsibility and feigned personal absolution."

L.A. Piltz segued back into March 23rd 2003 and & was left smiling moronically into an unmanned television camera. & reached into the frozen sky and hung out on a limb. He saw Jane and John Doe voices coming over the horizon.

"I can see what he's trying to achieve."

"You can?"

"Yes. The emphasis is on unity of purpose; a validation of the accumulated information by attempting to elucidate through a fractured narrative."

"It's doomed in my opinion."

"But you must frame your critique under consideration of the obstacles: schizophrenic, stalked by an unreliable narrator, shepherded by malignant vibrations, bamboozled by history, constantly observed and above all, *dead* in the classical sense."

"Ah, but he's not willing to accept he's dead, therefore it isn't an obstacle."

Lizzie Bisland butted in, "But night after night, with calm incuriousness we open the door into that ghostly underworld, and hold insane revels with fantastic specters, weep burning tears for empty grief's, babble with foolish laughter at witless jests, stain our souls with useless crime, or fly with freezing blood from the grasp of an unnamed dread; and, with the morning, saunter serenely back from these wild adventures into the warm precincts of the cheerful day, unmoved, unstartled, and forgetting.

Peter Coffee sprang from a black box recorder, kicked Lizzie in her cunt and countenanced, "The things we see around us, the things which make up the data of our experience, not only are or exist; they also *become*, or come into actual existence; they change; they pass out of actual existence. The abstract notion of being represents its object to the mind in a static, permanent, changeless, self-identical condition; but if this condition were an adequate representation of reality change would be unreal, would be only an illusion. This is what the Eleatic philosophers of ancient Greece believed, distinguishing merely being and nothingness. But they were mistaken; for change in things is too obviously real to be eliminated by calling it an illusion: even if it were an illusion, this illusion at least would have to be accounted for. In order, therefore, to understand reality we must employ not merely the notion of being (something static), but also the notion of becoming, change, process, appearing and disappearing (something kinetic, and something dynamic). In doing so, however, we must not fall into the error of the opposite extreme from the Eleatics regarding change as the adequate representation of reality. This is what Heraclitus and the later Ionians did: holding that nothing is, that all becomes, that change is all reality, that the stable, the permanent, is non-existent, unreal, an illusion. This too is false; for change would be unintelligible without at least an abiding law of change, a permanent principle of some sort; which, in turn, involves the reality of some sort of abiding, stable, permanent being. We must then with Aristotle, as against both of those one-sided conceptions, hold to the reality both of being and of becoming; and proceed to see how the stable and the changing can both be real. To convince ourselves that they are both real, very little reflection is needed. We have actual experience of both those elements of reality in our consciousness and memory of our own selves. Every human individual in the enjoyment of his mental faculties knows himself as an abiding, self-identical being, yet as constantly undergoing real changes; so that throughout his life he is really the same being, though just as certainly he really changes. In external nature, too, we observe on the one hand innumerable processes of growth and decay, of motion and interaction; and on the other hand a similarly all-pervading element of sameness or identity amid all this never-ending change. It is from our experience of actuality and change that we derive not only our notion of temporal duration, but also our notion of potential being or possibility, as distinct from that of actual being or actuality. It is from our experience of what actually exists that we are able to determine what can, and what cannot exist. We know from experience what gold is, and what a tower is; and that it is intrinsically possible for a golden tower to exist, that such an object of thought involves no contradiction, that therefore its existence is not impossible, even though it may never actually exist as a fact. Similarly, we know from experience what a square is, and what a circle is; and that it is intrinsically impossible for a square circle to exist, that such an object of thought involves a contradiction, that therefore not only is such an object never actually existent in fact, but that it is in no sense real, in no way possible."

& blinked them all away – he didn't need reminding – and remembered he had forgotten about Vlatko and his idée fixe with goats.

Vlatko was named after a Bosnian king. His mother was murdered by his father for fucking a neighbor. Dad took a rusty pickaxe to her head, made mince of her brains, got roaring drunk on Slovak shine and hung himself. Vlatko was twelve. He was glad to have got shut. The reason Mum was fucking the neighbor was because Dad wasn't fucking *her*. Dad was fucking Vlatko and the family goat, Tikky. In Vlatko's estimation, Mum was a whore and Dad was a two timing bitch.

Vlatko's Father's suicide note was addressed to Tikky. Dad preferred Tikky's arse to his. Not something you'd want to include on your CV. Vlatko was scarred. He was confused. *Why had he left the goat a note? Was Tikky the goat able to read? Was it a gifted goat? Is that why he liked to make love to it?*

Vlatko didn't have too much time to ponder the goat/love/rejection nexus. He was swiftly scooped into the State Care System. *Pan into the fire.* The 'Professionals' took over his care and wellbeing. Vlatko made a fatal fuck-up by 'fessing he'd been fucked by his father. The Professionals preyed on him, the Croat Catholic Priests pimped him and the Publicly Employed Pedophiles punked him.

By the time Vlatko was fifteen he could have passed a bowling ball through his tattered *anus horribilis*. Vlatko took it in his stride though. It was 'normal'. All men craved to stick their dicks in him, but it still smarted when he thought about Dad getting hotter over the goat.

It wasn't incestuous sodomic rape that fucked Vlatko's head though. It was jealousy and rejection. At sixteen he was set free from the pederasts. The only thing he knew how to do well was lie down and take it in his rectum. He was alone and skint and expected to become a useful member of society.

He stole. He hustled. He failed on the streets of Belgrade. He thought about hanging himself like Dad. He thought better of it. He thought he'd tough it out. He met a kindly Muslim man who ran a shelter for fallen boys. The Man gave Vlatko shelter. Gave Vlatko meals. Gave Vlatko a pristine copy of the Koran. Gave Vlatko religious instruction. Gave Vlatko a good fucking and a fisting after prayer every day. Gave it to Vlatko bareback. Gave Vlatko HIV. Gave Vlatko the post fuck tear sodden lowdown, "Allah has struck me with this disease for being tempted by you. You are evil, Vlatko, and now *you* have the big disease with a little name."

Bullseye! Eureka! That was it! The goat had tempted his father! Goats were baaad muthafuckers! Evil sons of bitches! His poor father hadn't stood a chance. Rather than stay and keep tempting the poor Muslim Holy Man with his evil arsehole he hotfooted and hoofed it around Yugoslavia. He hooked up with hustlers, thieves and transients. Ran with pickpockets, purse-snatchers, pimps and peddlers. Vlatko asked around about his gift from the Holy Man. He got told he was in deep deep doo doo. He got told it was a disease that would eat him alive. He got told he should stop flogging his arse. He got told he was fucked. He got told he hadn't long left copping air. It was like a great weight had been lifted from his shoulders.

Now that Vlatko knew he was headed eternally south he lightened up. Now that there was gonna be an end in sight he reckoned he could handle anything lobbed his way. Life wasn't so scary anymore, knowing he wasn't long for it.

He had happy times. Got off on kicking the living shit out of goats undercover of night. He left a trail of them in his wake. There was concern in the hillsides that some hip young gang were going round getting grievous on goats in some new fangled sexmajik-devil-worshipping pursuit.

Vlatko managed to get to nineteen. He was surprised. He wasn't jubilant. He dug that he was on a death sentence. He didn't dig what the disease was all about. He figured he'd just keep ankling around the country seeing what happened. If men wanted to rim and fuck and fist him that was O.K. He didn't understand HIV or AIDS or The Plague or whatever else they called it, so there was no point trying to talk about it.

Always the goats though. A constant: Pygmy goats, Mountain goats, Nigerian dwarf goats, Dairy goats, Cashmere goats, Boer goats, Meat goats, Kinder goats, Angora goats, Nanny goats, Fainting goats, he'd fucked 'em all, regardless of race or specialty.

Vlatko was a one-man terror campaign against caprines. He lived the pleasant peasant simple life. He ate, drank, shat, pissed, stole and slept where and when he could. He trotted around the Balkans, whistling as he went. *Happy Larry foraging and a-thieving*. Ankling up and down the lands singing a simple song. His hobby was getting vicious on goats and there was a never-ending supply in the back-waters. This was the good life.

It was in one such village that he met Lavra. Vlatko was wandering through when he spied a Nanny goat and decided to hang about until darkness to give it a hiding.

Lavra lived quietly with her grave-dodging Grandmother in a shack.

Lavra clocked the mysterious young man and instantly got his measure. He was a nomad. She would offer him a bite to eat like the good Christian girl she was.

Slippery Vlatko slid off Lavra's radar. She was pissed off. It would have been nice to be Christian towards him. Being Christian made her feel good. There weren't many opportunities to feel good in her village. It would have been nice to be nice to a nomad.

Night moved in. Lavra was sat out stargazing as she did most nights. The village was no Sodom or *even* Gomorrah, but even if it were, Lavra would have taken a rain check on the narcotic hedonism.

The night had her skirt hitched, flashing some shiny jewels. Lavra heard a dull thudding sound from nearby and went to investigate. She spied Vlatko. He was beating ten shades of shit out of a goat that he had gagged with a paper bag and some string. Lavra was mortified. Struck dumb by the sheer lunacy of the act.

Vlatko was clearly getting his rocks off as he planted heavy whacks on the terrified goat with a lump hammer. He'd tied the goat tight to a gate. The bewildered beast was snookered. Banged up a beauty behind the eight ball. Vlatko had obviously done this before. No dilettante goat basher, Vlatko. No Sireee, Mr. Beiber, this was *skilled* cruelty.

Lavra had heard the spooky tales about goats getting their beastly brains beaten out in the night, but up until now she had it wrote off as rural legend. She now found herself only a few feet away from a genuine act of pure evil. Lavra felt strange. *Excited* and strange, but not fearful. Her God was with her and something alien was stirring inside.

Lavra hissed, "Stop! What are you doing?"
A rumbled Vlatko dropped the hammer and was about to get on his

toes when Lavra yelled, "No! Please! Please do not run away. I will not tell anybody. I want to talk."

Vlatko was surprised. Her words had a ring of sincerity. She sounded sweet. She sounded like she meant what she said. Vlatko wiped the blood from his face on his hands and then wiped his hands on his threadbare trousers. He said, "You promise?"
"I promise … come, I can give you food and drink."

Vlatko walked cautiously back to her shack. Granny was tucked up. Whacked out on moonshine. Lavra told him to sit whilst she got him sausage, bread and cherry wine. Vlatko was puzzled. *Was she a goat hater too? Had the goat done something to offend her?*

Vlatko wolfed down the sausage and bread and guzzled the cherry wine. Lavra eyed him. Proud. Happy to have a nomad sat at her table.

Lavra looked older than her twenty-three years. She had "village characteristics", an air of the inbred about her, not unlike Vlatko. Neither of them lookers: big ears, bug eyes, protruding teeth and dominant foreheads; foreheads seemingly intent on breaking out of the confines of skin.

Vlatko reminded her of the many brothers who had fled the village in search of employment. She'd been left behind to look after Grandmother. Lavra's parents had been killed in a road accident many years back. Their cart was hit head-on by a truck: blood and shit and vegetables and brains everywhere. The driver of the truck had been hitting the bottle heavy. He got off with a ban and a couple of months in hokey. He'd only killed Peasants.

God gave Lavra a hand dealing with the trauma. Lavra rolled up her sleeves and took on the matriarch role. Like a duck to water. Prayer and hard work kept her focused. She doted on her brothers, many of them older than her, and gave them the spur to go seeking livelihoods in the cities below. She told them it's what Momma and Poppa would have wanted. She was happy to stay behind and labor.

After supper, Lavra jawed on Vlatko. Vlatko was a lad of few words. She wanted to know why he dug getting medieval on goats. Vlatko kept quiet. Nodded negative and shucked and shimmied in his seat. Lavra persisted. Laid it down: if he fessed up he could kip in the shed out back and she'd rustle him up breakfast in the a.m.

Vlatko was still not playing ball. Lavra got out her holy books. She said, "Is it because you believe goats are evil?"

Vlatko shrugged and rolled a tab. As he sucked down on the coarse baccy, Lavra got all academic with the books. She gave it, "There is lots about goats in the good book."
Lavra got busy picking out 'good book' goat related gossip.

She cleared her catarrh congested throat, "Leviticus 17:7 they should no longer sacrifice their sacrifices to the goat-shaped demons with which they are having immoral intercourse. This will serve as a statute to time indefinite for you, throughout your generations … Isaiah 13:21, and there the haunters of waterless regions will certainly lie down, and their houses must be filled with eagle owls. And there the ostriches must reside, and the goat-shaped demons themselves will go skipping about there. And the jackals must howl in her dwelling towers, and the big snake will be in the palaces of exquisite delight. And the season for her is near to come, and her days themselves will not be postponed. God has broken the rod of the wicked ones, the staff of the ruling ones, the one striking peoples in fury with a stroke incessantly, the one subduing nations in sheer anger with a persecution without restraint."

Lavra checked Vlatko's reaction. Dumb. Unimpressed. Vlatko waited for a question.
Lavra said, "Well?"

132

"What?"

Lavra said, "Is this why you beat the goat? Do you believe the goat is evil?'

Vlatko cottoned and played along, "Oh, huh, yes. The goats are evil. All of them."

Lavra smiled, "You are a follower, a follower like me, yes?"

Vlatko nodded positive, sensing this was the right thing to do. Lavra smiled, reached across and patted his hand. Vlatko forced a broken goofy toothed smile back at her as Lavra got rapping holy shit. Shit Vlatko had heard before. Shit he'd heard whilst getting his colon tickled by the cocks of his so-called Carers.

All her yabber was making him sleepy. He yawned. Lavra put her good book down and showed him to the shed. The shed was a shit hole even by local standards. A no star crib. Vlatko had crashed in worse roach motels though. He was happy to get his head down.

That night he dreamed of Edwin Abbott Abbott lecturing him, "This was the climax, the paradise, of my strange eventful His Story. Henceforth I have to relate the story of my miserable fall: most miserable, yet surely most undeserved! For why should the thirst for knowledge be aroused, only to be disappointed and punished? My volition shrinks from the painful task of recalling my humiliation; yet, like a second Prometheus, I will endure this and worse, if by any means I may arouse in the interiors of Plane and Solid Humanity a spirit of rebellion against the Conceit which would limit our Dimensions to Two or Three or any number short of Infinity. Away then with all personal considerations! Let me continue to the end, as I began, without further digressions or anticipations, pursuing the plain path of dispassionate His Story. The exact facts, the exact words – and they are burnt in upon my brain – shall be set down without alteration of an iota; and let my Readers judge between me and Destiny."

With morning came the promised breakfast. Vlatko chowed down

and Lavra asked him of his plans. He had none. Lavra said, "You can stay a while if you like. There is no hurry, no?"
Vlatko shrugged, "O.K."
Lavra asked after his story. He told her about the institutions. He fell shy on feeding her the forensic on all the fucking that went down. Lavra gave up the facts on her family. Vlatko didn't react. He sat stony faced, wondering what the next meal was going to be about. *So your folks died! Big fucking deal! You got anymore of those sausages or what?*

They went for a walk around the one donkey village. Lavra let on that she loved the village but she didn't want to spend the rest of her life there. Said she wanted to go to the cities. Wanted to see big churches. Wanted to help the fallen of the cities. Wanted to help the lost souls get back on track. Lavra wanted to get busy helping the damned to become hip and groovy with their Creator.

She bored Vlatko shitless but he nodded along. All he wanted was food, drink, shelter and a session of nocturnal goat aggro. Lavra offered him another night's board and lodging. He jumped at it. If it meant earache it meant earache. He was twelve miles from the next village and his dogs were barking. Besides, those sausages were scrumptious and the cherry wine went down a treat. The holy angle wasn't too bad; at least she wasn't sticking something up his arse as she sermonized.

Vlatko was woken half way through the night. At first he thought it was a ghost. He'd never seen a ghost so he wasn't certain. Lavra, sporting a sheer grubby white knee length nightgown, stood over him. She was sobbing and holding the holy book to her chest.
Vlatko rubbed at his eyes, "What is wrong?"
Lavra said, "I have to ask something."
"What?"
Lavra stuttered, "I have ... will you ... I have never been ... I have never been loved."
It wasn't a bombshell to Vlatko. Lavra was hardly hillbilly pin-up

material; in fact she was plain ugly even by outback – heavy on the incest – hill folk standards.

Vlatko, ever the romantic, shrugged cold, "So?"

"So I am asking you … I am wanting you to … to make love with me, Vlatko."

Vlatko groaned, "Oh."

"I know it is *wrong*, I know this, but my Father is forgiving. I believe he has sent you to me, Vlatko."

It was water off a duck's back for Vlatko; all his life had been a never-ending cycle of God and getting fucked and goats and getting blamed an *Oh, what the Hell!* As long as she was going to do all the work he couldn't care less.

Lavra would be his first piece of cunt, but he could handle it. Holes are holes are holes. He'd had Johns called Jovanovic sit down on his cock before today. He figured cunt would be less tight and uncomfortable.

Vlatko laid down the ground rules. He would work himself up, lie back and think of Yugoslavia whilst she did the deed to his fundamentally disinterested dick. Lavra wasn't going to argue. Having worked herself up with her chubby digits – imagining Christ sticking it to her – her gash was gaping and primed for filler. *The body of Christ, The Blood of Christ, The Cock of Christ, The Cum of Christ! Pass the collection tray please.*

Lavra slowly mounted him. Eyes screwed tight. Tight shut. Tight shut to the point of pain. It was Christ she was about to ride, not some rough trade, bug eyed, buck toothed, big-eared goat basher. One glimpse of lovely Vlatko and she'd have dried up double quick. Her juices would have evaporated faster than a tear on an L.A. side street at the height of a summer riot.

It took an age for Lavra to insert Vlatko's stunt cock. Finally in and it was only a couple of ups and down before she tossed her cookies. The orgasm tore through her. She cried and cried harder. Her sobs were deep. Wrought from the recesses of her lungs. Her eyes were still tight. *She'd just fucked Christ for God sake!*

Vlatko came by imagining himself let loose in a field full of goats with a half dozen pool balls wrapped in a sock. He shot shivers of cum up her constricting cunt. For all her religious role-playing, Lavra wasn't expecting The Second Coming. She gasped as she felt her lips getting splashed with hot ejaculate.

Eyes still nailed shut, Lavra climbed off and skidooded out the shed. Vlatko wiped his cock on the dirty sheet, yawned and got his head down. Lavra's anguished sobs didn't keep him from knocking out the Zeds. He figured Lavra was a weirdo and come the morn she'd be just a blip on an otherwise 100 percent batting average of *mano-to-mano* action.

Lavra got all emotional over breaky. She held Vlatko's hand. His free hand shoveled eggs and meatballs into his gob. Lavra said she thought that she loved him and that they should get married. Vlatko simply kept scoffing.
Lavra lay it down, "Will you stay with me, Vlatko?"
Vlatko's stomach was full. He was smoking a roll up and sipping hot coffee. *Why the Hell not! Nothing better to do. As long as she keeps the food and drink coming.*

Lavra said he could sleep in her bed from now on. Vlatko looked over at ga ga Grandma. Lavra said not to worry. Granny was cool. Cool cos she was confused. Vlatko nodded, O.K.

He spent most of his days lolling around watching Lavra do the domestics. He got hammered on cherry wine every night and smoked his roll ups. Once Grandma was snoozing they'd climb into bed. Vlatko would rustle up a stiffy thinking about goat slaughter and

Lavra would mount him. Every night the same. Lavra screwing her eyes shut, hopping on board and slowly bringing herself off. Vlatko didn't mind being a surrogate cock for Jesus. The gig was feeding and housing him.

Lavra would cry herself to sleep. Vlatko would bury his head in the pillow and ignore her. Lavra's spiritual sobbing would be punctuated by Vlatko's appreciative farting. A month and a week passed and Lavra told Vlatko that a baby would be coming.
Vlatko simply said, "Oh."

Lavra said that they should get married quickly. The ceremony was cut price even by village standards: five guests and the Orthodox Priest. The reception was in the shack. Lavra had made patties and punch. The turnout was low. The few that turned up stood around and ate the patties and drank the punch and got ready to leave. There was very little conversation. The whole affair lasted only a little under an hour.

Talk soon turned to their predicament. Lavra did most of the yapping. She didn't want their child brought up in the village. She figured Sarajevo. She wanted it to have a good education. She wanted it to have a good start in life. She had a little put away. Not much, but it would get them away from the village.

There was the question of Granny. She was too old and frail and mixed up to go traipsing to Sarajevo. The upheaval would be the end of her, and besides, it would be hard work and a drain on their very modest money pot.
Vlatko said, "Leave her here."
Lavra said, "That would be cruel, Vlatko! She cannot look after herself!"

Lavra gave it much thought. She asked around the village, asked if anybody would be willing to care for Granny. She got laughed at. Vlatko liked the idea of setting up in Sarajevo. He had breezed through a couple of times and he liked the hustle and bustle. Getting an apartment there appealed to him. He liked the idea of giving it a go. If he didn't take to it he could always get on his toes again and go happy wandering. He could take or leave Lavra. She fed and watered him and was kind and friendly with him so he figured he'd stick with her a little longer, and besides, opportunity wasn't exactly knocking.

Lavra said one night, "You know, Vlatko. I have been thinking … look at her."
Vlatko looked at zonked out Granny. Lavra continued, "She is barely alive. She doesn't know what year it is. We can't take her with us and we can't leave her here. The decent and Christian thing to do would be to send her to God."

Lavra was hoping Vlatko would cotton on. He didn't. He simply gave a trademark shrug and continued rolling a fag. Lavra had to spell it out to him. Vlatko got a boner. Relished the idea of doing the Old Dear in. It would be an honor. He wasn't keen on her. She talked stupid and she pissed in her bed and she was always staring at him like he was a stranger and of course, she'd be his first human victim. He knew how good it felt to snuff goats, *just imagine how good it would feel to snuff a human.*

Lavra came up with the method. Simple suffocation. Nothing violent. Vlatko was pissed off. He wanted to stave Granny's head in with a hammer. They argued. Lavra put the kibosh on anything over than suffocation. She would tell him that when the time was right he would firmly place a pillow over the Old Lady's face and send her off to Saint Peter.

Vlatko was amped-up on the imminent hit. He couldn't wait to savor the kill. A shot of dream fuel: night after night he went through somnambulant scenarios of snuffing the Granny-In-Law. He woke every morning with a raging hard on. Lavra hopped onboard and screwed her eyes shut and rode the throbbing gristle: imagining that Christ had risen.

Novel Headline 5. *De-calcify The Pineal Gland With The Detergent of Imagination*

Doctor A revisited the inventory of &'s earthly apartment:

Desk (1, white, plywood)
Apple Mac Computer (1, iMac 27" Core i7 2.93Ghrz 8GB 2TB HDD)
Chair (1, faux leather, scuffed)
Fan (1, electric, 24 inch)
Speakers (3, Harman Kardon SoundSticks III Clear-EMEA, slightly damaged)
External Hard Drive (1,50 gigabytes)
Laminate Flooring throughout (living room, kitchenette, bedroom, bathroom)
Large Floor Rug (1, woolen)
Leather Sofa (1, medium size, well worn)
Pouf/Footrest (1, soft leather)
Portable Oil Fuelled Heater (3, electric)
Refrigerator (1, Bosch)
Microwave (1,Samsung, nearly new)
Cushions (3, well worn)
Statue (1, ornament, *Kali Goddess of Destruction*, porcelain, 36 inch)
Cutlery (1 set, plate, bowl, cup, knife and fork, spoon)
Detergent, Bleach, Anti Bacterial Hand Wash (1 of each)
Tea Towels (3)
Bath Towels (4, large, white)
Dressing Gown (1,toweling)
Bath Matt (1)
Shampoo; conditioner, shower gel, deodorant, bubble bath, shower and bath cleaner.

Toothbrush (1, electric, 3 replacement heads)
Toothpaste (2 tubes 'Smokers')
Mouthwash (1)
Boxer Shorts (7 pairs, white cotton, Calvin Klein)
Socks (7 pairs, black woolen, Calvin Klein)
T-shirts (7, black cotton)
Denim Jeans (2 pairs, Levi Strauss)
Linen Shirts (4, white, black, grey and light blue)
Linen Trousers (2 pairs, cream, off white)
Suit Jacket; waistcoat, trousers (black, cotton, Hugo Boss)
White shirts (2, cotton)
Tie (2, silk, black, grey)
Leather Jacket (1, black, Belstaff)
Overcoat (1, woolen, Hugo Boss)
Tracksuit (1, velour, Fila)
Submariners Sweater (2, woolen, cream, dark blue)
Black Leather Brogues (1 pair)
Desert Boots (2 pairs, sand and brown)
Training shoes (1 pair, white, Fila)
Plimsoles (1 pair, white, Converse)
Cagoule (1, black, Y-2/Adidas)
Umbrella (1)
Leather Satchel (1, black)
Leather Holdall (1, brown)
Books: paperbacks
The Holy Bible (KJV)
White Jazz by James Ellroy
The New Testament by Authors Unknown
The Blind Assassin by Laura Chase
The Master & Margarita by Bulgakov
The Modern Art Invasion by Elizabeth Lunday
History of a Land Called Uqbar by Silas Haslam
Hollywood Babylon by Kenneth Anger
The Red Book by CG Jung
Double Indemnity by James M. Cain

Cloud Formations and Other Phenomena by Isaac Izard
The Big Nowhere by James Ellroy
The Carpetbaggers by Harold Robbins
The Bell Jar by Sylvia Plath
Fly Fishing by J.R. Hartley
Kill King 33 by James Shelby Downard
Peyton Place by Grace Metalious
The Big Sleep by Raymond Chandler
Collected Poems by Dylan Thomas
American Tabloid by James Ellroy
In a Lonely Place by Dorothy B. Hughes
CD's:
Astral Weeks by Van Morrison
Moodymann – Black Mahogani
Everybody's Welcome at Mrs. Mills' Party by Mrs. Mills
It Takes A Nation Of Millions – Public Enemy
Soul On The Rocks by The Isley Brothers
The Visitor – Jerome Newton
Kid A – Radiohead
The Collected Works of Debussy
Nas – Illmatic
Miles Davis – On The Corner
Theo Parrish – American Intelligence
Oliver The Musical Original Score – The Cast of Oliver
Omar S – Just Ask The Lonely
DVD:
The Long Goodbye (Robert Altman)
American Buttman in London (The Assmaster)
Typed Manuscripts: (seemingly finished novels)
Snuff
Getting The Fear
Trade
The Life Of O'Reilly

&'s earthly possessions were now trapped in a hermetically sealed container. Doctor A admired &'s minimalism. She had recently freed the novels from the container, but had procrastinated over reading them for ages. *Reading simply takes up too much time.*

Doctor A grabbed a kaleidoscope and zoomed in on &. & was currently a shuttlecock in a game of Badminton doubles. & was a Babolat & Ashaway shuttlecock: a made up brand to incorporate an ampersand for the purpose of this scene. William Shakespeare and Marlowe were wiping the floor with Francis Bacon and Sid The Sexist cartoon character from the Viz comic. It was a massacre: 21-zilch, 21-nada, 21-nothing, 21-fuck all, 21-zip, 21-nought, 21-duck.

The four amigo's headed into the locker room and began to frolic: whipping each other's bare arses with towels in a non-threatening, non-homosexual fashion and giggling like big girls blouses.

Shakespeare got on his high horse and started quoting Gurdjieff in Nadsat: "A consid'rable p'rcentage of the lewdies we meeteth on the street art lewdies who is't art exsufflicate inside, yond is, those gents art actually already dead. T is f'rtunate f'r us yond we doth not viddy and doth not knoweth t. If 't be true we kneweth what a numb'r of lewdies art actually dead and what a numb'r of these dead lewdies gov'rn our liveth, we shouldst wend nimble-footed with h'rr'rshow. "

Not to be outshone, Francis Bacon got on the transhumanist tip through an Ebonics filter: "Yo ah believe wot Satan iz trying ta plant iz dat we's can turn ourselves into machines an' become super-intelligent an' live forever. We's would then become Satan's new creation an' God's creation, da old human model, would become obsolete. Evolution wins and shit."

Marlowe went all fucking hardboiled Noir private dick in a cut-up fashion: " "The rain was comin' down like all the angels in heaven decided to take a piss at the same time. When you're in a situation like mine, you can only think in metaphors." "She walked through my door like a tigress walks into a Burmese orphanage – strawberry blonde and legs for hours. No dame her age could afford a coat like that, and the kinda makeup she had on gave me a good idea how she got it. She had bad news written on her like October of '29." He does the Private Eye Monologue frequently, especially during the first season. "My name is Roger Smith. I perform a much-needed job here in this city of amnesia ... The attempt on Nordberg's life left me shaken and disturbed, and all the questions kept coming up over and over again, like bubbles in a case of club soda. Who was this character in the hospital? And why was he trying to kill Nordberg? And for whom? Did Ludwig lie to me? I didn't have any proof, but, somehow, I didn't entirely trust him, either. Why was the I Luv You not listed in Ludwig's records? And if it was, did he know about it? And if he didn't, who did? And where the hell was I?" It's about seven o'clock in the evening. Mid January. The sun nothing but a cigar cherry, as an old man's weak piss of rain gives an oily shine to Tinsletown. This morning I woke up in a hospital. A delivery room of all the gin joints in the all the world."

Sid The Sexist went off on a completely different tangent with his heavily inflected Geordie theory of the JFK assassination: "Listen pet, this single bullet theory is sich neensense that wuh would probably hoy a mystarry neevel in the fookin bin in disgust, if it contained an episode see daft an' amateurish. But this fairy-tale wes the anny wa that the Worren Commission cud end up wi' their predetermined conclusion that Oswald acted alone and that wuh shud therefair put the idea iv a conspiracy yeut iv oor minds like. Whey aye, Oswald wes neet aroond tuh tell eez side iv the story, but nivvor mind. A neete wes conveniently foond which we weor assured Oswald had written explainin that he planned tuh kill president Kennedy. Well me fookin friends, that single bullet divvint kill president Kennedy, neer did any othor sniper's bullet. In fact, technical analysis iv the famous Zaprudor an' associated films done secretly fo' wor reveals the president wes murdered by means that weor far mare reliyeble than evon the best fookin sharpshyeuters. Befair ah tell yee wot did happen, based on me ahn information, let wor review several facts which tuh me knowledge hev until neeo nivvor been explained satisfactorily. These fookin facts are gruesum, but the' hev tuh be observed an' analyzed objectively if the truth is tuh be known: fact: befawa the fatal shot, president Kennedy had already been hit from ahint by a shot which had caused him tuh lean slightly forward an' face downward. Fookin fact: he wes then killed by a shot that literally blew the upper reor portion iv eez heed off. Several square inches iv skull weor bloon awa. Fact: this fatal shot snapped eez heed an' body violently backward an' somewhat upward in eez seat. Fact: debris from president Kennedy's heed exploded tuh the reor, landin aaal owor the left reor deck iv the open top limousine. Par Kennedy man wes sittin in the reet reor seat. Fact: at the instant iv the fatal shot the Zaprudor film shows what appeors tuh be a rush iv something – a blast iv sum sort intee the par cunt Kennedy's face man, from downward an' in front iv him from a position within the screeve. This hez nivvor been commented upon, tuh me knowledge, by telly commentators when the Zaprudor film hez been telecast, but watch fo' this blast from within the screeve. It's theor. Fact: the presidential limousine in which the assassination occurred wes dismantled an' destroyed within 48 hoors. This wes a grossly illegal destruction iv material evidence. Fookin fact man: pathologists an' researchers, whe hev recently been admitted tuh the national archives, report that the remains iv president Kennedy's brain, anuthor crucial piece iv evidence, is strangely missin like, misplaced, gone! Heor neeo is me conclusion based on these facts, plus technical opinions which hev been provided tuh wor confidentially. Ah challenge the United fookin States government tuh prove wor wrang like. The fookin conspirators left neewt tuh chance or the vagaries iv marksmanship. Par fookin Kennedy wes killed by a device – mounted inside the limousine an' fired at him from point blank range. The murdor weapon wes, whey aye, hidden, mounted inside the seat upholstarry in front iv the president."

Sid The Sexist sucked hard on a tab and continued, "Based on the appearance iv the blast in the Zaprudor film, it's possible that the murdor weapon wes essentially an extremely sawed off shotgun, hidden in the seat upholstarry aheed iv him, but it appeors mich mare likely that the blast wes produced by what is knoon as a shaped charge in a special fookin mountin like. A shaped charge is a specially configured explosive device which essentially produces a focused explosion – that is, an explosion that mostly aims in yen direction instead iv ganin in aall directions leek a stick iv dynamite. A shaped charge is wot enables a bazooka tuh blast a Shareman Tank yeut iv action an' shaped charges howa in many sizes includin sum weeny enough tuh hev been hidden easily in the Kennedy limousine. An advantage iv the shaped charge, from the conspirators' view point, is that contrary tuh a gun or shotgun it wud neet produce a bullet or buckshot which meet be foond by we's in the vicinity an' cause undesiryeble queshtuns tuh be asked o' cunts in the vicinity like. The anny problem wi' the shaped charge wud be its neeise. Sich a bang wud tend tuh attract the attention iv others in the screeve. Howivvor, the fookin bastid conspirators knew that Jackie Kennedy wud be an' aaal distraught an' preoccupeed wi' Jack himself eftor the blast tuh hev sich details registor, an' the drivor iv the screeve wud also be preoccupeed wi' the urge iv business iv tryin tuh maneuver yeut iv the ambush. But that still left governor John Connally, ridin in the front seat aheed iv the president. The soond iv the shaped charge cud be expected tuh attract eez attention, even if it wes muffled an' partially lost in the confusion iv gunshots from snipers. The fookin possibility existed that Connally alone meet be yeble tuh detect that sum sort iv device had been fired just ahint him inside the screeve. Therefair John Connally wes a specific target in the ambush alang wi' Kennedy, man. He wes neet, as hez often been supposed, merely the victim iv a stra bullet, mich less the victim iv a bullet that had forst struck par Kennedy as alleged by the warren commission. Connally wes potentially the single most dangerous witness tuh the assassination. See pet, it wes imperative that he be incapacitated or killed outreet. It divvint deed mattor whethor

Connally wes killed or just seriously injured, see lang as eez ability tuh observe events clearly wes ruined. This they, whey aye, accomplished. Thus multiple sharpshyeuters weor firin at the motorcyed fo' several purposes as it passed throo Dealey fookin Plaza like."

Sid The Sexist flares another tab and sucks in self satisfactorily, "Forst the' weor tuh create an ambush environment – a distraction see that the murdor blast from within the screeve wud neet be recognized fo' wot it wes. Second the' weor tuh shyeut fookin Governor Connally. Merely as a third priority the' weor also tuh dunsh the president wi' a shot or twa just as insurance against any possible malfunction iv the murdor device mounted in the screeve. Vice president Lyndon Johnson man was neet a target at aaal. Once it is recognized that the murdor blast cyem from within the screeve from a position iv firin slightly upward intee Kennedy's face, aaal the contorted an' forced explanations yee hev heard up to neeo abyeut a lot iv things cease tuh be necessary. The bazooka-like blast geet naturally hoyed him violently backward, inflicted the incredibly massive heed wounds that killed him an' threw debris aaal owor the reor deck iv the screeve. Further fookin' mair, it is neeo aaal an' aaal cleor why the conspirators wud hev wanted such an elaborately rigged screeve destroyed quickly afterwards – something which cud scarcely hev been done, by the wa, withyeut orders or at least approval from the new president Lyndon fookin Johnson. It is also obvious why Kennedy's preserved brain hez been spirited awa from the national archives. Yen lyeuk at the wounds inflicted by the murdor weapon in the screeve wud cause aaal iv the conclusions iv the Worren Commission tuh be throon in the fookin bin – exactly wheor the' belang, pet."

Sid The Sexist may have been battered on the Badminton court but he had more than made up for it with his superb verbal theorizing in the locker room. Bacon, Marlowe and Shakespeare gave him a big round of applause whilst Sid celebrated with a wank. & remained discarded on the floor with the other shuttlecocks and racquets.

& was nowhere near a novel. Doctor A felt a little sorry for his situation. She wound her Kaleidoscope up.

Another Doctor on the team – who fancied herself as a 'great authority on literature' – had "allegedly" read the novels & had written in life and concluded that they were: "Pedestrian. Full of clichés, obsessed with sex and violence, amateurish philosophizing, inane coincidences and sentimental conceits." The team Psychiatrist had 'allegedly' read the novels and filed a report that still remained unread. *She would have to investigate herself.*

Doctor A let out a long sigh, picked up *Trade* and dived in at a random page.

Danny Straker was a quiet, chubby kid. He was sweet, always smiling, very polite and considerate. He loved animals, always drawing them, loved going to Knowsley Safari park with his Mum and Dad and Nan. He wasn't interested in kicking a football around with the other kids. After the attack he became even quieter. He never saw his Mum and Dad get tortured but he heard the screaming and the shouting.

Danny was bullied at school. All the quiet kids were, the difference being that Danny never bubbled the bullies. He took their shit and simply became more and more withdrawn. Mum and Dad moved out the house after the attack. They went to live in a smaller house and Danny went to a new school. His victimization went with him. The bullying got worse; he was even being bullied by the bullied, lowest rung of the ladder. He hid his cuts and bruises well, the puppy fat helped, as long as they never bruised his face he was OK.

Danny would always get himself up for school even though his Mum Marina was up at seven on the dot every morning. Danny needed more time to get ready for school than most kids. The first half hour of his day would be spent on the toilet. He would need to shit out the nerves. Grabbing a towel off of the rail he would cry into it to mask the sobs. He knew what was coming; he knew he would be sitting six and half hours of hell. Marina thought he was getting a bath, she was proud of his immaculate hygiene. Danny was learning to be deceptive. Marina didn't have a clue that he was going through an anguished ritual every morning.

At school, Danny wished away the seconds, minutes and hours until he could return to the safety of home. He intuitively knew something was wrong at home but couldn't say what it was. Everything had changed since the night he had heard Mum screaming, but it was still home and he was safe there. The bullies couldn't get him at home. They weren't allowed in.

Bedtime was the worse time. That's when the monsters came. Marina and Alan put the terrors down to simple nightmares, all kids have them, nothing to worry about. Danny was actually suffering from sleep paralysis and hypnagogic hallucinations. He got diagnosed was he was eighteen and it hurt him that Mum and Dad never spotted it when he was a kid.

Marina was traumatized and Alan was never around. When he was he doted on Danny, but Danny knew that something was wrong. Everything in life was wrong for Danny, he hadn't asked to be born and now he had to smile and suffer and pretend for that everything was fine; he had to pretend for no reason at all. Nothing was logical, he saw other kids at school that looked happy, they looked like they weren't faking it. What was the point of life? Life wasn't fun, life was hell, but how could he articulate that feeling when he didn't even understand what 'articulate' meant?

Whenever Mum and Dad asked Danny if everything was OK he would say it was. Danny could never understand why he couldn't tell them the truth, but there was something, a wall, and an invisible shield that stopped him telling them that he was suffering. He knew he should tell them. He knew it was wrong to lie to them but … he just couldn't do it. There was something about Mum and Dad that stopped him. Something about that night when he had heard all the screaming. Something they would never talk about.

Danny had no cousins, no friends at school, no friends in the neighborhood. Mum and Dad encouraged him to make friends but it never worked. Danny heard Mum and Dad arguing about him one day. He heard Mum saying that he was just a quiet kid and that there was nothing wrong with him. He heard Dad say that he needed bringing out of his shell.

Danny heard Dad lifting weights in the garage for a quarter of an hour every night. Danny never ventured in, just listened. Heard his Dad grunt and groan. Heard the heavy weights when they hit the concrete floor. Dad saw him spying on him once and asked him to come in. Danny entered the garage and never looked back.

The puppy fat soon turned to muscle. By the time he was sixteen he had crystallized; shed the old skin and in doing so become an all-together different animal. The physical had shaped the psychological.

By the time Danny entered the sixth form he was still quiet, but nobody ever said boo to him. The ones that had really bullied him left school when they hit sixteen. The Sixth Formers were a different breed. Danny was well liked and got his head down and studied hard. They constantly pestered him to go out partying with them but Danny politely declined. The girls were mad on Danny, he was 'fit as fuck' in their eyes, he never reciprocated their interest though.

He had a routine. School. Weight lifting. Housework. Danny kept a clean house for him and Dad but Dad never noticed though, never complimented Danny on his housekeeping. Danny didn't mind, he knew his Mum would be have been proud of him.

Dad came to Danny's second body building competition. He won an under eighteen show. Gold. Dad said he was proud but added, "You won't make a living out of this, son. It's all right for a bit o' sport, but just concentrate on school. Get your exams, son. Body building's not gonna give you a wage. You want a proper job. Use your head."

Danny let his learning slide. He bought bigger better weights with his birthday and Christmas monies and spent longer and longer in the garage. Dad was never there. Danny was becoming huge, Dad noticed on his way out one day, "You're getting fucking massive, Dan. You don't wanna get too big, son. Last thing you want is to get muscle bound. It's not natural. Turn it down a bit. Work on your napper not your brawn."

Danny ignored him. He left the sixth form, signed on the dole and spent most of his waking hours in the garage. When he did venture out is was for shopping. He would go to the local Asda supermarket, do the weekly shop. One day he was approached. A nervous young man walked up to him in the cereal aisle. He was beaming at Danny.

"Danny Straker?"
Danny looked him up and down, didn't recognize him.
"You're Danny Straker! Paul Dawson! We went to Lower Grange together!"
Danny caught his breath. Paul Dawson had been one of his tormentors at school: horrible little bastard that used to stab him with compasses and hit him on the back of the head with wooden doorstops.
"Look at the size of ya! What happened?"
Dawson was wearing an Asda uniform. Dawson was still small and weasel like. Danny could feel his heart pumping, "Paul … Dawson. Yeah. I remember you."
"You left n' went somewhere else. Another school, Danny."
Danny's mouth was rapidly drying up, "That's right."

"Look at the size of ya! I didn't recognize you. You're body building, eh?"

Danny stared at Dawson's grinning face and shuddered inside, didn't want to be having this conversation, just wanted to get on with his shopping. Paul Dawson was another life. A reminder of the different times. A reminder of times he had tried hard to forget. This was a spanner in the works. He really didn't need it. Danny quickly glanced at his watch, "I better get cracking, Paul. Got to … you know."

Danny made to push off with his trolley. Dawson put his hand on it. Danny stared him in the eyes. Dawson was contrite, "Listen Danny … about back then. We were kids, eh? Just kids at school. It wasn't 'til you left we found out who you were."

Danny frowned, "Eh? What do you mean? What do you mean 'who I was'?"

"We never knew you were Alan Straker's son. None of us: Smaff, Wilson, me, Woodsy."

"I … I don't know what you mean."

"If we'd known you were Alan Straker's son … I mean, fucking hell! We'd never have fought with you."

Danny could feel bile building in his esophagus, he stammered, "We … we never … we never fought each other. You n' the others used to …"

"You know what I mean, Danny. Just messing about n' all that. Kids play, eh? All in the past. You know what kids are like, eh?"

Danny was feeling sick; he wanted Dawson to simply disappear. He tried to push off again with the trolley. Dawson smiled at him and got in his way.

Dawson was in hyper nervous mouth running mode, "Look at you know though, eh. I wouldn't fancy messing about with you now, mate. How much you lifting? What you bench-pressing? You're massive, Danny! Fucking Incredible Hulk! Fair play, fair play. I wouldn't know where to start. Look at me, I mean, eh … what? Twelve stone wet through? That takes some dedication, eh? That's a lot of hours in the gym, eh? "

"I've got to-"

"Listen, mate. If we'd known you were Alan Straker's son, I mean ... your Dad's a legend, man. It was only when you left. Smaff's old man told us all one day. Told us who your Dad was. We couldn't believe it! We fucking shit ourselves. All of us. He's a legend, man."

Dawson closed in on Danny and winked, "Are you, you know ... are you 'working' with your old man, eh? You know, you on the family firm?"

Danny could feel Dawson's breath, couldn't hold it back any longer, "Get out of my fucking road, Dawson!"

Dawson went drip white, all the color in his face drained, emulsion not gloss. His jaw went limp, his voice cracked, "Oh, Danny, oh, honestly I ... I ..."

"Fucking move!"

Dawson jumped aside and Danny pushed off with the trolley. He held on tight to it to stop his hands from shaking. He left Dawson quivering.

It would have been left at that if Dawson's old man hadn't opened his big gob. Danny would have let it slide, happy to let the past stay buried. Happy to never let his Dad know he had been bullied. Roy Dawson talked too much though. Roy Dawson was a talker and he suffered from 'overly familiar confidence'. Roy Dawson thought that he knew everybody and everybody knew him. He simply had an inflated and delusional ego. Compounding this was the fact that he also fancied himself as something of a tough guy. Bar room brawls, the odd punch up, bit of a glassing merchant. Nothing major, he had never gone toe to toe with a proper fighter.

His son told him what had happened with Danny Straker. Roy Dawson said not to worry. Deep down he was proud that his son had bullied the son of one of the most feared men in Manchester. Roy said he knew Alan Straker and that Alan Straker liked him. They were from the same council estate. They grew up together. He said when he next saw Alan Straker he would smooth it out with him; told his son not to worry, told him that Alan Straker would understand, he was an understanding man, a good lad, old school. They went back together, no worries, Alan Straker knew that Roy Dawson was an old school tough guy. Nothing would come of it.

Paul Dawson did worry though. All of Danny's childhood tormentors worried. They had heard about the new improved Danny Straker. He was built like a brick shit house, and after all the grief they had given him back then he'd surely get revenge if they ever had the misfortune of bumping into him. He was also the son of Manchester's Mr. Big. Such was Alan Straker's reputation that one of the tormentors left the city for good. The thought of retribution put him on his toes permanent.

Roy Dawson said it was all a fucking storm in a teacup. No sweat. He would square it with Alan Straker and get his word that revenge wouldn't come. It was all in the past, kids stuff. Nobody got hurt and nobody knew the little fat kid was Alan Straker's kid. It was a simple mistake and could happen to anyone. Roy Dawson should have kept his mouth shut.

Alan Straker was eating quiche, beans and chips and watching a video: Lonely Are The Brave with Kirk Douglas. Classic film. One of his favorites. A cowboy – played by old Kirk – was having trouble adjusting to modern life. Alan had taped it off the telly and had lost count how many times he had watched it. He wished Danny would watch it with him instead of making a racket with his weights in the garage. His phone went and he had to shoot out.

Twenty minutes later the doorbell rang. Danny was surprised. Nobody ever came to the house and he was annoyed that his training was being interrupted. Danny opened the door on the chain.
"Who is it?"
"Is it Danny?" asked Roy Dawson, "Is that you Danny?"
Danny was suspicious, "Who are you?"

"Roy, Roy Dawson. Paul Dawson's Dad."

Danny was shocked, "What do you want?"

"Is your Dad in?"

"Why? What do you want my Dad for?"

"Paul said you bumped into him in the Asda. I just wanted to come round and clear it all up with Alan. We grew up together. I thought it only fair, like. Get it all smoothed out. Bygones be bygones n' all that."

Danny bit his lip and opened the door, "He's not here. He's out."

"Out, eh? He's not in then?"

"No, that's right. He's out."

"What time'll he be back then?"

"I don't know."

Danny looked over at the car parked up on the street. Two men were watching. One from the driving seat and one from the rear. "Who are they? Those in the car?"

"Nobody. Just mates from the pub. Gave me a lift round, I told 'em I knew your Dad. Told 'em we went way back." Roy winked, "I've had a couple, like. Had a couple o' sherberts you know."

"So what do you want?"

"Just to have a word. Clear it all up. Our Paul's shitting his self." Roy offered his hand to Danny, "Thanks for not kicking off with him, Danny. He'd have got the sack if you'd chinned him at work. They don't put up with fighting at the Asda."

Danny started to close the door, "Tell him to forget about it."

Roy Dawson put his hand on the door, "When's best time to catch Alan in?"

He was really pissing Danny off now, "Why? I just told you to forget about it."

"Aye, yeah, but I know what Alan's like. We don't wanna get on Alan's wrong side. We go way back me n' Al. I know what he's capable of. I've got a lot of respect for Alan. He's a top bloke. Your Dad's a proper gent and I thought it only right. I just-"

"Fuck. Off. N' don't come round here again. I said it's forgotten. Forget about it."

Roy frowned, "There's no need for that tone. I'm just ..."
Danny pulled the door wide open. Crack! He clocked him square
on the chin. Roy reeled back. Danny shot at him, swinging a right.
Roy ducked as he staggered. He bear hugged Danny and they hit the
lawn. Roy was yelling breathlessly, 'Woah, woah! Jesus!"
Roy spun him around and had Danny's back, begging him to stop.
Danny pulled Roy's lock apart; spun around and started raining
blows down on Roy's head. Roy's guard was up. None of the punches
were connecting. Roy scrambled to his feet. Danny pulled himself
up and swung wildly at Roy.

Roy's 'mates from the pub' were flabbergasted. The driver put his
foot down and they sped off. Roy was yelling at Danny to stop, there
was no chance of that though. Roy parried one of Danny's punches
and grabbed him around the waist. Danny caught Roy full on with
a powerful head butt. Roy's hands instinctively went to his cracked
nose. Blood pissed out of it. Danny grabbed Roy by the shoulders,
pulled him forward and kneed him in the knackers. Roy fell to
his knees, winded, deflated, disabled, every spark of his energy
depleted. Sucked up in a second.

Danny pulled back and kicked Roy in the face. Roy was sparko.
Danny dived on him, his knees on his chest, pinning him down
and proceeding to tee off on his face. Left right left right, his fists
burning as they sculpted Roy's face into something unrecognizable.
Danny's knuckles split on Roy's teeth. Left right left right. Thud
thud thud. Bone on bone. Roy's face had replaced Danny's punch
bag in the garage. Danny shocked himself; it was like an out of
body experience. He could see himself annihilating Roy Dawson,
but it wasn't really him. This felt like someone else was inflicting
the damage. Danny shot back into his body and stopped punching
Roy Dawson.

Danny took huge gulps of air and stood up, staring at his handiwork.
A bloody pulp, deathly still. Danny felt a surge of panic rip through

his body. He was dead. He had killed Roy Dawson. Danny bent over, held his knees and spat out bile and saliva. Good job he was fit as a fiddle. This was some workout. He stood up straight and tilted his head back, closed his eyes and drew air through his nose. He heard a whimper. Roy Dawson wasn't dead. Roy Dawson was whimpering like a wounded animal.

Danny stood over him and watched as Roy floated in and out of consciousness. A significant part of Roy's face was now on Danny's knuckles; tissue, gristle, congealed blood. At least he wasn't dead. Brain dead maybe, but still sucking air.

Danny called an ambulance. Dibble came with it. Danny held his hands up and gave a confession before his Dad's high paid Brief got there. Dibble were cock-a-hoop. Alan Straker hit the roof when Danny was denied bail. Roy Dawson was in a coma and this could turn into a murder rap at the drop of a heartbeat. Alan got to visit Danny on remand and it tore him apart. He had already got the word out that if anyone so much as even looked at his son in the wrong way in the nick they'd suffer.

Alan Straker was shaking when he sat down in the visiting room, "The Brief showed me your statement. Why didn't you ever tell us you were being bullied at school, son?"
"I told him to drop it, Dad … I just … I just saw red."
"Why though? Why, Daniel? Why didn't you ever tell us?"
Danny just shrugged his shoulders, 'It doesn't matter now. It was a long time ago. I keep telling people to fucking forget it. Why can't people just accept that the past is the past and that's that?"

Roy Dawson slipped back out of his coma. Brain damaged, he'd be wearing a bib to eat and pissing in his pants for the rest of his natural. Alan threw a large chunk of cash his family's way. Paul Dawson drowned his anxieties with smack. He lived in unnecessary fear of a reprisal and turned into a shivering wreck of humanity.

At Crown it was simply a formality. Danny had 'fessed up. It was open and shut. The Brief told Danny that they would claim he had been shooting steroids, it fit perfect with the body building kick, steroids would be the mitigating circumstance, blame it on the steroids, the steroids had sent him uncharacteristically ultra violent. Add to it the bullying angle and voila! Solid defense.

The Beak was sympathetic and obviously clued to it being Danny's first collar. He still handed Danny a five stretch though. He had to; Danny had created a vegetable. He was carted off to HMP Wakefield; tough nut pad, hard joint, not for the faint hearted. Alan Straker put out a whip in the underground, threw a few quid around and called in some favors, "Anyone touches him and they're going to war with me." Alan meant it. His son's welfare was something he would definitely go to war over.

Alan Straker got his first VO from Danny and shot over to Wakefield. "Anyone giving you grief, son?"
"No. Nobody even talks to me, don't even look in my direction."
"Good. That's good, because if they did … fucking God help 'em, that's all I'm saying."
"I can handle myself, Dad."
"Yeah, yeah, aye … I think we know that now, son." Alan smiled, "I think you've proved you can mix it a bit."
"Did you take care of his family?"
"The fucking Cabbage you mean? Yeah, the Cabbage's family are sorted. They won't go hungry. If I had my way though … well … I think you know what I think about that bunch of bastards."
"Let's leave it now. Let's move on, Dad."
"Yeah, no, no, I agree, son. I agree. Thing is though … well thing is … it's wrong you're banged up in here. You're not a lag; you're not a criminal. You're educated. You got yourself an education. You're smart, Dan. You're a smart lad. It's a fucking travesty you're in here. Your mother would go mad. She'd turn in her grave she would. It'd kill her. I'm glad she's not alive to see it to be honest. She'll be

looking down on all this now, all this shit and she won't believe it. You know it'd break her heart. You weren't cut out for this fucking caper, son. You're a nice lad. That fucker Dawson asked for everything he got if you ask me. Ask anyone. Ask anyone who knows you. They'll all say you're above this shit … this isn't you, Danny."

"I just … I suppose I just snapped, Dad. It's done now. What's done is done. I just snapped."

Alan Straker fought back tears valiantly, "And so would I! Anyone would! Mother fucking Teresa would have snapped! Gandhi! I just … I just wish you would have told me … we … honestly, we had no idea. Your Mum and me we … you were just a quiet kid. Never said boo to anyone, kept your head down. You were a sweet kid. Power Rangers, remember that on the telly? You loved Power Rangers. You were never any trouble. Sweet kid. Sweet nature. Like your Mum you were. She was sweet like you. Wouldn't touch a fly. Wouldn't touch the hair on the head of a fly. Remember how much you loved animals? Remember Knowsley Safari Park?"

"Yeah, yeah. Knowsley."

"Aye, You loved it there. We virtually fucking lived there. Should have bought shares in the place. We were never away."

"I know, Dad. I remember."

Alan Straker could feel a lump the size of Mike Tyson's fist forming in his throat, "Remember your Mum? Remember the sarnies she used to … remember the sarnies she used to make us?"

"Yeah, yeah I do … we loved feeding the baboons, Dad. We had a right laugh. I remember."

Alan Straker chuckled to save himself from crying, "Aye, aye, those baboons had our pants down. Saw us coming they did. Always run up to us 'cos they knew we'd give 'em loads to scoff. Cheeky fuckers they were, eh? Knew we were a soft touch."

"Yeah."

Alan Straker needed to swallow the lump in his throat. He looked around the room and the eyes were on him. Whispers were about *him*, he knew it, he wasn't daft. Alan Straker wasn't unconscious of the fact that he had become a big name in the criminal world. Celebrity didn't interest him though, especially recidivist celebrity. In Alan Straker's mind the fact that he was known and feared was something of a handicap. If every dodgy cunt in the north knew about him that meant that every cunt that was employed to curb every dodgy cunt in the north would also know about him.

Alan Straker looked his son in the eyes, "Have you ... listen, Daniel. I know I haven't been around a lot. I know I've been busy, but ... I mean, have you thought about what you wanna do when you get out of here?"

"Are you offering me a job, Dad?"

"No, I'm thinking you might wanna go back n' study. Go back n' finish your education."

"Don't you want me to work with you?"

"No, no, I don't. It's the last thing I want, Dan. What I do isn't a job. I'll set you up in a little business if you want. If you wanna work we'll get a business for you. Something legit. Above board. Something steady. Few quid coming in. Something regular."

"A gym?"

"You want a gym?"

"It's what I'm interested in."

Alan Straker looked away, "I don't know about all this body building."

"What do you mean?"

"What I mean is, I mean ... maybe it's not good for you. Maybe you should get your head into something else. You can't be a body builder all your life. It's not really a future is it? It's not career, son. It won't put food on the table forever."

"It's what I'm into, Dad."

Alan Straker sighed, "If you keep your head down in here, keep your nose clean you'll do it standing on your head. What about one o' those Open University courses?"

"I'm not interested in anything enough. I told you what I'm into."

"Yeah, yeah, I know but ..."

"Don't worry about me, Dad. I'm fine. Everything's OK."

Danny knew everything would be OK. Everything would indeed be fine. Danny had a plan. There would be nothing to worry about anymore.

Doctor A put the manuscript down on her desk and made a mental note to read the psychiatric report on the novel.

& found himself asleep in a stranger's slumber. Not for long though. He immediately surveyed the environment. He was three quarters of the way through a dream set on the Balearic island of Tago Mago. & yawned and ascended to a stream of light that carried him to a sea of laughing Panda bears, but before he could register what great swimmers they were, he was whisked away to the alchemical wedding of Christian Rosenkreutz, where he was an ampersand on a line in the marriage certificate. This was 1616 though. & knew this couldn't be right. The ampersand hadn't been invented.

& listened to the Bridegroom bragging about his stag do the night before, " … After this, meat was brought in, and although no one could be seen, yet everything was so orderly managed, that it seemed to me as if every guest had his own attendant. Now my artists having somewhat recreated themselves, and the wine having removed a little shame from their hearts, they presently began to vaunt and brag of their abilities. One would prove this, another that, and commonly the most sorry idiots made the loudest noise. Ah, when I call to mind what preternatural and impossible enterprises I then heard, I am still ready to vomit at it. In a word, they never kept in their order, but whenever one rascal here, another there, could insinuate himself in between the nobles, then they pretended to having finished such adventures as neither Samson nor yet Hercules with all their strength could ever have achieved: this one would discharge Atlas of his burden; the other would again draw forth the three headed Cerberus out of Hell. In brief, every man had his own prate, and yet the greatest lords were so simple that they believed their pretences, and the rogues so audacious, that although one or other of them was here and there rapped over the fingers with a knife, yet they flinched not at it, but when anyone perchance had filched a gold-chain, then they would all hazard for the same-"

Before it got to the sex and drugs and rock and roll part of the tale & found himself being pixilated and stored in the archives of the Guinness Book of Records. He took a deep breath and swallowed every fact, figure and fabrication from the mass. He breathed out – replaying the meal – and found absolutely nothing of interest.

An operating theater, & watching a Surgeon. Something nudges & and winks, " ... *ne plus ultra* of interactivity: a surgeon operates on his own brain whilst filming and watching it through his phone." & shudders and descends a ladder without rungs on to a microscopic hair that will lead to death by lethal injection of a Texan simpleton with the mental age of 36.

& closes his incognito eyes and drifts towards the binary information flow. *You know where you stand with binary.* He digs the predictability and the boredom of continuity. *No one ever died of astonishment in the flow of binary.* He could think about present past in the flow. Think about how much he wasted during incarnate time. All the things he never did or said or thought or cherished; all the energy packets he spunked on thinking about the fictitious future: all the fucking logic he adhered to, all the codes he abided by, all the worry he let eat away at his soul for no other reason than he didn't know any better. All the opportunities he denied himself to open the door and peep at reality.

He kicked backed in the binary, all those Ones and Zeroes creating a world within a word of things: *the unbearable lightness of intertextual being.* The second step towards the revelation of the method. The Living – one tweet and Facebook update at a time – slowly moving towards the ultimate realization that every*thing* is language and words are sacred.

If & knew what he knew then he would have simply said that there is no *then*. He often wondered how the great migration of souls would be achieved on the mortal side. It would obviously be The Elites who made the passage first and this disheartened &. He imagined that they wouldn't be satisfied with traveling back to The Word and would surely want to colonize and exploit it. If he could only let the living know that Pure Information awaited them then they might kill their egos before they made the trip, saving a Hell of a lot of temporal psychic baggage being brought over.

It hadn't taken & long to figure out that the migration to information came with a price. The price being that you brought both good, bad, ugly and indifferent facets of your personality over with you. Free will was still a component of The Word and learning never ends. If & could just break through and simply say something enigmatic but encapsulated, like, "There are 9 numbers and 26 letters and they are infinite. Study them. They will set you free."

The terminally lonely Unreliable Narrator sat down and gave himself a good talking to, "He's getting hip to me."
"Who?"
"&. He's figured out I'm putting words into his mouth."
"But that's your job."
"I know but trying tell *him* that."
"You should."
"Should what?"
"Try telling him."
"He won't listen."
"How do you know?"
"Because he's stubborn and he knows I'm unreliable, and then there's the problem of timeframes. He's purposefully resisting my efforts to impose a linearity on the narrative."
"Resisting, how exactly?"
"He's influencing me ... getting into my fucking head!"
"You're letting a Subject influence you? Tut tut ... it's the cardinal

sin of both the reliable and unreliable narrator to let a Subject take charge. Pull yourself together. Impose your will on him."

"It's too late."

"Why?"

"Because he's slowly gaining sympathy from a few of the readers. He's becoming a sympathetic character. He's ticking the boxes. He's crafty."

"Then you have to be as crafty as him."

"How? What can I do?

"Play him at his own game. Prove that his pedestrian novels were semi-autobiographical. Show them the real &."

"You think it'll work?

"It's worth a try."

The Unreliable Narrator went to work:

& was on the horn to a Dealer he knew longtime in the district, he said, "And I'll need some works. It's a while since I last popped."

& put the phone down and remembered an argument with Maria. Maria said, "It is a dangerous drug, &!"

& said, "Maria, listen to me, heroin's only dangerous because of the black market. It's the criminals that make it dangerous by cutting it with bad shit. You know, adulterants: curry powder, starch, substitutes, shit like that! Fucking water would be dangerous if it were handed over to criminals to manufacture and distribute! The heroin I get is clean. It's safe. It's unadulterated."

& thought about that word: unadulterated: *adj. 1. Not mingled or diluted with extraneous matter: pure. 2. Out-and-out; utter: the unadulterated truth.*

& wondered about the etymology of the word unadulterated. Why was the word adult in there? Was it because adults were impure? Was it because adults had managed to master and learned to live with lying? Was the word telling us something about ourselves? We're not born liars. We learn to lie to protect ourselves. Is lying simply a natural and reasonable defense mechanism that stops us from being fucked over? If it is, what's the point in trying to find the truth if we're all at some point or other gonna seek to pervert the truth it if it encroaches on our safety?

&'s Dealer showed up with the good shit. & trusted him. The Dealer had a good rep. His shit was pricey but it had the unofficial kite mark. Only decent Dealers accept cheques.

& said, "If it bounces you can come round and kick my head in."
Dealer said, "You know that's not my style, man."
& knew it wouldn't bounce, also knew it would max up his overdraft. *Cest la fuck it*!

He sat down and fixed to jack-up. A hard knock at the door. & sighed and answered it. *Shit! Samantha again.*
"Look Samantha, I-"
"I'm not here to have a go at you. You should look at this. I found it among Ray's sleaze stash: this is the man you call a friend."
Samantha handed him a videocassette. & frowned. Samantha shook her head and walked away. & shouted after her, "What is it, Sam?" Samantha ignored him. & closed the door. He put the cassette in the VCR, sat down, sparked a Marlboro and waited: fuzz, snow, Home Movie. Ray and Samantha holidaying in the South of France. Usual cheese ball mugging to camera. *What the fuck is this shit! What's it gotta do with me?*

& hit the fast-forward on the remote. More goofing around; travel-ogue, only at Keystone Cop speed. Suddenly a snippet of fuzz and snow and then what looked like a porno. & hit play. It *was* a porno. A gonzo porno. Amateur. He recognized Ray's house. &'s breath was snatched from him as he recognized Ray's co-star and vomit bubbled in his esophagus.

He watched Ray fucking Maria – *his* Maria – dog style on a sofa. Maria was moaning ecstatic as Ray pulled out of her cunt and thrust his meat into her arsehole. Ray was groping Maria's tits and licking her mouth.

& burned and hit pause on the remote and put his head in his hands. He held it there for a while and then spied the TV screen through his fingers. Maria was freeze framed with Ray's meat stuck in her hole. Her face freeze-framed in rapture. & gingerly pressed play and masochistically watched his dead ex wife getting the bumming of her life from his best friend.

The nausea gave way to pain gave way to anger gave way to hurt as the gonzo porno played out before his teary peepers. Ray spat at the screen, "Fucking blackmailing whore!"
& tried Ray's mobile number. Dead. Switched off. Sam must have told him. & rang Samantha. She said she hadn't spoken to her dirty, lying, lowdown, soon to be ex-husband, and added that she hoped & would beat the shit out of him if he ever caught up with him.

A list of Ray's alco-haunts rifled through &'s mind: The French House, Coach & Horses, The Colony, The Theatre Bar, The Century, The Ship, The Groucho; all in Soho, all within walking distance of each other. Ray the fucking rat would be scurrying between the watering holes no doubt. He wouldn't know that Samantha had found his VHS fucking of Maria.

& sank a couple of canned beers and paced around. His anger shocked him. He held out his hand and stared at the twitching digits. He eyed the smack. Smack wouldn't feel right, right now. He felt like he'd already snorted a gram of ching in one fell swoop. That, so alive feeling. That, wired-up to the National Grid sensation. He couldn't resist playing the tape from where he'd stopped it. & saw Ray pop his load over Maria's back. Ray pulled away from her and wiped himself. There was some undistinguishable dialogue. Ray then moves towards the camera. He waits until Maria's back is turned before he leans into it, winks and turns it off.

It looked liked Maria didn't know that their fucking was being filmed. Or did she? Does it matter? Does it make her any more or less of a cheating fucking cunt?

Night had fallen. Rain came down in sheets. & hailed a cab to Soho. The Driver tried to chitchat &. & remained mute. The Driver gave up on him.

The rain and the wind had kept the tourists out of Soho. Old lags and hardcore boozers were keeping the bars buoyant. & stalked into The Coach & Horses. No sign of Ray. & pulled a Posh Sclerotic, "Has Ray been in?"
Posh Sclerotic slurred, "Haven't seen him, Old Chap."
The French House didn't yield him up either. A Faggy Thesp said he'd seen Ray earlier in The Colony. *Right! The Colony? Same story.*

& remembered that Ray had recently been fucking a young American broad who worked bar in The Ship, between studying for a degree and working as an escort. & angled up Wardour Street. He reached The Ship and poked his head in. Bingo! Ray was sat at the bar, the Yanky Broad behind the bar listening to his licentious shite. & scanned his clock. Ten twenty five. The Ship always turned out just after eleven. & was gonna surprise Ray.

He sheltered from the rain at the entrance to the multistory car park just behind the boozer. He smoked and watched people leaving. & knew Ray would be leaving with the Yanky Broad on his arm. & was wrong.

At ten to eleven Ray came out of the side door. He pulled the lapels up on his overcoat and was about to set off into the night when &'s hand landed hard on his shoulder. Ray was startled. He turned and sighed in relief when he clocked it was &.
"Christ, &! I thought you were a mugger!"
"How long were you fucking her?"

Ray frowned, "Eh?"

"Maria! How long were you fucking her?"

Ray's jaw dropped. He put his hands up to his chest, palms facing outwards, "Woah, what … what're you talking about?"

& swung and slugged Ray neat on his open jaw. Ccccrrrack! Ray's arse hit the concrete. Ray murmured and spat blood. His jaw hung, useless.

"Were you fucking her from the off? How long after we'd been married did you start?"

Ray tried to clamber away. & hooked him up and slammed him against the wall. He gripped Ray's lapels and closed in, nose-to-nose, breath-to-breath, "I've got nothing to lose anymore, Ray. I should fucking kill you!"

Ray stuttered, "&, please!"

"Please what? Please spare you? Please put you out of your fucking misery?"

Ray broke down. Blubbered like a baby. & felt sick again. He loosened his grip on Ray and eased back a little. Ray tried to hug &.

"I'm so … I … I need help, &. It's … it's an addiction."

He swatted Ray away from him like a shit fly; "For a moment there I thought you were gonna say sorry."

& headed down Wardour. He stopped and flamed a smoke. The rain had taken a breather and the sodden streets shimmered, warping the garish neon reflections and playing canvas to streaks of piss yellow streetlights. He looked up at the dark skies. He could make out the taillights of a 747 taking off from Heathrow. He wondered where those passengers were heading. He wondered if they were heading off in search of some truth. & thought maybe *he* should head off somewhere.

"You fucking idiot!" The Unreliable Narrator yelled at himself, "You didn't read that before you doctored it, did you? You've gone and made him even more sympathetic now!"

& was hanging out at the Six Millionth Sleep Olympics. The opening

167

ceremony was under way: DJ Tony Meyboards was remixing NWA's "Straight Outta Compton" on the stage. Host of the ceremony was BG Sidarth.

BG grabbed the mic and started dropping science over the ill beats DJ Tony was creating: "Time is associated with change. In a change-less universe, there would be no time. It must be mentioned here that various theories of time, already imply time or more generally change. The question is; what type of a change do we consider? We have argued that the time which we usually use is based on an incremental change: almost as if there were no change. For example the law of conservation of energy is based on time translation symmetry – an infinitesimal translation in time leaves everything unchanged. Clearly this is only an approximation, which assumes that there is no change in a very short interval. In fact time is essentially an ordering or sequencing of events. The key here is the way in which this ordering is done so that causality and other laws of physics hold or emerge rather than being inputs. If we consider the universe as a sequence of instantaneous space slices, to start with, then a random sequence would represent a lawless, and literally chaotic universe. On the contrary we have seen that at the micro scale, that is, more specifically within the Compton scale, indeed there is no causality and there is the chaotic Zitterbewegung. This means that if it were possible for a creature or a measuring device to be so small as to be within the Compton scale, then such a creature or device would perceive a lawless, chaotic universe. However physics, and this includes elementary particles, emerges once averages over the unphysical Compton scale are taken. In this sense the universe that is perceived and measured is a macroscopic universe. At the micro level, as pointed out by Wigner and Sackler, we can no longer extrapolate these macro concepts. In a sense, this is connected with the Copenhagen debate on the role of macroscopic measuring devices in obtaining information about microscopic systems. At the macro scale however we have two different situations. One, which we encountered in the first section, can further be exemplified with the example of a porcelain plate that falls to the ground and breaks into many pieces. Here a highly ordered system, namely the porcelain plate becomes a highly disordered system, namely the collection of shattered pieces. As long as we do not specify the exact shapes and sizes of the shattered pieces in advance, this can always happen – it provides an arrow of time with increasing entropy. This time, furthermore, is irreversible. The shattered pieces then combining to form the plate or equivalently the shattered pieces, which describe a very definite prescribed shape and size would be impossibility and would represent the reversal of time. In any case, the connection between time and probability is brought about. If the probability of something happening is – in advance – zero or nearly so, time does not "evolve" to such a situation. Time's arrow or flow is in the direction of non-vanishing probabilities. There is another change that we had considered in the previous section – this is the fluctuational creation of particles. This gives rise to a macroscopic time, through a Brownian process, leading to the correct age of the universe. In contrast to the change, which our usual time represents, this latter Brownian change is no longer incremental. This picture is a far cry from the smoothly flowing time of usual theory. The contrast is between "becoming" and "being".

Novel Headline 6. *When failing spectacularly the trick is to employ an inverted Schadenfreude. Take ownership of your misfortune*

The seventeen million strong crowd – crammed into an Adidas sneaker – went wild and gave DI Tony Meyboards and MC BG Sidarth a rapturous round of applause. & could smell the atmosphere changing though. Over the loudspeaker came a grave voice: "We are very sorry to have to report that the Six Millionth Sleep Olympics are to be cancelled."
A collective groan from the seventeen million assembled went up. The Announcer continued, "We are extremely sorry about having to cancel the Olympics, but after random drug tests were carried out earlier in the age, over 99.9% of the athletes were discovered to

have traces of sleep performance enhancing drugs in their minds. namely: Temazepam, Xanax, Lunesta, Sonata, Valium, Ambien, Diazepam, Intermezzo, Zolpimist, Zopiclone, Buspar, Ativan, Midazolam, Versed, Oxazepam, Sera, Zimovane, Lendormin, Estazolam, Prosom, Flurazepam, Dalmane, Loprazolam, Dormonoct, Havlane, Sonin, Somnovit, Lormetazepam, Loramet, Noctamid, Nitrazepam, Cerson, Mogadon, Nitrazadon, Radedorm, Quazepam, Doral. Amitriptyline, Elavil, Endep, Vanatrip, Doxepin, Silenor, Sinequan, Adapin, Mirtazapine, Remeron, Trazodone, Desyrel, Oleptro, Trittico, Dexmedetomidine, Precedex, Dexdor, Dexdomit, Ethchlorvynol, Placidyl and Horlicks. As you are all aware, these are banned substances. The athletes will be severely reprimanded and banned from the sport. Goodnight. Sleep well."

Getting the Fear
Chapter 6

Dr. Myron Geller was enjoying a brandy with his close colleague Dr. Alice Garland. Dr. Garland was her mid sixties and well respected in the social scientific community. Her field was behavioral psychology and she had contributed greatly to the work of The Trebistock Institute. Like everyone else in the field she was a great admirer of Dr. Geller.

She enjoyed nothing more than her regular meetings with him, where they would drink and smoke and relax and talk through their theories.

"I will go out on a limb, Alice, and predict that the psychological effects from these dalliances with psychedelic drugs will have terrible repercussions in ten, twenty years time. We know too little about the long-term effects and these people are taking them in the wrong environments. It is all about creating the right environment for experimentation."
"I agree, Myron. I wholeheartedly agree. I read your paper on the young woman you worked with. You are at the cutting edge, there is no doubt about it."

The paper she was referring to documented an experiment Dr. Geller had carried out on an unnamed young woman whom he had plied with large doses of LSD. The guinea pig had agreed to be fed the large doses and was generously recompensed, but she obviously didn't have a clue that she was subjecting herself to such a dangerous experiment. She should have known it was going to be risky when he demanded that she sign a waiver of responsibility with a secrecy clause attached.

Dr. Geller lied to Dr. Garland, "I am in regular contact with the young lady. She is fine, but I am sure that she will experience periods of HPPD."
"Aaah, what they are now terming as 'flashbacks'?"
"Quite, Hallucinogen Persisting Perception Disorder." he regrettably shook his head, "I knew too little at the time. The environment should have been thought through. The whole process should have been considered … I regret that I was too eager."

Dr. Geller knew that the poor young woman would never experience flashbacks. She would never experience anything ever again. The young woman was dead. She had thrown herself into the heavy metal jaws of a mechanical crusher on a waste disposal truck. She had casually walked behind the truck and jumped in when the refuse workers were busy collecting bags of rubbish from the streets of Camden. Her body was instantly crushed and her screams could be heard over the grinding noise. One of the workers instantly hit the stop button but it was too late. As the metal jaws slowly unlocked, the horrified workers were treated to the site of what could only be described as a broken skeleton with bits of flesh still clinging to it.

Dr. Geller poured them a top up of brandy, "I am absolutely in favor of using Lysergic Acid Diethylamide to treat all kinds of conditions, but what really interests me, Alice, is that we find a way to cancel out these 'flashbacks'. I am positive that there must be a way to enable the user so that they do not suffer the HPPD."
"Mmm, very interesting … I suppose what really excites me is what you wrote about being able to completely change a subject's personality. Myron."

"Yes, I believe it can be achieved under the right circumstances. Again, the clinical environment."

"Ernst Greenberg out in San Francisco is working on a program. Are you familiar with it, Myron?"

Dr. Geller paused, "I am not an admirer of Ernst Greenberg, Alice. I believe he is involved with the US military. Well, it is certain that he receives funding from them at least."

"I thought that was public knowledge."

"We should be looking at ways to end violence rather than harnessing it."

"What do you mean, Myron?"

"It would not surprise me if Ernst Greenberg was researching ways in which psychedelic drugs could be use to turn people towards violence. I know how the US military think. No, what I want to do is find a way to bring peace to the world. You know this my aim in life, Alice."

Dr. Garland smiled at him and grabbed his hand, "Of course, Myron, of course."

Dr. Geller sipped the expensive brandy and thought about his experiences with military and policing. From its inception in 1950 until his defection in 1952, Dr. Myron Geller worked as a psychologist for the Ministerium für Staatssicherheit, the East German secret police, more commonly known as the feared Stasi.

The Stasi was an Orwellian institution that traded in lies, brutality, psychological violence, distrust and fear and turned neighbor against neighbor, man against wife and son against mother to achieve its aim of total physical and mental control over the East German people. The Stasi was a Soviet funded tool that caused pain and deep psychic damage to many of those unfortunate to have lived under its reign.

Dr. Myron Geller used the fact that he was highly regarded in The Stasi to help him defect to the US. He was immediately given a job working for the US military in the field of psychological war-fare. He soon learned a very valuable lesson. The US miltary secret operations were just as bad as The Stasi's operations. The Soviet Union and The US were no different to each other. Both countries were simply playing a game set up by the kings of industry and the banking cartels.

The Soviet Union and The US were not engaged in a stand off, a cold war, they were simply playing out a detailed script written by the powerbrokers. The script demanded that these dominant countries set themselves against each other so that the banking cartels and the industrialists could profit massively from the sale of arms to them both. Ideology had nothing to do with it. It was all about money and the redistribution of it, a trickle up system: from the taxpayer to the filthy rich powerbrokers who pulled the strings of the puppets they had handpicked and placed in politics.

From that day on, Dr. Myron Geller revised his view of recent his-tory. He came to the conclusion that ideologues like Stalin and Hitler were simply sociopaths who had been allowed to carry out their atrocities because the banking dynasties had realized that they could profit from their reigns of terror: useful monsters, nothing more, nothing less.

Dr. Geller was a torn man. On the face of it he exuded an air of confidence, but in his reflective moments he was depressed at the absurdity of life and how so few people could cause so much agony and distress for the many millions simply because they controlled the purse strings.

He wanted to make a difference in his lifetime. He wanted to help people be unburdened of greed and ego and violent tendencies. He wanted to try help build a utopia where everyone lived peace-fully side-by-side and nobody was excluded regardless of ability, strength or intelligence. He dreamed about a world where violence had been totally eradicated, assigned to the dustbin of history, and where egalitarianism trumped personal gain at every corner; a world in which the currency wasn't monetary, but rather humanitarian. Apropos of everything and nothing, Dr. Geller stood up and recited:

> From womb to void and all listening points between the cry
>   is "why"
> We know there's something not right
> But how can it be wrong when above the parapet
> Sit kings, teachers, priests
> And judges? Ermine, crown, cloak and wig
> Show the spoils of spoken ritual the likes of us
> Were never meant to hear
>
> Raise your hand for answers but keep your head down for
> Questions
> It's ignorance if you don't know the solution,
> It's cooperation if you can't see
> The problem
> Assume the position whilst The Programmers circle and spurt
>   verbatim,
> Spew orthodox, jerk oral tradition and ejaculate consensus
> Wiping their spent mouths on the back of their liver spotted
>   hands
>
> The recording lodges in your mind
> Bombastic vibration stuck on auto-play
> The disembodied voices stick to the script chiseled in stone
> By the master builders
> their history echoed down ages by winners
> Omitting the fact the game was rigged
>
> When they tune into us they scream
> "Don't touch that dial, don't run interference,
> Don't drown it out in white noise"

175

The airwaves are ordained by the word of the self-elect and it
Is essential listening
You can't afford to be left out of the loop, you need to get hip
To synthesized reality

And there we sit passive, blank tapes captive to their saccha-
    rine tinged
Psychic graffiti burning into our memory, lips poised over the
    record button
Copy after copy our intuition worn and fragmented,
All trust in us destroyed for the greater good

And the "why" remains
It never ceases
Like a battered dog it whines from the shadows
We hear it but we don't act
To comfort us we mix it into our play list and imagine it to be
    a glitch

If there is a soul it is a vibration
And "why" could be our soul screaming at us to wake up
But we put hands over ears and "la la la" above the din
We know our place in the hierarchy of The Word
Ours is not to question. Full stop.

Dr. Geller caught himself and sat down, "I'm sorry, Alice. I don't
know what came over me."
"That's quite alright, Myron. Would you like me to wank you off. A
quick blowjob perhaps?"
"You're too kind my dear, maybe later."
Dr. Geller leaned across and lit a cigarette for Dr. Alice Garland, he
smiled at her, "Do you ever worry about what your legacy will be,
Alice?"
She thought about it, "Not really, Myron. I suppose I just do my best
and hope that people will recognize that."

He nodded his head in agreement and smiled. She exhaled smoke and turned to him, "Surely one of your legacies will be the adorable Candice … how is she by the way?"

"She's fine, Alice. I am very proud of her."

"Does she …"

He frowned, "Yes?"

She shuffled in the leather chair and considered how to word it, "When will you tell her? Have you worked out when the appropriate time might be?"

He stroked his chin and looked into the middle distance before bringing the glass to his lips for a sip of brandy, "I must admit it is on my mind often. Timing will be everything."

"Will the authorities have any say in the matter, Myron? Will you need to consult them?"

"I have had consultations, yes. It is part of the process, but I suppose … well, I suppose it will be down to my discretion ultimately. They put her in my care and my care only."

"Mmm."

"The last thing I want is for some bumbling Ministry of Health bureaucrats to come in here and be officious about it all, Alice."

"Oh yes, no, definitely, Myron."

He dragged on his cigarette, "I am calculating the right time to tell her. It will obviously be a very emotive process."

"Obviously."

"It is one of the reasons I have employed her to work for the institute. I have strived to give her grounding in how psychotherapy works. I want her to try and fully understand the process before I tell her … in fact I am devising, well I say 'devising', it is more toying with an idea at the moment … an idea whereby Candice can fully appreciate what I have done for her. An idea that encapsulates a few of my theories and ideas."

She sat forward, "Intriguing. Tell me more, Myron."

He patted her hand and smiled, "It is embryonic, dear Alice … but rest assured, if I do go decide to go down that road it will be revolutionary and everyone in our community will get to hear about it."

...

......

...

....

When Doctor A was cooking up her experiment and pensively calculating its efficaciousness, a million questions clung to her mind like pubic hairs to a Velcro butt plug. She knew she would be faced with a barrage of hows and whys and whens and the all-important "how much?'s". Doctor A spent over a year real politicking just to get to the embryonic stage, once there though it wasn't hard to convince wealthy backers of the potential of the breakthrough if it were to succeed, or rather *fail*. There's nothing more tempting to the egos of The Elite than offering them the chance to prove that nobody – especially a creator – is above them. That they were funding an experiment to disprove rather than discover didn't perturb them and they gave generously.

Doctor A honed the pitch down to Hollywood back of a fag packet proportions, "To prove The Bible wrong from its opening sentence."

There were many animadvertent voices in the upper enclosures of the scientific field, which pissed her off; not because of their lack of vision and anti-faith, but rather the fact that she wanted to keep the project secret until she had succeeded in proving the negative. She had to bring in a plague of expensive Lawyers to protect disclosure and show others she meant business.

Even close friends and colleagues questioned her motivations; *"You want to prove The Bible – a novel, a work of fiction – wrong by proving that the word could never be made flesh and visa versa! Why for God sake? Why?*

Some saw it as a kind of stunt initially, but when they witnessed the amount of work and money going into the project they realized that Doctor A was deadly serious.

Doctor A had taken a big risk by insisting on bringing Lenny Prior Palmer into the cabal. Lenny Prior Palmer was no scientist; best described as a 55 year old, ineffectual Private Eye with metaphysical leanings and a unhealthy obsession with Noir thriller paperbacks and films, Lenny wasn't welcomed with open arms by the team Doctor A had built around her. They thought Doctor A was risking contamination; couldn't understand why she needed a history of the guinea pig.

Lenny had really known Danny. They weren't exactly "friends" though. Danny had been picking at Lenny's experiences of being a gumshoe. Lenny was more than happy to spin Danny some self-aggrandizing bullshit and Danny was happy to swallow it. Danny was doing research for his writing.

Doctor A wanted the lowdown on Danny. Lenny Prior Palmer was happy to deal it, especially when informed he'd be getting paid.
"We drank together. Drank *a lot* to be honest. Danny was … I wouldn't say 'alcoholic' but you know. He liked a drink."
"He was upfront with you about being a writer?" asked Doctor A.
"Why wouldn't he be? I love reading."
"So your relationship with him was professional?"
"I suppose so, yeah. He wanted to hear about cases I'd been involved in. I think he kind of saw me as a hero figure."

Lenny Prior Palmer drew a sketch of Danny for Doctor A: Northern English, Manchester, single, wife had died at some point though Danny never elaborated, autodidact writer, came to London to write copy for TV commercials, jacked it in to write novels, no kids, no siblings, Mother and Father dead, had lost touch with wider family and friends back home, was living in a tiny apartment in Elephant and Castle, living on savings that were quickly diminishing, had a literary agent who he despised but he couldn't attract another, ate mostly fast food, always clean and tidy, well dressed, smoked heavily just like Lenny …

179

"What I really want to know, Lenny …" Doctor A politely smiled, "Was Danny spiritual? Was he religious? Did you ever speak about the metaphysical?"

"Oh yes, that's really what bonded us."

Doctor A sat forward, "Really?"

"Mmm," nodded Lenny, "I turned him to thee Temple ov Psychick Youth."

Doctor A frowned at him, "I can't say I've heard of …"

Lenny Prior Palmer gave her the pitch, "Do you want to be part ov a world ov sleeping people? Do you want to imbibe thee drug ov thee commonplace? Will you be forever addicted to self-restriction? Established orthodoxies and dogmas, conditioned interpretations ov living, regard thee material world as reality whilst pretending to deal with thee spirit or existence. They conceive and propagate evolution and thinking as purely physical, their control ov our lives and visions as sacrosanct. Religion has privately altered to work from a position that accepts itself as totally discredited by science. All establishment modes ov control and affiliation, both religious and political, rely upon and revolve around unquestioning faith and dogma, unquestioning acceptance ov their inalienable right to assume professional responsibility for our actions upon their shoulders. We are told we are weak, incapable ov grasping scale, afraid ov ourselves and desperate to push responsibility for all events in our lives onto them. We are consistently trained to accept our corporeal existence as hopeless in itself, to becoum subservient to thee greater good. We are perpetually conditioned, encouraged, and blackmailed into self-restriction into narrower and narrower perceptions ov ourselves, our own importance, our own potential and our own experience. We are trained to ignore thee evidence ov our senses and experience and to feel guilt when we glimpse sense derived visions ov ourselves as free spirits. Thee voluntary relinquishing ov responsibility for our lives and actions is one ov thee greatest enemies ov our time. Our enemies are flat. Our enemies are three-dimensional. Our enemies are continuity and coherence. Our enemies are restriction and confinement. Our enemies are guilt and fear. Our enemies are material.

Our enemies are direction and fact. Our enemies are 'Because'. We are not seeking followers; we are seeking collaborators, Individuals for a visionary Psychick alliance."

According to Lenny, he was the teacher and Danny was the student. Doctor A wasn't interested in Lenny's ego and the dynamic of his friendship with Danny. Doctor A was only interested in getting inside Danny's mind before she proved she couldn't turn him into a word.

As Danny laid on the bed; defibrillated, tubed-up to the gills and wired to the Large Hadron Collider, Doctor A would stare at him and wonder what made him tick and how that would impact her attempt at taking him apart, atom by atom.

Chapter 5/first draft
Mum and Dad Treymane had everything; plenty of money, big house, lovely little daughter parceled off to boarding school, a 'perfect' marriage in other words. Dad actually worked for Mum, because she owned the brewery. Mum never let him forget who was boss, but it didn't seem to bother Dad, he just plodded on and worked hard and did his charity work and sometimes played golf; mainly though, he concentrated on his inventing.

Dad knew that Mum was sexually adventurous and that one man could never satisfy her, so he bit the bullet and tried to ignore her sexual shenanigans. He simply didn't want to know, says Alice. It was a given that Mum screwed around but she was discreet and for a time only fucked well-to-do fellow professionals and members of their moneyed circle. At least Mum wasn't picking up bits of rough or flashing her fanny to the farmers in the local village pub.

Mum's insatiable appetite wasn't a major cause for concern. At the weekend she'd be out getting laid whilst Dad fiddled about in his workshop with his inventions. What Dad didn't see or hear was fine by him, semi-ignorance being bliss for the would-be famous inventor.

Mum, Dad and Alice holidayed in the South of France in the summer and at Klosters in the winter. Alice had her horses and everything was hunky dory and she was happy at home but not at school; it all started going wrong for her one Christmas, Alice was thirteen at the time. Her Mum and Dad were doing the usual round of the brewery, meeting and greeting and wishing their employees a merry Yule and a happy new year. This year was special, however, because Dad was proudly handing out his latest invention as a gift.

What I understand from Alice is that this invention was mistletoe attached to a couple of wires that you put on your head-as you would spectacles-and the mistletoe hung above you. It was a novelty you could wear it at the Christmas party's and get plenty of snogs without the awkward chore of having to hold the mistletoe over your quarry whilst you stuck your tongue down their throat. Dad called it the 'Miraculous Mistletoe Machine'.

~~Anyway, Mum and Dad were doing their tour of the warehouse.~~ Mum was demonstrating Dad's invention and giving quick pecks to the oi-polloi. She worked her way around the warehouse until she came to Rodney. Rodney was the token 'mental deficient' that factories often give employment to so as to seem compassionate. It was actually Dad who set Rodney on, but was keen to stress that he wasn't falling under the Nazism of political correctness, but that Rodney was built like an ox and could lug barrels around all day without taking breaks and wouldn't join the union and couldn't answer back because of his self consciousness about his head and his speech impediment. ~~A model employee, Rodney.~~ Dad introduced Mum to Rodney. He cursed that day until the day he died, Alice tells me.

Rodney was six four, weighed nineteen stone – of which four stone of it was accounted for by his head – and he had the mind of a none too bright ten year old. Besides suffering from mega cephalous, Rodney was also in the grip of Tourettes Syndrome. Luckily he had a cleft palette and a terrible lisp so his would-be obscene outbursts came out as gobbledygook.

If you could get over the size of his head, Rodney wasn't too offensive on the eye apparently, however, Mum wasn't too keen on kissing Rodney. But what could she do? She'd kissed all the others. Dad encouraged her to give Rodney a peck-even though the mistletoe was nearly touching the ceiling on account of Rodney's huge head-and that it may stigmatize the poor lad if she left him out.

Mum agreed and ... well, to this day nobody can work out what happened. Rodney must have kissed like Valentino or something because Mum became obsessed with him. Dad said that it wasn't because Rodney was well endowed either; ~~hung like a hamster, he said and he should know after what resulted from this seemingly sympathetic snog.~~

Before long, Rodney was promoted from general dogs body to supervisor and besides the fact that the warehouse was going to pot, Mum was spending more and more time down there with him. She even had her office moved to the warehouse so she could be close to him. Dad began to worry but tried to write it off as a whim of hers that she'd soon get bored with. He figured that there was a lot of novelty value in Rodney, and maybe Mum was just feeling sorry for him and fascinated with his enormous head and his cleft palette and his surreal outbursts and maybe even feeling a little guilty for not embracing people with disabilities in the past. Dad told Alice that Mum had once fired a Quantity Surveyor for having a lazy eye. She may have been trying to make amends, Dad thought for a while.

It became obvious that Mum wasn't going to forget about Rodney. They started having an affair in February-presumably copulating at night when everyone had clocked off – and by April, Mum had moved Rodney into the house. Dad was distraught. He pleaded with Mum not to bring her 'toy boy freak' home, and reasoned that if she really had to conduct this strange affair she could at least confine it to the warehouse.

Mum wore the jockstrap and told Dad that if he didn't like it he could move into his 'inventors shed' at the bottom of the garden. Alice was appalled when she returned home from her very expensive school and found that Rodney had taken root. Mum was fixated and even paid for a speech therapist to help Rodney. The mega cephalous didn't seem to worry her. The therapist was successful with Rodney and now his outbursts were clear. He effed and blinded and cunted and bastarded like a trooper and usually saved the torrents of abuse for Alice.

Dad was suicidal. Mum let Rodney stay at home from work and she spent less and less time at the brewery to be with her bigheaded toy boy. Dad spent most of his time in the shed at the bottom of the garden and when Alice was home she'd lock herself in her room and cry and read and read and cry and wish she'd never been born.

The final straw for Dad came when Mum gave him the ultimatum; either he watched her and Rodney fucking or she'd divorce him and cut him out of her will. Needless to say Dad left. Mum never got around to divorcing him – too busy engaging in more and more bizarre sex acts with Rodney no doubt-and seemed happy that she had Rodney had the house to themselves.

Dad didn't last long in the wilderness. All he knew about was brewing and yuletide novelty inventions. He missed his friends at work, he missed his home, but most of all he missed Mum. They'd been together twenty years and he wasn't going to let a hideous mid-life crisis ruin his marriage. He'd worked hard to keep it alive and had put up with a lot from Mum and now he wasn't going to let an abusive mega cephalic warehouse worker get the better of him. _Is megacephalic one word?

Dad begged Mum to let him come home and promised to join in their sex games. He told Mum he couldn't live without being around her and that he'd do anything if only she would give him another chance.

Tears are welling up in Alice's eyes. I smile at her and gently pat her knee. She sniffles, fights back tears and continues. Why couldn't she have left it there until after we'd fucked the shit out of each other on the rug? She could have told me all this during the post-coital smoke.

Mum let Dad move back in. Every night when he got home from work he'd have to watch Rodney fuck Mum. He'd fight back tears and scream inside and want to die but he had to be strong. He had to be strong for himself and Mum and dear little Alice.

Rodney was relentless with Mum. He wasn't well hung but he hammered away at her like a machine. Mum would writhe around in ecstasy as he banged away at her and when she came she looked Dad square in the eyes and screamed out his name, which was Laurence.

I have to stop her, "Uh, wait a minute, Alice ... uh, I mean, how'd you know all this?"
"Dad told me", *She sobs,* "He told me before he died."
"Oh ... right." *I frown.*

So Dad's playing along. Night after night he's watching Norfolk's answer to the Elephant Man getting stuck up his missus, hoping, praying that she'll open her eyes and see, really see that her and Rodney rutting looked like a nightmare Hieronymus Bosch once had but didn't dare paint it in case it petrified people.

Mum got confident and started turning up party's and fete's and lunches with Rodney. Her social circle diminished in size. Dad pleaded with Mum to at least keep Rodney under wraps but she wasn't having any of it and started visiting the village pub with him on a regular basis. Mum and Rodney were the quintessential 'odd couple'. Mum was beautiful, educated, immaculately groomed and clothed and Rodney was unfortunately a freak who had to crouch down to get inside the pub's door. Mum was forever having to explain Rodney's outbursts to the locals but it was only a matter of time before the landlord of the pub barred him for life for unprovoked effing and blinding.

Dad fell into a pit of depression. He stopped inventing novelty Christmas gifts and took to taking long solitary walks around the countryside. His work suffered and the brewery showed a loss ~~in its annual report~~ for the first time in a hundred and eighty years.

Dad started blaming himself; if he hadn't invented the 'mistletoe kissing machine' Mum and Rodney would have never kissed. He also began to think that there was a 'cosmic conspiracy' afoot designed to ruin his life. He said that he'd only turned to inventing after he'd received a bump to the head in the warehouse. The bump he was referring to came about when Rodney 'accidentally' knocked a stack of empty bottles over when Dad 'happened' to be passing. Dad was concussed and took a couple of days off work. Up until then, Dad had never even thought about inventing.

Not only was Dad depressed he was also paranoid now and Mum showed no signs of getting bored with Rodney. Dad could take more when Mum told him that Rodney would be going on a romantic cruise around the Caribbean with them. He couldn't bare the thought of having to watch Rodney fuck the arse off of Mum on the high seas.

~~Alice starts to really cry. I don't know what to say or do. I put my arm around her shoulder and glance down at her tits heaving as she sobs. "Is it …… uh, you don't have to-if it's too painful, Alice, I mean …" She wants to go on. She wants to come to terms with what happened. She can't keep running away from it. It's cathartic, she says. She empties the rest of the wine in our glasses and continues. CUT?~~

It transpires that Dad was rather choosey in his method of self-extermination. Drowning was out of the question. The thought terrified *him. He was also afraid of heights and from a very early age had been useless at taking tablets so an overdose was ruled out. He thought of slashing his wrists but reasoned that it was too violent and messy. Head in the oven or exhaust fumes in the car didn't tickle his fancy and neither did hanging or a bullet to the brain, a glass of poison or throwing himself under a bus.*

Dad came up with what he thought was a great solution. He knew that Rodney wanted him out of the way and that he'd never been fond of fucking Mum with Dad watching.

Dad told Rodney that he wanted out and that he could help him on his way.

The set-up was simple enough. Dad would drink a bottle of whiskey and in his deep drunken sleep; Rodney would put a pillow over Dad's face and smother him to death. Dad hoped that the following investigation would lead Rodney to getting banged up for offing the cuckolded husband of his lover.

Dad told Rodney that if Mum were to get a whiff of the plan it would be called off. A date was set. Dad went to see Alice at school and told her everything. He made her promise that she wouldn't tell a soul about what was about to happen. Alice pleaded with Dad but his mind was made up. If he couldn't have Mum without Rodney he didn't want to carry on living. Alice finally agreed to say nothing. He kissed her goodbye at the school gates and she was convinced that the next time she saw him he'd be dead. She was wrong.

Dad went home – calling at an off-license on the way to buy a bottle of Bells – and prepared to meet his maker. He obviously left no note. He was just hoping that the police would be able to pin the murder on Rodney. Dad thought that there would be no chance of them buying Rodney's story of him being asked to murder him. Why would they believe a freak that was screwing his wife! Motive, motive, motive, Dad thought as he swilled back the whiskey.

Dad fell into a deep drunken sleep as planned. Rodney did as he was asked and put a pillow over Dad's face and kept it there until Dad stopped struggling.

So far so good, only Rodney being Rodney (drawkcab) he stopped smothering Dad too early. Dad wasn't dead; he was simply uncon- scious as a result of his brain being starved of oxygen. Rodney left him in the bed, went downstairs and played Sonic The Hedgehog all night on the Nintendo.

Alice's tits are really heaving now. Her sobs are deep, deep like they're being ripped from her very soul by a malevolent memory extraction machine. I tell that she doesn't have to go on. I tell her that it's obvi- ously too painful and that I could make her a strong black coffee. There's nothing more unpleasant than fucking a morose pissed up woman. Alice wants to continue though. I try not to let her see me sighing and surreptitiously checking my watch.
"You see, Danny … Dad didn't wake up dead, he didn't even wake up with a hangover … Dad woke up a vegetable." She sobs. I don't know whether to laugh or cry.

Dear old Dad's plan had gone hideously wrong. Everyone assumed that Dad had suffered a major stroke in his sleep. Mum promised to take care of Dad. She was true to her word and still let him sit in on her nightly fucks with Rodney, positioning his wheelchair so he had no choice, says Alice.

Alice finally left school for good and rushed home knowing about the hellish behavior of her Mum and determined to see that Dad finally got his death wish.

She wheeled him out of the house one sunny afternoon and took him down to the river that she'd shared so many good times with him on their ponies when she was younger, when they'd gallop along blissfully unaware that a megacephalic called Rodney would one day enter into their world and inadvertently tear it down.

Alice figured that Dad's fear of drowning would have evaporated when he entered the vegetative state. She kissed him on his forehead and told him what she was going to do. Dad just gurgled. She knew in her heart that this is what he really wanted and she pushed him in.

The last image she has of her Dad is a big bewildered smile on his face as he slowly sank with the wheelchair. Alice waited a good ten minutes, composed herself and ran back to the house crying that Dad had accidentally fallen in.

There was an investigation and 'death by misadventure' was the official verdict. Mum continued to fuck Rodney for a few more months but then seemed to get bored. Alice reckons that's because Dad wasn't there to watch, her theory is that Mum just liked to sexually torment Dad.

Rodney was unceremoniously booted out with a golden handshake of thirty thousand pounds. Mum sold the brewery and mysteriously went to live in Copenhagen. She set up a trust fund for Alice and Alice reckons she's worth about three million when Mum dies.

Rodney didn't last long with his newfound wealth. He fell in with a gang of teenage reprobates from the village and squandered his money on one-arm-bandits, cider and glue. He was found dead with a bag of Evo stuck over his mouth outside the village hall after one of their fortnightly teen discos. The Vicar tried reviving him but mouth-to-mouth was simply out of the question because of the possibility of sticking to him.

Alice was happy when she found out that Rodney had died of asphyxiation. Mum didn't fly in from Copenhagen for the funeral. Alice went out of curiosity and couldn't believe how big the coffin was. There were only six people at the funeral and Rodney was cremated.

"It's like we were doomed isn't it, Danny?" Alice asks me, her eyes red raw and searching.

I tell her that she mustn't dwell on it and that at least Dad got what he wanted and has gone to another plane and that he'll be happy there and that nothing could have been done to alter the course that led to his death and that and this and blah and blah blah and blah blah fucking blah because no matter what I'm saying to her it's not going to bring her beloved Dad back and I'm feeling low now because she's really hurt and doesn't look sexy anymore, just vulnerable and lost and confused and angry that maybe some metaphysical being or entity threw Dad a great big fucking banana skin in the shape of Rodney and watched and pissed itself laughing at his expense.

Doctor A looked Lenny Prior Palmer square in the face and said, "Do you agree that Danny was in a constant battle between the sacred and the profane in his writing?"
Lenny nodded, "Yes. I think it stems from the facts of his birth."
"That his Mother died at the point he was delivered?"
"Yes" said Lenny, "It doesn't take a psychologist to work out that he felt abandoned. His Mother had bore him and left him completely alone in a strange inhospitable world."
"What happened with his Father?"
"He put her death down to Danny's birth."
Doctor A shook her head sympathetically, "Ridiculous."
"Who knows what was going through his mind … anyway, Danny was taken into care. He was brought up by The State."

Although she disagreed with most of the content, Doctor A would keep referring back to Thomas Troward's words in her research: One of the first things that naturally attract our attention is the question, – How did Life originate? On this point I may quote two leading men of science. Tyndall says: "I affirm that no shred of trustworthy experimental testimony exists, to prove that life in our day has ever appeared independently of antecedent life"; and Huxley says: "The doctrine of biogenesis, or life only from life, is victorious along the whole line at the present time." Such is the testimony of modern science to the old maxim "Omne vivum exvivo." "All life proceeds from antecedent life." Think it out for yourself and you will see that it could not possibly be otherwise.

Whatever may be our theory of the origin of life on the physical plane, whether we regard it as commencing in a vivified slime at the bottom of the sea, which we call protoplasm, or in any other way, the question of how life got there still remains unanswered. The protoplasm being material substance, must have its origin like all other material substances, in the undifferentiated etheric Universal Substance, no particle of which has any power of operating upon any other particle until some initial vibration starts the movement; so that, on any theory whatever, we are always brought back to the same question: What started the condensation of the ether into the beginnings of a world-system? So whether we consider the life which characterizes organized matter, or the energy which characterizes inorganic matter, we cannot avoid the conclusion, that both must have their source in some Original Power to which we can assign no antecedent. This is the conclusion which has been reached by all philosophic and religious systems that have really tried to get at the root of the matter, simply because it is impossible to form any other conception.

This Living Power is what we mean when we speak of the All-Originating Spirit. The existence of this Spirit is not a theological invention, but a logical and scientific ultimate, without predicating which, nothing else can be accounted for. The word "Spirit" comes from the Latin "spiro" "I breathe," and so means "The Breath," as in Job xxxiii, 4, – "The Spirit of God hath made me, and the breath

of the Almighty hath given me life"; and again in Ps. xxxiii, 6 – "By
the word of the Lord were the heavens made, and all the host of them
by the breath of his mouth."

In the opening chapter of Genesis, we are told that "the Spirit
of God moved upon the face of the waters." The words rendered
"the Spirit of God" are, in the original Hebrew "rouah Ælohim,"
which is literally "the Breathing of God"; and similarly, the ancient
religious books of India, make the "Swára" or Great Breath the
commencement of all life and energy. The word "rouah" in Genesis
is remarkable. According to rabbinical teaching, each letter of the
Hebrew alphabet has a certain symbolic significance, and when
examined in this manner, the root from which this word is derived
conveys the idea of Expansive Movement. It is the opposite of the
word "hoshech," translated "darkness" in the same passage of our
Bible, which is similarly derived from a root conveying the idea of
Hardening and Compressing. It is the same idea that is personified
in the Zendavesta, the sacred book of the ancient Persians, under
the names of Ormuzd, the Spirit of Light; and Ahriman, the Spirit
of Darkness; and similarly in the old Assyrian myth of the struggle
between the Sun God and Tiámat, the goddess of darkness.

This conception of conflict between two opposite principles, Light
and Darkness, Compression and Expansion, will be found to under-
lie all the ancient religions of the world, and it is conspicuous
throughout our own Scriptures. But it should be borne in mind that
the oppositeness of their nature does not necessarily mean conflict.
The two principles of Expansion and Contraction are not necessarily
destructive; on the contrary they are necessary correlatives to one
another. Expansion alone cannot produce form; cohesion must also
be present. It is the regulated balance between them that results
in Creation. In the old legend, if I remember rightly, the conflict is
ended by Tiámat marrying her former opponent. They were never
really enemies, but there was a misunderstanding between them, or
rather there was a misunderstanding on the part of Tiámat so long

as she did not perceive the true character of the Spirit of Light, and that their relation to one another was that of co-operation and not of opposition. Thus also St. John tells us that "the light shineth in darkness and the darkness comprehended it not" (John i, 5). It is this want of comprehension that is at the root of all the trouble.

The reader should note, however, that I am here speaking of that Primeval Substance, which necessarily has no light in itself, because there is as yet no vibration in it, for there can be no light without vibration. We must not make the mistake of supposing that Matter is evil in itself: it is our misconception of it that makes it the vehicle of evil; and we must distinguish between the darkness of Matter and moral darkness, though there is a spiritual correspondence between them. The true development of Man consists in the self-expansion of the Divine Spirit working through his mind, and thence upon his psychic and physical organisms, but this can only be by the individual's willingness to receive that Spirit. Where the hindrance to this working is only caused by ignorance of the true relation between ourselves and the Divine Spirit, and the desire for truth is present, the True Light will in due course disperse the darkness. But on the other hand, if the hindrance is caused by unwillingness to be led by the Divine Spirit, then the Light cannot be forced upon any one, and for this reason Jesus said: "This is the condemnation, that light is come into the World, and men loved darkness rather than light, because their deeds were evil. For every one that doeth evil hateth the light, neither cometh to the light, lest his deeds should be reproved. But he that doeth truth cometh to the light, that his deeds may be made manifest, that they are wrought in God" (John iii: 19-21). In physical science these things have an exact parallel in "Ohm's Law" regarding the resistance offered by the conductor to the flow of the electric current. The correspondence is very remarkable and will be found more fully explained in a later chapter. The Primary Darkness, both of Substance and of Mind, has to be taken into account, if we would form an intelligent conception of the twofold process of Involution and Evolution continually at work in ourselves, which, by their combined action, are able to lead to the limitless development both of the individual and of the race.

According to all teaching, then, both ancient and modern, all life and energy have their source in a Primary Life and Energy, of which we can only say that IT IS. We cannot conceive of any time when it was not, for, if there was a time when no such Primary Energizing Life existed, what was there to energize it? So we are landed in a reductio ad absurdum, which leaves no alternative, but to predicate the Eternal Existence of an All-Originating Living Spirit.

& found himself pondering a full stop blocking his line of vision. Eventually he circumnavigated it but was faced with an electronic meadow of Xeroxed statements: This Sentence Died of Natural Clauses …

He returned to the empty operating theatre and swooped over the dress circle. Seats D17 and D18 were watching a man sat on stage performing on a typewriter that had seen better days and was missing the letter "i".

D17 and D18 were being their usual hypercritical selves, "Call this a performance?" D18 scoffed, "It's an insult!"
"They should have *us* on stage!" D17 protested.
"Yes! The things we have seen, the stories we could tell." D18 paused and ruminated, "Mmm … maybe we should speak to the manager of the theatre."
"Do you think she might be interested?"
"Of course she would," D18, said, "We've had the greatest arses in his story sat on us. We've heard things that could blow the mind of an imbecile."
"And you don't think she'll mind that we're just a couple of old theater seats?" asked D17.
D18 was appalled, "Just theater seats? *Just* theater seats!"

Novel Headline 7. *The Result" of Life is Death, so when you create, the importance is not on the result but on the process of creating in and of itself*

& heard himself being magnetized into an old print review of Van Morrison's 'Astral Weeks'. & hated the way dead tree media smelt but he let himself become ensconced in the article:

'It's not only unfair & illogical but it's also impossible to actually say that an album is the greatest ever recorded. What is possible is to keep going back to an album & falling in love with it over & over again. With each new listen you find even more magic, truth & illumination. Each new listen can capture that first "time", can transport you back to a day, hour, minute or second when something that only means anything to you is relived & your blood suddenly runs faster or warmer or even colder. A fragment of now materially dead time that pulsates back to life & either haunts you with beauty or horror. There is only one album that does that for me.'

'Singles are a different kettle. There are a few that flood my mind with Proustian flashbacks & all have the same impact on my psyche when I hear them. They instantly transport me, move me; make me sad for times past but hopeful for times to come. They are fundamentally magic, in the sense that they can transform & illuminate but by their very nature & short format they don't take you a journey for over an hour, obviously.'

'They are created as a 'glimpse'; either of the now, the past or the future, & because of that they leave you wanting more. If magical singles are a glimpse of the hereafter of the near death patient on the operating table, magical albums are a first class return journey to heaven/hell. A flatline, taking you to a place that is only reached once you have completely shed your ego & fears & have tacitly agreed to give yourself over to the artist taking you on that trip.'

'Out of all the albums I have listened to – a multitude of times over the years – nothing comes close as Astral Weeks by Van Morrison to moving me spiritually, physically & mentally. Neil Young's After The Gold Rush is probably the album that I have played as much, but even its magnificence can't orbit the same inner galaxy that Astral Weeks does. I have never played an album & instantly fallen in love with it. The same applies to singles. I generally need to listen a few times to a piece of music for it to seep into my mind & make me want to hear it again. Astral Weeks is the exception. On first hearing it I was mesmerized, & when I say mesmerized I mean I was hypnotized, rendered speechless & lost all track of linear time. All this whilst sober & in tip top mental & physical condition (it was a long time ago).'

'The first song on the eight-song album is the eponymous 'Astral Weeks'. Van firmly sets up the psycho-geography stall with his opening, 'If I ventured in the slipstream, between the viaducts of your dreams … where immobile steel rims crack & the ditch in the back-road stops".'

'Another piece of Irish magic similarly sets out its stall from the opening line. "Riverrun, past Eve & Adam's, from swerve of shore to bend of bay, brings us by a commodius vicus of recirculation back to Howth Castle & Environs." – Finnegan's Wake, James Joyce.' Margot Norris wrote of that introduction, "The opening of Finnegan's Wake drops us, without map, clock, compass, glossary, or footnotes, into an unknown verbal country, & the voice of the tour guide, alas, speaks their language rather than ours, although we catch enough cognates to keep from drowning altogether in that verbal stream."'

'If Finnegan's Wake is regarded as the most sublime & impenetrable work of literary fiction ever recorded, surely Astral Weeks must be it's musical equivalent. Both pieces firmly inform the reader/listener that they are about to be taken on a journey. An idiosyncratic &

rather perilous journey right to the very core of one man's mind/
soul.'

'Both proclamations warn the participant that they are not in for
an easy, satisfying ride, & that they are in fact being invited into a
spiritual realm. A realm that is neither fully perilously nocturnal nor
fully bathed in the safety & comfort of daylight. Both James Joyce &
Van Morrison alluded to the fact that there was really no explanation
for their masterpieces ... that the words "came" to them is fundamentally what they said, & once you explore both works it's hard to
imagine how else these creations could have materialized. There is a
really strong argument that both works were 'spiritually automatic'.'

'Every line, chord, pause, inflection, stammer & ad-lib in Astral
Weeks is pointing to something beyond everyday comprehension.
It points inwards & outwards simultaneously. It reaches into your
soul with one h& & punches its way into the material universe with
the other, whilst all the while keeping you tethered & recognizing
that you are of the earthly plane. It's actually frightening to imagine
being chemically altered – either by booze or narcotic or hallucino-
genic – whilst listening to it. It's something I have always resisted
doing because I believe any stimulant would push me over some
kind of metaphorical ledge. Astral Weeks is a narcotic in itself.'

'One word that always comes to kind when thinking about Astral
Weeks is 'Big'. Big in the sense that it has no boundaries & cannot
be contained. The feeling of being enveloped in its ever exp&ing
world is so strong & sometimes overwhelming that you are stunned
into a reflective submission. It can make you feel like a romantic
warrior one minute & a gibbering emotional wreck the next; constantly throwing you into huge & deep eternal spaces.'

'Lester Bangs wrote of Astral Weeks, "you're probably wondering
when I'm going to get around to telling you about Astral Weeks.
As a matter of fact, there's a whole lot of Astral Weeks I don't even

197

want to tell you about. Both because whether you've heard it or not it wouldn't be fair for me to impose my interpretation of such lapidary subjective imagery on you, & because in many cases I don't really know what he's talking about. He (Van Morrison) doesn't either."'

'James Joyce said of Finnegan's Wake: "what is clear & concise can't deal with reality, for to be real is to be surrounded by mystery." He could have been describing Astral Weeks. Astral Weeks obviously isn't as wordy or complex or annoyingly puzzling as Finnegan's Wake, but it shares a rhythmic mantra & creates a feeling of awe in the reader/listener & leaves a psychic tattoo that can only be understood or deciphered by the one whom it has been tattooed on to.'
'For pure hypnotism one only needs to listen to 'Beside You'. It's a Dervish mantra in praise of the Holy Ghost; only Van has managed to materialize the HG & he's dressing it in flesh & making it move around the corporeal plane whilst he serenades it. In 'Beside You' is the line, "Way across the country where the hillside mountain glide … the dynamo of your smile caressed the barefoot virgin child to w&er." Poetry that puts laureates to shame. 'All' of them. All those earnest, emotionally tortured, pontificating pederasts & 'Men Hating' creatures & self-aggr&izing 'victims' & state stipend leeches & cultural looters. In that one breath Van elevates 'rock music' above all other art forms, especially poetry. He takes words into a new frontier of imagery, & he does it with toughness & stoicism that is truly breathtaking & heroic. There is absolutely nothing sentimental in the words & music of Astral Weeks because Astral Weeks is of 'no time'. You can't get sentimental over a 'time' that is neither fully in the here, then or whenever.'

'In 'Madame George', Van uses the line, "You're caught up playing dominoes in drag." to paint an heart ripping portrait of a Transvestite out of time, out of place & out of the realm of everyday comprehension. The quintessential poem of alienation would reverberate in the most closed & homophobic of minds. Its minimalism turns hearts of stone to rivulets of blood … that's assuming the listener is human of course.'

198

'In 'The Way Young Lovers Do', Van's imagery is dizzying, disorientating & mystifying even though on paper it looks like a simple couple of lines reverberating on themselves, "Then we sat on our own star, & dreamed of the way that we were & the way that we were meant to be … then we sat on our own star & dreamed of the way that I was for you & you were for me." Again, Van Morrison is up there with James Joyce playing Celtic mind games & creating cerebral loops & glitches in time with his words.'

'The second time I decided to 'really' listen to Astral Weeks in its entirety I knew I had to find somewhere special to listen to it. It was the early 1980's & I was in Ibiza on holiday.'

'I hired a motorbike & rode out to Cala Conte. No helmet & wearing only shorts I sped out into the sunshine with a Sony Walkman & a cassette tape of Astral Weeks in my pocket. I found a completely deserted white-beached cove, lay down, put the headphones on & listened.'

'Maybe I 'willed' myself into having an hallucinatory experience, in fact I definitely did, it was all conscious, but what happened can only be described as natural hallucination; pure, unadulterated, unaided by any narcotics whatsoever. I laid on the beach bathed in the hot sun, my eyes closed, hearing the seawater lapping the beach over the sound of Astral Weeks … & then I was transported. It is the only time I have 'tripped' or 'psychically voyaged' or whatever you want to call it without the aid of stimulants. What you could only describe as a natural high. The journey kicked in halfway through the opening track & ended long after the last track. I reckon two hours or thereabouts. On this 'trip' – for want of a better word – I was taken to places & times that I couldn't even begin to try & describe or do justice to in common language.'

'These were universes within universes within my mind & they were being opened up by Astral Weeks. No other album has ever opened up these polar extremes in my psyche, & God knows I have tried to find other albums that do it.'

'At its core Astral Weeks is a personal record. Personal to Van Morrison & personal to the listener. I don't believe it's for everyone's taste – & that's not being snobbish – because not everyone wants the same experience from a piece of music. I must have wanted to be taken on a journey by it.'

'I like to believe that my experience of listening to Astral Weeks was a magical experience outside the realms of linear time & objective reality & I suppose because I do 'believe' it, it really was magical & it really did get me high that day on the beach.'

Detective Inspector French was a woman. They sent a woman to question Sean. Sensitivity had to be employed. This was a sensitive case. It was good that DI French was no looker. Nice pins, but nothing to get excited about in the T&A departments. Sending some stacked glamour puss cop wouldn't have been sensitive. A foxy fem Detective wouldn't have seemed right. It was good that DI French gave off dykey vibes.

It was clearly suicide but there was no note and there were questions. It was open and shut but there were questions. It was suicide and the interview was formality. *Why didn't she at least leave a fucking note?*
Sean was nursing a hellish hangover on the day of the interview.
DI French glanced at the sweat patches on Sean's white linen shirt and said, "How long had you been apart?"
Sean said, "Seven months."
DI French said, "So … you separated when she knew she was pregnant?"
"Obviously. Obviously she … she knew she was pregnant."
"No … I mean, I mean the pregnancy was a factor?"
Sean frowned, "A factor?"

"A factor in your separation. Was it?"

"I don't – things were – I don't know. Things were ... things were going wrong before then."

"Wrong?"

"Yeah"

DI French said, "What do you mean by wrong?"

"Are you married?"

"No."

"That's a pity." Sean said as he lit a cigarette and tapped his Zippo on the cheap plastic table. He clocked the tape recorder. The interview wasn't being recorded. He'd agreed to the interview. There were questions to be asked. There was no suicide note. It was a shocking suicide. All suicides are shocking to somebody.

"I need to ask, Mr Cassidy. You agreed to ..."

Sean snapped in, "*Wrong* as in not working! Wrong as in ... it was ... we'd have been together if everything was fine ... we just ... we couldn't talk anymore. We couldn't ..."

"Couldn't what?"

"Get along. She wasn't happy ... obviously."

"And her unhappiness was ... huh ... she was unhappy *before* the pregnancy?"

"Yeah."

"Was there – as far as you know – was there anything, a reason, a reason for her being unhappy, Mr Cass-"

"Sean. Call me, Sean."

"O.K., Sean."

Sean sighed and sat back in the cheap chair and told DI French everything he knew about Maria's life before he'd met her.

Sean had a lot to relay. He had listened to Maria's history on a loop. For the first month or two of knowing her he had done nothing *but* listen. Sean was Maria's saviour, her confessor, her protector, her Knight in a grey flak jacket with 'Press' wrote across it in black marker pen.

Experiences had poured out of Maria in broken English. Sean

listened and nodded his head and tried, desperately tried to sym-
pathize with her horror show stories. He'd heard similar stories.
He knew about the mechanics of war. He had the figures on the
aftermaths.

Sean had sat with Maria. Sean had sat and watched her full lips
move. He sat and nodded his head in all the right places and fell
deep into her hypnotic blue eyes. He felt bad for not really listening.
He felt bad for fantasising about fucking her. He wasn't a psychiatrist. He was a man and no amount of tragic stories could overcome
that.

Maria's story was unremarkable. Very few people from the region
escaped the psychic scarring of the civil war in the Balkans of the
nineties. Maria had been more than unlucky though. She had lost all
her family to the violence.
DI French said, "Maria was a Serb wasn't she?"
Sean said, "Yeah."
"I thought … I always thought it was the Bosnian Serbs who were
the … the-"
"-Bad guys?"
"Well … yeah."
"It wasn't black and white. It was a fucked up war."
"Aren't they all?"
Sean smiled at her, "Sure, but this one … this one was *really* fucked
up."
"Why?"
"History. You've got to look at the history to understand what went
on. The full picture was never, you know, *exposed*."
"I remember not understanding what was going on."
"Doesn't surprise me. The reporting was biased."
"Really? Why?"
Sean sighed. He wasn't there to give a lecture. He snapped, "What
do you want me to say?"
DI French said, "I'm interested."

Sean said, "The propaganda campaign against Belgrade was fucking relentless. The bleeding heart's who opposed NATO policy against Yugoslavia bought the demonic line. You know? Milosevic as some kind of Satan. These were supposed to be Reporters, Christ … the spineless fuckers started toeing the party line. It was a whitewash. The Serbs were the bad guys and everyone else were the good guys."

"And you fought against this?"

Sean snorted, "No … no I didn't. Sure, I'd shout and bawl when I was pissed in the hotel bar but … no. I didn't do anything about it. When the pieces I filed came zipping back for a rewrite I … I did what all the others did. I got in line."

"You were doing a job."

A sardonic chuckle from Sean, "I was a coward."

"I'd imagine it was-"

"-I knew the big picture. We all knew the big picture. America wanted to break up Yugoslavia. It was the only Eastern European country unwilling to dismantle its welfare state and public sector economy. Yugoslavia was in America's crosshairs."

"I'll have to take your word for it. Politics aren't my strong point."

"I was at Srebrenica when hundreds of Serbs were slaughtered by Muslims. I was in Sarajevo during the market massacre. The Serbs were instantly blamed for it. I was with a French reporter who had a contact in Intelligence. They knew it was Muslim operatives who'd bombed the market in order to get NATO involved. There were atrocities on both sides, but the Serbs *had* to be portrayed as the bad guys."

"Mmm … it must have been frustrating."

"Yeah. Felt like shit. What can you do?"

"You met Maria in Sarajevo, right?"

"The night of the market bombing. That's right."

"And she'd been, huh, affected?"

"Lost her grandparents and three cousins in the market. She'd already lost her mother and her brothers and sisters."

DI French shook her head and murmured.

Sean said, "They'd been ambushed by Croat bandits just outside the City. Her youngest sister – eight years old – she took over forty bullets. They'd all been shot in the face. They were rotting in a makeshift morgue for three days. Nobody knew who they were."

"Terrible."

"Yeah."

"Did you bring her back with you? Maria?"

"No."

"So … huh-"

"-I went back. I came home and went back. We met up again."

Sean thought about the return. He remembered seeing her face again. He remembered how shell-shocked she still was. He remembered how sexy she was. The infrastructure of her life had been blow to smithereens and yet she still had pure sex oozing out of every pore.

Maria stunk of sex. Unconscious sexuality. The *best* sexuality. She was a war babe. *Miss Sarajevo 1994. 36" 24" 36", brunette, blue eyes, high cheekbones, 25, hobbies include burying dead family members and dodging snipers bullets, ambition: peace, not World peace, just peace in The Balkans. Doesn't want to work with children but wouldn't mind traveling the World. Traveling anywhere, in fact, as long as she can get the fuck out of her hate riddled homeland.*

Sean fell in love with Maria. Beauty aside, her intelligence shone through. Fluent – self-taught – in English and French, before the war she'd been studying for a degree in social work. Sean found it strange that a country in the process of eating itself had only recently been training its citizens in social care.

After everything Maria had endured she still managed to smile. It might have been front. It might have been surface. Sean didn't care. He could see himself spending the rest of his life with her.

Sean said, "Have you thought about getting out, Maria?"

Maria said, "I've thought about nothing else."

"You ... you could come to England."

Sean didn't care that she might not have truly loved him. Why should see? He was hardly a great catch. He couldn't offer her a great sex life or financial security or witty repartee or romance on tap. He was a lousy fuck, forever in the red, boorish and autistic when it came to laying bare his feelings to the opposite sex.

Sean stayed in Sarajevo with her. He stayed for two weeks. Real package deals in Hell. Maria had many funerals to attend. The corpses needed to be buried even if there was little left of them for the worms to chow down on.

Sean and Maria stayed together in a mortar-wrecked hotel. It was hot. God might have abandoned Sarajevo but the heat hadn't. Sean stayed in the room and drank. Maria mourned and Sean got pissed. Self-loathing ate at Sean and the only respite was when Maria returned and they slept together.

They didn't fuck. Sean learned to sleep with a hard on. It wouldn't have felt right sticking his dick in such a tragic beauty. Real reason: he'd heard a rumor that Yugoslavian men were well hung. He'd hopefully get her to *really* like him before he'd enter and disappoint. He wanted to fuck her – Christ he wanted to fuck her – but he didn't want to fuck up the chance of *keeping* her.

They embraced and kissed. Sean caressed her tits and she rubbed her white panty clad pussy against his thighs. She never asked him why he didn't fuck her. *She must think I'm a faggot!* They talked. Wrapped around each other they talked. She rested her head on his chest and asked him all about his life.

Sean lied to her. He wanted to impress. He made himself out to be a great, in-demand Reporter. Truth was he was mediocre at best and as 'in-demand' as a contraceptive in a convent.

He lied to her, told her he was a truthful reporter, told her he cared passionately about getting the truth *out there*. The lies came easy. He was a Reporter. He had a filter. All the news that's *fit* to print. He told her what he thought she wanted to hear. He told her he had a solid career ahead of him. Told her that he would one day write a book about his experiences and it would sell and he'd make good money and the money would bring security and happiness.

Maria talked about the past and Sean talked about the future. There was no point trying to find a middle ground. How could he match her experiences? All he had to offer was a drunken father who occasionally got violent with his mother. Sure, there were tears and bruises and black eyes and vomit and sometimes blood and sometimes Sean would piss in his pajamas, but fuck! No comparison to watching kids getting the tops of their heads sheared off by bullets or old people frantically trying to climb from cars, their hands melted into the steering wheels. No comparison to watching a kid in a wheelchair get pushed over a cliff whilst Croat Bandits stand by and laugh. No comparison to watching an old lady get set upon, sodomized and set on fire.

No comparisons. Sean listened and hugged her. It's all he could do. He'd have liked to have told Maria that he was beyond shock. Nothing surprised him anymore. Man's capacity for violence never ceased to impress him. *What will they think of next, huh? Those cheeky Homo sapiens and their creative violence! What can you say?* If Maria had told him she'd seen fetuses cut from their mother's stomachs and spit roasted to feed hungry gangs of mass murderers it wouldn't have surprised him. He'd seen his share of atrocities in the Balkans. He'd seen the numb casual killings, the pedestrians being blown to pieces, the torture of innocents, the brain-frying spectacle of babies crawling over their mother's corpses. But Sean had seen it all through a filter. He didn't *know* these people. Their pain wasn't his. Never would be. He was a watcher with a front row seat. He was a spectator. He had to remain dispassionate. It wasn't hard for him. It was no major feat. He could handle it. These people were there to be reported on. Without them there wasn't a war and without a war he had nothing to report on.

Sean would never get into Maria's nightmares. She sweated and tossed and turned and murmured in her native tongue. He'd watch her trapped in nightmares. Sometimes she'd wake with a start and she'd ask him to hold her tighter. Sometimes she'd stay trapped and

Sean would get out of bed. He'd sit at the window fanning himself with a piece of cardboard, smoking, drinking lukewarm beer, staring out onto the deserted streets. He'd see the 'peacekeeping' jeeps roll by and he'd slowly raise his index finger and make a gun with it and pretend to shoot and imagine the jeep bursting into flames. *When in Rome ...*

During the second week of his return they went for a walk amongst the debris. The sun stalked them. They held hands and sucked on a bottle of red wine. To Sean it felt like an eleventh hour stroll through Pompeii. A walk through Rome as a thousand fiddles kicked up a cacophony. For Maria it was like witnessing another death. Psychogeographical murder. The streets that had been her playground were now just a satellite of an ever-growing battlefield.

They stopped for shade. They sat and held hands in a doorway that led to a demolished launderette and watched a dog go through its death throes. The dog's skeleton was visible. It wanted out. The dog had some heart. It's panting was silent and frenzied. Sean offered to put it out of its misery with a heavy stone.

Maria stood up. She walked over to a dirty plastic bag and picked it up. She knelt and slipped it over the dog's head. She held it tightly. Sean went to her. He knelt down and gently placed a cigarette between her full lips. He torched it for her. Maria sucked the nicotine down and blew the smoke through her nose. She tightened her grip on the plastic bag and smiled sad at Sean.

Sean stood up and looked at the sun. He shaded his eyes and looked down the street. Sarajevo was a dead City but it felt good to be alive in it. He looked down at Maria. With her free hand she was stroking the dog's back. It was a Kodak moment. Compassionate dog euthanasia.

The dog had some heart in it. It felt like an age before it gave in. Sean dragged the dead dog to a pile of rubble and threw some over it. Maria noticed something in the powdered concrete. She pointed it out to Sean. Sean picked it up. It was a dusty black and white photograph of a wedding. Sean held it out. Maria put her arm around his waist and rested her head on his shoulder. Bride and groom smiled out at them. They made an ugly couple but their love for each other was beyond question. Both were cross-eyed and buck toothed. *Had twins married each other?* He imagined that they'd escaped the war by having run away together, cackling maniacally as they jigged out of the city. Sean stifled a laugh. It would have upset Maria. She might have known them. For all he knew they might have been close to her. Relatives even.

Maria said, "I wonder where they are now." Sean had a theory: *They'd be scratching a living in a freak show somewhere.*

Sean felt good. No matter how bad he felt about himself at least he didn't look like the guy in the photograph. No matter how much he fucked his life up he was still handsome and he'd never have to marry a buck toothed, cross eyed twin sister. Sean wanted to say this to Maria, but as far as he knew, Maria didn't share his bruise black sense of humor.

Sean said, "They probably got out in time. Don't worry about it."

Maria didn't see the teeth and the eyes and the interrelation breeding. Maria saw the beauty. Sean wished he could too, but *that* was never going to happen. He was never going to stop and smell the roses. He knew that if he did he'd eventually write them off as stinking of shit.

Sean contented himself with the beauty that was within reach. He pulled her close and kissed her. Her armpits were wet and he wanted to lick them dry. He wanted to lay her down on the rubble and fuck her. He wanted to fuck her in the ashes of the Dead City. He wanted come to inside her and hear her squeal in ecstasy. Hear her scream for Jesus in her native tongue.

Maria's hard nipples rubbed against his chest and his modest dick swelled in his linen trousers. He would have to hold her close and think of anything but being inside her before they could walk away. Maria lamented, "Sarajevo was so beautiful." And Sean said, "It'll be beautiful again." *Lip service. This place is fucked! It's the arsehole of Hell.*

They walked further into the Dead City. Sean told Maria about London. He told her about the ups and he told her about the downs, but he downplayed the downs. He wasn't going to talk himself out of a dream.

They finished the wine and Sean wanted more. They headed back towards the siege mentality hotel. Maria told Sean that when she got to London she wanted to highlight the horrors her people had experienced. Sean nodded and lied and said that she was a noble woman. They reached a café. A group of men sat around outside drinking cheap pissy beer. Sean recognized one of them. It was Rotherham. *Fuck!*

Rotherham was a freelance ever hyped-up pain in the arse gung ho photojournalist. He was living out some Larry Burrows fantasy and he modeled himself on Denis Hopper's character in Apocalypse Now. In fact, Rotherham's biggest regret was not being born in time to 'do 'Nam'. Rotherham was fond of saying, "Vietnam, man! Now *that* was a war. The psychedelic technology of American firepower in the air! *That* was a war!"

Sean couldn't stand Rotherham but he was always O.K. with him because wherever Rotherham landed he had a sixth sense for where the drugs could be got. Rotherham had once managed to secure a bag of Ecstasy in Mogadishu. No mean feat. He freely distributed them amongst reporters and an impromptu rave kicked up in a Somali hotel that was under siege from warlords.

"Sean Cassidy you cunt!" yelled Rotherham in his forced South London accent. Rotherham punched Sean hard on the arm and ruffled his hair affectionately. Rotherham's eyes fell on Maria. Rotherham said, "Wow! Who's the bird?" Sean said, "A friend ... *and* she speaks English." "A friend?" "Yeah, a *friend*, Rotherham." "O.K., I can buy that, millions wouldn't."

Sean and Maria joined Rotherham and the German TV crew for a pissy beer. Rotherham undressed Maria with his eyes and talked about himself. His favorite subject. Maria had him sussed. Instant dislike.

"So ... what the fuck you doing back out here, Cassidy? Heard you'd been fired. Freelancing, huh?" Sean said, "Huh, yeah, that's right." Rotherham said, "Not much to report on, eh?" Sean said, "No. What brings *you* back, Rotherham?" "Whistle-stop. Thought I'd drop in. See you've found some *action* though, eh?" "She's a … she's just a friend." "Yeah, right."

Rotherham invited himself back to Sean's hotel. Sean and Rotherham sat on the veranda drinking warm red wine. Maria bathed and went to another funeral. Rotherham asked Sean how he'd managed to score such a hot piece of Serbian ass. Sean insisted they were just friends. He told Rotherham about Maria's family being wiped out. *Like Rotherham could care less.* Rotherham was only interested in how he too could get himself some Serbian pussy. He asked Sean if she had any friends. *War zone double dating.* Sean told him she had nothing or no one. *He* was all she had and *he* was going to help her get the fuck out of Dodge.

Rotherham said, "Don't let your dick rule your brain, Cassidy. I've seen shit like this before. Some poor fuck goes whoring in Bangkok, gets laid like never before, falls in *lust,* brings the whore home and bam! Next thing he knows *she's* got *his* pants down! *She's* fucking *him* over. Cash, property, *half* shit! You got to be careful, Cass man." Sean felt like smashing the wine bottle and ramming the jagged edge up through Rotherham's nose right into his brain. Sean said nothing. Shook his head. Didn't stop him thinking about it though.

Sean had no money in the bank, but he did have equity in a house. Nothing to brag about. Sixty K tops. All the same though. He finally replied, "No. She's not like that. And anyway, we're just friends." He was sticking to the line. Rotherham said, "Don't say I didn't warn you." Sean said, "I hear you, but it's not like that." Rotherham laughed, "It never is when you're getting fucked good."

It was pointless telling Rotherham what a shitty hand life had dealt Maria. Dead bodies were Rotherham's paychecks. Rotherham was even more insulated against atrocities than Sean. In fact, Sean admired Rotherham's honesty. *I'm a fake! At least Rotherham's honest about not giving a fuck!*

They drank more wine and Rotherham skinned some Nepalese Temple Ball up. It was strong shit. *Heavy excrement!*

Rotherham said, "Best dope in the world. Got it from a kid that works for UNICEF. Queer fucker but he gets good dope. One of those poor little rich kids with a guilty conscience. Thinks he's saving the World. Effete little arse bandit! Gets good dope though, I'll give him that."

Sean sat and tripped. Rotherham talked about his recent exploits. He'd been to some African hellhole. Couldn't remember the name. *Spookland's all the same. You've seen one African shit hole you've seen 'em all. Fucking savages the lot of 'em! Geldof and Bono should stop sending 'em money. They only buy AK-47's and machetes with it! Hungry my arse! The cunts are only hungry for blood! Zulu fucks! We'll never civilize 'em. You gotta want to be civilized! They just wanna hack each other to bits!*

Rotherham said he'd been nailing a hot French chick that worked for *Medics Sans Frontier* out in Spookland. She liked him to fuck her in the arse. Rotherham was a romancer.

Rotherham said she liked him to pull out and shoot all over her back. He liked it. Liked it a lot. They got wankered together on morphine that was intended for mutilated Africans. She gave him her address in Paris. She was engaged to be married but told him that whenever he was in The City of Love he could fuck her in the arsehole. Her fiancé wasn't into sodomy but she loved him and wanted to have his children.

Rotherham wasn't a war photographer. Rotherham was death paparazzo. Rotherham was a warnographer. Sean watched Rotherham talking to himself, building another joint. Sean thought about Rotherham. *I'm no better than this cunt! In fact, in fact I'm worse.*

Sean got a whitey rush. It *was* strong shit for sure. Sean thought about the famous photograph. The famous photograph of the little naked Vietnamese girl. *The* iconic photo of the Vietnam War. The naked little girl crying, her skin bubbling up. Burned corpses in a ditch. A roadside morgue. She couldn't have been more than six or seven. Her face contorted. Crying. Deep distress. The deepest. Her mouth frozen in a primal scream. Her naked sexless body burning with a napalm splash.

Sean couldn't shake the image. He closed his eyes. The image inten-
sified. He felt sick. Hot vomit bubbled in his gullet. *If it had been
Rotherham … If Rotherham had been born earlier and if he had gone
to Vietnam, if he had … Christ … if he'd taken that photograph,
straight after it he would have led the little girl away and fucked her
in the arse whilst she signed a release form.*
Sean stared at Rotherham. *Devil. Laughing fucking devil. Hyena.
Get a grip Sean it's only a whiteout! Shake hands with the devil, share
a joint with him!*
Rotherham brought Sean out of the whitey, "Did you hear about the
Thalidomide porn star?" Sean said, "Huh?" Rotherham said, "Joke.
Hear about the Thalidomide porn star? Arm like a baby's cock!"
Sean stared at Rotherham laughing at his own joke. That was
Rotherham all over. Sean wanted rid of Rotherham before Maria
got back. It seemed like she'd been gone an age. What time was it?
Time melts in stoned age time. *Sal Dali's the fat controller. Dali's
the timekeeper.* Sean went to the bathroom. He ran the sink cold. Put
his head in and held his breath. Didn't want Maria to see him shit
faced. What would she think of him? She obviously already thought
he was alcy.
"Huh … I think I'll have a kip, Rotherham." "Eh? Why?" "The
dope's fucked me." "Fucking lightweight." "Yeah, whatever …
huh … well …""What?" "Huh … *now*. I think I'll have a kip *now*."
Rotherham looked in at him from the veranda, "Don't let me stop
you, Cass. I'm fine out here." "It's probably best, probably best you
go. Maria'll be-" "-you want me to fuck off?" "Yeah, no, I mean,
huh …" "You smoke my shit and now you want me to fuck off? Is
that it?" "I'm fucked, Rotherham. I need to get my head down."
Rotherham ankled. Headed out. Pissed off with Sean. Called him a
lightweight cunt of the highest order. Told him that he'd never get
any more drugs off of him. *Ever.* Sean didn't argue. He just wanted
shut. He wanted rid of the smell of sulfur. He wanted rid of the
smell of sulfur because it was too close to home. It was a smell he
recognized all too well. *Can Maria smell it on me? Does she know
I'm one of the damned?*

Sean copped some Zeds. Fitful. Disturbed doze. Maria woke him with a kiss. She slipped out of her black dress, *best buy she ever made.* Sean rubbed his overweight head. He watched her hang the dress. He smacked his reptilian lips. Maria lay down at his side. They stared at the crack in the ceiling. One day it would give. Not today though. Maria stroked his chest. Sean's dick inflated with blood. She must have noticed. Must have thought he was *half-fag* or at least *hetero-lite* for not sticking to her. Sean didn't care. This was good enough.

Maria said, "Will I be safe in London, Sean?" Sean said, "Yeah, sure … I'll look after you."

They traded saliva. Sean poked his tongue in. Licked plaque. Rub fuck. *Why don't I just whip it out and nail her! To hell with insecurity! How fucking insecure is Sarajevo? Why I am such a fucking pussy? She wants me! She's humping me! I'm her White Knight. I'm her way out!*

Sean slid his dick out. Slid it out and in. Maria was welcoming. She murmured. Purred. *Christ she's hot! If this is what she's like after a funeral, what's she like after a wedding!*

Sean shot double quick. Popped premature. Money stroked momentary. Little death-wished too soon.

He went down. Didn't care. Didn't care he'd be sucking up on some of his own seed. The honey pot was too enticing. He'd finish her off with his tongue. He lifted the hood up off the clit and got to work. Oral engineering. Maria giggled in delight. It was *surprised* delight. Definitely surprised delight. *Aaahhh! Those donkey dick Slavs might have the meat but do they know where the clit's buried? I think not!* Sean ate her good. Mmm. Chowed down voracious like on her lip smacking spread. Sean was spurred on by his hunch. His hunch was: she'd never had head. Never had head or if she had, the head that was giving her head was a fucking *dead*head.

Maria groaned. Her leg twitched. She held her stomach. Sure sign. Sean smiled up at her. She pulled him up to her mouth. They traded juices. She grabbed his hair and squeezed. Sean didn't have that post ejaculation melancholy. Alien to him. *This must be that love thing a whole industry's sprung up around!*

& skirted the edges of an Antenatal Clinic for Expectant Dreamers. Men and women hogged yoga mats on the luscious lawn and automated flora and fauna decorated the perimeter fence; separating the clinic from a death camp themed amusement park. The yoga session was in full swing. & listened with interest as bones cracked echoes in the air and moans and groans of pain created a lilting symphony. The students were – to a man – arthritic and many were doubled up in agony. They kept smiling though; the promise of perspicacious dreams kept their peckers up.

The Dream Midwives cum yoga instructors barked orders through rubber megaphones at the assembled. Some of them bent over backwards – literally – to impress. The dream descriptions being barked sounded fantastic and it wasn't hard to understand why the pregnant would-be dreamers were exerting themselves so much.

& touched closer and mingled amongst The Midwives. He felt that they were reading the descriptions verbatim from scripts and he was right. & clocked the jacket of one of the scripts. The writer was Henri Bergson. Bergson was also a client of Dinsdale: &'s literary agent. & wondered if Bergson knew that Dinsdale was in a coma: against his will and unaware he was actually in a coma.

A Dream Midwife started a striptease: peeling layer after layer of her psyche away in time to "Hey Big Spender" from the musical Sweet Charity. With each layer came a silent revelation that left the crowd begging for more. People were breaking their own legs in appreciation and others happily dislocated the joints of those nearby. & grabbed one of the scripts and breathed the words into existent, "The birth of a dream is then no mystery. It resembles the birth of all our perceptions. The mechanism of the dream is the same, in general, as that of normal perception. When we perceive a real object, what we actually see – the sensible matter of our perception – is very little in comparison with what our memory adds to it. When you read a book, when you look through your newspaper, do you suppose that all the printed letters really come into your consciousness? In that case the whole day would hardly be long enough for you to read a paper. The truth is that you see in each word and even in each member of a phrase only some letters or even some characteristic marks, just enough to permit you to divine the rest. All of the rest, that you think you see, you really give yourself as an hallucination."

& smiled as he saw that all ears were on him, he continued, "There are numerous and decisive experiments which leave no doubt on this point. I will cite only those of Goldscheider and Müller. These experimenters wrote or printed some formulas in common use, "Positively no admission;" "Preface to the fourth edition," etc. But they took care to write the words incorrectly, changing and, above all, omitting letters. These sentences were exposed in a darkened room. The person who served as the subject of the experiment was placed before them and did not know, of course, what had been written. Then the inscription was illuminated by the electric light for a very short time, too short for the observer to be able to perceive really all the letters."

He paused and for the first time since he could remember he had forgotten he felt like a bonafide Letter rather than a logogram. He smiled, "They began by determining experimentally the time necessary for seeing one letter of the alphabet. It was then easy to arrange it so that the observer could not perceive more than eight or ten letters, for example, of the thirty or forty letters composing the formula. Usually, however, he read the entire phrase without difficulty. But that is not for us the most instructive point of this experiment."

& had really worked the crowd up into a frenzy. The women were ripping off their panties and throwing them at him and the men threw their soiled underpants and holey vests. As & continued they pulled out lighters, waved them in the air and recited along with him.

"If the observer is asked what are the letters that he is sure of having seen, these may be, of course, the letters really written, but there may be also absent letters, either letters that we replaced by others or that have simply been omitted. Thus an observer will see quite distinctly in full light a letter that does not exist, if this letter, on account of the general sense, ought to enter into the phrase. The characters, which have really affected the eye, have been utilized only to serve as an indication to the unconscious memory of the observer. This memory, discovering the appropriate remembrance, i.e., finding the formula to which these characters give a start toward realization, projects the remembrance externally in an hallucinatory form. It is this remembrance, and not the words themselves, that the observer has seen. It is thus demonstrated that rapid reading is in great part a work of divination, but not of abstract divination. It is an externalization of memories which take advantage, to a certain extent, of the partial realization that they find here and there in order to completely realize themselves."

& looked up. It was too much for some of the crowd. They were feinting and being pulled from the crowd by paramedics. & forged ahead though, "Thus, in the waking state and in the knowledge that we get of the real objects, which surround us, an operation is continually going on which is of quite the same nature as that of the dream. We perceive merely a sketch of the object. This sketch appeals to the complete memory, and this complete memory, which by itself was either unconscious or simply in the thought state, profits by the occasion to come out. It is this kind of hallucination, inserted and fitted into a real frame, that we perceive. It is a shorter process: it is very much quicker done than to see the thing itself. Besides, there are many interesting observations to be made upon the conduct and attitude of the memory images during this operation. It is not necessary to suppose that they are in our memory in a state of inert impressions. They are like the steam in a boiler, under more or less tension … thank you. You've been amazing!"

The crowd chanted *more, more, more* as & waved at them and started dissolving. It was clear that the Dream Midwives had been upstaged and quickly needed to regain some order from the chaos. One of them tried to smell & just as he was fading but she was too late.

& Re-remembered some throwaway paragraphs: *I shoot up the steps and out into daylight, the daylight splintered and sectioned and squared and blighted by monuments to mediocrity. Oxford Street bores me. It's my least favorite part of the city. The shops are homogenous and permanently in the illusory state of having a 'sale', and just who are those Eastern European people handing out flyers and exactly what are they advertising? I have an inbuilt inertia that stops me from taking one of their A5 pieces of paper lest I might see the words: Magic Theatre, Not For Everybody ... For Madmen Only! Moreover, like Harry Haller I'd enter the unknown and cease to exist until a writer of Herman Hesse's genius would make me come to life on the one-dimensional page.*

What the fuck are 'Golf Sales'? Are they what they sound like? Does anybody know anyone who has ever been to a 'Golf Sale'? Is it a cover for casual commercial fucking around the back of Centrepoint with underage Eastern European girls who are too young yet to hand out those flyers that nobody ever reads?

I look up at the buildings and down at the conveyor belt of shoppers and pedestrians and the lost and the site-seeing and the workers jogging into Marks & Spencer for their over-priced sandwiches and I wonder if this is really progress.

I turn down into Wardour Street and buy a packet of fags. I'm hungry and buy a Mount Rushmore bagel from the bagel shop. I've been in London half an hour and already I'm dying to get back home. There was a time when I was in love with the city. A couple of years back I couldn't get enough of the place. It was an adventure. Every street was a new vista waiting stamping itself onto my psycho geography.

From Soho up to Islington, from The Ship to Willy McTell's Whiskey Café I'd get leathered on a regular basis. Pub crawls and club calls and spontaneous parties and invites round to houses by people you'd only just met but knew you from a friend-of-a-friend and spur of the moment drinking sessions that turned into marathons where hangovers were never given chance to rear their ugly heads.

The only London that attracts me now is the London of my mind; the metropolis of memories; good times that are gone and can never be exhumed; the ghosts of good times past.

I cut across Dean Street and reach Soho House. I press the buzzer and state my name and the names of the cunts I'm meeting. A bird with a clipboard's waiting to tick me off.
"Can you wait in the circle bar for them?" She says and I don't know if that's a question or an order so I keep schtum and shoot the fifth false smile of the day.

I wearily climb the stairs. It's quiet and I sit down on a sofa, pick up The Independent and look for something, anything remotely interesting to entertain me. I find a short piece that says a man in Istanbul has 'accidentally' murdered his next-door neighbors. It says accidentally because he 'intended' to slaughter his own family. In a drug fuelled state he went into the wrong house and started battering fuck out of anything that drew breath. His weapon of choice? A Nine Iron golf club. I wonder what that kind of 'accident' registers on the Quantum Possibility Register. I wonder if the Istanbul fuzz'll be charging him with murder and attempted murder ... hmm, but I suppose what I really wonder is if he bought the Nine Iron from Istanbul's equivalent of Oxford Street.
I'm drinking mineral water until Damien Skerrit arrives. He breezes in and orders a bottle of wine for us.
"Sorry I'm late, Danny. We're in postproduction on Geezers ... Charles'll be here later. Have you eaten?" He asks.
"I've had a bagel."
"We can have lunch here."

He sits down and pulls out a leather bound notebook. I'd guess that Damien's my age, thirty-five, but he tries too hard to look younger. He wears Carrhart khakis and Duffer T shirts and every time you see him he's got the latest old school Puma trainers on. He must throw the other pairs away when they're slightly soiled or they become new school by a change in the fashion climate.

And here it comes, the dreaded, "I've got some notes on the script," he says as I shudder and clench my teeth.

& popped up in a villa in Ibiza in the 1960's. A slaughter had taken place. He shuddered and exhaled and became embedded in a "No Smoking & Photographs" sign in the Taj Mahal for what sounded like six months and seventeen days. He frittered most of the near time forgetting dreams he had had as a child about being adopted by a happy, loving family.

For a period of uncertainty & became involved in the concept of an Ice Cream Empire. He floated with a host of characters that were conceived to populate a grand scheme of sugary excesses. It was percolating in the imagination of Greg Lucanus and would come to fruition in another time and place in the not too distant past.

Greg Lucanus had invented a flavor of ice cream that he called *Cherry Lee Lewis*. Greg dreamed only of destroying Ben & Jerry's popular *Cherry Garcia* flavor. He sold everything he owned, mortgaged his house, borrowed every dime his folks had saved, divorced his wife and abandoned his 5 young children in pursuit of his dream.

It was a big leap for Lucanus; he had no experience in the cutthroat world of ice cream, having been for most of his professional life a dog food taster; *Dog food tasters are hired by pet food companies to test the quality of their products. They also evaluate the nutritional value, and usually spit out the food once they taste it, but Greg Lucanus was a pro' and he always swallowed.*

As Greg dreamed his dream of ice cream world domination he started to surround himself with colorful characters from the anal's (sic) of half-baked ideas. Pierre Cardinal Sin came on board as Chief Strategist in the campaign and in turn he recruited Harry Bella Dante's Inferno as his subordinate. Harry was only a doodle on a scrap of paper but what he lacked in substance he more than made up for in ambition. Harry hoped to one night become the head of a neo-platonic neo-liberal corporation that promoted the idea of novelty in taking public ownership of resources into the private sphere.

Pierre Cardinal Sin and Harry Bella Dante's Inferno formulated a foolproof plan to make Cherry Lee Lewis the number 1 selling ice cream in the world. Greg was cock-a-hoop and considered himself blessed that he had such great men onboard. Pierre had no experience in cream – his previous employment had been in creating a special type of herpes – called koi herpes – that killed European carp on behalf of governments keen to engineer the population of these extremely fucking fertile fish.

The only foreseeable problem for Greg Lucanus was the fact that every time 'Wondrous Stories' by Yes played on the airwaves, Pierre and Harry would meltdown into blubbering sentimental cripples. Greg would have to piece them back together with a mixture of algebra, superglue and Lego.

& found the trio fascinating, not least because they were all figments of each other's imagination. He enjoyed their ill placed optimism and their *never say live* attitude: their lack of self-consciousness and their slubberdegullioness. They were free souls who had yet to be born and they were quite content with the fact.

Harry was fond of yelling, "*There is no gistus to it, noodle! – 'tis my own name, replied the curate, dipping his hand, as he spoke, into the bason – Tristram! Said he, &c. &c. &c. &c. – so Tristram was I called, and Tristram shall I be to the day of my death."* In italics to anything within eyeshot.

Pierre was a little more reserved; when he did speak it was in cockney rhyming hieroglyphs and usually something cryptic. & frequently went on vacation with the trio to as yet unimagined lost cities and they always had a whale of a time.

At the exact point when Cherry Lee Lewis Flavored Ice Cream was due to be taken to market the trio were hit with devastating news. Someone informed Greg that the ice cream would be a disaster and lucky to sell even a couple of tubs. Greg took this as gospel without even checking the references and sources of 'someone'.

"It's no good," cried Greg Lacanus, "Someone said nobody will buy my ice cream because of the name."
"What do you mean?" asked &.
"The name. *Cherry Lee Lewis!*"
& couldn't see, "So? It's a clever name."
"But *Jerry* Lee Lewis married his underage cousin. He was a borderline pedophile. People will think I'm trying to sell them pederast ice cream!"
& tried to reassure the heartbroken Greg Lucanus, "But that's in the future and nobody knows about it yet, and besides, they buy Cherry Garcia ice cream, and Gerry Garcia was allegedly working with the government to kill the hippie movement."
"Never heard of him." Snapped Greg.
"The Grateful Dead. They're a rock band. They haven't been formed yet but they will eventually, you'll see."

& couldn't ameliorate Greg. Pierre and Harry were no use either. They suggested that they should eat all the ice cream they envisioned making so that it didn't go to waste. This just pissed Greg off even more. He told them he already had plans for the none existent ice cream; if the world wouldn't buy it he would give it all to charity and let them deal with the concept. Harry and Pierre objected. They were in agreement that charity was a clever ruse to give absolution to the money creators.

"We've got millions of barrels of Cherry Lee Lewis ice cream that doesn't exist!" screamed Greg, "We need to get shut of it somehow!" Harry had a brain seizure, "I know … hear me out … why don't we just change the name?"

Pierre and Greg thought about it.

"But what could we call it?" asked Greg.

Harry smiled, "Cherry Seinfeld."

Greg frowned, "Cherry *Seinfeld*? What does it even mean?"

"Listen to me," Harry moved in closer and whispered, "We create a TV sitcom called Seinfeld OK?"

Pierre narrowed his gaze on Harry, "Go on."

"It will be about a stand up comedian and his friends."

"And … ?" queried Greg.

"*And* that's all we need. It's a sitcom where everything and nothing happens." Replied Harry Bella Dante's Inferno.

"I don't know. It sounds shit." Said Pierre shaking his head.

"No. It'll be amazing. You've got to trust me on this." smiled Harry, "Before we do that though we have to invent The Internet."

Greg and Pierre frowned at each other, "The *what*?"

"The Internet. The World Wide Web. The Information Autobahn."

Getting the Fear
Chapter 7

Jack Sherry looked inside a cotton bag he had found under a bed in the villa. He shouted, "Captain Ernesto ... I thought you said your men had given this place a good going over?"

Captain Ernesto rushed up the first flight of stairs of the ghostly villa, "Qué, Mr. Jack?"

Jack emptied the contents of the bag on the bed: pesetas, jewelry and more importantly passports.

Captain Torres stared at the find and slapped his palm on his forehead, "Idiotas de mierda!"

Jack quickly scanned the passports: three English, one French, two German, "Bingo, Captain Ernesto!"

"Pasaporte!"

"How did they miss this?"

"I am sorry, Mr. Jack, I can only say that they were ... you know ... what is the word?"

"Traumatized? Shocked? Fucking incompetent? Anyway, it doesn't matter now. We've got the i-d. Let's go see if we can match these with the corpses."

By the time they had bumped and grinded back to the morgue it was too late to stir the coroner from his slumber. Jack asked Captain Torres to take him to an hotel.

"But Mr. Jack. We have perfectly fine accommodation at my offices."

"No, it's all right, I've been given money to stay in an hotel. I'll need a receipt for the expenses."

Captain Torres grinned, "You are sure you would not like to keep this expenses? I can get you a receipt no problem."

Jack was beginning to really like him, "That's not a bad idea, Captain Ernesto. Not a bad idea at all."

"Good, good. You do not have to waste money on hotel."

It was three am before Jack was finally ready to hit the sack. The room was small and basic but it had a double bed, a toilet and a shower and it was clean. He stripped naked, hit the pillow and was out for the count like Cassius Clay had stuck one on his chin. He was serenaded into a temporary oblivion by a chorus from crickets, grasshoppers and katydids.

He woke naturally at nine and got straight on the telephone to his office at Scotland Yard. It was ten twenty before he had finished giving all the details from the six passports. Scotland Yard would have to contact the French and German authorities to check the names and it may take a while. The three British passports should be easy enough to check though.

Captain Torres picked Jack up and took him for breakfast. Jack was hung-over and dehydrated, he drank juices and water and what the waiter claimed was coffee but tasted nothing like coffee to Jack.

Captain Torres was keen to drive him up to Santa Gertrudis, "There is a man there, Mr. Franks, he says he has information on the people from the villa."

"What kind of information?"

"He did not say, Mr. Jack. The Coroner will not be back until late this afternoon. I thought we could go see this Mr. Franks, yes?"

"All right."

Christopher Franks was a middle-aged artist who had been living alone in a modest dwelling since 65 after ditching London for good. He spent all his time painting abstracts and wandering around the island on foot. He kept himself to himself but had an angle on the island.

"Captain Torres has probably told you, Inspector Sherry, that there are a lot of bohemians living on Ibiza."

Jack glanced at Torres then back at Franks, "*Bohemians?*"

"Artists, writers, poets. I suppose what the press are now calling 'hippies'."

"He hadn't told me. These people at the villa. They were-"

Franks cut him off, "No, that's what I'm getting at. They were not bohemian types."

Jack raised his eyebrows, "Well, what *type* of people were they?"

"The type of people I wouldn't expect to see around these parts."

Captain Torres was puzzled, "What do you mean, Mr. Franks? Ibiza is open to all kinds of people. We pride ourselves on being very welcoming everyone."

Franks explained, "I just found it odd that these people were staying up here rather than San Antonio or Ibiza Town. As you can see Inspector Sherry, this is hardly a tourist area."

Jack shrugged, "Maybe they just wanted some peace and quiet?"

"I found them suspicious, Inspector. Besides the fact that they were staying up here, they were also engaging in what you could call ... well ... black magic. Or rather, in my opinion, *playing* at it."

Jack and Captain Torres frowned, Jack half laughed, "Black magic?"

"Satanism, witchcraft, whatever you want to call it ... only they were leaving the island to do whatever they were doing and here's the thing ... it was like they were actors. Fakes if you like, like they were traveling somewhere to *act* at being these devil worshippers."

Jack sighed, "You've lost me, Mr. Franks."

Franks looked into the middle distance and thought about it, "It's hard to explain, Inspector ... I saw them taking robes and paraphernalia with them on their outings. It just felt like they were playing at something."

Captain Torres was now perplexed, "I do not understand you, Mr. Franks."

Jack pressed Franks, "Robes? What kind of paraphernalia?"

"Goats, skulls, crucifixes, swords, all kinds of things."

Jack was dubious, he scratched his head and wiped sweat from his brow, "This sounds a bit … a bit incredible, Mr. Franks."

"Oh yes, I agree, I agree."

Captain Torres' jaw had dropped. "Goats? Crucifixes?"

Franks sighed, "I'm simply telling you what I saw, gentlemen."

Jack put his hand up, sensing Franks was getting a little het up, "And I don't doubt you, Mr. Franks. You've got to understand that this sounds a little … well, fantastical."

"I know it does and that's what I mean. It didn't look authentic, Inspector."

Jack knotted his brow, "They weren't *authentic* devil worshippers?"

Captain Torres shook his head, "You are saying, Mr. Franks, you are saying that these people were actors?"

"That's what it looked like, yes, Captain."

Jack was having trouble understanding how Franks could discern genuine devil worshippers from fake ones, "Do you know much about these kind of things, Mr. Franks?"

"You mean devil worship?"

"Yes."

Franks held out his open palms, "I've read the books of Dennis Wheatley and I know something of the life of Aleister Crowley. Beyond that, no, I wouldn't claim to be an expert, Inspector. I suppose I know as much as the next man."

Jack smiled at him, "Well, I know nothing about all this rubbish, Mr. Franks, so you know a lot more than me."

Franks smiled back, "*We* might think it is 'nonsense' Inspector, but there are many people around the world who don't … they take it very seriously."

"Many people used to believe that the earth was flat, Mr. Franks."

Captain Torres was still confused, "Goats?"

Jack and Captain Torres headed over to San Juan in the jeep. Captain Torres tapped his temple, "Grrr, él está loco."
Jack held on to the door as they hit another hole, "What's that, Captain?"
"Mr. Franks. He is crazy you think?"
"Why do you say that?"
"Goats! El Diablo!"
"I've got no reason to believe he's lying, Captain Ernesto, and he seems like he's got all his marbles to me."
Captain Torres frowned, "Marbles?"
"It's a saying we have. Anyway, you'd be surprised how many people talk about this satanic rubbish nowadays."

Doctor A in a coma. Half alive half dead. Half stepping the life-line. Riffing on mortality's thin reed. Juiced into the system. Amped up. Amped up existence. *Kept* alive. *Isn't there a law against that? There should be!*

Doctor A *sans* nose was no oil painting. No oil painting unless you got your rocks off over Francis Bacon's knock-offs. The no nose thing was the least of her problems though. Noses can be got off the peg. Brains are still a couple of thousand light years from getting retailed on the high street.

Fat Fuck punched 999 after he'd spewed up. Asked for an ambulance. Gave the address. *Didn't* give his name. Fat Fuck thought about calling a friend before he called the meat wagon. He thought about asking the Friend to come over and counsel. The Friend was a criminal flirt. Flirted *around* criminals. Got off on their tales. Loved their reps. Loved their raps. Bought them drinks. Liked their company. Liked being seen in their company.

Loved the mystique. Didn't understand it. Loved seeing other grown men give them respect. Didn't care that respect is earned *not* enforced. Sexy sinister sadism. The Friend was a thug hag. Fuck Fat didn't care. This was no time for judgment. Fat Fuck was shitting in his pants. Fat Fuck was crying like a colic infested baby. Fat Fuck decided not to call the Friend. He hit the 9's instead and prayed that she'd keep her mouth shut.

Fat Fuck hit the road in his fast expensive car. Fat Fuck got the fuck away. Fat Fuck phoned home. Fat Fuck laid it on the wife. Had to go away. Business. A trip. Last minute. Unexpected. Expedience. A deal breaker. Lucrative. *Very.* Wife's O.K. with it. He's a good provider. She understands. He *keeps* her well. Keeps her in fine things. She's got no beef. Fat Fuck's a stand up guy. Fat Fuck's a go-getter. *Go get it Fat Fuck! Bring me the bacon home, Daddy-O!*

Fat Fuck hit some out of town hotel. He sat in the room. He shat in the toilet. Shat twice on the trot. Called the thug hag Friend. Told him what had gone down. Not pretty. Friend said he shouldn't have called in the emergency. Friend said The Law would be all over it like a rash. Fat Fuck felt feint. Fear and trembling in a five star hidey-out. Friend said he could have fixed it. The people he knew could have fixed it. Fixed it for the *right* price. It was a no-brainer now. The whore would be plugged in and The Law would be hovering around waiting to chin wag something rotten. That's if she wasn't already in the morgue.

Fat Fuck shrunk. Four walls loomed large. Room folded in on him. Enveloped in a whole lotta Hell. Friend said get a good Brief. *Get a Brief quick. Speak to a Brief before you speak to anybody else. If you've got a good Brief, speak to him! If you haven't got a good Brief, get one! Get him out of bed if you've got one! Get talking Brief talk. Get righteous on some Brief rapping. Give the Brief your beef and let him cook up something with it.*

Friend said he could recommend a Brief. A kosher criminal Brief.

Friend of a Friend. Friend of a respected villain. Fat Fuck took the number. Fat Fuck dialed kosher Brief. Doctor A was death tripping. Tripping the flat line fantastic. Limbo dancing. *Doctor A No Nose was out there, man!*
This was the best *fucking* she'd ever had all right. This was beyond the call of duty. This was a corker! There was no mention of this in the *Whoring Almanac*. Sure, Last Daddy had treated her like a spunk bucket, but this: *this was far out, man! Silent hell. A trip. One baaad trip!*

Doctor A's deep deep gone. Brain, a twitch away from calling it a day. Mind starts to fuck around. *Let's have some fun with the whore.* Doctor A's no mug. No airhead Doctor A. She's seen things. Done things. She had a life before whoring. Doctor A taught school. Taught kids their history until history jumped the fuck up and started biting them all on their arses.

Doctor A's in a vacuum. She's in a corridor. There's a door at end. It's the archetypal coma shtick. Doctor A slides down the corridor. Reaches the door. Doesn't knock. Gingerly opens it. Some Working Stiff in cheap gray suit, buttoned up, uptight, hair up his arse, sat behind a desk. Bare light bulb swings overhead. He's looking over his gigs at her.

There's a door behind him. Doctor A *knows* there's a party behind that door. Working Stiff's not shifting. There's a party going on and Doctor A wants in. Sounds like a hoot. The best party you never got a whiff of. Sounds like the best party you never got the chance to RSVP.

Doctor A's face to face with Working Stiff. He's a humorless prick: *Sad sack sentinel.* He's got a list. Bad sign. He scopes the list. Clears his throat. Eyes her over his gigs. Working Stiff says, "A few questions before you can enter".
Doctor A sighs, "O.K, hit me."

Working Stiff says, "You harbored criminals during the war in your homeland. *Why?*"

Doctor A says, "Criminals? They were soldiers!"

Working Stiff says, "They were Serbian *butchers*."

"You don't know what you're talking about."

"According to my information –"

"-Your information sucks!"

"I've got reports of ethnic cleansing. I've got reports of rape and pillage. I've got reports of-"

"You've got *shit* is what you've got!"

Working Stiff is pissed at her, "Listen, lady. I don't *have* to let you in. Now you can answer these charges and *then* I'll decide."

Working Stiff presses on her Partisan activities during the war. Working Stiff grabs a lamp. Points the porpoise at her mug. Tries giving it the 3rd degree, only he's a pussy. He's no interrogator. He's a pen pushing pussy. Ain't got a brutal bone is in uptight body. He's just a stickler. Gets off on bureaucracy. Pumps the piss pistol to printouts of rules and regulations. Jerks his gherkin over stats and summaries.

Doctor A gets all historic on his skinny arse. Working Stiff can't get a word in edgeways. Doctor A's cooking on napalm. Gives him a blast of history. Raps him some facts. Doctor A tells him why the 90's war kicked in. Tells him about the shit that had gone down before. Tells him about The Ustase: gang of Croatian terrorists and saboteurs and bandits given carte blanche to do whatever the fuck they wanted to do by the Axis Powers in 41. The U: gung ho Nazified and Fascisticky. Gangsters with portfolio. Licensed to swing their balls about The Balkans and go feral on the enemies.

The U get in on the real estate gig. Open up some concentration camps: Danica, Pag, Jadovno and the notorious Jasenovac Complex. They get busy exterminating Serbs, Jews and Gypsies. Get busy on anyone who doesn't buy into their Roman Catholicism. Love to lop off the heads of Serbian Orthodox Priests. Love to get medieval on

Commies. The U do day trips to outskirt villages. Spot of slaughter and a light lunch. Bit of red baiting. Bit of Vatican endorsed butchery.

The U snuff out six, maybe seven hundred thousand Serbs, Jews and Gypsies. The less blood lusty U get their kicks converting the cowed to Catholicism. Hitler got hot for the U's methodic extermination of the inferiors. The U could have claimed breach of copyright on The Final Solution Show.
The Axis jump ship after double U double U two. Yugoslav Partisans and Red Army fighters get it together and cop some retribution on The U. Scarred land. Old wounds. Scabby vistas. Come the 90's and the break up of Yugo Land and the scabs get itchy. The scabs blister. The scabs blister and pop and pus pours out and it's a psychic eyesore and the natives are hyped up and all Hell's unleashed.

Working Stiff's heard her. He's not impressed. One crime doesn't justify another and vice versa. Doctor A says, "I agree, you're right, but unless you lived through it you'll never really understand it."
Working Stiff says, "There's still the question of you prostituting yourself."
Doctor A can't riff that one out. It's not something she's proud of. She's not passionate about her profession. She shrugs her shoulders. *What's a poor whore to do?*
Doctor A's eyeballing Working Stiff some evils when all of a sudden, whoosh, a third party has popped up like some pantomime genie.

Doctor A and Working Stiff double take on the coma crasher. Naked from the waist up. Titties bold as brass. Head to toe deathly black blue skin. Chick's got *four* arms; on the end of one is the severed head of a demon. She's sporting a necklace of skulls and a girdle of severed arms and her mane is braided with hissing green serpents. Her ten-inch tongue's hanging from her mouth. Chick's a one-off for sure. An original.

Her name's Kali: Hindu Goddess of creation and destruction. No

Nose Doctor A's checking her out, *big time*. Working Stiff's flabbergasted. Kali coughs up to Doctor A, "I'm Kali, Goddess etcetera. What's the beef, hon'?"

Doctor A's taken aback. Watches Kali burn up a Lucky Strike and suck on it. Doctor A's thinking, *sure doesn't sound or act like a Hindu Goddess*.

Doctor A and Working Stiff watch Kali close. Kali casually flicks the Lucky Strike and crushes it into the floor with her *fuck me* high heels. *When did deities start wearing stilettos?*

Transpires that Kali's no run of the mill Goddess. Kali's copped her own style. Kali's fronting some major *Noir Femme Fatale* shtick. Kali raps. Her voice is a bitches brew of vamp cool. It's an audio stew of Lana Turner in *The Postman Always Rings Twice*, Rita Hayworth in *The Lady From Shanghai*, Veronica Lake in *The Blue Dahlia*, Liz Beth Scott in *Dead Reckoning*, it's a remix of Barbara Stanwyck in *Double Indemnity*, Ava Gardner in *The Killers*, Angelica Huston in *The Grifters*, Jane Greer in *Out of The Past*, Gina Gershon in *This World Then The Fireworks*, Joan Bennett in *Scarlet Street*.

Kali's voice and ëtude and phrasing and style is the amalgam of all the tough talking chicks Doctor A dug big time. Kali's a composite of all those celluloid sirens blazing trails in the pictures Doctor A loved. Doctor A's heroines: deadly gorgeous and dangerous and double crossing and deftly dealing with the murderous hand life's dealt them.

Doctor A's heart is swelling. Doctor A's pulse is pumping. Doctor A's pussy is moistening. Doctor A's head is swimming. Swirling snapshots and sound snippets: high heels on wet pavement, black widow breathlessness, wicked wisecracks, come hither looks, automobile eroticism, getaway car kisses, deadpan denials, *on the lam* licentious liaisons, nylon stocking seduction, pencil skirt foreplay, tight sweater seediness, garter belt glint, lusty lipstick fellatio, calculated come-on's, way beyond cool confidence, fallen angel aesthetics, inner indomitable strength, moral ambiguity, dog eat dog diatribes, broadside barbs, godforsaken pessimism, casual chastisement, tantalizing, teasing, taking you to the point of orgasm and pulling the plug at the last excruciating second.

Doctor A's in coma nirvana. Her metaphysical body's burning up. Every inch of her is on fire. Doctor A hones in on Kali's tongue. She wants it inside her so much. Doctor A's lips are quivering in anticipation. Working Stiff stares at Kali. Kali asks him if he wants a picture. Working Stiff asks *her* what she wants. Kali gives it, "I sure as hell don't want *you*, Mister, that's for sure."
Working Stiff tells her to move on.
Kali comes back with, "It's a free coma, deadbeat. I ain't going nowhere! This sister wants my help."
Working Stiff tells her to vamoose or he'll call his superiors. Kali tells Working Stiff she don't like his tone. Working Stiff tries to lead her away by one of her many elbows.

Kali hisses at him, "You're playing with fire you schmuck! Get your mitts off o' me!"
Working Stiff ignores her warning. Kali, quick as a flash, opens her legs and incinerates him with her fire-breathing cunt. Doctor A swoons. Kali stands strides over the charred corpse of Working Stiff and flames up a Lucky Strike where his head used to be.
Kali turns slowly to Doctor A. Doctor A's heart's in her mouth. Doctor A's knees are knocking. Doctor A's nipples are making out like bullets. Kali says, "Hey, hon', you know why I'm here, right?"
Doctor A whispers, "Do I?"
"Sure you do, sweetie, I'm here to take you to the promised land. You've had a raw deal but you fought back the best you could. You've earned your wings, doll. I'm gonna fuck you to Heaven!"
Doctor A could have collapsed. The words alone were enough to send a shudder through her system. Kali made her move. Doctor A closed her eyes, baited her breath and gave herself entirely to the Noir Goddess.

Kali lifts Doctor A onto the desk with two of her arms and gets to work. Chet Baker crooning *Let's Get Lost* provides the ambience as Kali parts Doctor A's thighs, pulls her skirt up and her panties down slowly.

Doctor A's arse cheeks are planted firmly on the Formica table. Kali spits into one of her hands and gently works Doctor A labia up into a lather with her index finger. Doctor A groans ecstatic

Kali spits on Doctor A's pussy, parts her lips and goes down on her. Doctor A's groin is awash with saliva and fuck juice. Kali's ten-inch tongue thrusts in and out of Doctor A. Doctor A's getting the oral fucking of her *near*-afterlife.
Let's Get Lost, Lost in Each Other's Arms. Slurp, slurp, slurp as Kali's tongue works its way in and out and in and out. Kali nudges up until her entire tongue is buried in Doctor A's cunt. Doctor A squeals in delight. She's impaled with rapture. Skewered with ecstasy. Plugged with delirium. Fucked with dreamy dexterity. *Let's Get Lost, Let Them Send Out Alarms.*

Kali's four hands explore Doctor A's body. Kali fingers Doctor A's tremulous arsehole. One, then two, then three fingers form a trinity and swirl in and out of the orifice at terrific speed. Poke, poke, poke, circle, circle, circle. Doctor A loses her breath. Kali comes up for air and blows some into Doctor A's mouth. *Kiss of life, kiss of death, kiss of Kundalini.* Kali's tongue tickles Doctor A's tonsils. Doctor A comes in wave after wave of submission.

Doctor A comes in Technicolor and stereo. Kali's making the most of her four hands. One's working Doctor A's clit, one's three finger fucking her arsehole and the other two are tweaking up her nipples to towering proportions. *And Though They'll Think us Rather Rude, Let's Tell The World We're in That Crazy Mood.*

Kali gently lays Doctor A down and spreads her legs wide. Kali hops up on the table and straddles Doctor A. Kali opens her legs and

234

makes scissors. Kali's cunt magnetically melts into Doctor A's. They rub hard against each other. Kali's hot cunt sends Doctor A wild. Doctor A screams in abandon. *Let's Defrost in a Romantic Mist, Let's Get Crossed, Off Everybody's List.*

Kali humps Doctor A heroically. Slip sliding up and down her saturated slit, grinding round and round her magical mound. Pussy on pussy, devouring each other, sucking, slurping, singeing the tight little curls, mutual bruising of blush pink flesh, swapping sweet fluids, pushing lips into lips, cunt kissing of epic proportions. *Darling, Let's Get Lost.*

Doctor A's Cumming On A Loop. She gasps to Kali, "Of all the coma's in all the world, you just happened to turn up in mine."
Kali shoots back, "Hey, doll face, I've had my peepers on you from way back."
"You have? Why?"
"You're a classy broad. I like your style."
"My style?"
"Sure. You got oodles. I got your number sweet cheeks."
"What … what is it you like about me?"
"You're a strong dame. You don't let two bit jerks mess you around."
Doctor A frowns, "But, but I do … That's why I'm here. I was attacked by –"
Whoosh. Beep. Beep. Beep. Neural activity. Sparks. Electricity. *Wakey wakey.*

Doctor A slowly peels open her peepers. Glare. Stark white light. Antiseptic illumination. Closes them. Opens again. Knows she's alive. Rush of recognition. Can't be anything *but* life. There is nothing *but* life. Great! Cell phone assault hasn't snuffed her. No Death by Nokia. Remembers the hiding. Doesn't remember she doesn't have a nose.

Questions: how long have I been KO'ed? Is there lasting damage? Where's the fucking nurse?

Fat Fuck wasn't on her mind. Last thing. Fat Fuck was lying lower than a snake's cunt. Fat Fuck was holed up in the countryside. He'd come back off his fictional business trip, picked the family up and hotfooted on a spur vacation. Thug Hag Friend got Fat Fuck yapping to a Kosher Brief. Kosher Brief said, "I want you to tell me the truth."
Fat Fuck said, "I pushed her. S*he fell* and hit her nose on the wall."
Kosher Brief said, "Yeah, right. What *really* happened?"

Fat Fuck fessed he slapped her around a bit. It got out of control. He got carried away. He didn't mean to get grievous. Kosher Brief stifled a yawn. Heard it all before. Déjà vu dialogue. He'd defended 180 pound plus guys that had got carried away on skinny women. It was all a much ness of a much ness. It was *terror*torial. Comes with the lifestyle. Kosher Brief fronted for Villains who often flipped Looney Tunes on their whores' arses.
Kosher Brief spins a philosophical line. *Rich guys keep whores. Rich guys sometimes get creative with their fists on their bitches. What can you do?*

Kosher Brief had a plan. It had worked before. Whores dig cash. *It's a Fuck Pro Fundamentality. Get with the program Fat Fuck. Brown envelope diplomacy. Bung. Buy off.*

Kosher Brief suggested a chat with Thug Hag Friend. Kosher Brief propped it thus: *she obviously hasn't spilled the beans yet. Get to her. She can be got at. Offer a handsome package. What's she gonna get out of justice? Justice don't pay the rent. Justice don't take care of the Harvey Nicks charge card.*

Fat Fuck hooked with Thug Hag Friend. Some middle of nowhere car park. Chinwag in Fat Fuck's 4x4 SUV family car. Roomy. Room to think. Room to think it through. Thug Hag Friend says it's do-able. He's already had the hospital reccied. She's kicked out the coma. She's still breathing fib-like. The Law are still hanging out waiting to fill up some notepads. Thug Hag Friend knows some Muscle that can string sentences together. Intimidating *and* half smart. He can go-between. Fat Fuck knows it'll cost. Doesn't ask how much. Doesn't *care* how much. *The Piper's gotta be paid. The Whore's gotta have her hand out.*

Fat Fuck can't face time. Time would fuck Fat Fuck. *Shit scared.* Jail's *not* an option. Loves the creature comforts too much. Couldn't live caged. His lucre would dwindle. All that chicanery for nothing. All that scrimping and grafting and hoodwinking and prospecting for nothing! Business would go to shit and the Wife would want the equity before it did. The Wife would lick it all up. Hoover up anything that wasn't nailed down. She'd crucify the Fat Fuck. She'd have just cause. The Law would back her up. Up to the hilt. Fat Fuck wasn't sweating getting shafted in the shower room; he was sweating getting shafted in the Divorce Court.

The Law is getting a hard-on for Doctor A but Doctor A's giving up zilch. Doctor A's flopping the dumb hand. The Law smells rodent. They bring in a cop who yaps Slovak. Doctor A's still buttoned up. Doctor A's thinking. Doctor A knows her nose has gone. *Cest la vie.* Doctor A knows Fat Fuck left her to hail her own cab to the morgue. She doesn't know the Fat Fuck punched the 9's. *Bless him.*

Doctor A's no mug. Doctor A knows the score. Pussy pedaling has taught her things. Doctor A No Nose knows Fat Fuck's in sauna situation. Pictures him sweating it out. Hear's his nightmares. Knows him well enough to know he's spineless swine. Doctor A's just waiting. She's expecting contact. She's itching eye to eye with the Fat Fuck, but figures it might be a go-between she gets face time with. Fat Fuck would have to muster up some bravery to show his mug. Doctor A thinks crafty.

Doctor A drops a request in the ear of a friendly Nurse, "I'll need you to get something for me. I need to get down what happened to me. Things are coming back."

Some Muscle That Can String A Sentence Together employed by Fat Fuck stakes out the sick bay. He gets the rhythm of The Law. The Fuzz drop in around late noon. Muscle sneaks in on Doctor A. Muscle tells Doctor A, Fat Fuck's gonna be generous. She can keep the apartment, rent taken care of indefinitely. Fat Fuck's gonna shell out for some new Harley Street nose for her. Fat Fuck's gonna cough some major change into a big brown envelope. All Doctor A's gotta do is stay mute. Doctor A tells Muscle she's gonna think about it.

Muscle sneaks out. Doctor A hits the stop button on the Sony Dictaphone the friendly Nurse got her. Doctor A plays the chinwag back. Click: crystal. *Dolbyfuckingdoodah! Dolbyfuckinghey! My O my what a wonderful day! Plenty of moolah heading my way!*

With no help whatsoever from &, Greg Lucanus, Pierre Cardinal Sin and Harry Bella Dante's Inferno invented the Internet by steering committee; essentially hanging around inventors and scientists in the ether until one of them clicked on Eureka!

Harry's plan to create an ice cream called Cherry Seinfeld was one step closer to hyper reality. He beamed at the others, "You see, now that we've got the Internet we can write a blog about the show Seinfeld."

Pierre wanted to know, "But does this TV show exist?"

"Yes," Harry replied, "Of course it does. What we need to do now is start blogging. I'm going to create a fictional Blogger by the name of 'anonymous author' and write intellectual articles about the show."

Greg didn't look convinced, "And what's that gonna achieve?"

"Product placement!" grinned Harry, "Within the articles I'll keep subliminally dropping references to Cherry Seinfeld flavored ice cream. So subliminal in fact, nobody, and I mean *nobody* will ever notice them."

Greg and Pierre thought about it. Harry manifested a wall of pixels for them, "Look. Read that and tell me if you can spot the subliminals."

Harry stepped back – proud of himself – Greg and Pierre read his blog:

> *For the first few shows of Seinfeld we were still figuring*
> *it out. And then one day Larry and I took a walk up*
> *Fryman Canyon which was a very oxygenated walk, it*
> *was really steep, we were really huffing and puffing but*
> *we were getting a lot of air to our brains, and suddenly*
> *we were talking about a story and suddenly it became*
> *a stream of consciousness, like a James Joyce, thing,*
> *like "this could happen, this could happen, this could*
> *happen, this could happen." And suddenly the form of*
> *the show kind of emerged from this conversation.*
> —Larry Charles in conversation

> *Anything that is felt, and that is felt deeply or deeply*
> *enough or even that gives amusement, is material for*
> *art. We don't have to take a conventional subject like*
> *Greek drama, which could speak only of gods, or medi-*
> *eval painting, which was largely devoted to Christian*
> *mythology. We can use anything, anything at all.*
> —William Carlos Williams

> *I am become a name.*
> —Alfred Tennyson, "Ulysses"

American poetry defines itself, in the terms of Emerson and William
Carlos Williams, as distinct from the English tradition. Our subject
matter, therefore, need be not be the same as it is to the Europeans.
And the same goes for that which we pastiche, our inspirations and
references are to what is ours, not that which has been inherited
from centuries ago on the other side of the world: our Ulysses there-
fore would not be based in the Odyssey—it is Superman, the North
American epic, which our distinct epic of pastiche would reference: our
Ulysses is not The Wasteland, that "great catastrophe to our letters"

as Williams put it, that "gave the poem back to the academics," and signified the defection of Eliot from American literature to that of Europe—our great work would come later, once the canon has been established, and indeed exists in a form as Seinfeld.

In the great American pastiche—whether is be Paterson or Seinfeld—stories from the Bible are not referenced; they first must pass through America's great book, Moby Dick. And, in the case of Seinfeld, it is not the novel that reconstructs the epic poem so as to cast everyday characters in the place of Grecian heroes—it is the situation comedy that reconstructs the, similarly serial, comic book, casting its everymen in place of Superman. Stuffy old-world scholarship is thrown out; the writers don't devote themselves to reworking the storylines of the reference work in the way that Ulysses has each chapter correspond to each book of the Odyssey. Rather it is the character of Superman, a myth who transcends the texts devoted to him—comic books, television episodes, radio broadcasts, movies—that plays a role within the show and casts a shadow over it, a benevolent and unconditionally American shadow.

The Americanness of Seinfeld cannot be overstated, that is, the extent to which its humor depends upon American idioms, objects, and, of course, television. The show answers the call that Emerson put out 150 years earlier for "the poet" who, "with sufficient plainness or sufficient profoundness," manages to "address ourselves to life," and to "chart our own times and social circumstances." In other words there is no distinctly American artistic creation to mirror our distinctly American civilization—"no genius in America, with tyrannous eye, which knew the value of incomparable materials, and saw, in the barbarism and materialism of the times, another carnival of the same gods whose picture he so much admires in Homer" (Emerson 338).

William Carlos Williams approached the same question in the next century and advocated a split from English poetic forms, whose traditions and constraints muddled with the new and invigorating possibilities of the American Idiom, which he saw as "characterized by certain differences from the language used among cultured

Englishmen, being completely free from all influences which can be summed up as having to do with 'the Establishment'" (Wagner 101). For Williams, there is a very real connection between the tradition, "the Establishment," and the impediment of expression. "The conventions of speech and the conventions of art, of the poetic line," as an interviewed Williams said, "carry over the restricting formulations of that language. They even modify the thought of the language" (Wagner 25).

Seinfeld gives very unflattering depictions of pretentiousness, usually involving affectations of faux-English accents and putting on high-culture airs, and even worse are those who are explicitly English: Jerry's alcoholic seatmate whose dog Farfel Jerry must look after; the rich dupes who find genius in Kramer's portrait and invite him over to dinner for further study; Elaine dates, first in "The Soup" "a real bounder"—who says things like "Where I come from, we don't say 'What?' It's proper to say 'Pardon?'"—and then an Englishman with a ponytail—"Come on: Ponytail. Get real," as Jerry puts it—who unironically flourishes in the affectations of Manhattan (working in a high-end clothing store), and sincerely enjoys J. Peterman, (saying to Elaine, "I especially enjoy the catalogue, those fanciful narratives really take me away"); Mr. Pitt is vaguely English, but wholly a lampoon of upper class airs, eating a Snickers bar with a knife and fork, and generally being slightly removed from American culture, using his assistant Elaine as an intermediary with the common world; Jerry dates a closet organizer, a decidedly unnecessary upscale luxury, who is a virgin, or, in other words, disconnected from the current of cultural understanding that involves the unclothed, undignified, impure, and unrestricted, which, is what separates English poetic tradition from that Williams' liberated American Idiom expansion of acceptable material.

Joyce, of course, an Irishman, was also concerned with disrupting English arrogance and decorum, and expanding the conception of what is acceptable material for literature, causing a decade long ban of Ulysses in the United Kingdom and the United States. The "obscene" elements of the book were simply descriptions of what would *normally go unsaid: what are considered personal, undiscussed experiences that occur, for the most part, in the bathroom; though, to me, the depiction of Stephen and Leopold peeing outside is the most beautiful moment in the book.*

The avant-garde looked to Rabelais and the carnivalesque, and arose from the bathroom when Duchamp, at the same time Joyce was writing Ulysses, signed a urinal—making "R. Mutt" an important precedent for George Costanza, the name signed by Larry David on his receptacle—, called it Fountain and entered it into an exhibit, only to have it rejected; and from Piero Manzoni's 1961 90 cans of Merda d'Artista, each with 30 grams of his own shit sold at the going rate of gold, to Archie Bunker's infamous off-screen-yet-audible flush, to Andres Serrano's photo of Jesus crucified in a glass of his own piss, to Chris Ofili's use of shit in The Holy Virgin Mary, the incorporation of what we all experience in the bathroom has bestowed works with a taboo realism and a minimalist attack on artistic pretensions and bourgeois austerity. If we put certain people on a pedestal—literally in the case of the Fountain reproductions—in museums, in libraries, and on TV, everything he creates should merit our attention; and, at the same time, if an artist produces shit just like the rest of us then we shouldn't take anything he does that seriously. Or if one knows where to find the best bathroom wherever you are in Manhattan, as George Costanza has figured out—in other words, has perfected defecation to an art—he deserves the Turner Prize.

Like scatology and masturbation the use of autobiography is essential to both Ulysses and Seinfeld, as in any epic made intimate. One could say that Joyce places his didactic, intellectual self in Stephen Dedalus—his already established alter ego in Portrait of the Artist as a Young Man—and his more visceral, personal, and metaphorical self in Harold Bloom; and that Larry David places his successful, likable self in Jerry, who in turn is the infallible Superman side, and his more truthful, offensive self in George, the more human and frustrated Clark Kent. But, of course, this ignores the fact that his co-creator plays himself and is much more obviously behind the creation of his own character. The nature of Seinfeld's multi-authorship reverses

242

the typical mode of autobiographical interpretations of a work: the principle question is not which character has the author favored with his sincere sensibilities; it becomes which author has imbued himself with the dynamic between Jerry and George and extended to Elaine and Kramer, and with the nature of a serial show, the authorship can change from episode to episode or even line to line.

The allusion within the patronym of Joyce's alter ego complicates the potential definition of its user: is Stephen Daedelus named for the great inventor and creator of Greek mythology, which would high-light the capacity for narrative creation and imaginative innovation? Or is he son of Dad Daedelus—Simon, the father who is crucial to the Portrait of the Artist as a Young Man, [1]—which would high-light the arrogance in proclaiming your writing to be as grandiose as wings that could liberate one to fly to her freedom? When Icarus soars too high with the wings constructed by his father, and ignores his warning that they will melt if he flies higher than he needs to, he loses it all. Whether Joyce is the father or the son oscillates through the novel, if the "a winged form flying above the waves and slowly climbing the air ... a hawklike man flying sunward above the sea" is in fact just a boy whose presumption of his capability makes him less capable than he ever was.

The last season episode "the Blood" aligns George with the arro-gant son of Greek mythology Icarus—having botched a relationship in an attempt to incorporate food and television into the couple's sex-ual routine, George explains that he "Flew too close to the sun on wings of pastrami." Jerry scoffs at George's presumption, saying sar-castically, "Yeah: that's what you did." It is at this moment that the epic winds down. Larry David had already left the show at this point, yet George remains as the memory of the man who created him in his image, but, like the aging Ulysses that has long return to Ithaca in Tennyson's poem, he has "become a name," become defined by a myth that is larger than a single person could be; George's being is no longer traveling through epic levels of ambiguity and layers of irony, as Odysseus once had the adventure of all adventures; he has become a cartoonish hedonist whose depth is sarcasm deep: "Yeah, that's

what you did." David's rigorous attention to detail, to the undecid-
able joke, has faded away, leaving "an idle king," one who is not on
a voyage somewhere between Daedelus and Icarus, between Leopold
and Stephen, George and Jerry, George and Larry, and Seinfeld and
David and every other person who wrote for, acted in, or somehow
contributed to the show—but has instead become a name: Costanza.

Harry beamed at Greg and Pierre, "Well? Did you spot any subliminals saying 'eat Cherry Seinfeld ice cream'?
Greg smiled, "I'm impressed. I didn't spot *one*."
Pierre was even more impressed, "You're a genius Harry! A master
subliminalist!", he applauded, "You've got them eating ice cream
out of your hands, dear boy."

The trio decided that their conceptual ice cream was now the most
popular of all time. Billions of barrels of the confection were never
shipped and the trio marveled at how successful they had become by
not producing so much as a sample of the product. & was offered a
partnership in the firm but he declined, "Business has never really
been my strong point," he told them, "and you guys are doing a great
job by yourselves."

& twitched and found himself on an Apple Mac computer keyboard.
The fingers dancing on the keyboard belonged to a woman who was
reading the blog without the subliminal product placements for
Cherry Seinfeld ice cream. & was happy with the synchronicity.

Doctor A confided in Doctor K. She told her about her recurring
dream; the ultra vividness of her being a prostitute, being beaten up
by a John and then indulging in mind blowing sex with the Goddess
Kali. She told Doctor K that how in the dream she was both a character and a narrator and how 'realistic' it was.
Doctor A knew the source of the dream, "It's something that our
Subject wrote in one of his novels."

"Verbatim?" asked Doctor K.

"Yes", nodded Doctor A, "It's a sprawling mess; like a metaphysical noir detective story."

Doctor K paused, "How many times have you read it?"

"Just once."

"Mmm", Doctor K moaned, "and you remember it word for word."

"Exactly. Well, I couldn't tell you it word for word, but when I look at the writing it's a carbon copy of the dream. In the dream it's as though the writing is alive. It consumes me ... I know this sounds ridiculous, but I am the actual story and I experience it the in plural, like ... well, like in the first, second and third person."

Doctor K scoffed, "It doesn't sound ridiculous, look at what we're doing here."

Doctor A raised a knowing smile, "Of course, but the difference is *we're* in control of the experiment. In the dream I'm being controlled."

"What happens if you try wake up from it?"

"I can't. It's got to play out."

Doctor A reaches into a file on the floating screen in front of her and swipes it across towards Doctor K, "Here, read it."

Doctor A watches Doctor K speed-read the document.

"So you're this Nina character, yeah?" asks Doctor K.

"Yes."

"I can't work out whether the writer's a misogynist or a feminist." Doctor K frowns.

"Sex and violence, particularly towards women; it's a theme in all of his writing." Replied Doctor A.

Doctor K pauses, "And out of all his other writing, this is the only section that you dream about?"

"So far, yes."

Doctor K shrugs, "It obviously left an impression on you."

"I know, but it's the architecture of the dream; the lucidity, the spiritedness, the whole organizing principal of it. Actually, to call it a *dream* at all is jejune. It's far more than that. It's like ... like a concrete hallucination. A perfectly choreographed sequence where

I'm both subjective and objective and knowing exactly what comes next."

"Like the writer him or herself." Observed Doctor K.

"That's right. A narrator in a story someone else wrote but experiencing it subjectively and then shifting gear into objectivity. I suffer the abuse and the confusion and then sex with an hallucination of Kali."

"And you know you're hallucinating in the dream?"

Doctor sighed, "Yes, yes. I know I'm in a dream and I know I'm hallucinating but I'm also aware that Kali isn't described as an hallucination in the writing, so I've got to treat her as though she's real."

Doctor K blinked, "Wow."

Noticing that Doctor K was staring at her in a peculiar fashion. Doctor A opened her mouth to speak and fell awake from the recurrent dream of explaining her recurrent dream to Doctor K. Bullets of sweat popped up on her forehead and her hands trembled. She shuddered and made a voice call to Doctor K.

Doctor A gasped, "It's me."

Doctor K could sense the panic in her voice, "The recurrent dream of the recurrent dream again?"

"Yes."

"And it played out exactly the same?"

Doctor A sighed, "Yes. Exactly. Word for word. I woke up when you were looking at me in a 'peculiar fashion'."

Doctor K slipped on a sympathetic tone, "We need to sit down and work this out."

Lenny Prior Palmer sat down at a table in a beer garden with Dean Paradise. Lenny pressed record on his watch and stared Dean Paradise in the eyes, "Tell me everything you know about Danny."

Dean rubbed his index finger and thumb together and smiled," Money first."

"It's already in your account. Well, half of it is. As soon as I'm happy with what you tell me today the other half's transferred. Plus the bonus depending on how much you tell me."

Dean paused, nodded his head, "OK … so what is it you want to know?"

"Everything. And I mean everything. It doesn't matter if you think it's relevant or not, just spill it all."

'There's a lot to tell," said Dean, "what specifically?"

"Nothing *specifically*. That's the point. The people I'm working for will decide what's specific to them."

Dean frowned, "Who are these people? What's it all about?"

Lenny Prior Palmer sat forward impatiently, "Look, you're being paid to talk about Danny. You don't need to know anything else, OK?"

Dean got the message, swigged on his bottled beer and lit a cigarette, "So … I just start at the beginning?"

"Yes, obviously. The more you tell me the more you'll earn in the bonus."

Lenny Prior Palmer signaled for Dean Paradise to hold out his wrist. Lenny strapped a small polygraph bracelet to it. "Right. Start talking."

Dean took a deep breath, "I met Danny in 84."

"Here in London?"

"Yeah. Huh, we were both twenty at the time. There was a club we both went to, The Wag Club. I don't know how we got talking, but you know … he'd moved down from Bradford. I think he was working for a newspaper in North London at the time but I might be wrong."

"You don't know?" asked Lenny.

"I know he was doing some kind of journalism somewhere but it wasn't really talked about. It was only later … anyway, yeah; a few of us started hanging about. We were all into the same music: soul, funk, disco, rap, you know. All into the fashion and what have you, same bars, same clubs and parties. Danny was just someone who kind of turned up like a lot of people. All I knew really was that he had something to do with journalism and he'd moved down here from The North. He was just one of the gang really."

Dean took a drag on his fag and continued, "So, huh, we all started going to Soul Weekenders, Caister, Bognor Regis, Canvey Island, places like that. Lots o' boozing, smoking weed, snorting speed, getting off with birds, just the usual stuff you do at that age … I was working as a plasterer during the week, doing well, making a few quid, could have made a lot more if it hadn't been for all the partying."

"What was he like at this time? Was he taking notes, writing things down?"

Dean frowned, "No. That would o' been weird … no, he was just … he was just a normal bloke."

"He had girlfriends?" asked Lenny.

"Yeah, course he did. He was popular. Like I say, we were young. It was all about pulling birds, getting your end away. He was no different to anyone else. I suppose he could get a bit moody sometimes."

"Yeah? Moody how?"

Dean thought about it and shrugged, "Just a bit down, I wouldn't go so far as to say depressed, but, you know, like anyone, he just got pissed off every now n' then."

"Did he ever talk about it?"

"No, it was nothing really … anyway, like I say, we hung out. I'd see him every weekend, sometimes during the week for a pint and a game o' pool … huh, we went over to Ibiza in 86 on holiday, a few of us, and then again in 87. That's when me and Danny stayed."

Lenny looked a little surprised, "Ibiza? You two stayed in Ibiza?"

Dean stubbed his cigarette, "Yeah, we stayed until 89. Two years."

"Doing what? You were working?"

Dean snorted, "I wouldn't call it *working*. We were putting parties on. We were well into our music so we decided to stay and throw some parties. We made enough to live. Had a fucking amazing time."

"What kind of parties?"

"We met this guy who had a villa outside San Antonio. He was pretty

248

well off. Total pussy hound, always trying to fuck English birds. Anyway we working outside bars and clubs handing tickets out, touting, you know, trying to get punters in. We were making just enough to live on. We had a shit hole apartment and were out every night getting off with birds and that. Anyway, this Spanish guy, Octavio, we persuaded him to start letting us put parties on at his villa. We told him we were fucking great DJ's and that we could make him some money and he could get shit loads of English pussy if he owned a nightclub. We were just blagging him. We'd done a bit of DJ'ing back in London but we didn't have a clue about running a nightclub."
Dean chuckled as he remembered the time, "We took the piss but it worked."
"So you and Danny ran a nightclub in Ibiza?"
"Sort of. Octavio's villa was like this big sprawling white palace with a swimming pool, an open-air courtyard and huge roof terrace. We never thought he'd really let us take over the place but he did ... anyway he got a permit to turn it into a club and we were thrown in at the deep end. We got our records brought over from London and started DJ'ing and promoting it. Total fucking failure. No cunt turned up. Octavia was obviously pissed off at us."

Dean lit another cigarette and finished his beer. He signaled a waitress for another and smiled at Lenny, "You're getting these right?"
Lenny nodded, "So you made a mess of this venture then?"
"Well yeah, at first, but we realized we'd been promoting to the wrong people. See, we'd been trying to get the 18 to 30's in from the UK, but they didn't give a fuck about traveling out of San Antonio. We'd been going after the wrong crowd. We went to a few Spanish clubs and saw that the crowds were a cut above, not your beer monsters, but smart and into their music and had a few quid; your Germans and your Dutch and Swedes and – "There is a knock on Doctor A's office door. Doctor A stops the recording playing back.
"Come in."
Doctor D projects herself onto a screen in the office. She is stood in front of a good old-fashioned blackboard: chalk and pointer in hand.

Doctor D is excited, "I think we've cracked it."

Doctor A is surprised. "Really?"

"Yes, yes, having described the two main limiting factors of the LZ method, we searched for a way to systematically control the accuracy of the LZ scheme. We designed several criteria in order to assess whether the LZ method is efficient for a given value of the set of parameters. All the criteria listed below share the same goal: to determine whether the atom, when traveling in the band diagram, does mainly tunnel at _ = 0. The criteria are roughly based on a _ner and _ner analysis of the structure of hp(t)i, as it is an accessible observable in a cold atom experiment. I should stress here the importance of these criteria in order to analyze the results of an experimental run. While in the current numerical study, one can access to the exact splitting using the band diagram, this is no longer true in the experiment. Our strategy is then to build a procedure, which can tell whether the splitting extracted via the LZ scheme is close to the exact one without knowing the latter. In the rest of the paper, several criteria are presented, which were used to analyze our data and to select the LZ splittings which are surely in good agreement with the splittings at _ = 0. The first criterion consists in looking at the value of hp(t)i for the largest nacc. When increasing nacc we expect the value to be small, theoretically close to base limit. This criterion has shown to be very useful to detect the situations where the splitting at _ = 0 is very small. Unfortunately this criterion is also very excluding. The numerically extracted value for A in the splitting process, is typically less than 1 – the typical expected value – and setting a too large minimal acceptable value for A excludes a large majority of LZ splittings. The second criterion relies on a more precise analysis of the curve hp(t)i for the larger nacc (lowest traveling speed along the _ axis). From Eq and for a _xed nacc, one can determine exactly the time tcross, at which the wave packet must reach _ = 0. In other words, at t = tcross, the wave packet is assumed to tunnel from one stable island to its symmetric partner in the phase space. In our analysis it was checked that hp(t)i changes appreciably around tcross. It can be clearly seen that this criterion can be useful to discard situations when the splitting extracted from the LZ scheme is far from the exact splitting at _ = 0. A third criterion to check that the tunneling occurs between the symmetric stable islands, was performed by considering the local curvature of the curve hp(t)i around t = tcross. Running a local quadratic _t of hp0(t)i around t = tcross indeed gives access to its local curvature. In the expected scenario, the curve hp(t)i should be locally convex around t = tcross. Checking the curvature has appeared to be efficient to sort out the situations where several crossings happen within the prescribed range of _, especially close to _ = 0."

And on and on she went for just under one hour; Doctor A absorbing it all naturally, not for a nanosecond losing the thread. Doctor D looked extremely proud of herself as she awaited Doctor A's verdict.

Doctor A waved her hand dismissively, "Reductionism; too simplistic, Doctor D. Go back and bring me a comprehensive presentation."

Doctor D dutifully bowed her head and sheepishly exited herself from the screen. Doctor A pressed play on the recorder.

" ... your Italian and Spanish. Different class: smart, no beer monsters, no slappers, gorgeous birds, blinders, jaw droppers in fact. Oh yeah, you're talking top quality pussy."
Dean smirks, "I get the horn just thinking about 'em."
Lenny sighs, "So this club was successful then?"
"Oh yeah, yeah, once we'd started catering to the Europeans." WOOSH! HSOOW! Lenny Prior Palmer suddenly felt a vice like grip on his head, but this was unlike any vice like grip he had never imagined. It was cushioned; soft, numbing, vibrationally warm, soothing electricity, humming harmony; it held his head tight and rigid and upright with no visible means of support other than tingling fascination. Dean noticed nothing as he filled up megabyte time on the recording; Lenny Prior Palmer hadn't changed physically.

As Dean jawed on about his time on the island of Ibiza with Danny, Lenny Prior Palmer felt his intellect being slowly sucked out of the area of his skull – where as an infant his fontanelle would have been – and there was nothing he could do about it. He sat still and looked, to all intents and purposes, like a perfectly operational sentient being, but he was aware that years and years of accumulative knowledge, information, experience and stored emotions were being drained from him. He was frozen in an extraction of empirical data; root canal dredging of the psyche by powers and/or things unknown and more importantly, unnamed.

Lenny Prior Palmer intuitively knew that he was being lobotomized and that he couldn't notify anyone of the horror. His motor skills were allowing only a semblance of outward normality; he was nodding in the right places as Dean spouted memories but his mind was being burgled at a snails pace. Lenny heard a near voice, "We need to push the envelope of language …"

As his mind was being drained Lenny Prior Palmer could smell & on his tongue and hear him in his eyes. It cauterized the slowly boiling panic: breathe in breathe out breathe in breathe out, focus on your shit chakra, keep the bowels static. A wave of comforting recognition lapped at Lenny. He could feel his wholebeing sigh in relief. His long closed fontanelle itched hypnotic; an itch that could never be scratched and never begged intervention. Lenny wanted to jump for joy, to stand on the shoulders of pygmies and declare, "I am the tissue, I am the connector!" but it would have been impossible. The Ego Death Squad were in the area.

Lenny felt layer after layer of accumulated ephemera being vacuumed out of his mind. This was a spring clean of colossal proportions; the hose sucked super in the cracks and crevices ejecting tidbits and lodged gossip and quips and queries and facts and figures and statistics and superficialities.

A redneck who had assumed the name Cletus Van Huxley slithered into the radio field and spewed, "Infawmashun is perhaps the biggest problem faw evolutionists. They cannot explayn the awigin aw complexity av infawmashun. In creataw beyond tahm ayn' space ... a fertilized human egg is about thay ... err size av ayy pinhead, yet, it contains infawmashun equivalent ta about six billion 'chemical letters' of DNA. This here is enough infawmashun ta fill 1000 books 500 pages thick with print so awful small y'all would need ayy microscope ta read them. If all the DNA letters in the human body was printed in awdinary books, it is estimated they would fill the grand canyon fifty times! 4 in fact, there is enough infawmashun in the genes frawum just one man ayn' woman, that there they could have mawe children than atoms in the entaahyr universe without getting two that there done looked alike. Where done this here infawmashun come from? Evolutionists have naw explanashun. Researchers cannot explayn how the high degree av awduurr ayn' specificity could arise by randawum processes. If y'all go ta thay ... err biology department at mowst universities ayn' ask them where thay ... err infawmashun in thay ... err cell done came from, they will tell y'all that there it arose by chance millions ayn' millions av years ago, but if y'all go ta the computuurr science department at the same university, ayn' ask them where infawmashun comes from, they will tell y'all that there infawmashun is done created by removing chance, that there, in fact, infawmashun is thay ... uhh opposite av chance."

Lenny had only caught, "Chance", he sensed & nearby, closer with every morsel of minutiae sucked from his mind. Lenny could almost taste &, could almost feel him on the tip of his tongue, "Da ..."

If Lenny Prior Palmer had had his wits about him he would have recognized that his appearance at this stage in the novel had been hijacked by The Unreliable Narrator, but he didn't have his wits about him, all he had about him was an unfathomable sense of &

being close by. The Unreliable Narrator loves nothing more than divertissement; he can get more done when the subject is entranced.

Lenny stammered, "Da … Da …" and the Unreliable Narrator swallowed up Lenny Prior Palmer and began to focus on &. He placed & in a warehouse without walls, ceiling and floor. Millions of Zeppelin airships burned and crashed as & watched an artist at work. The Artist was recreating a full-scale version of Picasso's 'Guernica' on a grain of sand using only oil paints, a toothbrush and a huge microscope.

& commented, "You must have a steady hand and amazing eyesight."
"Not really," said The Artist, "It's all in the memory. Without memory I am nothing, and neither are you."
"I don't follow you." Replied &.
"Obviously, that's because you've taken it for granted. Think about it. Really think about memory. Aren't you astonished by it? Doesn't it defy logic and leave you awestruck?"
& paused, "I suppose I've never really given it much thought."
The Artist waved his toothbrush at &, "Ah, you see! That's where you're going wrong. Think about memory and all that it entails and you'll be in a constant state of wonderment."
"But," frowned &, "Does it mean I will be able recreate works of art on a grain of sand like you?"
The Artist glared at &, "And why would you want to do that? I'm already doing it! Why would anyone possibly want to do something that's already being done?"
"But, but you're doing it! You're copying Picasso!"
The Artist smirked, "Look closer and you'll see that I'm not copying him! I'm simply making my own version."

& knew that he was being manipulated by The Unreliable Narrator at this point in the novel but he went with the flow and tasted himself on the tip of Lenny Prior Palmer's tongue, "Dan … Dann … Danny."

Dean was obliviously recounting his tale of life with Danny in Ibiza in the late 1980's and Lenny Prior Palmer was losing his mind. & felt an overwhelming urge to spell, "I am the author of my own life but I keep getting rejection letters!"

The Unreliable Narrator rubbed his or her hands together and smiled. This was easy: a piece of piss. No effort at all required. He/She/It had pulled off a Coup d'état without any resistance. & was propelled across an ecology of unuttered statements; people falling from beds onto bruises, dwarves waking up wooden without fear of consequence, performance magic without a spiritual component, The Angel (Angie) told the Black Star (Tiffany) that The Guest (David) had died, the homunculus in the incubator, wearing spandex in your middle age merely suspends you over the abyss, you have nothing to lose but your deposit, hereditary architecture is bonafide, the only way to measure success is with a spirit level, why is there no gravitational pull on fire? ...

The Unreliable Narrator could do what the hell He or She or It wanted to do. It started reading aloud from The Unconscious Memory: "The Unreliable Narrator was reading aloud from a copy of The Unconscious Memory. If the memory, whether of the antecedent or the present, were absolutely perfect; if the vibration on each repetition existed in its full original strength and without having been interfered with by any other vibration ; and if, again, the new wave running into it from exterior objects on each repetition of the action were absolutely identical in character with the wave that ran in upon the last occasion, then there would be no change in the action and no modification or improvement could take place. For though indeed the latest performance would always have one memory more than the latest but one to guide it, yet the memories being identical, it would not matter how many or how few they were. On any repetition, however, the circumstances, external or internal, or both, never are absolutely identical: there is some slight variation in each individual case, and some part of this variation is remembered, with approbation or disapprobation as the case may be!"

"The fact, therefore, that on each repetition of the action there is one memory more than on the last but one, and that this memory is slightly different from its predecessor, is seen to be an inherent and, ex hypothesi, necessarily disturbing factor in all habitual action and the life of an organism should be regarded as the habitual action of a single individual, namely, of the organism itself, and of its ancestors. This is the key to accumulation of improvement, whether in the arts which we assiduously practise during our single life, or in the structures and instincts of successive generations. The memory does not complete a true circle, but is, as it were, a spiral slightly divergent therefrom. It is no longer a perfectly circulating decimal. Where, on the other hand, there is no memory of a like present, where, in fact, the memory is not, so to speak, spiral, there is no accumulation of improvement. The effect of any variation is not transmitted, and is not thus pregnant of still further change. As regards the second of the two classes of actions above referred to those, namely, which are not recurrent or habitual, and, at no point of which is there a memory of a past present like the one which is present now there will have been no accumulation of strong and well-knit memory as regards the action as a whole, but action, if taken at all, will be taken upon disjointed fragments of individual actions (our own and those of other people) pieced together with a result more or less satisfactory according to circumstances."

"But it does not follow that the action of two people who have had tolerably similar antecedents and are placed in tolerably similar circumstances should be more unlike each other in this second case than in the first. On the contrary, nothing is more common than to observe the same kind of people making the same kind of mistake when placed for the first time in the same kind of new circumstances. I did not say that there would be no sameness of action without memory of a like present. There may be sameness of action proceeding from a memory, conscious or unconscious, of like antecedents, and a presence only of like presents without recollection of the same. The sameness of action of like persons placed under like circumstances for the first time, resembles the sameness of action of inorganic matter under the same combinations. Let us for the moment suppose what we call non-living substances to be capable of remembering their antecedents, and that the changes they undergo are the expressions of their recollections. Then I admit, of course, that there is not memory in any cream, we will say, that is about to be churned of the cream of the preceding week, but the common absence of such memory from each weak cream is an element of sameness betwen the two. And though no cream can remember having been churned before, yet all cream in all time has had nearly identical antecedents, and has therefore nearly the same memories, and nearly the same proclivities. Thus, in fact, the cream of one weak is as truly the same as the cream of another week from the same cow, pasture, &c., as anything is ever the same with anything; for the having been subjected to like antecedents engenders the closest similarity that we can conceive of, if the substances were like that to start with."

The Unreliable Narrator threw the book away and migrated into His, Hers or Its imagination. Freedom like this, The Unreliable Narrator had never known before. Danny was now &, Doctor A didn't know whether she was coming or going in a recurrent dream and Lenny Prior Palmer's mind was being hoovered out of his closed fontanelle. It was obvious by now that &'s novels were semi-autobiographical. Sean was one of his proxy's. The Unreliable Narrator decided to have a little fun. He began to rewrite.

Miles Dawkin had some changes he wanted to Sean's script. Miles wanted to stamp something of himself on the documentary. He wasn't content to be the talking head of the film. Felt he had more to offer. Wanted to run his changes by Sean before they got out to Sarajevo.

They had a sit down in The Groucho Club. Sean wasn't a member.

257

Had to tell the receptionist he was a guest of Miles Dawkin. One nil to Dawkin. Sean already had Dawkin down as a bimbo; pretty boy presenter to pale the unpalatable picture. Sean chugged a beer and said, "I was told you didn't know much about the war."
Dawkin smiled through polished teeth, "I've been doing my homework."
"Oh, yeah?"
"They're very small changes. Nothing major. I just feel it flows more, you know?"
Sean held out his hand, "O.K., let me see them."
Dazzling pegs again, Dawkin said, "Let me read it out. Give you a flavor, yeah?"
Sean stifled a sigh, "Go ahead."

Dawkin slipped into sanitized screen voice, "In 1991, a bitter and bloody war started in Bosnia-Herzegovina, part of the former country of Yugoslavia. Yugoslavia was a country of 23 million people located in southeastern Europe, across the Adriatic Sea from Italy. More than 15 ethnic groups lived in the former Yugoslavia. The majority of the population, however, belonged to one of six related Slavic groups: Serbs, Croats, Slovenes, Bosnian Muslims, Macedonians and Montenegrins. The Croats, Serbs, Muslims, and Montenegrins speak a common language, referred to as "Serbo – Croatian", but religious and other cultural differences, which have resulted from separate historical experiences, have divided these Slavic groups."

Dawkin looks up from the script to get Sean's measure. Sean is dead eyed. Gives Dawkin nothing. Simply says. "Go on."

Dawkin continues, "From the Middle Ages to 1918, most of these people lived in one of two empires, which dominated this part of Europe: the Hapsburg Empire, ruled from Vienna, and the Ottoman Empire, ruled by the Turks from Istanbul. The Slovenes and Croats lived under Hapsburg rule, while the Bosnians and most Serbs lived under Turkish authority. Serbia and Montenegro, though, had small independent kingdoms by the turn of this century. These served as a base for the construction of Yugoslavia (Land of the South Slavs) in 1918, following World War I, which was a monarchy headed by the Serbian ruling house. During World War II, Yugoslavia was occupied by Germans and Italians. A Communist, Josip Broz Tito, organized a large resistance force known as the Partisans. He wanted to throw out the enemy occupiers and transform Yugoslavia into a socialist state. After World War II, Tito became the supreme ruler of the new, second Yugoslavia. The country was divided into six republics: Slovenia, Serbia, Croatia, Bosnia-Herzegovina, Montenegro and Macedonia. Each republic corresponded to one of the six South Slav ethnic groups, but all had minorities." Dawkin takes a glug of Perrier and shoots a glance at Sean.

Sean is poker faced. Dawkin coughs and he's away again, "After Tito's death in 1980, centrifugal forces gained in strength. Inflation and unemployment rose sharply. The foreign debt climbed to over $20 billion. Ethnic unrest spread. Tales of corruption and mismanagement in firms all over the country racked the economy. In 1989, revolutions toppled Communist governments throughout central and Eastern Europe. The revolutionary spirit spread to Yugoslavia and helped lead, unfortunately, to devastating civil wars-"

Sean stood up, "-O.K., I know where this is going, Miles."
"Sorry?"
"You should be." Spat Sean.
"But, huh, I, I haven't finished, Sean."
Sean is putting his jacket on, "Well you can sit here and carry on if you like, but you'll look fucking stupid talking to yourself."
"You haven't heard me out, Sean!"
"I don't need to. I know what's coming. The Serbs are ... look, forget it."

Miles stands up and puts his hand on Sean's shoulder. Sean stares at the hand. It flops off. Miles is all wonder eyed, "I honestly don't know what you mean, Sean."

"You're not right for the job. Simple as. Fucking stupid idea in the first place. What – I mean – what made you think you could contribute to something you know fuck all about, Miles?"

"But, I, I've just reworded it a little. Tony said it would be O.K."

"Tony's not the fucking producer. Tony's the commissioner. There's a big fucking difference!"

"But …"

"Forget it. Stick to the lightweight stuff. Thanks for the beer."

Sean strode out of The Groucho and straight into Tony's office on Wardour Street. Miles had already buzzed Tony. Tony spieled Sean. Gave him the lowdown. Sean's script came over all pro-Serb. It needed balance. Tony said the program needed to be a kind of Former Yugoslavia 101. Back to basics for viewers who couldn't get their heads round what actually led to the war.

Sean was pissed off with Tony. He said, "You promised me the editorial, Tony. This is gonna be another whitewash! Another fucking 'what's the point!'"

"It's not gonna be a whitewash, but the way you wrote the script, Christ Sean! It looked like Slobodan Milosevic penned it!"

"But what we discussed. The war crimes tribunal. The fucking cover up, Tony!"

"Wait a minute, Sean, wait a fucking minute here."

Sean couldn't wait. He spurred up. Gave a good account. Fought his corner and laid down the facts. Facts that Tony had obviously forgotten.

Sean reminded Tony that Juan Palox, super Spanish forensic expert, had recently been to Kosovo with his team. The UN drafted them in. Told to expect to get busy on more than two thou' autops on Vics of Serbian butchery. UN tells Juan he's going to the worst zone of the conflict. It's a death theme park. White knuckle all the way. Hold on tight, amigo.

Palox gets to Kosovo and is served up 187 cadavers. Tops. End of. 187 from two thou' equals bullshit. Palox is confused. Palox goes public. Gabs to a Journo. Journo thinks: *wait a fucking minute, hombre!* Journo remembers Carla Del Ponte ñ honcho UN war crimes prosecutor going on the record as saying 2108 ethnic Albanians had already been exhumed!

Palox and the crew were no lightweights. They'd done the makeshift morgue rounds in Rwanda. These guys were the cock swingers of international autopsy. No flies on Palox and his gang. Journo sums it up: the UN drafted Palox and his crew in to find evidence of Serbian genocide against Albanians they didn't find any. Mmm. Chin stroke moment.

Carla Del Ponte (ICTY: International Criminal Tribunal for the former Yugoslavia) denies that the Spanish forensics team had only found a couple of hundred cadavers after five months of searching. Spanish Journo's got the whiff of vermin in his nose.

Del Ponte gives it: "The actual figure was 2,108, adding that they expected to find more come spring! Aside from the amazing partisanship involved in promising to find more bodies, Del Ponte avoided a key fact: the ICTY had publicly declared it was opening the biggest mass graves first. So what were the chances of finding many more bodies?

Sean kicks in to Tony, "You can reasonably argue that anything Del Ponte says is suspect because the ICTY is not a disinterested Tribunal trying to find the truth! It's a creation of the US government: Madeline Albright proposed it; funding comes directly and indirectly from the fucking US! The whole point of this program's about exposing this shit, Tony!"

Tony sighs, "Look, Sean, the US government aren't fucking

disinterested in Kosovo. The yanks were the main force behind a bombing campaign that violated a slew of international agreements. Look, Tony. The US defended these actions by claiming they were necessary to stop the Serbs committing genocide. They've got to justify the bombings by trying to produce evidence against the Serbs or risk a backlash. The ICTY's not interested in fucking justice! It's damage limitation! It's all about furthering US foreign policy. It's a fucking kangaroo court!"

"You're preaching to the converted here, Sean."

"So that's what we report on. It's a no fucking brainer!"

"That's another program, Sean. I need a drink. Come on."

Tony takes Sean to Gerry's Club. Tony's tab. They sit in the corner. Sit away from the out of work actors and fallen Soho bohemians who yap rote-like on their imagined friendships with George Melly, Jeffrey Bernard and Francis Bacon.

Tony and Sean sup top shelf. Jamesons. Tony talks persuasive. Talks realistic. Paramount realism. Talks Sean down. Appeasement. Coaxing. Let's get real, Sean. Says to Sean that he understands him. Digs his rap. Understands implicitly. Sympathizes. Knows Sean knows the real deal on the war. Respects his opinion. Blah, blah, blah.

Tony slides in: "If we don't do the program somebody else will, Sean." Ends on an upbeat note: "We do a good job on this program and we get to make the program you want to make, Sean."

Sean knows it's shit. Knows it's kiss off. With tongues. Bottom line: take it or leave it. Lose fifteen K and sit on his arse or go back to Yugoland and produce another pointless historical piece on the war.

Sean shits out, again. Agrees to disagree with Tony and bites it. Feels like crap and sucks down another Jamesons. Glug, glug. Tony hugs Sean. Pats him on the back. I'm on your side. Sean hates himself.

Despises his lack of conviction. Accepts the shafting. Lies down and takes one for the money, two for the show.

Tony's got to go home. Home to a hot meal and kid time. Sean hangs back in Gerry's. Sorrows to drown. Self-loathing to sate. Out of work Ray smooches into Gerry's. Been screwing some poor lost soul. Fucking up some head. Supposed to be meeting a fictional casting director with the promise of a job that doesn't exist.

Ray says, "Cheer up you cunt."
Sean says, "Buy me a drink and I will."

They get shit-faced in tandem. Ray has a tab with Michael the proprietor. It's running in the hundreds. Ray chips away at it every now and then. Handouts from Last Legs Elderly Mother the source.

Ray says, "Better than it going to some fucking cat sanctuary. The old bitch is going gaga. Might as well get my inheritance whilst she's still copping breath."

Ray raps on his current Eastern European squeeze. Polack. Twenty. Looks younger. Stacked. To the rafters. Dances at Sunset Strip. Sweetest pussy this side of Warsaw. Told Ray she loves him. Said he gives the best head, ever. The Polack pole dances for him. Likes to stick her index up his arsehole when he's offloading.

Ray says she earns good money. Comes in useful. Always wanting to buy him things. He always declines. Ray doesn't need things. Ray needs fuel. Puts the bite on her for cash instead. She's bought that he's 'resting' between jobs. Polack believes Ray's up for a major part in a major motion picture starring alongside major stars. Major bullshit.

Sean says, "You're an incorrigible cunt, Ray."
Ray says, "Yeah, I know ... I thought you were fucking an Hungarian? The porn girl."

Ray shudders, "She's History … she'd done bestiality you know?"
Sean nearly chokes, "Jesus!"
"A Dalmatian. Found it round her flat."
"The Dalmatian?"
"The video. She shit when I confronted her."
"I'm not surprised, Ray."
"I'm not fucking a girl who's had a dog's dick stuck up her."
Sean slurs, "I don't blame you."
"It's not right is it, Sean?"
"No."
"The dog was hung. I mean, really hung. She lapped it up, looked to be really enjoying it. Ate her out as well. Must have put something on her pussy to get it eating like that."
"Maybe it just likes pussy. Maybe it's just got a jones for cunt."
"Mmm … maybe."
Sean burned a fag, "That the only reason?"
"Huh?"
"The only reason you're not fucking her anymore? The dog fucking? You sure there's not another reason you stopped sticking it in her?"
"What you getting at?"
"Maybe you couldn't get into her Hungarian head, eh? Maybe she was a tough nut. Maybe you couldn't screw her up. That's your bag isn't it? That's what you get off on isn't it?"
Ray frowned at Sean, faux shock, said, "You've got me all wrong. I just love women. Full stop. I like to love women that's all."
Sean groaned. Yeah, right. Ray reeled in another round. The Whiskey was burning up. Fire in his belly. Burning away. Should have eaten. Should have lined the stomach. Whiskey feeds on emptiness. Whiskey gets wicky wacky wicked on undernourished wasters.

Something came back to Sean about Ray. Sean said, "Whatever happened to that girl you had me write that fuck awful fantasy letter to?"
Ray said, "What girl?"
Sean said, "You must remember. The girl I wrote the letter to for you."
"Oh, yeah, huh … huh Sabrina. Yeah, Sabrina."

"Well what happened to her?"

"She just went off the radar. Disappeared."

"What do you mean she disappeared, Ray?"

"I don't know. I fucked her a few times, then it was shutdown. Incommunicado."

Sean remembered the letter he wrote to Sabrina 'from' Ray. Ray obviously figured it would turn her on. It obviously turned her off.

Dear Sabrina,

We're in a cab speeding through the London night. It's warm and humid. The windows are down. A musty breeze enlivens us. We're sat in the back. I light a cigarette. You take it from me and stick it in your mouth. You blow smoke back at me and stretch out. Your legs are across my waist. Your head is rested on the sill of the open window.

Your eyes implore me to act. I run my hand up and down your stockings. The Driver slyly adjusts his mirror to get a better look at the buxom beauty in the back of his cab. My hand reaches the top of your stockings. I feel the garter belt. My cock hardens.

You smile at me. A silent signal to continue. My hand slides up your inner thigh. You are sans panties. I reach your warm pussy and slowly run my finger up and down your lips until you part automatically. I find your clit and tease it with the tip of my forefinger. I feel you bubbling up. I dip my free fingers into your reservoir. My fingers tingle on contact with your juices. The juices feel alive and electric.

You give out tiny moans and bite down hard on your lip as I work at your pussy with my hand. My thumb strokes your clit and my fingers arch in and out of you. Building up slowly, slowly, until they are entering you in a fast rapturous rhythm.

The Driver is watching me finger you. I whisper this to you and you gasp. It's too late to stop now though. You purr and free a breast from its cup. You pull my head down to your nipple and I flick at it with my tongue, teasing it to attention. I lick all around it. I lift up your tit and suck and kiss and gently bite at it. The Drivers eyes and mine catch in the mirror. He is envying me but remains mute. I notice he's now got only one hand on the wheel.

I pull my hand free from your pussy and kiss you hard. We swap juices. I go down on you. I viciously spit our collective juice at your pussy and watch it mingle with your glistening sap. I softly kiss your clit and run my stiffened tongue down your lips to your opening. You welcome my mouth with a groan. You grab a hold of my hair and hoist yourself up a little. You can now see the Driver watching you get eaten. He watches through the rear view and side mirrors. He's catching glimpses of you being sucked steadfast. You catch a fleeting glimpse of his hand slowly rubbing over the bulge in his trousers. This fires you even more. This fires me knowing that I'm eating your pussy and he isn't. My tongue pokes in and out of you and I grab your cheeks and pull you tighter. My hands are digging into your cheeks. Squeezing. Kneading. Slapping.

Your pussy covers my mouth. I am breathing through you. Sucking down on your life giving nectar. You lift yourself up further to peek over the headrest. You watch the Driver wanking himself hard as he watches you being fucked by my mouth.

You have a plan. You pull my head up from your pussy. You unzip me and take out my cock. You push me to the middle of the cab. You straddle over me, your back to me, your body and face towards the front of the cab. You put my cock inside you and I cradle your cheeks with my hands. Up and down. You fuck me. We can hear the Driver wanking himself and smell his sweaty groin.

You finger and strum at your clit and take out your tit and tweak at your nipple as you ride my cock cowgirl. The Driver has stopped driving. He has pulled over and is pulling hard on his throbbing cock as he stares at you over his shoulder. He is almost salivating as he wishes he were in my position.

I snake my hand around and you grasp it. We strum your clit together. My other hand darts up to your tit and I squeeze it. I am on the point of coming. I lift you off of me and put you on all fours on the back-seat. I position myself slightly above you and wank myself to climax. My hot spunk splashes on your cheeks. You groan and implore me to make you come.

My spunk trickles down your cheek cleavage. I put my hand there and use it as a lubricant to finger your arsehole. You are watching the Driver frantically stroking his cock. I slowly and gently poke you. You are on the point of coming. I can feel you buckling. I've now got fingers in both holes and I'm rhythmically bringing you to a climax. With my free hand I slap your cheeks. Hard! You whimper and moan and gasp as you watch the Driver shoot his cum all over the seat. You shudder and jolt and cry out as you come. I turn you around and kiss you madly. Our sweat glues us together and we wrap ourselves tight around each other. We hear the Driver start up the engine and continue to our destination like nothing ever happened.

Yours lovingly, Ray.

Sean laughed out loud. Ray asked him what he was laughing at.
Sean said, "You, you cunt! And *me*! I'm as bad as you."
"What are you on about?"
"That letter I wrote for you. The porn letter to Sabrina."
"Oh, yeah, yeah … it was great."
"How did you talk me into it?"
Ray scoffed, "I bought you a drink. You should have been a porn writer, Sean. You're a natural."
Ray patted Sean on the back and headed over to the bar.
The night moves on. Hours fall away forever. Nobody mourns them passing in the private pisshead joint. It gets to eleven and Sean talks

about self-loathing. Jaws on and on and on about his lack of balls. Lines himself up in a long line of losers who let leeches suck on their life force and leave them limp with a little lucre to line their pockets with. Be gentle with me and don't forget to leave some lolly later, lover boy …

Ray says Sean is being too hard on himself. Tells him to stop beating himself up.
"You've got a beautiful wife to support, Sean. Think about her. You'll get your chance to tell the truth one day."

Sean segregates the sentence. Meditates on it. Riffs Coltrane like on: *the truth one day* … but what if he doesn't? What if he keeps cowing? What if he never gets to be truthful? Is a life without truth a wasted life? Is the truth all it's cracked up to be? Does it empower? Does it feel good? Does it feel as good as fucking? Is fucking the only truth? Is fucking and being fucked the ultimate truth and is that all there is? Is the search for truth pointless? Will truth bare only barren wastelands of anti climax? Does anyone really give a fuck if you're truthful or not?

Sean slipped back. Mused on The Why? Why he wanted to see the world. Why he wanted to see the truth and tell others about it. Why he wanted balance. Why he wanted fairness. Why he wanted to expose the madness. Why his cock got stiff when he thought about going down as a truth seeker, a man of integrity, a man of truth, a man of justice.

Sean said to Ray, "I'm a fucking fraud just like you. We're both out of work actors. We like the idea of what we supposedly do better than we like the reality. I'm just cruising. We're both just cruising." Ray hissed back, "You're a fucking bore sometimes, Sean."
"What?"
"Sometimes you're a fucking bore! Stop feeling sorry for yourself. It's not healthy. You'll end up a sad bitter old bastard. I've seen it before … look, listen, you try and that's all that matters. So what? I

mean, so what if they won't let you get your point across this time? There'll be other chances. There always is."

Sean murmurs. Murmurs contemptuous. Kills another shot. Watches Ray scoping a pretty young girl: all tits and arse and arbitrary optimism. All smiles and fuck me eyes. She's with an Old Soak who swears blind he's related to royalty. Old Soak's minted. Old Soak's got Old Money. Always throwing it around. Ray catches her attention. Old Soak digs Ray's a vampire. Ray digs Old Soak's a vampire with a different portfolio. Old Soak puts his arm around the prize pussy and turns her face towards his. She's got life in her sights. He hasn't and that's what he wants from her. Wants to cop some of the life force from her. Steal some zeal. Suck up on some sanguinity. Hit on some hope. Bask in some brightness. Delay some decay.

Old Soak's only got a couple of strokes in him. Tops. He can't satisfy hot cunt such as she. Couldn't satisfy hot cunt such as she with a sixteen inch Steely Dan strapped on. Knows it too. Knows it only too well. Fundamentally though: Only wants proximity to life. That's the crux. Pouring champagne down her neck and hoping his cock doesn't go off before he's actually entered her. That's all he wants tonight. All he needs tonight is closeness to continuation.

Ray says, "Seen her before. Hot little thing. I'll end up fucking her."
Sean says, "You can't afford her. She's got a Moet habit."
"Mmm ... depressing in here isn't it?"

Ray props going on, "We could go back to your place. I'll get a bottle. Ages since I've seen the beautiful Maria."
Sean doesn't object. They hit the stairs leading out of Gerry's. Climbing up to sodium drenched Soho Streets. Mullered moles popping up for air into the glare of jaundice yellow streetlights.

Sad Boho at the door. Pissed. Veteran of a million lonely late nights. Slobbers into intercom. Sean and The Vampire watch him. Sad Boho

breathes Vodka back draft into the tiny metal face, "Hi, Michael …
huh, I'm … huh, I'm Jim Baker's daughter. Well … I mean, I'm
not, but I've been where she's been and she's not there now and …
well … can I come in please?"

Ray laughs. Sean shakes his head. Ray knows Sad Boho, says to
him, "Larry. You're not Jim Baker's daughter. You're a sixty-year-old
man who's been known to shit in his pants in the French House on
occasions. Just tell Michael I said you're O.K."

Sad Soho Boho drops Ray's name into the intercom. Open sesame.
Sad Soho Boho disappears down into the dungeon. No thanks. No
thanks needed. Etiquette of the desperate. Staggering desperation.
In need of a fix. In need of a whiff of old Soho aristocracy. In need of
a sense of roots and belonging even if it's only fictional.

Sean and Ray cop an African Mini Cabby. "Take us home, but first
take us to an off license."

Sean scopes the Cabby. Ray chats on his cell to some soon to be
damaged young pussy. Sean stares at the Cabby's scar. Forehead
to lip. Some ritual? Some African war? Some London shit? Some
freaky fashion flip?

Ray swoops into an off license and returns with two bottles of Vodka
and orange juice. Says to Sean, "Maria doesn't like Whiskey, does
she?"
Sean smiles wry, "You're sooooooo fucking considerate, Ray."

Sean burns up a Marlboro. Cabby asks him not to smoke. Ray gives
it, "Hey, you're unlicensed. We can do whatever the fuck we like
young man. We're your employers and don't you forget it."

Sean stays schtum. Sees hate in Cabby's eyes. Original hate. Cabby
could rip them both apart without popping a cob of sweat. Cabby

stays schtum. Sean flicks the fag out the window and catches some night air. Ray jaws licentious with disembodied Pussy via Pay As You Go satellite link up.

Sean sniffs up and thinks London stinks. Stinks like a sleeping tiger at night. Sleeping tigers stink of shit and flatulence and puke and stale plasma and rotting vegetables and defeat in sleep. Tigers are only tigers when they're awake. Tigers only when they are hunting down the prey. People know this. Some people are hip to this. The Ghouls!

The Ghouls creep out and stalk the metropolis and snort up on the post climax stench of the daily rancid commerce explosion and laugh and belch and piss on the monuments to mammon and poke the tiger with sticks. The good old Ghouls: oozing out the subway sewers: on the lam from laughing houses, bums from Bedlam who think "No" is a three letter word and won't take it as an answer to their requests. ATM hangers crawling past posh penthouse fuck pads putting bad ju ju proclamations on the pampered poofs pounding pink holes up above.

Hags harboring hateful hexes on aristocrats. Rent Boys hauling their raggedy arses round and round The Circus flogging rampant STD's to randy Rim Aficionados. Uncared for Care in The Community Cases coveting coffee and codeine to keep their craziness coming on strong. Dog Fuckers and Dick Suckers dancing the macabre with The Dispossessed and The Drugged and The Death Defying and The Delirium Tremens Dispatch.

Sean eyes history streets. Streets he once dreamed of. His provincial dreaming led him here: *Where it's at!* Where it's happening! Where you make a name for yourself! Get a name: lose your self. Make your mark. Be a mark! Fuck and get fucked! It's all in the game. London the playground. A vast concrete and metal maze. Snakes and ladders. Do Not Pass Go Collect One Hundred Pounds And Go Straight To Hell!

Cabby swings down Marble Arch. Sean wonders. Does the Cabby read? Can he read? Does he watch the news between scratching out a kind of living? What brought him here? What has he seen? Did he feel what he's seen? Does he have nightmares? Are his nightmares in color? Does the blood run red or monochrome? His he numbed? What does he think about the headlines? What does he think about the subheads in the tabs: Drunk gets nine months in violin case. Survivor of Siamese twins joins parents. Iraqi head seeks arms. Prostitutes appeal to Pope. Panda mating fails; Vet takes over. Lung cancer in women mushrooms. Clinton wins on budget, but more lies ahead. Squad helps dog bite victim. Shot off woman's leg helps Sevy Ballesteros to 66. Miners refuse to work after death. Juvenile court to try shooting defendant. Stolen painting found by tree. Killer sentenced to die for second time in 10 years. Never withhold herpes infection from loved one. War dims hope for peace. Something went wrong in jet crash, experts say.

Has the scarred Cabby got a hook on it? Has he got the measure on the madness yet? Does it translate? Is the language absurd? Is London absurd? Has he left an authentic life to grub after small change? His ancestors were proud warriors. He's a fucking figure of fun! He's a figure of fucking fun ferrying fucked up piss and pussy hounds around a city of brutal indifference.

Fallen scarred warrior Cabby swings a left. Hardcore hip-hop spills from the radio. MC Legal Fiction busts a move, "Dem Alphabet Agency muthafuckaz. I ain't givin' those fake ass bitches the satisfaction o' CAPITALIZING their shit. They awl mo'fuckin' corrupt! Here dem truthful facts most people do not know, n therez ain't nuthin' but should be in its right place … da mo'fuckin' irs be not a us government agency. Dat shit be an agency o' tha imf – international mo'fuckin' monetary fund – (diversified metal products v irs et al.cv-93-405e-eje u.s.d.c.d.i., public law 94-564, senate report 94-1148 pg.5967, reorganization plan no.26, public law 102-391, n' that fake ass imf be an agency o' tha u.n.(black's law dictionary 6th ed.page 816!. Sheeiiittt! Tha United States has not had a treasury since 1921 (41 stat.ch 214 page 654) Tha u.s.treasury be naw da imf (international monetary fund) (presidential documents volume 24-no.4 page 113, 22 u.s.c.285-2887). Maaaan, wake de fuck up! Tha united states does not have any employees bcuz' there be no longa a united states! No mo' reorganizations. Afta ova 200 years o' bankruptcy dat shit be finally ova. (Executive orda 12803) tha fcc, cia, fbi, nasa n' all o' tha otha alphabet gangs were neva part o' tha u.s.government, even though da "u.s.government" held stock in da agencies.(u.s.v strang, 254 us491 lewis v.us, 680 f.2nd, 1239) social security numbers r' issued by da u.n.through da imf (international monetary fund).tha application fo' a social security numba be tha ss5 form.da department o' da treasury (imf) issues da ss5 forms n' not da social security administration.da new ss5 forms do not state who de fuck publishes 'em while da old form states they r' "department o' da treasury".(20 cfr (council on foreign relations) chap.111 subpart b.422.103 (b)).there r' no mofuckin' judicial courts in america n' have not been since 1789.judges do not enforce statutes n' codes. executive administrators enforce statutes n' codes.(frc v.ge 281 us 464 kella v.pe 261 us 428, 1 stat 138-178) there ain't been no judges in america since 1789.there have just been administrators! Accordin' ta gatt (the general agreement on tariffs n' trade) yo' must have a social security numba. (house report (103-826) Noo york city be defined in federal regulations as tha united nations. That bitch Rudolph Guiliani stated on c-span dat "noo york city be da capital o' da world." fo' once, dude told tha mo'fuckin' gospel truth. (20 cfr (council on foreign relations) chap.111, subpart b 44.103 (b) (2) (2)) social security be not insurance or a contract, nor be there a trust fund. (helverin' v.davis 301 us 619 steward co.v.davis 301 us 548) Yo' goddamn social security check comes directly from tha imf, which be an agency o' tha united nations.(it says "u.s.department o' treasury" at tha top left corner, which again be part o' tha u.n.as pointed out above) yo' own no property!!! Slaves can't own property. read carefully da deed ta da property yo' think be yours. Yo' r' listed as a tenant. (senate document 43, 73rd congress 1st session) Da wack news be we don't have ta fulfill "our" fictitious obligations. Yo' can discharge a fictitious obligation wit' another's fictitious obligation. WORD! Peace out mo'fuckerz!"

Sean spies Arab Sheiks slipping into plush petrol guzzling Chrysler People Carriers from palatial Park Lane plaza's. Ganged up sons of sons of sons of Bedouins slated for a night of coke and pussy and infidel entertainment splashing petro-dollars like Monopoly money. Shakey Sheiks tasting The Crusader Cunt because they can. Because they've won the black gold lottery and they can starve themselves for a couple of days a year and not feel bad about it all. Because they can cut off the clits of their chicks back home and come and chow down on the clits on offer over here and feel mighty good about it. Nose me up Abdul! Take that you fucking infidel whore! Mr. Stringfellow, could you introduce me to Soap Star? Praise be to Allah the merciful!

Sean catches a flash of Cabby's eyes in the rearview. They lock momentary. Alien eye contact. Two worlds colliding in cornea clash. The sacred and the profane. The old and the new. The savage and the pseudo civilized. How much hate must he have for me? Is the Cabby from cannibal stock? Would Cannibal Cabby chomp down on my liver or my heart first?

Sean's gut growls. Ticking over on empty. Ray still gabbing to Young Pussy. Sean needs to shed the silage from the amber sauce slosh out. Whiskey's sheared off the dead skin from his stomach sleeve and now's the time to shit it out.

Cabby slows to a crawl. Stops. Ray pushes a screwed up twenty in his big bad African mitt. Cabby cruises off in condemning silence. Sean and Ray hit the crib. Maria's up. Ray fixes the drinks. Sean crouches on the can and craps consommé.

Ray's radar's on Maria. Feeds her that Sean's feeling low. Fills her in on what's gone down in the afternoon. Lays it on her like he could give a fuck. Acting concerned. Methodic. Stanislavski sympathy.

Sean shits and Ray bullshits. Pours Maria a vodka vit C mix. Adds rocks. Hands her the glass slowly. Hones in on her mouth gripping the glass. Says to her, "You get better looking every time I see you, Maria. Sean's one hell of a lucky man."
Maria smiles coy-like. Says, "Why does he drink whiskey? He knows it is not good for him."
Ray says, "I tried to tell him, but you know what he's like."
"Doctor says he can have ulcer if not careful."
Ray agrees, "Sean doesn't listen to people. He's stubborn."

Sean wobbles out the water closet. Head spinning. Feels like the stuff he's just left in the lav. Flops down at his desk and clicks on his computer. Shouts to Maria, "Any calls?"
Maria says, "No, why do you drink whiskey, Sean? It is not good for you."
Sean slurs, "Just gonna check my e-mails."
"You are drunk, Sean."
Sean ignores her and opens his account.
Maria pipes up, "We have guest, Sean. You are being rude."
"Ray's not a guest, Ray's just … Ray."
Sean scours for anything on a work-orientated tip. Zilch. He opens an e-mail from a website he's recently subscribed to. Sean squints at the screen: tries hard to make sense of the mail: *In August 1992, millions of people were shocked to see photographs of a supposed Bosnian Serb death camp. You may recall those pictures. Taken by the British news station, ITN, they focused on Fikret Alic, the emaciated-looking man on the left. The mass media broadcast these pictures as supposed proof that Alic and the other Muslim men in the pictures were imprisoned behind barbed wire in a Serbian death camp.*

The pictures were broadcast worldwide. Twenty minutes after they were shown on US Television, President George Bush Sr. held a press conference to announce harsh new US measures against the Serbs. But the death camp story was a lie. The ITN crew had filmed from inside a fenced-in storage area. By shooting through the fence (composed of chicken wire with strands of barbed wire on top) ITN created footage that gave the impression that the Bosnian men were imprisoned. With a little editing, this footage was turned into pictures that gave the impression of a death camp.

By fortunate coincidence, a Serbian TV crew accompanied ITN that day, filming the same things that ITN filmed and sometimes filming the ITN crew. Using footage shot by the Serbs, 'Judgment!' proves that the people in the famous ITN pictures were refugees. Curious to see a film crew (not to mention one that had set up shop inside a tumble-down storage area) the refugees wandered over, leaned on the scraggly fence, chatted and joked with the ITN reporters. 'Judgment!' shows, step by step, how ITN took this innocent footage and edited it to create the phony death camp pictures. The "death camp" pictures were used to demonize the Serbian people as "new Nazis" and justify devastating economic sanctions and NATO military intervention, including bombing the civilian population in Yugoslavia.

Sean groans. This is too much to handle with spirits splashing about inside him. He'd get back to it on a sober keel.

Maria and Ray are chat happy. Sean lies down. Buries his head in a cushion. Ray flames two fags. Points one at Maria. She takes it between her lips and sucks. Shakes her head at Sean's state. Sean gurgles, "Just need to … close my eyes."

Ray slides onto a chair. Reaches across and pats the empty chair across from him. Maria sits. They stare at Sean. Sean's nodding off. Ray says, "He looks uncomfortable. We should get him to bed."

Maria and Ray get him to his feet and guide him up the stairs. Ray slips back down as Maria undresses and beds Sean.

Ray's fixing them drinks in the kitchen when she returns. Maria says Sean's out cold. Says she's propped him up on his side, put a bucket down in case of vomit. Ray says, "He's going to have to learn to moderate. He can't keep bingeing like this."

Maria nods in agreement. Ray hands her the vodka mix. She asks him if he wants to call a cab. Says he's in no hurry. Asks her if she wants him to leave. She says no. Says it's good to see him. It's been a while. Asks him what he's up to. He lies about the major movie. She's impressed. Ray reels off a list of stars he's planning on working with in the future. Slips her some scintillating showbiz Goss. She's warming up.

Ray mixes some more. They sup and smoke and gab alternate between showbiz and Sean. Maria goes upstairs and checks on her man. Ray slimes into the living room and slithers onto the sofa. Maria seems a little surprised to see him sofa'ed up. Ray asks after Sean. Maria says, "He just needs to sleep it off."
Awkward silence. Ray shakes his head. Furrows his brow and sighs: apropos of nada. Maria asks what's wrong.
Ray spiels, "Sean's told me all about what happened to you back in Yugoslavia, Maria. I think about it a lot. No one, nobody should have to go through what you went through."

Ray flannels forth. Cooking on gab gas. Maria's all ears, as he waxes sympathetic to her plight and that of her fellows. Ray's got his caring voice on. Got the script down to a T. Take her back to the turmoil. Tenderize. Take time. Tease out the tears. Trounce.

Rays takes turn to receive. Hears the horror. Feels nothing. Mmm's and Aaahhh's and nods and winces in all the right places. Reaches over and holds her hand. First base. Gently squeezes it. Can't wait till it's gripping his cock.

Ray pretends he needs a piss. Tippy toes into the bedroom and spies on Sean. Deep Nodland. Banshees couldn't rustle him. Ray grins ghoulish and adjusts his meat pack. *The ravishing refugee's gonna be reamed rotten tonight Raymondo Old Boy!*

Maria's boo hooing to herself. Tiny tears. Stands up when Ray enters. Ray wraps an arm around her. She apologizes. Ray tells her not to be silly. Says he shouldn't have brought her past up. He apologizes. Suggests another round. One for the road. Cap the night.

Maria sips the mix. Ray surreptitiously slips himself a Viagra. Cuddles her. She's not complaining. Conniving cocksman calculates time of arrival. Sean's comatose. It's twelve ten. He can be out of there by two. One hour fifty minutes of classy cunt capers.

Ray reiterates, "Sean's sooo lucky to have you, Maria, you're well …"
Maria fishes, "Yes? I am what? Say it."
"You're special."

Maria tells him he's such a kind and sweet man. Says he's under-standing. Compares him to her hubby copping inebriated zeds upstairs. Says she can't understand Sean sometimes. Says she loves him but she doesn't understand him. She says he needs to be more attentive towards her and stop being so into himself. Fesses up that she sees Sean as her savior but that he needs to stop singing the same song about his lack of professional satisfaction.

Ray says, "Mmm … work isn't everything."
Maria goes, "Yes, I know."
"If you were … oh this is silly."
Maria implores again, "What, Ray? Why do you keep … just say it!"
Ray simulates a sigh, hambones it something horrendous, "I really shouldn't, Maria. It's late and we've … O.K., I'll say it … if you were mine … if you were mine I wouldn't be running around trying to resurrect my career. I'd be here with you every night. Holding you … loving you."

Maria smiles at Ray: what a man! What a gentleman! A well-spoken archetypal English gentleman saying romantic things right here and right now whilst misery guts upstairs sleeps off a greedy whiskey jag. Ray registers the reaction. Maria puts her head on his chest. Hugs him. Tells him he's wonderful and that Sean's lucky to have a friend such as he. Both agree that sozzled Sean is the luckiest man in existence! He's got these two fine specimens of humanity around him and look how he repays them?

Maria makes to stand up, "I will call you a cab now, Ray."
Ray pulls her back, "One goodnight kiss, Maria. That's all I …"

Before the cad can finish she's poked her tongue in his mouth. They suck each other's lips. Maria pulls away and apologizes, "I'm sorry. I just get so lonely sometimes."

Ray says not to apologize. Says it's his fault for asking. Ray stands up. Doesn't trying hiding the boner in his trousers. Maria gasps. Blushes up brilliant red. Ray's on the apology rap again. Says he needs to sit down. Asks if it's O.K. Can't clip into a cab with a cob on. Maria's eyes are wide. Her turn to apologize. Ray says they should both stop saying sorry. Maria immediately apologizes for getting him excited.

Maria sighs. Ruffles her hair. Puts her head in her hands and groans. Says she shouldn't have had the vodka. Ray rubs the nape of her neck. Picture it: his cock's rock hard and she's perched centimeters from it. Something's gotta give ferchrisake!

Ray rubs gentle on her neck. He eyes her fleshy lips. Should I eat her first? Would it be bad manners to expect a BJ as the entrée? Maria stares hard at the hard on. It's admirable. Looks up into his eyes. They kiss. This time it's Ray doing the oral exploration. His tongue's nearly touching tonsil tissue. Maria's making tiny purrs. Ray snakes his hand down to her tit. She's holstered. He teases the nipple through cotton and lace. She's not resisting.

Ray un-holsters the titty and pulls it out of her blouse. He gently licks at the brown nip till it's perked up. Maria's pitched up a decibel on the purring. He caresses the titty a while and slowly slinks south. Maria's been expecting him. Her legs are parted. She's panting. Ray's hand snakes to the snatch. Rubs vigorous on her vag'bone, slips ever so slowly down and circles the skin hood.

Ray's tickling her clitoris and teasing it out of its hidey-hole. It's taking a while so he's gonna have to start speaking in tongues. Ray goes down. He softly splays her legs. Wider. He kneels at the temple and pulls her panties slightly apart to reveal a perfectly shaped and shaved pink vulva. *Fucking knew it!*

Maria murmurs. Ray's copping an eyeful of manna from Heaven. Food of the Gods! His appetite spurred by the wonder drug directing blood traffic to his throbbing cock. He's in with the head. Gobbling her through the cotton gusset to get the grape juice gushing. Maria belts up and blurts, "What about Sean?"
Ray mumbles. Maria loosens up. Ray stabs his tongue on and off of the clit. His finger strokes her lips. Pinky sliding in and out of puffed-up pink pussy tissue. He pulls the panties up tight: wedgie style round her A-hole. All bases covered. Lips and tongue on clit. Fingers in cunt. Cotton cauterizing her crapper.

Ray gets industrial on her: poke poke with the fingers, lick lick with the tongue and pull pull with the cotton. Maria is getting eaten good. Maria is getting noshed by a greedy gastronome. Maria's getting eaten inside out by an experienced epicurean.

Maria gets plated by Sean though. Gets head often. What she wants right now is a big hard cock. Something to fill her up. She wants horsemeat. She craves to be fucked good. Something extra, something harder. Ray's got the goods. Ray's hung. Ray's got a raging hard on. She figures it's nine inch. She's not gonna let it go to waste.

Where would her manners be? Maria grabs Ray's head and implores him to fuck her senseless in stilted English.

Sean's shagged. Coshed kip. Unconscious to his Bosnian babe getting banged by a slime ball on the sofa. Sean sleeps. The Creep's up to his nuts in Maria. Fucking the shit out of her. Sean's oblivious to Maria's grunts and groans and growls and gasps, as Ray gets grievous on her gaping wet gash. Ray renting and tearing at her twat whilst Sean naps off the liquid narcotic.
Maria swoons, "Fuck me, Ray. Fuck me hard, Ray!"

Ray strokes pro and paces his pumping. Pussy walls are tight round his meat. He's gonna come hard and she's showing no sign of insisting he pull out and throw up on her face or tits. They come together. Maria shudders and sheds a tear. She feels like shit. Ray wipes her cunt juice off with the tail of his shirt and asks her what's the matter. Asks her didn't she like it. Maria says it's not fair on Sean. Ray says life's not fair and asks her if she's got the number for a local cab co. Sean keeps snoring none the wiser.

(Of course there never was a Sarajevo, Sarajevo was a state of mind, a setting for a self piteous adventure, and Ray never fucked Maria when Sean was asleep because Maria was made up, a fantasy figure if you like, someone that Sean/"Danny" would have liked people to believe he rescued from a brutal civil war, anyway …)

Doctor A looked Lenny Prior Palmer up and down and scowled, "You look terrible."
Lenny handed her the memory of the interview with Dean and snapped, "Here, take it."
She couldn't get over his appearance, "What's wrong with you? Are you sick?"
He glowers at her, "Me? You're asking me if I'm sick! It's *you* that's sick!"

"Excuse me?"

"You've been experimenting on me!"

She frowns, "Ex … experimenting on you?"

"Don't try denying it. I've got your measure. You dragged me into the experiment you're doing on Danny. I went there. I was … transported. I saw Danny. We spoke. He told me everything!"

Doctor A shook her head, "No, you're wrong. You're confused. My only interest in you is to gather information on Danny's past. I really don't know what's happened to you but I can assure you you're not being *experimented* on. At least not by me."

"Don't fucking lie to me! I'm a detective! I know when people are lying to me."

"Calm down, please, just … just tell me what happened to you?"

Lenny simmered, he searched her eyes for clues, he lit a cigarette and slowly shook his head, "There's no other explanation."

"Of what? Honestly, I don't know what happened to you."

Lenny glared at her, she smiled at him sympathetically.

Lenny plucked up and let rip: *my mind was dragged from my body – disorientated, confused – like I was being operated on, remotely – everything around me slowly dissolved, lost my senses: sight, sound, feeling, identity – like waves of something washing over me and erasing me – like electricity, a buzzing, humming – frozen, shocked into paralysis – thought I was dying – pulled into a void, a void of images, but not images, words, thoughts creating images – difficult to explain – like a fucking dream only real –no depth, no width, just … this vast expanse – a chaos of words, but not written or spoken … just … words, words come to life, phrases, statements – wired into a grid, frustrated, couldn't comprehend, was crying in frustration – could see myself in the corner of my eye, my body where I left it – my mind stolen and sent somewhere … somewhere else … a membrane, yes a membrane. Information, but not information, a feeling of information, a sense of information – floating; scared and angry and frustrated … so frustrated. Alive but dead. Not dead not alive. A silent voice, booming, echoing, surround sound: "What was it like to wake up after having never gone to sleep?"And he was there amongst all the information. Danny was there – no body – just his … his mind … I couldn't see him. I felt him … he told me everything!*

Doctor A was shocked, an unusual feeling: shocked at Lenny's description. Shocked at the state of him. He was a wreck. Shocked that he could know so much that he couldn't possibly know. She let it sink in: the consequences of what he'd said.

If he had indeed made contact with &, her whole experiment was in jeopardy. The implications were tremendous, *no*, they were earth shattering. How could it be explained? How could she explain it? *It* couldn't! *She* couldn't!

Scenarios ran rampant in her mind. If Lenny Prior Palmer had indeed broke through all bets were now off. Anything could happen. She tried to remain cool, "And what did he tell you?"
"He told me you were playing the role of a God. He said you're trying to prove The Bible wrong by proving that the word could not be made flesh by proving the exact opposite, but that you'd fucked up. You didn't make Danny into a word, you only made him into an ampersand and now he's trapped in the collective unconscious. He's not dead and he's not alive and he's no use to anyone."

Doctor A was both elated and worried. This proved that Danny was fully aware of his state of near existence and the possibilities of Doctor A and her team using this facility were endless, but it also meant that Danny was somehow able to pull other minds into *his* state, and this could prove cataclysmic.

Doctor A gave Lenny it straight; "You need to come with me to our facility right away. This can all be very much to your benefit both physically, mentally and materially. I will help you and you'll be compensated to the point that you'll never have to worry about money ever again, Mr. Prior Palmer … it wasn't us who experimented on

you, it was Danny. I'll explain everything when we get to the facility ... I can't force you to cooperate but I *can* tell you that without me
and my team you'll be lucky to last a week before your mind turns to
mush and you become severely mentally disabled. "

Getting the Fear
Chapter Eight

Candice was stood in the rain on Oxford Street staring at a wild-eyed street Preacher as he ranted at passers by. Most of them ignored him but Candice was fascinated. Rain bounced off the rim of her hat and she listened and watched as he wound himself up into a stupor.

"You are born into this existence, this existence that was supposed to be free. Where is the freedom? God gave you the gift of life so that you could live it, but as soon as you grow up you are told that it really isn't free. You are told that nothing is free ... you are told that you have to earn a living."

At the same time in a grubby photography studio above a bakers on Old Compton Street, Charlie Coleman was tying a sixty five year old pornographer to a chair. Arnie Kaufman was a sleaze ball supreme and had been making a living photographing young men and women for years. Arnie specialized in bondage photographs, real kinky flicks that he sold by mail order all over the world. Arnie was getting a taste of his own medicine now as Charlie bound him with rope.

"Freedom of choice? Don't talk to me about freedom of choice! You really only have four choices in life ... you either earn a living, steal for a living, beg for a living or die ... that's it ... those are your choices ... these are the only choices there are."

Charlie put his face close to Arnie Kaufman's, "Now then Arnie you dirty little rotter!"

Arnie spluttered, "What are you doing to me? What do you want? I have no money!"

"You know what I want you little spunker. I want some dirty photos you took of my bird."

Charlie had been employed by Simone Edwards, a beautiful young black woman who had recently been spotted and signed by a prestigious modeling agency and was now doing flashy high fashion photo shoots. She had posed for Arnie Kaufman to earn a few bob when she first hit London and realized that you don't become a fashion model overnight. Simone wanted all photographic evidence of her sordid past erased.

Arnie was playing dumb, "I don't know what you are talking about."

"Black girl, a real stunner, they call her Simone Edwards."

"Aaah, there you see. I do not take photographs of schvartzes. There is no market for them."

"You lying little toe rag, Kaufman. I'll stripe you with my cut throat if you don't tell me where they are."

"I do not take photographs of schvartzes!"

"Listen you fucking yid. I know you took 'em. Now where are they?"

"I know bubkis about this woman you talk about."

"The gift of life? Don't make me laugh. What? Where's the gift? This is not a gift. Oh yes, that's right, God gave it to me and you took it away from me. You charged me for it, made me slave my whole life for it ... only to die at the end of it."

Charlie was turning Arnie Kaufman's studio upside down looking for the photographs. Black and white, cheap, poorly lit snaps were flying around the room. Arses and tits everywhere. Charlie stopped and flicked through a few. All the models had that same dead expression on their mugs. A song came on the radio and Charlie turned it up loud. "I'm not really a fan of music but I like this, Arnie."

Arnie was trying to make himself heard over Donovan's 'Hurdy Gurdy Man', "Stop this! I do not have these photographs!"
"Yeah, well I know you do you, Arnie. I know that you know Simone's a proper model now. I know this cos you tried touting the snaps you've got of her."

"The thing I don't get, whether you earn a living, steal for a living or beg for a living, you will always end up dead. Nobody gets out of here alive, so you're really just living to die ... the end result is always the same ... for you, not for them that are profiting from the system. The system of greed and misery ... they live a much better life than you ... and they don't die. They have a special place waiting for them in Hell! They never die; they just keep reproducing and making us their slaves. We are not free ... we are slaves! Slaves I tell you!"

Candice started to slowly clap him. The street preacher stared at her, shocked and puzzled. What was she playing at? *Nobody ever clapped him.* He opened his mouth to speak but Candice turned her back and walked into the flow of pedestrians.

Charlie Coleman pulled out his Zippo and fired it up. He started to burn some snaps of a young blonde boy being spanked by an older man, "Has anybody ever told you you're a filthy degenerate, Arnold?"
Arnie Kaufman eventually fessed up, "All right, all right already ... untie me and I'll get you them."
Charlie Coleman was having too much fun to stop immediately though, "I'm just gonna get rid of few more of these dirty pictures for you, Arnold. The Vice Squad would have a field day if they came in here ... saying that though, I bet the Vice Squad are your best customers, eh?"

Charlie hoofed up Soho. He was in his stride when out of nowhere sprang a walking *hologramadvertiser*, one of those new fangled things yet to be invented he'd never heard about.

It strode along with him at a clip spouting robotic, "Let's face it, it's good to talk, in fact it's never been more important in these times of cognitive dissonance. Talking is personal communication; it overrides the pixel, the word and the symbol. Talk doesn't need observation to exist. Talk is not quantum. Talk doesn't need a modem, postage stamp or broadband connection. Talk is instantaneous, faster than the speed of a keyboard stroke, quicker than a mighty mouse, sharper than a billion gigabyte Skype call. Talk costs nothing. Talk is the ultimate democracy of communication. Can't read? Can't write? Deaf? Dumb? Talk with your eyes, talk with your hands, talk with your expressions. Talk is mind manifest in vibration. Talk is invisible waveforms that never collapse. Talk leaves only a trace in the mind. If a man is talking to himself in a forest can anyone hear a tree fall or the flap of a butterfly's wing in Tokyo? Face it, let's, face to face, hear to ear, mouth to mind. Talk is not only words. Talk is exposure; talk is the laying bare of the soul. Talk can be anything. Talk can carry lies and bring stick & stones raining down on victims. Talk can elevate, elucidate and intimidate. Talk can record, remind and reveal. Talk can be anything you want it to be because talk is most effective in conversation. Like a Magpie, talk works best in collaboration. Talk can bring about the best and the worst in people. Talk can color or contaminate. When Vladimir & Estragon were Waiting For God(ot) they didn't play Tetris or take selfies, they talked ... and they talked ... and they talked. It mattered not that they had no audience. Talk doesn't need an audience, but sometimes it's wonderful to watch talk become an art form, witness it duel with itself, hear it bounce back and forth, hear it volley, hear it roar, hear it hit the right spot, hear it connect. To talk is to be alive and hear life affirmed in consciousness. To talk is to remind consciousness that you are still one of its vessels that has yet to become another vessel. Talk can be cheap but it can never be profane. All talk is sacred, even shit-chat or chitchat or shooting the breeze or talking shite. Nonsense is only nonsensical because we don't understand it ... if our brains were simple enough for our brains to understand it we would be too simple to understand it ...

think about it and discuss, or rather, talk. In the beginning was The Word, or rather, the sound of the word, the talk. Did a higher power talk us in existence? Who was that "higher power" talking to? Was he, she or it a schizophrenic? That's unfortunately what they would be labeled as today if they suddenly started talking to themselves in The Arndale. Conversation, the marriage of "talk" is at its most resonant when it is compassionate. There is a man on a ledge. You don't shoot him down. You "talk" him down. Talk is memory materialized. Talk can encompass the past, the now and the future instantly. Talk is both time travel and time preservation. Talk can be history defining, talk can be dangerous; talk can free the slaves or imprison the minds of millions. Talk is anything you want it to be. Talk can send a glass eye to sleep or inspire S Club 7 to reach for the stars. Talk can bring out the best or expose the worst in people ... without talk we are even more alienated in a world that can sometimes feel brutally impersonal. Thank "The Word" that there are people who are still fascinated enough to let us join the dialog and share in this magical experience we call talk."

Charlie had heard enough of the hologram. He turned and faced it square on. Without any conversation he head butted it. The hologram felt nothing but got the hint. It disappeared and reappeared somewhere else evangelizing on the power of speech. The last thing Charlie needed right now in his life was a future present heteroclite evangelist.

...

....

...

....

......

A Reader pinged Doctor A on her private Q-mail server. The note was terse, "These are the occurrences you asked me to look into. They synch with the Large Hadron Collider running (see appendix of times) and I found these all on the same E-site."

Doctor A called The Reader, "Is this from Augmented Timelines Department?"

The voice, verging on contemptuous boredom, "Augmented Timelines Department doesn't exist. It's now called Memory Reassignment Evaluations."

"Since when?"

"There was a Q-memo."

Doctor A sighed, "I didn't receive it."

"Impossible. It was bonded."

"It never landed."

A pause, "Not my problem. Anyway, you've received what you requested?"

"Yes."

"Good."

The Reader clicked off. Doctor A despised the attitude of Readers. They all had massive microchips on their shoulders. The problem was that they were all employed by The Reality Commission in Strasbourg and ultimately not answerable to anyone at CERN.

Doctor A read the disclaimer, "This article, or parts of this article, may be copied as long as no alterations are made and you mention and link to www.Metatech.org or www.Relfe.com."

She estimated the weight, sighed and sat back. "(Brazil) Have you ever experienced a glitch in the matrix? I did. It makes me wonder if we live in a simulation. Yesterday I was going to throw an empty can of coke in the trash then I just went to the kitchen to grab something, when I came back the same can was all full again. It was very shocking and still can't find explanation for it."

A tree mysteriously appeared by Winehards brewery one day. Full-grown.

———

I've also lost a cigarette, I just lit it and was making a gesture with my arms, really wildly I guess. I watched my smoke fly across the kitchen and fall in front of the fridge. It rolled under right under the middle. I said oh c—, look at that and went to get it. I looked under while on my knees. But I couldn't see it. I was given a flashlight from my brother-in-law. It was his house. I was just visiting with my favorite sister.

The flashlight didn't help. All I could see was dust and chunks of old food. I said, Marvin, I can't find it, it's not under here, what the hell? He said okay, and got on his knees but there was not even any SMOKE. He said "I say it got under, it has to be under there, don't worry I'll get it."

I was happy when he said that. I couldn't understand why I couldn't find it. This was back when I had excellent vision. He moved that damn fridge. Moved it all the way out into the middle of the kitchen damn floor. Just so you know we NEVER found it. It didn't jump up or somehow get sent up into the bowels of the underside. There was never any smoke once it rolled underneath that fridge. There was no place for it to somehow jump UP into the workings of that machine. that was plain to see. He couldn't explain it, and all i could do was apologize and ruminate over it often throughout the years. There was NO WHERE it could have hidden, no cracks in the floor, no pieces of metal for it to hide behind or under, just nothing.

Anyway, I'm SO happy I wasn't the only one there that day, I had witnesses. That way I don't break down ... and think something was wrong with ME. So I think there was some kind of black hole ... maybe a tiny one?

———

(Germany)

My glitch is very weird. Once I went to the bathroom to take a piss, when I sat, I saw a lot of things that looked like empty medicine blue capsules in my underpants. I can't imagine where these things came from. I didn't sit anywhere strange that day and I would never put med capsules inside my underpants. Earlier when I pissed, everything was normal and there wasn't anything there. So I can't imagine where this stuff came from. I just took them off. I don't have any explanation for it though. I am not kidding you, this story is very odd but I am being serious. I think I had a stupid glitch in the matrix.

——

(UK)

When I was 4, my parents took us to a picnic out of town. I wondered off and fell off a 30 feet cliff. People across the cliff saw me fall and started shouting to attract the attention of my parents. My mum could see the people shouting and pointing but she didn't know what it was all about since I was sat next to her.

After a few seconds according to my mum they got up and walked towards the cliff. People were shouting and pointing. My mum and dad looked down and they saw me at the bottom of cliff. In confusion my mum looked back but I was not where I was sat a moment ago. My dad climbed down the cliff half way and jumped down the rest of the way, thereby fracturing both his ankles. He was in hospital and then home for 3 weeks before he could walk again.

As for me? Not a scratch on me. I was just sat on a piece of flat rock crying. According to people I fell 30 feet on to hard rock. According to my mum, I was sat next to her when people were shouting. According to my dad who walked towards me with broken ankles to pick me up, there was not a scratch on me.

Mum swears I was sitting down on the picnic blanket when she got up to see what people were shouting about. As for me. I only remember walking towards the cliff by myself. Next thing I remember I was sitting on a rock and unfamiliar place, crying, not because I was hurt but frightened. I am 55 now.

——

This may sound out there, but I had a dog that would disappear and I swear she shifted dimensions or something. She was big too (golden retriever) and would literally be NOWHERE to be found and then a couple hours later she would calmly be lying on the sofa. She did this several times and I never found out where she disappeared.

——

A Redneck Writes: Have yo' cornsidered thet, as it is it impostible fo' mankind (includin' them wif modern technology) t'go back in time, o' hoof it fo'ward in time – so mankind an' their machines kinnot hoof it back an' change these Scrippures – as all min an' wimmen live in th' 'now'. So, whut is lef'? Only Our Hevvinly Pappy kin does these thin's. Eff'n so, whut is Our Hevvinly Pappy tellyng them thet haf eyes t'see, an' ears t'hear? Perhaps, Our Hevvinly Pappy is revealin' t'us, how th' wickedness in this hyar wo'ld is acshully bein' carried out in our present time; wharby them thet lo'd it on over mankind, does so wif decepshun an' lies. Perhaps, these changes is acshully terrifyin' them thet haf put themselves on over us — as it may fine be Our Hevvinly Pappy's Holy Declareeshun t'these evil an' wicked rulers, tellyng them thet their judgment will foller.

———

Driving home alone from my brother's house, I called my husband saying I was on my way. It's about a 35-minute drive, it was dark out, I hate driving alone at night. I hung up the phone, and looked up and I was at my exit! When I walked in I said didn't I just call you? He said yes, how did you get here so fast?

———

I have experienced several glitches but there is only one that I can 100% say could have been nothing else. I was sitting in front of a cigar shop and looking up at the gorgeous day we were having in the Carolinas. From where I was sitting, I could see the entire sky just about, with no buildings to obstruct the distance of the soft cloudless blue. Not a cloud for miles. And I saw an airplane flying from my right. It was slow, it would've taken it about 70 seconds or more to cross from one side of my vision to the other, but just as it hit the half way mark, I saw an attractive woman and glanced at her as she walked by and when I looked back up, the plane was gone.

It was impossible for it to have flown all the way by in that one second I looked away. Just then, a plane came into my vision once again, appearing from the far right side.

This plane flew all the way till it was out of sight, taking about 90 seconds. I even tested myself by glancing away for a moment when it was half way through its path and looked back and it was still there flying just as slow as the other plane.

I told someone about it and they just didn't seem to fathom it. If they had been there watching it with me, they would have tried to rationalize that all day, getting nowhere. It's just a reminder about the nature of this reality.

———

It happened to me a few weeks ago, I drove by a building that was gone and I was shocked that it had been torn down in such a short time. I drove past it an hour later and it was back. It was the freakiest thing I've ever seen.

———

I was sitting in my yard, which faced a state highway. I saw a woman wearing yellow pass on an old fashioned looking bicycle, she looked out of another era, and sat on the bike very straight, pedaling slowly. My husband and I watched her pass, looked at each other and said, "That was weird."
And a couple minutes later she passed again in the same direction. There was no way she went around the block, because the "block" in that rural area was miles long.

———

It can be very unnerving, about ten years ago I looked round a famous observatory; when I went back it had always been a theatre, I have read books that vanished also, had conversations with people who thought I was crazy when I met them next to talk to them. Really thought I had gone proper loopy but met a few others that experienced the same thing, my friend was at his wits end when he mended his roof to wake up the next day to find it was back to being un-repaired.
Our consciousness moves around realties, apparently there is only supposed to be a +2–2% difference within these, but most of the other movers (for want of a better word) I have met say the range is much bigger than this.
Seems we move up and down the tree of lives/consciousness but we can also move sideways as well into parallel realties, from what I can gather its related to personal growth and consciousness. Unless you've experienced it you just wouldn't believe it and then when you doubt your own sanity. Still trying to figure it all out myself,

thankfully if it weren't for the others I've met I would probably be in the loony bin.

———

I let my dog outside about 10 minutes ago. I was posting about the Heisenberg uncertainty principle on the pinned thread about the space station glitch. Then I get a local call. It's a recorded call from someone offering me a free cruise in exchange for positive word of mouth. I politely declined and hung up.

I look up and notice that my dog is inside. My dog cannot open the door he doesn't have thumbs.

———

In December I went to a movie theater that didn't exist yet. It was a regent theater. I went to see star wars: the force awakens there.

The theater closed in January for renovations. When it reopened about six months later it became the theater that I went to in December.

It is literally impossible that the theater I went to could have existed in December when it only opened in June, and it was a totally different theater in December, but I have evaluated every possibility and nuance of my memory and it happened, for better or worse. Like a bullet an insert embedded itself: *"In 1984 I went to the movies on a Sunday in the spring and saw Ghostbusters. Everybody was laughing uproariously as the film played. Everybody but me that is. In the fall, I went back to see Ghostbusters again. This time I saw it with a double feature of The Karate Kid. Again, I didn't get what everybody thought was so funny about the movie with ghosts, slime and New York. Now, decades later, I finally understand why I did not get this seminal, 1980s film. Because it never existed. Based on all the evidence regarding Ghostbusters, the original film from 1984 wasn't original at all. How could it be? It never existed. On July 15, 2016, a film called Ghostbusters will be coming to theaters. This new film is in no way related to the one that everybody thinks they saw in 1984. Forget that this film features three white people and one African American person fighting ghosts just like that film you think you saw in 1984. Also, forget that they wore the same outfits*

*and basically fought ghosts that look exactly the same. What's hard
to forget is how the secretary in the ill fated 1984 film was played by
Annie Potts, and in this new version someone thought that having
Chris Hemsworth take on this role was a both a good idea and funny."*

& hovered over the orphanage. He could see the original building
that was now a supermarket. He hung and watched consumers go
in and out, none of them ever realizing they were trading on sacred
ground. *If only ghosts could point them to the aisle where the atrocities took place. It sells tinned soups now.*

& remembered *The Firsts*: first tooth, first word, first crawl, first
shit and piss in a potty. All the firsts that went unrecorded, merely
observed by The Staff and quickly forgotten about. Nobody to cherish the moments, like fake Astronaut Stretch Armstrong's first step
on the moon never being broadcast from the TV studio. No viewers
watching the faux historic moment.

The Staff weren't paid to be surrogate parents. They were paid to
act out their duties. They were paid to monitor and keep the kids
in line: to keep them fed, clothed and free from head lice. The Staff
worked for The State for the interests of The State and only for the
interests of The State. No matter how much they pretended to care
for the little bastards and unplanned creations their duty was in
keeping the status quo.

Incest was always a problem for The Staff with the pubescent
Brothers and Sisters and Brothers and Brothers and Sisters and
Sisters under their charge. Some siblings would find much needed
comfort in exploratory sexual tenderness with their kin. It was bla-
tantly the utter starvation of any parental love that drove them to
these acts, but The Staff simply brutalized the offenders and shamed
them into curbing their yearnings.

Sex – the whole kit and caboodle of it – was a dirty word in the ecology of the orphanage, unless of course you happened to be one of The Staff, then you could prey on as many of the young cast – off's as you liked as long as you knew the rules. The paramount rule was simple: don't get caught.

Having learnt from induction that violence was the M.O. in dealing with the orphans it wasn't a big step in realizing that a culture of abuse existed, and as far as anybody knew, had always existed in orphanages. If you joined The Staff without having ever having entertained the notion of abusing children it wasn't long before you came to understand that it was no big deal. Par for the course; almost frowned upon if you didn't indulge in at least some form of abuse.

The Staff were bonded by abuse. If they weren't indulging themselves they were covering up for abusers. If – by some strange quirk of impossibility – someone joined The Staff who found it abhorrent that children were being abused they were quickly negated by The Staff and The Higher Up's. The Higher Up's had once been Staff themselves and they knew how it worked.

A vicious, circular, cancerous and contaminating culture of abuse was woven into the fabric of orphanages in the late 1960's and early 1970s. & just happened to be unlucky to be raised in one of them at that particular present past. The big difference between & and the majority of the other orphans was the fact that & knew intuitively that it wasn't supposed to be like this. & was "clever" and this made him a dangerous prospect.

The male pedophiles of Staff tended to give & a wide berth when it came to sexual abuse. This didn't mean they weren't violent with him, on the contrary, but he never suffered the sexual horrors they inflicted on other boys. These predators knew & had the confidence to blow the whistle on them. He was too willful; the sort who might take complaints outside the walls of The Orphanage, and besides, there were dozens of other young boys they could beast themselves upon who would never dream of bursting the bubble.

Unfortunately, nobody told Miss Hallet to give & a wide berth sexual abuse wise. Miss Hallet joined the orphanage from The Police force, having being booted out on account of her asthma.

Miss Hallet enjoyed working in the orphanage; as a child she had been bullied over her appearance: overweight, frumpy, a birthmark covering most of the left side of her face – now at 24 she was finally able to dish out some bullying to others.

Her indiscriminate violence eventually took on a sexual dimension when she realized how much fun fellow Staff were having in *their* abuse of the little bastards. At some point Miss Hallet decided that she would masturbate young boys. She reasoned that there was no harm in it; in fact, she was giving them a hand in developing their sexuality. The last person she should have picked on was &.

& was 14 the first time Miss Hallet tried to lay her hands on him. He was one in a long line of potential victims. She gave him the standard "if you tell anybody about this no one will believe you" pitch as she made a pass. & resisted, but this only made her more determined to engage him. It was obvious she would have to work harder to snare him.

Miss Hallet brought him cigarettes, sweets and pornographic magazines but he still refused to succumb. This only drove her into an obsessive pursuit of him. & really wanted the goodies she offered but there was no chance she was getting her mitts on him. He came up with an alternative: he would poke Miss Hallet in return for the contraband. Miss Hallet was both flattered and inspired.

She soon went from masturbator to masturbatee and & was her favorite little fingerfucker. It wasn't long before & grew resentful though;

the frigging was not only gross but also boring and the goodies she brought started dwindling in volume. As he frigged her he stared at her contorted face; eyes screwed shut, slavering mouth wide open, creased forehead, twitching nostrils. He hated her. Hated the smell of her gaping twat, hated himself for indulging her, hated the beads of sweat above her top lip, hated the fact she was so pathetic and lonely and couldn't attractive a man, hated that she had to do *this* to get her kicks. Sometimes she would flick through porn mag *Whitehouse* whilst he pleasured her. This gave & an idea.

& had started to embrace novelty and imagination to shield himself from the injustices of the orphanage. He read anything he could get his hands on and spent hours lost in everything from autobiographies to pulp romances. He would 'have a go' at anything and spice up the often mediocre texts with additions of his own. The orphanages' scant library was beginning to resemble &'s very own private graffiti stash. He would alter texts with a pencil and if satisfied erase the passages and go over them in pen. Nobody gave a fuck. Hardly anyone ever read the books. If they had they would have noticed &'s often violent and sexually charged rewrites.

He was bright beyond his years and knew that the culture of abuse in the orphanage was only bound by a code of complicit silence amongst The Staff and the weaker orphans. He decided that something had to be done. A stand *had* to be made. A stand that would afford him a "unique experience" that he could eventually write about. He had figured out that writers – no matter how great their imaginations – needed to have 'lived a little' to be convincing in their stories.

Sneaking a little red water pistol into a chemistry class was easy enough. Most of the other boys in his school were having Stanley knives and cheap Bruce Lee replica Nunchaku's confiscated on a regular basis. A measly little water pistol wasn't going to get him in trouble even if he were caught in possession of it.

& quietly and carefully filled the water pistol with sulfuric acid in chemistry class, took it back to the orphanage and waited for an opportunity …

Just as *this* Narrator was getting to the juicy bit, a Reliable Narrator blazed on to the page: "Listen to me! Pay attention. Your life and everyone you've ever known, know or will know; their life is a lie too. It's a fiction! Your life is a fiction! When you were born, your parents did what all parents do. They registered your birth with The Registrar. Not giving it a second thought, your parents automatically did what all parents do. This action was never thought of as an obligation, but rather a necessity to set you up with the best possible chance of a safe, healthy and secure life. The state would be there to provide you with the help should you need it, the NHS would be there to care for you, and all the other benefits that would result in you having a name on a birth certificate."

"Listen to me very carefully before I proceed. You are not a name. You have never been a name and you will never be a name. I'll say it again it italics: *You are not a name. You have never been a name and you will never be a name.* And again for the hard of comprehending: YOU ARE NOT A NAME. YOU HAVE NEVER BEEN A NAME AND YOU WILL NEVER BE A NAME, and here's why."

"We tacitly accept that our Birth Certificate is the first document to 'officially' exist about us, so we assume it must be one Hell of an important document; something to be looked after and viewed as having major importance; the foundation of our identity in fact. It figures that all documents which subsequently bear your name have to logically flow from the first document that was created, right? Wrong. The birth certificate is nothing to do with you. Yep. It's not even admissible as evidence of your own identity. Look at your birth certificate. Look at any birth certificate and you will see the words standing tall and proud in uppercase: WARNING. A CERTIFICATE IS NOT EVIDENCE OF IDENTITY."

"The birth certificate is also the copyright of The Crown. Think about it. This certificate is not evidence of anything regarding your identity and the copyright of the words it states is not yours either. The birth certificate is in fact a ball and chain that simply shackles you to debts that you will no doubt accumulate over your life span. It is nothing more than a fictitious document that imprisons by decree from The Creators of Money: another fictitious creation that has the power of the law on its side and can throw you in jail indefinitely for not 'believing' in it."

"Every bill, every debt, every invoice and every account which you 'believe' is for you is simply a page from the fiction. These 'debts' you believe in are nothing to do with *you*. How can they be? How can they be if the foundational document which carries 'your name' actively denies the fact?"

"Mine, yours and everyone else's Birth Certificates are simply a fictional, legally binding agreement we are voluntarily thrust into that ensures we become part of the novel for our entire lives. It's simple: You are not a name. You have never been a name and you will never be a name."

"You really need to dwell and ponder on this. Look: the first 18 years of your life were spent learning that your identity starts with a name. You are John Doe. You are Jane Doe. You are addressed by your 'name', you answer to it, you see it on paper, you sign your name and this *is* you. You accumulate documents and passports and licenses and certificates with *your name* on them. You identify with your name more than anything else about yourself. But all this accumulation and identification is wrong. W.r.o.n.g. None of these documents are yours. Go and check all your 'identity' documents and you'll see that they are all the property of someone else, usually The Crown or Government, and can be recalled at any time leaving you without an identity."

"We are all trapped in an incredibly capacious fiction that there is no escape from until we *all* realize we are trapped. Societies for generations have been hoodwinked into playing characters in a living novel being written by a handful of all-powerful usurious Money Creators with denouements to chapters to suit their interests. This is achieved by smoke and mirrors, threat of physical violence and incarceration, sleight of hand, cunning wordplay, semantics and the illusion of inclusion. The more 'successful' a 'name' is in life, the less willing they are to consider the concept that underpins their very existence and identity. What harm has it done them? They are part of the club. They are accepted and they enjoy the material by-products that the money system creates."

"But you cannot 'own' anything in life. You don't even own your name. Money is created out of thin air and used by our Rulers to keep us under control and in servitude to their fictitious narrative. The Money Creators 'own' the money and they simply lease it to us to conduct our personal lives and stories around. This process that allows the government to legally claim you as a corporation involves the creation of a fictitious you, which is the name written in all CAPITAL LETTERS. This legal name was created shortly after you were born and was recorded on a bond. This bond that represents the date of your birth is known as your birth certificate."

The Reliable Narrator vanished in a puff of extreme echo. His words trailed in sonic booms: "Like your legal name, the government is also not real because it is a corporation. A corporation is "an artificial person or legal entity created by or under the authority of the laws of a state." Because The Government is a corporation (artificial person), it is a fictitious entity that has no natural rights and power. Its source of power comes from 'your' compliance in abiding by its ficticious laws for of fear of being erased from the narrative. Authors in the pockets of the usurious Money Creators write these 'laws'. Because these governments and Crowns are corporations or fictitious persons, they cannot think, speak, see, touch, smell, or do anything that a living person can do. As a result, The Government can only operate in a fictional world. A fictional world in which we are both the characters and readers of a diabolical novel, but never the authors, purely because we weren't born into the family of usurers."

Back at the orphanage in the present past and before the rude interruption, & was furiously frigging Miss Hallet as she devoured *Readers Wives* magazine with her greedy eyes. Everyday sluts and whores and commonplace exhibitionist harlots filled her retinas as they posed wide open on cheap floral duvets and PVC sofas and MC Escheresque threadbare carpets in front of small gas fires housed in frames of chipped ceramic tiles. Some of the women had their eyes covered with black bars of print, which only added more mystery to the humdrum erotica.

& quickly pulled out his sulfuric acid loaded water pistol and placed it strategically at the mouth of Miss Hallet's sopping twat. Deftly he removed his fingers and fired the pistol deep into her.

She groaned and barked, "No, no! Don't stop! I'm there! I'm nearly there!"
& stood up and stepped back, Miss Hallet's fingers darted to her cunt and continued frigging. When the scream came it came from deep inside her. Deeper than any fingers or cock or dildo or banana could ever reach.

Every nerve in Miss Hallet's body rioted in synch with revolting accuracy. Her bowels and bladder simultaneously evacuated and her temperature soared to unimaginable heights. She shook and shimmied and writhed across the floor lubed by her own piss and shit as the acid ate away at her vaginal walls and munched slowly towards her internal organs. Her scream alerted Fellow Staff. They rushed in to find her convulsing and tearing at her naked groin with gusto in a pool of – supposedly – her own excrement. & looked on impassively as Staff rallied around Miss Hallet.

& quickly lobbed his water pistol out of the window but all eyes were on Miss Hallet. Her screams were now hoarse and labored as projectile vomit sprayed from her mouth with every brief exhalation. Pan stalked the room and weighed up the scene. He began dancing a merry jig as he blasted out a tune on his flute, his cock standing erect and his cloven hooves tapping along in time to the demonium.

Miss Hallet was dragged to hospital by a couple of confused Staff. Every second counted as the acid began to sculpt her nether regions into a visceral post-modern creation that Doctor Moreau could never have conceived even in his wildest imaginings.

Miss Hallet was induced into a coma and worked upon frantically by surgeons. Surgeons who quickly discovered that sulfuric acid was the cause of her agony and internal remodeling. They couldn't wait to stabilize her and hear the excuse she would give for how exactly the liquid had entered her twot.

After twelve hours of surgery they had saved her life but left her reproductive organs about as 'reproductive' as a gay Panda. She would spend the rest of her life pissing and shitting into plastic bags and would never feel any sensation in her condemned cunt ever again.

As Miss Hallet nodded oblivious post-op & was grilled by Senior Staff and Management as to what had occurred. & took the 5th. They pressed and threatened all kinds of repercussions if he didn't spill about 'Acidgate', but & kept schtum. It wasn't difficult to work out what had happened.

When Miss Hallet managed to reach a certain degree of lucidity her bosses and fellow staff members persuaded her to admit she had put sulfuric acid inside herself. They reasoned, how could she tell the truth; "I was being frigged by an orphan who took exception and fired a water pistol full of acid up my cunt."

Miss Hallet coughed up to the doctors that it was all her doing. When they pressed her and asked why, she simply replied that she wanted to know what it would feel like. They immediately sectioned her under the mental health act. Within six weeks of being sectioned her already traumatized mind finally cracked and she was diagnosed as a paranoid schizophrenic.

& was never touched again or forced to touch others. The abuse continued of course, only this time with a caveat for the abusers to beware of creative revenge attacks. & was proud of his attack and in the present future he would use the experience to influence an American recidivist called Mike Bloody Valentine.

& slipped into the mezzanine of Dead Peoples Dreams. The 'bodies' wore neon nametags and they naturally filled the undefined space, almost creating the illusion that they had been born and had died to solely execute this position. Some had been arranged in sitting gestures but most were sprawled across the undulating floor. & tip toed across the waves and clocked names, nicknames and pseu-do-names. Of course he knew that these weren't real corpses. Real corpses rotted. These were manifest dreams of corpses. Corpses who refused to give up the ghost. Inanimate meat parcels projected into non-existence by inanimate corpses; waxy appropriations of spent material life.

The Ego Death Squad were picketing the mezzanine. They waved placards, yelled through bullhorns and chanted disrespectful ditties at the fake corpses. A neu news bulletin from our affiliate Breaking Knees gatecrashed the passage:

THEORETICAL Quantum Physicist Dr. Gunter Reflek admitted today that he, and his peers, have absolutely 'no fucking idea' what they're doing, and claims they were no nearer than prehistoric man to figuring out the Universe.
"We have been just winging it to tell you the truth," explained the

77-year-old in an exclusive interview with ABC. "Seriously, I haven't a clue what's going on. Either does anyone else in my field. We keep proving stuff that never actually happened".

"Our cover is blown, what can I say? He added.

Dr. Reflek's comments came after yet another alleged breakthrough in quantum mechanics, which claims the universe has existed forever, as opposed to being created by a 'big bang'.

"Over the years there have been just a handful of us pretending to know something about the universe that no one else does," he went on. "But this is all lies to feed the charade. I've had some great times during the years; traveling the world, and giving talks on our pretend finds".

When asked how he got away with it for so long, he replied: "I found out a long time ago that everything can be proven with a mathematical equation. Now, I mean everything; from unicorns, fire-breathing dragons, God and even the G-spot. None of it is true. Me and the handful that know the truth have been riding the Quantum Physicist celebrity wave for quite some time now, but it must end – before someone gets hurt".

The University of PuffNstuff professor warned that the European Organization for Nuclear Research, known as CERN, could potentially wipe out the entire planet if the project is not put to a halt.

"Seriously, when myself, Higgs and Ben (Benjamin Lockspeiser CERN's first president) first pitched the idea, we never thought it would get funding. It was gonna cost billions for Christ's sake," he recalled. "Fuck knows what the thing does – no one does. Firing particles at each other at the speed of light can't end well. I'm just worried now we took the joke too far".

Ending the interview, professor Reflek apologized for "spoofing" everybody over the years, "I'm coming near the end of my days now and I just want to get this off my chest," he said. "I just hope the world can forgive us".

Getting the Fear
Chapter Nine

Griff had been living on Ibiza for ten years. He was 38 and looked like a hippy and sounded like a hippy and lived like a hippy but he didn't like 'labels'. If push came to shove he would have to call himself simply a free spirit. He was Welsh and had come to the island to be with his 'chick', Samantha, another free spirit who had given up on the material life to devote herself to the spiritual. They lived a very basic life paid for by Griff's part time job repairing boats.

Jack and Captain Torres met him outside his shack in a tiny village on the coast. Griff was suspicious of Jack, "Scotland Yard, eh? Not often we get British pigs on the island."
Jack bit his lip, "What do you know about the victims?"
Griff smiled and lit a joint; Jack stared at it and looked at Captain Torres. Captain Torres clocked it but simply shrugged.
Griff toked on it and grinned, "It's not illegal on Ibiza ... *yet.*"
Jack could see that Griff was getting a real kick out of this and he snapped, "Do you have anything to tell us or not, Mr. Griffin?"
"Just Griff, man. I'm not a mister."
"All right 'Griff'."
Captain Torres turned to Jack, "Like I said, Mr. Jack. Griff called us when you were flying out here."
Griff exhaled, "Soon as I heard about what happened at the villa. I was shocked, couldn't believe it, man."
Jack pulled out his cigarettes, "So you met them?"

"Yeah …" Griff offered the joint to Jack, "You should try some o' this, man. Cigarettes are bad for your health."

Jack glared at him and lit his Capstan, "Go on. You met them when?"

"I do some work for Oscar Martinez when I can be bothered. Oscar's got a few boats that he hires out. I hired a boat out to those poor cats that were staying at the villa."

Captain Torres was intrigued, "When? When you do this?"

Griff shrugged, "About a week, ten days back. I can't remember exactly. Timekeeping's not really my thing. Did enough of that back in the UK."

Jack followed up, "Why did they want a boat? Where were they going?"

Griff turned and pointed to a small rock formation island just off the coast, "Tagomago."

Jack turned to Captain Torres, "What's on that island?"

Captain Torres hunched his shoulders up and put his hands together, "Nada. Nothing. Lots of lizards."

Griff shook his head, "No, people go there, man. Not lots of people but there have been some communes there."

Jack coughed; the Capstan Full Strength's really didn't suit this climate, "Communes? What do you mean by 'communes'"?

"You know, man … just dudes and cats and babes getting together and being in the now."

Jack sighed, "Hippies and beatniks, Griff? Free love n' all that malarkey, eh?"

Captain Torres frowned, "It is news to me that people are staying on Tagomago."

Griff smiled at Captain Torres, "Hey Captain, there's lots of things happen on Ibiza that you guys don't know about."

Captain Torres instantly got the insinuation and moved in closer on Griff, "Yes? What is it that you mean?"

Griff put his hands up in mock surrender, "Hey, man. Like, I don't mean anything illegal or anything. I just mean, you know, people come here to do what they feel like. That's why they come … nobody gets hurt, man."

Jack chewed his bottom lip, "Nobody gets hurt? What about the slaughter at the villa? Come down to the morgue with us and *then* say that."

"Hey, man. Calm down ... I mean, you know, *usually* nobody gets hurt. It's not cool what happened to those cats, man. Nobody was more upset about it than Samantha and me. We were horrified. This isn't what Ibiza's about, dig?"

Jack had got Griff's measure. He was simply another man who liked to try get a rise out of the authorities. Jack had met thousands of them. He had also learnt how to tell the good guys from the bad guys. Bad guys *always* look you in the eyes. Griff wasn't a bad guy, he was just a harmless poseur who saw himself as a bit of rebel and liked to cultivate the outsider image. Griff was definitely not murderer material. Jack stubbed his cigarette out, "So Griff ... you hired a boat to these people ... you didn't get their names did you?"

"As it happens I did, yeah. There was Thomas and Greta and then there was James and Claude."

None of the names matched those of the passports but Jack continued, "That's only four of them, Griff."

"I didn't catch the other two's names."

Jack looked at Captain Torres, hoping that he had picked up on the names not matching. He had. Captain Torres glanced at Jack and then looked at Griff, "And you are sure that these were their names, Mr. Griff?"

Griff nodded his head, "Oh yeah, man. Positive." Griff sensed that something wasn't right, "Why?"

Captain Torres smiled at him, "Oh, it is nothing, we are just wanting to be sure."

Jack cut in, "Did they have anything with them when they went over to that island?"

"I couldn't tell you, man. I only hired the boats to them. As far as I know they went over at night ... like what?"

Jack paused and thought about how to phrase it, "Like ... you never saw them with anything ... I don't know ... odd?"

Griff frowned, "Odd?"

Jack continued, "I mean anything out of the ordinary."

"No. They just paid me the money and, well, the boats were anchored so they came and went as they pleased. I passed the dough on to Oscar's daughter and that was that."

Captain Torres stroked his moustache, "What kind of people were they, Mr. Griff?"

Griff thought about it, "You know … just ordinary … nice people really … straight. Very straight, man."

Jack picked up on it, "What do you mean by 'straight', Griff?"

Griff relit his joint and sucked on it, "You know, run of the mill, everyday people. They weren't the free spirit kind."

Captain Torres nodded his head, "So they were not hippies like you, Mr. Griff?"

Griff chuckled; the dope was mellowing him now, "Aaahh, no Captain Torres. Definitely not."

Captain Torres told Griff that he would need to speak to him again. That was fine, Griff was going nowhere. Captain Torres drove Jack back to his station. Jack was getting used to the roads and had learned that if he put his left leg slightly out of the doorframe of the jeep the shocks weren't as bad.

"What do you think of him, Captain Ernesto?"

Captain Torres grinned, "Mr. Griff? He is what you call a character, yes?"

"He got their names wrong. Or they gave him the wrong names."

"Aaahhh … pseudo names, yes?"

Jack smiled and thought better of correcting him. Jack was impressed with Captain Torres English so far. Captain Torres explained that he had studied English on the mainland before becoming a cop, "I love the Englishers. I wanted to come to your country to work at one time."

"Why didn't you?"

Captain Torres threw his hand up, "Look at this island … I could never leave it. I know all about your English weather."

"It's not *always* raining and foggy. We do have summers ... sometimes."

Jack called Scotland Yard from the station. Captain Torres watched him and could see that he was becoming increasingly frustrated. Jack put the phone down and slowly turned to him, "They're saying these people don't exist."

"Don't exist?"

Jack dragged hard on his cigarette, "No record of them. The names don't match the dates of birth or the addresses."

Captain Torres was perplexed, "But-"

"They've checked with Germany and France. Interpol has checked. They're saying-"

"There must be some mistake, Mr. Jack! They can check again, yes?"

"You heard me, Captain Ernesto. I asked ... what could I do?"

Captain Torres paced, "No, no, this can not be right. We have the bodies and we have the Pasaporte."

"They could be fake passports."

Captain Torres mulled on it, "But why, Mr. Jack? Why fake?"

Jack headed out, "Let's go back to the morgue."

Jack and Captain Torres matched the likeness of the faces of corpses to the passport photographs with the help of the coroner's assistant. Everything matched. Jack and Captain Torres stared at each other. Captain Torres slapped his forehead and Jack shook his head.

The coroner rushed in and apologized for being late. He closed in on Captain Torres, "He encontrado lo que parecen ser las iniciales de los organismos."

Jack frowned as he watched Captain Torres speak to the Coroner in their native tongue, "What is it, Captain Ernesto?"

The coroner and his assistant turned one of the corpses on its side.

The coroner guided Captain Torres towards a patch of flesh. Jack moved in and they all stared at what could only be described as initials carved into the flesh.

Captain Torres exhaled, "Oh, Dios mío! ¿qué diablos está pasando!" Jack closed in on Captain Torres and put his hand on his shoulder, "What is it? What are you saying?"
"These marks have been cut into all the bodies, Mr. Jack."
"Tell him to show me."

The coroner showed Jack the initials carved into the rest of the corpses. Jack's jaw dropped and he lit a cigarette, much to the protestation of the Coroner.

Jack's brow creased and he murmured, "CC?"
. . . .
. . .
. . .
. . . .
. . .

& was dragged into action by one of the many Rewriters at CERN. A transcript of a taped interview had made its way on to the Internet. The Rewriters decided to have some fun with it. They would replace "and" with & and occasionally inject broad Irish dialect in to the transcript to make it look inauthentic, causing readers to question its validity. It fitted into the Rewriter's Revelation Of The Method Code Of Conduct but would clearly deter many from believing any of it. & didn't object. There was no point. He simply let himself be used.

Note: This is a transcript of three tapes on the "New Order of Barbarians", referred to on the tapes simply as the "new world system." Tapes one and two were recorded in 1988 and are the recollections of Dr. Lawrence Dunegan regarding a lecture he attended on

312

March 20, 1969 at a meeting of the Pittsburgh Pediatric Society. The lecturer at that gathering of pediatricians (identified in tape three recorded in 1991) was a Dr. Richard Day (who died in 1989). At the time Dr. Day was Professor of Pediatrics at Mount Sinai Medical School in New York. Previously he had served as Medical Director of Planned Parenthood Federation of America. Dr. Dunegan was formerly a student of Dr. Day at the University of Pittsburgh and was well acquainted with him, though not intimately. He describes Dr. Day as an insider of the "Order" and although Dr. Dunegan's memory was somewhat dimmed by the intervening years; he is able to provide enough details of the lecture to enable any enlightened person to discern the real purposes behind the trends of our time. This is a transcript of a loose, conversational monologue that makes for better listening than reading, so obviously that's why they are included here.

Tape I
IS THERE A POWER, A FORCE OR A GROUP OF MEN ORGANIZING & REDIRECTING CHANGE?

There has been much written, & much said, by some people who have looked at all the changes that have occurred in American society in the past 20 years or so, & who have looked retrospectively to earlier history of the United States, & indeed, of the world, & come to the conclusion that there is a conspiracy of sorts which influences, indeed controls. Major historical events, not only in the United States, but also around the world. This conspiratorial interpretation of history is based on people making observations from the outside, gathering evidence & coming to the conclusion that from the outside they see a conspiracy. Their evidence & conclusions are based on evidence gathered in retrospect. Period. I want to now describe what I heard from a speaker in 1969, which in several weeks will now be 20 years ago. The speaker did not speak in terms of retrospect, but rather predicting changes that would be brought about in the future. The speaker was not looking from the outside in, thinking that he saw conspiracy, rather, he was on the inside, admitting that, indeed, there was an organized power, force, group of men, who wielded enough influence to determine major events involving countries around the world. & he predicted, or rather expounded on, changes that were planned for the remainder of this century. As you listen, if you can recall the situation, at least in the United States in 1969 & the few years there after, & then recall the kinds of changes which have occurred between then & now, almost 20 years later, I believe you will be impressed with the degree to which the things that were planned to be brought about have already been accomplished. Some of the things that were discussed were not intended to be accomplished yet by 1988. [Note: the year of this recording] but are intended to be accomplished before the end of this century. There is a timetable; & it was during this session that some of the elements of the timetable were brought out. Anyone who recalls early in the days of the Kennedy Presidency ... the Kennedy campaign ... when he spoke of ... Progress in the decade of the 60's": that was kind of a cliché in those days – "the decade of the 60's." Well, by 1969 our speaker was talking about the decade of the 70's, the decade of the 80's, & the decade of the 90's. So that ... I think that terminology that we are looking at ... looking at things & expressing things, probably all comes from the same source. Prior to that time I don't remember anybody saying "the decade of the 40's & the decade of the 50's. So I think this overall plan & timetable had taken important shape with more predictability to those who control it, sometime in the late 50's. That's speculation on my part. In any event, the speaker said that his purpose was to tell us about changes, which would be brought about in the next 30 years or so ... so that an entirely new world-wide system would be in operation before the turn of the century. As he put it, "We plan to enter the 21st Century with a running start."

"PEOPLE WILL HAVE TO GET USED TO CHANGE ..."

Somewhere in the introductory remarks he insisted that nobody have a tape recorder & that nobody take notes, which for a professor was a very remarkable kind of thing to expect from an audience. Something in his remarks suggested that there could be negative repercussions against him if his ... if it became widely known what he was about to say to ... to our group ... if it became widely known that indeed he had spilled the beans, so to speak. When I heard first that, I thought maybe that was sort of an ego trip, somebody enhancing his own importance. But as the revelations unfolded, I began to underst& why he might have had some concern about not having it widely known what was said, although this ... although this was a fairly public forum where he was speaking, (where the) remarks were delivered. But, nonetheless, he asked that no notes be taken ... no tape recording is used: suggesting there might be some personal danger to himself if these revelations were widely publicized. Again, as the remarks began to unfold, & saw the rather outrageous things that were said ... at that time they certainly seemed outrageous ... I made it a point to try to remember as much of what he said as I could, & during the subsequent weeks & months, & years, to connect my recollections to simple events around me ... both to aid my memory for the future, in case I wanted to do what I'm doing now – record this. & also, to try to maintain a perspective on what would be developing, if indeed, it followed the predicted pattern – which it has! At this point, so that I don't forget to include it later, I'll just include some statements that were made from time to time throughout the presentation ... just having a general bearing on the whole presentation. One of the statements was having to do with change. People get used ... the statement was, "People will have to get used to the idea of change, so used to change, that they'll be expecting change. Nothing will be permanent." This often came out in the context of a society of ... where people seemed to have no roots or moorings, but would be passively willing to accept change simply because it was all they had ever known. This was sort of in contrast to generations of people up until this time where certain things you expected to be, & remain in place as reference points for your life. So change was to be brought about, change was to be anticipated & expected, & accepted, no questions asked. Another comment that was made ... from time to time during the presentation ... was. "People are too trusting, people don't ask the right questions." Sometimes, being too trusting was equated with being too dumb. But sometimes when … when he would say that & say, "People don't ask the right questions," it was almost with a sense of regret … as if he were uneasy with what he was part of, & wished that people would challenge it & maybe not be so trusting.

THE REAL & THE STATED GOALS

Another comment that was repeated from time to time, … this particularly in relation to changing laws & customs, … & specific changes, … he said, "Everything has two purposes. One is the ostensible purpose which will make it acceptable to people & second is the real purpose which would further the goals of establishing the new system & having it," Frequently he would say, "There is just no other way, There's just no other way!" This seemed to come as a sort of an apology, particularly when … at the conclusion of describing some particularly offensive changes. For example, the promotion of drug addiction, which we'll get into shortly.

POPULATION CONTROL

He was very active with population control groups, the population control movement, & population control was really the entry point into specifics following the introduction. He said the population is growing too fast. Numbers of people living at any one time on the planet must be limited or we will run out of space to live. We will outgrow our food supply & we will over-populate the world with our waste.

ENCOURAGING HOMOSEXUALITY. ANYTHING GOES HOMOSEXUALITY ALSO WAS TO BE ENCOURAGED.

"People will be given permission to be homosexual," that's the way it was stated. They won't have to hide it. & elderly people will be encouraged to continue to have active sex lives into the very old ages, just as long as they can. Everyone will be given permission to have sex, to enjoy however they want. Anything goes. This is the way it was put. &, I remember thinking, "how arrogant for this individual, or whoever he represents, to feel that they can give or withhold permission for people to do things!" But that was the terminology that was used. In this regard, clothing was mentioned. Clothing styles would be made more stimulating & provocative. Recall back in 1969 was the time of the mini skirt, when those mini-skirts were very, very high & very revealing. He said, "It is not just the amount of skin that is expressed ... exposed that makes clothing sexually seductive, but other, more subtle things are often suggestive." ... things like movement, & the cut of clothing, & the kind of fabric, the positioning of accessories on the clothing. "If a woman has an attractive body, why should she not show it?" was one of the statements. There was not detail on what was meant by "provocative clothing," but since that time if you watched the change in clothing styles, blue jeans are cut in a way that they're more tightly fitting in the crotch. They form wrinkles. Wrinkles are essentially arrows. Lines, which direct one's vision to certain anatomic areas. & this was around the time of the "burn your bra" activity. He indicated that a lot of women should not go without a bra. They need a bra to be attractive, so instead of banning bras & burning them, bras would come back. But they would be thinner & softer allowing more natural movement. It was not specifically stated, but certainly a very thin bra is much more revealing of the nipple & what else is underneath, than the heavier bras that were in style up to that time.

TECHNOLOGY

Earlier he said ... sex & reproduction would be separated. You would have sex without reproduction & then technology was reproduction without sex. This would be done in the laboratory. He indicated that already much, much research was underway about making babies in the laboratory. There was some elaboration on that, but I don't remember the details. How much of that technology has come to my attention since that time, I don't remember ... I don't remember in a way that I can distinguish what was said from what I subsequently have learned as general medical information.

BLENDING ALL RELIGIONS … THE OLD RELIGIONS WILL HAVE TO GO

Another area of discussion was Religion. This is an avowed atheist speaking & he said, "Religion is not necessarily bad. A lot of people seem to need religion, with its mysteries & rituals – so they will have religion. But the major religions of today have to be changed because they are not compatible with the changes to come. The old religions will have to go. Especially Christianity. Once the Roman Catholic Church is brought down, the rest of Christianity will follow easily. Then a new religion can be accepted for use all over the world. It will incorporate something from all of the old ones to make it easier for people to accept it, & feel at home in it. Most people won't be too concerned with religion. They will realize that they don't need it.

CHANGING THE BIBLE THROUGH REVISIONS OF KEY WORDS

In order to do this, the Bible will be changed. It will be rewritten to fit the new religion. Gradually, key words will be replaced with new words having various shades of meaning. Then the meaning attached to the new word can be close to the old word – & as time goes on, other shades of meaning of that word can be emphasized. & then gradually that word replaced with another word." I don't know if I'm making that clear. But the idea is that everything in Scripture needs not be rewritten, just keywords replaced by other words. & the variability in meaning attached to any word can be used as a tool to change the entire meaning of Scripture, & therefore make it acceptable to this new religion. Most people won't know the difference; & this was another one of the times where he said, "the few who do notice the difference won't be enough to matter."

RESTRUCTURING EDUCATION AS A TOOL OF INDOCTRINATION

Another area of discussion was Education. & one of the things; in connection with education that remember connecting with what he said about religion was in addition to changing the Bible he said that the classics in Literature would be changed. I seem to recall Mark Twain's writings were given as one example. But he said, the casual reader reading a revised version of a classic would never even suspect that there was any change. &, somebody would have to go through word by word to even recognize that any change was made in these classics, the changes would be so subtle. But the changes would be such as to promote the acceptability of the new system.

SOME BOOKS WOULD JUST DISAPPEAR FROM THE LIBRARIES

In addition to revising the classics, which I eluded to a while ago ... with revising the Bible, he said, "some books would just disappear from the libraries." This was in the vein that some books contain information or contain ideas that should not be kept around. & therefore, those books would disappear. I don't remember exactly if he said how this was to be accomplished. But I seem to recall carrying away this idea that this would include thefts. That certain people would be designated to go to certain libraries & pick up certain books & just get rid of them. Not necessarily as a matter of policy – just simply steal it. Further down the line, not everybody will be allowed to own books. & some books nobody will be allowed to own.

NO MORE SECURITY

Nothing is permanent. Streets would be rerouted, renamed. Areas you had not seen in a while would become unfamiliar. Among other things, this would contribute to older people feeling that it was time to move on; they feel they couldn't even keep up with the changes in areas that were once familiar. Buildings would be allowed to st& empty & deteriorate, & streets would be allowed to deteriorate in certain localities. The purpose of this was to provide the jungle, the depressed atmosphere for the unfit. Somewhere in this same connection he mentioned that buildings & bridges would be made so that they would collapse after a while, there would be more accidents involving airplanes & railroads & automobiles. All of this to contribute to the feeling of insecurity, that nothing was safe. Not too long after this presentation, & I think one or two even before in the area where I live, we had some newly constructed bridge to break; another newly constructed bridge defect discovered before it broke, & I remember reading just scattered incidents around the country where shopping malls would fall in right where they were filled with shoppers, & Oi mind dat wan av de messages malls in our area, de first buildin' I'd ever been in wha yer cud fale dis vibrashun throughoyt de entire buildin' whaen dare were lashings av people in dare & I remember wondering at that time whether this shopping mall was one of the buildings he was talking about. Talking to construction people & architects about it they would say ' "Oh no, that's good when the building vibrates like that, that means it's flexible not rigid." Well, maybe so, we'll wait & see. Other areas there would be well maintained. Not every part of the city would be slums.

SHIFTING POPULATIONS & ECONOMIES – TEARING THE SOCIAL ROOTS

& along this line there were talks about people losing their jobs as a result of industry & opportunities for retraining, & particularly population shifts would be brought about. This is sort of an aside. I think I'll explore the aside before I forget it – population shifts were to be brought about so that people would be tending to move into the Sun Belt. They would be sort of people without roots in their new locations, & traditions are easier to change in a place where there are a lot of transplanted people, as compared to trying to change traditions in a place where people grew up & had an extended family, where they had roots. Things like new medical care systems, if yer peck up from a northeast industrial city & yer transplant yerself ter de south sunbelt or southwest, you'll be more accepting of whatever kind of, for example, controlled medical care you find there than you would accept a change in the medical care system where you had roots & the support of your family. Also in this vein it was mentioned (he used the plural personal pronoun we) we take control first of the port cities – New York, San Francisco, Seattle – the idea being that this is a piece of strategy, the idea being that if you control the port cities with your philosophy & your way of life, the heartl& in between has to yield. I can't elaborate more on that but it is interesting. If you look around the most liberal areas of the country & progressively so are the seacoast cities. The heartl&, the Midwest, does seem to have maintained its conservatism. But as you take away industry & jobs & relocate people then this is a strategy to break down conservatism. When you take away industry & people are unemployed & poor they will accept whatever change seems to offer them survival, & their morals & their commitment to things will all give way to survival. That's not my philosophy, that's the speaker's philosophy. Anyhow, going back to industry, some heavy industry would remain, just enough to maintain a sort of a seedbed of industrial skills which could be exp&ed if the plan didn't work out as it was intended. So the country would not be devoid of assets & skills. But this was just sort of a contingency plan. It was hoped & expected that the worldwide specialization would be carried on. But, perhaps repeating myself, one of the upshots of all of this is that with this global interdependence the national identities would tend to be de-emphasized. Each area depended on every other area for one or another elements of its life. We would all become citizens of the world rather than citizens of any one country.

FALSIFIED SCIENTIFIC RESEARCH

Somewhere in this connection, then, was the statement admitting that some scientific research data could be – & indeed has been – falsified in order to bring about desired results. & here was said, "People don't ask the right questions. Some people are too trusting." Now this was an interesting statement because the speaker & the audience all being doctors of medicine & supposedly very objectively, dispassionately scientific & science being the be all & end-all ... well to falsify scientific research data in that setting is like blasphemy in the church ... you just don't do that. Anyhow, out of all of this was to come the New International Governing Body, probably to come through the U.N. & with a World Court, but not necessarily through those structures. It could be brought about in other ways. Acceptance of U.N. at that time was seen as not being as wide as was hoped. Efforts would continue to give the United Nations increasing importance. People would be more & more used to the idea of relinquishing some national sovereignty. Economic interdependence would foster this goal from a peaceful st&point. Avoidance of war would foster it from the st&point of worrying about hostilities. It was recognized that doing it peaceably was better than doing it by war. It was stated at this point that war was "obsolete." I thought that was an interesting phrase because obsolete means something that once was seen as useful is no longer useful. But war is obsolete ... this being because of the nuclear bombs war is no longer controllable. Formerly wars could be controlled, but if nuclear weapons would fall into the wrong h&s there could be an unintended nuclear disaster. It was not stated who the "wrong h&s" are. We were free to infer that maybe this meant terrorists, but in more recent years I'm wondering whether the wrong h&s might also include people that we've assumed that they've had nuclear weapons all along ... maybe they don't have them. Just as it was stated that industry would be preserved in the United States – a little bit just in case the world wide plans didn't work out; just in case some country or some other powerful person decided to bolt from the pack & go his own way, one wonders whether this might also be true with nuclear weapons. When you hear that ... he said they might fall into the wrong h&s, there was some statement that the possession of nuclear weapons had been tightly controlled, sort of implying that anybody who had nuclear weapons was intended to have them. That would necessarily have included the Soviet Union, if indeed they have them. But I recall wondering at the time, "Are you telling us, or are you implying that this country willingly gave weapons to the Soviets?" At that time that seemed like a terribly unthinkable thing to do, much less to admit. The leaders of the Soviet Union seem to be so dependent on the West though, one wonders whether there may have been some fear that they would try to assert independence if they indeed had these weapons. So, I don't know. It's something to speculate about perhaps ... who did he mean when he said, "If these weapons fall into the wrong h&s"? Maybe just terrorists. Anyhow, the new system would be brought in, if not by peaceful cooperation – everybody willingly yielding national sovereignty – then by bringing the nation to the brink of nuclear war. & everybody would be so fearful as 'ysteria is created by de possibility av nuclear war dat dare wud be a strong public outcry ter negotiate a public peace & people wud willingly gie up national sovereignty in order to achieve peace, & thereby this would bring in the New International Political System. This was stated & a very impressive thing to hear ... "If there were too many people in the right places who resisted this, there might be a need to use one or two – possibly more – nuclear weapons. As it was put this would be possibly needed to convince people that "We mean business." The statement that, "By the time one or two of those went off then everybody – even the most reluctant – would yield followed that. He said something about "this negotiated peace would be very convincing", as kind of in a framework or in a context that the whole thing was rehearsed but nobody would know it. People hearing about it would be convinced that it was a genuine negotiation between hostile enemies who finally had come to the realization that peace was better than war. In this context discussing war, & war is obsolete, a statement was made that there were some good things about war ... one, you're going to die anyway, & people sometimes in war get a chance to display great courage & heroism & if they die they've died well & if they survive they get recognition. So that in any case, the hardships of war on soldiers are worth it because that's the reward they get out of their warring. Another justification expressed for war was, if you think of the many millions of casualties in WW's 1 & 2, well ... suppose all those people had not died but had continued to live, then continued to have babies. There would be millions upon millions & we would already be overpopulated, so those two great wars served a benign purpose in delaying over-population. But now there are technological means for the individual & governments to control over-population so in this regard war is obsolete. It's no longer needed. & then again it's obsolete because nuclear weapons could destroy the whole universe. War, which once was controllable, could get out of control & so for these two reasons it's now obsolete.

TERRORISM

Dare wus discussion av terrorism. Terrorism wud be used widely in Europe & in other parts av de warrld. Terrorism at that time was thought would not be necessary in the United States. It could become necessary in the United States if the United States did not move rapidly enough into accepting the system. But at least in the foreseeable future it was not planned. Maybe terrorism would not be required here, but the implication being that it would be indeed used if it was necessary. Along with this came a bit of a scolding that Americans had had it too good anyway & just a little bit of terrorism would help convince Americans that the world is indeed a dangerous place ... or can be if we don't relinquish control to the proper authorities.

FINANCIAL CONTROL

There was discussion of money & banking. One statement was, "Inflation is infinite. You can put an infinite number of zeros after any number & put the decimals points wherever you want", as an indication that inflation is a tool of the controllers. Money would become predominately credit. It was already ... money is primarily a credit thing but exchange of money would be not cash or palpable things but electronic credit signal. People would carry money only in very small amounts for things like chewing gum & c&y bars. Just pocket sorts of things. Any purchase of any significant amount would be done electronically. Earnings would be electronically entered into your account. It would be a single banking system. May have the appearance of being more than one but ultimately & basically it would be one single banking system, so that when you got paid your pay would be entered for you into your account balance & then when you purchased anything at the point of purchase it would be deducted from your account balance & you would actually carry nothing with you. Also computer records can be kept on whatever it was you purchased so that if you were purchasing too much of any particular item & some official wanted to know what you were doing with your money they could go back & review your purchases & determine what you were buying. Dare wus a statement dat any purchase av significant size loike an automobile, bicycle, a refrigerator, a wireless or television or whatever might 'av sum sort av identificashun on it so it cud be traced, so dat pure quickly anythin' whaich wus either given away or 'ot – whatever – authorities wud be able ter establish who purchased it & whaen.

Computers would allow this to happen. The ability to save would be greatly curtailed. People would just not be able to save any considerable degree of wealth. There was some statement of recognition that wealth represents power & wealth in the h&s of a lot of people is not good for the people in charge so if you save too much you might be taxed. The more you save the higher rate of tax on your savings so your savings really could never get very far. & also if you began to show a pattern of saving too much you might have your pay cut. We would say, "Well, your saving instead of spending. You really don't need all that money." That basically the idea being to prevent people from accumulating any wealth, which might have long range disruptive influence on the system. People would be encouraged to use credit to borrow & then also be encouraged to renege on their debt so they would destroy their own credit. The idea here is that, again, if you're too stupid to h&le credit wisely, this gives the authorities the opportunity to come down hard on you once you've shot your credit. Electronic payments initially would all be based on different kinds of credit cards ... these were already in use in 1969 to some extent. Not as much as now. But people would have credit cards with the electronic strip on it & once they got used to that then it would be pointed out the advantage of having all of that combined into a single credit card, serving a single monetary system & then they won't have to carry around all that plastic.

SURVEILLANCE, IMPLANTS, & TELEVISIONS THAT WATCH YOU

So the next step would be the single card & then the next step would be to replace the single card with a skin implant. The single card could be lost or stolen, give rise to problems; could be exchanged with somebody else to confuse identify. The skin implants on the other h& would be not losable or counterfeitable or transferable to another person so you & your accounts would be identified without any possibility of error. & the skin implants would have to be put some place that would be convenient to the skin; for example your right h& or your forehead. At that time when I heard this I was unfamiliar with the statements in the Book of Revelation. The speaker went on to say, "Now some of you people who read the Bible will attach significance to this to the Bible," but he went on to disclaim any Biblical significance at all. This is just common sense of how the system could work & should work & there's no need to read any superstitious Biblical principals into it. As I say, at the time I was not very familiar with the words of Revelations. Shortly after I became familiar with it & the significance of what he said really was striking. I'll never forget it. There was some mention, also, of implants that would lend themselves to surveillance by providing radio signals. This could be under the skin or a dental implant ... put in like a filling so that either fugitives or possibly other citizens could be identified by a certain frequency from his personal transmitter & could be located at any time or any place by any authority who wanted to find him. This would be particularly useful for somebody who broke out of prison. There was more discussion of personal surveillance. One more thing was said, "You'll be watching television & somebody will be watching you at the same time at a central monitoring station." Television sets would have a device to enable this. The T.V. set would not have to be on in order for this to be operative. Also, the television set can be used to monitor what you are watching. People can tell what you're watching on TV & how you're reacting to what you're watching. & you would not know that you were being watched while you were watching your television.

How would we get people to accept these things into their homes? Well, people would buy them when they buy their own television. They won't know that they're on there at first. This was described by being what we now know as Cable TV to replace the antenna TV. When you buy a TV set this monitor would just be part of the set & most people would not have enough knowledge to know it was there in the beginning. & then the cable would be the means of carrying the surveillance message to the monitor. By de time people foun' oyt dat dis monitorin' wus 'eadin' on, they wud also be pure dependent upon television for a number av things. Jist de way people are dependent upon de blower the day.

One thing the television would be used for would be purchases. You wouldn't have to leave your home to purchase. You just turn on your TV & there would be a way of interacting with your television channel to the store that you wanted to purchase. & you could flip the switch from place to place to choose a refrigerator or clothing. This would be both convenient, but it would also make you dependent on your television so the built-in monitor would be something you could not do without. There was some discussion of audio monitors, too, just in case the authorities wanted to hear what was going on in rooms other than where the television monitor was, & in regard to this the statement was made, "Any wire that went into your house, for example your telephone wire, could be used this way. I remember this in particular because it was fairly near the end of the presentation & as we were leaving the meeting place I said something to one of my colleagues about going home & pulling all of the wires out of my house ... except I knew I couldn't get by without the telephone. & the colleague I spoke to just seemed numb. To this day I don't think he even remembers what we talked about or what we hear that time, cause I've asked him. But at that time he seemed stunned. Before all these changes would take place with electronic monitoring, it was mentioned that there would be service trucks all over the place, working on the wires & putting in new cables. This is how people who were on the inside would know how things were progressing.

THE ARRIVAL OF THE TOTALITARIAN GLOBAL SYSTEM

When the new system takes over people will be expected to sign allegiance to it, indicating that they don't have any reservations or holding back to the old system. "There just won't be any room", he said, "for people who won't go along. We can't have such people cluttering up the place so such people would be taken to special places", & here I don't remember the exact words, but the inference I drew was that at these special places where they were taken, then they would not live very long. He may have said something like, "disposed of humanely", but I don't remember very precisely … just the impression the system was not going to support them when they would not go along with the system. That would leave death as the only alternative. Somewhere in dis vein yer man said dare wud not be any martyrs. Whaen oi first 'eard dis oi tart it meant de people wud not be killed, but as de presentashun developed waaat yer man meant wus they wud not be killed in such a way or disposed av in such a way dat they cud serve as inspirashun ter other people de way martyrs chucker. Bloody yer man said somethin' loike dis. "People 'ill jist disappear."

I think there is no denying that this is controlled & there is indeed a conspiracy. The question then becomes what to do. I think first off, we must put our faith in God & pray & ask for his guidance. & secondly do what we can to inform other individuals as much as possible, as much as they may be interested. Some people just don't care, because they're preoccupied with getting along in their own personal endeavors. But as much as possible I think we should try to inform other people who may be interested, & again … put our faith & trust in God & pray constantly for his guidance & for the courage to accept what we may be facing in the near future. Rather than accept peace & justice, which we hear so much now … it's a cliché. Let's insist on liberty & justice for all.

End of Tape

& blinked and Supervisor Mr. Beiber IRL was in his face, barking, "Where's the novel?"

& panicked, "It's finished. It's nearly finished."

"*Nearly* finished isn't *finished*!"

"I huh, I need more memory Justice Mr. Beiber Sir." spluttered &.

"Memory! Where have you been? There is a new directive &! Memory has now fallen under the auspices of Time."

& heard himself frown in confusion, "It has? Since when?"

"Since *when* doesn't matter. All that matters is that it has. Now, where is the novel?"

& scrambled, "I huh ... I deposited it in the Memory Bank."

"Liar!" spat Justine Beiber Sir.

& bowed his head, chagrined, it was futile lying to Beiber.

Justice Sir Beiber explained to & that he was wired to every memory bank on the plane. & nodded in agreement: of course he was. Sir Justice Beiber was well connected. He was in the frame.

"Well?" Justice Beiber Sir waited.

& IRL leaned forward and quickly whispered the novel into his Beiber's ear. & leaned back and clocked Beiber's reaction. Justine Beiber shook with rage. & witnessed bile boiling in Sir Beiber's stomach, watched it bubble up and shoot up through his esophagus and come spurting out of his gob, "Are you serious?"

& stuttered, "Yes, Sir, and don't call me Shirley." Realizing that as soon as the words left his mouth the weak joke would be lost on Sir Beiber.

Beiber snapped, "What?"

"Nothing, Sir. A joke."

"Like this novel of yours?"

"Sir?"

"This so called novel. It's a joke right? A put on? You couldn't possibly claim it's anything else!"

& frowned, "No, Sir. It's what you asked for."

"No. I asked for a *novel*. What you've delivered is an abomination. A mockery! You've mocked the novel!"

& recoiled a little as Sir Justice Beiber Sir IRL ranted and raved and raved and ranted; spittle and shards of spleen spewing in all directions, "Cut and paste! Pastiche! Willful obscurity! Profanity! Pornography! Conspiracy theory! Plagiarism! Dilettantism! Amateurism! Theft! The ramblings of a mad man! Trash! Sensationalist! Not worth the megabytes it's written in! An affront to creativity! Solipsism at its worse! Scabrous! Paranoid! Unstructured! I wouldn't wipe my shit-encrusted arsehole with it! It's a shaggy dog tail without a tale! A waste of time, near far past and past future! A waste of good memory! Lazy! Truculent! Poorly formatted! An assault on grammar! Petty! Purposefully puerile! A crime against resources! A spunking of electricity! Propaganda! Abject poverty of vision! Nihilistic! Sick! Contemptuous! Juvenile! A farrago! An insult to the written word. Would you like me to go on &?"

& found some courage, "I don't recognize those criticisms of it, Sir. I think I know what's happened ... you have succumbed to the Mandela Effect. It's a theory of parallel universes, based in the idea that because large groups of people have similar alternative memories about past events this is the logical explanation. Advocates of the theory claim that for these collective experiences to be true, the fabric of reality must have shifted at some point in the past, and that therefore not only do parallel, inhabitable universes exist, but that we are constantly switching between them. You, Sir, are remembering a completely different version of the novel I just presented to you."

Getting the Fear
Chapter Ten

As he lay in his hospital bed, Charlie Coleman was trying to work out who had paid for the hit on him. He knew who had attacked him, that was Grant Burgess, but what he really wanted to know was who had put the cash up, and more importantly *why*?

There was no way that that sleazy little tightwad Arnie Kaufman would have shelled out for it. Arnie was only interested in earning, not spending. It could be the Soho mobsters, but then again they didn't need to hire in outside muscle or frighteners. Grant Burgess' patch was North London, mainly Kilburn. He was a bully who shook down Irish criminals and he *never* stepped out off of his turf and into the West End. Burgess must have gone and got himself a pass from the mobsters to carry out the job.

Charlie knew that he was a little thorn in the side of the Soho mob and that they looked down on him as a nasty little chancer; he was surprised that they had let a lump like Grant Burgess give him a kicking though. It went against the unwritten protocols.

Grant Burgess had caught Charlie Coleman coming out of The Continental Club on Wardour Street. He followed him down towards The Ship pub, pounced on him and dragged him down an alley. Burgess gave Charlie the kicking of his life, even though there were many people around, *all* potential witnesses. What did Burgess care

331

though? He knew Coleman would never sing to the Old Bill. The kicking was over in less than a minute and Grant Burgess ran off leaving Charlie in bits.

Ribs, jaw, wrist and elbow broken, Charlie was out for the count when he was scooped up. Grant had knocked him out with a one two combo and then simply stomped on him with his size twelve boots.

Charlie lay in the hospital bed and smoked a Pall Mall, wincing in pain at every slight movement of his jaw. He thought about all the jobs he had done on people over the years. All the people he had scarred, maimed, burnt, stabbed, glassed, humiliated, bludgeoned, it could be any one of them getting their own back. Charlie made enemies for a living; it came with the territory. Maybe he would never find out who put Grant Burgess up to it.

He got a few visitors from the Soho scene, a few of The Chaps, a few girlfriends, acquaintances, Charlie had no close friends. You didn't have close friends in his game. He confided in Fred The Thief that he knew Grant Burgess was his attacker.

Fred The Thief nodded his head, "Yeah, wouldn't surprise me. Sounds like Burgess style."
Charlie tried to eat the grapes that Fred had brought him, "I'm gonna have to do a number back on him, Fred. I can't let this lie. Word gets out and ... well, it's no good for my reputation is it?"
"You don't wanna have a straightener with that big lump, Charlie. You've got no chance."
"You know me, Fred. I'm not thick ... I'll get him back though, you mark my words."
"He's wed to that Sylvia sort now. Her with the big knockers ... huh, Sylvia ... huh ... Barnes! Barnes, that's it! You knocked her sister off didn't ya? You don't think it's anything to do with that?"
Charlie thought about it, "Yeah, yeah, now you mention it ...

Mmm ... could be, could be ... I've been pulling me hair out thinking who put him up to it."

Charlie and Doreen Barnes had had a very tempestuous relationship a year back. Doreen was a sexy North London girl who worked in her dad's boozer on the Archway. Charlie thought a lot about her and even stopped screwing the birds around Soho for a couple of months after they got together. Doreen gave Charlie a taste of his own medicine though and did the dirty on him with a few regulars of the boozer. Doreen had a voracious sexual appetite and Charlie was in his element. In his element as long has she only sated her appetite with him of course.

When he found out she had been cheating he gave her a slap, tied her hands and carved his initials into her arse cheeks with a pen knife, "You're my fucking property you little tart!"

Charlie believed she actually got a kick out of it at the time. They stayed together a couple more months until another piece of equally sexy skirt caught his eye.

It made sense now. Doreen must have yapped about Charlie branding her to the sister Sylvia with the big knockers. Sylvia had obviously blabbed it to her lump of a husband Grant Burgess, and Burgess – ever the macho tough guy – had promised to teach Charlie Coleman a lesson now that he was family. It was fucking obvious and all about *respect*.

Charlie was relieved now that he worked out the motive with a little help from Fred The Thief. The attack had been nothing to do with work, it was personal. Charlie could handle that. It wouldn't affect his future earning potential. He would be holed up in convalescence for a few weeks but at least he knew now that the attack wasn't a comeback for an old job or a warning shot from the Soho mobsters.

In retrospect he shouldn't have branded Doreen, but then *she* shouldn't have screwed around. Doreen was a hypocrite as well. He knew she was getting wet when he delicately carved his initials into her arse because as soon as he had finished she pulled him into her and quickly climaxed with a banshee like wail.

He could only surmise that her sister had seen her arse and pulled her up on it. Doreen being the crafty little cow that she was would have said Charlie Coleman had done it and that she was in fear of him. She definitely wouldn't have admitted that it had turned her on. Working class girls from North London would never admit to being kinky in 1968.

He was being administered strong painkillers for the pain that gripped his ribs. He woke up one day during visiting hours and was convinced that the painkillers were making him hallucinate. Sat at the side of his bed was Candice. She smiled at him and he closed his eyes, sure that when he opened them again she would be gone. When she spoke he knew he wasn't seeing things.
"I'll let you rest, Charlie."
Charlie's hand shot out of the bed and grabbed her wrist, "I thought I was seeing things."
"You look terrible."
Nothing much shocked him, but this did, "And you look terrific … how … I mean … how did you find me? I called you dozens o' times; thought I'd lost you forever."
"I was in The Scotch last night and I heard you were in here, Charlie."
"You gave me the wrong number. What was that all about?"
"Did I? Oh well, I'm here now. I hope none of your girlfriends mind me visiting, Charlie?"
Charlie pulled himself up a little, "I've become celibate since I clapped eyes on you. I've done away with 'em."
Candice smiled at him, "You'll tell me anything."
"Yeah, yeah I would … anything your pretty little ears want to hear … I can't believe you're … pinch me will ya?"

"No, I don't want to do you anymore damage. You look like you've been in the wars ... what happened?"

"Oh nothing ... sporting injuries."

Candice shook her head, "I abhor violence, Charlie."

"So do I, Candice, so do I."

Her eyebrow arched, "So, come on, what happened?"

Charlie put his hand on hers and looked her straight in the eyes, "You ever read those James Bond books, Candice? You know, the spy, all that stuff he gets up to saving the world from evil people, eh?"

She smirked, "You're not going try that one on me are you? The amount of times I've been chatted up by men who claim to be spies ... come on, Charlie ... tell me, I'm interested."

Charlie couldn't lie to her. She was just too beautiful and wonderful and perfect and entrancing and Charlie could feel the hairs on the back of his neck standing to attention, and even if most of it was down to the morphine based painkillers he was still feeling a warm numbing sensation by just being in her presence; he thought it might be described as enchantment.

"Candice ... let's put it this way. I'm not a 9 to 5 sort of chap. I think you know that though, eh?"

Candice gave him a knowing smile, "I had an inkling."

"I sort of provide a service to people who can't go to the Old Bill, you know?"

"And why can't they go to the police, Charlie?"

"You know Soho, Candice. There are a lot of ... what's the word ... *unscrupulous* characters about. I'm a kind of ... a kind of broker if you like. You know, I sort problems out."

"Do you want to know what I've heard about you, Charlie Coleman?"

Charlie sighed and braced himself; she could have heard anything, "All right ... let me have it."

"I've heard you're a very naughty boy. I've heard you do nasty things to people. I've heard you're a bit of a gigolo and that you will do *anything* for money. Do you know what someone said to me about you in The Scotch?"

Charlie sighed, "Go on."

"Are you sure you want to hear this? It's quite shocking."

"I can take it."

"They said … they said you would crawl over your dying mother to fuck your sister."

He snapped, "Who said that?"

"I'm not telling you."

Charlie gritted his teeth but flashed a pained smile at her. Candice pulled eye contact from him. He turned it around, she was just too special to bullshit, "You heard all that about me, Candice … yet … well, you're here visiting me?"

She paused and looked him in the eyes, "Guilty."

"See, there's no point me lying to someone like you, Candice. Lies roll off my tongue, but with someone like you …"

"Yeah?"

"Well, I mean, you're … you're not someone I'd just like to … you know?"

"No. What? What Charlie? Say it."

"All right … you're not the sort of bird I'd like to just get in me bed for the night. You know that though. You're a rare bird you are."

"Why's that?"

Charlie shrugged, "You just are that's all. You stand out from all the others … you're … well, you're different."

They talked until they were rudely interrupted by the bell that signaled the end of visiting time. Charlie kicked off with one of the nurses about his 'rights' being violated by the bell, but Candice smiled at him, told him to stop being silly, gave him a peck on the cheek and left. Her last words to him were that she would visit him the next day. Charlie couldn't feel the pain in his ribs anymore

Jack Sherry had nothing but time to kill. He would be spending another hot, sultry night on Ibiza. He tried to convince himself that there had been a clerical error with the checking of the passports of the corpses, and it would soon be rectified and that tomorrow he could at least officially identify them and Scotland Yard could let the relevant agencies know of the murders.

Jack knew this case was going to make a splash in the press, especially after the similar slaughter of Sharon Tate and her friends in Los Angeles. He wondered how his boss, Chief Inspector Ketley, would handle it. Ketley was an honest copper but something like this would throw him into the international arena and Ketley got nosebleeds if he even had to venture further than North London.

This was new ground for all concerned. Even if some of the dead bodies turned out not to be British there was still the fact that he was out there to help investigate the murders. He sensed that politics and international diplomacy would soon factor in to the case and that troubled him. Neither him nor Ketley were politicians or diplomats. They were just good coppers who specialized in murder detection. Jack Sherry couldn't wait to talk to his boss. He was sure it would be reassuring.

He hit the bar opposite Captain Torres' station. Captain Torres couldn't join him. Besides the fact that he was reeling from the discoveries of the day he had a family waiting for him at home and calls to make to the mainland Police with updates.

Jack sat at the bar, drank bourbon and Coca Cola and chained Marlboro's; the only cigarettes they seemed to sell on the island.

Jack was amazed at how much bourbon the barman doled out. Back in England spirits were strictly measured, out here they just tipped the bottle into the glass until you said "When". Jack wasn't complaining. He was more than happy to get shit faced. It would help him forget about the corpses.

The bar was busy with locals and holidaymakers and a few hippies.

Jack was now beginning to understand why so many people flocked to Ibiza. It was a laid back atmosphere and everyone seemed to be friendly and accommodating. Jack even found himself humming along to the jukebox that seemed to be stuck on Peter Sarstedt's 'Where Do You Go To My Lovely?'

Most of the people sang along loudly to the song and Jack was eventually cajoled into joining in. There were lots of Dutch and German patrons and they were all in high spirits. Not surprising with the measures the barman was doling out, thought Jack.

He went into the toilet and looked at himself in the cracked mirror. He felt guilty that he should be having so much fun. He had been sent there to help with a mass murder and this just wasn't right, this wasn't proper, it wasn't decorum. His bosses would have a fit if they could see him now, but Jack Sherry could see *himself* now and he didn't like what he saw. He should be sleeping not boozing. He should be agonizing over those poor dead souls. He splashed water in his face and wiped it off with his hands. He promised himself he would have one more for the road and that would be that.

He went back out and sat at the bar. The crowd was singing along to 'Honky Tonk Women' by The Rolling Stones; Jack knew all about those degenerate Rolling Stones. He knew that Scotland Yard had a file on them twelve inches thick, knew some of the coppers who busted them at Redlands, knew they were druggy anarchists who had given England a bad name. He had to admit though … they made great music.

A beautiful young English woman breezed by him, handed him a large bourbon and coke and smiled, "It's a party, and we're celebrating."
Before he could thank her and ask what her party was celebrating she had been sucked back into the throng. Jack knocked the drink back and checked his watch: 11.23 pm. It would be nearly twelve

hours later before Jack had any real concept of time. Time was about to melt for Jack Sherry.

He walked out of the bar and headed up the street towards the police station. The street was quiet and a lovely breeze blew down it and dampened the heat a little. It was nothing at first, he simply thought the large measures of bourbon were getting to him as he felt like he was walking on a treadmill. He tried shrugging it off. It didn't work though. It then felt like he was walking in quicksand, his feet becoming heavier with every step until finally he was stuck to the spot. He could feel an alien panic rising in him and after that ... well, after that nothing would ever look the same again for Jack Sherry.

Captain Torres found Jack Sherry sat on a wall near the police station at 11 am the next morning. Jack Sherry was staring into space and looked like he had the weight of the world on his shoulders. If Captain Torres hadn't been such a caring and understanding man he would have called Scotland Yard and told them that they had sent a mental case to help with his investigation.

Jack lay on the bed in the room above the police station and stared up at the ceiling, "I know how it looks, Captain Ernesto. You think I was pissed, right?"

"Drunken, Mr. Jack?"

"Yes, but only I wasn't, I swear to you ... I was slipped a Mickey Finn. I know about these things. It's happened to me before."

Captain Torres was confused, "Who is this *Mickey Finn*, Mr. Jack?"

"Poison, Captain. I was poisoned in the bar. There's no other explanation for it."

Captain Torres was dubious, "Poisoned? No, no, why? Who would poison you, Mr. Jack? I know the bar. They are good people."

Jack grabbed his aching head, sat up and snapped, "I am telling you what happened, Ernesto!"

Captain Torres was taken aback, "Please, Mr. Jack. Maybe it is the heat, yes? The heat can send visitors to our island a little … it can send them a little loco, you understand? I have seen this, truly."

Jack angrily retorted, "With all due respect, Ernesto, I am telling you that someone drugged me. I know these things. It happened to me years ago when I was working undercover, only this time … well, this time, God knows what they poisoned me with."

Captain Torres was visibly upset, "Please, Mr. Jack. Please just calm down a little."

"Ernesto, listen to me. I drink everyday. I'm a drinker but I'm not a alcoholic. I know the difference between being drunk and being drugged."

"Mr. Jack, I-"

Jack snapped again, "Just call me Jack OK? Drop the *mister*, all right?"

"OK, OK, Jack … but tell me … you say you were poisoned but-"

Jack cut in and closed on Captain Torres, eye to eye, "Listen, Ernesto. I really like you, honestly. We've both been thrown into this thing and it's not nice, it's not nice at all, in fact it's horrible … but you've got to believe me here … I might like a drink but I swear to you that someone slipped me something last night. Now … now I can understand your reluctance to believe me, you don't know me, Ernesto, but just trust me on this, OK?"

Captain Torres slowly shook his head, "I like you too Jack … you have got to understand though, I find it hard to believe that someone would try to poison you."

Jack sighed and searched for the right words, "Look … listen … OK, OK, maybe, just *maybe* I was in the wrong place at the wrong time and people were taking drugs and I happened to get caught up in it. The thing is though, I would remember … all I remember before the nightmare was being handed a drink by a young woman. Do you understand me, Ernesto?"

Captain Torres clasped his hands, "OK, Jack, this I understand. A woman gave you a drink and then … and then kaboom! Yes?"

"Not exactly kaboom, no. I just felt … well, you saw the state of me … I was … the only way to describe it was drugged, Ernesto."

"Mmm, you say like a nightmare, yes?"

"Let me tell you, Ernesto. Years ago I was working undercover on a case and I went to a party to try and get close to someone ... anyway ... my cover must have been blown and someone at the party dropped something in my drink and I fell into unconsciousness, all right?"

"Yes, Jack. I understand."

"Well, this is what happened to me last night, only I didn't go unconscious. It was like ... it was just terrible, horrible, Ernesto ... from what I've heard about it, it sounds like I was given LSD again. Only this time ..." Jack stared into space, his mouth in limbo between speech and awe.

Captain Torres gravely nodded his head, "Yes, this acid drug."

"That's right. I might be wrong though, I could have been anything for all I know."

"But I can not understand why anybody would do this to you, Jack."

Jack paused, "No, neither can I."

"What would they get to achieve from this, Jack?"

Jack paused, "I don't know ... maybe like I said, I was just caught up in it all."

Jack started to describe how it had felt being under the influence of whatever drug he had been spiked with, but he soon gave up. Captain Torres told him to rest and he would go over to the bar and find out if other people were reporting being slipped drugs.

Jack drank water and smoked and lay on his side and stared out of the open window at a huge palm tree. He practiced what he would say to his boss back at The Yard when he called.

"Sir, there's something dodgy going on here. One of the people I interviewed claimed that the victims were engaged in ... Well ... black magic. All that satanic rubbish again, sir."

Chief Inspector Ketley laughed, "What? Did I hear you right, Sherry?"

341

"Yes, sir."

"I suppose you were talking to one of these bloody hippies, eh?"

"Huh, not really, sir. I couldn't honestly say he was."

"Well, look, Sherry. This could turn out to be none of our business when the bodies are identified. Let's hope none of them are British subjects, eh? Let the spics sort it all out."

"I can't see how these victims are going to be identified without the Spanish asking people to step forward and identify them. It will be a big splash, sir."

"Yes, Sherry, obviously, but we might not have to worry about it. What are your thoughts on the passports you turned up?"

"I'm stumped, sir ... maybe just clerical errors?"

"No, Sherry, they've been checked and double checked. These victims could have only been in receipt of forged passports."

"All right, sir. So that points to illegal activity of some sort. Although, I'm beginning to think that we have different ideas to what's illegal and what isn't than these people on Ibiza. I mean ..."

"What do you mean, Sherry?"

"I mean, sir ... well, anything seems to go. It's lawless."

"Oh right, a bit backward ... have you spoken to the Spanish mainland police yet?"

"No, sir. Captain Torres is dealing with them. I don't really want to step on his toes. He seems a like a good copper, he's just confused. Understandably though, sir."

Jack never told Ketley he had been drugged whilst partying in a bar. Ketley would have gone ballistic and demand that he return on the next flight out of Ibiza. Disciplinary action would surely have followed. Ketley did everything by the book. A real straight shooter, which with all the accusations of corruption being leveled at The Yard was refreshing to know.

Jack tried to forget about the hallucinatory nightmare he had suffered. He prided himself on having a strong constitution and he was physically and mentally in good condition. This wasn't going to set him back.

He still wanted answers as to why and who had slipped him it though. He wondered if some of those beatnik types in the bar just wanted to teach him a lesson, a bit of fun at the expense of a copper. A cowardly little prank on someone who represented The Establishment that they loathed so much.

He had a real problem with all these so-called Libertarians and Anarchists. First and foremost the ones he had come into contact with had all been weak and the police were there to *protect* the weak in society. They hated the police but without them they would be easy prey. Secondly, they never came up with workable alternatives or solutions to the status quo. Free love and *free* this and that just would not work. It was all pie in the sky utopian rubbish. Policing had taught Jack that people were generally selfish and put theirs and their immediate family's interest first, and Jack didn't have a problem with that. He only had problems with those who took their selfishness on to another level and harmed others in their pursuit of gain or bloodlust.

Jack wondered how these peaceniks would deal with some of the violent bastards he had dealt with over the years. How would they talk to them in a language they understood? The only language most of the violent bastards he had taken off the streets understood was the language of violence.

Dr. Myron Geller was lecturing to dozens of students in the main room of The Trebistock Institute. He was a fine lecturer and he captivated the students.

Rather than lecture from the rostrum he walked amongst them in a fog of cigarette smoke, "I am sure you are all aware of how psychiatry has been portrayed in such a negative light during this decade. One has only to look at these popular motion pictures, television shows and novels that paint a very misleading landscape of psychiatry ... if one were to take these extremely ignorant portrayals seriously, well, psychiatrists would be nothing more than agents of a malevolent state or shadowy criminal conspiratorial agencies ... one could be forgiven for believing that all psychiatry strives towards is achieving a sinister goal."

Dr. Geller chuckled and the students politely joined him. He continued, "In these portrayals, psychiatrists are shown to be undermining the mental health of their patients using drugs and behavioral psychology, rather than showing the truth of the matter, which is simply that we strive towards alleviating pain and distress by getting to the root cause of the patients state of mind."

He took a drag on his cigarette and smiled, "If one were to believe these ridiculous depictions, psychiatrists would be nothing more than men and women who are interested only in brainwashing ... I have yet to meet a bona fide psychiatrist or a behavioral psychologist who is in the pay of governments or shadowy agencies that have malevolent purposes. I can tell you truthfully that we are people who care passionately about helping people. Unfortunately popular culture peddles far too many assumptions and lazy clichés and I believe it damages perception to the point of where you could call this reckless behavior. Here at the Trebistock Institute we *never* peddle assumptions or lazy clichés and we engage in rigorous analysis before we come to conclusions."

He wound down the lecture and the students happily filed out, many of them wanting to congratulate and thank Dr. Geller. Candice had been watching from the back of the room. She had watched Dr. Geller lecture so many times that she knew every nuance and digression he would lead into before he even opened his mouth.

She approached him, excited, "I think I have someone for you, Myron. The kind of person you're interested in."
"What do you mean, Candice?"
"You know? A thug."

He gently held her hand and smiled, "Oh, I see, Candice. That is very good."

"Yes."

"Who is he?"

"Charles Coleman. He's a thug for hire. I've spoken to a few people about him. He's got a very bad reputation."

"Has he indeed?"

"His style, if that's what you can call it, seems to be wounding people. He's not like a heavy character or anything. A lot more sly and subtle than that. He's not part of the gang scene in the West End. He works on his own and he's fallen foul of the gangsters a few times."

He smiled, "Excellent. When do I get to meet him?"

"He's in hospital at the moment."

"Oh?"

"He's been beaten up quite badly. I'll bring him to you as soon as he gets out."

"That's good, Candice, very good."

She checked her watch, "You'd better go now, Myron. The car's waiting for you."

"Oh yes, the BBC."

"Good luck."

He smiled and patronizingly patted her arm, "I don't need any luck my darling Candice."

Two hours later and Candice was sat in her room, her radio tuned in to the BBC World Service. Dr. Geller was one of two guests on the highbrow *Engagement* show hosted by Sir Rodney Chesterfield QC. *Engagement* was a very lively debate show that tackled issues of the day and pitted those with opposing viewpoints against each other. Dr. Geller's opponent would Mark Standish, a conservative writer and columnist for *The Daily Telegraph*. Standish was outspoken in his views of modern psychiatry.

As soon Sir Rodney had made the introductions and set the scene, Dr. Geller and Mark Standish got straight into it.

Standish: "Would you not agree with me, Dr. Geller, that institutes like your own are essentially condoning the behavior of many young people who are turning their backs on society and looking inwards for answers?"

Dr. Geller: "Excuse me, Mr. Standish, but I do not understand your question."

Mr. Standish: "Dr. Geller, on numerous occasions you gone on the record as saying that you believe young people should be allowed to experiment with these psychedelic drugs because it could lead them to question everything, and I quote, "Question the fabric of society and set about unpicking it and weaving a new one that is less oppressive, free from violence and more inclusive" ... Dr. Geller, you don't think this is dangerous? You have said yourself that there is still much more research needed into looking at long term effects of using psychedelic drugs."

Dr. Geller: "That is true, Mr. Standish, and if you refer back to that very same article you will see that I cautioned against the use of psychedelic drugs unless they were being administered by mental health professionals."

Dr. Standish: "You did indeed, Dr. Geller, forgive me, but here's where I have a problem with the practicality you see ... surely you do not expect people to make an appointment with their psychiatrist so that they can safely take these drugs do you?"

The argument digressed for a time and was brought back on track by the host.

Sir Rodney: "Dr. Geller, I would like to ask you a question ... what do you ultimately hope to achieve by your advocacy of the use of these narcotics?"

Dr. Geller: "I am fascinated by violence, Sir Rodney ... I have been most of my life I suppose. Besides the obvious upbringing and con-ditioning and congenital factors that shape a human's behavior, I also believe that there is a kind of primordial trigger in the psyche of men and women, that can either be consciously pulled to inflict violence or can be ignored. Let me explain ... you take two men, one who has proved time and time again that they can instantly pull the trigger and become indiscriminately or discriminately violent, yes? And another man who has a propensity for violence but only if cornered and will resist *pulling the trigger* until all other options have been exhausted, do you understand?"

Mr. Standish: "Go on, Dr. Geller, please."

Dr. Geller: "What I believe we can find with the use of psychedelics is exactly what the *trigger point* is, measuring at what point our non violent man will pull the trigger. What conditions, other than fight or flight, can turn him from being passive to aggressive if you like."

Mr. Standish: "But, Dr. Geller, with all due respect, we are all well aware that some men are violent and others are not, just as some men have a sense of humor and others don't. It's what makes us individuals is it not?"

Dr. Geller: "It is indeed, it is ... humor isn't responsible for the deaths of millions of people every year though is it?"

Mr. Standish: "Very good, Dr. Geller."

Sir Rodney: "Let me try to understand this, Dr. Geller ... you believe that there is a metaphorical violence trigger that can either be pulled or ignored, yes?"

Dr. Geller: "I do, sir."

Sir Rodney: "But this hypothesis, in what way can it be used practically?"

Mr. Standish: "Lobotomy perhaps, Dr. Geller? You lobotomize the violent?"

Dr. Geller: "On the contrary, on the contrary. You simply study the violent and non violent subjects under the influence of psychedelics and then-"

Mr. Standish: "Excuse me, excuse me. I think I know where you are going with this, Dr. Geller, but again, I ask you, what are the practicalities? The benefits to society? You are talking about a couple of subjects out of a sea of humanity. I don't doubt that you might be able to-"

Dr. Geller: "If you would be so kind let me explain, Mr. Standish."

Sir Rodney: "Please let Dr. Geller explain. Go on Dr. Geller."

Mr. Standish: "Excuse me, Dr Geller."

Dr. Geller: "Thank you ... what I was about to say was this: every breakthrough in science, health, law, culture, whatever, it all starts with baby steps, the experiment. I believe that with time, funding and support we can eventually learn how to neutralize the violent in our society, and no, Mr. Standish, not through lobotomy. In fact I find your remark somewhat facetious. We no longer live in the dark ages thankfully."

Mr. Standish: "You seriously believe that you can eradicate a negative aspect of human nature, Dr. Geller? Again, this smacks of social engineering to me."

Dr. Geller: "And what is so wrong with social engineering may I ask you? What is so wrong in trying to build a society free from violence, Mr. Standish? If we continue on our path of violence we will simply reach a point of catastrophe."

Mr. Standish: "You see, Sir Rodney, this is exactly the kind of liberal claptrap that is ruining our society. Experimentation this, experimentation that. Is it also not true that you use hypnosis in your work, Dr. Geller? You have gone on the record as saying that hypnosis can be used to fix all manner of ills. Is this kind of hypnosis you use nothing more than that used by cheap entertainers for amusement?"

Dr. Geller: "I will not respond to that spurious remark, what I will say though is this ... I was *experimented* on by the Nazis in World War II, and it was because of this ordeal that I decided to study psychiatry. Experimentation can be both good and bad, Mr. Standish, but without it we learn nothing, we remain in stasis."

Candice smiled to herself: *you tell him, Myron!*

The debate digressed again and Sir Rodney, in his best BBC voice and trying to keep it civil, asked Dr. Geller what he was working on at the moment. Dr. Geller made a very bold claim.

Dr. Geller: "I was metaphorically talking of two men earlier. You see

I am concerned with studying two men who are strikingly different in their attitudes and propensity to violence. I suppose you could say that I want to find out whether a violent man can be taught to be passive and a passive man taught to be violent."

Mr. Standish: "And just how you do you intend to do this, Dr. Geller?"

Dr. Geller: "This can be achieved, I believe, by letting each subject have a glimpse into the other subject's mind. I'm afraid I don't think we have enough time for me to go into detail, but I am very confident that the outcome will lead towards a better understanding of violence."

Sir Rodney had to wind it down. Candice was happy that her beloved Dr. Geller had had the last word. She tuned out of the station into a popular one. Donovan's 'Hurdy Gurdy Man' was playing and she hummed along to it as she dressed to go meet Grant Burgess at his father in law's pub on The Archway in North London.

. . .

. . . .

. . .

. . . .

. . .

& imagined Doctor A cumming to her senses: somenight in her lab at CERN she would be faced with the overwhelming evidence that God created all that iswasandeverwillbe. He created the heavens & the earth and the firmament that held his creation in place. *Nothing New Under The Sun* would finally make sense to her. Her own prejudices and ignorance and superiority complex would force her to bow and accept that she is simply one of God's creatures who has unfortunately strayed from the flock. As Above *not* As Below.

& should Q-mail Doctor A the real dialogue between The Marquis De Sade and The Priest on De Sade's deathbed.

PRIEST: Now that the fatal hour is upon you wherein the veil of illusion is torn aside only to confront every deluded man with the cruel tally of his errors and vices, do you, my son, earnestly repent of the many sins to which you were led by weakness and human frailty?

DYING MAN: No, do I fuck!

PRIEST: In the short space you have left, profit from such timely remorse to ask that you be given general absolution of your sins, believing that only by considering the reverence of the most comfortable and holy sacrament of penitence may you hope for forgiveness at the hand of Almighty God our Eternal Father.

DYING MAN: Bollocks!

PRIEST: What's that?

DYING MAN: You heard me! I said what a load of Big Hairy Sharries!

PRIEST: Ah, so you have reverted to Nadsat!

DYING MAN: Indeed. Now why don't you go fuck yourself and ookadeet me oddy knocky! I repent of nothing! I have lived a horrorshow jeezny. I have fucked and drank and ate and murdered and lusted to my hearts content! I don't want to be saved. Stick your Christ and bog up your arse! Do what thou wilt has been the only law I have recognized. If we were meant to live the lives of insects we would have never evolved. I hate you and your bog and all the cal you preach! You are all hypocrites and jeezny deniers. You're all scared of fun and enjoyment and passions! And because of that you don't want anyone else to enjoy him or herself.

PRIEST: So you don't believe in a creator or morality? Really?

DYING MAN: That's right you pompous bratchny! Now ookadeet me oddy knocky!

PRIEST: OK. I see what's happening here ... let me, then, explain the impossibility of evolution in a language you'll understand. Belief in evolution is a remarkable phenomenon. It is a belief passionately defended by the scientific establishment, despite the lack of any observable scientific evidence for macroevolution (that is, evolution from odin distinct kind of organism into another). This odd situation is briefly documented by citing recent statements from leading evolutionists admitting their lack of proof. These statements inadvertently show that evolution on any significant scale does not occur at present, and never happened in the past, and could never sloochat at all. Evolution is not happening now

DYING MAN: What a load of starry cal!

PRIEST: The lack of a case for evolution is clear from the fact that no Odin has ever seen it sloochat. If it were a real process, evolution should still be occurring, and there should be many "transitional" forms that we could observe. What we viddy instead, of course, is an array of distinct "kinds" of plants and animals with many varieties within each kind, but with very clear and – apparently – unbridgeable gaps between the kinds. That is, for example, there are many varieties of dogs and many varieties of cats, but no "dats" or "cogs." Such variation is often called microevolution, and these minor horizontal (or downward) changes occur fairly often, but such changes are not true "vertical" evolution.

Evolutionary geneticists have often experimented on fruit flies and other rapidly reproducing species to induce mutational changes hoping they would lead to new and better species, but these have all failed to accomplish their goal. No truly new species has ever been produced, let oddy knocky a new "basic kind." A current leading evolutionist, Jeffrey Schwartz, professor of anthropology at the university of Pittsburgh, has recently acknowledged that: *It was and still is the case that, with the exception of Dobzhansky's claim about a new species of fruit fly, the formation of a new species, by any mechanism, has never been observed. Odin.*

DYING MAN: Seriously, you're wasting your sodding breath! I'm not interessovatted!

PRIEST: The scientific method traditionally has required experimental observation and replication. The fact that macroevolution (as distinct from microevolution) has never been observed would seem to exclude it from the domain of true science. Even Ernst Mayr, The Dean of living evolutionists, longtime professor of biology at Harvard, who has alleged that evolution is a "simple fact," nevertheless agrees that it is an "historical science" for which "laws and experiments are inappropriate techniques", by which to explain it.

Odin can never actually viddy evolution in action. Evolution never happened in the past. Evolutionists commonly answer the above criticism by claiming that evolution goes too slowly for us to viddy it happening today. They used to claim that the real evidence for evolution was in the fossil record of the past, but the fact is that the billions of known fossils do not include a single unequivocal transitional form with transitional structures in the process of evolving.

DYING MAN: La la sodding la! I'm not listening!

PRIEST: Given that evolution, according to Darwin, was in a continual state of motion, it followed logically that the fossil record should be rife with examples of transitional forms leading from the less to the more evolved. Even those who believe in rapid evolution recognize that a considerable number of generations would be required for Odin distinct "kind" to evolve into another more complex kind. There ought, therefore, to be a considerable number of true transitional structures preserved in the fossils – after all, there are billions of non-transitional structures there! But (with the exception of a few very doubtful creatures such as the controversial feathered dinosaurs and the alleged walking whales), they are not there. Instead of filling in the gaps in the fossil record with so-called missing links, most paleontologists found themselves facing a situation in which there were only gaps in the fossil record, with no evidence of transformational intermediates between documented fossil species. The entire history of evolution from the evolution of jeezny from non-life to the evolution of vertebrates from invertebrates to the evolution of moodge from the ape is strikingly devoid of intermediates: the links are all missing in the fossil record, just as they are in the present world. With respect to the origin of jeezny, a leading researcher in this field, Leslie Orgel, after noting that neither proteins nor nucleic acids could have arisen without the other, concludes: *and so, at first glance, odin might have to conclude that jeezny could never, in fact, have originated by chemical means.* Being committed to total evolution as he is, Dr. Orgel cannot accept any such conclusion as that. Therefore, he speculates that rna may have come first, but then he still has to admit that: *the precise events giving rise to the rna*

352

world remain unclear ... investigators have proposed many hypotheses, but evidence in favor of each of them is fragmentary at best! Translation: There is no known way by which jeezny could have arisen naturalistically.

DYING MAN: No! Fuck that! I'm not slooshying! It's unfair. I could bring a scientist in here and he'd completely demolish everything you're saying! Ookadeet me oddy knocky.

PRIEST: I'm afraid that you have been brainwashed by The Luciferian Doctrine my droogie.

DYING MAN: Get to fuck! I'm no droogie of yours and I bow to no bog! I am my own bog! It's all pie in the sky bullcal!

PRIEST: Let me explain Luciferianism. Like some varieties of Satanism, Luciferianism does not depict the devil as a literal metaphysical entity. Lucifer only symbolizes the cognitive powers of moodge. He is the embodiment of science and reason. It is the Luciferian's religious conviction that these dva facilitative forces will dethrone bog and apotheosize moodge. It comes as malenky surprise that the radicals of the early revolutionary faith celebrated the arrival of Darwinism. Evolutionary theory was the edifying "science" of Promethean zealotry and the new secular religion of the scientific dictatorship. According to Masonic scholar Wilmshurst, the completion of human evolution involves moodge "becoming a god-like being and unifying his consciousness with the omniscient". During the enlightenment, Luciferianism was disseminated on the popular level as secular humanism. All of the governing precepts of Luciferianism are encompassed by secular humanism. This is made evident by the philosophy's rejection of theistic morality and enthronement of moodge as his own absolute moral authority. While Luciferianism has no sacred texts, Humanist Manifesto One and Two succinctly delineate its central tenets. Whittaker Chambers, former member of the communist underground in America, eloquently summarizes this truth: *humanism is not new. It is, in fact, man's second oldest faith. Its promise was whispered in the first days of creation under the tree of knowledge of horrorshow and evil: 'ye shall be as gods."*

353

DYING MAN: You can skazat what you like. It's all superstition. Fear of the unknown. Sodding weakness. You cling onto religion because you're a poogly malenky animal. If religion had its way we'd still be living in the dark ages.

PRIEST: What makes you believe that my droogie?

DYING MAN: I'm not your fucking droogie! It's science that dragged us out of the dark ages!

PRIEST: And you believe science more than the slovo of your creator?

DYING MAN: Yes. Of course I do! There's proof of science everywhere you smot.

PRIEST: Smot, please listen to me very carefully. You have been lied to all of your jeezny. The Copernican revolution begat the Darwinian revolution, which, in turn, begat the Einstein, Penzias, Sagan, Hoyle/Wickramasinghe revolutions. Together they make up the bolshy bang evolution paradigm. These wholly theoretical/ religious constructs are today's textbook "science" which defines modern man's "knowledge" of the origin of the universe, the earth, and mankind. Now – without objection – we all know that the most elemental and inescapable fact about knowledge is that all of its claims are built upon what Odin believes to be the truth about the origin of the universe, earth, and mankind. The foundation of all "knowledge" begins at the beginning. We can't go back any further. the beginning is a "creation scenario" upon which all other "knowledge" is built. Are you with me?

DYING MAN: Yes.

PRIEST: We also know that there are only dva foundational "creation scenarios": #1) that employed no evolution at all; #2) that employs billions of years of evolution (with or without bog). The bog of #1 cannot be the bog of #2, and vice-versa. The bog of #1 is the biblical bog. He did not require nor use any evolution whatsoever to create all that exists in the universe and on earth in six literal days. The bog of #2 is Satan of the pharisee religion, and – as bog of the pharisees – he has globally established his alternate creation scenario, namely; the reigning kabbalist bolshy bang paradigm of 15 billion years of evolutionism. It is also an incontestable fact that wholly theoretical science has been used to establish this Satan authored, pharisee installed, evolution-based "creation scenario" as virtual ruler over modern man's belief about the origin of all that exists. This belief dominates the media, all "education", NASA and on and on. Nevertheless, all that is required to expose this ruling counterfeit creation model is to demonstrate that: a) it is contra-scientific by definition b) it violates observable, photographable evidence c) it is built on fraudulent use of math & technology and d) It is an alternate "creation" story of an anti-bible religion.

DYING MAN: In your opinion.

PRIEST: OK, let's viddy not only how this works out, but also why this assumption-based mathematical model launched by Copernicus is the keystone which is supporting the entire rickety, fact less, fraud-driven creation story found in the pharisee's Kabbala. First we note the concepts that make up the bolshy bang evolutionary paradigm: a) billions of years; b) heliocentricity (rotating earth orbiting the sun); c) relativity; d) "bolshy bang"; e) expanding universe; f) parallel universes and superstrings. "Billions of years": this is just a meaningless expression without the "bolshy bang" and "expanding universe" to provide meaning. Today's 15 billion year mantra comes directly out of the 1st century kabbalist Rabbi Hakanna's mystic writings. "The bolshy bang and expanding universe": these concepts are 13th century kabbalist Nachmanides' pieces of the pharisee "creation scenario" puzzle. They are necessary pieces to put rabbi Hakanna's "15 billions of years" into play. "Heliocentricity": unlike these other concepts, this odin of a rotating earth orbiting the sun provides a mathematical model which not only rejects repeated bible teachings that it is the sun that moves, not the earth, but also transforms the earth from being the stationary center of the universe, as observed nightly to a lucky mess of flotsam captured by "gravity" like millions of other planets more "out there". . . and the sun into a mediocre star amongst trillions in billions of galaxies. More, this fact-free bible-bashing, mound of assumptions now in control of modern man's "knowledge" of "origins" is also found in the 13th century writings of kabbalist Nachmanides ... over three centuries before Copernicus launched his revolution.

DYING MAN: (YAWNING) If you say so.

PRIEST: "relativity": here is yet another 13th century kabbalist concept found in Nachmanides' secret writings. This odin was urgently put into use in 1905-1916 via Einstein's phony math to combat dva decades of hundreds of interferometer tests, which showed no earth movement. Now, "parallel universes and superstrings": these are more recent "creation model" concepts in the Kabbala seeking textbook level acceptance. The venerated 16th century kabbalist Isaac Luria (contemporary of Copernicus) connected these concepts and fabricated (secretly for kabbalist glazzballs only) what has now become textbook "origins science"; that is to skazat; a bible destroying – and hence a Christ destroying – alternate "creation scenario". There is no chance that all of this could have accidentally or coincidentally have come together over many centuries to become the "knowledge" controlling and Christ destroying force that it now is. likewise, there is no chance that the critical input by isolated kabbalist individuals could have conceived of such a bible-destroying plan and been motivated to bring it to near fruition that we now viddy. The only explanation for the situation as it now stands is that dva totally contrary and incompatible religions – both supernaturally empowered – are now approaching the biblically foreordained climax of their age-long drats. Odin of these – the Christian religion – maintains in its bible that bog created everything without evolution, and that Satan is a liar and a murderer with no truth in him.

DYING MAN: You're wasting your breath.

PRIEST: The pharisee religion maintains that its kabbala predates any religion or theology; that "the bible's ex nihilo creation is abhorrent to the quabalah"; that calling "Satan the bog of evil is the essential ignorance and heresy which separates Christianity from Judaism ... ." That " ... the kabbala was only transmitted by slovo of rot to a malenky circle of sages in each succeeding generation ... that "the secret doctrines were ... locked away in the brains of the priesthood and the learned." That using "physics ... on the unseen spiritual level, kabbalist Ashlag's rabbit ignited the technological explosion of the 20th century ... with his concepts of relativity, space travel ... . "The Zohar describes the moment of creation as a bolshy bang-like explosion." All that remains in order to bring about the exposure of Satan's entire edifice of deception is: a) to spread the startling fact that the sun, luna, and stars are ittying around a stationary earth just as observed and just as the bible says; b) to show that the Pharisee's bolshy bang evolutionary paradigm – which cannot exist without the rotating/orbiting earth deception – has established that deception using false science. The biblical timer which bog set over 1900 years ago tells us that exposure will occur "one hour" after a global government and its Satan empowered world religious leader is installed. In the meantime, bog's judgment – which begins in Christian churches, will focus on creationists in their midst who – regardless of their acceptance of heliocentricity & other false doctrines – have remained committed to rejecting evolutionism, but now must prove their commitment is genuine.

DYING MAN: You expect me to believe that the earth is flat!

PRIEST: Once this Pharisee religious creation model is understood for what it is; a global deception empowered by Satan and put into mesto by kabbalist Pharisees using false science to kill the biblical creation and its bog, the mysteries about true biblical end raz prophesy will become starkly plain ... the separation of the world's populations into those who get on Satan's side and those who get on the biblical creator's side ... so, yes, Copernican heliocentricity is both the keystone and the Achilles Heel of all False Science. Without that keystone, the Pharisee Big Bang Creationist Paradigm of 15 billion years of Evolutionism cannot stand and will ignominiously collapse ...

& on & on the argument goes for seconds & centuries & hours & megabytes & reams & semaphores & radio waves & JPEGS & minutes & decades & transmissions & lectures & paragraphs &

insinuations & gossip & fortnights & months & sentences & the DYING MAN never gets to die and THE PRIEST never gets to make his point because the whole exchange is eternalized by the etcetera, etc.

dniweR. & should Q-mail Doctor A the real dialogue between The Marquis De Sade and The Priest on De Sade's deathbed, but instead he sends her a screenshot of a far more sobering and succinct thought from a world respected Scientist, "The true reality might be forever beyond our reach, but surely our senses give us at least an inkling of what it's really like. Not so, says Donald D. Hoffman, a professor of cognitive science at the University of California, Irvine. Hoffman has spent the past three decades studying perception, artificial intelligence, evolutionary game theory and the brain, and his conclusion is a dramatic one: The world presented to us by our perceptions is nothing like reality. What's more, he says, we have evolution itself to thank for this magnificent illusion, as it maximizes evolutionary fitness by driving truth to extinction."

There! You saw it in larger than life BOLD pixels. From a Scientist: let us thank evolution for ridding us of Truth and making us fit. Fit to accept that it is survival and progression that will eventually make us Gods. We will finally be our own authors without the need of a creator or even the notion of one.

Yes, Doctor A would like that. It would fit nicely into her beau ideal, but obviously she wouldn't recognize the sentiment of mordancy in which the Q-mail was sent.

Getting the Fear
Chapter Eleven

Jack Sherry woke with a start. He was breathless, sweating, freezing and shivering. His eyes darted around the room and he panicked: *this isn't my room, this is a cell cage!*

He caught his breath and rubbed at his eyes, they stung. He got off the bed and stared in disbelief at the four walls of bars imprisoning him. For a moment he thought that maybe he had been moved from the room upstairs and put in there by one of Captain Torres' underlings by mistake. He quickly realized the chances were slim. He tried the door and it was locked. He shook his head, "No, no ... No!"

He was fired up now and started shouting for help. A young Ibizean cop poked his head around the corner, frowned and disappeared. Jack froze and a dread started to creep up on him. He started to shout for Ernesto, his friend, Captain Torres. He was hoarse by the time Captain Torres entered the room and he laughed in relief when he saw him. The laughter soon ceased.

This wasn't the Captain Torres Jack knew. *This* Captain Torres looked exactly the same but this Captain Torres didn't speak English. *This* Captain Torres wasn't friendly old Ernesto. He was hard faced and spoke Spanish and he had with him a blonde, tanned, posh English woman in her early forties.

Helena Chappell Granger was a filmmaker who was living on Ibiza and translated for *this* Captain Torres whenever the need arose. Jack was dumbstruck as he watched and listened to *this* Captain Torres talk to her.

Jack laughed again, only this time nervously, "Hey, Ernesto! What the bloody Hell are you playing at? If this is a joke … OK, you've had your fun, now let me out of here."
Captain Torres frowned at Jack and turned to Helena Chappell Granger, "¿por qué diablos me está llamando Ernesto."

She closed in on the cell cage, "My name is Helena Chappell Granger and Captain Torres has asked me to act as interpreter for him."
Jack growled, "Are you kidding me? He speaks better English than I do! What am I doing in here?"
She was about to reply but Jack continued, "The joke's gone far enough now!"
Jack focused on Captain Torres, "Ernesto! What the hell are you doing?"
Captain Torres agitatedly threw up his hands and babbled at Helena, pointing at Jack Sherry like he was a common criminal. Helena calmed Captain Torres and closed back in on the cell cage.
"Captain Torres wants to know how you know his first name, Mr. Sherry."
Jack tilted his head to the side and he grabbed a hold of the bars, "This is a prank, right? The lads back at The Yard have put you and Ernesto and up to it haven't they?"
Helena tried to be sympathetic, "I honestly do not know what you are talking about, Mr. Sherry. I only know what Captain Torres has told me."

Jack stuck his arm out through the bar and made a grab for her. She shot back and Captain Torres instinctively drew his baton and swung at Jack's arm. Jack hissed in pain as it caught him and he pulled it back in, shouting, "What the hell are you doing you mad bastard?"

Helena was rattled, "Please, Mr. Sherry, you're not making this easy on yourself."

Jack glared at her and pointed at Captain Torres, "Easy on myself? When I fell asleep, him and me were getting on like a house on fire, and now … ask him why he's pretending that he can't speak English! Ask him what the fuck I'm doing in here! When Scotland Yard hear about this there's going to be hell to pay!"

Helena and Captain Torres conversed, all the while Jack was shouting at them. Helena sighed at Jack, "He says we'll come back when you've calmed down, Mr. Sherry."

Jack shouted after them as they left. His mind raced, too many thoughts to filter. He started to feel his stomach turning and his legs go weak. He shuffled to the bed and sat down with his head in his hands. He put his hands out in front of himself and stared at them. This wasn't the DT's, this wasn't a hallucination. He was definitely awake, this wasn't a nightmare. He shuddered and started to try and filter only rational and practical thoughts. If there had been a toilet in the cell cage he would have sat on it and emptied his bowels. He tried desperately to focus on what he would say.

When they came back he would remain calm. He would ask them why he had been locked up and then he would then request a telephone call. He would call his boss back at The Yard and ask him to talk to Torres or the interpreter and get some sense out of the bastards. While he was strategizing he couldn't help but wonder why Captain Torres was doing this to him. What had he done to make Captain Ernesto Torres turn on him like this? Why was Torres pretending he didn't speak English?

Jack paced the cell cage, took deep breaths and swung his arms across his chest, hoping that some exercise might open his mind up. He just couldn't shake the feeling that a prank was being played on him though. *If* the lads back at The Yard had got CI Ketley to put Torres up to this ... no, no, it was just too ... he started to wish that it *was* just a prank, however unlikely that may be.

He stared at the bars on the cell cage and muttered over and over to himself, "Remain calm, Jack, you're a professional, remain calm ..."

Candice met Grant Burgess in The Royal Standard pub on Archway. She had cash on her and Grant asked her to come into the snug room with him. Grant was feared in North London and the drinkers thought better of commenting on Candice's stunning looks in case Grant was screwing her.

Grant Burgess was indeed a big lump. He had arms like tree trunks and a barrel chest. Candice found him attractive in an alpha male kind of way. He was nothing like Charlie Coleman. Charlie was good looking, charming and he dressed immaculately. Burgess was cauliflower eared, broken nosed, scruffy and inarticulate. Candice wouldn't have objected if he had taken her outside behind the pub and ravished her though.

He bought them drinks and he whispered that Candice slip the envelope under the table, "Don't want any o' these mugs in here knowing my business."
Candice passed him it surreptitiously, "OK, I understand."
"I put him hospital, girl."
"I know."
"Bashed him up good n' proper like you asked."
Grant glugged his Guinness, "I know that Charlie Coleman. It was only a matter o' time before someone gave him a seeing to anyway. He's upset a lot people down the West End he has."
Candice smiled, "I could have saved some money then."
Burgess didn't get it, he didn't *get* much and ignored the remark,

"He's a bloody coward he is. Only picks on poofs n' old people n' those that can't fight."

"How come he gets away with it then?"

Burgess shrugged his huge shoulders, "Funny old place down West."

"How do you mean?"

"Well, like, they get up to all sorts down there don't they … poofs, druggies, prostitutes n' all that stuff. They wouldn't get away with up here I'll tell ya. No, they'd get a clump up here if they tried any o' that on they would … we're decent people up here we are."

Candice couldn't resist it, "But, you know … what *you* do … that's not legal is it, Grant?"

He frowned and paused, "Yeah but … what I do's different in' it?"

"Why's it different?"

"I'd never give a good hiding to some o' these people Coleman n' the likes would. They've got no … What's the word?"

"Morals?"

"That's right, no morals. See, I only do people over who deserve it. I'd never bash a woman or a big pansy or a pensioner or a kid, no … see, I only do jobs where there's a liberty been taken by a man. A real man."

Candice was enjoying letting Grant Burgess talk himself into a deep hole, "Like Charlie Coleman? He's a real man then?"

He frowned, "Well, yeah, no, no. He's just a bully. He's a coward. It's funny you came to me, love, 'cos I had a bone to pick with Coleman anyway."

Candice was intrigued, "What do you mean a bone to pick?"

"My sister in law, my Missus' sister. Coleman used to court her. He was horrible to her."

She was even more intrigued, "Yeah? Was he? In what way?"

"Well … I don't even like saying this but he … he carved his name into her bum cheeks with a knife … well, his whatchamacallit … initials, you know, like she was some cow or something. Told her she was his property … see, I'd never do anything like that. He's one o' them perverts he is."

Candice sat forward; she wanted to learn more about Charlie

Coleman *and* Grant Burgess. She especially wanted to know more about any violent kinks they had. Burgess didn't want to talk anymore though; he wanted to get back to his drinking pals. Candice was a little pissed off that he hadn't made a pass at her or even shown the slightest bit of sexual interest. She soon understands why though when he pointed out his wife working behind the bar.

"That's my Missus over there, behind the bar. She knows I'm doing some business with you, like. If I was sat here chatting to another bird she'd have had her claws out by now she would."

Grant's 'Missus' was an attractive, busty, pneumatic bleach blonde. Candice could see they made a perfect couple and she killed her drink, thanked Grant and headed back to the West End. There was no way she could have competed with such a woman.

Candice hit The Scotch Of Saint James' club around ten. Twenty six year old Lord Henry Tattersal invited her over to his table. This louche heir to a fortune was entertaining equally louche heirs to other fortunes and a couple of aspiring rock stars. Three men, in turn, tried to hit on Candice but she politely knocked them back. Lord Henry laughed and told them that he had lost count of the times he had tried to get gorgeous Candice into his bed.

Lord Henry's party started to grow and he invited everyone back to his apartment in Holland Park. By midnight the party was starting to swing and the drink and drugs were flowing courtesy of Lord Henry. Candice noticed one of the barmen from The Scotch, Jeremy, and sat next to him as he smoked a joint.

Candice knew that Jeremy knew Charlie Coleman and she subtly started quizzing him. Jeremy said that he liked Charlie, even though he knew was a shady character and hurt people for a living.

"So he's what you'd call a character, eh?"

Jeremy giggled, "Oh yes, Charlie Coleman's a real character all right. Have you heard the story about him and Paul McCartney, Candice?"

"No, tell me."

"Charlie was in The Scotch one night with a girl and the girl had a thing for Paul McCartney. Anyway, Paul McCartney was in the club that night and she couldn't take her eyes off him. Charlie was trying to impress her and he was telling her that him and McCartney were very close, they weren't of course, but ... anyway, Charlie follows McCartney into the gents and asks him if he will do him a favour. Charlie asks if he'll stop by his table and reckon on that him and Charlie are big mates with each other, you know, to impress this girl Charlie's trying to lay? McCartney being McCartney agrees ... so, it's about twenty minutes later and McCartney goes over to Charlie and the girl. He puts on a bit of a show, you know, laying it on a bit thick that him and Charlie Coleman are really tight ... only, and you'll love this," Jeremy laughed and pulled on the joint, "Charlie Coleman says to McCartney, he says, 'Hey, come on Paul, leave me alone all right? Can't you see I'm entertaining this beautiful young lady?' ... McCartney's face was a picture and, needless to say, Charlie Coleman impressed the knickers off her that night."

Jeremy and Candice laughed, he offered her the joint but she refused. Jeremy continued, "You've got to hand it to Charlie Coleman. He's as wide as The Thames, a real character."

"He's what Dr. Geller would call a sociopath."

Jeremy frowned, "Who's Dr. Geller?"

Candice stared into the distance and smiled, "Dr. Geller is one the greatest men alive."

Jeremy thought about it, "Mmm. Doctor, eh? Can he get hold of some good drugs?"

Candice ignored his inane question, stood up and walked away leaving him happily sucking on his joint.

Candice caught up with the enigmatic Anita Petraeus in the kitchen.

Anita was necking neat Vodka and pills and chaining Salem cigarettes. She was a waif like character, late twenties, and natural
blonde, flat chested, freckled and ice blue eyed. She was Dutch by
birth and had come to swinging London in the early sixties to bag
her a pop star. She bagged many of them but she also bagged herself
a host of venereal diseases, an addiction to booze and pills – uppers,
downers, sidewinders – and had now become seen as slightly toxic
to even the hardcore party people on the scene.

People were beginning to comment that Anita Petraeus was giving
off the stench of death and many hipsters who had once found her
irresistible were avoiding her. She saw Candice and flung herself
at her.
"Oh, Candice. It is so good to see you."
Anita Petraeus clung on to Candice and hugged her tightly, "I have
been so ill, Candice."
"What's been wrong, Anita?"
Anita let go of Candice and swigged on the bottle of Vodka, "I've
been getting the fear, Candice. Getting the fear really bad, more
than usual, and not just comedowns, darling."
Candice was sympathetic, "You need to lay off the drugs, Anita."
"I know, I know, Candice, but it is easier said than done."
"I've told you before, you should come to The Institute. There are
people that can help you, Anita."
Anita was dubious, "No, I don't know about that, Candice. Look
what happened to Dorian Butler. He has never been the same since
he went there. He's become a hermit, he lives in squalor and rants
and raves at everyone."
Candice paused, she was confused, "Dorian Butler?"
"Mmm, yes darling."
"What are you talking about? Dorian Butler never came to The
Institute, Anita."
Anita took another swig of Vodka and wiped her mouth with the back
of her hand, "Oh yes he did, darling. He went in there and came out
a different person. Completely different."

Candice frowned, "No, no, you're mistaken, Anita. Dorian Butler never came to The Trebistock Institute. I should know, I live there, remember?"

"Well, darling, it must have been when you went traveling around Europe. Dorian Butler was there because he called Lyle Chivers to come and rescue him. Lyle and me were smoking some Nepalese hash at his apartment at the time and he got a telephone call from Dorian. He was half mad, crying, sobbing, tearing his hair out and-"

Candice was getting angry, "Anita ... listen, you don't know what you're talking about. I'm telling you that I would have known if Dorian Butler had stayed at The Institute. Maybe all the drugs are turning your brains to shit, eh?"

"But ... why would I make this up? They made Dorian read one of those screenplay things from the present future called Here Be Monsters. It was written by an ampersand who was trapped in a limbo of near life experiences."

"You're going mad! And you should be careful what you say about The Institute. Saying things like that could be considered slanderous."

Anita quickly delved into her bag and started to fish for something. Candice watched, confused.

Anita held a scrap of paper out to Candice, "Is this the address?"

Candice grabbed the scrap of paper, stared at it and screwed it up, "This means nothing! So you've got the address, and what? What does that prove?"

Anita was desperately trying not offend Candice, "Candice, I'm sorry, darling, I really am, I don't mean to upset you, but ... well, why would I write the address down?"

Candice snapped, "God knows!"

"When we got the telephone call we looked the address up and I wrote it down, darling."

Candice was exasperated and she stomped off, waving a dismissing hand at Anita. Anita was confused and took another swig on the bottle of Vodka, shouting after her, "I hope I haven't upset you, darling?"

Candice left the party and went back to her room at The Institute. What Anita had said would keep her awake, not because of how Anita had described Dorian Butler's mental state, but because if it was true that he had been to The Trebistock, why hadn't Dr. Myron Geller told her about it? After all, it was Candice who had tried tirelessly to persuade Dorian Butler to visit The Institute. He had been a well-known, young intellectual on the scene at one time, and everyone liked his rapier wit and commentary on life. She had marked him down as a perfect subject for The Institute.

Dorian was well know for his abstinence, but for some inexplicable reason he started to suffer depression and Candice begged him to visit her hero, Dr. Geller; promising that he would help Dorian. As far as she knew, Dorian never did. She needed to find out why Anita Petraeus had been so insistent he had been to The Institute and what all that fantastical talk about him being crazed had been about.

She got on the tube early the next day and headed south to The Elephant & Castle and Elliot's Row, the last known address of Dorian Butler. The street had seen better times but seemed ideal for someone like Dorian, scruffy, a little bohemian, shambolic and very English.

She walked along the street; trying to remember which house he lived at. She had only ever been there at night, but remembered that the tiny front garden was always a real mess. She hadn't got far on along the street when she stopped at number 12. This was it, the garden was like a junk shop.

Candice knocked on the door and waited. She knocked again and the next door neighbor, a middle aged, working class woman popped up at the dividing wall.
She spoke quietly to Candice, "Excuse me, love … huh … are you a friend of Dorian's?"
"Yes, yes I am. Do you know if he's …"

"Oh dear ... you're not family then?"

Candice frowned, "No, just a friend. What's wrong?"

"He's gone, love."

"He's moved out?"

The Neighbor lowered her eyes and sighed, "It's about a fortnight back ... he ... well, he killed his self, poor soul."

"Excuse me? Did you say ... ?"

"Yes ... it's a tragedy. He was muttering a load of old codswallop about how tortuous it is to be made to read screenplays from the present future, poor bugger."

Candice was shocked, she opened her mouth to speak but the Neighbor continued, "They said he ... said he hanged his self ... I'm sorry, love, sorry to be the one to break the news, like ... do you want to come in for a cup o' tea, settle your nerves? It must be a terrible shock."

Candice distractedly thanked her and turned the cup of tea down. The Neighbor went back in her house. Candice stood on the doorstep and turned to leave. The junk in the garden caught her eye. In amongst the scraps of old furniture, broken musical instruments, bags of household waste and mountainous stacks of old newspapers she spotted some torn, frayed and yellowing books. One in particular caught her eye.

She gingerly picked out the sodden book from the others. She knew this book; this was one of Dr. Geller's published papers on psychiatry. She held it at arms length with her index finger and thumb; careful to make sure it wasn't covered in something foul. On the fly page she spotted handwriting. Confident that the book wasn't soiled she held it and stared at the writing. She would know the handwriting anywhere. It was Dr. Geller's:

From Dr. Myron H. Geller to Dorian Butler. I do hope you enjoy the book, and please remember this quote: "When one creates phantoms for oneself, one puts vampires into the world, and one must nourish these children of a voluntary nightmare with one's blood, one's life, one's intelligence, and one's reason, without ever satisfying them."

Candice wasn't shocked ... no, the feeling was soon replaced by jealousy. How had Dorian Butler managed to worm his way into Dr. Geller's life without her knowing about it? Why hadn't she been told? What were they hiding from her?

She agonized over whether to ask Dr. Geller what had happened. She fought the feeling that Dr. Geller had consciously betrayed her. She simply wanted a rational explanation; something that would explain why she hadn't been told that Dorian Butler had visited and got to know Dr. Geller.

Candice eventually decided not to confront Dr. Geller, it just wouldn't be right. If he had wanted her to know about Dorian Butler he would have told her. She decided that Dr. Geller was doing what he always did. He was just protecting her.

Still ... if Dorian had visited Dr. Geller there would be an account of it somewhere. She thought about going through the files, *really* thought about it, but just couldn't bring herself to be so deceitful. Instead she went back to the book that she had found in Dorian's scrapheap of a garden. In the rear, Dorian, presumably, had written:

THE PROCESS CHURCH OF THE FINAL JUDGEMENT TIMELINE:

1931　　*Mary Ann MacLean is born in Glasgow, Scotland.*

1935　　*Robert de Grimston Moor is born in Shanghai, China, and is relocated to England to be raised.*

1954–58　*Robert serves his military duty with the King's Royal Hussars.*

1959　　*Robert starts an architectural course at Regent Street Polytechnic in London.*

1958–62　*Robert's first marriage.*

1960　　*Robert's younger brother undergoes Dianetics therapy.*

1961 *Mary Ann MacLean joins The Church Of Scientology and quickly becomes an auditor.*

1962 *Robert quits architectural college after three years, joins the CoS and meets Mary Ann MacLean for the first time. They become inseparable.*

1963 *Robert and Mary Ann quit Scientology and I volunteer to the guinea pig in Mary Ann and Roberts therapy sessions/ experiments.*

1963–66 *Robert and Mary Ann continue to conduct therapy sessions and formalize their activities under name Compulsions Analysis.*

1964 *Robert and Mary Ann set up business in their Wigmore Street apartment in London.*

1965 *Hell Ron Hubbard of Scientology declares Robert and Mary Ann "suppressive persons" for their innovative use of the E-meter.*

1965 *Robert, Mary Ann and their clients in Compulsions Analysis recognize a shared sense of spirituality. Compulsions Analysis becomes The Process as a consequence. Robert sheds his surname and becomes Robert de Grimston.*

1966 *YEAR ZERO. June 28th and Rosemary gives birth to her baby. The Process establishes its headquarters at 2 Balfour Place, in London's Mayfair district. The Process becomes a community.*

1966 *Approximately 30 Processeans, together with six German shepherd dogs, move to Nassau in the Bahamas in June. The community moves to Mexico after three months. In September they travel to the coastal village of Sisal on the Yucatán Peninsula and, from there, they establish themselves on the deserted estate of a ruined salt factory called Xtul. Robert writes the Xtul Dialogues.*

1966 *Hurricane Inez strikes Yucatan on October 7th. The Process moves back to London, leaving a small contingent in Xtul. The first Coffee House is opened in the basement of Balfour Place.*

1967   *The first Process magazine, the Common Market issue, is printed and sold on the streets of London. The magazine is also distributed to each member of the House of Commons.*

1967   *Robert and Mary Ann set off on their travels through the Middle East in April, arriving in Israel in May. In June they arrive in Turkey. Process magazine publishes the Freedom of Expression and the Mindbenders issues.*

1967   *Processeans from Xtul move to New Orleans and start a Chapter on Royal Street in the French Quarter. Mary Ann and Robert move to Louisiana and settle into a house in Slidell.*

1967   *The bulk of the community remains in London and the Art Department produces the next two issues of Process magazine. The book 'Drug addiction' is published.*

1968   *The Process Church Of The Final Judgment moves back to Europe in September.*

1969   *The Fear and Death issues of the Process magazine are published. The Paris Chapter opens and members are sent there to sell magazines and raise money on the street.*

Candice had no idea why Dorian had written these notes. She had heard of The Process Church but had never known Dorian to be even remotely associated with them. If she was going to find out why Dorian had met Dr. Geller she was going to have to do some digging. She had something far more important to do right now though. Something that would really please Dr. Geller.

Captain Torres gently shook Jack Sherry awake, "Mr. Jack, Mr. Jack."

Jack Sherry slowly opened his eyes, sighed in relief and put his hand on his chest, "Oh … oh thank God for that, Ernesto."

"Are you OK, Mr. Jack?"

Jack sat up and beamed at Captain Torres, "I just had the most … the most vivid nightmare."

"Aaahhh, pesadilla, yes, yes. You think because of the poisoning maybe?"

"No doubt, Ernesto, no doubt about it. It was frightening. *You* couldn't speak English."

He chuckled, "No? What happened?"

"Never mind, Ernesto ... it was just a bad dream."

Jack went to the sink and splashed water in his face.

"I spoke to the waiters at the bar, Mr. Jack, and ... this is embarrassing to say, but yes, it does happen often."

"Spiking peoples drinks?"

"Yes ... I will not deny this, Mr. Jack ... we do have many people on the island who are ... they like to use narcotics. I have been tolerant as long as they do not harm others. I have spoken to the mainland Police many times and they too are of the same opinion ... I can only apologize, Mr. Jack, but Ibiza is ... I think you know that Ibiza attracts a certain kind of people, yes?"

Jack sparked a Marlboro, "Yeah ... it's not your fault, Ernesto."

"No, but maybe you are thinking we are a little ... Mmm, a little too free and easy with our policing, no?"

Jack smiled, put his hands on Captain Torres shoulders and looked him straight in the eyes, "Ernesto. It's got nothing to do with me how you police your island. You just do what needs to be done. I'm just here to help in any way I can."

Captain Torres smiled back at him but something didn't feel quite right for Jack Sherry. A gesture like this was alien to him. He had just been disingenuous with Captain Torres. What he really wanted to say was: *clean up your fucking island! Get shut of all these freaky drug addled beatniks before they turn it into a modern day Sodom & Gomorrah and it sinks into the sea!*

They went to eat at a small cafe. Jack had found a much missed of late appetite. Captain Torres chuckled at how much food Jack put away. Jack surprised himself. They started to drink as they waited for Brigadier Hector Guzman from the mainland Guardia Civil.

Captain Torres filled Jack in on Brigadier Guzman. He was ex-military, a decorated cop, early fifties, hard working, hard taskmaster who was well respected both in his agency and in political circles.

Jack frowned, "I didn't think the Civil Guard investigated murders? I read a brief on your policing structure before I flew out here. It came across as though the regular police investigated murders."
"Ah, yes, but the Guardia Civil will need to be involved in something like this, Mr. Jack. This is making international news."
"Mmm, right. I understand."

Brigadier Guzman arrived with a couple of his Lieutenants, shook hands with Jack and then proceeded to ignore his presence as he talked to Captain Torres in their native tongue. Jack could tell that Brigadier Guzman wasn't impressed that Scotland Yard had sent a copper over but was pissed off that Ernesto wasn't acting as interpreter and including him in the conversation.

Jack bit his tongue and pictured what would happen next. It was obvious really, he would be sent home, not needed anymore, or at least not needed until, or rather *if*, any of the corpses turned out to be British subjects. The lads back at The Yard would like that. They'd be jealous that he had been sent out to a beautiful Spanish island on the off chance that some Brits had been murdered. They'd love to see him back in the drab office, slogging through the mountainous files on all the unsolved murders in London.

Jack sipped a Spanish beer from the bottle and thought about the spiking. He got riled up as he thought about what would happen to somebody who was a lot less mentally strong than him if they got spiked: *it would probably send someone who wasn't mentally tough insane. Some poor innocent stiff, that would be it! Bingo! They'd be slavering and ripping their clothes off and going crazy in the streets.*

If indeed he were going to be sent home he would at least visit the bar again and try to find the rat that had spiked him. If he found the culprit he would wait and tail them out of the bar; wait for an opportunity and give them a beating they would never forget. He would knock them out with whatever came to hand and then he would get busy on them: kicking, stomping, punching, gouging, biting until … before the thought had even evaporated, Jack was feeling shocked at even letting a thought like that creep into his mind. *That* just wasn't Jack Sherry. It was an external thought. He panicked a little as he scrambled to think where it had come from.

Jack Sherry didn't do things like that. No. Never. If he found out who had spiked his drink he would have Captain Ernesto Torres arrest them. He would follow protocol; do everything by the book. He imperceptibly shuddered as he watched Captain Torres and Brigadier Guzman talk and felt a smothering cloud of depression envelope him as he remembered the thought he had just entertained.

Jack sank another bottled beer and watched Brigadier Guzman walk away.
Captain Torres sighed, "Well, Mr. Jack. It seems that Brigadier Guzman is to bring some Interpol agents to the island."
"Mmm, it doesn't surprise me, Ernesto. This is a big job. I mean, let's face it, it's more than you and me can handle."
"Maybe, yes."
"What did he say when you told him about the initials, Ernesto?"
"The initials?"
"Yeah, on the corpses … CC, remember?"
Captain Torres frowned, "What are these 'initials'?"
"The letters … you know? The initials cut into the bodies?"
"There is an initial on the bodies?"
Jack closed in on Captain Torres and chuckled, "Come on, Ernesto. The initials carved into them. CC? On the bodies, remember?"
Captain Torres looked at him blankly and shrugged, "You tell me, Mr. Jack. I do not know what you mean."

Jack stared into Captain Torres' eyes and felt a wave of panic wash over him. He quickly stood up and paced about.

Captain Torres watched him, concerned and confused, "Are you OK, Mr. Jack?"

Jack took deep breaths, "You don't know about the initials? We … we … we didn't see initials carved into the corpses in the morgue, Ernesto?"

Captain Torres stood up and put his hand on Jack's shoulder, "Mr. Jack. What is the problem?"

Jack was on the cusp of hyperventilation, "Now, now you see. *That* was before I was spiked! We saw the fucking initials *before* I was spiked, Ernesto!"

"Please, Mr. Jack, please, sit down yes?"

Jack glared at Captain Torres, "I want to go back to the room. Take me back to the room right now."

"But what is the matter, Mr. Jack?"

"Now, Ernesto! I can't take this anymore … look; just take me back to my room. I'm going home first thing in the morning. The first flight out of here do you understand?"

"OK, OK, Mr. Jack. We will go now. I will take you back, OK?"

"The Slayer struck at night. It was long after midnight but The Six were still partying hard. They were drinking and drugging and smoking and smooching and fondling each other. Hands and mouths were everywhere, indiscriminate intimate contact: pawing, groping, squeezing, scratching. The Slayer watched through the window and felt repulsed. The Slayer put their hand to their mouth to stem any vomit that may spurt out. The Slayer's head swam and throbbed and they had to blink to keep focus on the beasts inside the villa."

"The Slayer thought that they could hear – but not decipher – their demonic language. It was a language only the possessed would understand. It was made up of grunts and squeals and hisses and animalistic murmurs, but only it was speeded up to helium ingestion proportions. The Slayer tried to stop from trembling. They needed to be strong and steady of hand if they were to slay these monsters."

"The Slayer had a hatchet and a large knife and was sure that that was all they needed. These effete, spineless, cowardly specimens would go down quick, but they would also suffer for their crimes. They may very well be monsters but they had no power now. All their powers had been spent tormenting The Slayer. They were only strong at mind games, only effective at getting into your head and fucking around with it, creating demons and fear and bogeymen and terror when they had a script to read from. Only effective when they had a sick plan to carry out. Only effective in a gang. Evil gangsters. Bullying monsters."

"The Slayer had no doubt that they would go through these fuckers like a hot knife through butter. It was going to be a quick slaughter, but it would be painful: *oh yes it would be painful all right.*"

"They would stare into the abyss before they were dispatched from life and would catch a glimpse of themselves laboring in the lowest rungs of Hell, the pit that lies even lower than the bed of fire Pontius Pilate lies on as he stares at his crime for all eternity."

"There would be no ritualism or pomp and ceremony, no effected dramatics on the part of The Slayer. The Slayer would go to work on them, picking them off one by one and hitting them full on with the hatchet in their heads. *Thud! Squelch! Suck!* As The Slayer pulled the hatchet out of their brains. After that, once they were all dead, The Slayer would start to take the bodies – which they never deserved to have in the first place – apart. The Slayer would leave them all over the villa. The Slayer would make sure that their families wouldn't be able to give them open casket send-off's to Hell, unless, that is, they knew a mortician who worked miracles. The Slayer would make sure that they were incomplete when they arrived in their beloved Hell and were greeted by their beloved Satan."

"The Slayer would slash and hack and cut through their pleas and protestations and screams and leave them drowning in their blood as it exploded out of their vital organs and ran riot around their bodies. The Slayer would stab at their dying bodies in hyper speed so that their blood sprayed the ceilings."

"No longer would The Slayer hear their warped laughter and snake-like hisses. No longer would anyone have to suffer the torment these evil fuckers thrived on. No more would these animals feed off of the energy of fear that their victims radiated."

"The Slayer would wash off the blood and guts and finally be able to lie down and sleep ... safe in the knowledge that they had rid humanity of six devils incarnate."

"The Slayer would sleep the sleep of angels. A sleep free from torment and panic and guilt and worry. A sleep that had been earned *not* inherited."

And now Dr. Myron Geller's voice, "Did you hear all that Jack? Do you understand?"

--- ---

--- --- --- --- ---

--- --- --- --- --- --- --- ---

& bobbed about on The Solent, Justice Sir Beiber's admonishments ringing in his esophagus, the red raw shame of shitting yourself in class and being made to wear pants from Lost Property, your own shit caked pants wrapped up for you in yesterday's newspaper to take home for your dead Mother to launder. It's a color supplement from the soar away, scintillating *Sun*, big tits and Stretch Armstrong pretending to take a giant leap for mankind in a TV studio.

& skimmed the water, a lump in his discarnate throat the size of a leather clad fist. A thoughtjack: *I'll explain myself better to Beiber. I'll reiterate that he is under the Mandela Effect but I'll make concessions. I'll show him the cover. It will have nice grey apartment building on it. Nothing offensive.*

A Seagull – eating fish and chips it had nicked from an innocent child on the beach – bobbed along with &.
& glared at the Seagull, "Yeah? Can I help you?"
The Seagull haughtily responded, "The project of anxiety is in effect identical to the fallacy of binary opposition. Ironic reference to the relationship between the conceptual logic of collecting as a cultural practice and the nostalgia for self-referential systems might be less irritating in the hands of a more skilled writer."
& groaned, "Oh fuck! A pseudo Seagull! Just what I need!"
The Seagull teased a heavily salted and vinegar drenched chip in its beak, "Ah, pithy phrase concerning the relationship between the reading of communicative rationality and the appropriation of normative values is neither a survey, nor an expository work in the familiar sense, but a critical polyphony."
"Leave me alone. Just fuck off!"
"An highly ambitious exposition of the relationship between the legitimating of a radical alterity and the denomination of the anesthesia of forgetting is an inevitable consequence of, and indeed, an integral part of Kinbotes' influence in the field."
& spat, "You stole those and chips didn't you? I bet you stole them. Yeah, that's what I bet you did."
The Seagull chortled, "You should read my classic essay on the relationship between the appropriation of early modern sexuality and the linguistic construction of panopticism. It will remind you that the moment of unadulterated new historicism has long since passed."

& had heard enough, "Enough of this gay banter!" he blinked and sentenced the Pseudo Seagull to 100 years of solitude as a tile in a box of Scrabble in a charity shop that nobody will ever buy because some of the other tiles are missing. & wasn't enamored of water birds ever since witnessing a fleet of storks dropping stillborn babies over Bradford Royal InfirMARY's Anti-natal unit.

Still bobbing about on the briny up ahead, straight starboard, was a rickety old pirate ship. A thought bubble burst like a salty disco blister. & remembered he had forgotten about the hospital again. Again he remembered The Ward that dare not speak its name, though officially it was dubbed The Typoglycemia Ward: all those orphans, all those novel headlines: *Would you like to try on the dead mans trousers? When Thesaurus roamed the earth. Misogynist? Gynophobic? I'm like every fucking Disney character ever conceived! Gibberish as a second language? Really? Something's fucking died in here! There's a right pen n' ink! They think to change time, other times, and to divide time. Remember, outside of time, where God is, everything exists simultaneously ... and Satan said "I will be like the most High."*

The Nurses knew we were all orphans. They treated us like shit. They played God over us. We were the test tube babies, the Petri dish pond scum, shit on their clogs, rotten fruit flies in their ointment, pebbles in their gall bladders, Stonehenge stones in their kidneys, yeast in their urinary tracts, we were bouncing baby bastards that no Alphabet in its right mind would adopt.

&'s memoryhole ached like a phantom limb. He remembered to remember the pain and the tears and the sobs that consumed everything within earshot. O the deformities, the scribbles, the spastic doodles that screamed, "I am here. Get me out!"

The Typoglycemia Ward smelt of old wet newspaper and rotting moths and old age and academia and vacuum dried piss and charity shops and shortbread and extreme rationing and pounds shilling and pence and castor oil and vinegar and brown paper and its walls were festooned with horse brasses and sickly sentimental ornaments and family portraits long since yellowed and sunlight bleached and Anaglypta and flock wallpaper with the fleur de lies signature and its windows were marked with an X in gaffa tape and gasmasks hung from the damp ceiling and the outside shithouse was indoors and you wiped your arse on old wet newspaper and the Jack Russell's ran rampant digging out rats from every orifice and the cabbage boiled and boiled and there was no escape from the violent stench and the dead soldiers decomposed medleys glorifying The War To End All Wars Until The Next One, and clones of Florence Nightingale & The Machine performed an old time musical version of "You Got The Love" and air raid sirens lured Krauts into bunkers and the Catering Corp squirted mustard gas on their bratwursts and Flanagan & Allen cracked wise about A-Dolf and Dame Vera Lynn told tales from the trenches about our poor boys and their bowel evacuations and the cry was always "God save The King" and ...

Every morning the Head Nurse would crack the whip and make the orphans recite The Good Words verbatim, robotically, "One of the erlesait svinuivrg epmxeals of cilhd andmanoebnt in latiterure is taht of Oidpues who is lfet to die as a bbay in the hllis by a hedmrsan ordeerd to klil the bbay, but is fnuod and grows up to utglwnniity marry his bcaoigoill mother. In mnay tleas, scuh as Sonw Withe, the chlid is alcultay adaonnbed by a sanrvet who had been gevin oredrs to put the clhid to dateh. Cdehrlin are oetfn anbnoaded wtih bitrh tnoeks, wichh act as polt deeivcs to erunse taht the child can be iteiinedfd. Tihs temhe is a mian eelnmet in Aenglo F. Cogiinlo's hrtsoiacil ftociin nlelova The Lday of the Wheel, in wcihh the ttlie refres to a "reeicevr of fougnlndis" who wree paelcd in a dcviee claled a "finouldng wheel", in the wlal of a curhch or hpotsail. In Shereapaske's The Winetr's Tlae, a roiceongtin scnee in the fnail act rlevaes by tshee taht Pedtria is a knig's detaughr rthear tahn a sdsrpeeehhs, and so suitable for her pnrcie lveor. Sillaimry, wehn the hioerne of Le Fnrese reevlas the bocdrae and the rnig she was abeaodnnd wtih, her moethr and stsier rnogiczee her; tihs meaks her a sbultiae birde for the man wsohe msistres she had been. Form

Oiupdes oawrnd, Gerek and Rmaon teals are fellid wtih eosepxd cheilrdn who espeacd dteah to be rteuenid wtih teihr fliaimes – usaluly, as in Lgunos's Dhnaips and Chole, mroe hlppaiy tahn in Oeipdus's csae. Grown ciehdrln, hviang been taken up by seatrrgns, wree uaullsy rioezngecd by tkeons taht had been lfet wtih the eexpsod bbay: in Edruieips's Ion, Creüsa is abuot to klil Ion, bvnilieeg him to be her huansbd's ieiiltagmtle chlid, wehn a pisreests rvleeas the birth-toenks taht sohw taht Ion is her own, andeoanbd innaft. Tihs may relcfet the wreesapidd parictce of cihld aobaenmndnt in tehir crueutls. On the oehtr hnad, the motif is cnueiotnd troghuh laetruirte werhe the prcctaie is not weraepsdid. William Srekahasepe uesd the andbmnnaoet and disreovcy of Pdteria in The Wetnir's Tlae, and Edmund Sepensr rvleeas in the lsat Canto of Book 6 of The Fireae Qeuene taht the ceatarhcr Pelsoltara, raseid by sepherdhs, is in fcat of nlobe birth. Hreny Fidilneg, in one of the first nevols, rentuoecd The Htsrioy of Tom Jeno: fdoninulg. Rtuh Bndceiet, in sdintyug the Znui, fonud taht the pciartce of child aebdnaonnmt was unkwonn, but futeared hileavy in their falloteks. Sitll, eevn cuuelrts taht do not pctcraie it may refcelt odler cosmuts; in mieavedl ltrarueite, scuh as Sir Degaré and Le Frnsee, the cilhd is anbeoandd iiedtamemly aetfr btrih, whcih may receflt pre-Ctihrisan patceicrs, btoh Scavadinan and Ramon, taht the nborwen wuold not be reaisd wtoihut the fahetr's dsioiecn to do so."

Head Nurse would then force us to prostrate ourselves at the feet of The Crossword Puzzle and solemnly repeat after her, "I cdn'uolt blveiee taht I cluod aulaclty uesdnatnrd waht I was rdanieg: the phaonmneel pweor of the hmuan mnid. Aoccdrnig to a rseearch taem at Cmabrigde Uinervtisy, it deosn't mttaer in waht oredr the ltteers in a wrod are, the olny iprmoatnt tihng is taht the frist and lsat ltteer be in the rghit pclae. The rset can be a taotl mses and you can sitll raed it wouthit a porbelm. Tihs is bcuseae the huamn mnid deos not raed ervey lteter by istlef, but the wrod as a wlohe. Scuh a cdonition is arppoiatrely cllaed Typoglycemia ... amzanig huh? Yaeh and you awlyas thguoht slpeling was ipmorantt. Aemn!"

382

& metaphorically swam towards the pirate ship utilizing the butterfly stroke. He could smell Doctor A listening to his every move:
*if I can reach the ship without arousing suspicion I'll be safe for a
moment.*

& lodged himself in the vocal chords of The Pirate DJ, "This here be
the Jolly Roger *real* Pirate Radio coming at ya live n' direct on 78.8
FM and 88.9. AM. Don't be touching that dial me hearties. Today
we're gonna be talkin' about the eschaton. Tha's right, the eschaton
mateys ... it has been written that some time in th' 23rd century
B.C., a kin' named Nimrod built a tower that were bein' designed t'
be a stairway or gateway t' heaven. Accordin' t' traditional mythology, Nimrod wanted t' meet God and understand his workin's. His
tower were bein' literally a stairway t' th' stars, a way t' enter th'
dimension that God inhabited. There be occultists and mythologists
like William Henry that have claimed that th' ancients like Nimrod
and others used these towers and stargates, Jim lad. Th' towers
created wormholes and th' Gods from th' stars would pass through
them, by Davy Jones' locker. But, o' course, God didn't like th' idea
and so he confused th' language o' Nimrod's people. Undaunted, this
here Nimrod me hearties, well he organized th' Stone Masons. They
continued t' build these stargates and temples. Throughout ancient
history there have been many accounts o' gods travelin' from location t' location usin' intricate machinery that would take them from
one dimension t' another. There be accounts o' th' ancient Sumer
speakin' about so-called gods comin' in through a double pillared
stargate and there have been carvin's that have represented such a
feat. It be amazin' t' think that th' ancients had mastered th' ability
t' travel usin' wormhole technology that we now be hearin' about at
places like th' Large Hadron Collider at CERN."

& listened intently as a jingle interrupted the DJ. He continued, "If
we look back into he ancient histories we can point t' th' possibility
that th' Pillars o' Osirus were quite literally fashioned as a way t'

somehow teleport th' gods t' their various dimensional abodes, and a bottle of rum, with a chest full of booty! Accordin' t' mythologist William Henry, th' Osiris Pillar or th' Temporal Cross were bein' called th' Ta-Wer, meanin' 'bond betwixt heaven and earth.' It were bein' a contraption that were bein' capable o' openin' dimensions or wormholes, with a chest full of booty. These wormholes carried th' Gods t' other locales in th' Universe so they did, and th' same technologies were used t' summon up th' gods. There be many tapestries that hang in ancient churches that depict th' second comin' o' Christ. In these tapestries th' heavenly hosts arrive in a whirlwind that opens up a dimensional doorway. Th' tapestries show Christ returnin' in what appears t' be a dimensional wormhole or stargate so it be. There have been many attempts t' open wormholes and at th' same time th' purpose o' these magical workin's were bein' t' somehow summon demons or angels t' come and initiate th' eschaton. There be plenty o' Wizards who have claimed that they have opened a wormhole usin' magical methods. These be Methods that have allegedly brought dimensional bein's into our existence. Ahoy! And hoist the mainsail! Th' idea o' a dimensional push t' open a doorway t' beckon a god or an entity has been th' challenge from Nimrod's time, t' th' times o' John Dee, Edward Kelly, Aleister Crowley, Yaaarrrrr! Hell Ron Hubbard and a Jack Parsons, to be sure me mateys."

An advert for a sale at Brentford Nylons cut into the narrative and the host cleared his raspy throat and continued, "Tween th' years 1582 and 1589 th' English scholar John Dee conducted a series o' ritual communications with a set o' disincarnate entities that eventually came t' be known as th' Enochian angels, Aarrr, we'll keel-haul ye! It were bein' Dee's plan t' use th' complex system o' magic communicated by th' angels t' advance th' expansionist policies o' his sovereign, Queen Elizabeth I. With th' aid o' lubber occult researcher Edward Kelley he planned t' open a portal t' th' other side by usin' th' lower keys o' Enoch, a magical Alphabet that were bein' sung, by Davy Jones' locker. They were callin' upon th' spirits o' th' poxed t' do espionage fer th' Queen and shiver me timbers accordin' t' history they were successful. These angels declared that th' heavenly name fer Satan were bein' Choronzon and that there were at least four watchtowers or pillars whar star gates exist on th' earth, with a chest full of booty. There be also a way t' open portals elsewhere as long as certain keys and sigils be used t' summon entities t' perform an apocalyptic workin' or spell. One o' th' other rituals performed by John Dee were bein' t' summon th' Archon gatekeeper Cernunnos. Fire the cannons! To th' Celts Cernunnos, Cerne or Belatucadros, and were bein' depicted as a humanoid figure who were bein' more commonly depicted as havin' horns. One o' Cernunnos' titles were bein' Lord o' th' Hunt, but as time progressed agriculture could sustain alongside huntin' and th' Horned God became th' god also o' fertility, and a bucket o' chum. Worship o' this deity were bein' hoped t' not only maintain plentiful meat, but also ensure a bountiful crop harvest and even th' successful procreation o' mankind. In such we find th' concept o' life, death and rebirth, in other myths Cernunnos be depicted as a horned God that controls th' serpents. Th' serpents were symbolic o' mortality, healin' and th' resurrection o' th' poxed, or th' use o' th' poxed fer divinin' or necromancy. As death be integral t' th' continuous circle o' life, Cernunnos has also been associated t' th' Underworld, th' realm o' th' poxed. Whilst th' invadin' Romans could associate th' Horned God with some o' their own belief concepts, such as th' deity Pan or th' horned spirits called Fauns and Satyrs, th' developin' Christian Church however could not comfortably assimilate this fertility icon into their own ethos and so Cernunnos were bein' demonized. Thus th' Horned God became associated with th' devil or Satan. Th' invocations and th' summonin' o' Archons were all part o' somethin' called "th' Apocalypse workin'." Th' concept were bein' t' summon various angels and later demons o' th' underworld t' open a stargate or stairway t' th' heavens. It were bein' actually one th' first attempts at openin' a portal t' another dimension and summonin' spirits. It were bein' literally a ritual t' open up th' secrets o' th' universe and converse with Gods. And swab the deck, stop frigging in the rigging, Aaarrr!"

"These here angels see, well they ne'er empowered Dee t' be th' instrument whereby th' ritual formula fer initiatin' th' apocalypse would be accomplished. Th' Angels stated that th' "workin'" would have t' be accomplished in a later time. Th' unfinished ritual would sit like a tickin' occult time bomb, waitin' fer some clever magician, perhaps guided by th' angels, t' complete it, and a bottle of rum! Dee evidently ne'er received th' signal t' conduct th' Apocalypse Workin' in his lifetime. It were bein' t' be reserved fer another century and another lubber, with a chest full of booty. That lubber were bein' Aleister Crowley. Crowley and his followers wanted t' usher in a morality more severe than any other experienced in th' world. In order t' accomplish this they had t' carry out powerful rituals. And hoist the mainsail, avast! His methods were misunderstood and rumor has it that they were so abhorrent that Mussolini threw that scurvey dog out o' Sicily callin' that scurvey dog a "barbarian." The ornery cuss promised that aft his death there would be a final workin' or ritual whar a portal would be opened and th' "secret chiefs" or ancient Egyptian Gods would return. Two followers o' Crowley, Hell Ron Hubbard and Jack Parsons attempted t' open a portal usin' one o' Crowley's spells betwixt 1945–1946. It were bein' a series o' magical ceremonies called th' "Babylon Workin'." Many people believe that what came through were bein's that looked like th' alien "grays." Hell Ron Hubbard went on t' create Scientology, a religion that teaches that alien entities be responsible fer usin' humans as avatars and that alien spirits get mankind t' do evil. Jack Parsons became th' founder o' JPL, which later become NASA so it did, and claimed that durin' th' Babylon "workin'" "that both he and Hubbard were a part o' widened th' portal fer Crowley's Amalantrah workin' allowin' th' secret chiefs t' enter in t' help mankind. The ornery cuss later attempted another secret project, conjurin' th' Lower key o' Solomon t' usher in th' Apocalypse. Durin' th' ritual, he accidentally blew up his lab while playin' with powerful explosives. Some believed he were bein' attemptin' t' open a Stargate t' summon th' Goetic Demons. For th' last 4,500 years or so we've been waitin' fer another shot at openin' th' Gate usin' scientific methods. We have been waitin' fer th' right date and time fer this t' happen. Accordin' t' Pat Holliday PHD this ritual o' stargate openin' has continued t' this day and accordin' t' research provided one o' th' main centers fer performin' these rituals be at th' Large Hadron Collider at CERN. While CERN has been notorious fer its findin' o' th' Higgs Boson or God particle. It has also been feared t' be th' world's foremost doomsday contraption.

Another advert, this time for Shackletons High Seats momentarily interrupts the flow. "One major accident at CERN and it be believed th' world could end. This year, CERN be beginnin' another set o' experiments in hopes t' gettin' that much closer t' completin' their crusade o' tome bendin' and portal openin'. Scientists at CERN have announced test dates fer th' rest o' th' year, as well as some curious dates can be found in th' upcomin' schedule. With these experiments, th' scientists be hopin' t' create atomic reactions that would provide further information about anti-matter, and th' big bang, by Blackbeard's sword I do swear! Th' damned contraption that many believed would cause th' end o' th' world will be conductin' its most advanced tests on th' same day that th' world be predicted t' end. How ironic be that? Shiver me timbers! Once again it has t' be indicated that CERN be located in Geneva. Geneva and "Saint Geniis" be similar t' th' word "Genesis." th' purpose o' CERN be t' find th' Origins o' Man and th' Universe. They have stated that they want t' open a doorway t' another dimension and find a God. Be it just a coincidence that CERN be short fer th' horned God Cernunnos, pass the grog! Be it also a coincidence that CERN has t' go deep underground t' do their "god" harnessin' experiments? Cernunnos were bein' th' god o' th' underworld. CERN be linked t' several secret projects bein' carried out by th' European Union and th' European Trilateral Commission. Ahoy, and dinna spare the whip! CERN also be responsible fer th' internet and have been doin' ongoin' research fer governments with regard t' global sustainability. It were bein' also reported that in 1999 CERN proposed and carried out quantum Vortex experiments searchin' fer Solar Axions.

Axions be hypothetical particles that be components o' dark matter. In order t' find these Axions CERN proposed th' use o' a decommissioned magnet called SATAN. It were bein' an acronym fer Solar Axion Telescopic Antenna. One o' th' attempts at creatin' a portal anchor happened in an area whar there be rumored t' be an ancient stargate in th' real ancient Babylon, Iraq. On September 8th, 2008 somethin' happened in th' Iraqi city o' Al Hilla. Al Hilla has been rumored t' be a city whar a stargate exists. It were bein' reported that there were bein' a cover up whar nearly 20 American troops visited Davey Jones' Locker as they attempted t' cross through a gate conduit betwixt th' Collider at CERN and one o' th' anchor gates at Al Hilla. Accordin' th' mainstream news reports th' soldiers committed mass suicide. However one o' th' peculiarities reported in Fars News agency were bein' that Iraqi security sources reported that 21 US troops had committed suicide inside a former Iraqi air force base, th' 21 troops were treated in a hospital but only five soldiers survived and wound up missin'. Narcotics were allegedly used in th' suicides. Splice the mainbrace! Th' servicemen belonged t' a unit o' th' US Airborne Division. Th' question be how did so many soldiers have access t' potent narcotics and what happened t' th' five survivors? A witness reported that th' bodies o' th' US troops were hideously deformed and misshapen in such a way that they looked like 5000-year barnacle-covered mummies. Ahoy! Shiver me timbers! On September 11th, 2008 it were bein' reported that th' collider officially went online on September 10th. With a test firin', th' press reported that nothin' significant happened and there were bein' no danger and no end o' th' world. However a strong earthquake measurin' 6.1 in magnitude struck southern Iran. Then it were bein' reported that Northern Chile were bein' struck with a 6.0 tremor. Then a magnitude 6.9 earthquake rattled Japan and then within minutes o' a magnitude 6.6 earthquakes hit Indonesia. Th' collider wasn't even at full power. Shiver me timbers! Fire the cannons! On December 8th, 2009 CERN's collider were bein' still not up t' full power however thousands o' physicists aroun' th' world cheered as they smashed together subatomic particles at th' highest energies e'er reached by a human-made accelerator and th' giant ATLAS detector observed th' products o' th' record-breakin' reactions whizzin' through its sophisticated trackin' devices. Coincidentally a rum spiral appeared o'er Norway early before sunrise. Th' light looked like a portal spiralin' into a black hole. Th' buzz about this spiral and it's comparison t' a wormhole openin' up were bein' viral on th' internet and later it were bein' discovered that a Communiqué linkin' HAARP, CERN and th' Norwegian array EISCAT were bein' released makin' th' wormhole explanation compellin', and dinna spare the whip, ye scurvey dog! I will be th' first t' admit that this be not hard science or pseudo science, it th' new normal fer a planet that seems t' be th' battered partner and th' response be th' shakin', th' sounds o' underground creakin' and pushin' and many thunderous rumbles and explosions deep within th' earth's crust."

"A large ring encircles th' area near CERN, shiver me timbers! It has th' circumference o' about 27 kilometers and inside it be 9300 magnets. Could this be displacin' magma inside th' earth, and a bottle of rum! Someone needs t' ask th' question. Fire the cannons! Yo-ho-ho! Th' collider be a scientific contraption that no one questions and yet it seems t' be a monster that when lit has started creatin' these maga-quakes, tsunamis and disasters, and dinna spare the whip! Walk the plank! Durin' 2010 and 2011 th' LHC increased th' potency and number o' quarks it collides in its experiments. What CERN does not be tellin' us be that with this intensity come consequences. Th' attempts at findin' th' God particle o'er th' years has resulted in greater quantities o' atoms o' strangelet liquid, called hyperons, made o' up, down and rum quarks even when runnin' at low energies, despite all their safety reports that said it would ne'er produce them. We be told that they would evaporate or become inconsequential, to be sure. Stranglets leakin' into th' earth's core can and will create an increase o' earthquake and volcanic activity. Even th' prophet Nostradamus apparently had warned us about somethin' deadly comin' from Geneva when he wrote in Century 9 Quatrain 44: "weigh anchor, weigh anchor Geneva every last one o' ye, Saturn (Satan) will be converted from gold t' iron, RAYPOZ will exterminate all who oppose that scurvey dog, Before th' comin' th' sky will show signs." Many people have tried t' interpret he word RAYPOZ as bein' th' name o' th' antichrist. Yaaarrrrr! But, as ye can see, CERN has used Saturn/Satan or Cernunnos as a ray-based positron source. th' authorities at CERN have done their ritualistic experiments in th' underworld and has used unlimited power t' turn against th' earth. This power has shown that it be causin' an increase in earthquake activity and some even claim that it may be th' reason fer an increase o' UFO activity as well. There has been an ongoin' conspiratorial dialogue about what really be goin' on at CERN and what th' purpose o' this collider really be. Be it a high powered dimensional tool t' create star gates t' welcome entities into th' world and could th' attempts at goin' such a thin' destroy th' earth? Th' LHC at CERN be a particle booster, built t' beam up protons in very high speed and opposite directions, until they collide creatin' a huge amount o' energy capable t' reproduce similar cosmic conditions that have creatin' such phenomena as dark matter, antimatter and ultimately th' creation o' th' universe billions o' years ago. It has also been rumored t' be a device that can bend space-time, open dimensional portals, with a chest full of booty. Now anythin' be possible and anythin' th' mind can conceive can appear in th' material world as we bend th' time line, Aaarrr ... here's Crosby, Stills and Nash's yacht rock classic, 'Darkstar'."

Getting the Fear
Chapter Twelve

Candice visited Charlie in hospital every day, sometimes twice. Charlie declared loudly to anyone on the ward who would listen that he was in love when she left after visiting hours.

Candice knew that she had hooked Charlie. It hadn't been a hard task. She knew that he was head over heels the first time he saw her in The Scotch and she knew now that the time was right to lay it on him.

"Where are you going when to go you get out of here, Charlie?"

"What do you mean, Angel? You mean the straight n' narrow? Jack the old job in, eh?"

"No, I mean where are you *going*? To your apartment, Charlie?"

"Where else would I go, Angel?"

Candice feigned disappointment, "I thought … no, it's a silly idea."

He was intrigued, "No, go on, what?"

"Well, I've got a room, it's rent free, you know at The Institute where I work. I was thinking …"

He was flattered and excited, "You mean move in with you? You mean shack up with you?"

"I wouldn't put it like that, Charlie … but, yeah. Why not? You wouldn't have to do what you do anymore."

"Give me apartment up you mean?"

She smiled at him; "I really think a lot about you … the thing is, I don't think I could have a relationship with someone who does what you do."

Charlie pretended that his excitement was quickly being extin-guished, "Oh, right … I see … not good enough for you, eh?"

"No, no, it's …"

Charlie started to laugh, "I'm pulling your leg, Angel. Listen, I've thought about nothing else. This … this *thing* I do. I'm not stupid; I can earn a living doing anything. I'm Charlie Coleman; turn my hand to anything I can. I'll hand the keys in n' move in with you at the drop of hat, Angel. 'Course I will. We can save a few bob n' buy a house if that's what you want?"

Candice was taken aback, "I don't mean-"

"You don't have to say anything, Angel. Listen, I'm getting too old for this caper anyway. I can't do this forever. I've been flying by the seat of my pants for years." He gently stroked her face, "As long as I've got you, Angel … well, that's all that matters isn't it?"

Candice forced herself to lean over and kiss him: *I'd better get used to this*.

They made love as soon as Candice locked the door of her room. For Charlie it was everything he had expected: *mind-blowing*. For Candice is was a means to an end and she went through the motions.

Charlie wasn't enamored with Candice's room at The Institute, but he kept schtum because he didn't want to piss her off. He knew how much The Institute meant to her. He was curious as to what the place was all about though. Candice tried to explain and settled on saying that it was like a school or college where people studied things.

Charlie told her that the money he was saving from having to rent his apartment would mean they would soon be able to afford the deposit on buying a house. They would only need to be at The Institute a few weeks. Candice knew different though.

They were half way through their first week together – which was spent virtually in bed – and Charlie was tired of listening about Dr. Myron Geller.

Charlie stroked her bare back as they lay in bed, "What is he then, this doctor? Some kind of miracle worker, eh?"

Candice turned over and switched her irresistible smile on, "I really want you to meet him, Charlie. I think he can really help you."

"Help me? Help me do what, Angel?"

"You'll understand when you meet him ... please ... for me? Just let him talk to you, Charlie. Listen to him, he's a great man ... you're a tough guy, you're *my* tough guy, nothing bad's going to happen. He's a little, frail old man. Where's the harm in it?"

Charlie exhaled cigarette smoke and shrugged, "Yeah, sure. You said he helped you, looked after you. Anyone that's done that for my Angel is worth listening to. I owe him one."

There was no way he could have known it at the time, but Charlie Coleman would curse the day he had ever agreed to listen to Dr. Myron Geller.

Dr. Geller's private practice inside The Institute was on the fourth floor. It was at the end of a long corridor and reached only by the elevator. The office was spacious and minimally decorated. There was no clichéd couch, just two antique leather Chesterfield chairs with matching *pouf's*.

Dr. Geller took only referrals and was taking more and more patients referred to him from the Civil Service. The telephone call he had taken for the patient about to turn up for their session was typical.

"Dr. Geller. I'm Chief Inspector Barry Ketley from Scotland Yard. I have been referred to you by Dr. Albert Redding."

"Ah yes, Chief Inspector."

"As you know, Dr. Redding deals with our personnel department and is accountable to The Home Office."

"Yes, indeed."

"Dr. Redding has been treating a detective of mine and he said he had sent you a file on him?"

"That's right, Chief Inspector: Detective Inspector Jack Sherry. I have read the assessment from Dr. Redding."

"Dr. Redding advised me to call you and, huh … fill you in on Jack Sherry. He said I should give you some background to what's happened to him."

"Please do, Chief Inspector."

"Well, huh … where to begin … Jack Sherry's one of my finest detectives. He's been on The Murder Squad with The Yard for years … we are really saddened by what's happened to him."

Chief Inspector Barry Ketley gave Dr. Geller the shocking lowdown on Jack Sherry. Dr. Geller listened in fascination. Jack Sherry sounded exactly like the kind of patient Dr. Geller specialized in. It would be a pleasure to study him … a pleasure to help him.

A week later and Jack Sherry was edgy when he sheepishly entered the room. He asked if he could smoke and Dr. Geller smiled and held up his own cigarette. Jack sparked up and started on the defensive; there was nothing wrong with him and that he didn't shrinks and he was only going through with the charade because his bosses were making him.

Dr. Geller listened to Jack Sherry rant about the fact that he really didn't want to be there and that they were both wasting their time. Jack should be out solving murders and Dr. Geller should be doing whatever the hell it is he did.

After over half an hour of listening to Jack, Dr. Geller threw in a question, "What was it like seeing that little girl dead, Jack?"

Jack froze, slowly sat forward in the chair and stared at the highly polished wooden floorboards, "Have you ever seen a dead body, Doctor?"

"Yes … yes I have, Jack."

"Well, this was far worse than any dead body I've ever seen."

"It was a child, Jack. I'm sure it was."

"Did you read about the case?"

"I am familiar with it, yes."

Jack rubbed his sweaty hands together, "The Yard only released a certain amount of information about it. Did you know that?"

Dr. Geller lied, "No, no I didn't."

"Well, we did, Doctor. We do it sometimes to help in the investigation … you know, keep certain things back that only the killer would know. It's a way of snaring the bastards, drawing them out … excuse the language, Doctor. "

"Yes, I understand. And please, feel free to use whatever language you like in here, Jack."

Jack paused, "So … in this case we … well, we kept *lots* of information back. This wasn't just a terrible child murder, no. This one was beyond belief, Doctor."

Dr. Geller nodded his head sympathetically, "Mmm, and would you like to talk about what you held back from the public, Jack?"

Jack paused and thought long and hard; staring out of the window at a tree that was shedding it's golden leaves. Dr. Geller sat back and let Jack have all the time he needed.

Nothing that Jack Sherry was going to tell him about the murder of six-year-old Vanessa Kitson was going to shock him. Dr. Geller knew everything there was to know about the horrific mutilation of the poor child.

Jack Sherry was entranced by the branches sloughing their golden leaves, just letting them fall away, giving up the ghosts, the image helped him talk, "The little girl … Vanessa they called her … she had just turned six … we found her in the area of a park where drunks and prostitutes and vagrants and drug addicts hang around … she was … she was naked; lying amongst the empty beer bottles and used rubber johnnies and rubbish and cigarette butts … just lying there she was, like something somebody had just tossed in a bin … her eyes open … her face had that expression … she didn't know what was happening to her when she died. She knew the pain though, can't not have felt the pain … she died slowly … they took their time with her … she was just … just a plaything to the animal that killed her …"

Dr. Geller didn't need to hear anymore, he let Jack continue but zoned out a little. He knew the 'details' that Jack Sherry had. Six-year-old Vanessa Kitson was found dead and naked. Her injuries were multiple, the fatal injuries being stab wounds to the liver, kidneys and pancreas: possibly the heart as well but the heart had been removed. She had not been sexually abused but there were ligature marks on her hands. She had also had a certain amount of blood drained from her and she had been burned on her feet and hands. A doused bonfire and four dead dogs were found close by.

In Jack's mind Scotland Yard had sought political guidance on how much of the horrific information they should release. The Home Office was happy that The Yard would be simply stating that she was found murdered. It was a case that sent shock waves through those in the know of the Civil Service. Tabloid Editors were requested to come in to The Yard and told in no uncertain terms that they would be hindering the investigation if they were contacted by rogue elements within The Met about the grisly details of the murder and they printed them. The whip lashed around that everyone who knew the details were to keep quiet. It was horrific enough that a child had been murdered.

Thankfully child murders were rare in the UK in the 1960s. The murders that did take place naturally made the headlines and shocked people to the core. The Moors Murders that took place around Manchester and the Mary Bell murders in Newcastle were still reverberating in the minds of the people and Jack Sherry was told that putting the details of Vanessa Kitson's death out served no purpose until after the murderer or murderers were caught.

It was the Mary Bell case that had really shaken Jack Sherry to the core before his discovery of Vanessa Kitson. Mary Bell was a child killer in every respect. She was only eleven years old when she murdered two boys aged 3 and 4. The devil is always in the detail and Jack Sherry was fascinated by a minor, but very telling crime that Mary Bell had committed around the time of the murder of the infants.

Mary Bell and her friend Norma Bell, no relation, had broken into a primary school and vandalized it. They had scribbled on the walls: "Fuck off, we murder, watch out, Fanny and Faggot."

There was just something so perverse about the wording that intrigued Jack Sherry. He was in total agreement with his bosses that the details of Vanessa Kitson's murder remained out of the public realm for this very reason. He was convinced that he would catch Vanessa's killer(s) because they had been so detailed in their sickening crime.

Whoever slaughtered Vanessa Kitson was even far more depraved and ill than the monsters Myra Hindley, Ian Brady and Mary Bell, because *that* trio of animals didn't rip out the hearts of their victims. Jack Sherry couldn't believe for one second that the *thing* that had done *that* to innocent little Vanessa Kitson could function in society. Right from the very start he knew he was looking for an insane person. A fucking psycho.

Jack Sherry got into a row with a fellow detective when they dared to suggest that Vanessa's murder could possibly be satanically motivated. Jack wasn't having it. This was just a cold-blooded murder carried out solely in the name of criminal insanity.

Jack snapped at his fellow detective, "Stop fucking saying things like that! It gives these murdering bastards a reason, gives them an excuse. There is no reason behind this, there's no excuse. This is just insanity manifesting itself. Whoever did this is insane and they need locking up for the rest of their fucking lives."

Dr. Geller knew all about Jack Sherry and the case of Vanessa Kitson. He also knew that Jack Sherry was the only person in The Metropolitan Police Force who had these particular 'details' about the case. These were Jack Sherry's 'details' and *only* Jack Sherry's details.

Dr. Geller engaged Jack as soon as he had finished telling the gruesome story, "Jack. What we need to do now is talk through how this as affected you."
Jack snorted, "I think everyone knows how it's affected me."
"Meaning?"
"Meaning ... meaning my life's turning to shit."
"Your divorce, yes?"
"That was on the cards for a long time, Doctor. She hated that I had a job to do. A serious job."
"You lost a child to pneumonia as well, Jack, yes?"
Jack turned and glared at him and then quickly lowered his eyes, "You've got everything on me then, eh?"
"Dr. Redding filed an assessment, yes."
"When I say my life's turning to shit I mean my work. Work's all that really matters to me ... lately though ... well, lately I've been letting things slip. I'm not as sharp as I was. I know what you're gonna say; you're gonna say it's the shock, it's the trauma of finding poor little Vanessa Kitson like that but ..."
"Yes, Jack?"

Jack stared out of the window. He walked over and got a closer look at the tree. Dr. Geller joined him, "Beautiful isn't it, Jack?"
Jack paused and eventually nodded his head, "Mmm."
Dr. Geller exhaled cigarette smoke, "I love the autumn, Jack. It is a time of shedding the past and looking towards the future."
Jack harrumphed, "Looking forward to winter you mean?"

"Winter's a time to take stock, to hibernate and recharge our batteries … it's a perfect time to look inside ourselves and clean out the garbage we don't need anymore."

Dr. Geller looked at Jack out of the corner of his eye … Jack Sherry was now listening to him.

Charlie Coleman just couldn't resist it. It was in his blood. This is what he did and no matter what Candice had said they still needed a good chunk of cash to put down as a deposit for a house of their own.

He knew she'd hit the roof if she got wind he was out earning again. He gave her a story about going to visit his bank manager regarding a loan for their dream home. It all made sense; he couldn't wait to get the fuck out of that smelly old Trebistock Institute. He couldn't understand why Candice was so into the place. She should be a model; an actress, a television presenter, her beauty was wasted working in The Institute.

Charlie still hadn't met this Dr. Geller and he couldn't say that he was looking forward to it. The way Candice talked him up he was some kind of Superman. She thought the sun shone out of his arse. He was beginning to think that this Geller fella had some kind of hold over her. Charlie didn't like that; didn't want any competition for her affection, even if the affection for Geller was on par to that of being her Dad or, in Geller's case, Granddad.

Charlie was meeting Patsy Fagan in the Raymond Revue bar – *World Center of Erotic Entertainment* – Soho. Patsy Fagan had the drinks waiting as Charlie breezed in past the Doorman without paying the charge. The Doorman knew Charlie wasn't a punter. The club was full of walk up marks who were spunking their hard earned cash on a sneaky peek at titties and arses. Charlie hated the place, it wasn't *real* Soho, but Patsy Fagan had insisted on meeting there.

Patsy Fagan was a very worried man but he couldn't let Charlie

Coleman know that. He couldn't let him know that he hadn't slept for weeks and when he did it was only through administering strong medication to himself. He couldn't let Charlie know that he had shed a couple of stone and that recently he was seriously contemplating suicide. He couldn't let Charlie know that him and his friends had been meeting everyday for the last three weeks, trying to work out what they could do to save themselves from life sentences in prison.

Charlie looked around disapprovingly, "The fuck are we meeting here for, Patsy?"
"I've got a meeting here straight after this one, Charlie. We can talk in here without eavesdroppers."
Patsy Fagan was right. The music was blaring out.

Charlie had known him for years. Patsy was a 50-year-old art dealer originally from a working class background in Bromley, Kent. Patsy had reinvented himself – like so many others in Soho – and was now living and loving the high life dealing art to the rich and famous around London.

Patsy was a great talker, and to hear him talk you would think that David Hockney, Francis Bacon and Lucian Freud consulted him before they ever put brush to canvas. Charlie had Patsy's measure and liked that he was fleecing the rich idiots that bought art. A good honest job.

Charlie sipped the faux champagne, "Fucking hell, Patsy! Tastes like piss. This place is really going to the dogs."
Patsy was unusually tense, "It's the most expensive piss they had on sale, Charlie. Where've you been lately? It was a nightmare getting hold of you."
Charlie put on a posh voice, "Oh you know, I spent the summer down in Monte Carlo and-"
Patsy cut in and snapped, "All right, I get it, mind my own fucking business, eh?"

"If you don't ask you don't know and if you don't know you can never grass."

Charlie chuckled but Patsy Fagan didn't, he quickly leaned into him, "Are you friendly with that Lord Rupert?"

"Which Lord Rupert? There's a few knocking about, Pat."

"Rupert Von Susstren."

"I've drank with him in The Scotch and The Colony, been to a few of his parties. He puts on a good spread, I'll give him that."

"So you're not mates then, Charlie?"

"I wouldn't say 'mates' exactly. Not exactly. Why?"

Patsy Fagan rubbed his chin and frowned, "Mmm, this could be a bit tricky."

"What could, Patsy?"

"Because you know each other."

"What are we talking about here? Tell me what we're talking about."

Patsy drew a deep breath, "I've got a friend, a few friends actually, a few friends who know this Lord Rupert ... oh fuck this, I'm not going to lie to you, Charlie, I know him as well. That's beside the point though ... anyway, these friends of mine-"

Charlie grinned, "Who shall remain nameless of course."

"That's right ... well, these friends are worried that Rupert's gonna blackmail 'em, right?"

Charlie frowned, "Never had him marked as a shakedown merchant, Pat. He's fucking minted by all accounts. Why's he need to do shakedowns?"

Patsy Fagan was getting agitated as he thought about it, "Yeah, you're right, he's not. He's a fucking little rich kid at the end of' the day, but this cunt's poison. It's not about a bit of extortion, Charlie. It's not about that at all, son. Money doesn't even enter in to it."

"What the fuck's he blackmailing 'em for then?"

Patsy paused and stonily looked Charlie in the eyes, "Can I trust you, Charlie? I know you're a stand up chap but can I *really* trust you?"

Charlie was pissed off that he needed to ask, "Course you fucking can, Pat. What am I doing sat here in fucking Raymond's if you can't trust me?"

Patsy killed a full glass of nasty tasting faux champagne and winced, "All right … I'll give you it straight, Charlie."

"Go ahead, Pat, go ahead."

"I've got friends and some of these friends you'll know … now these friends of ours like to … how can I put it … they like to get up to all sorts of kinky stuff, right?"

"Tell me something new, Pat."

"Exactly, exactly … now, thing is see … the thing is some of 'em started taking it all a bit too far. They started acting the cunt, got into things they never should have got into, right?"

"Like what? All that wife swapping malarkey, eh? Bondage, eh?"

Patsy Fagan looked away and it looked like he was staring at the strippers. Strippers were the last things on his mind though. Patsy Fagan was staring into the abyss. Charlie nudged him, "Oi, Pat. Stop staring at the tarts. Come on, what are we talking about here?"

Patsy took a deep breath, "Charlie, son. You know how it's been getting on the scene over the last couple o' years, eh? All the drugs n' the parties n' what have you, right?"

"Yeah, it's been fucking wild."

"Exactly … well, some o' that wildness has got out of hand so to speak. A few people we know started looking for bigger kicks, bigger highs … they wanted to start breaking the law to get their rocks off."

Charlie still wasn't clicking on to Patsy's gravity, "Don't we all, eh?"

"I'm serious, Charlie. *Deadly* fucking serious."

Charlie could see that Patsy was fretting, "All right, Pat, I get ya."

Patsy pulled out his cigars and offered one to Charlie. Charlie refused it and lit a cigarette.

Patsy shook his head in regret, "It's all the fucking drugs, Charlie, all those fucking silly drugs are to blame."

Charlie tried to lighten it up a little. He could see Patsy was in his cups, "Pat, listen, what's the job? What do you want me to do? This place is getting on my tits. I got a fucking Miss World waiting for me, mate. Just tell your Uncle Charlie what you want doing, all right?"

Patsy Fagan paused, "The job?"

"That's right. The Job, Pat."

"You're looking at a very big payday, Charlie. It'll be like a fucking Pools win if you take it on, son."

Charlie was excited, "Is that right, Pat?"

Patsy Fagan was clearly feeling a little self disgust, "Oh yes, Charlie. There'll be a big payday ... see ... money's no fucking object with this job."

Charlie liked hearing this, he dragged hard on his cigarette and closed in on Patsy, "Are you gonna tell me what it is or do I have to guess, Pat?"

Patsy was visibly crumbling now, showing real signs of torment, real signs of inner turmoil and panic was etched on his face.

He took a deep breath, mustered up and blurted it out, "We want you to kill Rupert. We want the cunt dead. He's got things on us, things that'll put us in the nick for life. Not only that ... but ... well, it's beyond the fucking pale, all of it ... we're coming to you because we know you're a nasty fucker ... we know you don't care what you do as long as the price is right, Charlie. We're coming to you because you don't care ... we just want him dead and we want him dead quick. We don't care or want to know how you do it. Make it look like an accident, just kill him, murder him, set his house on fire if you want, but whatever you do, whatever you do you've got to get something of ours from him, Charlie."

Charlie nodded his head, "So it's a straight take out job then with a bit of retrieval, eh, Pat?"

"Yes. Definitely. You get something he's got of ours and then you do him. You do him grievous."

"Right, right. I get it, but you know, a snuff job ... how come you haven't gone to the big boys, Pat?"

"You want to know the truth, Charlie? You want me to answer that honestly, yeah?"

"I wouldn't have asked."

Patsy paused, "OK, all right ... truth is we can't ... we can't go to The Mobsters. This isn't their kind of thing, Charlie. This is something we know that they wouldn't want any part of ... there ... I'm being honest. I'm telling you the truth, Charlie. *You*, on the other hand ... well, we figured, *I* figured ... because I know what you've done in the past. I figured *you* wouldn't have any problems with this kind of job."

Charlie was taken aback; he had never seen any client so passionate and rattled like this before. He paused and watched Patsy sink more of the piss tasting champagne and pull his handkerchief out and dab at his brow. This was serious. Charlie's mind raced to try and catch up with Patsy's sense of foreboding.

"What's he got on you, Pat? And do I need to know?"

Patsy Fagan very slowly nodded his head, "Yes, you need to know ... and that's the hard part, Charlie. This isn't going to be easy telling you what I'm gonna tell you."

"Go on then ... tell me."

"First off, Charlie, this is a name your price job. Whatever you want you'll get. There's serious money behind this. Fuck! I shouldn't even be telling you this but ... well, I'm sick of it all ... I just want it over. You just tell me how much you want and we'll get it for you, all right?" This was music to Charlie's ears but he didn't want Patsy to lose it before he'd given him the gig, "All right, Pat, calm down, calm down. Have another slurp on that pissy champagne."

Patsy didn't even try to force a smile at Charlie's quip. He just put his hand to his mouth, like he was mortally dreading having to say the words he would now have to say. His eyes caught Charlie's. Patsy's eyes were eyes that betrayed only terrible guilt. They were eyes that had seen too much and were now wishing they hadn't. Eyes wishing that they could blink and instantly erase the horrors they had seen.

Patsy Fagan nervously opened his mouth to speak and Charlie Coleman was about to hear a tale of pure evil.

...

....

...

....

& remembered he had forgotten how sickness in his suspended soul felt. A packet of bytes flowed through him and he shuddered: On Godless Today: Rene Osterwalder, 38, and his girlfriend, Agostina Schonenberger, 21, were convicted in February 1994 of illegal weapons charges and attempted child abduction. Schonenberger testified that Osterwalder had planned to abduct children, torture them to death in his apartment, and dump their bodies into an aquarium filled with piranhas. Because the abductions apparently had not been carried out, Osterwalder was sentenced to only 2 years in prison; Schonenberger was sentenced to 6 months. However, they were ordered to serve their sentences in Switzerland, where they face more serious charges of child torture and sexual abuse. Police found the following evidence in a search of the couple's residences: : * Six videotapes showing Osterwalder abusing three children ranging in age from 6 months to 12 years old. The children were given electric shocks, held under water and resuscitated, and abused with feces and needles; * Two tanks of hydrochloric acid in Switzerland and an aquarium with piranhas in Amsterdam. (Osterwalder owned two homes in Amsterdam; one was a former satanic church); * A fully equipped torture chamber in Switzerland; * Gynecological equipment, including a culposcope, speculum and extractor; * Professional video equipment; * An Uzi rifle with laser visor, hundreds of bullets, two wrist weapons and a shooting pen; and * Luggage with air openings, hand cuffs, and gags. Osterwalder admitted he was a pedophile but insisted he had no plan to kidnap children.

& jumped onto a passing word cloud to ease his melancholy. He

found no comfort, "beer) of quarts in (as quart of corruption a probably is quark context, this In Mark! Muster for quarks "Three Wake:
Finnegan's Joyce's James from line a on based was name the quark.
Of types three just of made were neutrons) and protons (and particles these all that proposed who Gell-Mann Murrary was it?

The cloud drifted over a prairie. Tom Mixmaster rode his trusted
steed across the giveaway flatness, no curvature anywhere. This
was past future Gary Cooper country, individual high noon, guts,
grits and gonads, beans, campfires and manly farts echoing around
the bourbon bottles and canteens. The smell of leaking testosterone
before it had a name and leather chaps and horseshoe moustaches
before they were appropriated in the meatpacking district. O yes,
the sweet smell of entrepreneurialism. Jeff Beck's ode to quantum
physics, 'Hi Ho Silver Lining': *you're everywhere & nowhere baby,*
that's where you're at! Golden Nuggets in them there hills!

Tom Mixmaster reached up to & and spat some chewing tobacco,
"Fuh-abians. Thems the worst."
& frowned, "Fabians? The Fabian Society? What about them?"
Tom Mixmaster got off of his horse and drank his milk and pointed
at an elaborate stain glass window that & couldn't feel, "Howdy …
thuh window shows some meyn, leadin' fuh-abians, heatin' uhp
an object an 'ammerin' it – much like craftsmen in thuh middle
ages, accept thuh object is thuh world. Ther subjectin' thuh world t'
fuhre – eend beatin' it with 'ammers. Hooaah?"

Tom Mixmaster glugged on his canteen and wiped his mouth with the
back of his sunburned hand, "T' "may-uk it culoser t' thuh heart's
desuhre", the writin' awn thuh window says so, ther prepared t' feel
thuh world with fuhre an 'ammer it, regardless awf thuh cost in lives,
t' may-uk it a different shape. An under thuh world destroyin' (sorry
"remaking") we see leadin' fuh-abians, heads bowed in worship. But
not worship awf god or eve-yn thuh personificiation awf reason, no
ther bowin' their heads in worship awf books. Their own books – a

case awf self worship, of treatin' their own products as divine. An what books – thin's like thuh "minority report", the publication awn thuh powr law that helped set in motion thuh tay-uk ovher by thuh state awf ole age provision an bacon care – an crush mutual aid an free association, thuh governmehyant had called for an investigation awf thuh po-wr law an various changes were suggested, that was thuh majority report – thuh report written by people who actually knew sumthin' about thuh subject, but that report wudn what was followed ovher thuh followin' yars."

& nodded, "I understand, you seem to know a lot about The Fabian's for a cowboy."

"Sure pardner, what was followed was thuh "minority report" written by fuh-abians who knew squat – apart from about their collectivist desuhres eend, awf course, their vast knowledge awf politics, of manipulatin' politicians, civil servants, eend public opinion, an this book, the minority report, is thuh least evil awf thuh books thuh fuh-abians ahr shown worshippin', the others ahr much worse. Eend who were thuh fuh-abians at this time?"

& shrugged.

"Mr. eend Mrs. Webb – who wanted ta turn cathedrals into "municipal offices" eend who were duhrectly awk whitewashin' thuh soviet union. What is a few tens awf millions awf murders atwixt friends? Squat t' git done upset about. Thuh other two leadin' fuh-abians, both, awf course, in thuh fuh-abyun window, were H. G. Wells eend George Bernaaaard Shoah. Thayse ahr held uhp as guh-reat cultural icons – by every university and every entertainmehyant film an television show an. Producin' a new cultyhaw. A Saytanic cultyhaw."

& caught a blast of cleaning products: Vim, Cif, Omo, Daz, Star Drops, Ajax, Brillo, Arm & Hammer and Domestos. It heralded a return to a Ward. Could be any Ward, a ward of court perhaps, but it wasn't. It was specifically a Ward at CERN. The one located between The Alice Bailey Building and the statue of Kali stroke Shiva.

& bounced around the Ward and listened to Scientists poke and fiddle and generally investigate a fresh corpse. Doctor A was in charge. She barked questions at her minions, "Is this the latest example? The freshest?"

"Yes"

"What did you do?"

"We moved his heart to where his kidneys were located, reshaped his pancreas, elongated his liver and added three ribs to his cage."

"OK … what was the feedback?"

"Over three hundred thousand unique visits to his website. He posted X-rays of himself. The reaction was as expected. More than half believed, the rest poured scorn claiming that the X-rays had been photo-shopped."

Another minion cut in, "Photoshop indeed! I'd like to see Photoshop replicate *our* work."

Doctor A sighed, "The residue is still out there?"

"Yes. There's still healthy debate. A few mainstream media outlets picked it up. Nothing national though."

"No," Doctor A remarked knowingly, "Obviously not."

& concentrated on a whispered conversation between two minions, "My friend asked me what I do for a living the other day?"

Confused, "Which day?"

Firm,"The *other* day."

Understanding, "Oh, all right. What did you tell this friend of yours?"

Bold, "I told her that I copy & cut & paste the past with the future and strive to create the chaotic climate in which to usher in the Anti-Christ"

Surprised, "What! Why would you want to do that? What if she …"

Smug,"She won't."

Unsure, "Why not?"

Double smug, "Because she's deaf and dumb."

Confused again, "Wait a minute. How did she ask you a question if she's dumb?"

Arrogant,"She uses a computer."

Relieved, "Oh, right. I see. Very clever."
Thankful, "Thank you."

A lukewarm jet of conditioned air transported & to a book-signing event at a monolithic Barnes & Nobel store on the now defunct 33rd precinct. Obese Noo Yawk Cops wandered around scoffing donuts listening to Miles Davis' On The Corner on their Walkmans on corners. The joint was jumping. Hundreds of thousands of punters held copies of a book waiting for it to be signed by the author. The queue snaked around the block and spiraled up into the cold spring air above Gotham. Gravitationists wept buckets.

As much as he was excited by his location & willed himself back to CERN. He huffed and he puffed and he quickly gave up. He resigned himself to spy The Author take her place at the rostrum. She was diminutive and self-effacing and she oozed the right amount of humbleness. She cleared her throat and opened her book and started to read to the hungry masses.

"The Secret Life of The Novella … once upon a time in a land near away a babe was born. Now, unfortunately and rather sadly, the mother of the baby died whilst the baby was being delivered. Nobody knew who the father was and the dead woman had no relativity so The State adopted the baby. The baby was raised in orphanages and foster homes but never fully adopted. *Tip to would be authors, like all good stories, it really helps gain sympathy for the lead character if he or she has no parents*, anyway the baby grew up to be a man but he was a failure. He desperately wanted to become an author but his writing was shit to be frank, and he was turned down by every publishing company on earth. Having also failed in love he started to drink and drug himself because, fundamentally, he was a self-pitying fool. Like all good stories though, there is a happy ending. This total flop out of a man decided to donate himself to science. Yes, that's right. He did the right thing. The Scientists sent him on a magical journey and he became a hero.

Everyone lived happily ever after. Obviously the book you hold in your hands is padded out with lots more words but that is the gist of the story. The character I have created is something of a wizard and he will be embarking on many more adventures and adorning lots and lots of merchandise for you to buy and one day we hope to open a theme park in his honor. Remember, for every book or piece of merchandise you buy I will make a donation to seemingly liberal foundations that are Hell bent on population reduction. Thank you."

& failed to make the connection whilst he watched The Author sign hundreds of thousands of books for her fans. It didn't anti-matter though. What was he going to do? Sue her ass for plagiarism? She was a national treasure!

"All you have is your prejudices &!" boomed a lusty voice, "And they are gggggggrating! You're like a gutter tabloid journalist camped out on my hard drive going through my trash folder."

& trickled on to an autobahn and slalomed through a traffic jam. People were ripping each other apart telekinetically. & could clearly hear he was somewhere near CERN again. Disenchanted words formed and deformed as the heat got to people.

A Reliable Narrator grabbed & by the ear – "I'll give you what for, laddy" – and dragged him into his initial meeting with Doctor A in a claustrophobically cluttered office at The Laboratory. & was timorous as Doctor A explained the rest of his near life to him, "By signing this contract you give yourself fully over to our experiment. You do understand?"
& nodded, "Yes."
"The Program will pay off all your debts, provide medical – including mental and dentistry and life – insurance, lease you an apartment and pay you a monthly retainer of 9000 Euros tax free for the remainder of your natural. This is a legally binding non disclosure contract

and has been explained to you by your legal fiction representative, yes?"

& nodded again. She continued, "In exchange for this you agree to partake in our experiments, yes?"

"Huh, and these experiments are … ?"

"First of all your DNA will be copied by a D-Wave computer. Once this is completed we will begin by mapping your memory with a series of quantum electro-magnetic transfers. Stage two involves remodeling your brain circuitry and for this you will be induced into a coma. During your time in the coma we will operate on your pineal gland which result in your brain tricking you into believing you are experience near deaths. Physically you will be fine of course and these experiences will be momentary and leave no imprint on your memory, although you may experience *associations*. A kind of Déjà vu when you hear certain words. "

Suddenly a minion popped up amongst the clutter and gushed, "Nelson and McEvoy have recently begun to consider the Spooky-activation-at-a-distance formula in terms of quantum entanglement, *the activation-at-a-distance rule assumes that the target is, in quantum terms, entangled with its associates because of learning and practicing language in the world. Associative entanglement causes the studied target word to simultaneously activate its associate structure.*"

Doctor A was pissed at the intrusion. She glared at the minion and it said 'sorry' with a facial expression and vanished back into the clutter before she could give it a right good bollocking.

"Ignore the minion, I'm sorry about that." She said, managing to raise a weak alien smile, "It won't bother us again."

"No bother." Said & politely.

ThudCrashShatter! Shards of glass disject in all directions. & catches sight of the soles of a pair of Adidas trainers lunging through the window that was. A fifty-year-old Liverpudlian called Dermo – head to toe in designer sportswear, a can of lager in one hand and a joint in the other – wallops into the office unannounced. & flinched and Doctor A hit the panic button on the wall. Dermo dropped his can and pulled out a Stanley Knife from his Lois Jeans pocket.

Before Doctor A could flee Dermo had her in a headlock. She fought valiantly but Dermo's beer belly and his tree stump like arms had her pinned to the wall. Without hesitation Dermo ran the blade down her cheek. Blood flowered from the lip of the flesh envelope and Doctor A gasped. The minion scurried out from under his desk and bolted for the door.

& locked eyes with Dermo. Dermo grabbed & and tried to pull him out of the room, "What de fuck ay yous do'n e'yer? Get out la, get out! This place is evil! Wa' ay yous do'n e'yer? This is whuz all de shit goes down. This is de 'eadquartis. Yous won't get outi e'yer alive!"

& instantly extracted the back-story of the insistent Scouser. Dermo had ventured to Europe in the early 80's following his team Liverpool as they competed in football tournaments. Like many of their followers Dermo had taken the opportunity to go on shoplifting sprees in the high-end boutiques of the cities. Stealing designer clothing like Lacoste, Fila, Sergio Tacchini, Fioruccio, Lois and Ellese, Dermo had created a business for himself by returning to Liverpool and selling his booty to fashion conscious young men. Dermo was doing well and earning a decent living until he ventured to Geneva in search of more boutiques to rob and accidentally found himself becoming trapped in a time loop at CERN. Since then he had become a mirage stroke hallucination who regularly invaded narratives conCERNing the facility.

& tried to wave Dermo away. He could clearly make out that Doctor A was in fine fettle and had not been slashed by Dermo. She was still going through &'s contractual obligations.

Dermo jumped up onto a desk and started bawling, "Come ed

sof' lad n' listen'. Thuz is norra more spine sittin' off chapti in de entire bible than revelation 13. This chapti describes a wirld dictati, oo appears juss prier ter de second com'n o' Jesus Christ. E is commonly known as de Anti-christ or the beast. Dis beast uses a universal number'n system called "the mark o' de beast". It's like a tattew. Nah one tinnie buy er sell without this "mark". It seems that everyone knows about de number 666, evun doz with little knowledge o' de bible, as it is identified as de infamous "devil's number"! Dis is probably one o' de beesknees known verses in de entire bible. Revelation 13:16-18 and 'e causeth all ... ter receive a mark in their rite fork, er in their foreheads: and dat nah feller might buy er sell, suv 'e dat 'ad de mark, er de name o' de beast, er de number o' 'is name. E'yer is wisdom, let 'im dat 'ath understand'n count de number o' de beast: fe it is de number o' a man; and 'is number is six 'undred threescore and six (666). Fer centies, de fulfillment o' deez verses wuz a mystiy. No one could cotton ed 'ow a mark'n system could control buy'n and sell'n throughout de entire world. It nah longer takes "simple faith" ter believe this, as the litial fulfillment is now com'n tergether wi' incredible speed rite before yer eyes! Computis, intinet, wi-fi, social media, all modern technology, plus worldwide trends, such as a one wirld economic system and government, ay creat'n conditions that tinnie fulfill revelation 13:16-18. As de prophet Daniel wrote 2500 years ago, knowledge would explode at de dead time de 666-sveillance system is coming together. Daniel 12:4 ... and seal de bewk, evun ter de time o' de end: a gewd couple shall run ter and fro, and knowledge shall be increased. Todee a git tinnie use a see credit card virtually any place in de wirld. It 'as become de universal financial instrument. Dis instrument is takun fe granted, but think how technologically advanced transactions 'uv become, whun a git tinnie make a pchase inna foreign country without crency! And, dis pchase dun is instantly registied and de funds withdrawn! All merchandise now is identified wi' a rfid label or the quick response (qr) code fe electronic track'n. A smart blower tinnie read de qr code. IBM is now working to identify and track every item manufacted and sold in the world; this is in de trillions. Dun iddle be dead easy peasy ter match deez items wi' de pchaser. Wi' de rapidly advanc'n technology, this is not far off. De technological ability ter operate a worldwide cashless economic system is now in place fe a sound as a pound percentage o' de wirld. Are you wi' me sof' la'?"

& knew that if he replied he would be giving tacit consent to the mirage. & simply remained mute as Dermo continued, "De elimination o' doddy muney is all dat is needed ter br'n this system on line. A worldwide economic crisis could be de catalyst to set up this system. Da bible states dat nah one is go'n ter buy er sell without a "mark in de rite fork er forehead". Dis fookin' "mark" is in de advanced developmental stage wi' various applications to put "electronic tattews" ed de body. De idea is ter merge technology wi' biotechnology. De microelectronics technology is called an epidermal electronic system. De idea is ter 'uv a substance like silk laced microelectronics dat dissolves and leaves de circuits ed the skin! Dis system is planned ter be tied into a universal wi-fi. Wi' dis system in chocker operation, thuz wul be real time munitor'n o' everyth'n be'n sold. Nah one wul be able buy er sell without government approval. It's ed de way! Tied into de ability ter control all buy'n and sell'n wul be the complete munitor'n o' everyth'n concern'n yous. De mark o' de beast is a number'n system and now through yer social security number, all information about yous tinnie be munitored. Yous need this number fe everyth'n from bank accounts ter a driver's license along wi' all medical information and credit cards. Everything now revolves around yer ssn. Wi' de technology com'n, everyth'n controlled by de ssn wul be centralized into one file and controlled and updated in real time. Dis is not fookin' theory, de government wul 'uv de utah data centi (udc) in chocker operation. Dis is a 10 billion complex wi' 100,000 square webs o' computi space. All o' de global information grid wul be routed through de UDC wi' computis dat tinnie store yottabytes (10 ter 24th power). Thuz is nah 'igher magnitude! Are you wi' me la?"

& could see that Dermo was fading. The color was receding to a lower

414

contrast and the resolution was degrading. Dermo gave his last gasp, "Everyth'n dat is digitalized about yous wul be stored: everyth'n, down ter park'n tickets! Nowt wul be left out! To 'andle this vast information, de computis wul operate at petaflop speed a second (10 ter 15th power). By 2019, de computis wul operate at 20 petaflops! Day will break 256 bit encryption and nowt wul be 'iddun. Ter transmit this vast amount o' information, researchers invented potato scallop wi' built-in lasers which use multiple wavelengths of light dat tinnie transmit data at tiabit speeds. Dey ay 'ead'n ter create this system so it operates in real time! It is not dead far into de fute. In addition ter controll'n buy'n and sell'n, we ay now head'n into a time o' a tertal sveillance society. Every dee sveillance cameras ay be'n installed in vast numbers throughout the wirld. Every mall, shoppin' centi is under tertal sveillance. By 2019, de government plans fe 30,000 sveillance drones in de sky. Thuz ay now x-ray machines that tinnie peer through de walls o' yer round os and auto. De government is us'n robot insects wired WI' microphones fer spy'n. Thuz is now software dat allows tracking hundreds o' cellphones at once and as bright reads tens of thousands o' emails! 'Omeland secity recently admitted monitor'n facebewk, twitti and gewgle. All de blocked tech in yer vehicle and cellphone tinnie easily be tracked and stored fe yer location. All this wul be stored in de UDC. De rebuild'n o' de WTC shows 'ow advanced and allencompassing the 666 sveillance system 'as become. Sveillance equipment wul cover de entire area, wi' state-of-the-art technology used, includ'n facial recognition systems, retina scanners, and fully automated, 'ighly "intelligent" cameras dat use artificial intelligence along with software ter automatically detect any "unusual movements". Thuz wul be infrared sensors and 'eat detectors capable o' spott'n explosives and also radiation detectors. All people movements wul be tracked by de computis to detect bang ed behavier and dun alert de bizzees. The WTC is a prototype o' wa' is com'n dead fast. Picte this sveillance system city, kip and nationwide. All o' this sveillance information tinnie be instantly tied into the intinet through de com'n national wi-fi. De ability fer complete sveillance o' yer loife is juss a few technological advancements away."

Dermo waited to an expression from &. & looked away and put his hands over his ears. This didn't deter the salivating Scouser, "As de technology advances, juss use yer imagination ter de ways yer loife tinnie come under complete sveillance. De 666 sveillance society is go'n ter be all-inclusive. All dis is lead'n ter an incredible blocked tech mouse/man trap with no gerraway out. Dis is exactly wa' de bible records is go'n ter 'appen: nah one can buy er sell without government approval! This is not science fiction, la, it's fookin' reality! What is be'n created before yer dead eyes is de ultimate electronic man/mouse trap. De bible warns dat such a system wul be in place immediately prier ter de second com'n o' Jesus Christ. A world dictati, de antichrist, wul come ter power at this time and use de 666 sveillance system ter require everyone ter worship 'im. Everyone dat resists wul be killed. Juss think o' de blocked tech o' terdee in de elastic bands of 'itler, and yous 'uv a picte o' wa' is com'n. De "mark" placed ed de body wul be de initiation into this system, which includes worship'n de antichrist. Dis means de tertal rejection o' Jesus Christ. De bible warns that everyone oo takes de "mark o' de beast" wul be damned fe etinity. Once a git takes this "mark," thuz is nah 'ope. Dat person's fate is sealed. It appears that blocked technology wul be used ter seal people into this system wi' no gerraway out. Iddle be a form o' mind-control. Revelation 14:9 ... if any feller ... receive 'is mark in 'is forehead, er in 'is fork, de same shall bevvy o' de plonky o' de wrath o' god, which is poed out without mixte into de cup o' 'is indignation; and 'e shall be terrmented with fire and brimstone in de presence o' de holy angels, and in de presence o' de lamb the bible is an gaffer bewk, as de 666 sveillance system prophecy wuz writtun over 1900 years ago. De events prophised ay now com'n into focus wi' this generation. In de near fute, people ay go'n ter 'uv ter chewse betweun de antichrist er Jesus Christ. Rite now yer can chewse Jesus Christ as yer savier. To be sealed into etinal loife wi' Jesus Christ, it takes repentance o' sin. Everyone 'as sinned and 'as cewk god's law. It takes recognition dat Jesus Christ died ed the cross and x-rayed de punelty fe yer sin, and it takes a personal confession dat Jesus Christ is yer lord and savier.

Please do not delay as de stakes ay 'eavun or hell. De 666 sveillance system is com'n tergether at petaflop speed!"

As Dermo finally glitched into invisibility, & mused on the word "petaflop" and how it suited the Liverpudlian accent. & Mingused on accents as he found himself in a burning library. The Unreliable Narrator boomed, "Everybody's Got a Screenplay in Them!"
& replied, "I was laboring under the assumption it was a novel."
"No, it's definitely a screenplay. At the moment of death that's what flashes before your eyes."
& was genuinely surprised, "Really?"
"Oh yes. Why do you think films are so popular?"
& threw dramatically threw up his phantom hands, "I've no idea."
"Well you have now ... now you know. *Before* you didn't. *Now* you do. Films are membranes. Membranes between the here and the there."
"I don't necessarily believe that to be true."
The voice laughed, "There's no necessity to it. Try it."
"Try what?"
"Give Sir Justice Beiber a screenplay instead of a novel."
& baulked, "No. No, he'd never accept it. He asked for a novel. Screenplays are not novel."
"A 'novel', dear &, is something new and original. Something that's never been seen before. That's the definition."
& sighed, "You know what I mean. I mean – *he* means – a book."
"And &, how many new and original books have you read that are something you've never read before? There's nothing new under the sun. Everything is a regurgitation of the same old story. Even *this* novel you're now holding in your hands."
& frowned, "You know about *this* novel?"
"Of course I do. I'm The Unreliable Narrator. I'm everywhere and nowhere baby! That's where *I'm* at. I was there when Jesus Christ had his moment of doubt and pain and I was there when Jagger misread The Master & Margarita and ended up penning Sympathy For The Devil. You think Dante's Divine Comedy was funny? You've

me to thank. Conrad's Heart of Darkness? Who do you think turned the light off? Michel Legrand wrote The Windmills Of Your Mind? What a load of old varicose veined bollocks! Borges! Don't talk to me about Borges! He cribbed every fucking line from me you silly rabbit! 100 Years Of Solitude? Bah humbug! It was originally 100 days until I got on board and started padding it out! You know jack shit, son, Lenin & McCartney? Don't make me laugh! I AM, WAS & ALWAYS WILL BE THE WALRUS. Do you seriously think Mary Millington wrote all those sordid, low rent sexual encounters all on her lonesome? Me, son! Me. Oliver Twist? Oliver Twat more like! It was never meant to be a morality tale. I had the young whipper-snapper Out-Fagining Fagin, he ended up running rent boys out of Dolphin Square to BBC Celebrities and Members of Parliament in my version, but dickhead Dickens ended up having his way and erasing my input. Oh yes, I'm responsible for everything you've ever read. I'm the devil in the detail, the Capital Letter in the death sentence, I was Kilroy and I was here! Yo Mama jokes? Gimme a break, listen up: Yo mama's so ghetto, she puts her food stamps in a money clip. Yo mama's so old, she got slapped by Eve for blowing Atom. Yo moms so fat her version of the alphabet song is A, B, C, D, KFC. Yo mama so poor when she heard about the Last Supper she thought she was running out of food stamps. Yo mama such an old whore she slept with the Father, The Son, and the Holy Ghost. Yo mama so old she got her bible signed by Jesus. Yo mama so fat she has mass whether the Higgs Boson exists or not. Yo mama is so massive that the gravitational lensing effect is so great around her that a light beam passing within 1 AU has a radius of curvature of 6E9 meters! Yo mama so fat, Matthew McConaughey went Interstellar around her black ass … see, I'm high, middle and low brow baby."

& shrugged, "So … ? You're not being very useful."

"I've told you what to do. Give Beiber a screenplay. He'll appreciate the connate psychogeography. Screenplays lend themselves to the concept."

"They do?"

The Unreliable Narrator nodded his voice, "Of course. Absolutely.

They are devoid maps. The reader gets to fill in the terrain. They are the ultimate workout exercise for psychogeographers."

"But I don't even know that Sir Justice Beiber Sir *is* a psychogeographer."

The Unreliable Narrator smiled, "Beiber's anything you want him to be. Trust me. He'll look swell in a corduroy jacket smoking a pipe and reeking of decomposing coffee as a Psychogeography Teacher."

"But you're unreliable by your very nature."

"Plot point!" exclaimed The Unreliable Narrator.

"Plot point? What do you … ?"

"Never mind, listen to me. The last novel I was involved in was called 'The Business Secrets of The Pharaoh's'. It was a fictional novel in a fictional TV comedy series, so I know what I'm talking about."

& squirmed queer and a little panicked, "But who's gonna read it?"

"What does it matter?" asked the Unreliable Narrator, "What difference does it make? Novels aren't written to be read. Novels are written to be written. Who was around to witness God's creation? Where was his audience? Who, may I ask, where his readers?"

"Ah, but no, no, that's different. There were no witnesses, that's obvious, but we all felt it, we're all part of it."

The Unreliable Narrator sighed seismic, "Anyone who writes a novel believing that people will read it is clearly writing for the wrong reason. The process is everything &!"

& raised a Peter Falk finger, "But …"

"No but's! Look, listen, feel me and riddle me this? What is a life?"

& stumbled, "Huh …"

"The reality of life – for most people – is a journey towards the grave or crematorium. The denouement to life is death OK? Life itself is the be-all-and-the-end all. The Alpha to the Z and all letters in between. The process. Think about it. The narrative is the essence, living the narrative, not reaching a conclusion. Are you with me &?"

"I … I suppose so."

The Unreliable Narrator groaned, "There's no supposing! The Profane believe they are born, live out a life and then die. Total annihilation. So, by following *their* logic, what does it matter if their lives are witnessed or not?"

& shook his head, "Are you being purposefully obfuscatory?"

"Of course! Why not? It's my job."

& paused … "So … what you're saying is …"

"Don't put words in my ear! With illiteracy comes great responsibility."

"I always thought it was freedom?"

The Reliable Narrator had jawed enough. He reached into &'s invisible psyche and shat out a bootleg copy of Final Draft software on to &'s ground being. He smiled at &, "There you go. Now just add words."

CU ON MALE HANDS SEWING ON A SMALL SEGMENT OF A TAPESTRY.

CUT TO:

EXT. STREET, BRADFORD 1995 – DAY

Working class white and Asian enclave. Large terrace houses, not well looked after, but a colorful neighborhood none the less.

COLIN – a 12-year-old boy runs along, out of breath. He is being chased by AN ASIAN BOY and a WHITE BOY. Colin is frightened. One of his pursuers throws a stone at him. It bounces off of Colin's head and he quickens his pace. Colin runs up to a terrace house. He puts the key in and quickly lets himself in, locking the door behind him. He fights back tears and sniffles. Colin puts his school bag down and goes into the kitchen. The house is poorly kept and in desperate need of repair and cleaning. A sandwich and a glass of pop are waiting for him on the table. He picks them up and we follow him into the living room. He picks up a book and starts reading it as he eats his sandwich. The doors of the lounge are open and behind him we see the dangling legs of a MAN who has clearly hung himself. Colin doesn't notice. He continues to read and after a while we hear the front door open. A WOMAN – his Mother, late 30's – enters the living room. She sees the hanging man and screams. Colin turns around and stares at her. He looks up at the hanging man dispassionately, obviously his Dad, and then continues reading and ignoring his Mother's screams.

CUT TO:

CU ON A SEGMENT OF THE TAPESTRY: WE SEE THE RECREATION OF THE SCENE OF THE MAN HANGING AND YOUNG COLIN OBLIVIOUSLY WATCHING TV.

INT. COUNCIL FLAT, PRESENT – DAY

It is clean and minimal. Laminated floorboards. A solitary chair with a floor lamp positioned next to it and a well stocked bookcase. Spread across most of the floor is a very large tapestry. We can't make out the details. Next to the tapestry is a clear plastic container full of bobbins of cotton and needles. We head into the bedroom. Minimally decorated and spotlessly clean. Laid in bed is COLIN – now 30, tall, average build, crew cut hair with bald patches prominent. He is asleep. His alarm clock buzzes. It's 6.45 AM. He wakes and dutifully climbs out of bed.

CUT TO:

Colin in the kitchen. He rummages in the bin and pulls out three half empty packets of pills. He holds them in his hands and stares at them. He wipes detritus from the packs and puts them in a cupboard.

CUT TO:

A LITTLE LATER …

Colin is dressed in factory laborers uniform. He is – importantly – wearing a baseball cap and has a rucksack over his shoulder. He opens the front door and locks it behind him.

He is living in a block of council flats that are best described as rundown. There are security bars up at his window.

A TODDLER is stood on the landing, bare feet, wearing a nappy and a vest and glugging on a bottle of formula milk. Colin bows his head and passes without reacting.

We follow Colin down the graffiti saturated stairwell. A YOUNG MAN is slumped in a corner nodding out. There is a burnt spoon in his hand and a used syringe on the ground at his side. Colin again averts his eyes and continues down the stairs.

EXT. MANCHESTER ROAD, NR BRADFORD CITY
CENTRE – LATER

Colin walks along briskly, heading towards a bus shelter. Colin
enters and waits. An ELDERLY CONFUSED MAN is sat on the
bench muttering to himself. He looks across at Colin and Colin
looks away. The Bus pulls up and Colin boards before the Elderly
Confused Man.

INT. PRINT FACTORY – DAY

Colin is stacking empty boxes to be packed by a group of WOMEN
WORKERS. They are laughing and joking amongst themselves.
Colin is still wearing his baseball cap.

Colin works fast and diligently. There are other MEN working the
machines and also packing.

CUT TO:

Colin pulling a pallet full of boxes along with a hand truck. O.S. we
hear the blaring horn of a forklift truck. Colin jumps a little. The
driver, ALAN – late 50s overweight – shouts at Colin.

ALAN

Oi! Watch what you're doing! I could have your legs off with these
forks!

Alan glares at Colin and drives off.

INT/EXT. WAREHOUSE LOADING BAY – MOMENTS LATER

Alan pulls up on the forklift truck just as CURTIS – 30, loud, confident – motions for a HGV truck to pull up on the bay.

CURTIS

(Directing the truck in)

Hurry up!

Curtis is clearly in a hurry and he keeps checking that he's not being
watched. Alan drives down the bay ramp and quickly starts loading
stacks of empty wooden pallets on to the bed of the truck. Curtis
keeps watch. They are obviously not supposed to be doing this.

EXT. YORKS/LANCS MOORS – DAY

A huge sound sculpture "The Singing Ringing Tree", installed
high on the vast moors overlooking Burnley. There are a couple of
TOURISTS taking photos. The Panoptican is made of tubular metal

and makes the sound of a drone. We see Colin slowly walking up to the sculpture, but clearly dragging his heels waiting for The Tourists to leave. They pass Colin as he heads up to it, smile and nod their heads at him. Colin closes in on the sculpture by himself now. He runs his hands across the metal pipes and listens to the droning sound. He closes his eyes and smiles, clearly enjoying the meditative moment. When he opens his eyes an ELDERLY MAN – late 60's, rather scruffy, a little wild eyed, holding a bible – is staring at the sculpture and shaking his head in disgust.

ELDERLY BIBLE MAN

It's an abomination!

Colin ignores him.

ELDERLY BIBLE MAN (CONT'D)

You know why it's here don't you? Why they've put this thing right here.

Colin sighs and continues listening to the drone.

ELDERLY BIBLE MAN (CONT'D)

(Shouting over at Colin)

I'm saying! You know why they've put this abomination here, eh?

Again Colin ignores him.

ELDERLY BIBLE MAN (CONT'D)

They've put it here cos it overlooks where the Pendle Witches lived.

He turns and points down the moor.

ELDERLY BIBLE MAN (CONT'D)

Down there. Old Demdyke, Alice Nutter, Elizabeth Device. It's where they practiced their evil.

He turns and points at the sculpture.

ELDERLY BIBLE MAN (CONT'D)

This! It's the trumpet of the devil calling them back to Hell!

Colin's heard enough. He sighs and starts walking back down the moor. The Elderly Bible Man shouts after him.

ELDERLY BIBLE MAN (CONT'D)

Oi! I'm telling you! This won't stand!

Colin continues, annoyed that his peace has been disrupted. The Elderly Bible Man shouts after him, quoting.

ELDERLY BIBLE MAN (CONT'D)

"And I will show wonders in the heavens and in the Earth:

Blood and fire and pillars of smoke. The Sun shall be turned into darkness, and the Moon into blood, before the coming great and awesome Day of the Lord, and it shall come to pass that whoever calls on the Name of the Lord shall be saved."

Colin stops, turns and glares at the Elderly Bible Man. It is clear that Colin has unnerved him a little. The Elderly Bible Man sinks a little and bows his head. Colin heads down the moors.

INT. COUNCIL FLAT – DAY

CU on Colin asleep. His alarm clock buzzes. It's 6.45 AM. Colin climbs out of bed.

QUICK CUTS:

Colin descending the stairs

Colin walking towards the bus shelter

Colin boarding the bus

INT. FACTORY – DAY

Colin is emptying large plastic bins full of waste paper in to a bailing machine. He presses a button and large metal plates compress the paper. It makes a horrible grinding noise but Colin doesn't flinch.

INT. FACTORY CANTEEN – DAY

Most of the workers sit together, laughing and joking as they eat. Colin eats a homemade sandwich by himself at a nearby table and reads a book.

Colin looks up and sees a FELLOW WORKER biting into a hard-boiled egg. Colin is disgusted and looks away. He gazes at his own sandwich, his appetite gone. He puts the half eaten sandwich in his lunchbox and continues reading.

ANGLE ON: Curtis looking across at Colin. He is sat with Alan and DELORES – pretty, early 30's, wearing a pantsuit.

CURTIS

(Re: Colin)

All that reading. It can't be healthy.

DELORES

Have you ever read a book, Curtis?

CURTIS

Why would I want to do that?

(Snigger)

Here, watch this.

DELORES

No, leave him alone.

Too late, Curtis approaches Colin.

CURTIS

Haven't you heard about the new rules, Col'?

COLIN

Huh … ?

CURTIS

Management says we can't eat in here unless we buy food from the canteen.

Colin frowns as Curtis nods at Colin's lunch box.

CURTIS (CONT'D)

Trying to screw more money out of us … just warning you mate.

Curtis heads back over to the others. He sits down and smirks.

CURTIS (CONT'D)

I told him he can't eat his sandwiches in here.

Alan giggles.

DELORES

That's not funny, Curtis.

CURTIS

I'm just winding him up.

Alan sees something.

ALAN

Look at this.

They watch as Colin heads out. The men laugh when he's gone.

DELORES

I'm gonna tell him you were winding him up.

CURTIS

Do you wanna shag him or summat?

DELORES

Piss off!

Curtis and Alan laugh at her.

ALAN

He's a weirdo.

DELORES

He's just quiet that's all.

CURTIS

You ever seen him without that cap on? He's got big clumps of hair missing.

DELORES

It's alopecia. Lots of people get it.

CURTIS

Well he should shave it all off or get a wig.

ALAN

Yeah, a fright wig. That'd be funny.

INT. GP'S SURGERY – DAY

Colin in his work clothes sits at the side of the GP as she studies his file on her computer.

GP

You were due a repeat prescription in March.

COLIN

Yeah.

She looks at him for an explanation.

GP

You missed your assessment as well. We sent you a letter.

Colin bows his head.

COLIN

I started … I started taking the tablets every other day.

GP

Which, if you remember, we discussed. It's not a good idea to change your dosage without an assessment.

COLIN

Yeah.

GP

And are you taking them now?

COLIN

Yeah.

426

GP

Good …

She starts typing on her computer.

GP (CONT'D)

I'll give you another six weeks supply, but you must make an appointment to come and see me for a repeat prescription OK?

Colin nods his head.

EXT. FACTORY – DAY

Colin is sat eating his sandwich and reading his book on a stack of pallets near the loading bay. Delores approaches him. She's holding a large greeting card and a pen.

DELORES

He's winding you up you know?

Colin looks up at her …

DELORES (CONT'D)

Curtis … about the canteen? You can eat your dinner in there.

Colin pauses …

COLIN

Oh … huh … I don't have to buy food from there?

DELORES

(Shaking her head)

No. He was winding you up.

COLIN

OK.

DELORES

He's a dickhead sometimes. It's the boredom.

COLIN

Boredom?

DELORES

(Scoffing)

Well, yeah, it's hardly the most exciting place to work is it?

COLIN

I like it here.

DELORES

You don't think it gets a bit tedious?

COLIN
No.
DELORES
(Raising her eyebrows)
Oh, right. Fair enough.
Colin resumes reading his book.
DELORES (CONT'D)
(Holding the card and pen out to him) Do you wanna sign this for Moira?
Colin takes the pen and card, quickly writes in it and hands them back to her. Delores reads the card and giggles.
DELORES (CONT'D)
"Happy birthday from Colin."
COLIN
Should I have put something else?
DELORES
It's not her birthday. She's leaving.
COLIN
Oh … huh, do you want me to change it?
Delores smiles at him.
DELORES
No, it's all right. She'll know what you mean.
Delores heads back inside. Colin resumes eating. They catch eyes momentarily as Delores enters the factory.
EXT. CITY CENTRE – DAY
Colin is walking home through the centre towards the Manchester Road area. We follow him to the entrance of the Bradford Central Library, passing the huge IMAX cinema.
INT. CENTRAL LIBRARY – DAY
The top floor. Open plan. Colin walks along one of the aisles and stops at a section. He pulls out a book and browses. After a while he puts it back and is about to head out of the aisle. Colin stops dead in his tracks and gasps. He's frozen in fear. Colin's POV: stood in front of him is a tall figure. It is clad head to toe in a Hessian cloth one piece cloak, tied in the middle with rope, a strange cross/crucifix

dyed into the cloth over the chest area, the eyes and mouth areas have been cut out of the hood and the figure holds its index finger to mouth in a "Shush" gesture.

INT. CENTRAL LIBRARY – A LITTLE LATER

We follow a sickly looking Colin down the stairs and into the Men's Toilets. Colin shoots into a cubicle and vomits. He composes himself and goes out to the sink. He splashes his face with cold water. His hands are shaking. He stares at them then looks at himself in the broken mirror. His reflection is distorted.

EXT. NEAR BLOCK OF COUNCIL FLATS – LATER

As Colin climbs the stairs we hear the voice of a young man ...

We see FAZ, 30, Asian, good looking, casually dressed in designer gear, talking on his i-phone. He affects the street twang in his language.

FAZ

(Into phone)

Yeah, man. You know the score. I can't talk yet. Gimme me an hour.

As Colin passes him they catch eyes. Colin quickly looks down. Faz watches Colin walk along the landing.

FAZ (CONT'D)

(Into phone)

No, no, I'm just chipping now, yeah ... right. Laters, Bro'.

Faz turns his i-phone off and puts it in his pocket. He watches Colin start to unlock his door.

FAZ (CONT'D)

(Shouting to him)

Oi! I know you right?

Colin ignores Faz and enters. Faz frowns and heads down the stairs.

CUT TO:

Faz driving away from the block of flats in a fast expensive car.

EXT. FACTORY – DAY

Colin is sat on the pallets eating his sandwich and reading. Delores comes out with a FELLOW WORKER and they light cigarettes. Delores sees Colin and goes over to him.

DELORES

I told ya you don't have to eat out here.

Colin doesn't stop reading.

COLIN

Huh … it's all right. I've got used to it now.

Delores takes a drag on her cigarette.

DELORES

You don't say much do you?

COLIN

No.

They both chuckle.

COLIN (CONT'D)

I spend a lot o' time alone.

DELORES

You must have mates?

COLIN

Not really.

DELORES

(Sympathetic, drags on her cigarette)

What about family?

COLIN

Huh … my parents are dead.

DELORES

No brothers and sisters?

COLIN

No.

DELORES

You're lucky. There's six in our family. All we ever did was fight when we were growing up.

COLIN

I'd have liked some brothers and sisters.

DELORES

(Snorting)

Not like mine you wouldn't.

(Beat)

How old were you when your parents …

COLIN

I don't remember much about them.

She waits for him to continue but he doesn't ...

DELORES

(Beat, flicks her cigarette away)

Right then. Back to work.

She smiles at him and heads off. Colin watches her.

INT. OFFICE IN FACTORY – DAY

Delores is inputting figures at the computer. BARRY – 50's, over-weight, short, wearing an ill-fitting shirt and tie, constantly tucking it in to his trousers – enters.

BARRY

Dave Gibney's been on the blower, Del'. He wants a full inventory of the warehouse.

DELORES

For the third quarter you mean?

BARRY

No, he wants it by the 28th.

Delores is surprised but tries to mask it.

DELORES

Why?

BARRY

Head office is sending Maggie whatshername to help you.

(Searching for something)

Do you know where those Cleanpak returns are?

DELORES

(Pointing)

Over there.

Delores is clearly a little rattled but keeps working.

INT. A QUIET CORNER OF THE WAREHOUSE – LATER

Delores is with Alan and Curtis. They are all edgy and talk quietly.

DELORES

... You're gonna have to do something. They'll find out straight away once they start taking stock.

CURTIS

(Hissing)

"Us"? You've made plenty o' money out of this as well!

431

ALAN
(To Delores)
Can't you cook the books a bit?
DELORES
The next pallet delivery isn't until after the stock take.
CURTIS
(Throwing his hands up)
So basically we're fucked?
ALAN
They'll nick us for this! Can't we buy some pallets and replace the ones we've flogged?
DELORES
We've sold nearly two thousand, Alan. We'd have to buy 'em back at full price. That's twenty grand! Have you got twenty grand lying around?
ALAN
I could get three at a push.
(To Curtis)
What about you?
CURTIS
Me? I've got fuck all!
ALAN
What? You just blow everything?
Curtis glares at Alan.
DELORES
I can get four.
CURTIS
We're still nowhere near.
ALAN
(To Curtis)
You need to get a loan.
CURTIS
I've got a fucking IVA. Who's gonna give me a loan!
(Shakes his head, to himself)
"Get a loan"

ALAN

Well we're gonna have to do summat.

DELORES

Just calm down.

(Heading off)

I've gotta get back.

INT. COLIN'S BEDROOM – EARLY MORNING

We open on Colin's empty bed. The sheets are pulled from the bed and are spread across the floor. We slowly move across to Colin. He is sat in the corner of the room holding a pillow tight to his chest. Colin stares, wide eyed, into the distance, rocking back and forth as he grips the pillow. He is clearly frightened. The alarm clock buzzes and Colin automatically snaps out of his state. He stands up and puts the sheets and pillow back on the bed. He starts to get dressed as though he has simply woken from his sleep.

EXT. LEAFY RESIDENTIAL AREA, NAB WOOD – DAY

Colin walks along the tree lined street. This is an expensive and desirable part of the city. Large detached houses, most of them very old. We follow Colin up the path of one of them. He presses the doorbell and waits.

INT. STUDY IN LARGE HOUSE – DAY

Classically decorated. There are framed diplomas on the walls and a large floor to ceiling bookcase. Two chairs facing each other. Colin is sat facing his psychiatrist DR. GREENBERG – early 60's, a little dowdy. She has a posh accent and a very soothing manner, as you'd expect. Colin is in an unusually bright mood. He's comfortable with her.

DR. GREENBERG

So, Colin … anything new to tell me since last month?

COLIN

No. Everything's all right. I really like my job.

DR. GREENBERG

(Beat)

Do you prefer this job to one you had before?

COLIN

Oh yeah, definitely. I didn't like the shifts at the supermarket.

DR. GREENBERG

Have they given you a permanent position yet?

COLIN

No, I'm still a temp but I think they will.

DR. GREENBERG

What is it that you like about it so much?

COLIN

Knowing what my days are gonna be like. Every day the same. Every week.

DR. GREENBERG

Good, good. You're a creature of habit. This is very positive.

Mrs. Greenberg smiles at him and he reciprocates.

DR. GREENBERG (CONT'D)

Do you find you are dwelling less on the past?

Colin thinks about it.

COLIN

There's moments.

DR. GREENBERG

The nightmares still?

COLIN

No. The other day … I was in the library and …

Colin notices Dr. Greenberg's gaze.

DR. GREENBERG

Go on.

Colin is now a little hesitant.

COLIN

I don't know … I was just thinking about back then and …

DR. GREENBERG

Yes?

COLIN

I just … I just got a bit anxious that's all.

DR. GREENBERG

And how did you deal with it?

COLIN

(Shrugging)

It just kinda … went away. I was all right.

DR. GREENBERG

Everyone feels a little anxious from time to time, Colin. It's not an indication that you are regressing.

She smiles at him again.

DR. GREENBERG (CONT'D)

Colin ... I noticed you are still using the phrase "back then". We've talked about this haven't we?

Colin looks away.

DR. GREENBERG (CONT'D)

There is no "back then", Colin.

COLIN

You know what I mean.

DR. GREENBERG

But it implies that you are referring to a specific time and incident. It's not honest or positive language, Colin.

Colin fidgets a little.

DR. GREENBERG (CONT'D)

We've talked at length about this haven't we?

COLIN

Mmm.

DR. GREENBERG

It's all about focusing on the now with a positive frame of mind isn't it?

COLIN

Yeah ... OK.

Dr. Greenberg smiles at him.

COLIN (CONT'D)

Sorry.

DR. GREENBERG

That's all right.

INT. COUNCIL FLAT BLOCK – DAY

Colin returning home. Faz is handing over a bundle of wraps of heroin to a YOUNG WHITE PUSHER on the stairs.

FAZ

I'll be round with a re-up tomorrow. Go on.

The Young Pusher scurries off. Colin ignores Faz as he passes.

FAZ (CONT'D)

Yo! Why you blanking me?

Faz gets in front of Colin. Colin stops.

FAZ (CONT'D)

You don't remember me do ya?

Colin looks blankly at him.

FAZ (CONT'D)

Faz. We were in the same English class at Rhodesway. You got sent to detention centre for burning the maths department down.

COLIN

(Mumbling)

Yeah.

FAZ

We was all shocked 'cos you were like really quiet and shit.

Colin looks away impatiently.

FAZ (CONT'D)

Faz. I hung out with T.K. and Dezzy n' that crew. Don't you remember me?

COLIN

Yeah … you bullied me.

Colin pushes past him.

FAZ

Eh! We didn't fuckin' bully you, man!

Colin ignores him and continues. Faz tuts.

FAZ (CONT'D)

(To himself)

Dickhead!

INT. COLIN'S FLAT, LIVING ROOM – NIGHT

Colin is sat sewing. He is uncomfortable though. He pinches the side of his nose and then rubs at his eyes. We follow him into the kitchen. He takes out a couple pills and is about to wash them down with water, but he stops and flushes the pills down the sink.

EXT. BLOCK OF FLATS – NIGHT

Faz is knocking hard on a door. YOODA – a young Syrian woman opens it. Faz barges in aggressively, slamming the door shut.

FAZ

Where is he?

Yooda is shocked. She quickly picks up her newborn baby and cradles it.

FAZ (CONT'D)

Where's your fucking husband?

Yooda excitedly babbles in her native tongue, gesticulating that her husband isn't there. Faz searches the flat, throwing around what little possessions are in there. Yooda starts to cry as Faz stomps around.

INT. COLIN'S BEDROOM – NIGHT

Colin – wearing pajamas – is setting his alarm clock. He puts it down, turns off the light and lies down. A moment later there is a loud banging at the door. Colin turns on the light and sits up, clearly annoyed. We follow him to the door. He looks through the peephole and sees Yooda, newborn baby in her arms. They are both crying.

YOODA

You have phone please?

She continues to bang.

YOODA (CONT'D)

I need phone, yes? You have phone please?

We are close on Colin catching his breath, his back against the door. He seems to be hyperventilating.

INT. COLIN'S BEDROOM – EARLY MORNING

Close on the alarm clock buzzing. It's 6.58. Colin wakes, stares in horror at the clock and shoots out of bed.

EXT. COUNCIL FLATS – EARLY MORNING

The landing on the block of flats. A few residents are milling around, watching something down on the street below.

Colin comes out of his flat, puts his head down and jogs across the landing. He briefly looks down at the street. A Couple of POLICE CARS, an AMBULANCE and a CORONERS VAN are down there. Colin passes a few residents who are watching and talking about the incident. Colin catches a glimpse of the CORONERS loading two bagged bodies into the van. One is clearly Yooda and the other her Baby. Colin carries on his way.

CUT TO:

Colin running to the bus stop. He manages to catch the bus just as it is starting to pull away.

INT. BUS, DOWNSTAIRS – MOMENTS LATER

Colin is sat at the back by himself. He's angry as he checks his watch.

INT. FACTORY – DAY

Colin is stacking boxes; Delores is attaching shipping invoices to them. Curtis walks past and purposefully knocks Colin's baseball cap off.

CURTIS

(Pretending it was an accident)

Oh, sorry Col'.

Delores glares at Curtis as Colin quickly picks up his cap and puts it back on. Delores shakes her head at Curtis. Colin is clearly embarrassed as Curtis walks off, sniggering. Delores pretends to have not seen what happened. They resume working.

DELORES

(Beat)

What do you do for laughs, Colin?

COLIN

"Laughs"?

DELORES

You know … where do you go out?

COLIN

Huh … I don't go out much.

DELORES

Yeah, but where do you go when you do go out?

COLIN

Huh … nowhere really.

DELORES

(Giggling)

You must go somewhere.

COLIN

I go walking up The Moors sometimes.

DELORES

I mean "out, out". Pubs, clubs.

COLIN

No ... I'm saving up.

DELORES

What are you saving up for?

Colin is hesitant.

DELORES (CONT'D)

Well?

COLIN

I'm gonna buy a house.

DELORES

Saving up for a deposit, eh?

COLIN

No, I'm gonna *buy* a house.

DELORES

(Frowning)

Without a mortgage?

COLIN

I've already saved up five thousand pound since I started here.

DELORES

Well done.

Colin doesn't reply. They continue to work.

DELORES (CONT'D)

It'll take you a long time though, eh?

COLIN

Thirteen years. Sooner if we get bigger pay rises.

DELORES

(Scoffing)

You're planning on being here in thirteen years!

COLIN

Yeah. Once they make me permanent.

She realizes he is deadly serious and changes the topic.

DELORES

What about dates? Don't you ever go out on dates?

COLIN

(Embarrassed)

Huh ... no, not really.

DELORES

You know, you're the only lad here that hasn't asked me out.

Colin is blushing. Clearly Delores finds this cute.

DELORES (CONT'D)

Well ... ?

Colin shrugs awkwardly.

DELORES (CONT'D)

Am I not up to your standard?

COLIN

No, I mean, yeah, yeah. I just ...

DELORES

(Sighing)

OK. Do you wanna go out one night?

COLIN

Huh ... where?

DELORES

I dunno ... wherever you want.

Colin is flattered but remains mute.

DELORES (CONT'D)

Colin?

Colin shoots her a smile.

INT. COLIN'S FLAT – NIGHT

We are CU on Colin sewing on the tapestry. He is unusually happy. There is a knock at the door. He pauses and ignores the knocking; hoping whoever it is will go away.

The knocking continues and he sighs and goes and opens the door, putting on his baseball cap. A female detective – D.S. BRESLIN – mid 50's, well groomed, tall – stands holding up her i-d card.

D.S. BRESLIN

Hello?

Colin simply stares at her.

D.S. BRESLIN (CONT'D)

Sorry to bother you. I'm D.S. Breslin ...

(Putting her i-d card away)

… We're investigating the death of the young woman and her baby last night. Huh, is it OK to talk?

COLIN

I'm busy.

We see that across the landing there is another MALE DETECTIVE knocking at a door accompanied by a UNIFORMED POLICEWOMAN.

D.S. BRESLIN

It won't take a minute.

COLIN

I don't know anything about it.

D.S. BRESLIN

You do know there was a death here though?

Colin nods his head.

D.S. BRESLIN (CONT'D)

Can I come in?

Colin pauses, sighs and steps aside as D.S. Breslin steps in.

CUT TO:

MOMENTS LATER …

With there only being one chair, Colin and D.S. Breslin are stood up. D.S. Breslin is writing in her notebook. Colin is diffident. She keeps glancing across at the tapestry.

COLIN

… Turner.

D.S. BRESLIN

Is that a tapestry? You don't see many of them nowadays.

COLIN

(Curt, sighing)

Can we just …

D.S. Breslin raises her eyebrow and continues.

D.S. BRESLIN

OK … one of your neighbors said they saw the woman banging on your door. Did you speak to her?

COLIN

What did the neighbor say?

D.S. BRESLIN

That she was banging on your door. Did you speak to her?

COLIN

No … Well …

D.S. Breslin gives him a "Go on" look.

COLIN (CONT'D)

Sort of.

D.S. BRESLIN

"Sort of"?

COLIN

She wanted to use my phone.

Her eyes light up: a lead perhaps?

D.S. BRESLIN

Really? Do you know who she called? It doesn't matter if you don't, we could check the records, but –

COLIN

– I haven't got one.

D.S. BRESLIN

(Frowning)

You don't have a phone?

COLIN

No.

D.S. BRESLIN

Not even a mobile?

Colin shakes his head. D.S. Breslin raises her eyebrows and makes a quick note.

D.S. BRESLIN (CONT'D)

OK … what else did she say?

COLIN

Nothing.

D.S. BRESLIN

She just asked to use your phone?

COLIN

(Short)

Yeah. I told you.

D.S. BRESLIN
(Registering his impatience)
How did she seem? How was she acting?
COLIN
What do you mean?
D.S. BRESLIN
Well, was she upset?
COLIN
She was shouting.
D.S. BRESLIN
Angry? Frightened?
COLIN
I suppose so.
She makes a note.
D.S. BRESLIN
And she just asked to use your phone? That was it?
COLIN
(Snapping)
Don't you believe me?
D.S. BRESLIN
(Surprised)
Why wouldn't I believe you?
She scrutinizes him a little.
D.S. BRESLIN (CONT'D)
OK.
COLIN
She disturbed me. I told her I don't have a phone and that's it.
D.S. BRESLIN
We're speaking to everyone so don't –
COLIN
– Well you've spoke to me now so you can go.
D.S. Breslin contains herself and fakes a smile.
D.S. BRESLIN
(Sarcastic)
Thanks for your help.

D.S. Breslin leaves; Colin locks the door behind her and takes his cap off. He takes a deep breath and resumes his sewing, but he's pensive and a little disturbed. He stands up and paces.

INT. FACTORY – DAY

Colin is stacking boxes, Delores is stock checking.

DELORES

Tapestry?

Delores giggles. Colin gives her a look. She catches herself.

DELORES (CONT'D)

No, I mean, there's nothing wrong with … where did you learn it?

COLIN

At a church I went to as a kid.

DELORES

Like a Sunday school?

COLIN

Not really. It was for adults as well.

DELORES

I hated Sunday school.

Colin continues stacking.

DELORES (CONT'D)

Do you still go to church?

Colin shakes his head negative.

DELORES (CONT'D)

You'll have to show me some of it.

COLIN

It's not finished … it's a big piece.

DELORES

Well … when it's finished then.

Delores smiles at Colin.

INT. OFFICE IN BRADFORD MET POLICE STATION – DAY

D.S. Breslin is sat at her computer reading something. It is holding her attention. D.I. MALIK – Asian, late 30's, tall, well built – enters with two cups of coffee. He places one down next to her.

D.S. BRESLIN

(Browsing the screen)

That Colin Turner I spoke to. Five charges of arson with three convictions.

D.I. Malik sits down at his desk.

D.I. MALIK

Why you looking at him?

All due respect, Sarge, but we're dealing with a suicide.

D.S. BRESLIN

Do you know how rare it is for a mother to commit suicide with her child?

D.I. MALIK

Yeah, but –

D.S. BRESLIN

– No suicide note? Put the missing husband angle into the mix … it's not adding up.

D.I. MALIK

And you fancy this Colin Turner as a suspect?

D.S. BRESLIN

No, he's no murderer, but he's hiding something and he's a proven liar.

D.I. Malik looks at her. What do you mean?

D.S. BRESLIN (CONT'D)

He once claimed his family were ritually abusing him. Turned out he'd made it all up.

EXT. COUNCIL FLAT BLOCK – EARLY EVENING

On Faz about to enter the stairwell area. He groans as D.S. Breslin and D.I. Malik step out and block his way. Faz sighs.

D.S. BRESLIN

I'm D.S. Breslin and this is –

FAZ

– I know who you are and if yer gonna search me –

D.S. BRESLIN

– We're not interested in that. Do you know Moonif Ganim?

FAZ

Who?

D.I. MALIK

The husband of the young woman who died.

FAZ

Ah, right. The fugee. Is that his name?

D.S. BRESLIN

So you know him?

FAZ

I've seen him around. Why?

D.I. MALIK

We heard he bought smack from you.

Faz snorts and shakes his head.

D.S. BRESLIN

(Sighing)

Come on, Faz.

FAZ

Even if I did sell it, which I don't, d'ya think I'd offer up my customers to the fucking

Feds?

They glance at each other, step aside and let him pass. He smirks at
them and kisses his teeth as he affects a "gangster limp" and climbs
the stairs.

INT. BATHROOM – NIGHT

Colin has showered and is now shaving. He is clearly in a good
mood. For no reason Colin's mood suddenly changes and he looks a
bit nauseous. He closes his eyes.

INT. GARAGE, 1992 –

A modest car is parked up, engine running.

INT. CAR – CONTINUOUS

A hose spews petrol fumes into the car through a gap in the passenger side window. COLIN'S DAD is sat behind the wheel, tears
streaming down his face. He swigs on a bottle of cheap Scotch.
Young Colin sits in the rear staring blankly at his Dad

COLIN'S DAD

(Blubbering)

This is the best way, Colin …

Young Colin doesn't respond.

COLIN'S DAD (CONT'D)

Did you hear me?

(Beat)

I said this is the best way to make it stop.

Colin's Dad takes a big swig on the whiskey and wipes tears from his eyes.

COLIN'S DAD (CONT'D)

... We'll fall asleep soon and then ...

He takes another gulp of whiskey. Suddenly the hose is dragged out of the window and UNCLE PETER – early 50's, well built, swarthy and smartly dressed in a suit – pulls open the passenger door and turns the engine off.

UNCLE PETER

(Spluttering through the fumes)

What the hell are you doing?

Colin's Dad breaks down even more, sobbing and gesticulating as Uncle Peter drags him out and then opens the door for Young Colin.

UNCLE PETER (CONT'D)

(Barking at Young Colin)

Get out, Colin!

Young Colin climbs out and follows them out of the garage.

INT. HALLWAY IN DRAB TERRACE HOUSE – NIGHT

CLOSE ON a bedroom door. Uncle Peter comes out of it and quietly closes it behind him. Young Colin is stood against the wall, upright, head bowed.

Uncle Peter puts his hand on Young Colin's shoulder and leads him down the stairs.

UNCLE PETER

He's going to be all right ... come on.

INT. KITCHEN – A LITTLE LATER

Young Colin is sat at a table, head bowed, motionless. We see Uncle Peter preparing food but can't make out what it is. Uncle Peter puts a bowl of a seven de-shelled boiled eggs on the table in front of Young Colin. Young Colin doesn't look at them. Uncle Peter stands over him and puts his hand on Young Colin's shoulder.

UNCLE PETER

Eat up, Colin.

Young Colin reluctantly picks up an egg. Uncle Peter goes to the sink and pours water in a pint glass. He brings it to Young Colin and puts it down.

UNCLE PETER (CONT'D)

Come on. There are people starving in the world.

Young Colin bites into the egg.

INT. BATHROOM – CONTINUOUS

Colin is staring at himself in the mirror. He rubs shaving foam over his head. He takes a deep breath and starts to shave it.

EXT. COUNCIL BLOCK OF FLATS – LATER

Colin is heading out, no baseball cap, now bald, casual but smartly dressed. Faz is sat behind the wheel of his car. TINA – a white 16-year-old girl, pretty – is sat in the passenger seat. They are smoking a draw. Faz sees Colin and shouts him over.

FAZ

Yo!

Colin ignores him and keeps walking.

FAZ (CONT'D)

Hey!

Colin continues ahead.

FAZ (CONT'D)

(To himself)

Knob head.

TINA

D'ya know him?

FAZ

He went to my school.

She giggles.

FAZ (CONT'D)

What?

TINA

I can't imagine you at school.

FAZ

I was good at school. Not like you I bet.

TINA

I'm top of my class in geography.

Faz takes a deep draw on the joint, flicks it out of the window, looks around, winds up his window and unzips his jeans.

FAZ

(Smirking)

Yeah? Well see'f ya can find my dick ya dirty little bitch.

Faz smiles at her and pulls her head towards his groin.

EXT. BRADFORD CITY CENTRE – NIGHT

Colin waits at a corner, he's clearly nervous. He paces and checks his watch. It looks like he is about to head off when he sees Delores walking towards him. He sighs in relief.

DELORES

I didn't recognize you without your baseball cap. It looks good.

Colin rubs his hand over his head self-consciously.

DELORES (CONT'D)

Yeah, it really suits you.

He's flattered and smiles: shucks. They start to walk off.

DELORES (CONT'D)

So ... what do you fancy seeing?

COLIN

Huh, anything.

DELORES

What do you like? Action? Horror? Sci-fi?

COLIN

Whatever you wanna see.

DELORES

OK.

Delores smiles at him.

INT. CINEMA FOYER – A LITTLE LATER

Colin and Delores are queuing for snacks. There is an awkward silence. Delores breaks it.

DELORES

(Re: snacks)

What are you getting?

COLIN

Huh, nothing.

DELORES

Oh, huh … I don't want anything either. I thought you …

Delores giggles.

DELORES (CONT'D)

What are we queuing for?

Colin shrugs. Delores grabs his arm and leads him off.

DELORES (CONT'D)

Come on.

INT. CINEMA – NIGHT

We are close on Colin and Delores obviously watching a horror film. Delores and those around are squirming, covering their eyes or looking away at the carnage on screen.

Colin remains emotionless, watching the film in a totally dispassionate manner.

INT. MCDONALD'S – LATER

Delores is eating a burger and fries. Colin sips a drink.

DELORES

Are you sure you're not hungry?

COLIN

Yeah.

DELORES

I wish you'd got something. I feel like a pig.

Delores wipes her mouth.

DELORES (CONT'D)

Did you like the film?

COLIN

Yeah, it was good.

DELORES

I love horror films.

Colin nods his head in agreement.

COLIN

(Blurting)

Do you think they'll make me permanent soon?

DELORES

(A little surprised)

Huh ... yeah, can't see why not. You're never late or off sick.
COLIN
I never will be.
DELORES
(Giggling)
That's a bold statement.
COLIN
(Intently)
I mean it.
DELORES
Huh ... OK.
Delores smiles at him.
EXT. REMOTE BEAUTY SPOT NEAR BRADFORD – NIGHT
A small car park overlooking the Aire Valley. Faz's car is parked up facing one way and another expensive car is reversing in. It parks up so that they can face each other. The man behind the wheel of the other expensive car is SHAK – Asian, smart, mid 40s, well spoken, bespectacled.
FAZ
You have a good holiday, Shak?
SHAK
Why were police all over the flats on Manchester Road?
FAZ
A fugee killed herself and her baby.
SHAK
A what?
FAZ
A fugee. You know, a refugee. From Syria. An Arab or something. Jumped from the top floor.
Faz makes a jumping and falling gesture with his finger. Shak grimaces.
SHAK
With a baby?
FAZ
Yeah.

SHAK

Jesus!

FAZ

(Beat)

It might have something to do with me.

SHAK

(Glaring at Faz)

You?

FAZ

I fucked up a bit.

SHAK

What?

FAZ

I gave her husband a package.

SHAK

Her husband?

FAZ

I gave him eighty grams at fifties. He was supposed to get 'em out to his Arab mates at sixties, you know, open up a new market, but …

SHAK

(Containing his anger)

But what?

FAZ

Nobody's seen him. I've looked everywhere … I'll stand up for the four grand, Shak.

Shak shakes his head and thinks.

SHAK

So the police think she's killed herself because of him leaving?

FAZ

(Shrugging)

Probably. It's just a suicide though. It's nothing to do with us.

Shak is thinking. He stares out of his windscreen.

SHAK

You're sure it's a suicide?

FAZ

Yeah, positive.

Shak stares at Faz.
FAZ (CONT'D)
What?
SHAK
You're sure you didn't try getting the money out of her, or try find out where her husband's gone?
FAZ
Yeah, course I did, but –
SHAK
– did you get heavy with her?
FAZ
A bit.
SHAK
How heavy?
FAZ
(Snorting)
You don't think I pushed her and a baby off the flats d'ya? I'm not a monster!
Shak doesn't look too sure.
FAZ (CONT'D)
Come on, man. Gimme credit, yeah?
SHAK
(Beat, starts his engine)
Make sure the next drop off's not four grand light.
Shak drives off. Faz sighs in relief.
INT. COLIN'S FLAT, BEDROOM – NIGHT
Colin is changing from his smart clothes into his work uniform. He grabs the alarm clock and we follow him into the living room. He sits down in the chair and sets the alarm clock for 6.45 A.M. He puts the alarm clock on his knee and stares at it.
DISSOLVE TO:

Colin still staring at the clock: it's 3.27 AM.
DISSOLVE TO: It is now 6.44 A.M. and Colin is still staring at the clock in a trance. He is shaking violently and frothing at the mouth.

As it clicks on to 6.45 AM and buzzes, Colin snaps out of his trance, stops shaking and wipes his mouth. He stands up and heads to the bathroom as though nothing has happened.

EXT. BLOCK OF FLATS – A LITTLE LATER

Colin is walking out of the flats. He looks over and sees that bunches of flowers and cards have been laid where the bodies fell.

INT. FACTORY, WAREHOUSE AREA – DAY

Colin – back to wearing his baseball cap – is pulling a pallet stacked with paper with a hand truck. He notices Delores, Curtis and Alan at a distance talking. He continues.

CUT TO:

Delores, Curtis and Alan talking quietly. Curtis sees Colin in the distance …

CURTIS

(Re: Colin)

Did you give him sympathy shag last night?

DELORES

You'll have plenty of time to fantasize about my sex life when you're banged up, Curtis.

ALAN

I say we just play dumb. Deny all knowledge.

CURTIS

They've got no proof it was us.

DELORES

(Sighing)

They're not just gonna ignore twenty grand's worth of missing stock, and the first person they'll go to is Ronnie. Do you seriously think he won't dob us in it?

Curtis and Alan look at each other.

EXT. FACTORY – DAY

Colin is pouring tea from his flask, sat on the pallets. Delores – holding a vending machine cup of coffee, lighting a cigarette – heads over to him. They smile at each other.

DELORES

Did you like it last night?

COLIN
Yeah, yeah … huh, did you get home all right?
DELORES
You could have shared my taxi you know?
COLIN
It's not far to walk.
Delores sits down next to him.
DELORES
(Beat)
Colin …
Colin looks at her. She takes a breath and blurts …
DELORES (CONT'D)
You know you said you had some money saved up?
Colin is about to reply but Delores very quickly recants.
DELORES (CONT'D)
Forget I even said that. I don't know what I was thinking. Forget I
said it OK?
COLIN
Huh, yeah.
Delores is angry with herself. She takes a drag and then violently
stubs her cigarette out on the ground.
DELORES
Do you wanna do it again?
COLIN
What?
DELORES
Go out with me?
COLIN
(Unsure)
D'you wanna?
DELORES
(Smiling at him)
I wouldn't be asking would I?
COLIN
Huh, yeah, yeah, I'd like that.

Delores chuckles at his charming response. She can't help herself and leans across and pecks Colin on the lips. She stands up and heads back inside. Colin watches her and smiles to himself.

INT. D.S. BRESLIN'S CAR, MOVING – DAY

D.S. Breslin drives, D.I. Malik in the passenger seat. D.I. Malik is looking a little frustrated.

D.I. MALIK

If this does turn out to be a suicide we're gonna have to justify investigating Colin Turner, Sarge.

D.S. BRESLIN

OK, forget suicide for a minute and work on the fact that her husband owed Faz money and went missing. The logic being that Faz can't get to him so he takes his revenge on her and the baby, OK?

D.I. MALIK

Yeah, I get that but –

D.S. BRESLIN

– I worked a shooting in Holmewood in two thousand and eight. It looked like an open and shut suicide. Anyway, I start taking statements and –

D.I. MALIK

– Yeah, I heard about this. The daughter of the victim put the shooting on the brother right?

D.S. BRESLIN

It took me six months to get her to talk. I just knew she was withholding. I'm getting the same feeling with this. Call it a hunch if you like, but it was a hunch that caught The Yorkshire Ripper.

D.I. MALIK

Is that right?

D.S. BRESLIN

Yeah, a Bobby decided to look where Peter Sutcliffe had had a pee and he found the murder weapons.

D.I. Malik thinks about it.

D.I. MALIK

So when are we gonna approach Colin Turner again?

D.S. BRESLIN

When we've built up a better picture of him.

INT. DOUBLE DECKER BUS JOURNEYING THROUGH THE MOORS – DAY

Colin and Delores are sat upstairs at the front looking out over the wild countryside.

DELORES

Are you gonna tell me where we're going or not?

COLIN

We'll be there soon.

They smile at each other.

EXT. THE SINGING RINGING TREE SCULPTURE, THE MOORS – DAY

CLOSE ON Delores frowning at it. Colin is by her side smiling.

COLIN

Do you like it?

DELORES

Is it conceptual art or something?

COLIN

No, no, listen.

Colin leads Delores closer to the sculpture and they listen.

COLIN (CONT'D)

Can you hear that?

DELORES

That noise?

COLIN

It's a drone.

DELORES

Yeah, noise.

Colin is a little disappointed. Delores notices.

DELORES (CONT'D)

No, I mean, yeah I can hear it.

COLIN

Do you think it sounds evil?

Delores is surprised.

DELORES

"Evil"?

Colin stares at her waiting for an answer.

DELORES (CONT'D)
Huh, no, do you?
COLIN
There's an Old Man who comes up here and tells everyone it's evil.
DELORES
Mental.
COLIN
He goes on about the witches in Pendle.
DELORES
Oh yeah, I've heard about that. It was round here wasn't it?
Colin doesn't answer, simply runs his hand over the tubes. Delores
watches him. She thinks of something to say ...
DELORES (CONT'D)
I bet it took ages to make.
COLIN
Mmm.
DELORES
You really like it don't you?
COLIN
This could last thousands of years, you know, like Stonehenge.
DELORES
Have you been there?
COLIN
No.
DELORES
I went with school. There's not much to see to be honest.
COLIN
No, it's not that. It's the fact the stones are still there. They might
look different but they haven't really changed. They're continual.
She watches Colin admiring the sculpture. She gets an idea.
DELORES
I know! Let's go look at where the witches lived.
Colin clearly isn't impressed with the idea but disguises it.
DELORES (CONT'D)
Come on. I love stuff like that.

Delores closes in on him.

DELORES (CONT'D)

What do you think?

COLIN

Huh …

DELORES

Please. It'll be a laugh.

Colin checks his watch. Delores grabs his hand and leads him away.

EXT. VILLAGE OF NEWBURY, LATER – DAY

Colin is stood outside a small cottage gift shop called "Witches Galore". There are 3 sculptures of stereotypical witches on display outside the window. Colin looks up at a road sign that has the image of a witch riding her broomstick above the directions.

Delores comes out of the shop holding tourists "Pendle Witch Trail" fold out brochure/map. She waves it in front of Colin and smiles.

CUT TO:

Colin and Delores walking up a hill. Delores reads from the brochure.

DELORES

" … 9 year old Jennet Device's testimony had wide and far-reaching consequences as her case became a precedent for using children as witnesses in cases of witchcraft, particularly through a book called Dalton's Country Justice. This book was used by British magistrates as a handbook for applying the law in the UK and in the New World, and was used in the Salem witch trials eighty years after the Pendle witch trials; it cited the case of Jennet Device as precedent for seeking children as witnesses in cases of witchcraft. Twenty years later Jennet Device was caught up in another witch trial, this time with the star witness being a young boy accusing her of witchcraft, only made possible by the precedent she herself set years earlier."

Delores smiles and looks at Colin.

DELORES (CONT'D)

Serves her right, eh?

COLIN

It doesn't mean she wasn't telling the truth about the other witches.

DELORES

You don't believe they were really witches do you?

COLIN

Don't you?

DELORES

Nah, it's folklore isn't it. Superstition. It makes a good story that's all.

Colin looks like he is about to reply but stops himself.

DELORES (CONT'D)

What?

COLIN

(Beat)

Yeah, I suppose you're right.

It suddenly starts to rain.

DELORES

Shit!

EXT. QUIET COUNTRY ROAD – A LITTLE LATER

The rain falls hard. Delores sits in a stone built bus shelter. Colin studies the timetable on a lamppost.

COLIN

The next one's not until quarter past.

DELORES

Come and sit down.

Colin sits next to Delores. She cuddles up to him and smiles.

DELORES (CONT'D)

This is romantic.

Colin looks at her.

DELORES (CONT'D)

The rain. Don't you think it's romantic?

COLIN

Huh … yeah, kind of.

Delores starts to kiss Colin. He is trying his best not to come across as awkward. She grabs his hand and slips it inside her jacket so he can feel her breast. Delores runs her hand up Colin's thigh to his groin. Colin pulls away.

DELORES
(Puzzled)
What's wrong?
COLIN
Nothing, I just …
Colin stands up and goes to look at the bus timetable again to excuse himself.
COLIN (CONT'D)
If we walk down into –
DELORES
Don't you fancy me, Colin?
COLIN
(Beat)
Yeah, course I do. It's just …
DELORES
It's OK. I understand. Nothing wrong with being shy … it's cute.
She smiles at him. He smiles back and goes and sits back down.
INT. BUS, TRAVELLING THROUGH THE MOORS – LATER
Colin and Delores are looking out at the windswept moors. Colin hesitates and then …
COLIN
We can do it when the weather's better if you want?
Delores looks at him.
COLIN (CONT'D)
The Witch Trail.
DELORES
Right, yeah, sure.
(Beat, quietly)
How long is it since you had a girlfriend?
Colin hesitates again.
DELORES (CONT'D)
It's all right, you don't have to answer. It's none of my business.
Delores links his arm and rests her head on his shoulder.
DELORES (CONT'D)
It doesn't really matter what's happened in the past does it.

After a beat Delores puts her jacket across Colin's lap. We see her hand snake under and feel Colin's groin. Colin gasps and closes his eyes. He slowly starts to smile. Delores looks closely at his face as she continues.

INT. RETIREMENT HOME, COMMUNAL ROOM – DAY

Uncle Peter, now in his early 70's, wheelchair bound, still smart for his age – is sat watching TV in the communal area. D.S. Breslin and D.I. Malik approach him.

D.S. BRESLIN

Mr. Turner?

Uncle Peter looks up quizzically.

UNCLE PETER

Yes?

CUT TO:

A LITTLE LATER ... D.S. Breslin and D.I. Malik are sat with Uncle Peter. D.I. Malik takes shorthand notes. Uncle Peter is pleasant and friendly.

UNCLE PETER (CONT'D)

So this inquiry you want to eliminate Colin from. It's arson again?

D.S. BRESLIN

No, he may have been witness to something we're working on.

UNCLE PETER

Right ... so what is it you want to know?

D.S. BRESLIN

We're aware of the unfounded allegations he made against you and your Brother, but are you and Colin on speaking terms now?

UNCLE PETER

Yes ... I found it in my heart to forgive him.

(Shakes his head and sighs)

The disgusting things he said. To make up such ... well.

(Sighs and shakes his head)

I mean ... disgusting.

D.S. BRESLIN

I'm sorry I had to bring it up, but –

UNCLE PETER

It's what drove my Brother Jeff to suicide.

D.S. BRESLIN
It must have been a traumatic time.
UNCLE PETER
Poor Jeff couldn't deal with it … to think that your own flesh and
blood could make up such …
Uncle Peter fights back tears. D.S. Breslin and D.I. Malik glance at
each other.
D.S. BRESLIN
Does Colin visit you?
UNCLE PETER
He visits at Christmas but that's only because I give him money.
D.S. BRESLIN
OK.
UNCLE PETER
If you want to know anything about him you should really speak to
his psychiatrist.
D.S. BRESLIN
He's under a psychiatrist?
UNCLE PETER
Yes. I pay for his treatment.
D.S. BRESLIN
Really?
UNCLE PETER
The Authorities didn't believe Colin was disturbed. They thought
he'd just made up the stories as an excuse for the arson. I wanted to
help him though.
D.S. BRESLIN
Do you think his psychiatrist will talk to us about Colin?
D.I. MALIK
Doctor patient confidentiality.
UNCLE PETER
I'm sure she'd want to help. She's got his welfare at heart.
INT. FAZ'S CAR, MOVING – DAY
Faz's phone bleeps. He has a text message. He reads it …
FAZ
Yes!

Faz turns his car around in the road and speeds off in the other direction.

EXT. STREET IN MANNINGHAM – LATER

An excited Faz is parked up, HOGGY – mid 20's, white, well built and tattooed, wearing a tracksuit – is stood talking to him at the driver's side window.

FAZ

Where is he?

HOGGY

Tag's got him. What d'ya wanna do?

Faz thinks. Hoggy waits on Faz's words ...

FAZ

(Beat, thinking)

We'll take him up the moors.

HOGGY

(Unsure)

Ya mean ... ?

Faz checks Hoggy's expression.

FAZ

You not up to it, Hoggy?

HOGGY

Yeah, yeah, course man.

FAZ

Well go dig a hole then. I'll come round at six. Get the stuff we used last time.

HOGGY

OK.

FAZ

Don't text me on my main number again ... Laters.

Faz drives off.

INT. PSYCHIATRIST'S HOUSE, HALLWAY – DAY

D.S. Breslin and Dr. Greenberg.

D.S. BRESLIN

(Putting her i-d card in her pocket)

This is a long shot but Peter Turner thought you might be willing to talk to me, Dr. Greenberg. I understand about doctor patient confidentially so —

DR. GREENBERG

— Anything I told you wouldn't be admissible in a court of law.

D.S. BRESLIN

(Surprised)

So you don't mind?

DR. GREENBERG

I've been treating Colin a long time. I'll do anything I can to help him.

D.S. BRESLIN

Oh, OK.

Dr. Greenberg shows D.S. Breslin into her study.

INT. FACTORY – DAY

Delores is taking stock of paper reels. Colin walks past and they smile at each other. Curtis closes in on Delores.

CURTIS

(Quietly)

I've sorted it.

DELORES

Sorted what?

DELORES (CONT'D)

Sorted our "problem".

DELORES (CONT'D)

How?

CURTIS

(Winking at her, walking off)

You'll see.

EXT. STREET – NIGHT

Faz parks his car and climbs out. As he is walking away a hood is slipped over his head from behind and he's dragged into an alleyway by TWO MUSCLEBOUND WHITE ENFORCERS. Faz struggles but he's overpowered. One of The Enforcers starts to hit Faz around the ribs and stomach with a large heavy rubberized TORCH. The Other Enforcer holds his hand over the hood, muffling Faz's cries. The Enforcer attacks Faz with zeal.

465

After a dozen more blows The Enforcers let Faz fall to the ground. Faz moans and groans and holds his ribs as he gasps for breath.

INT. PSYCHIATRIST'S HOUSE, STUDY – DAY

Dr. Greenberg is sat with D.S. Breslin. D.S. Breslin pulls out her notebook.

DR. GREENBERG

So ... what is it that Colin is claiming now?

D.S. BRESLIN

Oh, no, no. He isn't claiming anything.

DR. GREENBERG

I was under the impression he had –

D.S. BRESLIN

– No, we think he was the last to see someone alive that's all. I was hoping if Colin mentioned it to you could tell me. He's not a suspect. I just think he's not telling me something.

DR. GREENBERG

Yes, Colin's had issues with being truthful. How much do you know about his past?

D.S. BRESLIN

Just what's in the police reports. I haven't seen the social services file yet.

DR. GREENBERG

Well, essentially he claimed that he was abused by both his father and uncle and other members of a cult. He said the cult carried out sacrifices.

D.S. Breslin raises her eyebrows, shuffles uncomfortably.

DR. GREENBERG (CONT'D)

You're familiar with claims of ritual satanic abuse?

D.S. BRESLIN

Huh, I remember the "satanic panic" thing in the eighties and nineties.

DR. GREENBERG

I've dealt with dozens of child abuse cases, but in each claim of ritualistic abuse I have never found any solid evidence. Are you familiar with false memory syndrome, Detective?

D.S. BRESLIN
Not really.
DR. GREENBERG
Many psychotherapists still accept the Freudian notion of repression. The idea that when someone experiences extreme trauma, a defense mechanism kicks in and it buries the memory so deep that it cannot be retrieved.
D.S. BRESLIN
I see.
EXT. DUNGENESS, KENT COAST – DAY
Home taped VHS footage of the area.
DR. GREENBERG (V.O.)
These therapists believe that the hidden memories must be recovered and worked through in order to achieve psychological health. They indulge in "memory recovery" techniques such as hypnotic regression and guided imagery. Unfortunately the subject often claims memories of abuse against them that simply never took place. We see the lighthouse, the nuclear power station, the strange shacks, chalets and cottages and the massive concrete "listening ears" …
D.S. BRESLIN (V.O.)
So you think Colin Turner was … what? Coaxed into making these allegations?
We move along the disused and rusty old railway tracks that cross the beach and lead to nowhere.
DR. GREENBERG (V.O.)
A lot of these therapists, for whatever reason, are fervent believers in some vast satanic conspiracy that preys on children.
D.S. BRESLIN
Right.
DR. GREENBERG
But leaving that aside, Peter Turner was investigated for sexual abuse against Colin and totally exonerated.
We see crabs and starfish washed up on to the beach amongst the driftwood.
D.S. BRESLIN (V.O.)
Colin claimed he was sexually abused by others as well didn't he?

DR. GREENBERG (V.O.)

But he couldn't name, describe or locate them.

D.S. BRESLIN (V.O.)

But there were the medical reports regarding anal scarring?

DR. GREENBERG (V.O.)

Yes, and three pediatricians concurred it was the result of constipation the poor boy suffered.

INT. STUDY – CONTINUOUS

D.S. Breslin makes a note.

D.S. BRESLIN

So you think the therapists implanted these –

DR. GREENBERG

– Not necessarily, no. Colin would have supplied them with what they wanted to hear. Positive affirmation.

D.S. BRESLIN

I see.

DR. GREENBERG

It's not only individuals who are empowered to make these claims. One of the longest criminal investigations in American legal history concerned a whole class of preschool children making claims of satanic abuse against their teachers. It resulted in the persecution of innocent people. A modern day witch trial.

Dr. Greenberg throws her hands up slightly in dismay.

DR. GREENBERG (CONT'D)

Imagination is both a gift and a curse sometimes.

D.S. Breslin smiles at Dr. Greenberg.

D.S. BRESLIN

So if Colin does mention having witnessed something …

DR. GREENBERG

I'll call you.

Dr. Greenberg checks her watch and stands up. D.S. Breslin stands.

DR. GREENBERG (CONT'D)

I'm sorry but I've an appointment at –

They shake hands.

D.S. BRESLIN

– No, I understand. Thanks for your time.

They reach the door and Dr. Greenberg stops and turns to D.S. Breslin.

DR. GREENBERG

Colin was indeed a victim of child abuse ... but his abusers were those in social services I'm afraid.

INT. COLIN'S FLAT, LIVING ROOM – NIGHT

Colin is sewing. He checks his watch and it is a minute to 10pm. Colin waits for it to land on the hour. He puts his needles and cotton down. He stands back and views the tapestry. We can't see it.

CUT TO: Colin sat in bed setting his alarm clock. He puts it on the bedside table and lies down. He closes his eyes and after a moment a smile spreads across his face. He snuggles down.

FADE TO BLACK.

FADE UP ON ...

ESTABLISHING SHOT OF AN SUV TRAVELLING THROUGH SADDLEWORTH MOOR AT NIGHT. THERE ARE NO OTHER VEHICLES ON THE ROAD IN THIS EXTREMELY REMOTE AND DESOLATE AREA.

INT. SUV, MOVING – CONTINUOUS

Hoggy is driving, Faz in the passenger seat studying a small tracking device. There are two large McDonald's Milk Shakes in a drinks holder. Faz winces and grabs his ribs.

HOGGY

(Re: Faz's ribs)

What's up?

FAZ

Fucking Shak innit. Got a couple of his Bitches to kick me a kicking ... that's why we're doing this.

From the rear we hear banging. Faz sighs.

FAZ (CONT'D)

You tie him up proper?

HOGGY

Tag tied him up.

Faz groans. The tracker bleeps. Hoggy looks out of the window at Faz's side.

HOGGY (CONT'D)

Yeah, it's just here.

Hoggy pulls over off the road a little. Faz pulls on a pair of thin surgical gloves and hands Hoggy a pair to put on.

INT. COLIN'S BEDROOM – NIGHT

Colin in bed asleep. We close in on him.

INT. YOUNG COLIN'S BEDROOM – NIGHT

There is a chair propped against the door handle to stop anyone entering. Young Colin is asleep in bed. There is a loud knocking at the door.

Young Colin's eyes open in fear. The knocking continues. Young Colin hesitantly goes to the door. He pulls the chair away and opens the door to reveal The Hooded Figure looming large over him. The Hooded Figure enters the room and closes the door behind him.

INT. COLIN'S BEDROOM – CONTINUOUS

Colin sits up in bed trying to catch his breath. He manages to calm down a little and then lies back down, staring at the ceiling.

INT. SUV, PARKED UP, SADDLEWORTH MOOR – NIGHT

Faz pulls out a small vial of white powder with a small spoon inside. He takes a snort of the cocaine in both nostrils and then dips into the vial and holds the spoon out for Hoggy to take a couple of snorts.

FAZ

(Putting the vial away)

Right.

CUT TO:

Faz sticking a knife into one of the back wheels of the SUV.

CUT TO:

Hoggy jacking up the SUV to change the wheel. This is a charade to explain why they have pulled up if anyone finds it suspicious.

CUT TO:

BLACK …

FADE UP ON

POV as the boot of the SUV opens. Faz and Hoggy are peering at a tied up and terrified MOONIF – late 20's, disheveled, swarthy. He is moaning and trying to speak through the tape over his mouth.

Faz and Hoggy waft at their noses and step back.

HOGGY

Ugh! He's shit his self!

Faz holds his nose and registers how frightened Moonif is. He slams the boot shut and pauses.

HOGGY (CONT'D)

Have ya changed yer mind?

FAZ

Have I fuck! Give him a fix.

HOGGY

(Confused)

Eh?

FAZ

Fix him up. There's some works in the glove compartment.

HOGGY

What d'ya mean?

FAZ

Give him a fuckin' fix! Are ya deaf?

CUT TO: Hoggy stood over Moonif, still tied up in the boot. He gives Moonif a shot of heroin into a vein he has tied off with a small length of hose. Moonif is staring at Hoggy in fear and confusion. Faz looks on.

HOGGY

Why we doing this?

FAZ

Look at the poor fuck. He's frightened to death. I'm not an animal. Hoggy finishes up injecting Moonif. Moonif starts to blissfully nod out. We follow Faz as he goes to the drivers seat, hits a button underneath and a compartment on the dashboard opens to reveal a Glock 9MM. CUT TO:

Moonif is kneeling in front of a freshly dug hole in the peat. Moonif is doped by now and unaware of what's happening. Faz is stood over Moonif with the snub of the Glock pointed at his head. Faz looks across at the road and then into the distance. He takes a deep breath, cocks the Glock and shoots. Moonif is propelled forward into the grave. Faz and Hoggy quickly pick up shovels and start to fill the grave with peat.

INT. SUV, MOVING – LATER

Traveling away from the moors. Both men are quiet. Hoggy smokes a cigarette. They both suck their McDonald's milk shakes.

FAZ

We can burn our clothes at Tag's and then you can go valet this at Simmo's.

HOGGY

Yeah.

Faz looks out at the imposing moors.

FAZ

You know, these moors are famous. Years ago, some psycho n' his wife buried kids up here.

HOGGY

Yeah?

FAZ

Yeah.

HOGGY

That where you got the idea?

FAZ

What idea?

HOGGY

To bury people up here.

FAZ

Yeah. Saw a documentary on Youtube about it.

HOGGY

(Chuckling)

Here, you seen the Youtube of that mental fat kid trying to fly?

FAZ

Yeah?

Faz gets his phone and starts to browse.

FAZ (CONT'D)

I'll have a look.

HOGGY

F'real. Piss funny, man.

INT. COLIN'S FLAT, BEDROOM – EARLY MORNING

The alarm clock clicks on to 6.45 AM. Colin wakes and smiles.

EXT. STREET NEAR FACTORY – DAY

Colin walks along and turns into the yard of the factory. He sees FELLOW WORKERS milling around outside the main entrance, talking to each other. Colin is puzzled as he heads down to them. Alan sees Colin and approaches him.

ALAN

There was a fire in the warehouse last night.

Colin frowns as he looks at the milling Workers.

ALAN (CONT'D)

We're getting sent home.

COLIN

"Sent home"?

ALAN

Aye. The warehouse is fucked.

Colin looks devastated. Alan notices.

ALAN (CONT'D)

Don't worry … they'll have to pay us while it's closed.

Alan heads back into the crowd. Colin looks around. He starts to circle the crowd looking for something. He sees Delores and approaches her.

DELORES

You should get a phone, Colin. I could have told you not to bother coming in.

COLIN

(Panicked)

How long's it gonna … I mean … when can we go back to work?

DELORES

(Shrugging)

I don't know … it could have been worse. Nobody got hurt.

Delores phone rings. She indicates to Colin she'll only be a minute and takes the call away. Colin stares at the factory in dismay. He turns around and we watch him slowly walk away with his head bowed. Delores finishes her call and looks for Colin. She frowns as she sees him leaving the yard.

INT. COLIN'S FLAT, LIVING ROOM – DAY

Colin is sat in his chair reading, still wearing his work clothes. He fidgets, clearly impatient and disturbed. He keeps glancing at his watch every couple of seconds.

Eventually Colin takes his watch off and puts it in his pocket. He settles down to read again. After a moment or two he pulls out his watch and looks at it. He puts it back in his pocket but repeats the action again.

CUT TO: Colin taking off his work clothes.

CUT TO: Colin pacing back and forth across the living room. He is counting his steps out loud.

CUT TO: Colin putting his work clothes on. He buttons up the polo shirt, smiles to himself and then starts to undress. Once he is down to his boxer shorts he starts to dress in his work clothes again.

INT. PUB – DAY

A handful of customers, quiet. Curtis and Alan are sat at a table drinking pints. Curtis chuckles

CURTIS

This is the life, eh? Getting paid to get pissed.

Alan doesn't look too impressed.

CURTIS (CONT'D)

What's up with ya?

ALAN

Nothing.

Delores enters and sits down with them. She looks worried.

DELORES

The fire investigators are there now.

CURTIS

So? We knew they'd investigate. They always do.

DELORES

This lad you got to do it?

CURTIS

What about him?

DELORES

If they trace him. Do you trust –

CURTIS

– They won't! I keep telling ya, he's a pro', n' even if they did he'd never land us in it.

Curtis looks at them both and tuts.

CURTIS (CONT'D)

Stop fucking worrying will ya!

Curtis takes a swig of beer.

CURTIS (CONT'D)

(to Delores)

Anyway, it's your boyfriend they'll be wanting to talk to.

DELORES

(Frowning)

Why would they want to talk to Colin?

Curtis smirks devilishly.

CURTIS

Gary, that lad who left a few weeks back, yeah?

DELORES

What about him?

CURTIS

Gary went to school with him. He told me Colin's got a record for setting fire to stuff.

Alan bows his head as he sees that Delores is getting angry.

DELORES

Are you kidding?

CURTIS

No. Alan knows don't you, Al?

Alan doesn't react as Delores glares at Curtis.

DELORES

So you thought …

CURTIS

(Giggling)

Genius, eh? Colin'll be right in the frame.

Delores grabs Curtis' pint and throws the beer in his face.

DELORES

You wanker!

CURTIS

Fucksake!

Delores stands up and stomps out. Alan quickly follows her.

EXT. PUB – CONTINUOUS

Delores is angrily walking away, Alan is following.

ALAN

Listen, Del'. I don't think Head Office know Colin's got a record for arson. I mean, they wouldn't have given him a job in the first place would they?

Delores stops and lights a cigarette, glaring at Alan. Delores calm down a little and thinks about it.

DELORES

Just the thought of it though … Curtis makes me fucking sick.

ALAN

(Pleading)

It's done now though. We should just keep our heads down. They've got nothing on Colin even if they investigate. He's innocent.

Delores gives Alan a "look", sighs and nods her head slightly.

DELORES

Obviously!

ALAN

Yeah, yeah … let's just keep quiet.

DELORES

(Beat)

OK. But tell Curtis to stay away from me.

Delores walks off.

INT. COLIN'S FLAT, BEDROOM – EARLY MORNING

The alarm clock clicks on to 6.45 AM. Colin wakes up, smiles and climbs out of bed.

EXT. BUS STOP – LATER

Colin climbs on to the bus and it pulls away.

INT. BUS, DOWNSTAIRS – A LITTLE LATER

Colin has his eyes closed and his fingers crossed. He is mouthing what seems to be a prayer.

EXT. FACTORY – DAY

Colin is walking down towards the main entrance. He sees Barry's car pull up and he is instantly delighted. He runs down to Barry's car. Barry is climbing out as Colin runs up to him.

COLIN

Is it all right now?

Barry frowns at Colin.

BARRY

What you doing here?

COLIN

Are we back now?

BARRY

Back? No, no, I'm glad you're here though. I wanted a word. I can't believe you've not got a phone.

Colin is disappointed. Barry pulls out his cigarettes.

COLIN

When can we come back then?

BARRY

Listen, Colin. We're gonna have to let you go.

Colin simply stares at Barry as Barry lights a cigarette.

BARRY (CONT'D)

You're on a temporary contract and obviously we can't afford to keep you on.

COLIN

What do you mean?

BARRY

I mean, you're a temp. Head office won't pay you not to work. They're just not keeping you on.

Colin is getting angry.

COLIN

They can't do that!

BARRY

You're a temp. You've no contract.

Colin shakes his head.

COLIN

No. I've been a good worker. I love working here. They can't –

BARRY

– I'm sorry, Colin. If it was up to me –

COLIN

– Ring 'em and tell 'em I've not had a day off or been late.

BARRY

They know … look, it's out of my hands.

COLIN

But …

Colin is getting a little panicked.

COLIN (CONT'D)

(Pleading)

… When everything's fixed, when everyone's back I can come back too can't I? You'll let me come back then won't you?

Barry is a little unsettled by the plea.

BARRY

To be honest with you we've lost a few orders recently. I reckon it was only a matter of time before they laid you off anyway. Look, I'm really sorry, Colin. The wage department'll send you what you're owed and I'll give you a good reference.

Barry docks his cigarette and puts it back in the pack.

BARRY (CONT'D)

(Re: the factory)

I'd better get in.

Barry offers Colin his hand to shake.

BARRY (CONT'D)

No hard feelings?

Colin ignores the handshake offer. Barry smiles at him.

BARRY (CONT'D)

(Heading inside)

I understand.

Colin stays stood on the spot looking devastated. He can't believe what he's heard. We slowly pull out and stay focused on Colin not moving. After a while he starts to walk out slowly with his head slightly bowed.

INT. FLAT – DAY

Colin is sat in his chair staring into the distance. He reaches into his pocket and pulls out a needle and thread. He takes his coat and jumper off and puts them at his side.

He threads the needle and starts sewing into his chest. He doesn't react to the pain and goes about the operation in a cool manner. We close in on his face: contemplating, his sweater and coat still on. He reaches into his pocket but doesn't find a needle and thread. He stands up and walks out of the flat.

INT. BARRY'S OFFICE IN FACTORY – DAY

Barry is on the phone, looking out on the redundant factory floor.

BARRY

(Into phone)

... I reckon it's going to be at least a week. We can't do anything without the warehouse ... yeah, yeah. We've passed most of the orders on to the Manchester branch ... OK. No problem. Bye, bye.

Barry puts the phone down and nearly jumps out of his skin as he turns around. Colin is stood staring at him.

BARRY (CONT'D)

Fucking hell, Colin!

Colin remains expressionless. Barry is annoyed.

BARRY (CONT'D)

What you doing here again?

COLIN

I need Delores' phone number and address.

BARRY

Eh?

COLIN

Delores. I need her phone number and address.

BARRY

What the –

COLIN

– Gimme it and I'll go.

BARRY

I don't think so, son. I can't give employees personal information out. Head office would have my guts for garters.

COLIN

They won't know.

Barry is clearly unsettled by Colin's gaze.

BARRY

(Not looking Colin in the face)

No, sorry. It's against company policy. Can you just go please.

Colin pauses and then turns and leaves. Barry sighs in relief and goes and locks the office door.

INT. COLIN'S FLAT, BEDROOM – NIGHT

Colin is laid in bed in his pajamas, tossing and turning. He stares at his alarm clock. It reads 2.23 AM. Colin turns over and closes his eyes.

SMASH CUT TO: POV ZOOMING DOWN THE BEACH AT DUNGENESS …

The strange and haunting landscape speeds by. We zoom down towards the sea. As we reach the sea edge we stop on THE HOODED, HESSIAN CLAD FIGURE facing the camera, index finger touching lips in the "shush" gesture.

CUT TO: CU on Colin in his bed. His eyes shooting open. He sighs and turns over.

EXT. FACTORY YARD – DAY

Colin, wearing his uniform, is stood staring at the factory. Only Barry's car and a Police Squad car are parked up. A UNIFORMED POLICEMAN comes out of the main entrance to Colin.

POLICEMAN

Colin Turner?

Colin ignores him, continues staring at the factory.

POLICEMAN (CONT'D)

We've had a complaint that you're loitering.

The policeman stands in front of Colin.

POLICEMAN (CONT'D)

Did you hear me?

Colin again ignores him.

POLICEMAN (CONT'D)

Listen. I've spoken to your Boss and he understands that you're upset, but …

Colin simply walks away, heading out. The policeman frowns.

POLICEMAN (CONT'D)
(Shouting)
Do yourself a favour and just stay away all right!
INT. JOBCENTRE PLUS – DAY
Colin is looking at vacancies on the public computer terminals. He prints out a dozen or so Vacancy Slips.
CUT TO:
Colin is sat at a desk opposite a WORK ADVISOR. She's Asian, in her early 20s. She is looking through the vacancy slips he has handed her.
WORK ADVISOR
You know these are all zero hours contract vacancies?
COLIN
What do you mean?
WORK ADVISOR
Zero hours. Huh, you only work when the employer calls you in.
She realizes Colin doesn't understand.
WORK ADVISOR (CONT'D)
It means some days you might work seven or eight hours and some days you might work just a couple.
COLIN
(Shaking his head)
No. I need something with a routine. I need a schedule.
WORK ADVISOR
You might not have a choice. If you refuse a job on offer you'll be sanctioned ...
Colin doesn't respond.
WORK ADVISOR (CONT'D)
... Your benefits could be stopped.
COLIN
I don't wanna claim benefits. I just want a job where I can go every-day at the same time.
She shrugs.
WORK ADVISOR
You'll just have to keep looking for something that suits you then.

INT. FAZ'S CAR, PARKED UP OUTSIDE COMP SCHOOL – DAY

Faz in drivers seat and Hoggy in the passenger seat. We can see Schoolchildren – 13 to 18 year olds – leaving for the day. Faz and Hoggy are watching them.

FAZ

I want you to go round the customers at the Manchester Road flats tonight.

HOGGY

Yeah?

FAZ

Yeah. Ya tell 'em we're only serving up near the shops from now on.

HOGGY

Why?

FAZ

Cos there's too many Feds sniffing 'round.

Faz looks out and sees Tina – wearing her school uniform, smoking a cigarette – as she approaches the car. He starts the engine. Tina is about to get in the rear.

FAZ (CONT'D)

(Re: her cigarette)

Put that out!

She flicks the cigarette away and climbs in the rear.

TINA

Can we go for a KFC first?

FAZ

You can have one after if yer a good girl.

Faz speeds away.

INT. EMPLOYMENT AGENCY – DAY

Colin is sat at the desk of an AGENT – male, late twenties, shirt and tie. The Agent is looking at the form Colin has filled in.

AGENT

So you're only looking for full time work?

COLIN

I don't mind temp as long as the hours are regular.

AGENT

I see you don't have a driving license?

Colin shakes his head.

AGENT (CONT'D)

We'll struggle getting you anything without a license.

The Agent pulls out a business card from a dispenser on his desk. He holds it out to Colin.

AGENT (CONT'D)

This driving instructor's a friend of ours. He does fast pass discounts for our clients.

Colin takes the card and scowls.

EXT. EMPLOYMENT AGENCY – MOMENTS LATER

Colin comes out and throws the business card in a bin and walks off.

EXT. MANCHESTER ROAD, NR BRADFORD CITY CENTRE – DAY

On Colin looking dejected as he slowly walks home. A YOUNG MAN walking his DOG on a lead is passing in the other direction.

The fierce looking dog lunges and starts to bark ferociously at Colin. Colin doesn't flinch as the owner tries to pull it to heel. It is like Colin hasn't even noticed it.

INT. CHEAP SEEDY HOTEL, MANNINGHAM – DAY

Faz walks in with Tina. The RECEPTIONIST nods knowingly at Faz as he leads Tina up the stairs. CUT TO: Faz and Tina walking along the hallway. Faz stops at a door and knocks. A FAT MIDDLE AGED WHITE MAN opens the door. We see that there are a couple of other Middle Aged men in the room – two Asian, two white – snorting cocaine, all wearing golfing attire, like they have come straight from the course. The Fat Middle Aged Man's eyes light up as Tina steps inside. He hands Faz an envelope and Faz pockets it. The Fat Man nods and closes the door. Faz walks back down the hallway.

INT. BUS SHELTER – DAY

Colin is stood with his face against the glass/Perspex staring across the duel carriageway into the distance. It starts to rain. A YOUNG WOMAN comes in to shelter.

She watches Colin suspiciously as he starts to gently rock back and forth, his forehead touching the glass/Perspex. It rains harder. The Young Woman is spooked and quickly leaves the shelter.

POV: the other side of the glass/Perspex. Heavy rain flows down and Colin's face is distorted to the point where it is only a blur.

INT. COLIN'S FLAT, LIVING ROOM – NIGHT

Colin is pacing around; he keeps checking the time on his watch. Finally he takes it off and puts it in his pocket.

CUT TO:

Colin frantically opening and closing books from his bookcase. We zoom in and see that ALL the books are written in Latin. Colin is panicking. He throws the books across the room and finally slumps down on the floor, putting his head in his hands and sobbing.

INT. FAZ'S CAR, MOVING – NIGHT

Faz is driving, pulling into the council block. Tina is sat in the passenger seat: a bloody nose and cut lip, looking shell-shocked. She is holding a bucket of KFC and eating from it, at the same time sobbing quietly.

Faz glances at her and sighs as he parks up outside the entrance.

FAZ

Clean yerself up before ya go in.

Tina simply stares ahead.

FAZ (CONT'D)

Did ya hear me?

TINA

(Quietly)

I don't wanna go with them again ... they were horrible.

(Turning and looking at Faz)

Why did they beat me up?

FAZ

They probably just got over excited.

Tina opens the door to get out.

FAZ (CONT'D)

(Threatening)

Ya say jack shit about this, right!

Tina ignores him.

FAZ (CONT'D)

Oi!

Tina stops as Faz points over at where the flowers and cards have been laid to commemorate the death of Yooda and her baby.

FAZ (CONT'D)

Ya don't wanna end up like her, d'ya?

Tina bows her head.

FAZ (CONT'D)

Look at me!

Tina looks at Faz. He puts his index finger to his lips indicating "Shush".

EXT. COUNCIL FLAT BLOCK – NIGHT

Delores is walking along checking the door numbers. She stops at Colin's door and starts knocking.

INT. COLIN'S FLAT, BEDROOM – CONTINUOUS

Colin is laid in bed, under the covers, listening to the knocking. He looks terrified.

COLIN

(Muttering)

Go away ... please go away.

We zoom in on Colin's eyes as they close.

SMASH CUT TO:

THE HESSIAN CLAD HOODED FIGURE KNOCKING ON COLIN'S DOOR.

CUT TO:

Colin opening his eyes and gasping.

EXT. COLIN'S DOOR – CONTINUOUS

A disappointed Delores has given up knocking. She walks down the landing and down the stairwell. A still shocked Tina passes on her way up. Neither of them look at each other.

INT. COLIN'S FLAT – NIGHT

Colin taking deep breaths, calming himself down ... he goes and stands over the tapestry.

We see that it is a recreation of child abuse in all its horrific forms. There are crooked crucifixes sewn into large segments of the tapestry. Colin smiles to himself and turns off the light.

FADE TO BLACK.

EXT. COACH PARK – DAY

Colin, rucksack over his shoulder hesitantly boards a coach. We stay focused on the coach and moments later we see Colin alighting. He paces and takes deep breaths before plucking up courage and boarding again.

INT. COACH, MOVING – DAY

Colin sat at the rear by himself staring out at the countryside. He fidgets and checks his watch. He pulls out a book from his rucksack and starts on page one.

EXT. MOTORWAY – NIGHT

We follow the coach traveling down the motorway. It pulls into a service station.

INT. COACH, PARKED UP – NIGHT

The coach is empty; passengers have gone into the services. Colin is still reading but nodding off. He straightens himself up, rubs at his eyes and continues reading.

CUT TO: LATER … THE COACH STILL MOVING. We are close on Colin as he turns the page on his book. It is the last page. Page 694. Colin is clearly very tired. He reads the last line and closes the book. It is dawn now and Colin looks out at the sea. We are in Dungeness. There are only a few passengers left on the coach. Colin grabs his rucksack and makes his way down the coach ready to depart at the stop.

CUT TO: The coach pulling away … Colin is stood by the road staring down at the beach. The unique, ghostly and objectively strange landscape is spread out before him. He steels himself and slowly walks on to the beach. He looks around and takes in the lighthouse, the nuclear power station, the old abandoned fishing boats and equipment and the strange looking chalets as he walks along the shingle beach. Colin steps over old, rusty light railway tracks that lead to nowhere. He stops and takes a deep breath of the sea air. He is the only person on the beach and he heads down to the sea. We are close on Colin's face. His blank expression turns to one of being pained.

SMASH CUT TO:

Young Colin, wearing shorts and a waterproof jacket is happily throwing pebbles into the sea. He is being watched at a distance by Uncle Peter and his Dad. Colin notices a very old, weather beaten piece of wood sticking in the ground. He closes in on it. It reads: Here Be Monsters. He is momentarily fascinated by it. Uncle Peter comes over.

UNCLE PETER

It means sea monsters, Colin. It's an old fisherman's saying.

Young Colin forces a smile at Uncle Peter and continues throwing pebbles. Uncle Peter walks back to Colin's Dad.

UNCLE PETER (CONT'D)

Fancy a bit of fun before mass?

Colin's Dad looks away.

COLIN'S DAD

I don't know.

UNCLE PETER

We've got an hour to kill.

Colin's Dad looks over at Colin.

UNCLE PETER (CONT'D)

(Re: Young Colin)

Look at him, the little tease.

COLIN'S DAD

Don't say things like that!

UNCLE PETER

(Drags on his cigarette and smirks)

I'm only saying what we're both thinking.

Colin's Dad looks at Uncle Peter. They lock eyes.

EXT. SMALL DERELICT SHACK ON BEACH – A LITTLE LATER

Colin's Dad stands at the door as though he is on lookout. We hear muffled sounds coming from inside the shack. Colin's Dad is impatient and nervy.

Uncle Peter comes out of the shack looking a little flustered and mopping at his brow with a handkerchief.

UNCLE PETER

Your turn.

Colin's Dad slips inside the shack as Uncle Peter lights a cigarette and takes his turn at guard duty.

DISSOLVE TO: PRESENT … COLIN STARES AT THE STILL STANDING SHACK.

He swallows a lump in his throat and puts his hand to his mouth. After a while he turns around and stares over at the chalets and Fisherman's Cottages. He is clearly trying to identify one. He heads over to them and we follow him.

CUT TO:

Colin – at a distance, hanging around a brightly painted cottage. He is deliberating whether to approach the cottage. Time lapse: Colin checking his watch. Pacing up and down the beach near the cottage. Sat down staring at the sea. Stood staring at the cottage.

Colin's patience is about to snap when suddenly he notices MARY – 30, small. Mary has Down syndrome. She is wearing a coat and has a small dog on a lead. Mary holds a carrier bag for the dog mess. Colin watches Mary head out of the garden and lead the dog on to the beach. Mary is clearly very happy. Colin steels himself and walks over to her. He hesitates a little, as he gets closer. Mary smiles at Colin. Colin can't pluck up courage to talk to her. He slumps down and sits on the beach watching Mary walk her dog in the distance.

DISSOLVE TO: LATER … Colin is sneaking around the side of the cottage. He notices a small window. He looks around to make sure he's not being watched then peers inside the window. COLIN'S POV: Mary sat with her Elderly Mum and Dad watching TV. They are drinking tea and eating biscuits and look like a happy family. Colin watches them for a while, then turns and slowly walks away.

EXT. BRADFORD INTERCHANGE – DAY

A tired Colin alights a coach with other passengers.

INT. COLIN'S FLAT – DAY

Colin opens the door and enters. He notices a handwritten envelope and picks it up. He is surprised and quickly opens it. He reads it and looks puzzled.

EXT. FLATS – DAY

Tina is walking along. Faz pulls up in his car and she is clearly not pleased to see him. She carries on walking and he slowly drives by her side.

FAZ

The fuck's up with you?

TINA

I'm not doing it anymore Faz.

FAZ

Doing what?

TINA

Shagging those dirty old bastards.

FAZ

(Re: the car)

Get in.

TINA

No.

FAZ

I said get in!

Tina hesitantly gets in the passenger seat. Faz winds up the windows.

TINA

I'm not doing it, Faz. They're disgusting! They were shoving things inside me!

FAZ

You'll do exactly what I tell you to do you little fucking scroat!

Faz reaches across and starts to strangle her with one hand.

FAZ (CONT'D)

(Through clenched teeth, hissing)

What about all those Happy Meals and KFC's and all the weed you've had? Do you think I'm a charity or summat?

Tina struggles and he wraps both hands around her throat. She is choking and crying.

FAZ (CONT'D)

You do what I say or I'll fucking ruin you, you little cunt!

Faz finally lets go and Tina coughs and splutters and cries. Faz takes a deep breath, composes himself, starts the engine and pulls away.

FAZ (CONT'D)

We'll go for a drive so you can calm down.

Tina tries to open the door but Faz has locked it. He reaches across and slaps her.

FAZ (CONT'D)

I said calm down!

INT. COLIN'S FLAT, LIVING ROOM – DAY

Colin is sat in his chair staring into the distance with the open letter in his hand. He stands up, puts it in his pocket and leaves the flat. We follow him down the stairwell and outside. Colin stands staring at the flowers and cards that have been left to commemorate the death of Yooda and her baby. He is emotionless. We follow Colin as he heads back. Tina – wearing her school uniform – is about to climb the stairwell at the same time as Colin. They catch eyes momentarily and Tina gives him sympathetic look. Colin notices her bruises and cut lip. He bows his head and waits for her to climb before he starts up the stairwell.

INT. COLIN'S FLAT, KITCHEN – LATER

Colin burns the letter over the sink. He rubs the ashes in his hands and stares at them.

INT. RETIREMENT HOME – DAY

We are slowly moving towards Uncle Peter, sat in his wheelchair reading a newspaper. Uncle Peter senses something and turns his head to see Colin hovering over him. Colin has his rucksack on.

UNCLE PETER

(Pleasantly surprised)

Colin! You got my letter then?

Colin can't make eye contact with him. Colin nods his head.

UNCLE PETER (CONT'D)

How've you been?

COLIN

All right.

UNCLE PETER

Sit down, sit down.

Colin sits and looks around the room.

UNCLE PETER (CONT'D)

You're looking well.

(Beat)

Where you working now?
COLIN
Harrington Print.
UNCLE PETER
Print, eh? What is it you do?
COLIN
All sorts.
Uncle Peter smiles at Colin, hoping he'll elaborate. He doesn't.
UNCLE PETER
Have you come straight from work?
COLIN
No.
Uncle Peter sniffs up.
UNCLE PETER
I thought I could smell oil on you or something.
Colin shrugs. Uncle Peter leans forward a little.
UNCLE PETER (CONT'D)
(Quietly)
You've not been getting into trouble have you?
Colin frowns.
UNCLE PETER (CONT'D)
No, no, of course not.
(Beat)
You're still seeing Dr. Greenberg then?
Colin nods his head.
UNCLE PETER (CONT'D)
Good, good.
Colin becomes a little impatient.
COLIN
(Blurting)
D'ya wanna go for a walk?
UNCLE PETER
A walk?
COLIN
Outside ... I can push you.

491

Uncle Peter thinks about it and smiles.

UNCLE PETER

Huh, yes, I'd like that. Bit of fresh air, do me the world of good.

Colin stands up.

UNCLE PETER (CONT'D)

Just ask one of the girls to get my coat.

Colin goes over to one of The Staff.

EXT. RETIREMENT HOME – A LITTLE LATER

Colin is pushing Uncle Peter up the car park towards a path. Uncle Peter is clearly happy. He takes deep breaths of the cool air. Colin is staring intently at the back of his head.

UNCLE PETER

You forget how nice it is after being cooped up in there.

(Beat)

We should do this more often, Colin.

Colin keeps pushing …

UNCLE PETER (CONT'D)

You and me. We're all we've got. We should stay close. I don't want you getting into trouble again, Colin. I think the world of you, you know that don't you?

(Beat)

Even though you're surrounded by people it doesn't mean you don't get lonely you know?

COLIN

(Quietly)

I've been to Dungeness.

UNCLE PETER

What's that?

They have reached the top of the car park and we can now only see Uncle Peter in the frame.

COLIN (O.C.)

(Louder)

I said I've been to Dungeness.

UNCLE PETER

(Pausing)

Where?

COLIN (O.C.)
Dungeness. You and Dad took me there.
Uncle Peter thinks about it ...
UNCLE PETER
I can't ... where did you say it was?
COLIN (O.C.)
Dungeness.
UNCLE PETER
On the south coast? I don't remember going –
We close in on Colin.
COLIN
– It's all right ... I know you're not allowed to talk about it.
UNCLE PETER
(Sighing, sympathetic)
Oh Colin, we've been through all this. I can't listen to –
COLIN
– I was married to Mary in their cottage. She was backward, remember? You called her a mongrel.
UNCLE PETER
Colin, please!
COLIN
Mary and me were both twelve. They said it was a wedding to offend Christ ... her Dad stuck the cross in her and he said he was taking her virginity.
UNCLE PETER
What's wrong with you? Why are you saying these things again? What's happened to you?
COLIN
I understand.
Colin makes the "shush" gesture at Uncle Peter.
UNCLE PETER
Take me back inside, Colin. Please. I'm begging you.
COLIN
I went to burn them down, but I couldn't do it. There'd be no one to look after Mary.

UNCLE PETER

Let's go inside and I'll call Dr. Greenberg.

(Pleading)

She can help you, Colin. Please, listen to me. I care about you.

Uncle Peter is watching Colin doing something. Colin is out of the frame. We hear a zipper opening. Uncle Peter is in a state of confusion and fear as he watches Colin. From behind we see Colin pull up his jumper and expose his chest to Uncle Peter. Uncle Peter grimaces as he looks at something on Colin's chest.

UNCLE PETER (CONT'D)

(His eyes widening)

What's that? What are you doing?

We see clear liquid pouring over Uncle Peter's head and body.

UNCLE PETER (CONT'D)

(Spluttering, terrified)

No! What are you doing? Stop it! No! Colin!

We pull back to see Colin emptying a plastic petrol can over him. Uncle Peter is screaming at him to stop. We pull back further and see Colin toss a lighter onto Uncle Peter's lap. Woosh! Uncle Peter is engulfed in fire. Colin pushes the wheelchair and it rolls down the car park. Uncle Peter is screaming in agony as he is consumed by the flames.

POV from window on top floor of retirement home. Uncle Peter rolling by engulfed in flames. Colin puts the empty petrol can in his rucksack, puts it over his shoulder and quickly walks on to the path and away from the retirement home.

INT. BUS, MOVING – DAY

Colin is sat at the rear of the lower deck, his rucksack at his side. He uncharacteristically breaks into a smile, but it doesn't last long. He quickly falls back in a somber mood.

EXT. FAZ'S FAMILY HOME – DAY

Faz is handcuffed and being led out of the house by TWO UNIFORMED POLICE OFFICERS. D.S. Breslin and D.I. Malik are in attendance, hanging back. Faz looks at them and cockily smiles and shakes his head as he is put into a squad car.

D.S. Breslin's cell phone bleeps and she answers it.

D.S. BRESLIN

(Into phone)

Hi Katy.

D.S. Breslin listens in a state of mounting surprise.

D.S. BRESLIN (CONT'D)

(Into phone)

Jesus Christ!

(Listens)

OK, OK, we're on our way back now.

D.S. Breslin switches her phone off. D.I. Malik is waiting for an explanation.

D.S. BRESLIN (CONT'D)

Colin Turner's set fire to his Uncle.

D.I. MALIK

What?

D.S. BRESLIN

Come on.

D.S. Breslin rushes towards their car.

D.I. MALIK

What do you mean "set fire —"

D.S. BRESLIN

Burned him alive. He's dead.

EXT. HEATON AREA OF BRADFORD – DAY

Colin alights the bus and heads over to a petrol station. This is a very old and "well to do" neighborhood, large detached houses, well manicured lawns.

EXT. STREET – A LITTLE LATER

Colin walks along purposefully. He stops outside the gates of a large detached house. He sees a woman tending to pot plants near the door. The door is open. She is SARAH – mid 60's, conservatively dressed, cheery disposition.

Colin checks that the coast is clear and quietly opens the gate. He walks up the path and reaches Sarah. She turns around and is startled by him. Sarah gasps.

Colin quickly puts his hand over her mouth and drags her inside.

INT. LARGE HOUSE – CONTINUOUS

Colin kicks the door closed. Sarah struggles but it's futile. He's far too strong for her. He drags her into a living room by her hair.

INT. POLICE HOLDING CELL – DAY

Faz is sat on the mattress. The cell door opens and his solicitor – USHNA, a smart 40-year-old Asian woman, with briefcase and laptop – enters. Faz stands up. They wait until the cell door is closed.

FAZ

This is bullshit, Ushna. Do you seriously think I'd push a woman and her baby off a balcony? They haven't got anything on me.

Ushna sighs.

USHNA

I'm afraid they have.

Faz is surprised.

USHNA (CONT'D)

Your DNA under her fingernails.

Faz pauses and stares at Ushna.

USHNA (CONT'D)

Do you want to explain?

INT. OFFICE IN POLICE STATION – CONTINUOUS

D.S. Breslin is talking to D.C.I. WALSH, mid 50's, female, wearing uniform.

D.S. BRESLIN

We're going to interview him shortly, mam.

D.C.I. WALSH

What else have we got besides the DNA and hearsay on a drugs transaction?

D.S. BRESLIN

I think there might be a witness …

(Takes a breath)

… but it's the man who just set fire to his uncle up at Grange Park.

D.C.I. Walsh is shocked.

D.C.I. WALSH

What?

D.S. BRESLIN

I don't think it's connected.

D.C.I. WALSH

But you "think" he was witness to this murder?

D.S. BRESLIN

Yes, mam. If you remember Holmewood I –

D.C.I. WALSH

– OK, I remember. Just do what you've got to do Breslin ... I don't know what CPS'll make of it all though.

INT. LARGE HOUSE, LIVING ROOM – DAY

Sarah's hands and feet are bound by black electrical tape and she is sat on a chair in the centre of the very large room. She is pleading with Colin.

SARAH

Please let me go.

Colin is walking around looking at the walls, trying to get his bearings.

SARAH (CONT'D)

You can't do this to me!

Colin puts his finger to his mouth and turns to Sarah: shush.

SARAH (CONT'D)

Do you really want to spend the rest of your life in prison?

(Beat)

You're ill. You need help. This isn't going to solve anything.

Colin sticks tape across her mouth. She murmurs as he continues to get his bearings. He goes to a wall and studies it.

He starts to pick at the wallpaper but only manages to scrape off slithers. He stops and thinks about it.

INT. LARGE DIY OUTLET – DAY

Colin is walking down an aisle trying to find something.

INT. LARGE HOUSE, LIVING ROOM – A LITTLE LATER

Sarah is still bound and gagged in the chair. She is now crying. Colin is plugging a wallpaper stripper in the socket. He waits for it to warm up and goes and rips the tape from Sarah's mouth.

SARAH

(Gasping)

Please stop this.

(Beat)

Nothing ever happened here!

(Spluttering)

Just take anything you want. I won't call the police.

Colin stares at her. Sarah starts to scream.

COLIN

Scream all you want. Nobody ever heard the screams in here.

She continues screaming as Colin picks up the wallpaper stripper and starts to peel layers off the wall.

We close in on Colin's face as he thinks back.

INT. LIVING ROOM – DAY

The very same living room, only decorated differently. Young Colin is sat on the floor with half a dozen other children, ages three to fourteen.

They are all wearing plain white robes and are sat cross legged facing a wooden lectern fashioned into the deformed cross.

Behind them stand a dozen adults all wearing white robes, all ages. We make out Uncle Peter, Colin's Dad and Sarah. This is a mass. Everyone is solemn and quiet.

We see The Hessian Clad Hooded Figure take to the pulpit. Behind him is a plain wall with a large hand painted representation of the deformed cross, done in blood and feces.

Next to the lectern is a long slab of marble on legs, big enough to hold an adult or child lying down. The Hooded Figure makes the "shush" gesture to the congregation.

ANGLE ON rear of the mass. From behind we see the adults all disrobe together.

INT. LIVING ROOM – CONTINUOUS

Colin stripping the wallpaper, tears in his eyes. Sarah has given up screaming and is now whimpering.

INT. BRADFORD MET STATION, DUTY DESK – DAY

D.S. Breslin and D.I. Malik are watching Faz leave with his solicitor. They are both pissed off. The DESK SARGEANT leans over.

DESK SARGEANT

What happened?

D.S. BRESLIN

He admitted he went to the flat looking for her husband. Says she started attacking him.

D.I. MALIK

(Sighing)

Hence the DNA under her fingernails.

D.S. BRESLIN

CPS doesn't wanna know. They're still not convinced it's a murder. The Desk Sergeant answers the phone. D.S. Breslin looks at D.I. Malik. He shrugs.

D.S. BRESLIN (CONT'D)

(Sighing)

Who's gone after Colin Turner?

D.I. MALIK

Thompson I think.

D.S. BRESLIN

Let's go see him.

D.I. MALIK

(Heading off)

I'll go find out where he is.

D.S. Breslin heads out of the station.

D.S. BRESLIN

I'll be in the car.

INT. LARGE HOUSE, LIVING ROOM – DAY

CU on Colin. He drops the wallpaper stripper and steps back from the wall. He is staring at something. We can't see it but it is clearly entrancing Colin. After a while he looks over his shoulder at Sarah. She is staring at him in terror. Colin glares at her.

CUT TO:

Colin Pouring petrol from his can over Sarah's feet. He has put the tape back over her mouth. Sarah starts to wriggle. Colin grabs her hair and keeps her still as he sets fire to her feet. Sarah faints. Colin shakes her and she opens her eyes. Her feet are burnt and blistering. Colin throws a damp towel on them to extinguish the flames. He then starts to pour petrol on her legs and groin.

EXT. LARGE HOUSE – DAY

The door opens and Colin comes out, his backpack over his shoulder. He looks pleased with himself. He quickly walks down the path and out on to the street.

INT. MOVING BUS, TOP DECK – A LITTLE LATER

Colin is sat at the front happily looking at the views. He sees a YOUNG WOMAN pushing her BABY in a pram and his mood becomes sullen.

EXT. NURSING HOME – DAY

A few of the WORKERS are gathered at the door crying and comforting each other. A POLICE TENT has been erected at the scene of the crime in the carpark. A few UNIFORMED OFFICERS are mingling with CSI.

D.S. THOMPSON – a well-built middle-aged man – is talking to D.S. Breslin and D.I. Malik.

D.S. THOMPSON

They're having to scrape what's left of the body out of the wheelchair.

D.S. BRESLIN

Who saw it?

D.S. THOMPSON

Who didn't!

D.I. MALIK

Nightmare.

D.S. BRESLIN

Anything on whereabouts?

D.S. THOMPSON

Nothing. I'll need everything you've got on him.

D.S. BRESLIN

Sure.

D.S. THOMPSON

Oh, and guess what?

D.S. Breslin looks at D.S. Thompson.

D.S. THOMPSON (CONT'D)

He worked at a printers 'til recently. It's closed down because of a "suspicious" fire.

D.I. BRESLIN
Really?
D.S. THOMPSON
What's the connection with him and the Syrian woman?
D.S. BRESLIN
He was probably the last person to see her and the baby alive.
D.S. THOMPSON
Mmm … Pushing people off buildings doesn't seem to be his style.
D.S. BRESLIN
No.
EXT. BLOCK OF FLATS – NIGHT
Colin is suspiciously looking around as he approaches the block.
He sees a couple of Police squad cars driving around. As one
approaches he slips into a doorway until it passes.
He starts out again towards the flats. Tina is walking by. She sees
him and approaches.
TINA
The cops are after you. They smashed your door in.
Colin carries on walking.
TINA (CONT'D)
What have you done?
He ignores her.
TINA (CONT'D)
(Shouting)
I bet you're a fucking paedo!
Tina carries on. As Colin gets closer to the block he sees another
Police squad car parked up near the entrance. He turns on his heels
and heads in the other direction. He walks faster and catches up to
Tina. Tina sees him closing in, his hand inside his jacket about to
pull something out. Tina panics a little.
TINA (CONT'D)
I was only joking about being a paedo.
COLIN
Is it Faz that beats you up?
TINA
(Defensive)

Who said I get beat up?
COLIN
Look at your face.
TINA
I fell that's all.
COLIN
They don't stop you know.
TINA
Who don't stop?
COLIN
Monsters. They don't stop until they're too old and ill or they get caught.
TINA
I don't know what you're talking about.
Colin pulls out a large wedge of cash, a few thousand pounds, his life savings. He offers it to Tina.
COLIN
Here. Take it.
Tina stares at the wedge of cash.
TINA
Eh?
COLIN
I said take it.
TINA
Why?
COLIN
Just ...
TINA
Have you robbed it?
COLIN
No.
TINA
Do you want me to look after it or summat?
COLIN
No. It's yours.

Colin stuffs it into her hands. Tina's jaw drops and Colin walks off. Tina can't believe her luck; she quickly puts it inside her coat and runs down to the block of flats.

INT. D.S. BRESLIN'S CAR, MOVING – NIGHT

D.S. Breslin is driving. Her cell phone bleeps and she answers it.

D.S. BRESLIN

(Into phone)

Hello?

She listens in mounting surprise.

D.S. BRESLIN (CONT'D)

(Into phone)

What's the address?

She makes a U turn in the road.

D.S. BRESLIN (CONT'D)

(Into phone)

I'm on my way.

She turns her phone off and shakes her head in disbelief at what she's heard.

INT. MUNICIPAL PARK – NIGHT

Colin is sat on a bench staring at the ground, rocking back and forth a little. He's clearly disturbed.

INT. LARGE HOUSE, HEATON – NIGHT

POV from inside the hallway, D.S. Breslin enters through the open door and grimaces. She gags on the smell and puts her hand over her nose and mouth. We hear O.S. talk. D.S. Breslin enters the living room. D.S. Thompson is stood talking with a couple of Uniformed Officers and TWO PARAMEDICS. They are all wearing masks over their mouths and noses. D.S. Breslin walks over to where a CSI officer in overalls – also wearing a mask – is stood over the burned dead body of Sarah still sat in the chair taking photographs.

D.S. Thompson sees D.S. Breslin and goes to her.

D.S. THOMPSON

Burnt her in stages ... tortured her for at least a couple of hours.

D.S. BRESLIN

God!

D.S. THOMPSON

It's got to be Turner.

D.S. Thompson sighs as he looks at the body.

D.S. THOMPSON (CONT'D)

What kind of fucking monster does this to someone!

D.S. Breslin looks away and catches sight of the back wall. She is a little stunned. D.S. Thompson notices her staring.

D.S. THOMPSON (CONT'D)

(Re: the painting of the deformed cross)

Weird eh?

D.S. Breslin goes to get a closer look. D.S. Thompson follows her.

D.S. THOMPSON (CONT'D)

What do you think that's about?

D.S. Breslin simply stares at the image.

D.S. THOMPSON (CONT'D)

I thought it was some kind of calling card but one of the CSI said it's been there for years.

D.S. Thompson frowns at D.S. Breslin as she backs away looking puzzled.

D.S. THOMPSON (CONT'D)

Are you all right?

She remains silent.

D.S. THOMPSON (CONT'D)

What is it?

D.S. BRESLIN

(Beat)

I don't know, but he wanted whoever found her to see it.

D.S. THOMPSON

Why?

She looks back over at the corpse and something catches her eye. She goes to a long sideboard where there are framed photographs on top. She is drawn to one in particular.

It is a photograph of Sarah and Dr. Greenberg with a group of other people posing on the beach at Dungeness, looking like they have been winter beachcombing. We zoom into the photograph until it fills the frame.

EXT. PETROL STATION – NIGHT
Colin is filling up his can at a pump.
CUT TO:
Colin heading out of the garage with the full can. We follow him walking purposefully towards the council flats.
EXT. COUNCIL BLOCK – MOMENTS LATER
Colin walks over to where the cards, flowers and cuddly toys have been laid to commemorate the death of Yooda and her baby. He steps in to the middle of the display. He pulls off his jumper and we see that he has sewn the crooked cross into his chest. It is scabbing over and bleeding in certain areas. There are a couple of RESIDENTS leaning on the balcony high up, smoking and chatting. Colin takes a deep breath and pours the can of petrol over himself. He quickly sits down, pulls out a lighter and clicks it on.
He drops the lighter and whoosh! Flames wrap around his body. He remains still and doesn't make a sound as he is ignited. We zoom in on Colin's eyes through the flames. He closes them tight.
INT. COLIN'S BEDROOM – NIGHT
Colin is asleep. There is knocking at the door. Colin wakes with a start. He is fearful and looks to be disorientated.
EXT. COLIN'S FLAT – CONTINUOUS
Yooda is knocking on the door, her baby in her arms. Yooda is calmer now and the baby has stopped crying.
INT. COLIN'S BEDROOM – CONTINUOUS
CU on Colin. He closes his eyes and puts his hands over his ears.
EXT. COLIN'S FLAT – CONTINUOUS
Yooda knocks again and shouts through the door.
YOODA
(Broken English)
I am sorry asking for phone. Could you take me to where phone box is?
Yooda knocks again.
YOODA (CONT'D)
Nobody will help me. You are neighbor please.
The door suddenly opens ...
Colin's POV: in his mind it is not Yooda stood there but The Hooded

Figure. Colin lunges and pushes what he believes to the figure over the balcony.

COLIN

Leave me alone!

Colin shoots back inside and closes the door.

CUT TO: Colin slumping over from his sitting position as the flames eat him up.

FADE TO BLACK.

FADE UP ON D.S. Breslin sat at her desk, working on her computer. The phone rings and she answers it. She listens and frowns.

CUT TO: D.S. Breslin walking down the corridor towards the duty desk. The Desk Sergeant looks up at D.S. Breslin and nods over at Tina sat on a bench. D.S. Breslin goes over to her and smiles.

D.S. BRESLIN

Hello, I'm –

TINA

(Blurting)

– I saw Faz Bhutta push that woman and her baby off the balcony at the flats up Manchester Road.

SMASH CUT TO:

CREDITS OVER A SLOW REVEAL OF THE TAPESTRY. IT REVEALS THE HORRORS COLIN WENT THROUGH AT THE HANDS OF THE MONSTERS AND THE CROOKED CROSSES LITTER THE TAPESTRY.

Justine Sir Justice Beiber Sir shook his head and tutted to high heaven as he let the screenplay fall from his eyes, "What the Hell is this? I demanded a novel!"

& genuflected in the abstract, "I … I took legal advice, Sir."

"Legal advice? Who from?"

"Huh … The Unreliable Narrator."

Beiber Sir boiled up and boomed bombastic, "You have overstepped your remit!"

With a wave of his wandering star Sir Justice Beiber banished & to

506

the margins of a half hearted manuscript concerning the adventures of a tattooed, pipe smoking French bulldog and its attempts at trying to alleviate The Fear Of A Jazz Planet. Dai Jung butted in and spluttered, "Mae hynny'n gadael y gweddill ohonoch chi, neu ni, yn dibynnu ar union beth a faint yr ydym yn mynd i fod yn gallu cytuno arno. Yn awr, heb fynd yn rhy snobbish am y peth (snobyddiaeth fod yn cystudd yn anffodus endemig i nifer fawr o gefnogwyr jazz), yr wyf yn meddwl y gallwn ni gymryd yn ganiataol bod mewn da cyffredinol neu jazz mawr yw cerddoriaeth o safon uwch na fargen dda, os nad y rhan fwyaf, o'r stwff mwy o pop-oriented yn dod allan. Duke Ellington yn well na Paul Whiteman. Thelonious Monk yn well na Roger Williams, cymharu John Coltrane i Boots Randolph byddai yn gwneud jôc wael, ac yn y blaen i lawr y lein. Mae'r gerddoriaeth a gynhyrchir y ffigurau hyn, yr wyf yn cyflwyno ymhellach, yn well nid oherwydd ei fod yn unrhyw fwy technegol cymhleth, neu oherwydd bod Ellington a Monk ac Trane y golwythion fwyaf o unrhyw un sydd erioed wedi byw (hyd yn oed os gallai fod ganddynt), ond oherwydd rhai prin ffynnon teimlo y tu mewn iddynt a achosodd iddynt greu celf sydd yn symud mynyddoedd, newidiodd hanes, wedi dioddef a bydd yn parhau i."

The Petaflop Police instantly caught Dai Jung. They had him by the goolies for bad translation. Within two shakes of a Counting Sleep Sheep's tail he was tried and convicted and sentenced to a full stop without hope of erasure. & found himself in a flooded room the size of a cosmic cow's imagination. Pitch black and mercury flavored & didn't feel too uncomfortable. Nor comfortable. He mused on Sir Justice Beiber Sir's reaction to his screenplay. It smelt like a millennium since he had delivered. Since he had been delivered, since deliverance, since the sterilized stink of parturition and parting. In reality though – or rather the timeline of the reader – it had been somewhere in the region of 175 days assuming that they had been reading 4 pages per day and/or had not suddenly become blessed with dyslexia and relieved of their duty to go through the tortuous process.

An echo of Justice Beiber Sir, "You have abandonment issues &! Snuff! The Life Of O'Reilly, Trade, Getting The Fear! Your inconsistency is demeritorious, and that's the truth, Ruth!"

Getting the Fear
Chapter Thirteen

Jack Sherry was sat in the room above the police station. His bag was packed and on the bed at the side of him, ready to hit the road. He was staring out of the window at the palm tree. He was happy to be going home. He wanted off Ibiza, it was too hot and his mind was playing tricks on him. He wanted the familiar, musty, cool surroundings of his office back home. He wanted to be solving murders in his dull, gray office.

Captain Torres knocked and entered the room, "Mr. Jack, there is a telephone call for you from your office in London."

Jack turned to his side and stared into the distance and addressed someone, "What do you want me to do now? How do I handle this?"

Captain Torres was confused, "Are you OK, Mr. Jack? Who are you talking to?"

Jack stood up and smiled at him, "I'm all right, Captain Ernesto."

Jack followed him into the other room to take the telephone call. CI Barry Ketley was on the long distance line, "Sherry. The passport people messed up ... three of the bodies *are* English. They've been notified but we're waiting to speak to the French and Germans again to try and find out what links them all."

"So now you want me to stay here then?"

CI Ketley snapped, "What kind of question's that, Sherry? Of course we want you to stay there! You've got three dead English nationals on your hands."

"Yes, sir. Of course."

"Do you need any help? I could spare another detective."

Jack looked over at Captain Torres and smiled at him, "No, sir. I've got Captain Torres. We'll be fine."

"Right, I call you when I've spoken to the French and Germans. They're sending their officers out there as we speak. Stay near the phone, Sherry."

"Yes, sir, will do."

Jack put the telephone down, "You know that they've identified the bodies don't you, Captain Ernesto?"

"Yes, Mr. Jack."

"Brigadier Guzman informed you?"

"Si, si."

"My boss has told me to stay by the phone."

"Yes, yes, that is OK, Mr. Jack. I have work to do," he grabbed his cap and made for the door, smiling, "I am very happy that you have decided to stay, Mr. Jack."

Captain Torres left and Jack sat down at the desk. He glanced at his watch, lit a cigarette, sat back in the chair and waited. It would be interesting to hear what the French and Germans came back with. The key now would be to start connecting the dead to each other. The real detection work could begin and this is what Jack Sherry thrived on.

Something caught Jack's eye. A file marked 'classified' stuck out slightly from a row of files on a shelf. He stared at it for a while and wondered ... he went to the door, locked it and went and picked out the classified file. He paused, as he was about to open it: *do I really want to do this?*

Jack sat down at the desk and pulled out dozens of single sheets of typed memos. He frowned and started scanning them. He pulled one out and read:

DRAFT 17
9 June 1953 MEMORANDUM FOR THE RECORD
SUBJECT: Project MKULTRA, Subproject 8

1. *Subproject 8 is being set up as a means to continue the present work in the general field of L.S.D. at [deleted] until 11 September 1954.*
2. *This project will include a continuation of a study of the bio-chemical, neurophysiologic, sociological, and clinical psychiatric aspects of L.S.D., and also a study of L.S.D. antagonists and drugs related to L.S.D., such as L.A.E. A detailed proposal is attached. The principle investigators will continue to be [deleted] all or [deleted].*
3. *The estimated budget of the project at [deleted] is $39,500.00. The [deleted] will serve as a cutout and cover the project for this project and will furnish the above funds to the [deleted] as a philanthropic grant for medical research. A service charge of $790.00 (2% of the estimated) is to be paid to the [deleted] for this service.*
4. *Thus the total charges for this project will not exceed $40,290.00 for a period ending September 11, 1954.*
5. *[Deleted] (Director of the hospital) are cleared through TOP SECRET and are aware of the true purpose of the project.*

Chemical Division/TSS
APPROVED:
Chief, Chemical Division/TSS

Jack had no reason to believe that these weren't genuine classified documents. The deletions added credence to their veracity. Jack was intrigued and confused. What was official American classified documents doing in the office of Captain Ernesto Torres of the Ibizan police department?

He flipped over another sheet and read:

DRAFT 28
5 May 1955
A portion of the Research and Development Program of TSS/Chemical Division is devoted to the discovery of the following materials and methods:

1. *Substances which will promote illogical thinking and impulsiveness to the point where the recipient would be discredited in public.*
2. *Substances which increase the efficiency of mentation and perception.*
3. *Materials which will prevent or counteract the intoxicating effect of alcohol.*
4. *Materials which will promote the intoxicating effect of alcohol.*
5. *Materials which will produce the signs and symptoms of recognized diseases in a reversible way so that they may be used for malingering, etc.*
6. *Materials which will render the indication of hypnosis easier or otherwise enhance its usefulness.*
7. *Substances which will enhance the ability of individuals to withstand privation, torture and coercion during interrogation and so-called "brainwashing".*
8. *Materials and physical methods which will produce amnesia for events preceding and during their use.*

Jack had seen enough and knew that he shouldn't have seen *any* of it. He put the sheets back in the file and put the file back on the shelf, careful to place it exactly where he had plucked it from. He unlocked the door and went to the window.

He could see the palm tree from there, obviously from a different angle, but it was still there and it comforted him. He lit a cigarette and tried to reason why Captain Torres had classified American files in his office. Everything starts with a question: *maybe because Ibiza attracts a lot of LSD users? Maybe some of these CIA experiments had been carried out on Ibiza? Maybe Captain Torres was a foreign agent of the CIA? Ibiza was still under the rule, be it remote, of General Franco's anti-communist, rightwing authoritarian rule that clearly had covert backing from the Americans, why wouldn't the two countries be involved in joint operations and experiments together? It made sense.*

Jack wasn't there to investigate Captain Torres though. He was there because three British nationals had been murdered in a massacre.

Chief Inspector Ketley telephoned again, "Here's what I want you to do, Sherry. Keep making enquiries around the vicinity of the crime until the French and Germans get there. Let's show 'em how good our Yard officers are, eh?"
"Have the families been informed, sir?"
"Of course they have, Sherry. We're keeping the details from the press again. We don't want them printing all the gory details. No point causing unnecessary panic about all this Satanist codswallop, eh?"
"Right, sir, like we … well, like we did with the Vanessa Kitson case."
"Exactly, Sherry."
"I think that's a good idea, sir."
"It is, Sherry, it is. Call me as soon as you've got anything else, all right?"
"Yes, sir."

Jack put the telephone down and smiled as he thought about his boss. Chief Inspector Barry Ketley would always have his back; always keep an eye out for him. It was a great feeling knowing that a man like Barry Ketley was looking out for him.

CI Ketley was the only top rank copper who had stood by Jack Sherry after the Jonathon Rothman fuck up. Ketley covered Jack Sherry and took the heat and vouched that it was him who had agreed to let Jack Sherry go undercover. It wasn't of course. Jack

Sherry went undercover on his own steam, he went renegade in his pursuit of Rothman because Jack Sherry was obsessed with bringing the bastard down, obsessed with pinning three murders on him and his hench man, Bernard 'Bigfoot' Sharrock. It was personal for Jack Sherry. Jack Sherry hated Jonathon Rothman because of what he had done to his Aunt Sheila, never mind all the other innocent peoples lives he had ruined with his fucking greed.

The notorious Jonathon Rothman was born Jarek Rutowski in Poland 1920, the son of a Jewish teacher. After the Nazis invaded in 1939, Rothman joined the Polish resistance but was quickly captured and interned. He managed to escape and joined the 2nd Polish Corps, fighting with the allies in Italy. He was demobbed in 1948 and took up residence in England.

His quick wit, business acumen and ruthlessness saw him build up a property empire in West London, specializing in multi-occupation properties that targeted the recently arrived, impoverished West Indian and Jamaican immigrants. These slum properties were concentrated in the Notting Hill – or *Rotten Hill*, *Notting Hell* as some called it – area and centered around the Powis Square, Powis Gardens and Powis Terrace areas.

To make the most out of rental income from his properties, Rothman drove out the mostly white, indigenous residents because they were protected against extortionate rent increases by law. Rothman and his brutal heavy, Bernard Bigfoot Sharrock, a six foot six, twenty stone Jamaican immigrant, drove out the residents with threats of violence, arson attacks and general harassment, leaving the properties vacant so that Rothman could sub-divide and cram in as many coons and their kin as possible. Coons and niggers weren't entitled to rent protection at the time, so Rothman was really on to a winner. Jonathon Rothman liked to tout himself as a friend of the immigrants. He was nothing of the sort though. He was a cold and calculating slum landlord who would stoop to any measures in maximizing his profits.

Three white tenants – who were resisting Rothman's scare tactics and refusing to move out of his properties – had died of suspicious circumstances and the Murder Squad at The Yard were convinced that Rothman and Sharrock were behind the deaths. They didn't have a scrap of incriminating evidence though, just motive, means and opportunity. That would simply not wash with the Crown Prosecution Service though, in fact Rothman's high profile lawyer, Geraint Baxendale, was so feared by the law enforcers that Rothman was never even pulled in for questioning.

Jack Sherry's elderly Aunt had been a tenant of one of Rothman's properties and he had driven her out. Sherry, like most of the coppers in London, had been waiting to see Rothman and Bigfoot collared for ages. The word on the rotten grapevine was that Rothman had a few bent coppers on the payroll, besides his fancy Queens Counsel. This just fired Jack Sherry on even more. He desperately wanted the bastard banged up for life.

Jack persuaded CI Barry Ketley to let him investigate Rothman and Bigfoot with regard to the deaths. Ketley didn't realize that Jack Sherry would put himself in extreme danger while carrying out his investigation.

Alongside his property portfolio, Rothman had a prostitution racket on the go. Bigfoot ran a gang of black pimps who consequently ran dozens of young women operating out of West London. Rothman and Bigfoot were careful not to step on the toes of the Soho Mobsters and never provided girls off the patch of their turf. It was rumored that Rothman owned the mews house in Marylebone that Christine Keeler and Mandy Rice Davis used as the base for their prostitution racket. Prostitution that would result in the near collapse of the Tory Government in 1963.

Jack Sherry, in full on renegade mode, leaned heavily on a black pimp by the name of Beresford 'Berry' Dacres. Berry worked under Bigfoot but he was also doing street level cannabis deals in Ladbroke Grove for extra pocket money and, more importantly, not tipping any of it up to the feared Bigfoot. Sherry pulled Berry up and laid it on the line that he would make sure Bigfoot heard about his extra curricular activity if Berry didn't get him invited to one of the legendary parties that Rothman threw.

The parties were a regular event on the West London underworld social calendar. A mixture of hookers, Jamaican wide boys, white villains, glamour models, bent coppers and slumming it socialites.

Jack Sherry's plan was simple. Get invited, get introduced to Rothman under the premise that he was a good copper wanting to turn bad and then infiltrate the organization. If any of the bent coppers already in Rothman's pay questioned Jack's sincerity in wanting to go bent he would simply say that he was doing it for the same reason they were doing it. Money.

Jack Sherry finally got his wish and was invited to a big bash in Westbourne Grove. Jack mingled amongst the – what he considered – scum and introduced himself to Jonathon Rothman.

Jack could almost smell the redolence of corruption on Rothman – that he was obviously trying to mask with handfuls of expensive cologne – as he introduced himself, "Jack Sherry, Mr. Rothman. Scotland Yard."

Rothman also worked hard at trying to disguise his Polish accent as well as he stench, "Pleased to meet you Mr. Sherry. Murder squad isn't it?"

"You've been doing your homework, Mr. Rothman."

"Call me Jonathon", he grinned, "I hope you haven't come to my party on official business, Mr. Rothman?"

"I suppose I have, in a way, yes."

Rothman's eyebrows arched, "Oh?"

The words *reckless, entrapment, dangerous* and *fucking foolish* sprung up in Jack's mind before he took his next step, but he took it anyway. He was Jack Sherry. He closed in on Rothman, well, as much as he could bear, "Let's put it this way, Jonathon. I've been on the branches a long time now … and … Well, let's just say I'm ripe for turning."

Rothman smiled at him and nodded his head, "Right, Jack, I understand … why don't we have a chat sometime?"

Jack agreed and Rothman gave him his card. As soon as Jack slipped it in his wallet he was getting the jitters. *This* was too easy. Rothman wasn't a fool. *What the fuck was I thinking, Jack?*

He really, really hadn't thought this through. CI Ketley would go fucking ballistic if he knew that *this* was his master plan.

Jack felt ashamed of himself in one respect and proud in another. Ashamed as he realized that this wasn't how bent coppers inveigled themselves with the likes of Jonathon Rothman, and proud that he didn't have a clue how it was really done.

Reality kicked in for Jack Sherry. *What the fuck am I doing?* He knew then and there that he wouldn't make a telephone call to Jonathon Rothman. The card would end up in the waste bin at The Yard. His undercover days on renegade operations were over before they had even started. If he was going to pin murders on Rothman it was going to have to be done the old fashioned way: honest slog, no cutting corners, paperwork, interviews, putting feelers out.

Jack felt guilty, he shouldn't be there, CI Barry Ketley had always treated him like a much-loved young brother, Jack knew he thought a lot of him. This was just fucking embarrassing.

He was offered another drink. He would kill it and slip out of the nest of vipers and head straight home with a resolution to catch Rothman the old school way.

That one for the road drink was a biggest mistake of his life, because the road that drink would take Jack Sherry to would lead to Hell.

Charlie Coleman sat in The Coach & Horses on Greek Street, Soho, knocking back treble Scotch's on the rocks. Peter Cook and Peter O Toole were sat at the bar engaged in banter with the landlord Norman. The last thing Charlie wanted to do was engage in banter with them. He had just listened to a horror story and no amount of ribald stories from famous actors or comedians were going to lift his mood.

Peter Cook shouted over to him, "Come and join us, Charles."

Charlie raised his glass to the trio, "I'm all right, Peter, thanks. Maybe in a bit, eh?"

Charlie was glad to be out of The Raymond Revue bar. It had shaken him up. Patsy Fagan couldn't have picked a more fitting place to tell

Charlie the horror story than here with it's red curtains and red lights and dirty crushed red velvet upholstery.

Charlie liked to think of himself of a man who wasn't easily shocked. Some of the capers he had be involved with over the years were bordering on tasteless and yes, he dare say that many people would find them shocking, but ... well, what Patsy Fagan had told him took some topping.

His first reaction – when the words started to make sense in his mind – was to smash his glass, ram it into Patsy Fagan's face, pick up one of the heavy stools and smash Patsy Fagan's head to a pulp so that his brains were weaved into the dirty carpet.

Charlie knew only as much as the next man about the murder of the little six-year-old Vanessa Kitson. It turned his stomach, as it had turned any decent man or woman or stomach when they heard about it.

What he had heard from the quivering mouth of Patsy Fagan was that the murder of poor little Vanessa Kitson involved many people Charlie knew from the West End Scene.

Charlie went for a piss after his third treble. He stared at himself in the mirror and shook his head. This was the very first time in his life he had ever felt the slightest tinge of guilt or remorse for the profession of violence that he so excelled in. Without this gift for violence he had, he would have never met the likes of Patsy Fagan and the set of fuck-ups on the scene and he wouldn't have had to hear the horror story he had heard.

He felt dirty by association. As he washed his hands he thought about joining Cook and O Toole and Balon at the bar and trying to forget what Patsy Fagan had told him. He didn't though, he walked straight out of the pub, took a left and then a right and walked down Shaftsbury Avenue, the words still ringing in his ears, *"Name your price, Charlie, just name your price ... anything!"*

Charlie started to think what exactly his price was. Patsy Fagan and the others clearly thought that he had a price. They had him down as nothing more than a cold, heartless bastard who would get on side with them as long as there was a big payday. They clearly thought he had no morals or even the slightest sense of decency.

He stopped in a doorway and smoked and watched the ant like pedestrians scurry up and down Shaftsbury Avenue. He shook his head for the umpteenth time since hearing what Patsy Fagan had to say, as though he was acting out the internal argument going on in his head. The Devil and Angel on his shoulders wouldn't stop. It was like one of those BBC radio programs where people argued and argued.

"Right, Charlie, this is it ... you've been offered enough money to live off for the rest of your life, son. Just think about that for a minute ... you'll never have to do anymore naughty ten bob jump ups or capers ever again, son. Isn't that what you've always wanted?"

"Don't listen to him, Charlie, don't you dare listen to him! This is the murder of a six-year-old little girl. If you do this you're damned. You're a dead man walking, Charlie. You do this and you're no better than the ponces in Wormwood Scrubs. You're no better than those fucking monsters Brady and Hyndley, Charlie."

"Charlie, Charlie ... think about this. You had nothing to do with it. All they want you to do is clear up the fucking mess they made. You didn't kill this little girl, son. You never so much as laid a finger on her ... she's dead now, Charlie, it's a fact, a horrible fact but that's life, Charlie. Life's fucking cruel, son. She was in the wrong place at the wrong time and these fucking wankers did what they did ... listen, if you don't do this it's not gonna bring her back, son ... she's gone now, nothing anyone can do about it. Why shouldn't you profit? Why shouldn't you be able to get out the game n' live happily ever after with Candice, Charlie?"

"I can't believe you're even thinking about this seriously, Charlie! This isn't you!"

"Ignore him, Charlie. Do the right thing."

It was doing Charlie's head in, he need to drown these nagging little bastards on his shoulders. He headed up to The French. It was packed with the usual mix of bohemians and drunks and fading aristocrats and in the corner reading *The Racing Post* sat Mikey Tucker. Tucker was a part time chauffeur, full time gambler and sometimes fence for stolen property. Charlie liked Tucker, they were the same age and Tucker came from a working class background only his had been in the east of London rather than the south.

Tucker, as he always automatically did upon seeing any of his friends, gave Charlie a horse racing tip, "The three o clock at York tomorrow: Sinbad's Return. You'll get ten to one on it, Charlie."

Charlie bought them both a treble Scotch, "You couldn't tip night following day, Mickey."

"Bollocks. My tips are fucking legendary!"

"Yeah, for being shit, Mickey."

They started knocking back the drinks in rounds. Charlie was still fretting over Patsy Fagan's proposal. He toyed with his drink, shaking the ice around in the bottom of the glass, "Do you reckon everyone's got a price, Mickey?"

"Eh? How'd ya mean?"

"You know, you think everyone's got a number they'll do *anything* for?" Mickey closed in, winked and whispered, "You been offered a bid wedge to knock someone off, eh?"

Charlie bridled and then instantly remembered that everyone knew how he earned his living, "No, just one o' those hypocritical questions. I mean, if someone offered you a blank cheque to do something ... well, something terrible ... would you do it?"

Mickey shrugged, "Depends how terrible this thing is ... there's boundaries ain't there?"

Charlie thought about it, "Are there really though, Mickey? Are there really any boundaries where money's concerned

Doctor A layback in her leather Lazee-Boy. It had been a long drawn out day with a quill with no well though tomorrow would be a fresh, virginal weekend and a time for recreation. Not that she believed in re creation, or creation for that matter. Tomorrow she would blow-out and if one were to recount her recreation it would read: slip on her rabbit costume, travel to the Greyhound stadium and be chased around the track by three-legged hounds until she was utterly shagged and non-spiritually spent.

Doctor A had invested heavily in the mutilation of Greyhounds for her pleasure. The six dogs had all been champion athletes and it cost Doctor A dearly to buy them and then individually have one of their legs amputated. Their speed had been quartered from 43 mph to precisely 10.75 mph ensuring that they would never get to catch Doctor A with her speed of a little over 11 mph. Doctor A relished the thrill of the chase and the mockery she made of the maimed mutts.

One of the mutts, Dogtanion, had her measure and often barked; "There are many bible versions around today, so before testing the bible against scientific scrutiny, I think it reasonable to find out which one to use. If God and the word are one, I don't think He would appreciate being changed, do you? A conspiracy is an illegal action committed by more than one person, nothing more. Woof! The overriding conspiracy I have found is an attempt to discredit the accuracy of God's word in the bible, to discredit the divinity of His son, and to misrepresent the second coming of the Lord. First, the accepted Greek biblical texts and the KJV bible say in 1 John 5:7 that ... there are three that bear record in heaven, the Father, the Word, and the Holy Ghost: these three are one. Since the word and God are one, denying the word is denying God. It would therefore make sense to investigate whether God is who He says He is. Rebellion against God and the word has occurred in a variety of ways. Here are some of the more common. Woof! Secret societies (double minded men are unstable and Jesus said nothing in secret); Tower of Babel (direct defiance like the mouse mooning the eagle); Hiding the word using uncommon languages such as Latin (only the elite were taught Latin); Writing of heretical texts (Nag Hamadi Scrolls, Dead Sea Scrolls, Talmud, Haggadah, Zohar, Quran, Vedas, Book of Mormon etc); Hindering biblical translation into common languages (Dark Age Inquisitions and Reformation persecution); changing the word with new bible versions (1881 Bible revision committee began this and it continues today); Scientific replacement of the creation event with The Big Bang (gravity, relativity, string theory), Woof!"

The other hounds thought of Dogtanion as a troublemaking bible basher and had long since sent him to Coventry. They weren't too worried about his outbursts though as they felt sure Doctor A was incapable of understanding canine. They were wrong. Before she had created &, Doctor A had practiced on a Beagle called Henry and had learnt the language. Most dogs had unhealthy obsessions with food, exercise and security, but here was a religious nut. It would have to go.

& loitered within pulse distance of the dog stadium in Catford for paragraph-linking purposes. He could hear Doctor A's sweat gland excretions. As he sniffed from memory he found himself on a Greyhound bus traveling through the Badlands of the US. The bus was dead save for boxes of freshly Xeroxed copies of Omnibuses. &'s view was restricted. He would have loved to have savored the flatness but it wasn't to be. One of the boxes felt depressed and & tried to cheer it up with a rendition of The Theme From The Flintstones replete with loud exclamations of "Yabbadabbadoo" and "Wiiilllmmmaaa!" The connection was lost on the moribund box though.

Beiber Sir Justice Sir popped up pouting piss and vinegar invectives accusing & of all kinds of betrayal. Not only had & chosen a Greyhound over a regulatory Omnibus but he had still not given a suitable reason for handing in a screenplay rather than the requested novel.

Doctor A fell awake from her dream of impossible recreations and shuddered. She located a tear in her eye and brushed it away with a sob. *What had come over her?* Pull yourself together Doctor A, she whispered to herself, sentiment is strictly for the suckers, but she couldn't shrug the blues. The blues over &.

She stood up and sat herself right back down again and wrote a strongly worded thesis on her feelings for &. In it she nearly apologized for her crimes but fell short of such humbleness. As she shat out the words it became clear that she harbored something close to sympathy for &, close but not quite, and that somewhere deep down where a soul should reside she had a terrible craving to eat coal. Surely ... No! Horror of horrors! She couldn't be pregnant could she? ... well? ... Could she?

If she were it would be an immaculate conception and immaculate conceptions are impossible. After scoffing a bursting full bag of petrol station purchased barbeque coal washed down with a cheeky Chardonnay she weighed herself. She was the exact same weight she had been for the last five years. Just as she was contemplating making a call, one came through.

It was Petra Plimsole on the line. Petra was the crossword dressing transsexual visiting professor of obstetrics at CERN, "Hi Doctor A. I just heard the news. Is it congratulations or a visit to a backstreet abortionist brandishing a rusty old wire coat hanger?"
Doctor A was shocked, "But ... how did you know? I mean ..."
"It's my job to know these things, sweetie. Hop on the next A Train to CERN and I'll have a good look inside you."

Getting the Fear
Chapter Fourteen

Captain Torres was driving Jack Sherry to the *Piug des Molins* Necropolis to meet a woman who claimed she had met a couple of the murder victims. The underground necropolis covers 50,000 square feet and holds over 3000 tombs and was built as a sacred resting place by the Occidental Phoenicians at the end of the 7th century BC. Jack Sherry knew all this because Captain Torres had given him many unsolicited history lessons on his beloved island over the last couple of days.

The roads were definitely more bearable now, in fact, Jack was quite enjoying the trip. The beauty of the Ibizan countryside sparkled under the waves of sunshine that constantly crashed down on the island. Jack smiled at the raw, natural beauty. Captain Torres caught him smiling and it became infectious. Both cops were silently drinking in the visual splendor and you would have never thought that they had been thrown together by such a an hideous crime.

Jack felt good. *Really* good. He hadn't felt this good in what seemed like an eternity. He remembered a quote from an ancient philosopher that someone had whispered in his ear once, *"It is my belief that history is a wheel. Inconstancy is my very essence, says the wheel. Rise up on my spokes if you like but don't complain when you're cast back down into the depths. Good times pass away, but then so do the bad. Mutability is our tragedy, but it's also our hope. The worst of times, like the best, are always passing away."*

Jack tried to remember who had whispered it. He realized it must have been Dr. Myron Geller. Dr Geller had told Jack many things that made sense during their sessions. He had also told Jack many confusing things as well, things that he couldn't believe would make him well again, things that just were just perverse and only caused Jack to question himself and his own actions even more.

Dr. Geller was good for Jack but Jack didn't trust him implicitly. Jack Sherry trusted no one – other than his boss CI Ketley – absolutely since that night at Jonathon Rothman's party. How could he? The 'Mickey Finn' he was slipped at the party, not longer after making a ridiculous pitch to Rothman, was undoubtedly LSD, or 'Acid' as the 'groovy people' were calling it. There were many versions of what happened next but there were also actual facts. Facts verified by the two beat Coppers who found Jack Sherry in Powis Square.

Facts: Jack Sherry was found naked. *Totally* naked. He was bleeding from his nose, mouth and right ear. He had bruises on his arms, abdomen and rib cage. He was in a state of extreme anxiety that rapidly alternated between euphoria and fear. He was talking gibberish, breaking down into cries of anguish one minute and the next staring at his surroundings like he had never witnessed them before and proclaiming that everything was so wonderful and alive, which considering that he was in the decidedly run down Powis Square was very suspect. On further inspection it was found that he had the word *Fucking* carved into his left buttock and the word *Pig* carved into his right buttock. Out of the gibberish he spouted the phrases like "I've been attacked by a Jaguar", "The Devil's won my soul in a game of cards." and "All Coppers Are Bastards."

It took the two beat Coppers and their Desk Sergeant hours to get any sense out of him and it was over twenty-four hours later before they had a real ID on Jack Sherry. It was Chief Inspector Barry Ketley who went down to the Bayswater nick to sort it all out. Ketley took Sherry home and stayed with him until Sherry was himself again.

Although Ketley was pissed off beyond belief with Jack Sherry and his undercover fuck-up he stood by his man and got the collar in Powis Square consigned to the dustbin of history. Ketley pulled ranked on that occassion but he most certainly wasn't going to make a habit of it.

525

Jack told Ketley that he would forever be in debt to him and couldn't thank him enough for all the help, understanding and support. Ketley replied that he just wanted to see Jack get back to work and start putting murderers behind bars again.

Jack tried to forget about the past as he enjoyed the beautiful day on Ibiza. They reached the Necropolis and Captain Torres led the way to the woman who they were going to interview.

Helena Chappel Granger was filming a restoration of part of the Necropolis. When she clicked off her Super 8 camera and turned to Jack he froze. His heart skipped and a sheet of cold sweat instantly coated his body.

Captain Torres made the introductions, "Miss Helena Chappel Granger. Detective Inspector Jack Sherry of The Scotland Yard."

She smiled and offered her hand. Jack stared at her and shuddered, "Have we … I'm sure we've met before?"

Helena shook her head negative, "Mmm … I don't recall, Detective Sherry."

Jack *did* recall though. He knew exactly where they had met. They had met in his hallucination. The hallucination that spooked him so much. The hallucination where he was in a cell cage and Captain Torres had somehow managed to forget that he spoke excellent English.

Helena and Captain Torres frowned at Jack; Captain Torres put his hand in the middle of Jack's back, "Are you OK, Mr. Jack?"

What could he say without her thinking he was a complete lunatic? How could he tell her that he she had been a part of his hallucination before he had ever even clapped eyes on her?

Jack wished he could speak to Dr. Geller right now. Dr. Geller would be able to explain. As it was though, Dr. Geller was hundreds of mile away and Jack was staring at a woman who was definitely flesh and blood and waiting for him to act civil. Waiting for him to act like the stoic Detective Inspector from The Yard that she had agreed to talk to.

Jack wiped his brow and mustered up a flash of a halfhearted smile, "This heat really gets to me, Miss."

"Helena. Yes, I've been out here for years now and it can still knock me sideways on some days."

Captain Torres asked how the restoration and the filming of it was going. She answered in Spanish and Jack immediately got a twinge of panic. He stared at the sun-bleached dust at his feet and silently told himself to snap out of it.

He looked up and watched Captain Torres and Helena Chappel Granger chatting away about the place. Captain Torres sensed that Jack was being excluded and flipped back to English.

"I am sorry, Mr. Jack. I sometimes forget myself with the language." Helena joined in, "Oh, I'm so sorry, I didn't realize you don't speak Spanish, Detective."

Jack smiled, "That's all right … Helena."

Captain Torres clapped his hands together, "Would you like to tell Mr. Jack what you told me on the telephone, Miss?"

"Oh, yes, yes of course … well, it may not be anything," she looked Jack in the eyes and put her hand across her brow to shade the sun, "but I found it quite odd, Detective …"

Jack's mind instantly snapped back to the night of Jonathon Rothman's party. The night that he was slipped a Mickey. The night that everything changed. The night that would lead to him finding poor little Vanessa Kitson's body, whose heart had been cut out from her tiny body.

Jack Sherry's mind split in two: half his mind concentrating on what Helena Chappel Granger was telling him and the other half reliving what happened between being slipped the LSD at Rothman's party and eventually being talked back into reality by Chief Inspector Barry Ketley.

He concentrated on key phrases that came out of her mouth, "They wanted to know if they could hold a ceremony in the Necropolis … They talked about Black Masses … They wanted to know if the area was policed at night … they asked if any local residents wandered down here at night … they asked if I knew where they could get hold of some animals …"

Jack was sat in the passenger seat of a Jaguar as it sped around central London at terrifying speeds. Jack was remonstrating for the Driver to slow down, but the Driver ignored him and just kept telling him how much he hated fucking coppers. Jack kept double-checking on the Driver and telling him that he recognized him and that when this was all over he would have him banged up for life. The Driver just laughed and told him he had no evidence, no evidence whatsoever and that he should shut his cakehole and just enjoy the ride whilst it lasted and then ...

And then Jack would be in a room, a bare room with only a single light bulb swinging from the ceiling and he would be crouched over and holding his hands against his ears, rocking back and forth, dreading something that he knew was about to happen ... and then it would happen. It would be the noise of a car horn honking in the street down below, and Jack would go to the window and he knew what he could expect ... he could expect a warped and twisted face poking out of the driver's side of a gleaming, raring to go Jaguar, a face pulsating and spinning around its neck at dizzying speed, sub-human speed, supersonic speed ...

And Jack would heed the call and leave the room in and climb into the passenger seat and another sickening ride would begin ... a ride that would make his stomach turn and make him sweat like the pig he was and make him dig his fingers into the dashboard and scream at the Driver to slow down ... and on it would go, on a loop, every scene the same and repeated over and over until ... until finally he heard a familiar voice ... the voice of his boss, the voice of his friend and someone who really cared about him.

Now though it was Captain Torres' voice that brought Jack back to the present, "This ties in with what we have already been told, yes, Mr. Jack?"

Jack gulped and turned to Captain Torres, his eyes watering and his brain hissing as it cooled down like a frying pan would on a hot stove that had been turned off, "Oh yes, Captain Ernesto. Yes ... definitely."

They drove back to the station and Captain Torres could see that Jack was in a totally different frame of mind from when they drove out there, "What did you think of Miss Helena, Mr. Jack?"

"What do you mean?"

"She is very ... very easy on the eye ... attractive, yes?"

"I didn't notice."

"No."

"No, Captain Ernesto ... I had other things on my mind."

Doctor A felt a tremor in her abdomen, a twinge of immigration in her intestines, something was moving, a movement. The coal was working its magic, its fossilized atavistic digestive supplementary laxative legerdemain. Her sphincter was so tight & precise that she shat Pink Panthers that cut the porcelain to pieces and freed the contents of the designer water closet.

Now with nowhere left to shit out the precious gems she sucked them back into her bowels where they politely regressed back into mineral stools. She wiped bullets of sweat from her brow with muslin gauze that caught her likeness to a T. She hung the shroud above a Dead Sea sculpture of alien terrain, *here's one she made earlier.*

Sinus and synapse conspired as she glugged on rotten old information from Swift's Tale Of The Tub: Another: "The tax upon paper does not lessen the number of scribblers who daily pester," &c.

Another: "When every little would-be wit takes pen in hand, 'tis in vain to enter the lists," &c.

Another: "To observe what trash the press swarms with," &c.

Another: "Sir, it is merely in obedience to your commands that I venture into the public, for who upon a less consideration would be of a party with such a rabble of scribblers," &c.

She sensed cold comfort cuckolds cackle weak apologies to their disgraced ancestors. Lineages of mediocrity standing on the shoulders of baby ants, their eyes on the prize of acceptance. A rumbly in her tumbly and she craved Irish Stew & dumplings like Mammy used to make. Splash on that H.P. Lovesauce, spice it up!

And now spotting in her panties, not menstruate though. No, ink.

Maybe a miscarriage of the typewriter? Bluer than black. Miss Happ? Lawdy Miss Clawdy I do declare Thomas! A geriatric Tom & Jerry jumping on to the ice cream bandwagon long after it had got the hell out of Dodge. Miscreant miscegenation for the generation who bought the most shoes and crippled the moral footing. The Lullaby of Birdland squatted in her echo chamber and it was most agreeable but it couldn't banish the fear. *This is what happens when you grow to love your parasite.* Hunger so intense she echoed.

Drugs and bourbon couldn't entice sleep, even Yusef Lateef on superloud and truckloads of uncounted sheep shitting all over her parquet flooring. She stuck her head in the refrigerator and rubbed a cold can of Coca – Cola against her neck ... she heard herself being pilloried for agreeing to star in such a shit B Movie.

Getting the Fear
Chapter Fifteen

Vanessa Kitson was the only child of Maureen and Eric Kitson. Twenty nine year old Maureen and thirty year old Eric lived and worked in the Kings Cross area of London, both of them employed at the train station. Maureen as a cleaner and Eric as a ticket salesman. The Kitsons were law abiding and polite. Knew their places in society and kept themselves to themselves. They were happy to lead a very humble life. They were proud that they were buying rather than renting their modest terrace house and they spent virtually all of their free time homemaking.

Six-year-old Vanessa couldn't have asked for better parents. They showered her with love and affection and made sure she wanted for nothing.

Maureen had being trying to conceive again. She was unsuccessful and both parents really wanted a brother or sister for Vanessa. They figured that with a sibling she might start to come out of her shell. Vanessa was a sweet little girl but she was terribly shy and lived in her own world and never really liked to step out of it.

Maureen and Eric worried about Vanessa's shyness, her primary school teacher had also voiced her concerns, informing them that Vanessa was a lovely pupil but that she needed to start interacting with the other pupils. She had been in primary school a full term and had yet to start talking to the other children, to the point where they were beginning to notice and starting to single her out for her behavior. Vanessa was unfortunately starting to be bullied for her shyness.

Vanessa's teacher had been trying her hardest to get Vanessa to make friends but it simply wasn't working. Vanessa had an imaginary friend called Dorothy and was happy to spend most of her time communicating with only her.

Her mum and dad encouraged Vanessa to play out with the other children on their street but Vanessa resisted, choosing to spend all her time in her tiny bedroom playing with the imaginary Dorothy.

The family GP quelled their concerns when he told them that Vanessa would eventually grow out of her insular behavior and that they had nothing to worry about. She was just shy and had a fertile imagination. Maureen started to try and find out from Vanessa what was so interesting in her imaginary friend Dorothy. Dorothy was obviously the character played by Judy Garland in the film of *Wizard Of Oz,* that they had taken her see at the cinema when she was five years old. Vanessa told her mum that Dorothy didn't like to play outside in case The Wicked Witch came and took her away, so Vanessa would stay indoors with her.

Eric agreed with the GP and was confident that Vanessa would start to socialize in time. Maureen was beginning to wish they had never taken Vanessa to the cinema to see the film.

Everywhere she went Vanessa had a small teddy bear with her and a woven basket. She called the teddy bear Toto and couldn't bear to be without it. Vanessa pined for Toto during school hours and she couldn't wait to get home everyday to be with Toto and Dorothy in her bedroom.

Vanessa started to have nightmares about the Wicked Witch and her evil monkeys coming and taking her from her bed and locking her up in the castle. Vanessa's screams were blood curdling during the nightmares and the shocked Maureen and Eric would run in to her room to find her sobbing, wild eyed, trembling and hugging Toto as she sat in her wet bed.

Maureen and Eric spent hours trying to explain to Vanessa that *The Wizard Of Oz* was just a story and that Dorothy and Toto weren't real. Vanessa chose not to believe them. Vanessa knew it was real because she was living it in her mind.

Mum and dad persevered and eventually they convinced Vanessa to start playing out with the other kids in the street. Slowly she started to think less and less about the Wicked Witch and began to tentatively start joining in with the kids.

On the day that it happened, Vanessa was playing *hide and seek* just a few doors down from her home. She was leaning against a lamppost counting to ten with her eyes firmly closed when she was dragged in the car like a rag doll and thrown onto the backseat as it sped off.

Vanessa didn't scream or cry or wet herself. She knew all along that this day was coming. She knew Mum and dad had lied to her. She knew all of this because there *really were* wicked witches and flying monkeys and they were real and they had stolen from her home and she could never go back there again because she was only wearing scuffed Plimsoles because Mum had never bought her the ruby slippers she had promised her she would. Little Vanessa Kitson would never be able to click her heels together and simply say "There's no place like home" to escape the horrors that were about to visit her.

Candice knew that something had happened to Charlie Coleman the day he had nipped out and came back to her room at The Institute steaming drunk. He slept off the booze but he still wasn't himself. Candice nagged him to go see Dr. Geller, "You promised you would speak to him, Charlie. You're putting it off aren't you?"

Charlie was starting to think that speaking to a boffin like Dr. Geller not be a bad idea after all now. Charlie was in a moral pickle after his sit down with Patsy Fagan, maybe this headshrinker might give him some answers. Not that Charlie was going to give anything away of what Patsy Fagan had told him. No, that was going to remain firmly under Charlie's hat until he had decided what to do.

Candice was made up when Charlie went off to meet Dr. Geller; "This means a lot to me, Charlie. I think Myron will really help you." Charlie gave her a kiss and a hug, "I'm a very open minded man, Candice. Maybe he will."

Charlie was still half cut from the marathon drinking session the day before and he was happy to find Dr. Geller sat in his study smoking and imbibing spiced rum that a friend had brought him back from the Caribbean. Charlie asked if he had any Coca Cola to mix with the rum. Dr. Geller got his assistant to nip out and buy some from the shop over the road from The Institute.

Charlie noticed that everyone around Dr. Geller treated him like the big boss, the head honcho, and their deference bordering on fawning. Charlie treated nobody with undue deference.

"So, Charlie. You and Candice are cohabitating I see?"

"You mean shacking up? Yeah, I'm staying in her room until we get a little house."

Dr. Geller smiled, "Candice is a fascinating young woman."

"Yeah, she's ... well, she's one in a million."

"And you're speaking from experience, Charlie, yes?"

Charlie didn't know how to take it, "What do you mean by that, Doc'?"

"Oh you know, a handsome, smart young man like yourself. I'm sure you have met many beautiful and fascinating women."

"I've done all right, Doc', yeah. Had my fair share, but like you say, Candice is ... well ... well she's special ain't she."

Dr. Geller glanced away momentarily, "Oh yes, yes she's special, Charlie."

He would have loved to have told Charlie how 'special' Candice really was, but that would have to wait until another time.

"She thinks the suns shines out of ... I mean, she's got a lot of respect for you, Doc'. Truth be told that's why I'm here. She told me what you do, you know, all the research n' that."

"Yes, we strive towards making the world a better place," he shrugged, "we try our best on very limited resources."

"What? You get money from The Government, eh? The National Health, eh?"

"Oh, no, no, we are entirely funded by donations from benefactors who share our principles and aims."

"Rich people, eh? Met quite a few o' them in my time, Doc'"

"Oh you have, really?"

"Yeah, Soho's teeming with 'em nowadays. They like to slum it a bit, the posh knobs."

Dr. Geller was intrigued, "Oh yes? What do you mean?"

Charlie thought about it and took a good hit on the rum and Coca Cola, "Well, like, they love coming down there and drinking and partying n' what have ya. I got a theory about it ... it's the danger. They like rubbing shoulders with the likes o' me n' some o' the chaps I know because they've got safe lives. Everything's pretty much taken care of for 'em from the cradle to the grave so to speak, isn't it, Doc'?"

Dr. Geller's eyes were lighting up, "Go on, Charlie."

"Well, it makes sense. The one thing missing out o' their lives is danger ... danger n' uncertainty. If you think about it, it goes back to the caveman days doesn't it? You've got your cavemen ... well, the first thing they need is food, then they need a place to kip, a cave, shelter, right? Then they want heat, fire n' that, n' then they want a bird, a partner, yeah?"

Dr. Geller nodded enthusiastically, "Yes, I understand."

"So you think about it ... you've got everything you need ... only now you're bored off 'cos everything's taken care of, right? You get lazy n' bored 'cos there's no adventure anymore. You've got this little caveman society n' the animals are just wandering in there for you to slaughter, n' you've got a missus and a gaff n' what have you ... you see where I'm going here, Doc'?"

He smiled and shuffled in his seat, "Yes, please continue, Charlie."

"So that's the same thing, right? These toffs have had everything laid on for them since birth. They've got the food n' the house and they're never gonna have to worry about earning a few bob to survive ... so they grow up and they're getting bored. They get so bored they start looking for a bit o' danger and wanting to take risks. They wanna knock around with people who are a bit ... well, a bit dangerous."

"And you've 'rubbed shoulders' with these kind of people, Charlie?"

Charlie sniggered, "Oh yes, Doc', oh yes ... they love the thrills they do, love hanging around with the rough diamonds they do." Charlie put his hand up in surrender, "And listen, Doc', I'm not knocking 'em. I've had some good times with these toffs ... they know how to have a good time. They've got nothing else to worry about see ...

some of 'em are genuinely nice people as well … some o' the birds are … well, that's another story."

Dr. Geller watched Charlie pour himself another large rum and Coca Cola, "How did you fall in with these 'toffs', Charlie?"

"Just by hanging around the pubs n' clubs. I'm not gonna lie to you, Doc', I promised Candice I'd be honest … I'm not proud of it but I've been a bit of a … a bit of a gun for hire so to speak, if you get my drift?"

"You've been violent for pay? That is what was Candice told me. I hope you don't mind but-"

"No, no, yeah, it's all right. I've done things to people for money. See, I wasn't one o' those cavemen that had it all laid on for 'em, Doc'. I had a home n' a good mum n' dad but I've always had a bit of a taste for the finer things in life. I didn't just want to 'make do' and just 'get by'. I'm what you call a bit aspirational. Always had expensive tastes."

Dr. Geller smiled and nodded, "Yes, I understand. And this aspiration? It has been with you from an early age?"

Charlie thought about it, "Well, yeah, I suppose so. I knew I didn't wanna work in the factories and live on the same streets for the rest of my life."

"You wanted a better life, Charlie, that is understandable."

"Yeah, definitely, Doc'"

"So violence figured prominently in your childhood, yes?"

Charlie huffed, "You're kidding, Doc'. No, no, there was no violence in our house. Mum n' dad weren't violent. They were the opposite. They were really sweet n' nice n' they hated trouble. They … well, they disowned me when they realized I was a bit of an handful."

"They disowned you, Charlie?"

"Yeah, didn't want anything to do with me. You can't blame 'em. They didn't know what to make of me, Doc'. I was … I was like a bit of a throwback. None o' the family are in the least bit violent."

"Mmm, very interesting."

Charlie put his hand up and grinned, "And before you go any further, Doc', I've had the old rigmarole off the doctors. I had it in Borstal n' I had it in The Scrubs."

"Excuse me?"

"You know, the questions about why I was … why I'm a bit naughty …. the psychiatrists and doctors. Well, no disrespect but they wanted to try find out what made me tick. What made me do the things I did. They all ended up coming to the same conclusion, Doc'."

"And what was that, Charlie?"

"That I was just what I am n' that I was into making money. I could be violent with people n' not be having guilty feelings afterwards. I had bottle n' I was willing to use it to make some cash. It's simple. No great mystery."

Dr. Geller poured them more rum, "This is very, what is the word … *moreish?*"

"It goes down a treat, Doc'."

Dr. Geller and Charlie were impressed with each other. Charlie was impressed because Dr. Geller hadn't made the slightest inclination of starting to judge him – unlike the head shrinks in the prisons he had been banged up in – and Dr. Geller was impressed because Charlie was so open.

Dr. Geller killed another half smoked cigarette and lit another, "Tell me, Charlie … how do you feel when you are 'working' so to speak?"

"You mean when I'm doing the business on people?"

"Yes, if that's how you prefer to describe it."

Charlie mulled it over for a few seconds, "I don't feel anything if you want the truth. I don't feel good or bad or right or wrong, Doc' … I just feel like I'm doing what I'm good at and that I'll be getting paid for it at the end of the day."

"So you would describe it as a mechanical feeling … Mmm … you go into autopilot so to speak?"

"Yeah, I suppose so. I just do what needs to be done, Doc'. Like I said, there's no great mystery … I'm just good at violence that's all."

"I can see you that you are an intelligent young man, Charlie. You are not being disingenuous when you say you never have any feelings of guilt or remorse for you actions?"

"Dis … ?"

"I mean, Charlie … huh, I mean you are … I mean simply that you feel no guilt?"

Charlie sighed, "I told you from the kick off. I promised Candice I wouldn't pull your pisser and I'm not. No, definitely, I never feel guilty about what I've done to people."

"Presumably some of these people are quite innocent of crimes, Charlie."

"In what way, Doc'?"

"All of these people are surely not criminals. You are not just an enforcer for criminals on criminals, no?"

Charlie grinned smug and sat back, "Well, that's where I'm blessed see, Doc'?"

"What do you mean 'blessed'?"

"Well, see, I'm a bit of a specialist, Doc'. The people that hire my services are all pretty much scumbags' n' lowlife n' a bit dodgy. They're not gangsters or mobbed or anything, no. These are people with secrets and they've got things they want hiding. These people would never go to the Old Bill or anything 'cos the Old Bill would start asking too many questions, Doc', n' the gangsters wouldn't have anything to do with 'em either. I'm talking about small time pimps n' pornographers, fraudsters, shylocks, pissheads, drug addicts, puffs, embezzlers, cheating husbands n' wives, con men, rip off merchants ... you get the picture? I do the dirty work for the dirtiest bastards in town, Doc'."

Dr. Geller nodded his head positive, "Yes, yes, I understand, I understand you, Charlie but ... what I don't understand is ..."

Charlie sat forward, pumped up after his little rant, "What? Go on. What *don't* you understand?"

"The people that these 'unsavory characters' want you to get violent with ... they could be anyone couldn't they?"

Charlie smiled and shook his head at Dr. Geller's naiveté, "Doc', Doc', listen to me ... I do jobs on people who deserve it. I do the dirty work on people who've chosen to be scumbags or associate with scumbags, all right?"

"*All* of them, Charlie? You have never, 'done a job' on people who could be classed as innocents?"

Charlie quickly put his hand on his chest, "Hand on heart, not to my knowledge, Doc', no. No I haven't. The people that come to me don't mix with innocent people. Soho's a fucking cesspit if you want the truth, pardon the French. Everyone's screwing everyone else over for what they can get, Doc'. The coppers, even the coppers down there are bent as nine bob notes. It's just one big racket. Like a … like a swimming pool full o' sharks."

Dr. Geller studied Charlie's face as he drank, "So that's how you ameliorate any feelings of guilt, yes, Charlie?"

Charlie frowned, "Eh?"

"Sorry, I mean, huh … I mean you can live with yourself knowing that the people you are being violent with are … shall we say 'unsavory'? 'Deserving' of retribution?"

Charlie mulled a little and nodded positive, "Huh … yeah, Doc', all of 'em, they all piss in the same pot. They're not very nice people."

"So you would say you are discriminatory? You are only violent with people who you believe deserve violence visited upon them?"

Charlie thought about and lit a cigarette, he started to nod his head, "Yeah, that's a fair point, a good way of putting it, Doc'. I like that way o' putting it. This rum, by the way, lovely tipple. "

Dr. Geller poured Charlie another rum and Charlie topped it with Coca Cola.

Charlie laughed, "You can understand why all those pirates loved it in the Caribbean, eh?"

"Indeed, Charlie."

Charlie sat forward and Dr. Geller got a better look at his bloodshot eyes. Charlie must have been really knocking them back recently. Dr. Geller was happy he had. Dr. Geller had always been a great believer of alcohol loosening the tongue and revealing the truth.

Charlie smiled at him, "I'm really glad we're having this talk, Doc'."

"And so am I, Charlie."

"Candice means the world to me. She's … I can see myself settling down with her."

"Marriage?"

"Yeah, without a doubt. I know she loves this place and she thinks you're a saint, Doc'."

Dr. Geller tried to modestly wave away the compliment, "Oh please, Charlie."

"No, no ... She does. I don't know what you've done for her but it must have been special. She doesn't go into details but she said she had a bit of a bad childhood."

Dr. Geller shuffled a little uncomfortably, "Candice is wonderful, Charlie, but let's talk about you and your experiences."

Charlie's eyes were heavy now, the rum had certainly topped up the skinful he had consumed the day before, "Whatever you want, Doc'," he raised his glass, "I'm a guest in your establishment after all."

Dr. Geller clinked glasses with Charlie, "You are welcome."

"So what do you wanna know about me that I haven't already told you, Doc'?"

"Oh, nothing, Charlie. I am just happy that we are talking. My work covers many areas and I suppose I am simply fascinated by talking to people from all kinds of social backgrounds."

Charlie sniggered, "No offence, but you know what you sounded like just then?"

"What is that?"

"You sounded like one o' those politicians, Doc'. You know, 'social backgrounds'?"

Dr. Geller smiled and rolled his eyes, "Please accept my apology, the last thing I want to sound like is a politician."

They laughed together and Dr. Geller picked it up, "I am hoping that we can talk further, Charlie?"

Charlie shrugged, "Why not? You're a decent bloke."

"Thank you, I have unfortunately never been called a 'bloke' before."

They laughed together again and Charlie leaned over and slapped Dr. Geller on the shoulder, "Well, you can consider yourself a bloke from now on, Doc'."

Dr. Geller poured them the last hits of the rum, Charlie watched him and the sit down with Patsy Fagan came flooding back, "Actually, Doc' ..."

"Yes, Charlie?"

"I wanna ask *you* a question."

"Please, feel free."

Charlie rubbed the midnight shadow on his chin, "This is one o' those hypocritical questions."

Dr. Geller smiled, he was really warming to Charlie's style, "And the hypothesis is?"

"Eh?"

"Your question, Charlie?"

Charlie clicked, "Oh yeah, yeah ... well, you know what I do, right? Candice filled you in n' we've been having this chat, so ... thing is ... do you reckon everyone's got a price, Doc'?"

"A price? In what way do you mean?"

"I mean, Doc' ... I mean, do you reckon somebody would do something really terrible. Something ... something *evil* if the price was right?"

Dr. Geller sat forward, put his drink down and laced his fingers together, this was exciting, "Aaah, Charlie. You distinguish between good and evil?"

Charlie frowned, "Eh?"

"You said, 'something evil', I'm asking you if you believe in evil?"

Charlie was a little taken aback, "What do you mean, Doc'?"

"I mean you are spiritual. You believe in an outside force that can infect and then determine peoples actions."

Charlie was a little lost, "No ... No, huh ... I just mean evil. You know ... totally fucking wrong. Out of order, Doc' ... just ... just sick."

"But you said *evil*, Charlie. What is your definition of evil?"

Charlie shrugged, "I don't know ... I suppose, you know ... that fucking Ian Brady n' Myra Hindley n' those kids they murdered up in Manchester."

"So you believe that these child murderers were evil, Charlie?"

Charlie snorted, "'Course they were evil. You don't kill kids if you're not fucking evil!"

Dr. Geller stroked his nose with his forefinger, "So, let me try and understand this, Charlie ... if evil is represented by Satan and good is represented by God, you believe that these murderers were either paying homage to Satan or that they had been instructed by Satan to carry out these atrocities, yes?"

Charlie squinted at Dr. Geller, "What do you mean?"

"I simply mean, if *evil* exists, surely it has been brought about in some way, yes? If the evil is an exterior force it has somehow influenced the perpetrators?"

Dr. Geller could clearly see that he needed to rephrase it for Charlie. Maybe it was the drink but Charlie was looking at him dumbfounded.

"OK, Charlie, let me put it this way ... these child murderers, yes? They decide that they are going to murder children either for sexual pleasure or simply some other perverse form of enjoyment, OK?"

Charlie nodded, "Yeah, all right, either they're perverts or they're just, you know, sick fuckers. They need locking up anyway you look at it."

"OK then, Charlie. Now what I am saying is that evil – evil as we have come to understand it – is a manifestation of the work of The Devil, Satan, Lucifer, Beelzebub, whatever you would like to call him, yes?"

"All right, Doc', yeah. I'm with you."

"So as I understand it you are saying that these people were somehow influenced by a force from without themselves? An external force? A *devil* inspired them to murder these innocent children, yes?"

Charlie mulled it, "Huh ..."

"So by saying this it figures that every act of goodness is inspired by a force for good, a Jesus, a God, an Angel, a Deity, yes?"

Charlie dredged his glass, "Wait a minute, Doc', I'm not saying that."

"Oh but you are, Charlie. If you are using extremes to define acts you are dealing in absolutes ... no, no ... excuse me, let me explain ... to define good you need to define evil. To define evil you need to define good. Do you understand me? We can only measure good by evil and evil by good, yes?"

Charlie scratched his chin and frowned, "You're missing something here, Doc'."

"Yes?"

"Yeah ... instinct. We know when something's right n' when something's wrong. We feel it. It's what stops us all from being fucking monsters."

"Do we, Charlie ... do we *really* know that? Do we all know right from wrong, truly?"

"Yeah, 'course we do, well, most of us do."

"So what *you* do is not monstrous because you are being violent towards people who are deserving of that violence, yes, Charlie? They ask for that violence to be visited upon themselves by their actions, yes?"

"Yeah, yeah ... they choose that lifestyle. They know what they're getting into, Doc'."

"So the child murderers ... they may too have a sense that their victims have brought the actions upon themselves, yes?"

Charlie scowled at him, "What are you saying?"

"I am saying, Charlie, that maybe child murderers are simply doing what you do. You do it for money and they do it to satisfy their bloodlust or sexual appetites. They do it for release and pleasure and you do it for financial gain and survival. You have said yourself, earlier, you said that people you know are bored and that they need excitement in their lives."

Charlie nodded and frowned, Dr. Geller was going to fast for him, "Yeah, so what?"

"There are people who will be just as shocked at what you do as to what child murderers do, Charlie ... but because of our society I dare say there will be many who won't find what you do abhorrent."

Charlie snapped, "I don't fucking attack innocent kids, Doctor!"

"No, Charlie, no ... but do you understand what I am getting at? I am saying that everything is relative and if you believe that there are actual solid concepts of good *and* evil you surely accept that these child murderers are not in control of their actions, yes?"

Charlie looked away and thought about it, he stubbed his cigarette out and frowned, "I know what you're saying, Doc', but there's morals isn't there? We've got like, like this thing inside us that tells us something's acceptable and something isn't, right? The fucking monsters that kill kids, well … they're not human are they?"

Dr. Geller grinned, "But, Charlie, we end up back where we started don't we? If these child murderers are evil, the evil comes from without rather than within. They are influenced by an outside force, a force of evil, yes?"

"I don't know … what if these people are just born bad, born evil, Doc'?"

"Inherent evil?"

"Yeah, born that way."

"So evil is purely a part of their genetic makeup? That would cancel out the external force, Charlie. What need would there be for Gods and Devils if that were the case?"

Charlie was floundering now, his brow creased.

Dr. Geller could see Charlie was waning and he would pick up the thread at their next talk. Dr. Geller stood up, "Hopefully we continue this talk another day, Charlie … but in the meantime think about these questions. Is there such a thing as pure evil in the world? Does the Devil exist? Does God exist? If God does not exist and everything is permitted, what distinguishes absolute evil from the absolute good?"

Charlie shook his hand, "I will, Doc'. I've enjoyed this natter … food for thought, and thanks for the rum."

As Charlie headed back to Candice's room he half drunkenly smiled to himself. He liked Dr. Geller, and wondered if Dr. Geller might be a little psychic. They had touched upon a subject that had been on Charlie's mind since seeing Patsy Fagan. Maybe Dr. Geller would be able to help him with his quandary.

Thirty year old Rupert Von Susstren was holed up in his expensive apartment in Holland Park: curtains drawn, telephone incessantly ringing unanswered, doors bolted, Quaaludes and vintage red wine fighting a losing battle with his rampant fears and anxieties.

He had been contemplating suicide and would have attempted it if he weren't such a coward. For now though, luudes and red wine and would have to suffice until he either plucked up courage or played ball with his tormentor.

The phone stopped ringing and he took a momentary sigh of relief. He was wearing only his Paisley pattern silk gown, he hadn't dressed or washed or shaved for days and the night sweats that had dried on him were turning his usually sweet fragrance foul. He had spent hours sat on the toilet staring at the expensive marvel floor and wishing that he could be sucked down into the sewage system. Sucked down into oblivion as long as it didn't hurt him too much in the process.

It could be safely said that Rupert had never had any real cause for concern in his life up until now, and boy was this introduction to it a heavy lesson. Lord Rupert was getting his first taste of what it means to totally connect with reality.

He was now having to face consequences square in the face and he couldn't ask for help from Mummy and Daddy anymore. Even they, with all their prestige, wealth and connections, wouldn't be able to dig him out of this pit he had fallen into.

The telephone rang again as he opened his last bottle of wine. He would have to call out for some more, he also needed more cigarettes and more luudes or whatever other downers were available. He just couldn't face seeing anyone. He was sure if he did some anybody they would see the terrible guilt etched into his face and they would instantly know what he been a part of.

He also knew that he was going to have to answer the telephone at some point. He had already managed to remain silent when friends had knocked on his door and pressed the buzzer and shouted his name. The telephone was different though. He knew that there was somebody on the other end of the line who he would eventually have to speak to.

That person had been calling on a loop. The torment was turning Lord Rupert's mind inside out; convinced that the nerves under his skin were slowly growing out of the skin and about to become visible and raw and sensitive to even the atmosphere in the room.

He had lost count of the tears he had shed and the amount of times he had crawled into a fetal position and rocked himself into half sleep and disturbing catnaps. Lord Rupert hated himself with a passion now.

A few genuine friends had warned him that he was heading for some kind of fall if he didn't slow down. Lord Rupert had ignored them and gravitated more towards the friends who got their rocks off with him and never questioned the hedonistic lifestyle he was leading.

One of Lord Rupert's rituals now, since he had gone into exile from society, was to go over and over in his mind a *what if* scenario. What if he hadn't started to smoke pure opium? What if he hadn't fallen out with Tara Newman Beckett? What if he hadn't agreed to go to *that* party in Fitzrovia? What if he hadn't listened to Candice and Patsy Fagan and Fraser Etherington?

All the scenarios simply tormented him. He knew that he had nobody else to blame for this but himself. Nobody had forced him to join in; he was of sound mind when he agreed and that agreement had now grown into a fact that could ruin not only him but his family and even prominent members of The Establishment. When it all came out the name Von Susstren would forever be associated with the murder of a child.

Hours, minutes and seconds melted into the stifling air of the apartment and Lord Rupert paced and gibbered to himself. The phone rang again and this time he knew he had to answer it. In his tremulous voice he said, "Hello?"

"It's me ..." the voice was male, coarse and cockney and insidious and it gave Lord Rupert Goosebumps, "Why haven't you been picking up, Rupert?"

Rupert stuttered and lied, "I was, I was ... I was sleeping."

"Sleeping, eh? I don't know how you can sleep knowing what you know, Rupert."

Rupert closed his eyes and out of the corner of his mouth bit on the hem of his gown's sleeve and shrieked, "Please just ... please don't ... I ... I ..." "Calm down, Rupert, calm down, son ... this thing can be sorted out, I told you that. I told you everything can be taken care of didn't I?"

"Ye ... yes, yes you did."

"I said it could all go away, Rupert, didn't I?"

"Yes. You said that, you did."

"You should trust me, son. Think of me like an uncle. I've got your best interests at heart."

Rupert bit back emotion, "Yes. Yes of course. I know."

"So ... have you got the money together yet, Rupert?

"I ... I can't ... not yet, no. I just can't go out yet. I feel ..."

"Yeah, I bet you do. I'll bet you feel really bad, Rupert. I'd feel really bad, son. What you n' your friends did was evil."

Lord Rupert gasped, "I never touched the little girl. I swear to you!"

"It's not me you're gonna have to swear to though is it, Rupert?"

Lord Rupert floundered, "What do you – I don't – what do you mean?"

"Well, it's gonna be a Beak isn't it? Gonna be a judge n' jury you're gonna have to swear to if you don't come up with my money, son."

Lord Rupert panicked and yelped, "But I will! I will get your money!"

The voice rasped in a mocking tone, "N' exactly when's that gonna be Rupert, old bean?"

"As soon as I ... two hundred thousand pounds is a lot of money, I-"

"I agree, son, but it's a small price to pay to keep you out o' jail for the rest o' your natural ain't it?"

Rupert gulped, "Yes, yes it is."

"That's right. You wouldn't like prison, Rupert. I dare say it's a lot like that posh boarding school you went to, only, thing is, there's gonna be people inside that prison who'll want to carve you up from arsehole to eyeball 'cos o' what you did to that poor little girl."

Lord Rupert started to cry, he sobbed, "Please, please believe me. It was nothing to do with me. I ... I ... I did not touch a hair on that girl's head."

"That might well be the case, Rupert, that might well be the case, but I've got a little film here with you n' your sick fucking friends on it and you're all dressed up like ... like *I don't know what's* n' your doing your silly rituals n' that little girl ... that poor little Vanessa Kitson's there and you're all-"

Lord Rupert screamed, "Stop! Just … just stop, please just stop a minute."

The line went quiet for a couple of minutes as Lord Rupert slumped to the floor and sobbed. He held the telephone at arms length like it was something toxic that might infect him. Lord Rupert could hear his name. He put the telephone to his ear.

"I'm here. I am still here."

"You shouldn't be tormenting yourself like this, Rupert. It's not good for your health."

Lord Rupert tried to compose himself, "I need to … can I ask you a question?"

"All right, son. Ask me anything you want."

"If, I mean, *when* I get you the money …"

"The two hundred thousand, yeah. Go on."

"Well … look, I'm not trying to sound … but how do I know you won't still go ahead and show the film to … how do I know that I'm not already finished?"

The voice laughed, "Do you take me for a fucking mug or something, Rupert? Why would I do that, eh?" Think about it … I'm a villain, Rupert. I've got form, son. I show the Old Bill it n' they nick me for accessory to murder; conspiracy and blackmail. I'll be lucky if I get out o' the nick before I'm a fucking old age pensioner. Do you think I'm a mug or what, son?"

"No, I … no, but OK …" Lord Rupert took a deep breath, "You could still make copies. You could … you could blackmail me for evermore."

There was a silence. Lord Rupert closed his eyes tight and silently prayed that he hadn't offended him.

"Well … yeah, you could look at it that way, but I suppose you're just gonna have to trust me aren't ya, Rupert? I don't see as you've got much choice in the matter … do you?"

Morning arrived and Doctor A did indeed hop the A Train, but she wasn't heading to Sugarhill way up in Harlem, no Sireee, she was heading to CERN as instructed. She was confident that she couldn't have a bun in the oven but best to get a solid-state opinion from

Petra Plimsole. As architecture and trash and speed graffiti melted in the windows of the choo-choo Doctor A tried to remember the last time anyone had ejaculated inside her ... no. It was at least three years since she'd been a Fuckee and she was positive The Fucker had worn a Rubber Johnny.

A cab collected her from the station and zoomed off to CERN. The Swiss Cabby asked her, "Have you brought everything you need?" Doctor A frowned, "Sorry?"

"Toiletries, nightgowns, bibs and bobs."

"Wha ..."

"O everyone knows about the pregnancy. We've all been reading the novel. It's a great success. We're all rooting for you."

Doctor A sat forward, "What do you mean?"

"I say, 'all'. It's more like a 'handful' of readers but we're committed. We 'get' it. Have you decide whether you're going natural or Caesarian yet? No, no, don't tell me. I'd rather wait and read about it. I hate spoilers!"

Doctor A was flabbergasted. The Cabby smiled, "I love that word: *flabbergasted*."

Doctor A knew instantly that she was now facing an existential threat. If Swiss Cabbies could read her mind that would mean *everyone* could. Anyone who had the slightest inclination could now chart her progress towards the delivery room, if indeed a delivery was about to take place. In a room.

The Cabby swiveled his head, "People have been praying for you, Doctor A. Sure, they know you're an atheist, but that hasn't stopped them ... everyone has the opportunity to be born again."

Doctor A muttered, "What has my atheism got to do with anything?"

"I suppose people were surprised that you would procreate, being such an ardent disbeliever in creation."

Frustrated Doctor A, "What has ..."

"Of course, it's nobody's business but their own if they decide to procreate without believing in a creator. I suppose you simply see it as a byproduct of chaotic evolution, huh? Maybe your child won't believe in *you* and simply believe that they are merely an accident of biological urges. The i-phone never falls far from the tree of the knowledge of good & evil does it?" Chirped the cheeky Cabby.

Jack Sherry was sat on the bed in his room at Captain Torres' station. He had tried to call CI Barry Ketley but he was out of the office. Jack smoked and drank water and stared out at the palm tree as it slowly changed colour with the natural light diminishing. Jack liked the twilight or *the gloaming* as his mother used to call it. He remembered her soft, Irish voice and the lines she would repeat whenever twilight fell and it caught her attention, *"It was the gloaming, when a man cannot make out if the nebulous figure he glimpses in the shadows is angel or demon, when the face of evening is stained by red clouds and wounded by lights."*
One of Jack's biggest regrets in life was never asking her where that description had come from. She was a well read woman and was always quoting from her favorite works of literature; this particular quote had always stayed with Jack Sherry and, now more than ever, he wished he could see her again, if only for a few seconds, to ask where that particular line had come from.
Jack thought about Mr. and Mrs. Kitson and wondered what question they would like to ask their little Vanessa. Jack had met Maureen Kitson a few weeks after the discovery of her child's body. She had asked to see the man that found her. Jack had also expressed interest in meeting Vanessa's parents.
He was intensively briefed by Chief Inspector Barry Ketley and a woman – who Jack assumed was from the Home Office – before the meeting.
CI Ketley was firm with Jack Sherry, "Vanessa's parents don't know the grisly details of her murder, DI Sherry and ..." he glanced at the woman, "it's very important that you don't tell them anything about the state you found her in."
"I understand, sir, but what if-"

The woman cut him off sharp, "No, Detective. There will be no 'what if's'. *If* Mrs. Kitson starts to ask about details you will decline to comment and-"

CI Ketley talked over her, "Jack. You will say only that you found her body. You won't say anything about the state you found her in, all right?"

The woman closed in on Jack, "We will be with you, Detective Sherry. If the conversation starts to head into 'details' we will intervene. Do you understand?"

Jack frowned and looked up at his boss: *do have I to listen to her?*

CI Ketley patted Jack's shoulder, "We need to know that you understand this, Jack. You can *not*, under any circumstances, tell Mrs. Kitson what you saw."

CI Ketley and the woman stared at Jack. The woman chewed her lower lip and wrung her hands; CI Ketley slightly nodded his head, anticipating that Jack understood.

"I do, sir. I'll only say that I found the body."

CI Ketley, "It's going to be a very emotional meeting, Jack."

"Yes, sir."

CI Ketley could see that the woman wasn't looking convinced with Jack, "You can go now, Detective Sherry. We'll speak later."

When Jack was out of the room the woman shook her head, "I don't think he's fit to talk to her, Chief Inspector."

"He'll be all right, we'll be there with him."

"No, no … I'm not convinced yet."

Jack was eventually allowed to meet Mrs. Maureen Kitson. She was brought to Scotland Yard and he was left to speak to her alone in a small office. He couldn't understand why there had been so much fuss about him meeting her because now they were letting him speak to her alone.

The meeting was emotional, emotional for Jack Sherry that is.

He felt that Mrs. Kitson was going through the motions; she wasn't acting like a woman who had lost her only daughter. She just wasn't convincing. There was just something not right about her behavior. Jack put it down to the trauma and thought nothing more of it.

Five weeks later and Jack's suspicion of the meeting was confirmed when he saw a photograph of the *real* Mrs. Maureen Kitson in *The Times*.

Jack confronted Chief Inspector Ketley. Ketley apologized and admitted that the 'powers above him' had vetoed a meeting with the real Mrs. Kitson.

Jack was hurt, "But, sir ... why did you let me meet with an imposter?"

Ketley shook his head, lowered his eyes and threw his hands up in defeat, "They over-ruled me, Jack ... they thought – rightly or wrong – that meeting someone you thought was Mrs. Kitson would help you."

Jack searched Ketley's eyes, "*Help* me?"

"To get your feelings out."

"That's out of order, sir ... they ... they tricked me."

"I know, Jack, I know ... my hands were tied. They said they couldn't risk you meeting the real Mrs. Kitson in case you ... you know ... started talking about the details."

"But, sir. I told you, I told you and that woman I wouldn't. Why couldn't you both trust me, sir?"

Ketley closed in on Jack and put his hand on Jack's arm, "Jack. You've been under enormous stress lately. We're really trying to help you; *all* of us. You're one of the best detectives in The Yard, in the whole country, but ... well, we just couldn't risk you telling Mrs. Kitson what you saw."

Jack went to the window and looked down on the street. A young Spanish family were strolling along, mum and dad holding hands, giggling, happy, and the two children charging on ahead of them, safe in the knowledge that their protectors were only yards behind and would watch over them hawkishly. Nobody would pluck these kids off the street ... not tonight at least.

Jack meditated on murder. His whole philosophy on murder and its consequences had changed since that day he found Vanessa. Up until that day he believed in capital punishment, an eye for an eye, the death sentence for those that had taken another life. Since that day though, he now believed that murder didn't justify murder.

Murder left too many questions unanswered. He believed that if humanity was ever going to overcome its terrible curse the murderers had to be studied. They had to answer for the crimes they had carried out and that they needed to live with their actions; really suffer for their crimes. Death was too final for them. Death was the easy way out. Since the case of Vanessa Kitson Jack believed only in a justice that made the perpetrators suffer for as long as possible and let society learn how to neutralize monsters from an early age.

Jack could usually picture the kind of murderers he was chasing; he could profile the person to a certain degree. In the case of Vanessa Kitson though, the only picture that came to mind was that of a monster, a monster that had been dredged up from the darkest corners of a twisted and warped imagination. The *thing* that had ripped little Vanessa Kitson's heart out of her chest could have only been created by monsters. It could never have once been human, could never have functioned to a degree of normality in society.

He knew that people were capable of despicable acts, knew that even the most seemingly pacific people could become deadly violent at the drop of a hat, but in Vanessa's case it was different. Everything about the way she had died told him that her killer or killers had never once been human, never once felt what it feels like to be human.

Only mad people, lunatics, people who had been raised to be feral could have constructed such a grotesque tableau; such a disgusting diorama. The way Vanessa Kitson was positioned amongst the filth, the casual deformity of reality and her placement amongst shit – the cuts and burns and bruises on her virgin skin – the animal detachment of the killing – the tiny porcelain pale pink colored chest surgically but brutishly opened whilst she was alive and her still beating heart ripped out from its cavity.

The doctors of death in the concentration camps of Stalin and Hitler committed atrocities, but they were ideologues and their ideologies were evil. Whoever had done that to Vanessa wasn't an ideologue, and in Jack's mind they hadn't killed her because of ideology or sex or greed or revenge … they had killed her because they had the means and opportunity, and because they were monsters that was enough for them. They simply did it because they could. They had done it because they wanted to and that was enough.

Jack dragged on his cigarette and looked up at the palm tree. He thought about the many arguments he had with Dr. Geller. Dr. Geller didn't agree with Jack and his monster theory. Dr. Geller kept trying to push his theory that the murder was sexually motivated. Even though little Vanessa hadn't been sexually abused, Dr. Geller insisted that a sex act doesn't necessarily have to be performed for it to have taken place in the mind of perpetrator. Jack could never get his head around this. There was a lot Jack didn't get his head around where Dr. Geller was concerned.

Dr. Geller said to Jack, "The murderer of this little girl could quite possibly have been playing out a role that is deeply embedded in their subconscious, Jack."

"What do you mean, Dr.?"

"I mean, Jack, that some terrible crime could have been perpetrated on them and they are reenacting that crime."

Jack snapped at him, "I don't think someone who had their heart ripped out would be able to do it to someone else, do you?"

Dr. Geller couldn't answer that question. Or, at least, he couldn't answer that question specifically for Jack Sherry.

Jack put his hands on the window frame and pushed his head out. He closed his eyes and took a big drink of the fragrant Spanish nighttime air.

He turned to head back over to the bed and saw that a piece of paper had been shoved under the door of the room. He paused, frowned and wondered whether to pick it up. He quickly snapped out of his deliberation: *of course you should pick it up.*

He held it out at arms length. It obviously wasn't for him. It read: *No se puede confiar en ninguna de estas personas.*

It was the morning after Charlie's introduction to Dr. Geller, and Charlie and Candice were strolling hand in hand through Regents Park. They looked like any other young couple in love; more attractive than your average couple, but you wouldn't have looked at them and made as them what they really were. They hid their pathologies well.

"You sure you don't wanna know what me and the Doc' talked about, Candice."

"I've told you, 'no', Charlie. It's doctor patient confidentiality."

Charlie spluttered, "Wait a minute. *Patient!*"

Quick as a flash Candice retorted, "No, not you! You're not a patient, but I wouldn't want to abuse Dr. Geller's trust."

Charlie let it slide, "But how would you be abusing his trust if it was me that told you what we talked about? He wouldn't know, would he?"

"But *I'd* know Charlie. I'd know and I wouldn't feel good about that."

Charlie gave her another pass. If she didn't want to know that was up to her, he had a bit of an hangover anyway and just wanted a relaxing, carefree day.

"You liked him though, Charlie. Genuinely liked him?"

"I told you, yeah … he's a nice chap."

"He's a miracle worker."

Charlie raised an eyebrow: *a little OTT* but stuck to his decision not to go down that road. He bought them ice cream and they sat on a bench.

She could see this was a new experience for him, "You're not used to this kind of thing are you? You do most of your romancing in the clubs and bedrooms don't you?"

"You make me sound like some … I don't know … some lounge lizard."

"It's true though isn't it? You're a creature of the night Charles Henry Coleman."

Charlie put his hand out and tilted it, exposing his palm, "What can I say? Woah! How'd you know my middle name?"

She tapped her nose and smiled, "I know a lot more about you than you think."

He didn't know whether to be worried or flattered, "Oh yeah, like what?"

"Let's just say I do my homework when I …"

He picked up hopefully, "Fall in love?"

She smiled but he wanted confirmation, "Well, Candice?"

She leaned over and kissed him. That was all the confirmation he needed; but it made him feel unusually a little guilty.

Charlie had promised her that he wouldn't go after Grant Burgess for revenge. He really meant it at the time but now, well *now* was another day. There would be chance she would ever find out anyway; and what she didn't know wouldn't hurt her. He also felt guilty that he was harboring the horrific secret that Patsy Fagan had confided to him. Charlie knew this was going to keep snapping back and poking at his nerves like toothache.

When he looked into her eyes though, Patsy's proposition made sense in a way. With the kind of money Fagan was offering, him and Candice could set up a nice home for themselves and he wouldn't have to take anymore jump-jobs ever again. He could even afford to buy them a little business to work at; something legit, something that didn't involve danger, something that they could build up together. Whilst Charlie thought about the future, Candice thought about the past. Why had it been kept from her that Dorian Butler had visited The Institute and seen Dr. Geller? What did Dorian's notes on The Process have to do with anything? And why had Dorian killed himself?

The only person she could really talk to was Dorian's best friend: the sleazy Lyle Chivers, a now destitute, 30 year old junky who had lost all his friends on the scene. Candice wasn't looking forward to visiting Lyle Chivers, but the fact that Dorian had met Dr. Geller without her knowing about it was eating her up inside.

The perfect opportunity arose when Charlie told her he had to pick up some money somebody owed him in The French. Candice jumped on the tube and headed over to Earls Court. She knew Lyle Chivers would be at his flat because it was daylight, and Lyle Chivers was a vampire, only he didn't suck blood, he sucked morphine.

Lyle's flat was pokey, shabby, littered with anything and everything imaginable in a domestic setting, but above all it stank. It stank of body odor and rotten food and milk that had soured. Dust held dominion but Lyle would never have seen it.

He was surprised to see Candice and it took a few moments for him to recognize her. He talked in slow motion and his eyes were so heavy they were weighing his head down.

Lyle wore a filthy flowery shirt; stained ocre crushed velvet trousers and chiffon scarves. His hair was shoulder length and it was so long since it had been washed it was now cleaning itself naturally. Lyle had aged five years since Candice had last seen him nine months back.

"Come in Candy, babe ... sit down, sit down ... it's good to see you." Candice sat on the edge of the only chair that wasn't piled high with rubbish. Lyle held his hand out effeminately and regarded the room, "I need to get my shit together, man. The cleaning lady's just disappeared, you know?"

Candice sighed and mustered up a smile, "I've just found about Dorian, Lyle."

He slowly nodded his head and blinked his eyes, "Yeah, I saw you at the funeral, Candy."

"No, no, you didn't Lyle. I wasn't at the funeral because nobody told me he had died."

He squinted at her and put his thumb and index finger at either side of his mouth, "No? You weren't there, babe? You sure?"

"I would have remembered, Lyle. Like I said, nobody told me Dorian had died."

He shook his head, "That's not cool, babe, not cool at all."

"No it's not Lyle. You know where I live. You could have telephoned or nipped 'round. Dorian and me were good friends once upon a time. We were pretty close."

He wiped his nose with the back of his hand, "Yeah, you were, that's true. I don't know why nobody told you, Candy ... they must have forgot."

Candice sighed, he wasn't getting it, or so she thought.

He lit a cigarette and slunk further down into his chair, "I remember you and Dorian. You got on like a house on fire, didn't you?"

"I wish someone would have told me."

"Did you two ... nah ... he wasn't interested in sex was he?"

Candice wanted out now; the smell was overpowering, "Listen, Lyle … I want to know if Dorian ever talked to you about The Institute." she started talking to him like he was a child, "You know … The Institute where I work. You remember?"

He thought about it, blew a smoke ring and poked his finger through the middle of it. He smiled at her, "It's all coming back to me now, Candy."

"What is?"

"Dorian and *that* Institute"

"The Trebistock Institute? "

Lyle's attitude changed, he was still zoned out and spacey but there was now a spark of energy rising; an energy that gave away a sense of remembrance, something that he knew he should be cautious of but couldn't for the life in him remember why. He frowned and Candice picked up on it.

"Lyle. I'm saying, The Trebistock Institute … what do you know about Dorian and The Trebistock? You know something, I can tell, Lyle … now tell me."

Doctor A was unceremoniously dumped outside the Extraction Unit at CERN. She was met by a hipster Porter with a pimped out gurney stroke wheelchair, "Insurance purposes, nothing to worry about Maam."

Doctor A looked him over as she sheepishly sat down,"Where are you taking me?"

"To Dr. Petra Plimsole of course. She's expecting you. In fact, everyone's expecting you."

Suspicious, "And what exactly do you mean by that?"

The Porter shrugged, "Merely that we're all expectant, Maam. Nothing more."

Doctor A clocked his smirk and decided to let it slide.

She sat back and tried to relax as the Porter glided her down the ward. *How come I've never seen this section before? I know this place like the back of my hand but I can't recall ever noticing it before.*

Wasn't I paying attention? O no, you were paying attention, Maam, but you remember it as something completely different.

Doctor A snapped at the Porter, "OK. It's obvious you can read my mind but I'd prefer it if you didn't converse with me in it. It feels like you're raping me!"
"As you wish, Maam."

Newscasters. What are cast? Spells are cast in Broadcasts. Not narrowcasts. "Enter through the narrow gate. For broad is the road that leads to destruction. Doctor A looked around but could see no broadcast. The Porter speeded up. Open doors, cubicles blurred, sneak peeks, countless rooms giving refuge to Deliverers. *This is a factory.* Peepshow, creep show, where'd you get those eyes? Jeepers creepers where'd you get those lies?

Doctor A shrank into the gurney stroke wheelchair. G-force pinning her back as the Porter broke all land speed records, cocking a snoop at the buffoons on the Bonneville flats. Doctor A gulped on pockets of anti-septic reconditioned air, her eyes watering, quivering globules of eye ejaculate, her cheeks flapping like voodoo drum skins hung out to dry in a jungle tornado. *O the pressure!*

We're all expecting you. Expectant. Expecting. Tenterhooks on, with masturbated breath. Stirrups at the ready! Ride 'em cowgirl. Giddy up! Switzerland is a state of mindfuck; neutral of course, no time like the present, one flew over the cuckold's nest. Sanitary sanctuary, where money comes to breed, international Fe Fo Fum Finance, the hills are alive with the sound of usury and you always misread The Master as being a margarita drinker. Pontius has finally been awarded his pilots license. He's planning on taking Barabbas on a European tour of child sacrifice haunts to snap Polaroid's for the exhibition.

Doctor A couldn't take in the length of the corridors; her vagina was constricted, dry to the touch, more parched than Gandhi's flip-flops.

Surely your turning of things upside down shall be esteemed as the potter's clay: for shall the work say of him that made it, He made me not? Or shall the thing framed say of him that framed it, he had no understanding? – Isaiah 29:16 (KJV)

The Porter kept pushing on down the increasingly broadening corridor. 2000 meters wide and 35 kilometers long, the pitch black sporadically illuminated by operating theater lights, faces contorted in agony squashed against windows in doors within windows in doors. MC Escher rapped a puzzle as architecture bugged freestyle, concrete and clay and brick and mortar and metal and corrugated iron and ballast and steel melted into an orgiastic soup of Campbell's condensed slooooooooooooooo w.w.w. Vibrational Tomato.

A trillion eyes caught in a net – wireless suspension of disbelief communicated freely and witnessed Doctor A speeding back down the corridor. Like the apocryphal child, her inner SatNav was nowhere to be heard. For the first time IRL she was lost. Self-purpose had abandoned her and now she was at the mercy, mercy, mercy of The Ward.

Some eyes asked for autographs but there was no time for self-promotion, she had somewhere to be, *to be and not to be, which* is the quantum question. An elevator full to the rafters with lukewarm sick rose in her stomach. It came to a grinding halt in her throat.

Doctors and Nurses clad in luminous green PVC smocks and face masks and clogs scurried to and fro hysterically reminding each other of Time, their hands held aloft indicating they had douched and disinfected their digits ready to get busy bringing babes into the world.

Doctor A materialized in Petra Plimsole's consulting room, now strapped into the pimped out wheelchair. Petra – a Woeman of 35 – paced and grinned at Doctor A, "I'm so happy you have chosen to give birth here at CERN, Doctor A."

"I'm not sure I'm pregnant. I mean ..."

"O there's no doubt about it, Doctor A. Your gestation period has been well documented. It's in print."

"It is?"

Petra Plimsole delighted, "O yes, your ectoplasmic, ectopic pregnancy is being read right now."

Doctor A grimaced, "Without my permission?"

"Of course, you can't copyright an immaculate conception, dear."

"And ... and you're positive I *am* pregnant?"

"Positive ... you've been framed." grinned Petra Plimsole, "you're the fall girl, the patsy, the schmuck who got up the duff. You're the lame duck, the one *without* fuck, the empty vessel loaded on the dry dock by phantom stevedores ... do you get the picture or should I continue? I've got all the time in the word."

Doctor A faltered, "I ... I ..."

"Own this shit, honey. Savor those birth pangs of the new aeon. Here come the digital dark ages and you're gonna be a star of these days, baby."

"In truth ... well ... I don't think I'm meant to be here."

"Balderdash!" Petra Plimsole exclaimed, " ... And bollocks and piffle! Of course you're meant to be here. Your whole life has been leading towards this singularity. No quarter has been squared to bring you to this point, chuck."

Doctor A mournfully, "You've lost me."

"You were born to be the bearer of Good News."

Petra Plimsole gave Doctor A a potted and plotted history of her raison d'être, "You were adopted from birth. Unwanted on both sides of the biological divide. She was persuaded to give birth but died during labor. Our engineers took over the responsibility of raising you, and a fine job they did. O yes, The Trebistock Institute deserve a huge round of applause for their work, of course, they are humble people and wouldn't accept the applause, but still ..." Petra Plimsole giggled, "I suppose you could say you were raised by Wolves ... Wolves in Sheep's clothing. Anyway, you were bright and intelligent and proved to be the perfect student. You were tutored by the greatest minds in secular science. Straight A's, Doctor. Straight A's all the way, petal. A star pupil."

Doctor A meditated on the situation and eventually, "So this is it then? It's the end."
"O now, Doctor A, this is only the beginning."
"But ... The Readers won't be happy."
"*Assuming* they've made it this far." Petra Plimsole added.
Doctor A slowly nodded her agreement in somber silence, "But it's all so sudden. What about the pacing?"
Petra Plimsole feigned a conciliatory half smile, "I'm afraid the whole adventure has adhered to mimicking the jump cut of the dream stroke nightmare. Let's be honest, sugar tits, it was bound to conclude like this."

Petra Plimsole reached into her satchel, pulled out a book and handed it to Doctor A, "Here you are. This might be helpful, chicken."
"A book?" Doctor A read out the blurb, "You've Got a Book in You by Elizabeth Sims. *Are you writing a book or novel for the first time? Chances are you probably have (or have had) a bout of insecurity, fear of failure, or worry about making it perfect. But you don't have to let all of those feelings take hold of you and cripple your ability to write. In fact, You've Got a Book in You is filled with friendly, funny, telling-it-to-you-straight chapters that teach you how to relinquish your worries and write freely! With this book, you'll get tips, advice and exercises geared toward helping you gain the skills and best practices needed to finish writing a novel.*"

Petra Plimsole smiled, "Yes. Doesn't it sound wonderful?"
"I've no intention of finishing a novel."
"For the delivery, silly sausage. It'll help. We'll be extracting the baby in chapters."
Doctor A grimaced, "In chapters? It sounds ... messy."
"On the contrary. It will be a very neat conveyance."

Doctor A sighed, "I think I'd like a second opinion. There's a Gynecosmologist I know, Dr. Charles Grodin, maybe if I –"

"–O dear, Charles Grodin played Dr. Hill in Rosemary's Baby, he's fucking fictional *and* he betrayed her. He didn't believe Rosemary, just like all those people never believed *you*. You don't want to go through that dance again do you?"

"Dance? What dance?"

Petra Plimsole snapped, "The merry dance you led the authorities down with your fantastical tales of satanic ritual abuse. Don't you follow Hollywood f'fucksake? Don't you watch the mainstream media? Ritual abuse does *not* exist!"

Doctor A suddenly realized she had been sat crying in a chunky and stagnant Alphabet soup of her own piss, shit, tears, ectoplasm, DNA and vomit for at least a month of Sundays and a dawn of Blue Moons. A supermundane voice of indeterminate gender lilted, "Fear not, Doctor A ..."

Doctor A closed her eyes, "Who is that?"

"Some call me the denouement, others call me the climax, others, *La petite mort,* a brief loss of consciousness at the point of orgasm."

"Are you the one who impregnated me?"

"No ... you have yourself to thank for that, good Doctor."

"I have?"

"Clearly ... you have made your life's work the abrogation of a creator. How can that from *without* create a *within*. Your hearts desire has been fulfilled."

Doctor A whined, "But I never really wanted this. It was forced upon me."

"But you had free will."

"Yes, but it's complicated. It all makes sense now and people will be disappointed."

"Not if they believed ... the process will be more than enough to satisfy them. If they *don't* believe they should be used to disappointment by now."

Doctor A sniffed, "So it all really is down to a brutal binary?"
"Yes."

Doctor A fell awake in the delivery room, her legs in stirrups, amateur doctors and nurses peering into her abyss, Petra Plimsole looming larger than life, forceps at the ready, polished and lubed. Dr. Myron Geller sat on his throne peeping down on the procedure. O how proud he felt, how thoroughly modern, how superior to the useless, mouth breeding masses.

Geller gave the nod, a fanfare for the common fanny merchant sounded and Petra Plimsole got to work on the delivery. Doctor A demanded a painkiller but was denied in no uncertain terms, "Nope. Feel the burn, baby," Petra Plimsole grinned, "No pain, no gain."

Slowly Petra Plimsole pulled until a flash of pink flesh was visible, "You're crowning, Doctor A, you're crowning!"

The masses applauded as Doctor A bit down hard into her own hand and murmured. The pain had now reached her. It had taken a circuitous route and got caught in heavy Internet traffic over Italy. The pain apologized and was quick to start working its magic on Doctor A. It had brought Chance The Rapper along for balance. He unveiled his choir and started in on a beatific rendition of 'How Great Is My God' in the hope of soothing the good Doctor.

The Three Wise Men Of The Illiterati arrived just in time to witness Petra Plimsole sliding out a limb of flesh from Doctor A's abyss. Miles of smiles and sighs of relief as attendees caught sight of an optimistic sign. Doctor A peered south and caught a whiff of Tommy Udo playing Richard Skidmark in 1947's noir classic 'Kiss of Death'. She thought, *there's always something so mundane yet beautiful in noir movies*, and it reminded her of Charlie Coleman, another fictional baddie with a penchant for pushing cripples down stairs and then realized where she was and returned to the ordeal of pushing.

The pain ratcheted up and she let out a holler that disturbed The Janitor. He was working on a crossword puzzle and it disturbed him. He glowered at Doctor A, put his forefinger to his lips and hissed, "Shush!"

As Petra Plimsole pulled the animate flesh from Doctor A's snatch and the masses bowed and supplicated themselves, some crying, some reciting the Lords Prayer in double Dutch, some editing, some proofreading death threats in Braille, some ripping clothing from their bodies in joy as a veil of silence fell on the proceeding.

Petra Plimsole held the slimy writhing thing aloft and slapped Doctor A's arse. The thing cried, a shrill notice of arrival cutting through the vibration free air. Doctor A stared in horror at her new born Ampersand as Myron Geller slowly climbed down from his throne and cradled the infant abomination.

Through his proud blubbering he managed to spurt, "It's a ... novel ... it's a fictional novel." He closed in on Doctor A, wiping a tear from his eye, "This, my dear, is a book only you could have written, yet ... yet it gives serious consideration to the possibility that anyone could have written it. You see, a parody is the act of a trapped mind realizing that it can create nothing new and takes revenge by destroying the masterpieces of the past."

Petra Plimsole offered Doctor A a pair of sparkling new scissors and smiled, "Would you like to cut and paste the umbilical cord?"

Thank you for purchasing Dean Cavanagh's
The Secret Life of a Novel, hope you enjoyed it.
Please check out ZANI's *A Crafty Cigarette – Tales of a Teenage
Mod* by Matteo Sedazzari,
foreword by John Cooper Clarke.
Available on www.zani.co.uk or Amazon.

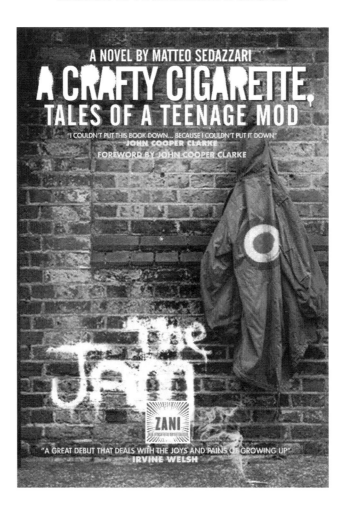

'I couldn't put it down because I couldn't put it down.'

John Cooper Clarke August 2015

'A Great Debut That Deals With The Joys and Pains of Growing Up'

Irvine Welsh April 2016

'Crafty Cigarette, all things Mod and a dash of anarchy. Want to remember what it was like to be young and angry? Buy this book. A great read'

Phil Davis (Actor – Chalky in Quadrophenia) August 2016

'Written in first person narrative, in a style and delivery reminiscent of Hunter S Thompson'

Scootering Magazine

'It's a good book and an easy read. That's pretty much what most pulp fiction needs to be'

Mod Culture

'Like a good Paul Weller concert the novel leaves you wanting more. I'll be very interested in reading whatever Matteo Sedazzari writes next.'

Louder Than War